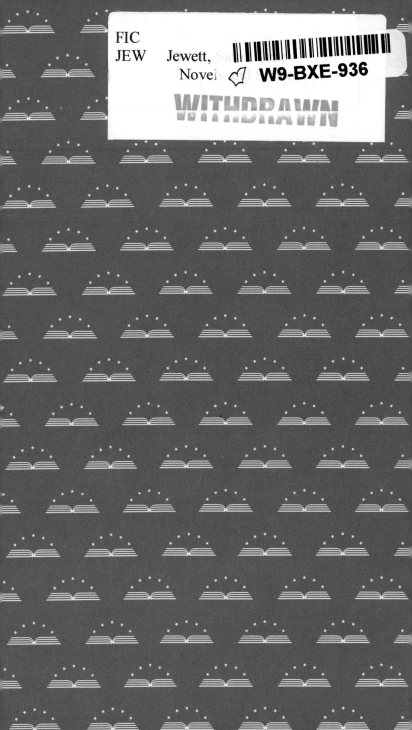

SARAH ORNE JEWETT

SARAH ORNE JEWETT

NOVELS AND STORIES
Deephaven
A Country Doctor
The Country of the Pointed Firs
Dunnet Landing Stories
Selected Stories and Sketches

THE LIBRARY OF AMERICA

The paper used in this publication meets the
minimum requirements of the American National Standard for
Information Sciences—Permanence of Paper for Printed
Library Materials, ANSI Z39.48—1984.

Distributed to the trade in the United States
by Penguin Books USA Inc
and in Canada by Penguin Books Canada Ltd.

Library of Congress Catalog Number: 93–24167
For cataloging information, see end of Notes.
ISBN 0–940450–74–7

First Printing
The Library of America—69

Manufactured in the United States of America

MICHAEL DAVITT BELL
SELECTED THE CONTENTS AND WROTE
THE NOTES FOR THIS VOLUME

Grateful acknowledgment is made to the National Endowment for the Humanities and the Ford Foundation for the grants that created this series and to the Andrew W. Mellon Foundation for having helped many public libraries acquire the volumes.

Contents

DEEPHAVEN

Preface

THIS book is not wholly new, several of the chapters having already been published in the "Atlantic Monthly."

It has so often been asked if Deephaven may not be found on the map of New England under another name, that, to prevent any misunderstanding, I wish to say, while there is a likeness to be traced, few of the sketches are drawn from that town itself, and the characters will in almost every case be looked for there in vain.

I dedicate this story of out-of-door life and country people first to my father and mother, my two best friends, and also to all my other friends, whose names I say to myself lovingly, though I do not write them here.

S. O. J.

Contents

Kate Lancaster's Plan

I HAD been spending the winter in Boston, and Kate Lancaster and I had been together a great deal, for we are the best of friends. It happened that the morning when this story begins I had waked up feeling sorry, and as if something dreadful were going to happen. There did not seem to be any good reason for it, so I undertook to discourage myself more by thinking that it would soon be time to leave town, and how much I should miss being with Kate and my other friends. My mind was still disquieted when I went down to breakfast; but beside my plate I found, with a hoped-for letter from my father, a note from Kate. To this day I have never known any explanation of that depression of my spirits, and I hope that the good luck which followed will help some reader to lose fear, and to smile at such shadows if any chance to come.

Kate had evidently written to me in an excited state of mind, for her note was not so trig-looking as usual; but this is what she said: —

DEAR HELEN, — I have a plan — I think it a most delightful plan — in which you and I are chief characters. Promise that you will say yes; if you do not you will have to remember all your life that you broke a girl's heart. Come round early, and lunch with me and dine with me. I 'm to be all alone, and it 's a long story and will need a great deal of talking over.

K.

I showed this note to my aunt, and soon went round, very much interested. My latch-key opened the Lancasters' door, and I hurried to the parlor, where I heard my friend practising with great diligence. I went up to her, and she turned her head and kissed me solemnly. You need not smile; we are not sentimental girls, and are both much averse to indiscriminate kissing, though I have not the adroit habit of shying in which Kate is proficient. It would sometimes be impolite in any one else, but she shies so affectionately.

"Won't you sit down, dear?" she said, with great ceremony,

and went on with her playing, which was abominable that morning; her fingers stepped on each other, and, whatever the tune might have been in reality, it certainly had a most remarkable incoherence as I heard it then. I took up the new Littell and made believe read it, and finally threw it at Kate; you would have thought we were two children.

"Have you heard that my grand-aunt, Miss Katharine Brandon of Deephaven, is dead?" I knew that she had died in November, at least six months before.

"Don't be nonsensical, Kate!" said I. "What is it you are going to tell me?"

"My grand-aunt died very old, and was the last of her generation. She had a sister and three brothers, one of whom had the honor of being my grandfather. Mamma is sole heir to the family estates in Deephaven, wharf-property and all, and it is a great inconvenience to her. The house is a charming old house, and some of my ancestors who followed the sea brought home the greater part of its furnishings. Miss Katharine was a person who ignored all frivolities, and her house was as sedate as herself. I have been there but little, for when I was a child my aunt found no pleasure in the society of noisy children who upset her treasures, and when I was older she did not care to see strangers, and after I left school she grew more and more feeble; I had not been there for two years when she died. Mamma went down very often. The town is a quaint old place which has seen better days. There are high rocks at the shore, and there is a beach, and there are woods inland, and hills, and there is the sea. It might be dull in Deephaven for two young ladies who were fond of gay society and dependent upon excitement, I suppose; but for two little girls who were fond of each other and could play in the boats, and dig and build houses in the sea-sand, and gather shells, and carry their dolls wherever they went, what could be pleasanter?"

"Nothing," said I, promptly.

Kate had told this a little at a time, with a few appropriate bars of music between, which suddenly reminded me of the story of a Chinese procession which I had read in one of Marryat's novels when I was a child: "A thousand white elephants richly caparisoned,—ti-tum tilly-lily," and so on, for a page or two. She seemed to have finished her story for that time, and while it was dawning upon me what she meant, she sang a bit from one of Jean Ingelow's verses:—

> "Will ye step aboard, my dearest,
> For the high seas lie before us?"

and then came over to sit beside me and tell the whole story in a more sensible fashion.

"You know that my father has been meaning to go to England in the autumn? Yesterday he told us that he is to leave in a month and will be away all summer, and mamma is going with him. Jack and Willy are to join a party of their classmates who are to spend nearly the whole of the long vacation at Lake Superior. I don't care to go abroad again now, and I did not like any plan that was proposed to me. Aunt Anna was here all the afternoon, and she is going to take the house at Newport, which is very pleasant and unexpected, for she hates housekeeping. Mamma thought of course that I would go with her, but I did not wish to do that, and it would only result in my keeping house for her visitors, whom I know very little; and she will be much more free and independent by herself. Beside, she can have my room if I am not there. I have promised to make her a long visit in Baltimore next winter instead. I told mamma that I should like to stay here and go away when I choose. There are ever so many visits which I have promised; I could stay with you and your Aunt Mary at Lenox if she goes there, for a while, and I have always wished to spend a summer in town; but mamma did not encourage that at all. In the evening papa gave her a letter which had come from Mr. Dockum, the man who takes care of Aunt Katharine's place, and the most charming idea came into my head, and I said I meant to spend my summer in Deephaven.

"At first they laughed at me, and then they said I might go if I chose, and at last they thought nothing could be pleasanter, and mamma wishes she were going herself. I asked if she did not think you would be the best person to keep me company, and she does, and papa announced that he was just going to suggest my asking you. I am to take Ann and Maggie, who will be overjoyed, for they came from that part of the country, and the other servants are to go with Aunt Anna, and old Nora will come to take care of this house, as she always does. Perhaps you and I will come up to town once in a while for a few days. We shall have such jolly housekeeping. Mamma and I sat up very late last night, and everything is planned. Mr. Dockum's house is very near Aunt Katharine's, so we shall not be lonely; though I know you're no more afraid of that than I. O Helen, won't you go?"

Do you think it took me long to decide?

Mr. and Mrs. Lancaster sailed the 10th of June, and my Aunt Mary went to spend her summer among the Berkshire Hills, so I was at the Lancasters' ready to welcome Kate when she came home, after having said good by to her father and mother. We meant to go to Deephaven in a week, but were obliged to stay in town longer. Boston was nearly deserted of our friends at the last, and we used to take quiet walks in the cool of the evening after dinner, up and down the street, or sit on the front steps in company with the servants left in charge of the other houses, who also sometimes walked up and down and looked at us wonderingly. We had much shopping to do in the daytime, for there was a probability of our spending many days in doors, and as we were not to be near any large town, and did not mean to come to Boston for weeks at least, there was a great deal to be remembered and arranged. We enjoyed making our plans, and deciding what we should want, and going to the shops together. I think we felt most important the day we conferred with Ann and made out a list of the provisions which must be ordered. This was being housekeepers in earnest. Mr. Dockum happened to come to town, and we sent Ann and Maggie, with most of our boxes, to Deephaven in his company a day or two before we were ready to go ourselves, and when we reached there the house was opened and in order for us.

On our journey to Deephaven we left the railway twelve miles from that place, and took passage in a stage-coach. There was only one passenger beside ourselves. She was a very large, thin, weather-beaten woman, and looked so tired and lonesome and good-natured, that I could not help saying it was very dusty; and she was apparently delighted to answer that she should think everybody was sweeping, and she always felt, after being in the cars a while, as if she had been

taken all to pieces and left in the different places. And this was
the beginning of our friendship with Mrs. Kew.

After this conversation we looked industriously out of the
window into the pastures and pine-woods. I had given up my
seat to her, for I do not mind riding backward in the least,
and you would have thought I had done her the greatest favor of her life. I think she was the most grateful of women,
and I was often reminded of a remark one of my friends once
made about some one: "If you give Bessie a half-sheet of
letter-paper, she behaves to you as if it were the most exquisite of presents!" Kate and I had some fruit left in our lunch-
basket, and divided it with Mrs. Kew, but after the first
mouthful we looked at each other in dismay. "Lemons with
oranges' clothes on, are n't they?" said she, as Kate threw hers
out of the window, and mine went after it for company; and
after this we began to be very friendly indeed. We both liked
the odd woman, there was something so straightforward and
kindly about her.

"Are you going to Deephaven, dear?" she asked me, and
then: "I wonder if you are going to stay long? All summer?
Well, that 's clever! I do hope you will come out to the Light
to see me; young folks 'most always like my place. Most likely
your friends will fetch you."

"Do you know the Brandon house?" asked Kate.

"Well as I do the meeting-house. There! I wonder I did n't
know from the beginning, but I have been a trying all the
way to settle it who you could be. I 've been up country some
weeks, stopping with my mother, and she seemed so set to
have me stay till strawberry-time, and would hardly let me
come now. You see she 's getting to be old; why, every time
I 've come away for fifteen years she 's said it was the last time
I 'd ever see her, but she 's a dreadful smart woman of her age.
'He' wrote me some o' Mrs. Lancaster's folks were going to
take the Brandon house this summer; and so you are the
ones? It 's a sightly old place; I used to go and see Miss
Katharine. She must have left a power of china-ware. She set
a great deal by the house, and she kept everything just as it
used to be in her mother's day."

"Then you live in Deephaven too?" asked Kate.

"I 've been here the better part of my life. I was raised up among the hills in Vermont, and I shall always be a real up-country woman if I live here a hundred years. The sea does n't come natural to me, it kind of worries me, though you won't find a happier woman than I be, 'long shore. When I was first married 'he' had a schooner and went to the banks, and once he was off on a whaling voyage, and I hope I may never come to so long a three years as those were again, though I was up to mother's. Before I was married he had been 'most everywhere. When he came home that time from whaling, he found I'd taken it so to heart that he said he'd never go off again, and then he got the chance to keep Deephaven Light, and we've lived there seventeen years come January. There is n't great pay, but then nobody tries to get it away from us, and we've got so's to be contented, if it is lonesome in winter."

"Do you really live in the lighthouse? I remember how I used to beg to be taken out there when I was a child, and how I used to watch for the light at night," said Kate, enthusiastically.

So began a friendship which we both still treasure, for knowing Mrs. Kew was one of the pleasantest things which happened to us in that delightful summer, and she used to do so much for our pleasure, and was so good to us. When we went out to the lighthouse for the last time to say good by, we were very sorry girls indeed. We had no idea until then how much she cared for us, and her affection touched us very much. She told us that she loved us as if we belonged to her, and begged us not to forget her,—as if we ever could!—and to remember that there was always a home and a warm heart for us if she were alive. Kate and I have often agreed that few of our acquaintances are half so entertaining. Her comparisons were most striking and amusing, and her comments upon the books she read—for she was a great reader—were very shrewd and clever, and always to the point. She was never out of temper, even when the barrels of oil were being rolled across her kitchen floor. And she was such a wise woman! This stage-ride, which we expected to find tiresome, we enjoyed very much, and we were glad to think, when the coach stopped, and "he" came to meet her with great satisfaction, that we had one friend in Deephaven at all events.

I liked the house from my very first sight of it. It stood behind a row of poplars which were as green and flourishing as the poplars which stand in stately processions in the fields around Quebec. It was an imposing great white house, and the lilacs were tall, and there were crowds of rose-bushes not yet out of bloom; and there were box borders, and there were great elms at the side of the house and down the road. The hall door stood wide open, and my hostess turned to me as we went in, with one of her sweet, sudden smiles. "Won't we have a good time, Nelly?" said she. And I thought we should.

So our summer's housekeeping began in most pleasant fashion. It was just at sunset, and Ann's and Maggie's presence made the house seem familiar at once. Maggie had been unpacking for us, and there was a delicious supper ready for the hungry girls. Later in the evening we went down to the shore, which was not very far away; the fresh sea-air was welcome after the dusty day, and it seemed so quiet and pleasant in Deephaven.

The Brandon House and the Lighthouse

I DO not know that the Brandon house is really very remarkable, but I never have been in one that interested me in the same way. Kate used to recount to select audiences at school some of her experiences with her Aunt Katharine, and it was popularly believed that she once carried down some indestructible picture-books when they were first in fashion, and the old lady basted them for her to hem round the edges at the rate of two a day. It may have been fabulous. It was impossible to imagine any children in the old place; everything was for grown people; even the stair-railing was too high to slide down on. The chairs looked as if they had been put, at the furnishing of the house, in their places, and there they meant to remain. The carpets were particularly interesting, and I remember Kate's pointing out to me one day a great square figure in one, and telling me she used to keep house there with her dolls for lack of a better play-house, and if one of them chanced to fall outside the boundary stripe, it was immediately put to bed with a cold. It is a house with great possibilities; it might easily be made charming. There are four very large rooms on the lower floor, and six above, a wide hall in each story, and a fascinating garret over the whole, where were many mysterious old chests and boxes, in one of which we found Kate's grandmother's love-letters; and you may be sure the vista of rummages which Mr. Lancaster had laughed about was explored to its very end. The rooms all have elaborate cornices, and the lower hall is very fine, with an archway dividing it, and panellings of all sorts, and a great door at each end, through which the lilacs in front and the old pensioner plum-trees in the garden are seen exchanging bows and gestures. Coming from the Lancasters' high city house, it did not seem as if we had to go up stairs at all there, for every step of the stairway is so broad and low, and you come half-way to a square landing with an old straight-backed chair in each farther corner; and between them a large, round-topped window, with a cushioned seat, looking out on the garden and the village, the hills far inland, and the sunset be-

yond all. Then you turn and go up a few more steps to the
upper hall, where we used to stay a great deal. There were
more old chairs and a pair of remarkable sofas, on which we
used to deposit the treasures collected in our wanderings.
The wide window which looks out on the lilacs and the sea
was a favorite seat of ours. Facing each other on either side
of it are two old secretaries, and one of them we ascertained
to be the hiding-place of secret drawers, in which may be
found valuable records deposited by ourselves one rainy day
when we first explored it. We wrote, between us, a tragic
"journal" on some yellow old letter-paper we found in the
desk. We put it in the most hidden drawer by itself, and flat-
ter ourselves that it will be regarded with great interest some
time or other. Of one of the front rooms, "the best chamber," we stood rather in dread. It is very remarkable that
there seem to be no ghost-stories connected with any part of
the house, particularly this. We are neither of us nervous;
but there is certainly something dismal about the room. The
huge curtained bed and immense easy-chairs, windows, and
everything were draped in some old-fashioned kind of white
cloth which always seemed to be waving and moving about
of itself. The carpet was most singularly colored with dark
reds and indescribable grays and browns, and the pattern,
after a whole summer's study, could never be followed with
one's eye. The paper was captured in a French prize somewhere some time in the last century, and part of the figure
was shaggy, and therein little spiders found habitation, and
went visiting their acquaintances across the shiny places. The
color was an unearthly pink and a forbidding maroon, with
dim white spots, which gave it the appearance of having
moulded. It made you low-spirited to look long in the mirror; and the great lounge one could not have cheerful associations with, after hearing that Miss Brandon herself did not
like it, having seen so many of her relatives lie there dead.
There were fantastic china ornaments from Bible subjects on
the mantel, and the only picture was one of the Maid of
Orleans tied with an unnecessarily strong rope to a very
stout stake. The best parlor we also rarely used, because
all the portraits which hung there had for some unaccountable reason taken a violent dislike to us, and followed us

suspiciously with their eyes. The furniture was stately and very uncomfortable, and there was something about the room which suggested an invisible funeral.

There is not very much to say about the dining-room. It was not specially interesting, though the sea was in sight from one of the windows. There were some old Dutch pictures on the wall, so dark that one could scarcely make out what they were meant to represent, and one or two engravings. There was a huge sideboard, for which Kate had brought down from Boston Miss Brandon's own silver which had stood there for so many years, and looked so much more at home and in place than any other possibly could have looked, and Kate also found in the closet the three great decanters with silver labels chained round their necks, which had always been the companions of the tea-service in her aunt's lifetime. From the little closets in the sideboard there came a most significant odor of cake and wine whenever one opened the doors. We used Miss Brandon's beautiful old blue India china which she had given to Kate, and which had been carefully packed all winter. Kate sat at the head and I at the foot of the round table, and I must confess that we were apt to have either a feast or a famine, for at first we often forgot to provide our dinners. If this were the case Maggie was sure to serve us with most derisive elegance, and make us wait for as much ceremony as she thought necessary for one of Mrs. Lancaster's dinner-parties.

The west parlor was our favorite room down stairs. It had a great fireplace framed in blue and white Dutch tiles which ingeniously and instructively represented the careers of the good and the bad man; the starting-place of each being a very singular cradle in the centre at the top. The last two of the series are very high art: a great coffin stands in the foreground of each, and the virtuous man is being led off by two disagreeable-looking angels, while the wicked one is hastening from an indescribable but unpleasant assemblage of claws and horns and eyes which is rapidly advancing from the distance, open-mouthed, and bringing a chain with it.

There was a large cabinet holding all the small curiosities and knick-knacks there seemed to be no other place for, — odd china figures and cups and vases, unaccountable Chinese carvings and exquisite corals and sea-shells, minerals and Swiss wood-work, and articles of *vertu* from the South Seas. Underneath were stored boxes of letters and old magazines; for this was one of the houses where nothing seems to have been thrown away. In one parting we found a parcel of old manuscript sermons, the existence of which was a mystery, until Kate remembered there had been a gifted son of the house who entered the ministry and soon died. The windows had each a pane of stained glass, and on the wide sills we used to put our immense bouquets of field-flowers. There was one place which I liked and sat in more than any other. The chimney filled nearly the whole side of the room, all but this little corner, where there was just room for a very comfortable high-backed cushioned chair, and a narrow window where I always had a bunch of fresh green ferns in a tall champagne-glass. I used to write there often, and always sat there when Kate sang and played. She sent for a tuner, and used to successfully coax the long-imprisoned music from the antiquated piano, and sing for her visitors by the hour. She almost always sang her oldest songs, for they seemed most in keeping with everything about us. I used to fancy that the portraits liked our being there. There was one young girl who seemed solitary and forlorn among the rest in the room, who were all middle-aged. For their part they looked amiable, but rather unhappy, as if she had come in and interrupted their conversation. We both grew very fond of her, and it seemed, when we went in the last morning on purpose to take leave of her, as if she looked at us imploringly. She was soon afterward boxed up, and now enjoys society after her own heart in Kate's room in Boston.

There was the largest sofa I ever saw opposite the fireplace; it must have been brought in in pieces, and built in the room. It was broad enough for Kate and me to lie on together, and very high and square; but there was a pile of soft cushions at one end. We used to enjoy it greatly in September, when the evenings were long and cool, and we had many candles, and a fire—and crickets too—on the hearth, and the dear dog lying on the rug. I remember one rainy night, just before Miss Tennant and Kitty Bruce went away; we had a real drift-wood fire, and blew out the lights and told stories. Miss Margaret

knows so many and tells them so well. Kate and I were unusually entertaining, for we became familiar with the family
record of the town, and could recount marvellous adventures
by land and sea, and ghost-stories by the dozen. We had never
either of us been in a society consisting of so many travelled
people! Hardly a man but had been the most of his life at sea.
Speaking of ghost-stories, I must tell you that once in the
summer two Cambridge girls who were spending a week with
us unwisely enticed us into giving some thrilling recitals,
which nearly frightened them out of their wits, and Kate and
I were finally in terror ourselves. We had all been on the sofa
in the dark, singing and talking, and were waiting in great
suspense after I had finished one of such particular horror that
I declared it should be the last, when we heard footsteps on
the hall stairs. There were lights in the dining-room which
shone faintly through the half-closed door, and we saw something white and shapeless come slowly down, and clutched
each other's gowns in agony. It was only Kate's dog, who
came in and laid his head in her lap and slept peacefully. We
thought we could not sleep a wink after this, and I bravely
went alone out to the light to see my watch, and, finding it
was past twelve, we concluded to sit up all night and to go
down to the shore at sunrise, it would be so much easier than
getting up early some morning. We had been out rowing and
had taken a long walk the day before, and were obliged to
dance and make other slight exertions to keep ourselves awake
at one time. We lunched at two, and I never shall forget the
sunrise that morning; but we were singularly quiet and ab-
stracted that day, and indeed for several days after Deephaven
was "a land in which it seemed always afternoon," we breakfasted so late.

As Mrs. Kew had said, there was "a power of china." Kate
and I were convinced that the lives of her grandmothers must
have been spent in giving tea-parties. We counted ten sets of
cups, beside quantities of stray ones; and some member of the
family had evidently devoted her time to making a collection
of pitchers.

There was an escritoire in Miss Brandon's own room,
which we looked over one day. There was a little package of
letters; ship letters mostly, tied with a very pale and tired-

looking blue ribbon. They were in a drawer with a locket holding a faded miniature on ivory and a lock of brown hair, and there were also some dry twigs and bits of leaf which had long ago been bright wild-roses, such as still bloom among the Deephaven rocks. Kate said that she had often heard her mother wonder why her aunt never had cared to marry, for she had chances enough doubtless, and had been rich and handsome and finely educated. So there was a sailor lover after all, and perhaps he had been lost at sea and she faithfully kept the secret, never mourning outwardly. "And I always thought her the most matter-of-fact old lady," said Kate; "yet here's her romance, after all." We put the letters outside on a chair to read, but afterwards carefully replaced them, without untying them. I'm glad we did. There were other letters which we did read, and which interested us very much,— letters from her girl friends written in the boarding-school vacations, and just after she finished school. Those in one of the smaller packages were charming; it must have been such a bright, nice girl who wrote them! They were very few, and were tied with black ribbon, and marked on the outside in girlish writing: "My dearest friend, Dolly McAllister, died September 3, 1809, aged eighteen." The ribbon had evidently been untied and the letters read many times. One began: "My dear, delightful Kitten: I am quite overjoyed to find my father has business which will force him to go to Deephaven next week, and he kindly says if there be no more rain I may ride with him to see you. I will surely come, for if there is danger of spattering my gown, and he bids me stay at home, I shall go galloping after him and overtake him when it is too late to send me back. I have so much to tell you." I wish I knew more about the visit. Poor Miss Katharine! it made us sad to look over these treasures of her girlhood. There were her compositions and exercise-books; some samplers and queer little keepsakes; withered flowers and some pebbles and other things of like value, with which there was probably some pleasant association. "Only think of her keeping them all her days," said I to Kate. "I am continually throwing some relic of the kind away, because I forget why I have it!"

There was a box in the lower part which Kate was glad to find, for she had heard her mother wonder if some such things were not in existence. It held a crucifix and a mass-book and some rosaries, and Kate told me Miss Katharine's youngest and favorite brother had become a Roman Catholic while studying in Europe. It was a dreadful blow to the family; for in those days there could have been few deeper disgraces to the Brandon family than to have one of its sons go over to popery. Only Miss Katharine treated him with kindness, and after a time he disappeared without telling even her where he was going, and was only heard from indirectly once or twice afterward. It was a great grief to her. "And mamma knows," said Kate, "that she always had a lingering hope of his return, for one of the last times she saw Aunt Katharine before she was ill she spoke of soon going to be with all the rest, and said, 'Though your Uncle Henry, dear,'—and stopped and smiled sadly; 'you'll think me a very foolish old woman, but I never quite gave up thinking he might come home.'"

Mrs. Kew did the honors of the lighthouse thoroughly on our first visit; but I think we rarely went to see her that we did not make some entertaining discovery. Mr. Kew's nephew, a guileless youth of forty, lived with them, and the two men were of a mechanical turn and had invented numerous aids to housekeeping,—appendages to the stove, and fixtures on the walls for everything that could be hung up; catches in the floor to hold the doors open, and ingenious apparatus to close them; but, above all, a system of barring and bolting for the wide "fore door," which would have disconcerted an energetic battering-ram. After all this work being expended, Mrs. Kew informed us that it was usually wide open all night in summer weather. On the back of this door I discovered one day a row of marks, and asked their significance. It seemed that Mrs. Kew had attempted one summer to keep count of the number of people who inquired about the depredations of the neighbors' chickens. Mrs. Kew's bedroom was partly devoted to the fine arts. There was a large collection of likenesses of her relatives and friends on the wall, which was interesting in the extreme. Mrs. Kew was always much pleased to tell their names, and her remarks about any feature not exactly perfect were very searching and critical.

"That's my oldest brother's wife, Clorinthy Adams that was.
She's well featured, if it were not for her nose, and that looks
as if it had been thrown at her, and she wasn't particular
about having it on firm, in hopes of getting a better one. She
sets by her looks, though."

There were often sailing-parties that came there from up
and down the coast. One day Kate and I were spending the
afternoon at the Light; we had been fishing, and were sitting
in the doorway listening to a reminiscence of the winter Mrs.
Kew kept school at the Four Corners; saw a boatful coming,
and all lost our tempers. Mrs. Kew had a lame ankle, and
Kate offered to go up with the visitors. There were some girls
and young men who stood on the rocks awhile, and then
asked us, with much better manners than the people who usually came, if they could see the lighthouse, and Kate led the
way. She was dressed that day in a costume we both frequently wore, of gray skirts and blue sailor-jacket, and her
boots were much the worse for wear. The celebrated Lancaster complexion was rather darkened by the sun. Mrs. Kew
expressed a wish to know what questions they would ask her,
and I followed after a few minutes. They seemed to have finished asking about the lantern, and to have become personal.

"Don't you get tired staying here?"

"No, indeed!" said Kate.

"Is that your sister down stairs?"

"No, I have no sister."

"I should think you would wish she was. Aren't you ever
lonesome?"

"Everybody is, sometimes," said Kate.

"But it's such a lonesome place!" said one of the girls. "I
should think you would get work away. I live in Boston.
Why, it's so awful quiet! nothing but the water, and the
wind, when it blows; and I think either of them is worse than
nothing. And only this little bit of a rocky place! I should
want to go to walk."

I heard Kate pleasantly refuse the offer of pay for her services, and then they began to come down the steep stairs
laughing and chattering with each other. Kate stayed behind
to close the doors and leave everything all right, and the girl
who had talked the most waited too, and when they were on

the stairs just above me, and the others out of hearing, she said, "You're real good to show us the things. I guess you'll think I'm silly, but I do like you ever so much! I wish you would come to Boston. I'm in a real nice store,—H——'s, on Winter Street; and they will want new saleswomen in October. Perhaps you could be at my counter. I'd teach you, and you could board with me. I've got a real comfortable room, and I suppose I might have more things, for I get good pay; but I like to send money home to mother. I'm at my aunt's now, but I am going back next Monday, and if you will tell me what your name is, I'll find out for certain about the place, and write you. My name's Mary Wendell."

I knew by Kate's voice that this had touched her. "You are very kind; thank you heartily," said she; "but I cannot go and work with you. I should like to know more about you. I live in Boston too; my friend and I are staying over in Deephaven for the summer only." And she held out her hand to the girl, whose face had changed from its first expression of earnest good-humor to a very startled one; and when she noticed Kate's hand, and a ring of hers, which had been turned round, she looked really frightened.

"O, will you please excuse me?" said she, blushing. "I ought to have known better; but you showed us round so willing, and I never thought of your not living here. I didn't mean to be rude."

"Of course you did not, and you were not. I am very glad you said it, and glad you like me," said Kate; and just then the party called the girl, and she hurried away, and I joined Kate. "Then you heard it all. That was worth having!" said she. "She was such an honest little soul, and I mean to look for her when I get home."

Sometimes we used to go out to the Light early in the morning with the fishermen who went that way to the fishing-grounds, but we usually made the voyage early in the afternoon if it were not too hot, and we went fishing off the rocks or sat in the house with Mrs. Kew, who often related some of her Vermont experiences, or Mr. Kew would tell us surprising sea-stories and ghost-stories like a story-book sailor. Then we would have an unreasonably good supper and afterward climb the ladder to the lantern to see the lamps lighted, and sit there for a while watching the ships and the sunset. Almost all the coasters came in sight of Deephaven, and the sea outside the light was their grand highway. Twice from the lighthouse we saw a yacht squadron like a flock of great white birds. As for the sunsets, it used to seem often as if we were near the heart of them, for the sea all around us caught the color of the clouds, and though the glory was wonderful, I remember best one still evening when there was a bank of heavy gray clouds in the west shutting down like a curtain, and the sea was silver-colored. You could look under and beyond the curtain of clouds into the palest, clearest yellow sky. There was a little black boat in the distance drifting slowly, climbing one white wave after another, as if it were bound out into that other world beyond. But presently the sun came from behind the clouds, and the dazzling golden light changed the look of everything, and it was the time then to say one thought it a beautiful sunset; while before one could only keep very still, and watch the boat, and wonder if heaven would not be somehow like that far, faint color, which was neither sea nor sky.

When we came down from the lighthouse and it grew late, we would beg for an hour or two longer on the water, and row away in the twilight far out from land, where, with our faces turned from the Light, it seemed as if we were alone, and the sea shoreless; and as the darkness closed round us softly, we watched the stars come out, and were always glad to see Kate's star and my star, which we had chosen when we were children. I used long ago to be sure of one thing,—that, however far away heaven might be, it could not be out of sight of the stars. Sometimes in the evening we waited out at sea for the moonrise, and then we would take the oars again and go slowly in, once in a while singing or talking, but oftenest silent.

My Lady Brandon and the Widow Jim

WHEN it was known that we had arrived in Deephaven, the people who had known Miss Brandon so well, and Mrs. Lancaster also, seemed to consider themselves Kate's friends by inheritance, and were exceedingly polite to us, in either calling upon us or sending pleasant messages. Before the first week had ended we had no lack of society. They were not strangers to Kate, to begin with, and as for me, I think it is easy for me to be contented, and to feel at home anywhere. I have the good fortune and the misfortune to belong to the navy,—that is, my father does,—and my life has been consequently an unsettled one, except during the years of my school life, when my friendship with Kate began.

I think I should be happy in any town if I were living there with Kate Lancaster. I will not praise my friend as I can praise her, or say half the things I might say honestly. She is so fresh and good and true, and enjoys life so heartily. She is so childlike, without being childish; and I do not tell you that she is faultless, but when she makes mistakes she is sorrier and more ready to hopefully try again than any girl I know. Perhaps you would like to know something about us, but I am not writing Kate's biography and my own, only telling you of one summer which we spent together. Sometimes in Deephaven we were between six and seven years old, but at other times we have felt irreparably grown-up, and as if we carried a crushing weight of care and duty. In reality we are both twenty-four, and it is a pleasant age, though I think next year is sure to be pleasanter, for we do not mind growing older, since we have lost nothing that we mourn about, and are gaining so much. I shall be glad if you learn to know Kate a little in my stories. It is not that I am fond of her and endow her with imagined virtues and graces; no one can fail to see how unaffected she is, or not notice her thoughtfulness and generosity and her delightful fun, which never has a trace of coarseness or silliness. It was very pleasant having her for one's companion, for she has an unusual power of winning people's confidence, and of knowing with surest instinct how to meet them on their own ground. It is the girl's being so genuinely sympathetic and interested which makes every one ready to talk to her and be friends with her; just as the sunshine makes it easy for flowers to grow which the chilly winds hinder. She is not polite for the sake of seeming polite, but polite for the sake of being kind, and there is not a particle of what Hugh Miller justly calls the insolence of condescension about her; she is not brilliantly talented, yet she does everything in a charming fashion of her own; she is not profoundly learned, yet she knows much of which many wise people are ignorant, and while she is a patient scholar in both little things and great, she is no less a teacher to all her friends,—dear Kate Lancaster!

We knew that we were considered Miss Brandon's representatives in Deephaven society, and this was no slight responsibility, as she had received much honor and respect. We heard again and again what a loss she had been to the town, and we tried that summer to do nothing to lessen the family reputation, and to give pleasure as well as take it, though we were singularly persistent in our pursuit of a good time. I grew much interested in what I heard of Miss Brandon, and it seems to me that it is a great privilege to have an elderly person in one's neighborhood, in town or country, who is proud, and conservative, and who lives in stately fashion; who is intolerant of sham and of useless novelties, and clings to the old ways of living and behaving as if it were part of her religion. There is something immensely respectable about the gentlewomen of the old school. They ignore all bustle and flashiness, and the conceit of the younger people, who act as if at last it had been time for them to appear and manage this world as it ought to have been managed before. Their position in modern society is much like that of the King's Chapel in its busy street in Boston. It perhaps might not have been easy to approach Miss Brandon, but I am sure that if I had visited in Deephaven during her lifetime I should have been very proud if I had been asked to take tea at her house, and should have liked to speak afterward of my acquaintance with her. It would have been impossible not to pay her great deference; it is a pleasure to think that she must have found this world a most polite world, and have had the highest opinion of its good manners. *Noblesse oblige:* that is true in more ways than one!

I cannot help wondering if those of us who will be left by and by to represent our own generation will seem to have such superior elegance of behavior; if we shall receive so much respect and be so much valued. It is hard to imagine it. We know that the world gains new refinements and a better culture; but to us there never will be such imposing ladies and gentlemen as these who belong to the old school.

The morning after we reached Deephaven we were busy up stairs, and there was a determined blow at the knocker of the front door. I went down to see who was there, and had the pleasure of receiving our first caller. She was a prim little old woman who looked pleased and expectant, who wore a neat cap and front, and whose eyes were as bright as black beads. She wore no bonnet, and had thrown a little three-cornered shawl, with palm-leaf figures, over her shoulders; and it was evident that she was a near neighbor. She was very short and straight and thin, and so quick that she darted like a pickerel when she moved about. It occurred to me at once that she was a very capable person, and had "faculty," and, dear me, how fast she talked! She hesitated a moment when she saw me, and dropped a fragment of a courtesy. "Miss Lan'k'ster?" said she, doubtfully.

"No," said I, "I'm Miss Denis: Miss Lancaster is at home, though: come in, won't you?"

"O Mrs. Patton!" said Kate, who came down just then. "How very kind of you to come over so soon! I should have gone to see you to-day. I was asking Mrs. Kew last night if you were here."

"Land o' compassion!" said Mrs. Patton, as she shook Kate's hand delightedly. "Where'd ye s'pose I'd be, dear? I ain't like to move away from Deephaven now, after I've held by the place so long, I've got as many roots as the big ellum. Well, I should know you were a Brandon, no matter where I see you. You've got a real Brandon look; tall and straight, ain't you? It's four or five years since I saw you, except once at church, and once you went by, down to the shore, I suppose. It was a windy day in the spring of the year."

"I remember it very well," said Kate. "Those were both

visits of only a day or two, and I was here at Aunt Katharine's funeral, and went away that same evening. Do you remember once I was here in the summer for a longer visit, five or six years ago, and I helped you pick currants in the garden? You had a very old mug."

"Now, whoever would ha' thought o' your rec'lecting that?" said Mrs. Patton. "Yes. I had that mug because it was handy to carry about among the bushes, and then I'd empt' it into the basket as fast as I got it full. Your aunt always told me to pick all I wanted; she couldn't use 'em, but they used to make sights o' currant wine in old times. I s'pose that mug would be considerable of a curiosity to anybody that wasn't used to seeing it round. My grand'ther Joseph Toggerson —my mother was a Toggerson—picked it up on the long sands in a wad of sea-weed: strange it wasn't broke, but it's tough; I've dropped it on the floor, many's the time, and it ain't even chipped. There's some Dutch reading on it and it's marked 1732. Now I shouldn't ha' thought you'd remembered that old mug, I declare. Your aunt she had a monstrous sight of chiny. She's told me where 'most all of it come from, but I expect I've forgot. My memory fails me a good deal by spells. If you hadn't come down I suppose your mother would have had the chiny packed up this spring,—what she didn't take with her after your aunt died. S'pose she hasn't made up her mind what to do with the house?"

"No," said Kate; "she wishes she could: it is a great puzzle to us."

"I hope you will find it in middling order," said Mrs. Patton, humbly. "Me and Mis' Dockum have done the best we knew,—opened the windows and let in the air and tried to keep it from getting damp. I fixed all the woollens with fresh camphire and tobacco the last o' the winter; you have to be dreadful careful in one o' these old houses, 'less everything gets creaking with moths in no time. Miss Katharine, how she did hate the sight of a moth-miller! There's something I'll speak about before I forget it: the mice have eat the backs of a pile o' old books that's stored away in the west chamber closet next to Miss Katharine's room, and I set a trap there, but it was older 'n the ten commandments, that trap was, and the spring's rusty. I guess you'd better get some new ones

and set round in different places, 'less the mice 'll pester you.
There ain't been no chance for 'em to get much of a living
'long through the winter, but they 'll be sure to come back
quick as they find there 's likely to be good board. I see your
aunt 's cat setting out on the front steps. She never was no
great of a mouser, but it went to my heart to see how pleased
she looks! Come right back, did n't she? How they do hold to
their old haunts!"

"Was that Miss Brandon's cat?" I asked, with great interest.
"She has been up stairs with us, but I supposed she belonged
to some neighbor, and had strayed in. She behaved as if she
felt at home, poor old pussy!"

"We must keep her here," said Kate.

"Mis' Dockum took her after your mother went off, and
Miss Katharine's maids," said Mrs. Patton; "but she told me
that it was a long spell before she seemed to feel contented.
She used to set on the steps and cry by the hour together, and
try to get in, to first one door and then another. I used to
think how bad Miss Katharine would feel; she set a great deal
by a cat, and she took notice of this as long as she did of
anything. Her mind failed her, you know. Great loss to Deephaven, she was. Proud woman, and some folks were scared of
her; but I always got along with her, and I would n't ask for
no kinder friend nor neighbor. I 've had my troubles, and I 've
seen the day I was suffering poor, and I could n't have
brought myself to ask town help nohow, but I wish ye 'd ha'
heared her scold me when she found it out; and she come
marching into my kitchen one morning, like a grenadier, and
says she, 'Why did n't you send and tell me how sick and poor
you are?' says she. And she said she 'd ha' been so glad to help
me all along, but she thought I had means, — everybody did;
and I see the tears in her eyes, but she was scolding me and
speaking as if she was dreadful mad. She made me comfortable, and she sent over one o' her maids to see to me, and got
the doctor, and a load o' stuff come up from the store, so I
did n't have to buy anything for a good many weeks. I got
better and so 's to work, but she never 'd let me say nothing
about it. I had a good deal o' trouble, and I thought I 'd lost
my health, but I had n't, and that was thirty or forty years
ago. There never was nothing going on at the great house

that she did n't have me over, sewing or cleaning or company; and I got so that I knew how she liked to have things done. I felt as if it was my own sister, though I never had one, when I was going over to help lay her out. She used to talk as free to me as she would to Miss Lorimer or Miss Carew. I s'pose ye ain't seen nothing o' them yet? She was a good Christian woman, Miss Katharine was. 'The memory of the just is blessed'; that 's what Mr. Lorimer said in his sermon the Sunday after she died, and there was n't a blood-relation there to hear it. I declare it looked pitiful to see that pew empty that ought to ha' been the mourners' pew. Your mother, Mis' Lancaster, had to go home Saturday, your father was going away sudden to Washington, I 've understood, and she come back again the first of the week. There! it did n't make no sort o' difference, p'r 'aps nobody thought of it but me. There had n't been anybody in the pew more than a couple o' times since she used to sit there herself, regular as Sunday come." And Mrs. Patton looked for a minute as if she were going to cry, but she changed her mind upon second thought.

"Your mother gave me most of Miss Katharine's clothes; this cap belonged to her, that I 've got on now; it 's 'most wore out, but it does for mornings."

"O," said Kate, "I have two new ones for you in one of my trunks! Mamma meant to choose them herself, but she had not time, and so she told me, and I think I found the kind she thought you would like."

"Now I 'm sure!" said Mrs. Patton, "if that ain't kind; you don't tell me that Mis' Lancaster thought of me just as she was going off? I shall set everything by them caps, and I 'm much obliged to you too, Miss Kate. I was just going to speak of that time you were here and saw the mug; you trimmed a cap for Miss Katharine to give me, real Boston style. I guess that box of cap-fixings is up on the top shelf of Miss Katharine's closet now, to the left hand," said Mrs. Patton, with wistful certainty. "She used to make her every-day caps herself, and she had some beautiful materials laid away that she never used. Some folks has laughed at me for being so particular 'bout wearing caps except for best, but I don't know 's it 's presuming beyond my station, and somehow I feel more respect for myself when I have a good cap on. I can't get over your mother's rec'lecting about me; and she sent me a handsome present o' money this spring for looking after the house. I never should have asked for a cent; it's a pleasure to me to keep an eye on it, out o' respect to your aunt. I was so pleased when I heard you were coming long o' your friend. I like to see the old place open; it was about as bad as having no meeting. I miss seeing the lights, and your aunt was a great hand for lighting up bright; the big hall lantern was lit every night, and she put it out when she went up stairs. She liked to go round same's if it was day. You see I forget all the time she was sick, and go back to the days when she was well and about the house. When her mind was failing her, and she was up stairs in her room, her eyesight seemed to be lost part of the time, and sometimes she'd tell us to get the lamp and a couple o' candles in the middle o' the day, and then she'd be as satisfied! But she used to take a notion to set in the dark, some nights, and think, I s'pose. I should have forty fits, if I undertook it. That was a good while ago; and do you rec'lect how she used to play the piano? She used to be a great hand to play when she was young."

"Indeed I remember it," said Kate, who told me afterward how her aunt used to sit at the piano in the twilight and play to herself. "She was formerly a skilful musician," said my friend, "though one would not have imagined she cared for music. When I was a child she used to play in company of an evening, and once when I was here one of her old friends asked for a tune, and she laughingly said that her day was over and her fingers were stiff; though I believe she might have played as well as ever then, if she had cared to try. But once in a while when she had been quiet all day and rather sad—I am ashamed that I used to think she was cross—she would open the piano and sit there until late, while I used to be enchanted by her memories of dancing-tunes, and old psalms, and marches and songs. There was one tune which I am sure had a history: there was a sweet wild cadence in it, and she would come back to it again and again, always going through with it in the same measured way. I have remembered so many things about my aunt since I have been here," said Kate, "which I hardly noticed and did not understand when they happened. I was afraid of her when I was a little girl, but I think if I had grown up sooner, I should have enjoyed her heartily. It never used to occur to me that she had a spark of tenderness or of sentiment, until just before she was ill, but I have been growing more fond of her ever since. I might have given her a great deal more pleasure. It was not long after I was through school that she became so feeble, and of course she liked best having mamma come to see her; one of us had to be at home. I have thought lately how careful one ought to be, to be kind and thoughtful to one's old friends. It is so soon too late to be good to them, and then one is always so sorry."

I must tell you more of Mrs. Patton; of course it was not long before we returned her call, and we were much entertained; we always liked to see our friends in their own houses. Her house was a little way down the road, unpainted and gambrel-roofed, but so low that the old lilac-bushes which clustered round it were as tall as the eaves. The Widow Jim (as nearly every one called her in distinction to the widow Jack Patton, who was a tailoress and lived at the other end of the town) was a very useful person. I suppose there must be her counterpart in all old New England villages. She sewed, and she made elaborate rugs, and she had a decided talent for making carpets,—if there were one to be made, which must have happened seldom. But there were a great many to be turned and made over in Deephaven, and she went to the Carews' and Lorimers' at house-cleaning time or in seasons of great festivity. She had no equal in sickness, and knew how to brew every old-fashioned dose and to make every variety of herb-tea, and when her nursing was put to an end by her patient's death, she was commander-in-chief at the funeral, and stood near the doorway to direct the mourning friends to their seats; and I have no reason to doubt that she sometimes even had the immense responsibility of making out the order of the procession, since she had all genealogy and relationship at her tongue's end. It was an awful thing in Deephaven, we found, if the precedence was wrongly assigned, and once we chanced to hear some bitter remarks because the cousins of the departed wife had been placed after the husband's relatives,—"the blood-relations ridin' behind them that was only kin by marriage! I don't wonder they felt hurt!" said the person who spoke; a most unselfish and unassuming soul, ordinarily.

Mrs. Patton knew everybody's secrets, but she told them judiciously if at all. She chattered all day to you as a sparrow twitters, and you did not tire of her; and Kate and I were never more agreeably entertained than when she told us of old times and of Kate's ancestors and their contemporaries; for her memory was wonderful, and she had either seen everything that had happened in Deephaven for a long time, or had received the particulars from reliable witnesses. She had known much trouble; her husband had been but small satisfaction to her, and it was not to be wondered at if she looked upon all proposed marriages with compassion. She was always early at church, and she wore the same bonnet that she had when Kate was a child; it was such a well-preserved, proper black straw bonnet, with discreet bows of ribbon, and a useful lace veil to protect it from the weather.

She showed us into the best room the first time we went to see her. It was the plainest little room, and very dull, and there was an exact sufficiency about its furnishings. Yet there was a certain dignity about it; it was unmistakably a best room, and not a place where one might make a litter or carry one's every-day work. You felt at once that somebody valued the prim old-fashioned chairs, and the two half-moon tables, and the thin carpet, which must have needed anxious stretching every spring to make it come to the edge of the floor. There were some mourning-pieces by way of decoration, inscribed with the names of Mrs. Patton's departed friends,— two worked in crewel to the memory of her father and mother, and two paper memorials, with the woman weeping under the willow at the side of a monument. They were all brown with age; and there was a sampler beside, worked by "Judith Beckett, aged ten," and all five were framed in slender black frames and hung very high on the walls. There was a rocking-chair which looked as if it felt too grand for use, and considered itself imposing. It tilted far back on its rockers, and was bent forward at the top to make one's head uncomfortable. It need not have troubled itself; nobody would ever wish to sit there. It was such a big rocking-chair, and Mrs. Patton was proud of it; always generously urging her guests to enjoy its comfort, which was imaginary with her, as she was so short that she could hardly have climbed into it without assistance.

Mrs. Patton was a little ceremonious at first, but soon recovered herself and told us a great deal which we were glad to hear. I asked her once if she had not always lived at Deephaven. "Here and beyond East Parish," said she. "Mr. Patton, —that was my husband,—he owned a good farm there when I married him, but I come back here again after he died; place was all mortgaged. I never got a cent, and I was poorer than when I started. I worked harder 'n ever I did before or since to keep things together, but 't was n't any kind o' use. Your mother knows all about it, Miss Kate,"—as if we might not be willing to believe it on her authority. "I come back here a widow and destitute, and I tell you the world looked fair to me when I left this house first to go over there. Don't you run no risks, you 're better off as you be, dears. But land sakes alive, 'he' did n't mean no hurt! and he set everything by me when he was himself. I don't make no scruples of speaking about it, everybody knows how it was, but I did go through with everything. I never knew what the day would bring forth," said the widow, as if this were the first time she had had a chance to tell her sorrows to a sympathizing audience. She did not seem to mind talking about the troubles of her married life any more than a soldier minds telling the story of his campaigns, and dwells with pride on the worst battle of all.

Her favorite subject always was Miss Brandon, and after a pause she said that she hoped we were finding everything right in the house; she had meant to take up the carpet in the best spare room, but it did n't seem to need it; it was taken up the year before, and the room had not been used since, there was not a mite of dust under it last time. And Kate assured her, with an appearance of great wisdom, that she did not think it could be necessary at all.

"I come home and had a good cry yesterday after I was over to see you," said Mrs. Patton, and I could not help wondering if she really could cry, for she looked so perfectly dried up, so dry that she might rustle in the wind. "Your aunt had been failin' so long that just after she died it was a relief, but

I 've got so 's to forget all about that, and I miss her as she used to be; it seemed as if you had stepped into her place, and you look some as she used to when she was young."

"You must miss her," said Kate, "and I know how much she used to depend upon you. You were very kind to her."

"I sat up with her the night she died," said the widow, with mournful satisfaction. "I have lived neighbor to her all my life except the thirteen years I was married, and there was n't a week I was n't over to the great house except I was off to a distance taking care of the sick. When she got to be feeble she always wanted me to 'tend to the cleaning and to see to putting the canopies and curtains on the bedsteads, and she would n't trust nobody but me to handle some of the best china. I used to say, 'Miss Katharine, why don't you have some young folks come and stop with you? There 's Mis' Lancaster's daughter a growing up'; but she did n't seem to care for nobody but your mother. You would n't believe what a hand she used to be for company in her younger days. Surprisin' how folks alters. When I first rec'lect her much she was as straight as an arrow, and she used to go to Boston visiting and come home with the top of the fashion. She always did dress elegant. It used to be gay here, and she was always going down to the Lorimers' or the Carews' to tea, and they coming here. Her sister was married; she was a good deal older; but some of her brothers were at home. There was your grandfather and Mr. Henry. I don't think she ever got it over, — his disappearing so. There were lots of folks then that 's dead and gone, and they used to have their card-parties, and old Cap'n Manning — he 's dead and gone — used to have 'em all to play whist every fortnight, sometimes three or four tables, and they always had cake and wine handed round, or the cap'n made some punch, like 's not, with oranges in it, and lemons; *he* knew how! He was a bachelor to the end of his days, the old cap'n was, but he used to entertain real handsome. I rec'lect one night they was a playin' after the wine was brought in, and he upset his glass all over Miss Martha Lorimer's invisible-green watered silk, and spoilt the better part of two breadths. She sent right over for me early the next morning to see if I knew of anything to take out the spots, but I did n't, though I can take grease out o' most any material. We tried clear alcohol, and saleratus-water, and hartshorn, and pouring water through, and heating of it, and when we got through it was worse than when we started. She felt dreadful bad about it, and at last she says, 'Judith, we won't work over it any more, but if you 'll give me a day some time or 'nother, we 'll rip it up and make a quilt of it.' I see that quilt last time I was in Miss Rebecca's north chamber. Miss Martha was her aunt; you never saw her; she was dead and gone before your day. It was a silk old Cap'n Peter Lorimer, her brother, who left 'em his money, brought home from sea, and she had worn it for best and second best eleven year. It looked as good as new, and she never would have ripped it up if she could have matched it. I said it seemed to be a shame, but it was a curi's figure. Cap'n Manning fetched her one to pay for it the next time he went to Boston. She did n't want to take it, but he would n't take no for an answer; he was free-handed, the cap'n was. I helped 'em make it 'long of Mary Ann Simms the dressmaker,—she 's dead and gone too,—the time it was made. It was brown, and a beautiful-looking piece, but it wore shiny, and she made a double-gown of it before she died."

Mrs. Patton brought Kate and me some delicious old-fashioned cake with much spice in it, and told us it was made by old Mrs. Chantrey Brandon's receipt which she got in England, that it would keep a year, and she always kept a loaf by her, now that she could afford it; she supposed we knew Miss Katharine had named her in her will long before she was sick. "It has put me beyond fear of want," said Mrs. Patton. "I won't deny that I used to think it would go hard with me when I got so old I could n't earn my living. You see I never laid up but a little, and it 's hard for a woman who comes of respectable folks to be a pauper in her last days; but your aunt, Miss Kate, she thought of it too, and I 'm sure I 'm thankful to be so comfortable, and to stay in my house, which I could n't have done, like 's not. Miss Rebecca Lorimer said to me after I got news of the will, 'Why, Mis' Patton, you don't suppose your friends would ever have let you want!' And I says, 'My friends are kind,— the Lord bless 'em!—but I feel better to be able to do for myself than to be beholden.' "

After this long call we went down to the post-office, and coming home stopped for a while in the old burying-ground, which we had noticed the day before; and we sat for the first time on the great stone in the wall, in the shade of a maple-tree, where we so often waited afterward for the stage to come with the mail, or rested on our way home from a walk. It was a comfortable perch; we used to read our letters there, I remember.

I must tell you a little about the Deephaven burying-ground, for its interest was inexhaustible, and I do not know how much time we may have spent in reading the long epitaphs on the grave-stones and trying to puzzle out the inscriptions, which were often so old and worn that we could only trace a letter here and there. It was a neglected corner of the world, and there were straggling sumachs and acacias scattered about the enclosure, while a row of fine old elms marked the boundary of two sides. The grass was long and tangled, and most of the stones leaned one way or the other, and some had fallen flat. There were a few handsome old family monuments clustered in one corner, among which the one that marked Miss Brandon's grave looked so new and fresh that it seemed inappropriate. "It should have been dingy to begin with, like the rest," said Kate one day; "but I think it will make itself look like its neighbors as soon as possible."

There were many stones which were sacred to the memory of men who had been lost at sea, almost always giving the name of the departed ship, which was so kept in remembrance; and one felt as much interest in the ship Starlight, supposed to have foundered off the Cape of Good Hope, as in the poor fellow who had the ill luck to be one of her crew. There were dozens of such inscriptions, and there were other stones perpetuating the fame of Honourable gentlemen who had been members of His Majesty's Council, or surveyors of His Majesty's Woods, or King's Officers of Customs for the town of Deephaven. Some of the epitaphs were beautiful, showing that tenderness for the friends who had died, that longing to do them justice, to fully acknowledge their virtues and dearness, which is so touching, and so unmistakable even under the stiff, quaint expressions and formal words which were thought suitable to be chiselled on the stones, so soon to be looked at carelessly by the tearless eyes of strangers. We often used to notice names, and learn their history from the old people whom we knew, and in this way we heard many stories which we never shall forget. It is wonderful, the romance and tragedy and adventure which one may find in a quiet old-fashioned country town, though to heartily enjoy the every-day life one must care to study life and character, and must find pleasure in thought and observation of simple things, and have an instinctive, delicious interest in what to other eyes is unflavored dulness.

To go back to Mrs. Patton; on our way home, after our first call upon her, we stopped to speak to Mrs. Dockum, who mentioned that she had seen us going in to the "Widow Jim's."

"Willin' woman," said Mrs. Dockum, "always been respected; got an uncommon facility o' speech. I never saw such a hand to talk, but then she has something to say, which ain't the case with everybody. Good neighbor, does according to her means always. Dreadful tough time of it with her husband, shif'less and drunk all his time. Noticed that dent in the side of her forehead, I s'pose? That's where he liked to have killed her; slung a stone bottle at her."

"*What!*" said Kate and I, very much shocked.

"She don't like to have it inquired about; but she and I were sitting up with 'Manda Damer one night, and she gave me the particulars. I knew he did it, for she had a fit o' sickness afterward. Had sliced cucumbers for breakfast that morning; he was very partial to them, and he wanted some vinegar. Happened to be two bottles in the cellar-way; were just alike, and one of 'em was vinegar and the other had sperrit in it at haying-time. He takes up the wrong one and pours on quick, and out come the hayseed and flies, and he give the bottle a sling, and it hit her there where you see the scar; might put the end of your finger into the dent. He said he meant to break the bottle ag'in the door, but it went slant-wise, sort of. I don' know, I'm sure" (meditatively). "She said he was good-natured; it was early in the mornin', and he hadn't had time to get upset; but he had a high temper naturally, and so much drink hadn't made it much better. She had good prospects when she married him. Six-foot-two and red cheeks and straight as a Noroway pine; had a good property from his father, and his mother come of a good family, but he died in debt; drank like a fish. Yes, 't was a shame, nice woman; good consistent church-member; always been respected; useful among the sick."

Deephaven Society

IT WAS curious to notice, in this quaint little fishing-village by the sea, how clearly the gradations of society were defined. The place prided itself most upon having been long ago the residence of one Governor Chantrey, who was a rich ship-owner and East India merchant, and whose fame and magnificence were almost fabulous. It was a never-ceasing regret that his house should have burned down after he died, and there is no doubt that if it were still standing it would rival any ruin of the Old World.

The elderly people, though laying claim to no slight degree of present consequence, modestly ignored it, and spoke with pride of the grand way in which life was carried on by their ancestors, the Deephaven families of old times. I think Kate and I were assured at least a hundred times that Governor Chantrey kept a valet, and his wife, Lady Chantrey, kept a maid, and that the governor had an uncle in England who was a baronet; and I believe this must have been why our friends felt so deep an interest in the affairs of the English nobility: they no doubt felt themselves entitled to seats near the throne itself. There were formerly five families who kept their coaches in Deephaven; there were balls at the governor's, and regal entertainments at other of the grand mansions; there is not a really distinguished person in the country who will not prove to have been directly or indirectly connected with Deephaven. We were shown the cellar of the Chantrey house, and the terraces, and a few clumps of lilacs, and the grand rows of elms. There are still two of the governor's warehouses left, but his ruined wharves are fast disappearing, and are almost deserted, except by small barefooted boys who sit on the edges to fish for sea-perch when the tide comes in. There is an imposing monument in the burying-ground to the great man and his amiable consort. I am sure that if there were any surviving relatives of the governor they would receive in Deephaven far more deference than is consistent with the principles of a republican government; but the family became extinct long since, and I have heard,

39

though it is not a subject that one may speak of lightly, that the sons were unworthy their noble descent and came to inglorious ends.

There were still remaining a few representatives of the old families, who were treated with much reverence by the rest of the townspeople, although they were, like the conies of Scripture, a feeble folk.

Deephaven is utterly out of fashion. It never recovered from the effects of the embargo of 1807, and a sand-bar has been steadily filling in the mouth of the harbor. Though the fishing gives what occupation there is for the inhabitants of the place, it is by no means sufficient to draw recruits from abroad. But nobody in Deephaven cares for excitement, and if some one once in a while has the low taste to prefer a more active life, he is obliged to go elsewhere in search of it, and is spoken of afterward with kind pity. I well remember the Widow Moses said to me, in speaking of a certain misguided nephew of hers, "I never could see what could 'a' sot him out to leave so many privileges and go way off to Lynn, with all them children too. Why, they lived here no more than a cable's length from the meetin'-house!"

There were two schooners owned in town, and 'Bijah Mauley and Jo Sands owned a trawl. There were some schooners and a small brig slowly going to pieces by the wharves, and indeed all Deephaven looked more or less out of repair. All along shore one might see dories and wherries and whale-boats, which had been left to die a lingering death. There is something piteous to me in the sight of an old boat. If one I had used much and cared for were past its usefulness, I should say good by to it, and have it towed out to sea and sunk; it never should be left to fall to pieces above high-water mark.

Even the commonest fishermen felt a satisfaction, and seemed to realize their privilege, in being residents of Deephaven; but among the nobility and gentry there lingered a fierce pride in their family and town records, and a hardly concealed contempt and pity for people who were obliged to live in other parts of the world. There were acknowledged to be a few disadvantages,—such as living nearly a dozen miles from the railway,—but, as Miss Honora Carew said, the tone of Deephaven society had always been very high, and it was very nice that there had never been any manufacturing element introduced. She could not feel too grateful, herself, that there was no disagreeable foreign population.

"But," said Kate one day, "would n't you like to have some pleasant new people brought into town?"

"Certainly, my dear," said Miss Honora, rather doubtfully; "I have always been public-spirited; but then, we always have guests in summer, and I am growing old. I should not care to enlarge my acquaintance to any great extent." Miss Honora and Mrs. Dent had lived gay lives in their younger days, and were interested and connected with the outside world more than any of our Deephaven friends; but they were quite contented to stay in their own house, with their books and letters and knitting, and they carefully read Littell and "the new magazine," as they called the Atlantic.

The Carews were very intimate with the minister and his sister, and there were one or two others who belonged to this set. There was Mr. Joshua Dorsey, who wore his hair in a queue, was very deaf, and carried a ponderous cane which had belonged to his venerated father,—a much taller man than he. He was polite to Kate and me, but we never knew him much. He went to play whist with the Carews every Monday evening, and commonly went out fishing once a week. He had begun the practice of law, but he had lost his hearing, and at the same time his lady-love had inconsiderately fallen in love with somebody else; after which he retired from active business life. He had a fine library, which he invited us to examine. He had many new books, but they looked shockingly overdressed, in their fresher bindings, beside the old brown volumes of essays and sermons, and lighter works in many-volume editions.

A prominent link in society was Widow Tully, who had been the much-respected housekeeper of old Captain Manning for forty years. When he died he left her the use of his house and family pew, besides an annuity. The existence of Mr. Tully seemed to be a myth. During the first of his widow's residence in town she had been much affected when obliged to speak of him, and always represented herself as having seen better days and as being highly connected. But she was apt to be ungrammatical when excited, and there was a whispered tradition that she used to keep a toll-bridge in a town in Connecticut; though the mystery of her previous state of existence will probably never be solved. She wore mourning for the captain which would have befitted his widow, and patronized the townspeople conspicuously, while she herself was treated with much condescension by the Carews and Lorimers. She occupied, on the whole, much the same position that Mrs. Betty Barker did in Cranford. And, indeed, Kate and I were often reminded of that estimable town. We heard that Kate's aunt, Miss Brandon, had never been appreciative of Mrs. Tully's merits, and that since her death the others had received Mrs. Tully into their society rather more.

It seemed as if all the clocks in Deephaven, and all the people with them, had stopped years ago, and the people had been doing over and over what they had been busy about during the last week of their unambitious progress. Their clothes had lasted wonderfully well, and they had no need to earn money when there was so little chance to spend it; indeed, there were several families who seemed to have no more visible means of support than a balloon. There were no young people whom we knew, though a number used to come to church on Sunday from the inland farms, or "the country," as we learned to say. There were children among the fishermen's families at the shore, but a few years will see Deephaven possessed by two classes instead of the time-honored three.

As for our first Sunday at church, it must be in vain to ask you to imagine our delight when we heard the tuning of a bass-viol in the gallery just before service. We pressed each other's hands most tenderly, looked up at the singers' seats, and then trusted ourselves to look at each other. It was more than we had hoped for. There were also a violin and sometimes a flute, and a choir of men and women singers, though the congregation were expected to join in the psalm-singing. The first hymn was

> "The Lord our God is full of might,
> The winds obey his will,"

to the tune of St. Ann's. It was all so delightfully old-fashioned; our pew was a square pew, and was by an open window looking seaward. We also had a view of the entire congregation, and as we were somewhat early, we watched the people come in, with great interest. The Deephaven aristocracy came with stately step up the aisle; this was all the chance there was for displaying their unquestioned dignity in public.

Many of the people drove to church in wagons that were low and old and creaky, with worn buffalo-robes over the seat, and some hay tucked underneath for the sleepy, undecided old horse. Some of the younger farmers and their wives had high, shiny wagons, with tall horsewhips,—which they sometimes brought into church,—and they drove up to the steps with a consciousness of being conspicuous and enviable. They had a bashful look when they came in, and for a few minutes after they took their seats they evidently felt that all eyes were fixed upon them; but after a little while they were quite at their ease, and looked critically at the new arrivals.

The old folks interested us most. "Do you notice how many more old women there are than old men?" whispered Kate to me. And we wondered if the husbands and brothers had been drowned, and if it must not be sad to look at the blue, sunshiny sea beyond the marshes, if the far-away white sails reminded them of some ships that had never sailed home into Deephaven harbor, or of fishing-boats that had never come back to land.

The girls and young men adorned themselves in what they believed to be the latest fashion, but the elderly women were usually relics of old times in manner and dress. They wore to church thin, soft silk gowns that must have been brought from over the seas years upon years before, and wide collars fastened with mourning-pins holding a lock of hair. They had big black bonnets, some of them with stiff capes, such as Kate and I had not seen before since our childhood. They treasured large rusty lace veils of scraggly pattern, and wore sometimes, on pleasant Sundays, white China-crape shawls with attenuated fringes; and there were two or three of these shawls in the congregation which had been dyed black, and gave an aspect of meekness and general unworthiness to the aged wearer, they clung and drooped about the figure in such a hopeless way. We used to notice often the most interesting scarfs, without which no Deephaven woman considered herself in full dress. Sometimes there were red India scarfs in spite of its being hot weather; but our favorite ones were long strips of silk, embroidered along the edges and at the ends with dismal-colored floss in odd patterns. I think there must have been a fashion once, in Deephaven, of working these scarfs, and I should not be surprised to find that it was many years before the fashion of working samplers came about. Our friends always wore black mitts on warm Sundays, and many of them carried neat little bags of various designs on their arms, containing a precisely folded pocket-handkerchief, and a frugal lunch of caraway seeds or red and white peppermints. I should like you to see, with your own eyes, Widow Ware and Miss Exper'ence Hull, two old sisters whose personal appearance we delighted in, and whom we saw feebly approaching down the street this first Sunday morning under the shadow of the two last members of an otherwise extinct race of parasols.

There were two or three old men who sat near us. They were sailors, — there is something unmistakable about a sailor, — and they had a curiously ancient, uncanny look, as if they might have belonged to the crew of the Mayflower, or even have cruised about with the Northmen in the times of Harold Harfager and his comrades. They had been blown about by so many winter winds, so browned by summer suns, and wet by salt spray, that their hands and faces looked like leather, with a few deep folds instead of wrinkles. They had pale blue eyes, very keen and quick; their hair looked like the fine sea-weed which clings to the kelp-roots and mussel-shells in little locks. These friends of ours sat solemnly at the heads of their pews and looked unflinchingly at the minister, when they were not dozing, and they sang with voices like the howl of the wind, with an occasional deep note or two.

Have you never seen faces that seemed old-fashioned? Many of the people in Deephaven church looked as if they must be — if not supernaturally old — exact copies of their remote ancestors. I wonder if it is not possible that the features and expression may be almost perfectly reproduced. These faces were not modern American faces, but belonged rather to the days of the early settlement of the country, the old colonial times. We often heard quaint words and expressions which we never had known anywhere else but in old books. There was a great deal of sea-lingo in use; indeed, we learned a great deal ourselves, unconsciously, and used it afterward to the great amusement of our friends; but there were also many peculiar provincialisms, and among the people who lived on the lonely farms inland we often noticed words we had seen in Chaucer, and studied out at school in our English literature class. Everything in Deephaven was more or less influenced by the sea; the minister spoke oftenest of Peter and his fishermen companions, and prayed most earnestly every Sunday morning for those who go down to the sea in ships. He made frequent allusions and drew numberless illustrations of a similar kind for his sermons, and indeed I am in doubt whether, if the Bible had been written wholly in inland countries, it would have been much valued in Deephaven.

The singing was very droll, for there was a majority of old voices, which had seen their best days long before, and the bass-viol was excessively noticeable, and apt to be a little ahead of the time the singers kept, while the violin lingered after. Somewhere on the other side of the church we heard an acute voice which rose high above all the rest of the congregation, sharp as a needle, and slightly cracked, with a limitless supply of breath. It rose and fell gallantly, and clung long to the high notes of Dundee. It was like the wail of the banshee, which sounds clear to the fated hearer above all other noises. We afterward became acquainted with the owner of this voice, and were surprised to find her a meek widow, who was like a thin black beetle in her pathetic cypress veil and big black bonnet. She looked as if she had forgotten who she was, and spoke with an apologetic whine; but we heard she had a temper as high as her voice, and as much to be dreaded as the equinoctial gale.

Near the church was the parsonage, where Mr. Lorimer lived, and the old Lorimer house not far beyond was occupied by Miss Rebecca Lorimer. Some stranger might ask the question why the minister and his sister did not live together, but you would have understood it at once after you had lived for a little while in town. They were very fond of each other, and the minister dined with Miss Rebecca on Sundays, and she passed the day with him on Wednesdays, and they ruled their separate households with decision and dignity. I think Mr. Lorimer's house showed no signs of being without a mistress, any more than his sister's betrayed the want of a master's care and authority.

The Carews were very kind friends of ours, and had been Miss Brandon's best friends. We heard that there had always been a coolness between Miss Brandon and Miss Lorimer, and that, though they exchanged visits and were always polite, there was a chill in the politeness, and one would never have suspected them of admiring each other at all. We had the whole history of the trouble, which dated back scores of years, from Miss Honora Carew, but we always took pains to appear ignorant of the feud, and I think Miss Lorimer was satisfied that it was best not to refer to it, and to let bygones be bygones. It would not have been true Deephaven courtesy to prejudice Kate against her grand-aunt, and Miss Rebecca cherished her dislike in silence, which gave us a most grand respect for her, since we knew she thought herself in the right; though I think it never had come to an open quarrel between these majestic aristocrats.

Miss Honora Carew and Mr. Dick and their elder sister, Mrs. Dent, had a charmingly sedate and quiet home in the old Carew house. Mrs. Dent was ill a great deal while we were there, but she must have been a very brilliant woman, and was not at all dull when we knew her. She had outlived her husband and her children, and she had, several years before our summer there, given up her own home, which was in the city, and had come back to Deephaven. Miss Honora — dear Miss Honora! — had been one of the brightest, happiest girls, and had lost none of her brightness and happiness by growing old. She had lost none of her fondness for society, though she was so contented in quiet Deephaven, and I think she enjoyed Kate's and my stories of our pleasures as much as we did hers of old times. We used to go to see her almost every day. "Mr. Dick," as they called their brother, had once been a merchant in the East Indies, and there were quantities of curiosities and most beautiful china which he had brought and sent home, which gave the house a character of its own. He had been very rich and had lost some of his money, and then he came home and was still considered to possess princely wealth by his neighbors. He had a great fondness for reading and study, which had not been lost sight of during his business life, and he spent most of his time in his library. He and Mr. Lorimer had their differences of opinion about certain points of theology, and this made them much fonder of each other's society, and gave them a great deal of pleasure; for after every series of arguments, each was sure that he had vanquished the other, or there were alternate victories and defeats which made life vastly interesting and important.

Miss Carew and Mrs. Dent had a great treasury of old brocades and laces and ornaments, which they showed us one day, and told us stories of the wearers, or, if they were their own, there were always some reminiscences which they liked to talk over with each other and with us. I never shall forget the first evening we took tea with them; it impressed us very much, and yet nothing wonderful happened. Tea was handed round by an old-fashioned maid, and afterward we sat talking in the twilight, looking out at the garden. It was such a delight to have tea served in this way. I wonder that the fashion has been almost forgotten. Kate and I took much pleasure in choosing our tea-poys; hers had a mandarin parading on the top, and mine a flight of birds and a pagoda; and we often used them afterward, for Miss Honora asked us to come to tea whenever we liked. "A stupid, common country town" some one dared to call Deephaven in a letter once, and how bitterly we resented it! That was a house where one might find the best society, and the most charming manners and good-breeding, and if I were asked to tell you what I mean by the word "lady," I should ask you to go, if it were possible, to call upon Miss Honora Carew.

After a while the elder sister said, "My dears, we always have prayers at nine, for I have to go up stairs early nowadays." And then the servants came in, and she read solemnly the King of glory Psalm, which I have always liked best, and then Mr. Dick read the church prayers, the form of prayer to be used in families. We stayed later to talk with Miss Honora after we had said good night to Mrs. Dent. And we told each other, as we went home in the moonlight down the quiet street, how much we had enjoyed the evening, for somehow the house and the people had nothing to do with the present, or the hurry of modern life. I have never heard that psalm since without its bringing back that summer night in Deephaven, the beautiful quaint old room, and Kate and I feeling so young and worldly, by contrast, the flickering, shaded light of the candles, the old book, and the voices that said Amen.

There were several other fine old houses in Deephaven beside this and the Brandon house, though that was rather the most imposing. There were two or three which had not been kept in repair, and were deserted, and of course they were said to be haunted, and we were told of their ghosts, and why they walked, and when. From some of the local superstitions Kate and I have vainly endeavored ever since to shake ourselves free. There was a most heathenish fear of doing certain things on Friday, and there were countless signs in which we still have confidence. When the moon is very bright and other people grow sentimental, we only remember that it is a fine night to catch hake.

The Captains

I SHOULD consider my account of Deephaven society incomplete if I did not tell you something of the ancient mariners, who may be found every pleasant morning sunning themselves like turtles on one of the wharves. Sometimes there was a considerable group of them, but the less constant members of the club were older than the rest, and the epidemics of rheumatism in town were sadly frequent. We found that it was etiquette to call them each captain, but I think some of the Deephaven men took the title by brevet upon arriving at a proper age.

They sat close together because so many of them were deaf, and when we were lucky enough to overhear the conversation, it seemed to concern their adventures at sea, or the freight carried out by the Sea Duck, the Ocean Rover, or some other Deephaven ship,—the particulars of the voyage and its disasters and successes being as familiar as the wanderings of the children of Israel to an old parson. There were sometimes violent altercations when the captains differed as to the tonnage of some craft that had been a prey to the winds and waves, dry-rot, or barnacles fifty years before. The old fellows puffed away at little black pipes with short stems, and otherwise consumed tobacco in fabulous quantities. It is needless to say that they gave an immense deal of attention to the weather. We used to wish we could join this agreeable company, but we found that the appearance of an outsider caused a disapproving silence, and that the meeting was evidently not to be interfered with. Once we were impertinent enough to hide ourselves for a while just round the corner of the warehouse, but we were afraid or ashamed to try it again, though the conversation was inconceivably edifying. Captain Isaac Horn, the eldest and wisest of all, was discoursing upon some cloth he had purchased once in Bristol, which the shopkeeper delayed sending until just as they were ready to weigh anchor.

"I happened to take a look at that cloth," said the captain, in a loud droning voice, "and as quick as I got sight of it, I spoke onpleasant of that swindling English fellow, and the crew, they stood back. I was dreadful high-tempered in them days, mind ye; and I had the gig manned. We was out in the stream, just ready to sail. 'T was no use waiting any longer for the wind to change, and we was going north-about. I went ashore, and when I walks into his shop ye never see a creatur' so wilted. Ye see the miser'ble sculpin thought I'd never stop to open the goods, an' it was a chance I did, mind ye! 'Lor,' says he, grinning and turning the color of a biled lobster, 'I s'posed ye were a standing out to sea by this time.' 'No,' says I, 'and I've got my men out here on the quay a landing that cloth o' yourn, and if you don't send just what I bought and paid for down there to go back in the gig within fifteen minutes, I'll take ye by the collar and drop ye into the dock.' I was twice the size of him, mind ye, and master strong. 'Don't ye like it?' says he, edging round; 'I'll change it for ye, then.' Ter'ble perlite he was. 'Like it?' says I, 'it looks as if it were built of dog's hair and divil's wool, kicked together by spiders; and it's coarser than Irish frieze; three threads to an *armful*,' says I."

This was evidently one of the captain's favorite stories, for we heard an approving grumble from the audience.

In the course of a walk inland we made a new acquaintance, Captain Lant, whom we had noticed at church, and who sometimes joined the company on the wharf. We had been walking through the woods, and coming out to his fields we went on to the house for some water. There was no one at home but the captain, who told us cheerfully that he should be pleased to serve us, though his women-folks had gone off to a funeral, the other side of the P'int. He brought out a pitcherful of milk, and after we had drunk some, we all sat down together in the shade. The captain brought an old flag-bottomed chair from the woodhouse, and sat down facing Kate and me, with an air of certainty that he was going to hear something new and make some desirable new acquaintances, and also that he could tell something it would be worth our while to hear. He looked more and more like a well-to-do old English sparrow, and chippered faster and faster.

"Queer ye should know I'm a sailor so quick; why, I've

been a-farming it this twenty years; have to go down to the shore and take a day's fishing every hand's turn, though, to keep the old hulk clear of barnacles. There! I do wish I lived nigher the shore, where I could see the folks I know, and talk about what's been a-goin' on. You don't know anything about it, you don't; but it's tryin' to a man to be called 'old Cap'n Lant,' and, so to speak, be forgot when there's any-thing stirring, and be called gran'ther by clumsy creatur's goin' on fifty and sixty, who can't do no more work to-day than I can; an' then the women-folks keeps a-tellin' me to be keerful and not fall, and as how I'm too old to go out fishing; and when they want to be soft-spoken, they say as how they don't see as I fail, and how wonderful I keep my hearin'. I never did want to farm it, but 'she' always took it to heart when I was off on a v'y'ge, and this farm and some consider-'ble means beside come to her from her brother, and they all sot to and give me no peace of mind till I sold out my share of the Ann Eliza and come ashore for good. I did keep an eighth of the Pactolus, and I was ship's husband for a long spell, but she never was heard from on her last voyage to Singapore. I was the lonesomest man, when I first come ashore, that ever you see. Well, you are master hands to walk, if you come way up from the Brandon house. I wish the women was at home. Know Miss Brandon? Why, yes; and I remember all her brothers and sisters, and her father and mother. I can see 'em now coming into meeting, proud as Lucifer and straight as a mast, every one of 'em. Miss Katharine, she always had her butter from this very farm. Some of the folks used to go down every Saturday, and my wife, she's been in the house a hundred times, I s'pose. So you are Hathaway Brandon's grand-daughter?" (to Kate); "why, he and I have been out fishing together many's the time,—he and Chantrey, his next younger brother. Henry, he was a disapp'intment; he went to furrin parts and turned out a Catholic priest, I s'pose you've heard? I never was so set ag'in Mr. Henry as some folks was. He was the pleasantest spoken of the whole on 'em. You do look like the Brandons; you really favor 'em consider'ble. Well, I'm pleased to see ye, I'm sure."

We asked him many questions about the old people, and

found he knew all the family histories and told them with great satisfaction. We found he had his pet stories, and it must have been gratifying to have an entirely new and fresh audience. He was adroit in leading the conversation around to a point where the stories would come in appropriately, and we helped him as much as possible. In a small neighborhood all the people know each other's stories and experiences by heart, and I have no doubt the old captain had been snubbed many times on beginning a favorite anecdote. There was a story which he told us that first day, which he assured us was strictly true, and it is certainly a remarkable instance of the influence of one mind upon another at a distance. It seems to me worth preserving, at any rate; and as we heard it from the old man, with his solemn voice and serious expression and quaint gestures, it was singularly impressive.

"When I was a youngster," said Captain Lant, "I was an orphan, and I was bound out to old Mr. Peletiah Daw's folks, over on the Ridge Road. It was in the time of the last war, and he had a nephew, Ben Dighton, a dreadful high-strung, wild fellow, who had gone off on a privateer. The old man, he set everything by Ben; he would disoblige his own boys any day to please him. This was in his latter days, and he used to have spells of wandering and being out of his head; and he used to call for Ben and talk sort of foolish about him, till they would tell him to stop. Ben never did a stroke of work for him, either, but he was a handsome fellow, and had a way with him when he was good-natured. One night old Peletiah had been very bad all day and was getting quieted down, and it was after supper; we sat round in the kitchen, and he lay in the bedroom opening out. There were some pitch-knots blazing, and the light shone in on the bed, and all of a sudden something made me look up and look in; and there was the old man setting up straight, with his eyes shining at me like a cat's. 'Stop 'em!' says he; *'stop 'em!'* and his two sons run in then to catch hold of him, for they thought he was beginning with one of his wild spells; but he fell back on the bed and began to cry like a baby. 'O, dear me,' says he, 'they've hung him,—hung him right up to the yard-arm! O, they oughtn't to have done it; cut him down quick! he didn't think; he means well, Ben does; he was hasty. O my God, I can't bear

to see him swing round by the neck! It's poor Ben hung up
to the yard-arm. Let me alone, I say!' Andrew and Moses,
they were holding him with all their might, and they were
both hearty men, but he 'most got away from them once or
twice, and he screeched and howled like a mad creatur', and
then he would cry again like a child. He was worn out after a
while and lay back quiet, and said over and over, 'Poor Ben!'
and 'hung at the yard-arm'; and he told the neighbors next
day, but nobody noticed him much, and he seemed to forget
it as his mind come back. All that summer he was miser'ble,
and towards cold weather he failed right along, though he
had been a master strong man in his day, and his timbers held
together well. Along late in the fall he had taken to his bed,
and one day there came to the house a fellow named Sim
Decker, a reckless fellow he was too, who had gone out in the
same ship with Ben. He pulled a long face when he came in,
and said he had brought bad news. They had been taken prisoner and carried into port and put in jail, and Ben Dighton
had got a fever there and died.

" 'You lie!' says the old man from the bedroom, speaking as
loud and f'erce as ever you heard. 'They hung him to the
yard-arm!'

" 'Don't mind him,' says Andrew; 'he's wandering-like, and
he had a bad dream along back in the spring; I s'posed he'd
forgotten it.' But the Decker fellow he turned pale, and kept
talking crooked while he listened to old Peletiah a-scolding to
himself. He answered the questions the women-folks asked
him,—they took on a good deal,—but pretty soon he got up
and winked to me and Andrew, and we went out in the yard.
He began to swear, and then says he, 'When did the old man
have his dream?' Andrew couldn't remember, but I knew it
was the night before he sold the gray colt, and that was the
24th of April.

" 'Well,' says Sim Decker, 'on the twenty-third day of April
Ben Dighton was hung to the yard-arm, and I see 'em do it,
Lord help him! I didn't mean to tell the women, and I
s'posed you'd never know, for I'm all the one of the ship's
company you're ever likely to see. We were taken prisoner,
and Ben was mad as fire, and they were scared of him and
chained him to the deck; and while he was sulking there, a

little parrot of a midshipman come up and grinned at him, and snapped his fingers in his face; and Ben lifted his hands with the heavy irons and sprung at him like a tiger, and the boy dropped dead as a stone; and they put the bight of a rope round Ben's neck and slung him right up to the yard-arm, and there he swung back and forth until as soon as we dared one of us clim' up and cut the rope and let him go over the ship's side; and they put us in irons for that, curse 'em! How did that old man in there know, and he bedridden here, nigh upon three thousand miles off?' says he. But I guess there was n't any of us could tell him," said Captain Lant in conclusion. "It's something I never could account for, but it's true as truth. I've known more such cases; some folks laughs at me for believing 'em, — 'the cap'n's yarns,' they calls 'em, — but if you'll notice, everybody's got some yarn of that kind they do believe, if they won't believe yours. And there's a good deal happens in the world that's myster'ous. Now there was Widder Oliver Pinkham, over to the P'int, told me with her own lips that she—" But just here we saw the captain's expression alter suddenly, and looked around to see a wagon coming up the lane. We immediately said we must go home, for it was growing late, but asked permission to come again and hear the Widow Oliver Pinkham story. We stopped, however, to see "the women-folks," and afterward became so intimate with them that we were invited to spend the afternoon and take tea, which invitation we accepted with great pride. We went out fishing, also, with the captain and "Danny," of whom I will tell you presently. I often think of Captain Lant in the winter, for he told Kate once that he "felt master old in winter to what he did in summer." He likes reading, fortunately, and we had a letter from him, not long ago, acknowledging the receipt of some books of travel by land and water which we had luckily thought to send him. He gave the latitude and longitude of Deephaven at the beginning of his letter, and signed himself, "Respectfully yours with esteem, Jacob Lant (condemned as unseaworthy)."

Danny

DEEPHAVEN seemed more like one of the lazy little English seaside towns than any other. It was not in the least American. There was no excitement about anything; there were no manufactories; nobody seemed in the least hurry. The only foreigners were a few stranded sailors. I do not know when a house or a new building of any kind had been built; the men were farmers, or went outward in boats, or inward in fish-wagons, or sometimes mackerel and halibut fishing in schooners for the city markets. Sometimes a schooner came to one of the wharves to load with hay or firewood; but Deephaven used to be a town of note, rich and busy, as its forsaken warehouses show.

We knew almost all the fisher-people at the shore, even old Dinnett, who lived an apparently desolate life by himself in a hut and was reputed to have been a bloodthirsty pirate in his youth. He was consequently feared by all the children, and for misdemeanors in his latter days avoided generally. Kate talked with him awhile one day on the shore, and made him come up with her for a bandage for his hand which she saw he had hurt badly; and the next morning he brought us a "new" lobster apiece,—fishermen mean that a thing is only not salted when they say it is "fresh." We happened to be in the hall, and received him ourselves, and gave him a great piece of tobacco and (unintentionally) the means of drinking our health. "Bless your pretty hearts!" said he; "may ye be happy, and live long, and get good husbands, and if they ain't good to you may they die from you!"

None of our friends were more interesting than the fishermen. The fish-houses, which might be called the business centre of the town, were at a little distance from the old warehouses, farther down the harbor shore, and were ready to fall down in despair. There were some fishermen who lived near by, but most of them were also farmers in a small way, and lived in the village or farther inland. From our eastern windows we could see the moorings, and we always liked to watch the boats go out or come straying in, one after the other, tipping and skimming under the square little sails; and we often went down to the fish-houses to see what kind of a catch there had been.

I should have imagined that the sea would become very commonplace to men whose business was carried on in boats, and who had spent night after night and day after day from their boyhood on the water; but that is a mistake. They have an awe of the sea and of its mysteries, and of what it hides away from us. They are childish in their wonder at any strange creature which they find. If they have not seen the sea-serpent, they believe, I am sure, that other people have, and when a great shark or black-fish or sword-fish was taken and brought in shore, everybody went to see it, and we talked about it, and how brave its conqueror was, and what a fight there had been, for a long time afterward.

I said that we liked to see the boats go out, but I must not give you the impression that we saw them often, for they weighed anchor at an early hour in the morning. I remember once there was a light fog over the sea, lifting fast, as the sun was coming up, and the brownish sails disappeared in the mist, while voices could still be heard for some minutes after the men were hidden from sight. This gave one a curious feeling, but afterward, when the sun had risen, everything looked much the same as usual; the fog had gone, and the dories and even the larger boats were distant specks on the sparkling sea.

One afternoon we made a new acquaintance in this wise. We went down to the shore to see if we could hire a conveyance to the lighthouse the next morning. We often went out early in one of the fishing-boats, and after we had stayed as long as we pleased, Mr. Kew would bring us home. It was quiet enough that day, for not a single boat had come in, and there were no men to be seen along-shore. There was a solemn company of lobster-coops or cages which had been brought in to be mended. They always amused Kate. She said they seemed to her like droll old women telling each other secrets. These were scattered about in different attitudes, and looked more confidential than usual.

Just as we were going away we happened to see a man at work in one of the sheds. He was the fisherman whom we knew least of all; an odd-looking, silent sort of man, more sunburnt and weather-beaten than any of the others. We had learned to know him by the bright red flannel shirt he always wore, and besides, he was lame; some one told us he had had a bad fall once, on board ship. Kate and I had always wished we could find a chance to talk with him. He looked up at us pleasantly, and when we nodded and smiled, he said "Good day" in a gruff, hearty voice, and went on with his work, cleaning mackerel.

"Do you mind our watching you?" asked Kate.

"No, *ma'am!*" said the fisherman emphatically. So there we stood.

Those fish-houses were curious places, so different from any other kind of workshop. In this there was a seine, or part of one, festooned among the cross-beams overhead, and there were snarled fishing-lines, and barrows to carry fish in, like wheelbarrows without wheels; there were the queer round lobster-nets, and "kits" of salt mackerel, tubs of bait, and piles of clams; and some queer bones, and parts of remarkable fish, and lobster-claws of surprising size fastened on the walls for ornament. There was a pile of rubbish down at the end; I dare say it was all useful, however,—there is such mystery about the business.

Kate and I were never tired of hearing of the fish that come at different times of the year, and go away again, like the birds; or of the actions of the dog-fish, which the 'longshore-men hate so bitterly; and then there are such curious legends and traditions, of which almost all fishermen have a store.

"I think mackerel are the prettiest fish that swim," said I presently.

"So do I, miss," said the man, "not to say but I've seen more fancy-looking fish down in southern waters, bright as any flower you ever see; but a mackerel," holding up one ad-miringly, "why, they're so clean-built and trig-looking! Put a cod alongside, and he looks as lumbering as an old-fashioned Dutch brig aside a yacht.

"Those are good-looking fish, but they an't made much ac-count of," continued our friend, as he pushed aside the mack-erel and took another tub. "They're hake, I s'pose you know. But I forgot,—I can't stop to bother with them now." And he pulled forward a barrow full of small fish, flat and hard, with pointed, bony heads.

"Those are porgies, are n't they?" asked Kate.

"Yes," said the man, "an' I'm going to sliver them for the trawls."

We knew what the trawls were, and supposed that the porgies were to be used for bait; and we soon found out what "slivering" meant, by seeing him take them by the head and cut a slice from first one side and then the other in such a way that the pieces looked not unlike smaller fish.

"It seems to me," said I, "that fishermen always have sharper knives than other people."

"Yes, we do like a sharp knife in our trade; and then we are mostly strong-handed."

He was throwing the porgies' heads and backbones—all that was left of them after slivering—in a heap, and now several cats walked in as if they felt at home, and began a hearty lunch. "What a troop of pussies there is round here," said I; "I wonder what will become of them in the winter,—though, to be sure, the fishing goes on just the same."

"The better part of them don't get through the cold weather," said Danny. "Two or three of the old ones have been here for years, and are as much belonging to Deephaven as the meetin'-house; but the rest of them an't to be depended on. You'll miss the young ones by the dozen, come spring. I don't know myself but they move inland in the fall of the year; they're knowing enough, if that's all!"

Kate and I stood in the wide doorway, arm in arm, looking sometimes at the queer fisherman and the porgies, and sometimes out to sea. It was low tide; the wind had risen a little, and the heavy salt air blew toward us from the wet brown ledges in the rocky harbor. The sea was bright blue, and the sun was shining. Two gulls were swinging lazily to and fro; there was a flock of sand-pipers down by the water's edge, in a great hurry, as usual.

Presently the fisherman spoke again, beginning with an odd laugh: "I *was* scared last winter! Jack Scudder and me, we were up in the Cap'n Manning storehouse hunting for a half-bar'l of salt the skipper said was there. It was an awful blustering kind of day, with a thin icy rain blowing from all points at once; sea roaring as if it wished it could come ashore and put a stop to everything. Bad days at sea, them are; rigging all froze up. As I was saying, we were hunting for a half-bar'l of salt, and I laid hold of a bar'l that had something heavy in the bottom, and tilted it up, and my eye! there was a stir and a scratch and a squeal, and out went some kind of a creatur', and I jumped back, not looking for anything live, but I see in a minute it was a cat; and perhaps you think it is a big story, but there were eight more in there, hived in together to keep warm. I car'd 'em up some new fish that night; they seemed short of provisions. We hadn't been out fishing as much as common, and they hadn't dared to be round the fish-houses much, for a fellow who came in on a coaster had a dog, and he used to chase 'em. Hard chance they had, and lots of 'em died, I guess; but there seem to be some survivin' relatives, an' al'ays just so hungry! I used to feed them some when I was ashore. I think likely you've heard that a cat will fetch you bad luck; but I don't know 's that made much difference to me. I kind of like to keep on the right side of 'em, too; if ever I have a bad dream there's sure to be a cat in it; but I was brought up to be clever to dumb beasts, an' I guess it's my natur'. Except fish," said Danny after a minute's thought; "but then it never seems like they had feelin's like creatur's that live ashore." And we all laughed heartily and felt well acquainted.

"I s'pose you misses will laugh if I tell ye I kept a kitty once myself." This was said rather shyly, and there was evidently a story, so we were much interested, and Kate said, "Please tell us about it; was it at sea?"

"Yes, it was at sea; leastways, on a coaster. I got her in a sing'lar kind of way: it was one afternoon we were lying alongside Charlestown Bridge, and I heard a young cat screeching real pitiful; and after I looked all round, I see her in the water clutching on to the pier of the bridge, and some little divils of boys were heaving rocks down at her. I got into the schooner's tag-boat quick, I tell ye, and pushed off for her, 'n' she let go just as I got there, 'n' I guess you never saw a more miser'ble-looking creatur' than I fished out of the water. Cold weather it was. Her leg was hurt, and her eye, and I thought first I'd drop her overboard again, and then I didn't, and I took her aboard the schooner and put her by the stove. I thought she might as well die where it was warm. She eat a little mite of chowder before night, but she was very slim; but next morning, when I went to see if she was dead, she fell to licking my finger, and she did purr away like a dolphin. One of her eyes was out, where a stone had took her, and she never got any use of it, but she used to look at you so clever with the other, and she got well of her lame foot after a while. I got to be ter'ble fond of her. She was just the knowingest thing you ever saw, and she used to sleep alongside of me in my bunk, and like as not she would go on deck with me when it was my watch. I was coasting then for a year and eight months, and I kept her all the time. We used to be in harbor consider'ble, and about eight o'clock in the forenoon I used to drop a line and catch her a couple of cunners. Now, it is cur'us that she used to know when I was fishing for her. She would pounce on them fish and carry them off and growl, and she knew when I got a bite,—she'd watch the line; but when we were mackereling she never give us any trouble. She would never lift a paw to touch any of our fish. She did n't have the thieving ways common to most cats. She used to set round on deck in fair weather, and when the wind blew she al'ays kept herself below. Sometimes when we were in port she would go ashore awhile, and fetch back a bird or a mouse, but she would n't eat it till she come and showed it to me. She never wanted to stop long ashore, though I never shut her up; I always give her her liberty. I got a good deal of joking about her from the fellows, but she was a sight of company. I don' know as I ever had anything like me as much as she did. Not to say as I ever had much of any trouble with anybody, ashore or afloat. I'm a still kind of fellow, for all I look so rough.

"But then, I han't had a home, what I call a home, since I was going on nine year old."

"How has that happened?" asked Kate.

"Well, mother, she died, and I was bound out to a man in the tanning trade, and I hated him, and I hated the trade; and when I was a little bigger I ran away, and I've followed the sea ever since. I was n't much use to him, I guess; leastways, he never took the trouble to hunt me up.

"About the best place I ever was in was a hospital. It was in foreign parts. Ye see I'm crippled some? I fell from the topsail yard to the deck, and I struck my shoulder, and broke my leg, and banged myself all up. It was to a nuns' hospital where they took me. All of the nuns were Catholics, and they wore big white things on their heads. I don't suppose you ever saw any. Have you? Well, now, that's queer! When I was first there I was scared of them; they were real ladies, and I wasn't used to being in a house, any way. One of them, that took care of me most of the time, why, she would even set up half the night with me, and I couldn't begin to tell you how good-natured she was, an' she'd look real sorry too. I used to be ugly, I ached so, along in the first of my being there, but I spoke of it when I was coming away, and she said it was all right. She used to feed me, that lady did; and there were some days I couldn't lift my head, and she would rise it on her arm. She give me a little mite of a book, when I come away. I'm not much of a hand at reading, but I always kept it on account of her. She was so pleased when I got so's to set up in a chair and look out of the window. She wasn't much of a hand to talk English. I did feel bad to come away from there; I 'most wished I could be sick a while longer. I never said much of anything either, and I don't know but she thought it was queer, but I am a dreadful clumsy man to say anything, and I got flustered. I don't know's I mind telling you; I was 'most a-crying. I used to think I'd lay by some money and ship for there and carry her something real pretty. But I don't rank able-bodied seaman like I used, and it's as much as I can do to get a berth on a coaster; I suppose I might go as cook. I liked to have died with my hurt at that hospital, but when I was getting well it made me think of when I was a mite of a chap to home before mother died, to be laying there in a clean bed with somebody to do for me. Guess you think I'm a good hand to spin long yarns; some-how it comes easy to talk to-day."

"What became of your cat?" asked Kate, after a pause, dur-ing which our friend sliced away at the porgies.

"I never rightfully knew; it was in Salem harbor, and a windy night. I was on deck consider'ble, for the schooner pitched lively, and once or twice she dragged her anchor. I never saw the kitty after she eat her supper. I remember I gave her some milk,—I used to buy her a pint once in a while for a treat; I don't know but she might have gone off on a cake of ice, but it did seem as if she had too much sense for that. Most likely she missed her footing, and fell overboard in the dark. She was marked real pretty, black and white, and kep' herself just as clean! She knew as well as could be when foul weather was coming; she would bother round and act queer; but when the sun was out she would sit round on deck as pleased as a queen. There! I feel bad sometimes when I think of her, and I never went into Salem since without hoping that I should see her. I don't know but if I was a-going to begin my life over again, I'd settle down ashore and have a snug little house and farm it. But I guess I shall do better at fishing. Give me a trig-built topsail schooner painted up nice, with a stripe on her, and clean sails, and a fresh wind with the sun a-shining, and I feel first-rate."

"Do you believe that codfish swallow stones before a storm?" asked Kate. I had been thinking about the lonely fisherman in a sentimental way, and so irrelevant a question shocked me. "I saw he felt slightly embarrassed at having talked about his affairs so much," Kate told me afterward, "and I thought we should leave him feeling more at his ease if we talked about fish for a while." And sure enough he did seem relieved, and gave us his opinion about the codfish at once, adding that he never cared much for cod any way; folks up country bought 'em a good deal, he heard. Give him a haddock right out of the water for his dinner!

"I never can remember," said Kate, "whether it is cod or haddock that have a black stripe along their sides—"

"O, those are haddock," said I; "they say that the Devil caught a haddock once, and it slipped through his fingers and got scorched; so all the haddock had the same mark afterward."

"Well, now, how did you know that old story?" said Danny, laughing heartily; "ye must n't believe all the old stories ye hear, mind ye!"

"O, no," said we.

"Hullo! There's Jim Toggerson's boat close in shore. She

sets low in the water, so he's done well. He and Skipper Scudder have been out deep-sea fishing since yesterday."

Our friend pushed the porgies back into a corner, stuck his knife into a beam, and we hurried down to the shore. Kate and I sat on the pebbles, and he went out to the moorings in a dirty dory to help unload the fish.

We afterward saw a great deal of Danny, as all the men called him. But though Kate and I tried our best and used our utmost skill and tact to make him tell us more about himself, he never did. But perhaps there was nothing more to be told.

The day we left Deephaven we went down to the shore to say good by to him and to some other friends, and he said, "Goin', are ye? Well, I'm sorry; ye've treated me first-rate; the Lord bless ye!" and then was so much mortified at the way he had said farewell that he turned and fled round the corner of the fish-house.

Captain Sands

OLD Captain Sands was one of the most prominent citizens of Deephaven, and a very good friend of Kate's and mine. We often met him, and grew much interested in him before we knew him well. He had a reputation in town for being peculiar and somewhat visionary; but every one seemed to like him, and at last one morning, when we happened to be on our way to the wharves, we stopped at the door of an old warehouse which we had never seen opened before. Captain Sands sat just inside, smoking his pipe, and we said good morning, and asked him if he did not think there was a fog coming in by and by. We had thought a little of going out to the lighthouse. The cap'n rose slowly, and came out so that he could see farther round to the east. "There's some scud coming in a'ready," said he. "None to speak of yet, I don't know's you can see it,—yes, you're right; there's a heavy bank of fog lyin' off, but it won't be in under two or three hours yet, unless the wind backs round more and freshens up. Were n't thinking of going out, were ye?"

"A little," said Kate, "but we had nearly given it up. We are getting to be very weather-wise, and we pride ourselves on being quick at seeing fogs." At which the cap'n smiled and said we were consider'ble young to know much about weather, but it looked well that we took some interest in it; most young people were fools about weather, and would just as soon set off to go anywhere right under the edge of a thunder-shower. "Come in and set down, won't ye?" he added; "it ain't much of a place; I've got a lot of old stuff stowed away here that the women-folks don't want up to the house. I'm a great hand for keeping things." And he looked round fondly at the contents of the wide low room. "I come down here once in a while and let in the sun, and sometimes I want to hunt up something or 'nother; kind of stow-away place, ye see." And then he laughed apologetically, rubbing his hands together, and looking out to sea again as if he wished to appear unconcerned; yet we saw that he wondered if we thought it ridiculous for a man of his age to have treasured up so much trumpery in that cobwebby place. There were some whole oars and the sail of his boat and two or three killicks and painters, not to forget a heap of worn-out oars and sails in one corner and a sailor's hammock slung across the beam overhead, and there were some sailor's chests and the capstan of a ship and innumerable boxes which all seemed to be stuffed full, besides no end of things lying on the floor and packed away on shelves and hanging to rusty big-headed nails in the wall. I saw some great lumps of coral, and large, rough shells, a great hornet's nest, and a monstrous lobster-shell. The cap'n had cobbled and tied up some remarkable old chairs for the accommodation of himself and his friends.

"What a nice place!" said Kate in a frank, delighted way which could not have failed to be gratifying.

"Well, no," said the cap'n, with his slow smile, "it ain't what you'd rightly call 'nice,' as I know of: it ain't never been cleared out all at once since I began putting in. There's nothing that's worth anything, either, to anybody but me. Wife, she's said to me a hundred times, 'Why don't you overhaul them old things and burn 'em?' She's al'ays at me about letting the property, as if it were a corner-lot in Broadway. That's all women-folks know about business!" And here the captain caught himself tripping, and looked uneasy for a minute. "I suppose I might have let it for a fish-house, but it's most too far from the shore to be handy—and—well—there are some things here that I set a good deal by."

"Isn't that a sword-fish's sword in that piece of wood?" Kate asked presently; and was answered that it was found broken off as we saw it, in the hull of a wreck that went ashore on Blue P'int when the captain was a young man, and he had sawed it out and kept it ever since,—fifty-nine years. Of course we went closer to look at it, and we both felt a great sympathy for this friend of ours, because we have the same fashion of keeping worthless treasures, and we understood perfectly how dear such things may be.

"Do you mind if we look round a little?" I asked doubtfully, for I knew how I should hate having strangers look over my own treasury. But Captain Sands looked pleased at our interest, and said cheerfully that we might overhaul as much as we chose. Kate discovered first an old battered wooden figure-head of a ship,—a woman's head with long curly hair falling over the shoulders. The paint was almost gone, and the dust covered most of what was left: still there was a wonderful spirit and grace, and a wild, weird beauty which attracted us exceedingly; but the captain could only tell us that it had belonged to the wreck of a Danish brig which had been driven on the reef where the lighthouse stands now, and his father had found this on the long sands a day or two afterward. "That was a dreadful storm," said the captain. "I've heard the old folks tell about it; it was when I was only a year or two old. There were three merchantmen wrecked within five miles of Deephaven. This one was all stove to splinters, and they used to say she had treasure aboard. When I was small I used to have a great idea of going out there to the rocks at low water and trying to find some gold, but I never made out no great." And he smiled indulgently at the thought of his youthful dream.

"Kate," said I, "do you see what beauties these Turk's-head knots are?" We had been taking a course of first lessons in knots from Danny, and had followed by learning some charmingly intricate ones from Captain Lant, the stranded mariner who lived on a farm two miles or so inland. Kate came over to look at the Turk's-heads, which were at either end of the rope handles of a little dark-blue chest.

Captain Sands turned in his chair and nodded approval. "That's a neat piece of work, and it was a first-rate seaman who did it; he's dead and gone years ago, poor young fellow; an I-talian he was, who sailed on the Ranger three or four long voyages. He fell from the mast-head on the voyage home from Callao. Cap'n Manning and old Mr. Lorimer, they owned the Ranger, and when she come into port and they got the news they took it as much to heart as if he'd been some relation. He was smart as a whip, and had a way with him, and the pleasantest kind of a voice; you couldn't help liking him. They found out that he had a mother alive in Port Mahon, and they sent his pay and some money he had in the bank at Riverport out to her by a ship that was going to the Mediterranean. He had some clothes in his chest, and they sold those and sent her the money,—all but some trinkets they supposed he was keeping for her; I rec'lect he used to speak consider'ble about his mother. I shipped one v'y'ge with him before the mast, before I went out mate of the Day-light. I happened to be in port the time the Ranger got in, an' I see this chist lying round in Cap'n Manning's storehouse, and I offered to give him what it was worth; but we was good friends, and he told me take it if I wanted it, it was no use to him, and I've kept it ever since.

"There are some of his traps in it now, I believe; ye can look." And we took off some tangled cod-lines and opened the chest. There was only a round wooden box in the till, and in some idle hour at sea the young sailor had carved his initials and an anchor and the date on the cover. We found some sail-needles and a palm in this "kit," as the sailors call it, and a little string of buttons with some needles and yarn and thread in a neat little bag, which perhaps his mother had made for him when he started off on his first voyage. Besides these things there was only a fanciful little broken buckle, green and gilt, which he might have picked up in some foreign street, and his protection-paper carefully folded, wherein he was certified as being a citizen of the United States, with dark complexion and dark hair.

"He was one of the pleasantest fellows that ever I shipped with," said the captain, with a gruff tenderness in his voice. "Always willin' to do his work himself, and like's not when the other fellows up the rigging were cold, or ugly about something or 'nother, he'd say something that would set them all laughing, and somehow it made you good-natured to see him round. He was brought up a Catholic, I s'pose; anyway, he had some beads, and sometimes they would joke him about 'em on board ship, but he would blaze up in a minute, ugly as a tiger. I never saw him mad about anything else, though he would n't stand it if anybody tried to crowd him. He fell from the main-to'-gallant yard to the deck, and was dead when they picked him up. They were off the Bermudas. I suppose he lost his balance, but I never could see how; he was sure-footed, and as quick as a cat. They said they saw him try to catch at the stay, but there was a heavy sea running, and the ship rolled just so's to let him through between the rigging, and he struck the deck like a stone. I don't know's that chest has been opened these ten years,—I declare it carries me back to look at those poor little traps of his. Well, it's the way of the world; we think we're somebody, and we have our day, but it isn't long afore we're forgotten."

The captain reached over for the paper, and taking out a clumsy pair of steel-bowed spectacles, read it through carefully. "I'll warrant he took good care of this," said he. "He was an I-talian, and no more of an American citizen than a Chinese; I wonder he hadn't called himself John Jones, that's the name most of the foreigners used to take when they got their papers. I remember once I was sick with a fever in Chelsea Hospital, and one morning they came bringing in the mate of a Portugee brig on a stretcher, and the surgeon asked what his name was. 'John Jones,' says he. 'O, say something else,' says the surgeon; 'we've got five John Joneses here a'ready, and it's getting to be no name at all.' Sailors are great hands for false names; they have a trick of using them when they have any money to leave ashore, for fear their shipmates will go and draw it out. I suppose there are thousands of dollars unclaimed in New York banks, where men have left it charged to their false names; then they get lost at sea or something, and never go to get it, and nobody knows whose it is. They're curious folks, take 'em altogether, sailors is; specially these foreign fellows that wander about from ship to ship. They're getting to be a dreadful low set, too, of late years. It's the last thing I'd want a boy of mine to do,—ship before the mast with one of these mixed crews. It's a dog's life, anyway, and the risks and the chances against you are awful. It's a good while before you can lay up anything, unless you are part owner. I saw all the p'ints a good deal plainer after I quit followin' the sea myself, though I've always been more or less into navigation until this last war come on. I know when I was ship's husband of the Polly and Susan there was a young man went out cap'n of her,—her last voyage, and she never was heard from. He had a wife and two or three little children, and for all he was so smart, they would have been about the same as beggars, if I hadn't happened to have his life insured the day I was having the papers made out for the ship. I happened to think of it. Five thousand dollars there was, and I sent it to the widow along with his primage. She hadn't expected nothing, or next to nothing, and she was pleased, I tell ye."

"I think it was very kind in you to think of that, Captain Sands," said Kate. And the old man said, flushing a little, "Well, I'm not so smart as some of the men who started when I did, and some of 'em went ahead of me, but some of 'em didn't, after all. I've tried to be honest, and to do just about as nigh right as I could, and you know there's an old sayin' that a cripple in the right road will beat a racer in the wrong."

The Circus at Denby

KATE and I looked forward to a certain Saturday with as much eagerness as if we had been little school-boys, for on that day we were to go to a circus at Denby, a town perhaps eight miles inland. There had not been a circus so near Deephaven for a long time, and nobody had dared to believe the first rumor of it, until two dashing young men had deigned to come themselves to put up the big posters on the end of 'Bijah Mauley's barn. All the boys in town came as soon as possible to see these amazing pictures, and some were wretched in their secret hearts at the thought that they might not see the show itself. Tommy Dockum was more interested than any one else, and mentioned the subject so frequently one day when he went blackberrying with us, that we grew enthusiastic, and told each other what fun it would be to go, for everybody would be there, and it would be the greatest loss to us if we were absent. I thought I had lost my childish fondness for circuses, but it came back redoubled; and Kate may contradict me if she chooses, but I am sure she never looked forward to the Easter Oratorio with half the pleasure she did to this "caravan," as most of the people called it.

We felt that it was a great pity that any of the boys and girls should be left lamenting at home, and finding that there were some of our acquaintances and Tommy's who saw no chance of going, we engaged Jo Sands and Leander Dockum to carry them to Denby in two fish-wagons, with boards laid across for the extra seats. We saw them join the straggling train of carriages which had begun to go through the village from all along shore, soon after daylight, and they started on their journey shouting and carousing, with their pockets crammed with early apples and other provisions. We thought it would have been fun enough to see the people go by, for we had had no idea until then how many inhabitants that country held.

We had asked Mrs. Kew to go with us; but she was half an hour later than she had promised, for, since there was no wind, she could not come ashore in the sail-boat, and Mr.

Kew had had to row her in in the dory. We saw the boat at last nearly in shore, and drove down to meet it: even the horse seemed to realize what a great day it was, and showed a disposition to friskiness, evidently as surprising to himself as to us.

Mrs. Kew was funnier that day than we had ever known her, which is saying a great deal, and we should not have had half so good a time if she had not been with us; although she lived in the lighthouse, and had no chance to "see passing," which a woman prizes so highly in the country, she had a wonderful memory for faces, and could tell us the names of all Deephaveners and of most of the people we met outside its limits. She looked impressed and solemn as she hurried up from the water's edge, giving Mr. Kew some parting charges over her shoulder as he pushed off the boat to go back; but after we had convinced her that the delay had not troubled us, she seemed more cheerful. It was evident that she felt the importance of the occasion, and that she was pleased at our having chosen her for company. She threw back her veil entirely, sat very straight, and took immense pains to bow to every acquaintance whom she met. She wore her best Sunday clothes, and her manner was formal for the first few minutes; it was evident that she felt we were meeting under unusual circumstances, and that, although we had often met before on the friendliest terms, our having asked her to make this excursion in public required a different sort of behavior at her hands, and a due amount of ceremony and propriety. But this state of things did not last long, as she soon made a remark at which Kate and I laughed so heartily in lighthouse-acquaintance fashion, that she unbent, and gave her whole mind to enjoying herself.

When we came by the store where the post-office was kept we saw a small knot of people gathered round the door, and stopped to see what had happened. There was a forlorn horse standing near, with his harness tied up with fuzzy ends of rope, and the wagon was cobbled together with pieces of board; the whole craft looked as if it might be wrecked with the least jar. In the wagon were four or five stupid-looking boys and girls, one of whom was crying softly. Their father was sick, some one told us. "He was took faint, but he is coming to all right; they have give him something to take: their name is Craper, and they live way over beyond the Ridge, on Stone Hill. They were goin' over to Denby to the circus, and the man was calc'lating to get doctored, but I d' know 's he can get so fur; he 's powerful slim-looking to me." Kate and I went to see if we could be of any use, and when we went into the store we saw the man leaning back in his chair, looking ghastly pale, and as if he were far gone in consumption. Kate spoke to him, and he said he was better; he had felt bad all the way along, but he hadn't given up. He was pitiful, poor fellow, with his evident attempt at dressing up. He had the bushiest, dustiest red hair and whiskers, which made the pallor of his face still more striking, and his illness had thinned and paled his rough, clumsy hands. I thought what a hard piece of work it must have been for him to start for the circus that morning, and how kind-hearted he must be to have made such an effort for his children's pleasure. As we went out they stared at us gloomily. The shadow of their disappointment touched and chilled our pleasure.

Somebody had turned the horse so that he was heading toward home, and by his actions he showed that he was the only one of the party who was glad. We were so sorry for the children; perhaps it had promised to be the happiest day of their lives, and now they must go back to their uninteresting home without having seen the great show.

"I am so sorry you are disappointed," said Kate, as we were wondering how the man who had followed us could ever climb into the wagon.

"Heh?" said he, blankly, as if he did not know what her words meant. "What fool has been a turning o' this horse?" he asked a man who was looking on.

"Why, which way be ye goin'?"

"To the circus," said Mr. Craper, with decision, "where d' ye s'pose? That 's where I started for, anyways." And he climbed in and glanced round to count the children, struck the horse with the willow switch, and they started off briskly, while everybody laughed. Kate and I joined Mrs. Kew, who had enjoyed the scene.

"Well, there!" said she, "I wonder the folks in the old North burying-ground ain't a-rising up to go to Denby to that caravan!"

We reached Denby at noon; it was an uninteresting town which had grown up around some mills. There was a great commotion in the streets, and it was evident that we had lost much in not having seen the procession. There was a great deal of business going on in the shops, and there were two or three hand-organs at large, near one of which we stopped awhile to listen, just after we had met Leander and given the horse into his charge. Mrs. Kew finished her shopping as soon as possible, and we hurried toward the great tents, where all the flags were flying. I think I have not told you that we were to have the benefit of seeing a menagerie in addition to the circus, and you may be sure we went faithfully round to see everything that the cages held.

I cannot truthfully say that it was a good show; it was somewhat dreary, now that I think of it quietly and without excitement. The creatures looked tired, and as if they had been on the road for a great many years. The animals were all old, and there was a shabby great elephant whose look of general discouragement went to my heart, for it seemed as if he were miserably conscious of a misspent life. He stood dejected and motionless at one side of the tent, and it was hard to believe that there was a spark of vitality left in him. A great number of the people had never seen an elephant before, and we heard a thin little old man, who stood near us, say delightedly, "There's the old creatur', and no mistake, Ann 'Liza. I wanted to see him most of anything. My sakes alive, ain't he big!"

And Ann 'Liza, who was stout and sleepy-looking, droned out, "Ye-es, there's consider'ble of him; but he looks as if he ain't got no animation."

Kate and I turned away and laughed, while Mrs. Kew said confidentially, as the couple moved away, "*She* need n't be a reflectin' on the poor beast. That's Mis Seth Tanner, and there is n't a woman in Deephaven nor East Parish to be named the same day with her for laziness. I'm glad she did n't catch sight of me; she'd have talked about nothing for a fortnight."

There was a picture of a huge snake in Deephaven, and I was just wondering where he could be, or if there ever had been one, when we heard a boy ask the same question of the man whose thankless task it was to stir up the lions with a stick to make them roar. "The snake's dead," he answered good-naturedly. "Did n't you have to dig an awful long grave for him?" asked the boy; but the man said he reckoned they curled him up some, and smiled as he turned to his lions, who looked as if they needed a tonic. Everybody lingered longest before the monkeys, who seemed to be the only lively crea-tures in the whole collection; and finally we made our way into the other tent, and perched ourselves on a high seat, from whence we had a capital view of the audience and the ring, and could see the people come in. Mrs. Kew was on the lookout for acquaintances, and her spirits as well as our own seemed to rise higher and higher. She was on the alert, mov-ing her head this way and that to catch sight of people, giving us a running commentary in the mean time. It was very pleas-ant to see a person so happy as Mrs. Kew was that day, and I dare say in speaking of the occasion she would say the same thing of Kate and me, — for it was such a good time! We bought some peanuts, without which no circus seems com-plete, and we listened to the conversations which were being carried on around us while we were waiting for the perfor-mance to begin. There were two old farmers whom we had noticed occasionally in Deephaven; one was telling the other, with great confusion of pronouns, about a big pig which had lately been killed. "John did feel dreadful disappointed at hav-ing to kill now," we heard him say, "bein' as he had calc'lated to kill along near Thanksgivin' time; there was goin' to be a new moon then, and he expected to get seventy-five or a hun-dred pound more on to him. But he did n't seem to gain, and me and 'Bijah both told him he'd be better to kill now, while everything was favor'ble, and if he set out to wait something might happen to him, and then I've always held that you can't get no hog only just so fur, and for my part I don't like these great overgrown creatur's. I like well enough to see a hog that'll weigh six hunderd, just for the beauty on't, but for my eatin' give me one that'll just rise three. 'Bijah's accu-rate, and he says he is goin' to weigh risin' five hundred and fifty. I shall stop, as I go home, to John's wife's brother's and see if they've got the particulars yet; John was goin' to get the scales this morning. I guess likely consider'ble many'll gather there to-morrow after meeting. John did n't calc'late to cut up till Monday."

"I guess likely I'll stop in to-morrow," said the other man; "I like to see a han'some hog. Chester White, you said? Consider them best, don't ye?" But this question never was answered, for the greater part of the circus company in gorgeous trappings came parading in.

The circus was like all other circuses, except that it was shabbier than most, and the performers seemed to have less heart in it than usual. They did their best, and went through with their parts conscientiously, but they looked as if they never had had a good time in their lives. The audience was hilarious, and cheered and laughed at the tired clown until he looked as if he thought his speeches might possibly be funny, after all. We were so glad we had pleased the poor thing; and when he sang a song our satisfaction was still greater, and so he sang it all over again. Perhaps he had been associating with people who were used to circuses. The afternoon was hot, and the boys with Japanese fans and trays of lemonade did a remarkable business for so late in the season; the brass band on the other side of the tent shrieked its very best, and all the young men of the region had brought their girls, and some of these countless pairs of country lovers we watched a great deal, as they "kept company" with more or less depth of satisfaction in each other. We had a grand chance to see the fashions, and there were many old people and a great number of little children, and some families had evidently locked their house door behind them, since they had brought both the dog and the baby.

"Does n't it seem as if you were a child again?" Kate asked me. "I am sure this is just the same as the first circus I ever saw. It grows more and more familiar, and it puzzles me to think they should not have altered in the least while I have changed so much, and have even had time to grow up. You don't know how it is making me remember other things of which I have not thought for years. I was seven years old when I went that first time. Uncle Jack invited me. I had a new parasol, and he laughed because I would hold it over my shoulder when the sun was in my face. He took me into the side-shows and bought me everything I asked for, on the way home, and we did not get home until twilight. The rest of the family had dined at four o'clock and gone out for a long drive, and it was such fun to have our dinner by ourselves. I sat at the head of the table in mamma's place, and when Bridget came down and insisted that I must go to bed, Uncle Jack came softly up stairs and sat by the window, smoking and telling me stories. He ran and hid in the closet when we heard mamma coming up, and when she found him out by the cigar-smoke, and made believe scold him, I thought she was in earnest, and begged him off. Yes; and I remember that Bridget sat in the next room, making her new dress so she could wear it to church next day. I thought it was a beautiful dress, and besought mamma to have one like it. It was bright green with yellow spots all over it," said Kate. "Ah, poor Uncle Jack! he was so good to me! We were always telling stories of what we would do when I was grown up. He died in Canton the next year, and I cried myself ill; but for a long time I thought he might not be dead, after all, and might come home any day. He used to seem so old to me, and he really was just out of college and not so old as I am now. That day at the circus he had a pink rosebud in his buttonhole, and—ah! when have I ever thought of this before!—a woman sat before us who had a stiff little cape on her bonnet like a shelf, and I carefully put peanuts round the edge of it, and when she moved her head they would fall. I thought it was the best fun in the world, and I wished Uncle Jack to ride the donkey; I was sure he could keep on, because his horse had capered about with him one day on Beacon Street, and I thought him a perfect rider, since nothing had happened to him then."

"I remember," said Mrs. Kew, presently, "that just before I was married 'he' took me over to Wareham Corners to a caravan. My sister Hannah and the young man who was keeping company with her went too. I have n't been to one since till to-day, and it does carry me back same 's it does you, Miss Kate. It does n't seem more than five years ago, and what would I have thought if I had known 'he' and I were going to keep a lighthouse and be contented there, what's more, and sometimes not get ashore for a fortnight; settled, gray-headed old folks! We were gay enough in those days. I know old Miss Sabrina Smith warned me that I'd better think twice before I took up with Tom Kew, for he was a light-minded young man. I speak o' that to him in the winter-time, when he sets reading the almanac half asleep and I'm knitting, and the wind's a' howling and the waves coming ashore on those rocks as if they wished they could put out the light and blow down the lighthouse. We were reflected on a good deal for going to that caravan; some of the old folks didn't think it was improvin'— Well, I should think that man was a trying to break his neck!"

Coming out of the great tent was disagreeable enough, and we seemed to have chosen the worst time, for the crowd pushed fiercely, though I suppose nobody was in the least hurry, and we were all severely jammed, while from somewhere underneath came the wails of a deserted dog. We had not meant to see the side-shows, and went carelessly past two or three tents; but when we came in sight of the picture of the Kentucky giantess, we noticed that Mrs. Kew looked at it wistfully, and we immediately asked if she cared anything about going to see the wonder, whereupon she confessed that she never heard of such a thing as a woman's weighing six hundred and fifty pounds, so we all three went in. There were only two or three persons inside the tent, beside a little boy who played the hand-organ.

The Kentucky giantess sat in two chairs on a platform, and there was a large cage of monkeys just beyond, toward which Kate and I went at once. "Why, she isn't more than two thirds as big as the picture," said Mrs. Kew, in a regretful whisper; "but I guess she's big enough; doesn't she look discouraged, poor creatur'?" Kate and I felt ashamed of ourselves for being there. No matter if she had consented to be carried round for a show, it must have been horrible to be stared at and joked about day after day; and we gravely looked at the monkeys, and in a few minutes turned to see if Mrs. Kew were not ready to come away, when to our surprise we saw that she was talking to the giantess with great interest, and we went nearer.

"I thought your face looked natural the minute I set foot inside the door," said Mrs. Kew; "but you 've—altered some since I saw you, and I could n't place you till I heard you speak. Why, you used to be spare; I am amazed, Marilly! Where are your folks?"

"I don't wonder you are surprised," said the giantess. "I was a good ways from this when you knew me, was n't I? But father he run through with every cent he had before he died, and 'he' took to drink and it killed him after a while, and then I begun to grow worse and worse, till I could n't do nothing to earn a dollar, and everybody was a coming to see me, till at last I used to ask 'em ten cents apiece, and I scratched along somehow till this man came round and heard of me, and he offered me my keep and good pay to go along with him. He had another giantess before me, but she had begun to fall away consider 'ble, so he paid her off and let her go. This other giantess was an awful expense to him, she was such an eater; now I don't have no great of an appetite,"—this was said plaintively,—"and he 's raised my pay since I 've been with him because we did so well. I took up with his offer because I was nothing but a drag and never will be. I 'm as comfortable as I can be, but it 's a pretty hard business. My oldest boy is able to do for himself, but he 's married this last year, and his wife don't want me. I don't know 's I blame her either. It would be something like if I had a daughter now; but there, I 'm getting to like travelling first-rate; it gives anybody a good deal to think of."

"I was asking the folks about you when I was up home the early part of the summer," said Mrs. Kew, "but all they knew was that you were living out in New York State. Have you been living in Kentucky long? I saw it on the picture outside."

"No," said the giantess, "that was a picture the man bought cheap from another show that broke up last year. It says six hundred and fifty pounds, but I don't weigh more than four hundred. I have n't been weighed for some time past. Between you and me I don't weigh so much as that, but you must n't mention it, for it would spoil my reputation, and might hender my getting another engagement." And then the poor giantess lost her professional look and tone as she said, "I believe I 'd rather die than grow any bigger. I do lose heart sometimes, and wish I was a smart woman and could keep house. I 'd be smarter than ever I was when I had the chance; I tell you that! Is Tom along with you?"

"No. I came with these young ladies, Miss Lancaster and Miss Denis, who are stopping over to Deephaven for the summer." Kate and I turned as we heard this introduction; we were standing close by, and I am proud to say that I never saw Kate treat any one more politely than she did that absurd, pitiful creature with the gilt crown and many bracelets. It was not that she said much, but there was such an exquisite courtesy in her manner, and an apparent unconsciousness of there being anything in the least surprising or uncommon about the giantess.

Just then a party of people came in, and Mrs. Kew said good by reluctantly. "It has done me sights of good to see you," said our new acquaintance; "I was feeling down-hearted just before you came in. I 'm pleased to see somebody that remembers me as I used to be." And they shook hands in a way that meant a great deal, and when Kate and I said good afternoon the giantess looked at us gratefully, and said, "I 'm very much obliged to you for coming in, young ladies."

"Walk in! walk in!" the man was shouting as we came away. "Walk in and see the wonder of the world, ladies and gentlemen,—the largest woman ever seen in America,—the great Kentucky giantess!"

"Would n't you have liked to stay longer?" Kate asked Mrs. Kew as we came down the street. But she answered that it would be no satisfaction; the people were coming in, and she would have no chance to talk. "I never knew her very well; she is younger than I, and she used to go to meeting where I did, but she lived five or six miles from our house. She 's had a hard time of it, according to her account," said Mrs. Kew. "She used to be a dreadful flighty, high-tempered girl, but she 's lost that now, I can see by her eyes. I was running over in my mind to see if there was anything I could do for her, but I don't know as there is. She said the man who hired her was kind. I guess your treating her so polite did her as much good as anything. She used to be real ambitious. I had it on my tongue's end to ask her if she couldn't get a few days' leave and come out to stop with me, but I thought just in time that she'd sink the dory in a minute. There! seeing her has took away all the fun," said Mrs. Kew ruefully; and we were all dismal for a while, but at last, after we were fairly started for home, we began to be merry again.

We passed the Craper family whom we had seen at the store in the morning; the children looked as stupid as ever, but the father, I am sorry to say, had been tempted to drink more whiskey than was good for him. He had a bright flush on his cheeks, and he was flourishing his whip, and hoarsely singing some meaningless tune. "Poor creature!" said I, "I should think this day's pleasuring would kill him." "Now, wouldn't you think so?" said Mrs. Kew, sympathizingly; "but the truth is, you couldn't kill one of those Crapers if you pounded him in a mortar."

We had a pleasant drive home, and we kept Mrs. Kew to supper, and afterward went down to the shore to see her set sail for home. Mr. Kew had come in some time before, and had been waiting for the moon to rise. Mrs. Kew told us that she should have enough to think of for a year, she had enjoyed the day so much; and we stood on the pebbles watching the boat out of the harbor, and wishing ourselves on board, it was such a beautiful evening.

We went to another show that summer, the memory of which will never fade. It is somewhat impertinent to call it a show, and "public entertainment" is equally inappropriate, though we certainly were entertained. It had been raining for two or three days; the Deephavenites spoke of it as "a spell of weather." Just after tea, one Thursday evening, Kate and I went down to the post-office. When we opened the great hall door, the salt air was delicious, but we found the town apparently wet through and discouraged; and though it had almost stopped raining just then, there was a Scotch mist, like a snow-storm with the chill taken off, and the Chantrey elms dripped hurriedly, and creaked occasionally in the east-wind.

"There will not be a cap'n on the wharves for a week after this," said I to Kate; "only think of the cases of rheumatism!"

We stopped for a few minutes at the Carews', who were as much surprised to see us as if we had been mermaids out of the sea, and begged us to give ourselves something warm to drink, and to change our boots the moment we got home. Then we went on to the post-office. Kate went in, but stopped, as she came out with our letters, to read a written notice securely fastened to the grocery door by four large carpet-tacks with wide leathers round their necks.

"Dear," said she, exultantly, "there's going to be a lecture to-night in the church,—a free lecture on the Elements of True Manhood. Wouldn't you like to go?" And we went.

We were fifteen minutes later than the time appointed, and were sorry to find that the audience was almost imperceptible. The dampness had affected the antiquated lamps so that those on the walls and on the front of the gallery were the dimmest lights I ever saw, and sent their feeble rays through a small space the edges of which were clearly defined. There were two rather more energetic lights on the table near the pulpit, where the lecturer sat, and as we were in the rear of the church, we could see the yellow fog between ourselves and him. There were fourteen persons in the audience, and we were all huddled together in a cowardly way in the pews nearest the door: three old men, four women, and four children, besides ourselves and the sexton, a deaf little old man with a wooden leg.

The children whispered noisily, and soon, to our surprise, the lecturer rose and began. He bowed, and treated us with beautiful deference, and read his dreary lecture with enthusiasm. I wish I could say, for his sake, that it was interesting; but I cannot tell a lie, and it was so long! He went on and on, until it seemed as if I had been there ever since I was a little girl. Kate and I did not dare to look at each other, and in my desperation at feeling her quiver with laughter, I moved to the other end of the pew, knocking over a big hymn-book on the way, which attracted so much attention that I have seldom felt more embarrassed in my life. Kate's great dog rose several times to shake himself and yawn loudly, and then lie down again despairingly.

You would have thought the man was addressing an enthusiastic Young Men's Christian Association. He exhorted with
fervor upon our duties as citizens and as voters, and told us a
great deal about George Washington and Benjamin Franklin,
whom he urged us to choose as our examples. He waited for
applause after each of his outbursts of eloquence, and presently went on again, in no wise disconcerted at the silence,
and as if he were sure that he would fetch us next time. The
rain began to fall again heavily, and the wind wailed around
the meeting-house. If the lecture had been upon any other
subject it would not have been so hard for Kate and me to
keep sober faces; but it was directed entirely toward young
men, and there was not a young man there.

The children in front of us mildly scuffled with each other
at one time, until the one at the end of the pew dropped a
marble, which struck the floor and rolled with a frightful
noise down the edge of the aisle where there was no carpet.
The congregation instinctively started up to look after it, but
we recollected ourselves and leaned back again in our places,
while the awed children, after keeping unnaturally quiet, fell
asleep, and tumbled against each other helplessly. After a time
the man sat down and wiped his forehead, looking well satisfied; and when we were wondering whether we might with
propriety come away, he rose again, and said it was a free
lecture, and he thanked us for our kind patronage on that
inclement night; but in other places which he had visited
there had been a contribution taken up for the cause. It
would, perhaps, do no harm,—would the sexton—

But the sexton could not have heard the sound of a cannon
at that distance, and slumbered on. Neither Kate nor I had
any money, except a twenty-dollar bill in my purse, and some
coppers in the pocket of her water-proof cloak which she assured me she was prepared to give; but we saw no signs of
the sexton's waking, and as one of the women kindly went
forward to wake the children, we all rose and came away.

After we had made as much fun and laughed as long as we
pleased that night, we became suddenly conscious of the pitiful side of it all; and being anxious that every one should have
the highest opinion of Deephaven, we sent Tom Dockum
early in the morning with an anonymous note to the lecturer,

whom he found without much trouble; but afterward we were disturbed at hearing that he was going to repeat his lecture that evening,—the wind having gone round to the northwest,—and I have no doubt there were a good many women able to be out, and that he harvested enough ten-cent pieces to pay his expenses without our help; though he had particularly told us it was for "the cause," the evening before, and that ought to have been a consolation.

Cunner-Fishing

ONE of the chief pleasures in Deephaven was our house-keeping. Going to market was apt to use up a whole morning, especially if we went to the fish-houses. We depended somewhat upon supplies from Boston, but sometimes we used to chase a butcher who took a drive in his old canvas-topped cart when he felt like it, and as for fish, there were always enough to be caught, even if we could not buy any. Our acquaintances would often ask if we had anything for dinner that day, and would kindly suggest that somebody had been boiling lobsters, or that a boat had just come in with some nice mackerel, or that somebody over on the Ridge was calculating to kill a lamb, and we had better speak for a quarter in good season. I am afraid we were looked upon as being in danger of becoming epicures, which we certainly are not, and we undoubtedly roused a great deal of interest because we used to eat mushrooms, which grew in the suburbs of the town in wild luxuriance.

One morning Maggie told us that there was nothing in the house for dinner, and, taking an early start, we went at once down to the store to ask if the butcher had been seen, but finding that he had gone out deep-sea fishing for two days, and that when he came back he had planned to kill a veal, we left word for a sufficient piece of the doomed animal to be set apart for our family, and strolled down to the shore to see if we could find some mackerel; but there was not a fisherman in sight, and after going to all the fish-houses we concluded that we had better provide for ourselves. We had not brought our own lines, but we knew where Danny kept his, and after finding a basket of suitable size, and taking some clams from Danny's bait-tub, we went over to the hull of an old schooner which was going to pieces alongside one of the ruined wharves. We looked down the hatchway into the hold, and could see the flounders and sculpin swimming about lazily, and once in a while a little pollock scooted down among them impertinently and then disappeared. "There is that same big flounder that we saw day before yesterday," said I. "I know

84

him because one of his fins is half gone. I don't believe he can get out, for the hole in the side of the schooner isn't very wide, and it is higher up than flounders ever swim. Perhaps he came in when he was young, and was too lazy to go out until he was so large he couldn't. Flounders always look so lazy, and as if they thought a great deal of themselves."

"I hope they will think enough of themselves to keep away from my hook this morning," said Kate, philosophically, "and the sculpin too. I am going to fish for cunners alone, and keep my line short." And she perched herself on the quarter, baited her hook carefully, and threw it over, with a clam-shell to call attention. I went to the rail at the side, and we were presently much encouraged by pulling up two small cunners, and felt that our prospects for dinner were excellent. Then I unhappily caught so large a sculpin that it was like pulling up an open umbrella, and after I had thrown him into the hold to keep company with the flounder, our usual good luck seemed to desert us. It was one of the days when, in spite of twitching the line and using all the tricks we could think of, the cunners would either eat our bait or keep away altogether. Kate at last said we must starve unless we could catch the big flounder, and asked me to drop my hook down the hatchway; but it seemed almost too bad to destroy his innocent happiness. Just then we heard the noise of oars, and to our delight saw Cap'n Sands in his dory just beyond the next wharf. "Any luck?" said he. "S'pose ye don't care anything about going out this morning?"

"We are not amusing ourselves; we are trying to catch some fish for dinner," said Kate. "Could you wait out by the red buoy while we get a few more, and then should you be back by noon, or are you going for a longer voyage, Captain Sands?"

"I was going out to Black Rock for cunners myself," said the cap'n. "I should be pleased to take ye, if ye'd like to go." So we wound up our lines, and took our basket and clams and went round to meet the boat. I felt like rowing, and took the oars while Kate was mending her sinker and the cap'n was busy with a snarled line.

"It's pretty hot," said he, presently, "but I see a breeze coming in, and the clouds seem to be thickening; I guess we shall have it cooler 'long towards noon. It looked last night as if we were going to have foul weather, but the scud seemed to blow off, and it was as pretty a morning as ever I see. 'A growing moon chaws up the clouds,' my gran'ther used to say. He was as knowing about the weather as anybody I ever come across; 'most always hit it just about right. Some folks lay all the weather to the moon, accordin' to where she quarters, and when she's in perigee we're going to have this kind of weather, and when she's in apogee she's got to do so and so for sartain; but gran'ther he used to laugh at all them things. He said it never made no kind of difference, and he went by the looks of the clouds and the feel of the air, and he thought folks couldn't make no kind of rules that held good, that had to do with the moon. Well, he did use to depend on the moon some; everybody knows we aren't so likely to have foul weather in a growing moon as we be when she's waning. But some folks I could name, they can't do nothing without having the moon's opinion on it. When I went my second voyage afore the mast we was in port ten days at Cadiz, and the ship she needed salting dreadful. The mate kept telling the captain how low the salt was in her, and we was going a long voyage from there, but no, he wouldn't have her salted nohow, because it was the wane of the moon. He was an amazing set kind of man, the cap'n was, and would have his own way on sea or shore. The mate was his own brother, and they used to fight like a cat and dog; they owned most of the ship between 'em. I was slushing the mizzen-mast, and heard 'em a disputin' about the salt. The cap'n was a first-rate seaman and died rich, but he was dreadful notional. I know one time we were a lyin' out in the stream all ready to weigh anchor, and everything was in trim, the men were up in the rigging and a fresh breeze going out, just what we'd been waiting for, and the word was passed to take in sail and make everything fast. The men swore, and everybody said the cap'n had had some kind of a warning. But that night it began to blow, and I tell you afore morning we were glad enough we were in harbor. The old Victor she dragged her anchor, and the fore-to'-gallant sail and r'yal got loose somehow and was blown out of the bolt-ropes. Most of the canvas and rigging was old, but we had first-rate weather after that, and didn't bend near all the new sail we had aboard, though the cap'n was most afraid we'd come short when we left Boston. That was 'most sixty year ago," said the captain, reflectively. "How time does slip away! You young folks have n't any idea. She was a first-rate ship, the old Victor was, though I suppose she would n't cut much of a dash now 'longside of some of the new clippers.

"There used to be some strange-looking crafts in those days; there was the old brig Hannah. They used to say she would sail backwards as fast as forwards, and she was so square in the bows, they used to call her the sugar-box. She was master old, the Hannah was, and there was n't a port from here to New Orleans where she was n't known; she used to carry a master cargo for her size, more than some ships that ranked two hundred and fifty ton, and she was put down for two hundred. She used to make good voyages, the Hannah did, and then there was the Pactolus; she was just about such another,—you would have laughed to see her. She sailed out of this port for a good many years. Cap'n Wall he told me that if he had her before the wind with a cargo of cotton, she would make a middling good run, but load her deep with salt, and you might as well try to sail a stick of oak timber with a handkerchief. She was a stout-built ship: I should n't wonder if her timbers were afloat somewhere yet; she was sold to some parties out in San Francisco. There! everything's changed from what it was when I used to follow the sea. I wonder sometimes if the sailors have as queer works aboard ship as they used. Bless ye! Deephaven used to be a different place to what it is now; there was hardly a day in the year that you did n't hear the shipwrights' hammers, and there was always something going on at the wharves. You would see the folks from up country comin' in with their loads of oak knees and plank, and logs o' rock-maple for keels when there was snow on the ground in winter-time, and the big sticks of timber-pine for masts would come crawling along the road with their three and four yoke of oxen all frosted up, the sleds creaking and the snow growling and the men flapping their arms to keep warm, and hallooing as if there wan't nothin' else goin' on in the world except to get them masts to the ship-yard. Bless ye! two o' them teams together would stretch from here 'most up to the Widow Jim's place,—no such timber-pines nowadays."

"I suppose the sailors are very jolly together sometimes," said Kate, meditatively, with the least flicker of a smile at me. The captain did not answer for a minute, as he was battling with an obstinate snarl in his line; but when he had found the right loop he said, "I've had the best times and the hardest times of my life at sea, that's certain! I was just thinking it over when you spoke. I'll tell you some stories one day or 'nother that'll please you. Land! you've no idea what tricks some of those wild fellows will be up to. Now, saying they fetch home a cargo of wines and they want a drink; they've got a trick so they can get it. Saying it's champagne, they'll fetch up a basket, and how do you suppose they'll get into it?"

Of course we did n't know.

"Well, every basket will be counted, and they're fastened up particular, so they can tell in a minute if they've been tampered with; and neither must you draw the corks if you could get the basket open. I suppose ye may have seen champagne, how it's all wired and waxed. Now, they take a clean tub, them fellows do, and just shake the basket and jounce it up and down till they break the bottles and let the wine drain out; then they take it down in the hold and put it back with the rest, and when the cargo is delivered there's only one or two whole bottles in that basket, and there's a dreadful fuss about its being stowed so foolish." The captain told this with an air of great satisfaction, but we did not show the least suspicion that he might have assisted at some such festivity.

"Then they have a way of breaking into a cask. It won't do to start the bung, and it won't do to bore a hole where it can be seen, but they're up to that: they slip back one of the end hoops and bore two holes underneath it, one for the air to go in and one for the liquor to come out, and after they get all out they want they put in some spigots and cut them down close to the stave, knock back the hoop again, and there ye are, all trig."

"I never should have thought of it," said Kate, admiringly.

"There is n't nothing," Cap'n Sands went on, "that'll hender some masters from cheating the owners a little. Get them off in a foreign port, and there's nobody to watch, and they most of them have a feeling that they ain't getting full pay, and they'll charge things to the ship that she never seen nor heard of. There were two shipmasters that sailed out of Salem. I heard one of 'em tell the story. They had both come into port from Liverpool nigh the same time, and one of 'em, he was dressed up in a handsome suit of clothes, and the other looked kind of poverty-struck. 'Where did you get them clothes?' says he. 'Why, to Liverpool,' says the other; 'you don't mean to say you come away without none, cheap as cloth was there?' 'Why, yes,' says the other cap'n,—'I can't afford to wear such clothes as those be, and I don't see how you can, either.' 'Charge 'em to the ship, bless ye; the owners expect it.'

"So the next v'y'ge the poor cap'n he had a nice rig for himself made to the best tailor's in Bristol, and charged it, say ten pounds, in the ship's account; and when he came home the ship's husband he was looking over the papers, and 'What's this?' says he, 'how come the ship to run up a tailor's bill?' 'Why, them's mine,' says the cap'n, very meaching. 'I onderstood that there wouldn't be no objection made.' 'Well, you made a mistake,' says the other, laughing; 'guess I'd better scratch this out.' And it wasn't long before the cap'n met the one who had put him up to doing it, and he give him a blowing up for getting him into such a fix. 'Land sakes alive!' says he, 'were you fool enough to set it down in the account? Why, I put mine in, so many bolts of Russia duck.'"

Captain Sands seemed to enjoy this reminiscence, and to our satisfaction, in a few minutes, after he had offered to take the oars, he went on to tell us another story.

"Why, as for cheating, there's plenty of that all over the world. The first v'y'ge I went into Havana as master of the Deerhound, she had never been in the port before and had to be measured and recorded, and then pay her tonnage duties every time she went into port there afterward, according to what she was registered on the custom-house books. The inspector he come aboard, and he went below and looked round, and he measured her between decks; but he never offered to set down any figgers, and when we came back into the cabin, says he, 'Yes—yes—good ship! you put one dou-

bloon front of this eye, *so!* says he, 'an' I not see with him;
and you put one more doubloon front of other eye, and how
you think I see at all what figger you write?' So I took his
book and I set down her measurements and made her out
twenty ton short, and he took his doubloons and shoved 'em
into his pocket. There, it is n't what you call straight dealing,
but everybody done it that dared, and you 'd eat up all the
profits of a v'y 'ge and the owners would just as soon you 'd
try a little up-country air, if you paid all those dues according
to law. Tonnage was dreadful high and wharfage too, in some
ports, and they 'd get your last cent some way or 'nother if ye
were n't sharp.

"Old Cap'n Carew, uncle to them ye see to meeting, did a
smart thing in the time of the embargo. Folks got tired of it,
and it was dreadful hard times; ships rotting at the wharves,
and Deephaven never was quite the same afterward, though
the old place held out for a good while before she let go as ye
see her now. You 'd 'a' had a hard grip on 't when I was a
young man to make me believe it would ever be so dull here.
Well, Cap'n Carew he bought an old brig that was lying over
by East Parish, and he began fitting her up and loading her
for the West Indies, and the farmers they 'd come in there by
night from all round the country, to sell salt-fish and lumber
and potatoes, and glad enough they were, I tell ye. The rigging was put in order, and it was n't long before she was
ready to sail, and it was all kept mighty quiet. She lay up to
an old wharf in a cove where she would n't be much noticed,
and they took care not to paint her any or to attract any attention.

"One day Cap'n Carew was over in Riverport dining out
with some gentlemen, and the revenue officer sat next to him,
and by and by says he, 'Why won't ye take a ride with me this
afternoon? I 've had warning that there 's a brig loading for
the West Indies over beyond Deephaven somewheres, and
I 'm going over to seize her.' And he laughed to himself as if
he expected fun, and something in his pocket beside. Well, the
first minute that Cap'n Carew dared, after dinner, he slipped
out, and he hired the swiftest horse in Riverport and rode for
dear life, and told the folks who were in the secret, and some
who were n't, what was the matter, and every soul turned to

and helped finish loading her and getting the rigging ready and the water aboard; but just as they were leaving the cove—the wind was blowing just right—along came the revenue officer with two or three men, and they come off in a boat and boarded her as important as could be.

" 'Won't ye step into the cabin, gentlemen, and take a glass o' wine?' says Cap'n Carew, very polite; and the wind came in fresher,—something like a squall for a few minutes,—and the men had the sails spread before you could say Jack Robi-'son, and before those fellows knew what they were about the old brig was a standing out to sea, and the folks on the wharves cheered and yelled. The Cap'n gave the officers a good scare and offered 'em a free passage to the West Indies, and finally they said they would n't report at headquarters if he 'd let 'em go ashore; so he told the sailors to lower their boat about two miles off Deephaven, and they pulled ashore meek enough. Cap'n Carew had a first-rate run, and made a lot of money, so I have heard it said. Bless ye! every shipmaster would have done just the same if he had dared, and everybody was glad when they heard about it. Dreadful foolish piece of business that embargo was!

"Now I declare," said Captain Sands, after he had finished this narrative, "here I 'm a telling stories and you 're doin' all the work. You 'll pull a boat ahead of anybody, if you keep on. Tom Kew was a-praisin' up both of you to me the other day: says he, 'They don't put on no airs, but I tell ye they can pull a boat well, and swim like fish,' says he. There now, if you 'll give me the oars I 'll put the dory just where I want her, and you can be getting your lines ready. I know a place here where it 's always toler'ble fishing, and I guess we 'll get something."

Kate and I cracked our clams on the gunwale of the boat, and cut them into nice little bits for bait with a piece of the shell, and by the time the captain had thrown out the killick we were ready to begin, and found the fishing much more exciting than it had been at the wharf.

"I don't know as I ever see 'em bite faster," said the old sailor, presently; "guess it 's because they like the folks that 's fishing. Well, I 'm pleased. I thought I 'd let 'Bijah take some along to Denby in the cart to-morrow if I got more than I could use at home. I did n't calc'late on having such a lively crew aboard. I s'pose ye would n't care about going out a little further by and by to see if we can't get two or three haddock?" And we answered that we should like nothing better.

It was growing cloudy, and was much cooler,—the perfection of a day for fishing,—and we sat there diligently pulling in cunners, and talking a little once in a while. The tide was nearly out, and Black Rock looked almost large enough to be called an island. The sea was smooth and the low waves broke lazily among the seaweed-covered ledges, while our boat swayed about on the water, lifting and falling gently as the waves went in shore. We were not a very long way from the lighthouse, and once we could see Mrs. Kew's big white apron as she stood in the doorway for a few minutes. There was no noise except the plash of the low-tide waves and the occasional flutter of a fish in the bottom of the dory. Kate and I always killed our fish at once by a rap on the head, for it certainly saved the poor creatures much discomfort, and ourselves as well, and it made it easier to take them off the hook than if they were flopping about and making us aware of our cruelty.

Suddenly the captain wound up his line and said he thought we'd better be going in, and Kate and I looked at him with surprise. "It is only half past ten," said I, looking at my watch. "Don't hurry in on our account," added Kate, persuasively, for we were having a very good time.

"I guess we won't mind about the haddock. I've got a feelin' we'd better go ashore." And he looked up into the sky and turned to see the west. "I knew there was something the matter; there's going to be a shower." And we looked behind us to see a bank of heavy clouds coming over fast. "I wish we had two pair of oars," said Captain Sands. "I'm afraid we shall get caught."

"You need n't mind us," said Kate. "We are n't in the least afraid of our clothes, and we don't get cold when we're wet; we have made sure of that."

"Well, I'm glad to hear that," said the cap'n. "Women-folks are apt to be dreadful scared of a wetting; but I'd just as lief not get wet myself. I had a twinge of rheumatism yesterday. I guess we'll get ashore fast enough. No. I feel well enough to-day, but you can row if you want to, and I'll take the oars the last part of the way."

When we reached the moorings the clouds were black, and the thunder rattled and boomed over the sea, while heavy spatters of rain were already falling. We did not go to the wharves, but stopped down the shore at the fish-houses, the nearer place of shelter. "You just select some of those cunners," said the captain, who was beginning to be a little out of breath, "and then you can run right up and get under cover, and I'll put a bit of old sail over the rest of the fish to keep the fresh water off." By the time the boat touched the shore and we had pulled it up on the pebbles, the rain had begun in good earnest. Luckily there was a barrow lying near, and we loaded that in a hurry, and just then the captain caught sight of a well-known red shirt in an open door, and shouted, "Halloa, Danny! lend us a hand with these fish, for we're nigh on to being shipwrecked." And then we ran up to the fish-house and waited awhile, though we stood in the door-way watching the lightning, and there were so many leaks in the roof that we might almost as well have been out of doors. It was one of Danny's quietest days, and he silently beheaded hake, only winking at us once very gravely at something our other companion said.

"There!" said Captain Sands, "folks may say what they have a mind to; I didn't see that shower coming up, and I know as well as I want to that my wife did, and impressed it on my mind. Our house sets high, and she watches the sky and is al'ays a worrying when I go out fishing for fear something's going to happen to me, 'specially sence I've got to be along in years."

This was just what Kate and I wished to hear, for we had been told that Captain Sands had most decided opinions on dreams and other mysteries, and could tell some stories which were considered incredible by even a Deephaven audience, to whom the marvellous was of every-day occurrence.

"Then it has happened before?" asked Kate. "I wondered why you started so suddenly to come in."

"Happened!" said the captain. "Bless ye, yes! I'll tell you my views about these p'ints one o' those days. I've thought a good deal about 'em by spells. Not that I can explain 'em, nor anybody else, but it's no use to laugh at 'em as some folks do. Cap'n Lant—you know Cap'n Lant?—he and I have talked it over consider'ble, and he says to me, 'Everybody's got some story of the kind they will believe in spite of everything, and yet they won't believe yourn.' "

The shower seemed to be over now, and we felt compelled to go home, as the captain did not go on with his remarks. I hope he did not see Danny's wink. Skipper Scudder, who was Danny's friend and partner, came up just then and asked us if we knew what the sign was when the sun came out through the rain. I said that I had always heard it would rain again next day. "O no," said Skipper Scudder, "the Devil is whipping his wife."

After dinner Kate and I went for a walk through some pine woods which were beautiful after the rain; the mosses and lichens which had been dried up were all freshened and blooming out in the dampness. The smell of the wet pitch-pines was unusually sweet, and we wandered about for an hour or two there, to find some ferns we wanted, and then walked over toward East Parish, and home by the long beach late in the afternoon. We came as far as the boat-landing, meaning to go home through the lane, but to our delight we saw Captain Sands sitting alone on an old overturned whale-boat, whittling busily at a piece of dried kelp. "Good evenin'," said our friend, cheerfully. And we explained that we had taken a long walk and thought we would rest awhile before we went home to supper. Kate perched herself on the boat, and I sat down on a ship's knee which lay on the pebbles.

"Didn't get any hurt from being out in the shower, I hope?"

"No, indeed," laughed Kate, "and we had such a good time. I hope you won't mind taking us out again some time."

"Bless ye! no," said the captain. "My girl Lo'isa, she that's Mis Winslow over to Riverport, used to go out with me a good deal, and it seemed natural to have you aboard. I missed Lo'isa after she got married, for she was al'ays ready to go anywhere 'long of father. She's had slim health of late years. I tell 'em she's been too much shut up out of the fresh air and sun. When she was young her mother never could pr'vail on her to set in the house stiddy and sew, and she used to have great misgivin's that Lo'isa never was going to be capable. How about those fish you caught this morning? good, were they? Mis Sands had dinner on the stocks when I got home, and she said she would n't fry any 'til supper-time; but I cal-c'lated to have 'em this noon. I like 'em best right out o' the water. Little more and we should have got them wet. That's one of my whims; I can't bear to let fish get rained on."

"O Captain Sands!" said I, there being a convenient pause, "you were speaking of your wife just now; did you ask her if she saw the shower?"

"First thing she spoke of when I got into the house. 'There,' says she, 'I was afraid you would n't see the rain coming in time, and I had my heart in my mouth when it began to thunder. I thought you'd get soaked through, and be laid up for a fortnight,' says she. 'I guess a summer shower won't hurt an old sailor like me,' says I." And the captain reached for another piece of his kelp-stalk, and whittled away more busily than ever. Kate took out her knife and also began to cut kelp, and I threw pebbles in the hope of hitting a spider which sat complacently on a stone not far away, and when he suddenly vanished there was nothing for me to do but to whittle kelp also.

"Do you suppose," said Kate, "that Mrs. Sands really made you know about that shower?"

The captain put on his most serious look, coughed slowly, and moved himself a few inches nearer us, along the boat. I think he fully understood the importance and solemnity of the subject. "It ain't for us to say what we do know or don't, for there's nothing sartain, but I made up my mind long ago that there's something about these p'ints that's myster'ous. My wife and me will be sitting there to home and there won't be no word between us for an hour, and then of a sudden we'll speak up about the same thing. Now the way I view it, she either puts it into my head or I into hers. I've spoke up lots of times about something, when I did n't know what I was going to say when I began, and she'll say she was just thinking of that. Like as not you have noticed it sometimes? There was something my mind was dwellin' on yesterday, and she come right out with it, and I'd a good deal rather she had n't," said the captain, ruefully. "I did n't want to rake it all over ag'in, *I*'m sure." And then he recollected himself, and was silent, which his audience must confess to have regretted for a moment.

"I used to think a good deal about such things when I was younger, and I'm free to say I took more stock in dreams and such like than I do now. I rec'lect old Parson Lorimer—this Parson Lorimer's father who was settled here first—spoke to me once about it, and said it was a tempting of Providence, and that we had n't no right to pry into secrets. I know I had a dream-book then that I picked up in a shop in Bristol once when I was there on the Ranger, and all the young folks were beset to get sight of it. I see what fools it made of folks, bothering their heads about such things, and I pretty much let them go: all this stuff about spirit-rappings is enough to make a man crazy. You don't get no good by it. I come across a paper once with a lot of letters in it from sperits, and I cast my eye over 'em, and I says to myself, 'Well, I always was given to understand that when we come to a futur' state we was goin' to have more wisdom than we can get afore'; but them letters had n't any more sense to 'em, nor so much, as a man could write here without schooling, and I should think that if the letters be all straight, if the folks who wrote 'em had any kind of ambition they'd want to be movin' back here again. But as for one person's having something to do with another any distance off, why, that's another thing; there ain't any nonsense about that. I know it's true jest as well as I want to," said the cap'n, warming up. "I'll tell ye how I was led to make up my mind about it. One time I waked a man up out of a sound sleep looking at him, and it set me to thinking. First, there was n't any noise, and then ag'in there was n't any touch so he could feel it, and I says to myself, 'Why could n't I ha' done it the width of two rooms as well as one, and why could n't I ha' done it with my back turned?' It could n't have been the looking so much as the thinking. And then I car'd it further, and I says, 'Why ain't a mile as good as a yard? and it's the thinking that does it,' says I, 'and we've got some faculty or other that we don't know much about. We've got some way of sending our thought like a bullet goes out of a gun and it hits. We don't know nothing except what we see. And some folks is scared, and some more thinks it is all nonsense and laughs. But there's something we haven't got the hang of.' It makes me think o' them little black polliwogs that turns into frogs in the fresh-water puddles in the ma'sh. There's a time before their tails drop off and their legs have sprouted out, when they don't get any use o' their legs, and I dare say they're in their way consider'ble; but after they get to be frogs they find out what they're for without no kind of trouble. I guess we shall turn these fac'lties to account some time or 'nother. Seems to me, though, that we might depend on 'em now more than we do."

The captain was under full sail on what we had heard was his pet subject, and it was a great satisfaction to listen to what he had to say. It loses a great deal in being written, for the old sailor's voice and gestures and thorough earnestness all carried no little persuasion. And it was impossible not to be sure that he knew more than people usually do about these mysteries in which he delighted.

"Now, how can you account for this?" said he. "I remember not more than ten years ago my son's wife was stopping at our house, and she had left her child at home while she come away for a rest. And after she had been there two or three days, one morning she was sitting in the kitchen 'long o' the folks, and all of a sudden she jumped out of her chair and ran into the bedroom, and next minute she come out laughing, and looking kind of scared. 'I could ha' taken my oath,' says she, 'that I heard Katy cryin' out mother,' says she, 'just as if she was hurt. I heard it so plain that before I stopped to think it seemed as if she were right in the next room. I'm afeard something has happened.' But the folks laughed, and said she must ha' heard one of the lambs. 'No, it wasn't,' says she, 'it was Katy.' And sure enough, just after dinner a young man who lived neighbor to her come riding into the yard post-haste to get her to go home, for the baby had pulled some hot water over on to herself and was nigh scalded to death and cryin' for her mother every minute. Now, who's going to explain that? It wasn't any common hearing that heard that child's cryin' fifteen miles. And I can tell you another thing that happened among my own folks. There was an own cousin of mine married to a man by the name of John

Hathorn. He was trading up to Parsonsfield, and business run down, so he wound up there, and thought he'd make a new start. He moved down to Denby, and while he was getting under way, he left his family up to the old place, and at the time I speak of, was going to move 'em down in about a fortnight.

"One morning his wife was fidgeting round, and finally she came down stairs with her bonnet and shawl on, and said somebody must put the horse right into the wagon and take her down to Denby. 'Why, what for, mother?' they says. 'Don't stop to talk,' says she; 'your father is sick, and wants me. It's been a worrying me since before day, and I can't stand it no longer.' And the short of the story is that she kept hurrying 'em faster and faster, and then she got hold of the reins herself, and when they got within five miles of the place the horse fell dead, and she was nigh about crazy, and they took another horse at a farm-house on the road. It was the spring of the year, and the going was dreadful, and when they got to the house John Hathorn had just died, and he had been calling for his wife up to 'most the last breath he drew. He had been taken sick sudden the day before, but the folks knew it was bad travelling, and that she was a feeble woman to come near thirty miles, and they had no idee he was so bad off. I'm telling you the living truth," said Captain Sands, with an emphatic shake of his head. "There's more folks than me can tell about it, and if you were goin' to keel-haul me next minute, and hang me to the yard-arm afterward, I couldn't say it different. I was up to Parsonsfield to the funeral; it was just after I quit following the sea. I never saw a woman so broke down as she was. John was a nice man; stiddy and pleasant-spoken and straightforrard and kind to his folks. He belonged to the Odd Fellows, and they all marched to the funeral. There was a good deal of respect shown him, I tell ye.

"There is another story I'd like to have ye hear, if it's so that you ain't beat out hearing me talk. When I get going I slip along as easy as a schooner wing-and-wing afore the wind.

"This happened to my own father, but I never heard him say much about it; never could get him to talk it over to any length, best I could do. But gran'ther, his father, told me about it nigh upon fifty times, first and last, and always the same way. Gran'ther lived to be old, and there was ten or a dozen years after his wife died that he lived year and year about with Uncle Tobias's folks and our folks. Uncle Tobias lived over on the Ridge. I got home from my first v'y'ge as mate of the Daylight just in time for his funeral. I was disapp'inted to find the old man was gone. I'd fetched him some first-rate tobacco, for he was a great hand to smoke, and I was calc'latin' on his being pleased: old folks like to be thought of, and then he set more by me than by the other boys. I know I used to be sorry for him when I was a little fellow. My father's second wife she was a well-meaning woman, but an awful driver with her work, and she was always making of him feel he was n't no use. I do' know as she meant to, either. He never said nothing, and he was always just so pleasant, and he was fond of his book, and used to set round reading, and tried to keep himself out of the way just as much as he could. There was one winter when I was small that I had the scarlet-fever, and was very slim for a long time afterward, and I used to keep along o' gran'ther, and he would tell me stories. He'd been a sailor,—it runs in our blood to foller the sea,—and he'd been wrecked two or three times and been taken by the Algerine pirates. You remind me to tell you some time about that; and I wonder if you ever heard about old Citizen Leigh, that used to be about here when I was a boy. He was taken by the Algerines once, same's gran'ther, and they was dreadful f'erce just then, and they sent him home to get the ransom money for the crew; but it was a monstrous price they asked, and the owners would n't give it to him, and they s'posed likely the men was dead by that time, any way. Old Citizen Leigh he went crazy, and used to go about the streets with a bundle of papers in his hands year in and year out. I've seen him a good many times. Gran'ther used to tell me how he escaped. I'll remember it for ye some day if you'll put me in mind.

"I got to be mate when I was twenty, and I was as strong a fellow as you could scare up, and darin'!—why, it makes my blood run cold when I think of the reckless things I used to do. I was off at sea after I was fifteen year old, and there was n't anybody so glad to see me as gran'ther when I came home. I expect he used to be lonesome after I went off, but then his mind failed him quite a while before he died. Father was clever to him, and he'd get him anything he spoke about; but he wasn't a man to set round and talk, and he never took notice himself when gran'ther was out of tobacco, so sometimes it would be a day or two. I know better how he used to feel now that I'm getting to be along in years myself, and likely to be some care to the folks before long. I never could bear to see old folks neglected; nice old men and women who have worked hard in their day and been useful and willin'. I've seen 'em many a time when they couldn't help knowing that the folks would a little rather they'd be in heaven, and a good respectable headstone put up for 'em in the burying-ground.

"Well, now, I'm sure I've forgot what I was going to tell you. O, yes; about grandmother dreaming about father when he come home from sea. Well, to go back to the first of it, gran'ther never was rugged; he had ship-fever when he was a young man, and though he lived to be so old, he never could work hard and never got forehanded; and Aunt Hannah Starbird over at East Parish took my sister to fetch up, because she was named for her, and Melinda and Tobias stayed at home with the old folks, and my father went to live with an uncle over in Riverport, whom he was named for. He was in the West India trade and was well-off, and he had no children, so they expected he would do well by father. He was dreadful high-tempered. I've heard say he had the worst temper that was ever raised in Deephaven.

"One day he set father to putting some cherries into a bar'l of rum, and went off down to his wharf to see to the loading of a vessel, and afore he come back father found he'd got hold of the wrong bar'l, and had sp'ilt a bar'l of the best Holland gin; he tried to get the cherries out, but that wasn't any use, and he was dreadful afraid of Uncle Matthew, and he run away, and never was heard of from that time out. They supposed he'd run away to sea, as he had a leaning that way, but nobody ever knew for certain; and his mother she 'most mourned herself to death. Gran'ther told me that it got so at last that if they could only know for sure that he was dead it was all they would ask. But it went on four years, and gran'ther got used to it some; though grandmother never would give up. And one morning early, before day, she waked him up, and says she, 'We're going to hear from Matthew. Get up quick and go down to the store!' 'Nonsense,' says he. 'I've seen him,' says grandmother, 'and he's coming home. He looks older, but just the same other ways, and he's got long hair, like a horse's mane, all down over his shoulders.' 'Well, let the dead rest,' says gran'ther; 'you've thought about the boy till your head is turned.' 'I tell you I saw Matthew himself,' says she, 'and I want you to go right down to see if there isn't a letter.' And she kept at him till he saddled the horse, and he got down to the store before it was opened in the morning, and he had to wait round, and when the man came over to unlock it he was 'most ashamed to tell what his errand was, for he had been so many times, and everybody supposed the boy was dead. When he asked for a letter, the man said there was none there, and asked if he was expecting any particular one. He didn't get many letters, I s'pose; all his folks lived about here, and people didn't write any to speak of in those days. Gran'ther said he thought he wouldn't make such a fool of himself again, but he didn't say anything, and he waited round awhile, talking to one and another who came up, and by and by says the store-keeper, who was reading a newspaper that had just come, 'Here's some news for you, Sands, I do believe! There are three vessels come into Boston harbor that have been out whaling and sealing in the South Seas for three or four years, and your son Matthew's name is down on the list of the crew.' 'I tell ye,' says gran'ther, 'I took that paper, and I got on my horse and put for home, and your grandmother she hailed me, and she said, "You've heard, have n't you?" before I told her a word.'

"Gran'ther he got his breakfast and started right off for Boston, and got there early the second day, and went right down on the wharves. Somebody lent him a boat, and he went out to where there were two sealers laying off riding at anchor, and he asked a sailor if Matthew was aboard. 'Ay, ay,' says the sailor, 'he's down below.' And he sung out for him, and when he come up out of the hold his hair was long, down over his shoulders like a horse's mane, just as his mother saw it in the dream. Gran'ther he did n't know what to say,—it scared him,—and he asked how it happened; and father told how they'd been off sealing in the South Seas, and he and another man had lived alone on an island for months, and the whole crew had grown wild in their ways of living, being off so long, and for one thing had gone without caps and let their hair grow. The rest of the men had been ashore and got fixed up smart, but he had been busy, and had put it off till that morning; he was just going ashore then. Father was all struck up when he heard about the dream, and said his mind had been dwellin' on his mother and going home, and he come down to let her see him just as he was and she said it was the same way he looked in the dream. He never would have his hair cut—father would n't—and wore it in a queue. I remember seeing him with it when I was a boy; but his second wife did n't like the looks of it, and she come up behind him one day and cut it off with the scissors. He was terrible worked up about it. I never see father so mad as he was that day. Now this is just as true as the Bible," said Captain Sands. "I have n't put a word to it, and gran'ther al'ays told a story just as it was. That woman saw her son; but if you ask me what kind of eyesight it was, I can't tell you, nor nobody else."

Later that evening Kate and I drifted into a long talk about the captain's stories and these mysterious powers of which we know so little. It was somewhat chilly in the house, and we had kindled a fire in the fireplace, which at first made a blaze which lighted the old room royally, and then quieted down into red coals and lazy puffs of smoke. We had carried the lights away, and sat with our feet on the fender, and Kate's great dog was lying between us on the rug. I remember that evening so well; we could see the stars through the window plainer and plainer as the fire went down, and we could hear the noise of the sea.

"Do you remember in the old myth of Demeter and Persephone," Kate asked me, "where Demeter takes care of the child and gives it ambrosia and hides it in fire, because she loves it and wishes to make it immortal, and to give it eternal youth; and then the mother finds it out and cries in terror to hinder her, and the goddess angrily throws the child down and rushes away? And he had to share the common destiny of mankind, though he always had some wonderful inscrutable grace and wisdom, because a goddess had loved him and held him in her arms. I always thought that part of the story beautiful where Demeter throws off her disguise and is no longer an old woman, and the great house is filled with brightness like lightning, and she rushes out through the halls with her yellow hair waving over her shoulders, and the people would give anything to bring her back again, and to undo their mistake. I knew it almost all by heart once," said Kate, "and I am always finding a new meaning in it. I was just thinking that it may be that we all have given to us more or less of another nature, as the child had whom Demeter wished to make like the gods. I believe old Captain Sands is right, and we have these instincts which defy all our wisdom and for which we never can frame any laws. We may laugh at them, but we are always meeting them, and one cannot help knowing that it has been the same through all history. They are powers which are imperfectly developed in this life, but one cannot help the thought that the mystery of this world may be the commonplace of the next."

"I wonder," said I, "why it is that one hears so much more of such things from simple country people. They believe in dreams, and they have a kind of fetichism, and believe so heartily in supernatural causes. I suppose nothing could shake Mrs. Patton's faith in warnings. There is no end of absurdity in it, and yet there is one side of such lives for which one cannot help having reverence; they live so much nearer to nature than people who are in cities, and there is a soberness about country people oftentimes that one cannot help noticing. I wonder if they are unconsciously awed by the strength and purpose in the world about them, and the mysterious creative power which is at work with them on their familiar farms. In their simple life they take their instincts for truths, and perhaps they are not always so far wrong as we imagine. Because they are so instinctive and unreasoning they may have a more complete sympathy with Nature, and may hear her voices when wiser ears are deaf. They have much in common, after all, with the plants which grow up out of the ground and the wild creatures which depend upon their instincts wholly."

"I think," said Kate, "that the more one lives out of doors the more personality there seems to be in what we call inanimate things. The strength of the hills and the voice of the waves are no longer only grand poetical sentences, but an expression of something real, and more and more one finds God himself in the world, and believes that we may read the thoughts that He writes for us in the book of Nature." And after this we were silent for a while, and in the mean time it grew very late, and we watched the fire until there were only a few sparks left in the ashes. The stars faded away and the moon came up out of the sea, and we barred the great hall door and went up stairs to bed. The lighthouse lamp burned steadily, and it was the only light that had not been blown out in all Deephaven.

Mrs. Bonny

I AM sure that Kate Lancaster and I must have spent by far the greater part of the summer out of doors. We often made long expeditions out into the suburbs of Deephaven, sometimes being gone all day, and sometimes taking a long afternoon stroll and coming home early in the evening hungry as hunters and laden with treasure, whether we had been through the pine woods inland or alongshore, whether we had met old friends or made some desirable new acquaintances. We had a fashion of calling at the farm-houses, and by the end of the season we knew as many people as if we had lived in Deephaven all our days. We used to ask for a drink of water; this was our unfailing introduction, and afterward there were many interesting subjects which one could introduce, and we could always give the latest news at the shore. It was amusing to see the curiosity which we aroused. Many of the people came into Deephaven only on special occasions, and I must confess that at first we were often naughty enough to wait until we had been severely cross-questioned before we gave a definite account of ourselves. Kate was very clever at making unsatisfactory answers when she cared to do so. We did not understand, for some time, with what a keen sense of enjoyment many of those people made the acquaintance of an entirely new person who cordially gave the full particulars about herself; but we soon learned to call this by another name than impertinence.

I think there were no points of interest in that region which we did not visit with conscientious faithfulness. There were cliffs and pebble-beaches, the long sands and the short sands; there were Black Rock and Roaring Rock, High Point and East Point, and Spouting Rock; we went to see where a ship had been driven ashore in the night, all hands being lost and not a piece of her left larger than an axe-handle; we visited the spot where a ship had come ashore in the fog, and had been left high and dry on the edge of the marsh when the tide went out; we saw where the brig Methuselah had been wrecked, and the shore had been golden with her cargo of lemons and oranges, which one might carry away by the wherryful.

Inland there were not many noted localities, but we used to enjoy the woods, and our explorations among the farms, immensely. To the westward the land was better and the people well-to-do; but we went oftenest toward the hills and among the poorer people. The land was uneven and full of ledges, and the people worked hard for their living, at most laying aside only a few dollars each year. Some of the more enterprising young people went away to work in shops and factories; but the custom was by no means universal, and the people had a hungry, discouraged look. It is all very well to say that they knew nothing better, that it was the only life of which they knew anything; there was too often a look of disappointment in their faces, and sooner or later we heard or guessed many stories: that this young man had wished for an education, but there had been no money to spare for books or schooling; and that one had meant to learn a trade, but there must be some one to help his father with the farm-work, and there was no money to hire a man to work in his place if he went away. The older people had a hard look, as if they had always to be on the alert and must fight for their place in the world. One could only forgive and pity their petty sharpness, which showed itself in trifling bargains, when one understood how much a single dollar seemed where dollars came so rarely. We used to pity the young girls so much. It was plain that those who knew how much easier and pleasanter our lives were could not help envying us.

There was a high hill half a dozen miles from Deephaven which was known in its region as "the mountain." It was the highest land anywhere near us, and having been told that there was a fine view from the top, one day we went there, with Tommy Dockum for escort. We overtook Mr. Lorimer, the minister, on his way to make parochial calls upon some members of his parish who lived far from church, and to our delight he proposed to go with us instead. It was a great satisfaction to have him for a guide, for he knew both the country and the people more intimately than any one else. It was a long climb to the top of the hill, but not a hard one. The sky was clear, and there was a fresh wind, though we had left

none at all at the sea-level. After lunch, Kate and I spread
our shawls over a fine cushion of mountain-cranberry, and
had a long talk with Mr. Lorimer about ancient and modern
Deephaven. He always seemed as much pleased with our enthusiasm for the town as if it had been a personal favor and
compliment to himself. I remember how far we could see,
that day, and how we looked toward the far-away blue
mountains, and then out over the ocean. Deephaven looked
insignificant from that height and distance, and indeed the
country seemed to be mostly covered with the pointed tops
of pines and spruces, and there were long tracts of maple
and beech woods with their coloring of lighter, fresher
green.

"Suppose we go down, now," said Mr. Lorimer, long before Kate and I had meant to propose such a thing; and our
feeling was that of dismay. "I should like to take you to make
a call with me. Did you ever hear of old Mrs. Bonny?"

"No," said we, and cheerfully gathered our wraps and baskets; and when Tommy finally came panting up the hill after
we had begun to think that our shoutings and whistling were
useless, we sent him down to the horses, and went down ourselves by another path. It led us a long distance through a
grove of young beeches; the last year's whitish leaves lay thick
on the ground, and the new leaves made so close a roof overhead that the light was strangely purple, as if it had come
through a great church window of stained glass. After this we
went through some hemlock growth, where, on the lower
branches, the pale green of the new shoots and the dark green
of the old made an exquisite contrast each to the other. Finally we came out at Mrs. Bonny's. Mr. Lorimer had told us
something about her on the way down, saying in the first
place that she was one of the queerest characters he knew.
Her husband used to be a charcoal-burner and basket-maker,
and she used to sell butter and berries and eggs, and choke-
pears preserved in molasses. She always came down to Deephaven on a little black horse, with her goods in baskets and
bags which were fastened to the saddle in a mysterious way.
She had the reputation of not being a neat housekeeper, and
none of the wise women of the town would touch her butter
especially, so it was always a joke when she coaxed a new

resident or a strange shipmaster into buying her wares; but the old woman always managed to jog home without the freight she had brought. "She must be very old, now," said Mr. Lorimer; "I have not seen her in a long time. It cannot be possible that her horse is still alive!" And we all laughed when we saw Mrs. Bonny's steed at a little distance, for the shaggy old creature was covered with mud, pine-needles, and dead leaves, with half the last year's burdock-burs in all Deephaven snarled into his mane and tail and sprinkled over his fur, which looked nearly as long as a buffalo's. He had hurt his leg, and his kind mistress had tied it up with a piece of faded red calico and an end of ragged rope. He gave us a civil neigh, and looked at us curiously. Then an impertinent little yellow-and-white dog, with one ear standing up straight and the other drooping over, began to bark with all his might; but he retreated when he saw Kate's great dog, who was walking solemnly by her side and did not deign to notice him. Just now Mrs. Bonny appeared at the door of the house, shading her eyes with her hand, to see who was coming. "Landy!" said she, "if it ain't old Parson Lorimer! And who be these with ye?"

"This is Miss Kate Lancaster of Boston, Miss Katharine Brandon's niece, and her friend Miss Denis."

"Pleased to see ye," said the old woman; "walk in and lay off your things." And we followed her into the house. I wish you could have seen her: she wore a man's coat, cut off so that it made an odd short jacket, and a pair of men's boots much the worse for wear; also, some short skirts, beside two or three aprons, the inner one being a dress-apron, as she took off the outer ones and threw them into a corner; and on her head was a tight cap, with strings to tie under her chin. I thought it was a nightcap, and that she had forgotten to take it off, and dreaded her mortification if she should suddenly become conscious of it; but I need not have troubled myself, for while we were with her she pulled it on and tied it tighter, as if she considered it ornamental.

There were only two rooms in the house; we went into the kitchen, which was occupied by a flock of hens and one turkey. The latter was evidently undergoing a course of medical treatment behind the stove, and was allowed to stay with us, while the hens were remorselessly hustled out with a hemlock broom. They all congregated on the doorstep, apparently wishing to hear everything that was said.

"Ben up on the mountain?" asked our hostess. "Real sightly place. Goin' to be a master lot o' rosbries; get any down to the shore sence I quit comin'?"

"O yes," said Mr. Lorimer, "but we miss seeing you."

"I s'pose so," said Mrs. Bonny, smoothing her apron complacently; "but I'm getting old, and I tell 'em I'm goin' to take my comfort; sence 'he' died, I don't put myself out no great; I've got money enough to keep me long 's I live. Beckett's folks goes down often, and I sends by them for what store stuff I want."

"How are you now?" asked the minister; "I think I heard you were ill in the spring."

"Stirrin', I'm obliged to ye. I was n't laid up long, and I was so 's I could get about most of the time. I've got the best bitters ye ever see, good for the spring of the year. S'pose yer sister, Miss Lorimer, would n't like some? she used to be weakly lookin'." But her brother refused the offer, saying that she had not been so well for many years.

"Do you often get out to church nowadays, Mrs. Bonny? I believe Mr. Reid preaches in the school-house sometimes, down by the great ledge; does n't he?"

"Well, yes, he does; but I don't know as I get much of any good. Parson Reid, he's a worthy creatur', but he never seems to have nothin' to say about foreordination and them p'ints. Old Parson Padelford was the man! I used to set under his preachin' a good deal; I had an aunt living down to East Parish. He'd get worked up, and he'd shut up the Bible and preach the hair off your head, 'long at the end of the sermon. Could n't understand more nor a quarter part what he said," said Mrs. Bonny, admiringly. "Well, we were a-speaking about the meeting over to the ledge; I don't know 's I like them people any to speak of. They had a great revival over there in the fall, and one Sunday I thought 's how I'd go; and when I got there, who should be a-prayin' but old Ben Patey,—he always lays out to get converted,—and he kep' it up diligent till I could n't stand it no longer; and by and by says he, 'I've been a wanderer'; and I up and says, 'Yes, you have, I'll back ye up on that, Ben; ye've wandered around my wood-lot and spoilt half the likely young oaks and ashes I've got, a-stealing your basket-stuff.' And the folks laughed out loud, and up he got and cleared. He's an awful old thief, and he's no idea of being anything else. I wa'n't a-goin' to set there and hear him makin' b'lieve to the Lord. If anybody's heart is in it, I ain't a-goin' to hender 'em; I'm a professor, and I ain't ashamed of it, week-days nor Sundays neither. I can't bear to see folks so pious to meeting, and cheat yer eye-teeth out Monday morning. Well, there! we ain't none of us perfect; even old Parson Moody was round-shouldered, they say."

"You were speaking of the Becketts just now," said Mr. Lorimer (after we had stopped laughing, and Mrs. Bonny had settled her big steel-bowed spectacles, and sat looking at him with an expression of extreme wisdom. One might have ventured to call her "peart," I think). "How do they get on? I am seldom in this region nowadays, since Mr. Reid has taken it under his charge."

"They get along, somehow or 'nother," replied Mrs. Bonny; "they've got the best farm this side of the ledge, but they're dreadful lazy and shiftless, them young folks. Old Mis' Hate-evil Beckett was tellin' me the other day—she that was Samanthy Barnes, you know—that one of the boys got fighting, the other side of the mountain, and come home with his nose broke and a piece o' one ear bit off. I forget which ear it was. Their mother is a real clever, willin' woman, and she takes it to heart, but it's no use for her to say anything. Mis' Hate-evil Beckett, says she, 'It does make my man feel dreadful to see his brother's folks carry on so.' 'But there,' says I, 'Mis' Beckett, it's just such things as we read of; Scriptur' is fulfilled: In the larter days there shall be disobedient children.' "

This application of the text was too much for us, but Mrs. Bonny looked serious, and we did not like to laugh. Two or three of the exiled fowls had crept slyly in, dodging underneath our chairs, and had perched themselves behind the stove. They were long-legged, half-grown creatures, and just at this minute one rash young rooster made a manful attempt to crow. "Do tell!" said his mistress, who rose in great wrath, "you need n't be so forth-putting, as I knows on!" After this we were urged to stay and have some supper. Mrs. Bonny assured us she could pick a likely young hen in no time, fry her with a bit of pork, and get us up "a good meat tea"; but we had to disappoint her, as we had some distance to walk to the house where we had left our horses, and a long drive home.

Kate asked if she would be kind enough to lend us a tumbler (for ours was in the basket, which was given into Tommy's charge). We were thirsty, and would like to go back to the spring and get some water.

"Yes, dear," said Mrs. Bonny, "I 've got a glass, if it 's so 's I can find it." And she pulled a chair under the little cupboard over the fireplace, mounted it, and opened the door. Several things fell out at her, and after taking a careful survey she went in, head and shoulders, until I thought that she would disappear altogether; but soon she came back, and reaching in took out one treasure after another, putting them on the mantel-piece or dropping them on the floor. There were some bunches of dried herbs, a tin horn, a lump of tallow in a broken plate, a newspaper, and an old boot, with a number of turkey-wings tied together, several bottles, and a steel trap, and finally, such a tumbler! which she produced with triumph, before stepping down. She poured out of it on the table a mixture of old buttons and squash-seeds, beside a lump of beeswax which she said she had lost, and now pocketed with satisfaction. She wiped the tumbler on her apron and handed it to Kate, but we were not so thirsty as we had been, though we thanked her and went down to the spring, coming back as soon as possible, for we could not lose a bit of the conversation.

There was a beautiful view from the doorstep, and we stopped a minute there. "Real sightly, ain't it?" said Mrs. Bonny. "But you ought to be here and look across the woods some morning just at sun-up. Why, the sky is all yaller and red, and them low lands topped with fog! Yes, it 's nice weather, good growin' weather, this week. Corn and all the rest of the trade looks first-rate. I call it a forrard season. It 's just such weather as we read of, ain't it?"

"I don't remember where, just at this moment," said Mr. Lorimer.

"Why, in the almanac, bless ye!" said she, with a tone of pity in her grum voice; could it be possible he did n't know, — the Deephaven minister!

We asked her to come and see us. She said she had always thought she 'd get a chance some time to see Miss Katharine Brandon's house. She should be pleased to call, and she did n't know but she should be down to the shore before very long. She was 'shamed to look so shif'less that day, but she had some good clothes in a chist in the bedroom, and a boughten bonnet with a good cypress veil, which she had when "he" died. She calculated they would do, though they might be old-fashioned, some. She seemed greatly pleased at Mr. Lorimer's having taken the trouble to come to see her. All those people had a great reverence for "the minister." We were urged to come again in "rosbry" time, which was near at hand, and she gave us messages for some of her old customers and acquaintances. "I believe some of those old creatur's will never die," said she; "why, they 're getting to be ter'ble old, ain't they, Mr. Lorimer? There! ye 've done me a sight of good, and I wish I could ha' found the Bible, to hear ye read a Psalm." When Mr. Lorimer shook hands with her, at leaving, she made him a most reverential courtesy. He was the greatest man she knew; and once during the call, when he was speaking of serious things in his simple, earnest way, she had so devout a look, and seemed so interested, that Kate and I, and Mr. Lorimer himself, caught a new, fresh meaning in the familiar words he spoke.

Living there in the lonely clearing, deep in the woods and far from any neighbor, she knew all the herbs and trees and the harmless wild creatures who lived among them, by heart; and she had an amazing store of tradition and superstition, which made her so entertaining to us that we went to see her many times before we came away in the autumn. We went with her to find some pitcher-plants, one day, and it was wonderful how much she knew about the woods, what keen observation she had. There was something so wild and unconventional about Mrs. Bonny that it was like taking an afternoon walk with a good-natured Indian. We used to carry her offerings of tobacco, for she was a great smoker, and advised us to try it, if ever we should be troubled with nerves, or "narves," as she pronounced the name of that affliction.

In Shadow

Soon after we went to Deephaven we took a long drive one day with Mr. Dockum, the kindest and silentest of men. He had the care of the Brandon property, and had some business at that time connected with a large tract of pasture-land perhaps ten miles from town. We had heard of the coast-road which led to it, how rocky and how rough and wild it was, and when Kate heard by chance that Mr. Dockum meant to go that way, she asked if we might go with him. He said he would much rather take us than "go sole alone," but he should be away until late and we must take our dinner, which we did not mind doing at all.

After we were three or four miles from Deephaven the country looked very different. The shore was so rocky that there were almost no places where a boat could put in, so there were no fishermen in the region, and the farms were scattered wide apart; the land was so poor that even the trees looked hungry. At the end of our drive we left the horse at a lonely little farm-house close by the sea. Mr. Dockum was to walk a long way inland through the woods with a man whom he had come to meet, and he told us if we followed the shore westward a mile or two we should find some very high rocks, for which he knew we had a great liking. It was a delightful day to spend out of doors; there was an occasional whiff of east-wind. Seeing us seemed to be a perfect godsend to the people whose nearest neighbors lived far out of sight. We had a long talk with them before we went for our walk. The house was close by the water by a narrow cove, around which the rocks were low, but farther down the shore the land rose more and more, and at last we stood at the edge of the highest rocks of all and looked far down at the sea, dashing its white spray high over the ledges that quiet day. What could it be in winter when there was a storm and the great waves came thundering in?

After we had explored the shore to our hearts' content and were tired, we rested for a while in the shadow of some gnarled pitch-pines which stood close together, as near the sea as they dared. They looked like a band of outlaws; they were such wild-looking trees. They seemed very old, and as if their savage fights with the winter winds had made them hard-hearted. And yet the little wild-flowers and the thin green grass-blades were growing fearlessly close around their feet; and there were some comfortable birds'-nests in safe corners of their rough branches.

When we went back to the house at the cove we had to wait some time for Mr. Dockum. We succeeded in making friends with the children, and gave them some candy and the rest of our lunch, which luckily had been even more abundant than usual. They looked thin and pitiful, but even in that lonely place, where they so seldom saw a stranger or even a neighbor, they showed that there was an evident effort to make them look like other children, and they were neatly dressed, though there could be no mistake about their being very poor. One forlorn little soul, with honest gray eyes and a sweet, shy smile, showed us a string of beads which she wore round her neck; there were perhaps two dozen of them, blue and white, on a bit of twine, and they were the dearest things in all her world. When we came away we were so glad that we could give the man more than he asked us for taking care of the horse, and his thanks touched us.

"I hope ye may never know what it is to earn every dollar as hard as I have. I never earned any money as easy as this before. I don't feel as if I ought to take it. I've done the best I could," said the man, with the tears coming into his eyes, and a huskiness in his voice. "I've done the best I could, and I'm willin' and my woman is, but everything seems to have been ag'in' us; we never seem to get forehanded. It looks sometimes as if the Lord had forgot us, but my woman she never wants me to say that; she says He ain't, and that we might be worse off,—but I don' know. I haven't had my health; that's hendered me most. I'm a boat-builder by trade, but the business's all run down; folks buys 'em second-hand nowadays, and you can't make nothing. I can't stand it to foller deep-sea fishing, and—well, you see what my land's wuth. But my oldest boy, he's getting ahead. He pushed off this spring, and he works in a box-shop to Boston; a cousin o' his mother's got him the chance. He sent me ten dollars a spell ago and his mother a shawl. I don't see how he done it, but he's smart!"

This seemed to be the only bright spot in their lives, and we admired the shawl and sat down in the house awhile with the mother, who seemed kind and patient and tired, and to have great delight in talking about what one should wear. Kate and I thought and spoke often of these people afterward, and when one day we met the man in Deephaven we sent some things to the children and his wife, and begged him to come to the house whenever he came to town; but we never saw him again, and though we made many plans for going again to the cove, we never did. At one time the road was reported impassable, and we put off our second excursion for this reason and others until just before we left Deephaven, late in October.

We knew the coast-road would be bad after the fall rains, and we found that Leander, the eldest of the Dockum boys, had some errand that way, so he went with us. We enjoyed the drive that morning in spite of the rough road. The air was warm, and sweet with the smell of bayberry-bushes and pitch-pines and the delicious saltness of the sea, which was not far from us all the way. It was a perfect autumn day. Sometimes we crossed pebble beaches, and then went farther inland, through woods and up and down steep little hills; over shaky bridges which crossed narrow salt creeks in the marsh-lands. There was a little excitement about the drive, and an exhilaration in the air, and we laughed at jokes forgotten the next minute, and sang, and were jolly enough. Leander, who had never happened to see us in exactly this hilarious state of mind before, seemed surprised and interested, and became unusually talkative, telling us a great many edifying particulars about the people whose houses we passed, and who owned every wood-lot along the road. "Do you see that house over on the pi'nt?" he asked. "An old fellow lives there that's part lost his mind. He had a son who was drowned off Cod Rock fishing, much as twenty-five years ago, and he's worn a deep path out to the end of the pi'nt where he goes out every hand's turn o' the day to see if he can't see the boat coming in." And Leander looked round to see if we were not amused, and seemed puzzled because we did n't laugh. Happily, his next story was funny.

We saw a sleepy little owl on the dead branch of a pine-tree; we saw a rabbit cross the road and disappear in a clump of juniper, and squirrels run up and down trees and along the stone-walls with acorns in their mouths. We passed straggling thickets of the upland sumach, leafless, and holding high their ungainly spikes of red berries; there were sturdy barberry-bushes along the lonely wayside, their unpicked fruit hanging in brilliant clusters. The blueberry-bushes made patches of dull red along the hillsides. The ferns were whitish-gray and brown at the edges of the woods, and the asters and golden-rods which had lately looked so gay in the open fields stood now in faded, frost-bitten companies. There were busy flocks of birds flitting from field to field, ready to start on their journey southward.

When we reached the house, to our surprise there was no one in sight and the place looked deserted. We left the wagon, and while Leander went toward the barn, which stood at a little distance, Kate and I went to the house and knocked. I opened the door a little way and said "Hallo!" but nobody answered. The people could not have moved away, for there were some chairs standing outside the door, and as I looked in I saw the bunches of herbs hanging up, and a trace of corn, and the furniture was all there. It was a great disappointment, for we had counted upon seeing the children again. Leander said there was nobody at the barn, and that they must have gone to a funeral; he could n't think of anything else.

Just now we saw some people coming up the road, and we thought at first that they were the man and his wife coming back; but they proved to be strangers, and we eagerly asked what had become of the family.

"They 're dead, both on 'em. His wife she died about nine weeks ago last Sunday, and he died day before yesterday. Funeral 's going to be this afternoon. Thought ye were some of her folks from up country, when we were coming along," said the man.

"Guess they won't come nigh," said the woman, scornfully;

" 'fraid they'd have to help provide for the children. I was half-sister to him, and I've got to take the two least ones."

"Did you say he was going to be buried this afternoon?" asked Kate, slowly. We were both more startled than I can tell.

"Yes," said the man, who seemed much better-natured than his wife. She appeared like a person whose only aim in life was to have things over with. "Yes, we're going to bury at two o'clock. They had a master sight of trouble, first and last."

Leander had said nothing all this time. He had known the man, and had expected to spend the day with him and to get him to go on two miles farther to help bargain for a dory. He asked, in a disappointed way, what had carried him off so sudden.

"Drink," said the woman, relentlessly. "He ain't been good for nothing sence his wife died: she was took with a fever along in the first of August. I'd ha' got up from it!"

"Now don't be hard on the dead, Marthy," said her husband. "I guess they done the best they could. They weren't shif'less, you know; they never had no health; 't was against wind and tide with 'em all the time." And Kate asked, "Did you say he was your brother?"

"Yes. I was half-sister to him," said the woman, promptly, with perfect unconsciousness of Kate's meaning.

"And what will become of those poor children?"

"I've got the two youngest over to my place to take care on, and the two next them has been put out to some folks over to the cove. I dare say like's not they'll be sent back."

"They're clever child'n, I guess," said the man, who spoke as if this were the first time he had dared take their part. "Don't be ha'sh, Marthy! Who knows but they may do for us when we get to be old?" And then she turned and looked at him with utter contempt. "I can't stand it to hear men-folks talking on what they don't know nothing about," said she. "The ways of Providence is dreadful myster'ous," she went on with a whine, instead of the sharp tone of voice which we had heard before. "We've had a hard row, and we've just got our own children off our hands and able to do for themselves, and now here are these to be fetched up."

"But perhaps they'll be a help to you; they seem to be good little things," said Kate. "I saw them in the summer, and they seemed to be pleasant children, and it is dreadfully hard for them to be left alone. It's not their fault, you know. We brought over something for them; will you be kind enough to take the basket when you go home?"

"Thank ye, I'm sure," said the aunt, relenting slightly. "You can speak to my man about it, and he'll give it to somebody that's going by. I've got to walk in the procession. They'll be obliged, I'm sure. I s'pose you're the young ladies that come here right after the Fourth o' July, ain't you? I should be pleased to have you call and see the child'n if you're over this way again. I heard 'em talk about you last time I was over. Won't ye step into the house and see him? He looks real natural," she added. But we said, "No, thank you."

Leander told us he believed he wouldn't bother about the dory that day, and he should be there at the house whenever we were ready. He evidently considered it a piece of good luck that he had happened to arrive in time for the funeral. We spoke to the man about the things we had brought for the children, which seemed to delight him, poor soul, and we felt sure he would be kind to them. His wife shouted to him from a window of the house that he'd better not loiter round, or they wouldn't be half ready when the folks began to come, and we said good by to him and went away.

It was a beautiful morning, and we walked slowly along the shore to the high rocks and the pitch-pine trees which we had seen before; the air was deliciously fresh, and one could take long deep breaths of it. The tide was coming in, and the spray dashed higher and higher. We climbed about the rocks and went down in some of the deep cold clefts into which the sun could seldom shine. We gathered some wild-flowers; bits of pimpernel and one or two sprigs of fringed gentian which had bloomed late in a sheltered place, and a pale little bouquet of asters. We sat for a long time looking off to sea, and we could talk or think of almost nothing beside what we had seen and heard at the farm-house. We said how much we should like to go to that funeral, and we even made up our minds to go back in season, but we gave up the idea: we had no right there, and it would seem as if we were merely curious, and we were afraid our presence would make the people ill at ease, the minister especially. It would be an intrusion.

We spoke of the children, and tried to think what could be done for them: we were afraid they would be told so many times that it was lucky they did not have to go to the poor-house, and yet we could not help pitying the hard-worked, discouraged woman whom we had seen, in spite of her bitter-ness. Poor soul! she looked like a person to whom nobody had ever been very kind, and for whom life had no pleasures: its sunshine had never been warm enough to thaw the ice at her heart.

We remembered how we knocked at the door and called loudly, but there had been no answer, and we wondered how we should have felt if we had gone farther into the room and had found the dead man in his coffin, all alone in the house. We thought of our first visit, and what he had said to us, and we wished we had come again sooner, for we might have helped them so much more if we had only known.

"What a pitiful ending it is," said Kate. "Do you realize that the family is broken up, and the children are to be half strangers to each other? Did you not notice that they seemed very fond of each other when we saw them in the summer? There was not half the roughness and apparent carelessness of one another which one so often sees in the country. Theirs was such a little world; one can understand how, when the man's wife died, he was bewildered and discouraged, utterly at a loss. The thoughts of winter, and of the little children, and of the struggles he had already come through against poverty and disappointment were terrible thoughts; and like a boat adrift at sea, the waves of his misery brought him in against the rocks, and his simple life was wrecked."

"I suppose his grandest hopes and wishes would have been realized in a good farm and a thousand or two dollars in safe keeping," said I. "Do you remember that merry little song in 'As You Like It'?

> 'Who doth ambition shun
> And loves to live i' the sun,
>   Seeking the food he eats,
>   And pleased with what he gets';

and

> 'Here shall he see
> No enemy
> But winter and rough weather.'

That is all he lived for, his literal daily bread. I suppose what would be prosperity to him would be miserably insufficient for some other people. I wonder how we can help being conscious, in the midst of our comforts and pleasures, of the lives which are being starved to death in more ways than one."

"I suppose one thinks more about these things as one grows older," said Kate, thoughtfully. "How seldom life in this world seems to be a success! Among rich or poor only here and there one touches satisfaction, though the one who seems to have made an utter failure may really be the greatest conqueror. And, Helen, I find that I understand better and better how unsatisfactory, how purposeless and disastrous, any life must be which is not a Christian life! It is like being always in the dark, and wandering one knows not where, if one is not learning more and more what it is to have a friendship with God."

By the middle of the afternoon the sky had grown cloudy, and a wind seemed to be coming in off the sea, and we unwillingly decided that we must go home. We supposed that the funeral would be all over with, but found we had been mistaken when we reached the cove. We seated ourselves on a rock near the water; just beside us was the old boat, with its killick and painter stretched ashore, where its owner had left it.

There were several men standing around the door of the house, looking solemn and important, and by and by one of them came over to us, and we found out a little more of the sad story. We liked this man, there was so much pity in his face and voice. "He was a real willin', honest man, Andrew was," said our new friend, "but he used to be sickly, and seemed to have no luck, though for a year or two he got along some better. When his wife died he was sore afflicted, and couldn't get over it, and he didn't know what to do or what was going to become of 'em with winter comin' on, and—well—I may's well tell ye; he took to drink and it killed him right off. I come over two or three times and made some gruel and fixed him up 's well 's I could, and the little gals done the best they could, but he faded right out, and did n't know anything the last time I see him, and he died Sunday mornin', when the tide begun to ebb. I always set a good deal by Andrew; we used to play together down to the great cove; that 's where he was raised, and my folks lived there too. I 've got one o' the little gals. I always knowed him and his wife."

Just now we heard the people in the house singing "China," the Deephaven funeral hymn, and the tune suited well that day, with its wailing rise and fall; it was strangely plaintive. Then the funeral exercises were over, and the man with whom we had just been speaking led to the door a horse and rickety wagon, from which the seat had been taken, and when the coffin had been put in he led the horse down the road a little way, and we watched the mourners come out of the house two by two. We heard some one scold in a whisper because the wagon was twice as far off as it need have been. They evidently had a rigid funeral etiquette, and felt it important that everything should be carried out according to rule. We saw a forlorn-looking kitten, with a bit of faded braid round its neck, run across the road in terror and presently appear again on the stone-wall, where she sat looking at the people. We saw the dead man's eldest son, of whom he had told us in the summer with such pride. He had shown his respect for his father as best he could, by a black band on his hat and a pair of black cotton gloves a world too large for him. He looked so sad, and cried bitterly as he stood alone at the head of the people. His aunt was next, with a handkerchief at her eyes, fully equal to the proprieties of the occasion, though I fear her grief was not so heartfelt as her husband's, who dried his eyes on his coat-sleeve again and again. There were perhaps twenty of the mourners, and there was much whispering among those who walked last. The minister and some others fell into line, and the procession went slowly down the slope; a strange shadow had fallen over everything. It was like a November day, for the air felt cold and bleak. There were some great sea-fowl high in the air, fighting their way toward the sea against the wind, and giving now and then a wild, far-off ringing cry. We could hear the dull sound of the sea, and at a little distance from the land the waves were leaping high, and breaking in white foam over the isolated ledges.

The rest of the people began to walk or drive away, but Kate and I stood watching the funeral as it crept along the narrow, crooked road. We had never seen what the people called "walking funerals" until we came to Deephaven, and there was something piteous about this; the mourners looked so few, and we could hear the rattle of the wagon-wheels. "He's gone, ain't he?" said some one near us. That was it, —*gone*.

Before the people had entered the house, there had been, I am sure, an indifferent, business-like look, but when they came out, all that was changed; their faces were awed by the presence of death, and the indifference had given place to uncertainty. Their neighbor was immeasurably their superior now. Living, he had been a failure by their own low standards; but now, if he could come back, he would know secrets, and be wise beyond anything they could imagine, and who could know the riches of which he might have come into possession?

To Kate and me there came a sudden consciousness of the mystery and inevitableness of death; it was not fear, thank God! but a thought of how certain it was that some day it would be a mystery to us no longer. And there was a thought, too, of the limitation of this present life; we were waiting there, in company with the people, the great sea, and the rocks and fields themselves, on this side the boundary. We knew just then how close to this familiar, every-day world might be the other, which at times before had seemed so far away, out of reach of even our thoughts, beyond the distant stars.

We stayed awhile longer, until the little black funeral had crawled out of sight; until we had seen the last funeral guest go away and the door had been shut and fastened with a queer old padlock and some links of rusty chain. The door fitted loosely, and the man gave it a vindictive shake, as if he thought that the poor house had somehow been to blame, and that after a long desperate struggle for life under its roof and among the stony fields the family must go away defeated.

It is not likely that any one else will ever go to live there. The man to whom the farm was mortgaged will add the few forlorn acres to his pasture-land, and the thistles which the man who is dead had fought so many years will march in next summer and take unmolested possession.

I think to-day of that fireless, empty, forsaken house, where the winter sun shines in and creeps slowly along the floor; the bitter cold is in and around the house, and the snow has sifted in at every crack; outside it is untrodden by any living creature's footstep. The wind blows and rushes and shakes the loose window-sashes in their frames, while the padlock knocks —knocks against the door.

Miss Chauncey

T HE Deephaven people used to say sometimes complacently, that certain things or certain people were "as dull
as East Parish." Kate and I grew curious to see that part of the
world which was considered duller than Deephaven itself; and
as upon inquiry we found that it was not out of reach, one
day we went there.

It was like Deephaven, only on a smaller scale. The village
—though it is a question whether that is not an exaggerated
term to apply—had evidently seen better days. It was on the
bank of a river, and perhaps half a mile from the sea. There
were a few old buildings there, some with mossy roofs and a
great deal of yellow lichen on the sides of the walls next the
sea; a few newer houses, belonging to fishermen; some dilapidated fish-houses; and a row of fish-flakes. Every house
seemed to have a lane of its own, and all faced different ways
except two fish-houses, which stood amiably side by side.
There was a church, which we had been told was the oldest in
the region. Through the windows we saw the high pulpit and
sounding-board, and finally found the keys at a house near
by; so we went in and looked around at our leisure. A rusty
foot-stove stood in one of the old square pews, and in the
gallery there was a majestic bass-viol with all its strings
snapped but the largest, which gave out a doleful sound when
we touched it.

After we left the church we walked along the road a little
way, and came in sight of a fine old house which had apparently fallen into ruin years before. The front entrance was a
fine specimen of old-fashioned workmanship, with its col-
umns and carvings, and the fence had been a grand affair in
its day, though now it could scarcely stand alone. The long
range of out-buildings were falling piece by piece; one shed
had been blown down entirely by a late high wind. The large
windows had many panes of glass, and the great chimneys
were built of the bright red bricks which used to be brought
from over-seas in the days of the colonies. We noticed the
gnarled lilacs in the yard, the wrinkled cinnamon-roses, and a

flourishing company of French pinks, or "bouncing Bets," as Kate called them.

"Suppose we go in," said I; "the door is open a little way. There surely must be some stories about its being haunted. We will ask Miss Honora." And we climbed over the boards which were put up like pasture-bars across the wide front gateway.

"We shall certainly meet a ghost," said Kate.

Just as we stood on the steps the door was pulled wide open; we started back, and, well-grown young women as we are, we have confessed since that our first impulse was to run away. On the threshold there stood a stately old woman who looked surprised at first sight of us, then quickly recovered herself and stood waiting for us to speak. She was dressed in a rusty black satin gown, with scant, short skirt and huge sleeves; on her head was a great black bonnet with a high crown and a close brim, which came far out over her face. "What is your pleasure?" said she; and we felt like two awkward children. Kate partially recovered her wits, and asked which was the nearer way to Deephaven.

"There is but one road, past the church and over the hill. It cannot be missed." And she bowed gravely, when we thanked her and begged her pardon, we hardly knew why, and came away.

We looked back to see her still standing in the doorway. "Who in the world can she be?" said Kate. And we wondered and puzzled and talked over "the ghost" until we saw Miss Honora Carew, who told us that it was Miss Sally Chauncey.

"Indeed, I know her, poor old soul!" said Miss Honora; "she has such a sad history. She is the last survivor of one of the most aristocratic old colonial families. The Chaunceys were of great renown until early in the present century, and then their fortunes changed. They had always been rich and well-educated, and I suppose nobody ever had a gayer, happier time than Miss Sally did in her girlhood, for they entertained a great deal of company and lived in fine style; but her father was unfortunate in business, and at last was utterly ruined at the time of the embargo; then he became partially insane, and died after many years of poverty. I have often heard a tradition that a sailor to whom he had broken a promise had cursed him, and that none of the family had died in their beds or had any good luck since. The East Parish people seem to believe in it, and it is certainly strange what terrible sorrow has come to the Chaunceys. One of Miss Sally's brothers, a fine young officer in the navy who was at home on leave, asked her one day if she could get on without him, and she said yes, thinking he meant to go back to sea; but in a few minutes she heard the noise of a pistol in his room, and hurried in to find him lying dead on the floor. Then there was another brother who was insane, and who became so violent that he was chained for years in one of the upper chambers, a dangerous prisoner. I have heard his horrid cries myself, when I was a young girl," said Miss Honora, with a shiver.

"Miss Sally is insane, and has been for many years, and this seems to me the saddest part of the story. When she first lost her reason she was sent to a hospital, for there was no one who could take care of her. The mania was so acute that no one had the slightest thought that she would recover or even live long. Her guardian sold the furniture and pictures and china, almost everything but clothing, to pay the bills at the hospital, until the house was fairly empty; and then one spring day, I remember it well, she came home in her right mind, and, without a thought of what was awaiting her, ran eagerly into her home. It was a terrible shock, and she never has recovered from it, though after a long illness her insanity took a mild form, and she has always been perfectly harmless. She has been alone many years, and no one can persuade her to leave the old house, where she seems to be contented, and does not realize her troubles; though she lives mostly in the past, and has little idea of the present, except in her house affairs, which seem pitiful to me, for I remember the housekeeping of the Chaunceys when I was a child. I have always been to see her, and she usually knows me, though I have been but seldom of late years. She is several years older than I. The town makes her an allowance every year, and she has some friends who take care that she does not suffer, though her wants are few. She is an elegant woman still, and some day, if you like, I will give you something to carry to her, and a message, if I can think of one, and you must go to make her a call. I hope she will happen to be talkative, for I am sure you would enjoy her. For many years she did not like to see strangers, but some one has told me lately that she seems to be pleased if people go to see her."

You may be sure it was not many days before Kate and I claimed the basket and the message, and went again to East Parish. We boldly lifted the great brass knocker, and were dismayed because nobody answered. While we waited, a girl came up the walk and said that Miss Sally lived up stairs, and she would speak to her if we liked. "Sometimes she don't have sense enough to know what the knocker means," we were told. There was evidently no romance about Miss Sally to our new acquaintance.

"Do you think," said I, "that we might go in and look around the lower rooms? Perhaps she will refuse to see us."

"Yes, indeed," said the girl; "only run the minute I speak; you'll have time enough, for she walks slow and is a little deaf."

So we went into the great hall with its wide staircase and handsome cornices and panelling, and then into the large parlor on the right, and through it to a smaller room looking out on the garden, which sloped down to the river. Both rooms had fine carved mantels, with Dutch-tiled fireplaces, and in the cornices we saw the fastenings where pictures had hung, —old portraits, perhaps. And what had become of them? The girl did not know: the house had been the same ever since she could remember, only it would all fall through into the cellar soon. But the old lady was proud as Lucifer, and wouldn't hear of moving out.

The floor in the room toward the river was so broken that it was not safe, and we came back through the hall and opened the door at the foot of the stairs. "Guess you won't want to stop long there," said the girl. Three old hens and a rooster marched toward us with great solemnity when we looked in. The cobwebs hung in the room, as they often do in old barns, in long, gray festoons; the lilacs outside grew close against the two windows where the shutters were not drawn, and the light in the room was greenish and dim.

Then we took our places on the threshold, and the girl

went up stairs and announced us to Miss Sally, and in a few minutes we heard her come along the hall.

"Sophia," said she, "where are the gentry waiting?" And just then she came in sight round the turn of the staircase. She wore the same great black bonnet and satin gown, and looked more old-fashioned and ghostly than before. She was not tall, but very erect, in spite of her great age, and her eyes seemed to "look through you" in an uncanny way. She slowly descended the stairs and came toward us with a courteous greeting, and when we had introduced ourselves as Miss Carew's friends she gave us each her hand in a most cordial way and said she was pleased to see us. She bowed us into the parlor and brought us two rickety, straight-backed chairs, which, with an old table, were all the furniture there was in the room. "Sit ye down," said she, herself taking a place in the window-seat. I have seen few more elegant women than Miss Chauncey. Thoroughly at her ease, she had the manner of a lady of the olden times, using the quaint fashion of speech which she had been taught in her girlhood. The long words and ceremonious phrases suited her extremely well. Her hands were delicately shaped, and she folded them in her lap, as no doubt she had learned to do at boarding-school so many years before. She asked Kate and me if we knew any young ladies at that school in Boston, saying that most of her intimate friends had left when she did, but some of the younger ones were there still.

She asked for the Carews and Mr. Lorimer, and when Kate told her that she was Miss Brandon's niece, and asked if she had not known her, she said, "Certainly, my dear; we were intimate friends at one time, but I have seen her little of late."

"Do you not know that she is dead?" asked Kate.

"Ah, they say every one is 'dead,' nowadays. I do not comprehend the silly idea!" said the old lady, impatiently. "It is an excuse, I suppose. She could come to see me if she chose, but she was always a ceremonious body, and I go abroad but seldom now; so perhaps she waits my visit. I will not speak uncourteously, and you must remember me to her kindly."

Then she asked us about other old people in Deephaven, and about families in Boston whom she had known in her early days. I think every one of whom she spoke was dead, but we assured her that they were all well and prosperous, and we hoped we told the truth. She asked about the love-affairs of men and women who had died old and gray-headed within our remembrance; and finally she said we must pardon her for these tiresome questions, but it was so rarely she saw any one direct from Boston, of whom she could inquire concerning these old friends and relatives of her family.

Something happened after this which touched us both inexpressibly: she sat for some time watching Kate with a bewildered look, which at last faded away, a smile coming in its place. "I think you are like my mother," she said; "did any one ever say to you that you are like my mother? Will you let me see your forehead? Yes; and your hair is only a little darker." Kate had risen when Miss Chauncey did, and they stood side by side. There was a tone in the old lady's voice which brought the tears to my eyes. She stood there some minutes looking at Kate. I wonder what her thoughts were. There was a kinship, it seemed to me, not of blood, only that they both were of the same stamp and rank: Miss Chauncey of the old generation and Kate Lancaster of the new. Miss Chauncey turned to me, saying, "Look up at the portrait and you will see the likeness too, I think." But when she turned and saw the bare wainscoting of the room, she looked puzzled, and the bright flash which had lighted up her face was gone in an instant, and she sat down again in the window-seat; but we were glad that she had forgotten. Presently she said, "Pardon me, but I forget your question."

Miss Carew had told us to ask her about her school-days, as she nearly always spoke of that time to her; and, to our delight, Miss Sally told us a long story about her friends and about her "coming-out party," when boat-loads of gay young guests came down from Riverport, and all the gentry from Deephaven. The band from the fort played for the dancing, the garden was lighted, the card-tables were in this room, and a grand supper was served. She also remembered what some of her friends wore, and her own dress was a silver-gray brocade with rosebuds of three colors. She told us how she watched the boats go off up river in the middle of the summer night; how sweet the music sounded; how bright the moonlight was; how she wished we had been there at her party.

"I can't believe I am an old woman. It seems only yesterday," said she, thoughtfully. And then she lost the idea, and talked about Kate's great-grandmother, whom she had known, and asked us how she had been this summer.

She asked us if we would like to go up stairs where she had a fire, and we eagerly accepted, though we were not in the least cold. Ah, what a sorry place it was! She had gathered together some few pieces of her old furniture, which half filled one fine room, and here she lived. There was a tall, handsome chest of drawers, which I should have liked much to ransack. Miss Carew had told us that Miss Chauncey had large claims against the government, dating back sixty or seventy years, but nobody could ever find the papers; and I felt sure that they must be hidden away in some secret drawer. The brass handles and trimmings were blackened, and the wood looked like ebony. I wanted to climb up and look into the upper part of this antique piece of furniture, and it seemed to me I could at once put my hand on a package of "papers relating to the embargo."

On a stand near the window was an old Bible, fairly worn out with constant use. Miss Chauncey was religious; in fact, it was the only subject about which she was perfectly sane. We saw almost nothing of her insanity that day, though afterward she was different. There were days when her mind seemed clear; but sometimes she was silent, and often she would confuse Kate with Miss Brandon, and talk to her of long-forgotten plans and people. She would rarely speak of anything more than a minute or two, and then would drift into an entirely foreign subject.

She urged us that afternoon to stay to luncheon with her; she said she could not offer us dinner, but she would give us tea and biscuit, and no doubt we should find something in Miss Carew's basket, as she was always kind in remembering her fancies. Miss Honora had told us to decline, if she asked us to stay; but I should have liked to see her sit at the head of her table, and to be a guest at such a lunch-party.

Poor creature! it was a blessed thing that her shattered reason made her unconscious of the change in her fortunes, and incapable of comparing the end of her life with its beginning. To herself she was still Miss Chauncey, a gentlewoman of high family, possessed of unusual worldly advantages. The remembrance of her cruel trials and sorrows had faded from her mind. She had no idea of the poverty of her surroundings when she paced back and forth, with stately steps, on the ruined terraces of her garden; the ranks of lilies and the conserve-roses were still in bloom for her, and the box-borders were as trimly kept as ever; and when she pointed out to us the distant steeples of Riverport, it was plain to see that it was still the Riverport of her girlhood. If the boat-landing at the foot of the garden had long ago dropped into the river and gone out with the tide; if the maids and men who used to do her bidding were all out of hearing; if there had been no dinner company that day and no guests were expected for the evening,—what did it matter? The twilight had closed around her gradually, and she was alone in her house, but she did not heed the ruin of it or the absence of her friends. On the morrow, life would again go on.

We always used to ask her to read the Bible to us, after Mr. Lorimer had told us how grand and beautiful it was to listen to her. I shall never hear some of the Psalms or some chapters of Isaiah again without being reminded of her; and I remember just now, as I write, one summer afternoon when Kate and I had lingered later than usual, and we sat in the upper room looking out on the river and the shore beyond, where the light had begun to grow golden as the day drew near sunset. Miss Sally had opened the great book at random and read slowly, "In my Father's house are many mansions"; and then, looking off for a moment at a leaf which had drifted into the window-recess, she repeated it: "In my Father's house are many mansions; if it were not so, I would have told you." Then she went on slowly to the end of the chapter, and with her hands clasped together on the Bible she fell into a reverie, and the tears came into our eyes as we watched her look of perfect content. Through all her clouded years the promises of God had been her only certainty.

Miss Chauncey died early in the winter after we left Deephaven, and one day when I was visiting Kate in Boston Mr. Lorimer came to see us, and told us about her.

It seems that after much persuasion she was induced to go to spend the winter with a neighbor, her house having become uninhabitable, and she was, beside, too feeble to live alone. But her fondness for her old home was too strong, and one day she stole away from the people who took care of her, and crept in through the cellar, where she had to wade through half-frozen water, and then went up stairs, where she seated herself at a front window and called joyfully to the people who went by, asking them to come in to see her, as she had got home again. After this she was very ill, and one day, when she was half delirious, they missed her, and found her at last sitting on her hall stairway, which she was too feeble to climb. She lived but a short time afterwards, and in her last days her mind seemed perfectly clear. She said over and over again how good God had always been to her, and she was gentle, and unwilling to be a trouble to those who had the care of her.

Mr. Lorimer spoke of her simple goodness, and told us that though she had no other sense of time, and hardly knew if it were summer or winter, she was always sure when Sunday came, and always came to church when he preached at East Parish, her greatest pleasure seeming to be to give money, if there was a contribution. "She may be a lesson to us," added the old minister, reverently; "for, though bewildered in mind, bereft of riches and friends and all that makes this world dear to many of us, she was still steadfast in her simple faith, and was never heard to complain of any of the burdens which God had given her."

Last Days in Deephaven

WHEN the summer was ended it was no sorrow to us, for we were even more fond of Deephaven in the glorious autumn weather than we had ever been before. Mr. Lancaster was abroad longer than he had intended to be at first, and it was late in the season before we left. We were both ready to postpone going back to town as late as possible; but at last it was time for my friend to re-establish the Boston housekeeping, and to take up the city life again. I must admit we half dreaded it: we were surprised to find how little we cared for it, and how well one can get on without many things which are thought indispensable.

For the last fortnight we were in the house a good deal, because the weather was wet and dreary. At one time there was a magnificent storm, and we went every day along the shore in the wind and rain for a mile or two to see the furious great breakers come plunging in against the rocks. I never had seen such a wild, stormy sea as that; the rage of it was awful, and the whole harbor was white with foam. The wind had blown northeast steadily for days, and it seemed to me that the sea never could be quiet and smooth and blue again, with soft white clouds sailing over it in the sky. It was a treacherous sea; it was wicked; it had all the trembling land in its power, if it only dared to send its great waves far ashore. All night long the breakers roared, and the wind howled in the chimneys, and in the morning we always looked fearfully across the surf and the tossing gray water to see if the lighthouse were standing firm on its rock. It was so slender a thing to hold its own in such a wide and monstrous sea. But the sun came out at last, and not many days afterward we went out with Danny and Skipper Scudder to say good by to Mrs. Kew. I have been some voyages at sea, but I never was so danced about in a little boat as I was that day. There was nothing to fear with so careful a crew, and we only enjoyed the roughness as we went out and in, though it took much manœuvring to land us at the island.

It was very sad work to us—saying good by to our friends,

and we tried to make believe that we should spend the next
summer in Deephaven, and we meant at any rate to go down
for a visit. We were glad when the people said they should
miss us, and that they hoped we should not forget them and
the old place. It touched us to find that they cared so much
for us, and we said over and over again how happy we had
been, and that it was such a satisfactory summer. Kate laughingly proposed one evening, as we sat talking by the fire and
were particularly contented, that we should copy the Ladies
of Llangollen, and remove ourselves from society and its distractions.

"I have thought often, lately," said my friend, "what a
good time they must have had, and I feel a sympathy and
friendliness for them which I never felt before. We could have
guests when we chose, as we have had this summer, and we
could study and grow very wise, and what could be pleasanter? But I wonder if we should grow very lazy if we stayed
here all the year round; village life is not stimulating, and
there would not be much to do in winter,—though I do not
believe that need be true; one may be busy and useful in any
place."

"I suppose if we really belonged in Deephaven we should
think it a hard fate, and not enjoy it half so much as we have
this summer," said I. "Our idea of happiness would be making long visits in Boston; and we should be heart-broken
when we had to come away and leave our lunch-parties, and
symphony concerts, and calls, and fairs, the reading-club and
the childrens' hospital. We should think the people uncongenial and behind the times, and that the Ridge road was stupid
and the long sands desolate; while we remembered what delightful walks we had taken out Beacon Street to the three
roads, and over the Cambridge Bridge. Perhaps we should
even be ashamed of the dear old church for being so out of
fashion. We should have the blues dreadfully, and think there
was no society here, and wonder why we had to live in such a
town."

"What a gloomy picture!" said Kate, laughing. "Do you
know that I have understood something lately better than I
ever did before,—it is that success and happiness are not
things of chance with us, but of choice. I can see how we

might so easily have had a dull summer here. Of course it is our own fault if the events of our lives are hindrances; it is we who make them bad or good. Sometimes it is a conscious choice, but oftener unconscious. I suppose we educate ourselves for taking the best of life or the worst, do not you?"

"Dear old Deephaven!" said Kate, gently, after we had been silent a little while. "It makes me think of one of its own old ladies, with its clinging to the old fashions and its respect for what used to be respectable when it was young. I cannot make fun of what was once dear to somebody, and which realized somebody's ideas of beauty or fitness. I don't dispute the usefulness of a new, bustling, manufacturing town with its progressive ideas; but there is a simple dignity in a town like Deephaven, as if it tried to be loyal to the traditions of its ancestors. It quietly accepts its altered circumstances, if it has seen better days, and has no harsh feelings toward the places which have drawn away its business, but it lives on, making its old houses and boats and clothes last as long as possible."

"I think one cannot help," said I, "having a different affection for an old place like Deephaven from that which one may have for a newer town. Here—though there are no exciting historical associations and none of the veneration which one has for the very old cities and towns abroad—it is impossible not to remember how many people have walked the streets and lived in the houses. I was thinking to-day how many girls might have grown up in this house, and that their places have been ours; we have inherited their pleasures, and perhaps have carried on work which they began. We sit in somebody's favorite chair and look out of the windows at the sea, and have our wishes and our hopes and plans just as they did before us. Something of them still lingers where their lives were spent. We are often reminded of our friends who have died; why are we not reminded as surely of strangers in such a house as this,—finding some trace of the lives which were lived among the sights we see and the things we handle, as the incense of many masses lingers in some old cathedral, and one catches the spirit of longing and prayer where so many heavy hearts have brought their burdens and have gone away comforted?"

"When I first came here," said Kate, "it used to seem very

sad to me to find Aunt Katharine's little trinkets lying about
the house. I have often thought of what you have just said. I
heard Mrs. Patton say the other day that there is no pocket in
a shroud, and of course it is better that we should carry nothing out of this world. Yet I can't help wishing that it were
possible to keep some of my worldly goods always. There are
one or two books of mine and some little things which I have
had a long time, and of which I have grown very fond. It
makes me so sorry to think of their being neglected and lost. I
cannot believe I shall forget these earthly treasures when I am
in heaven, and I wonder if I shall not miss them. Isn't it
strange to think of not reading one's Bible any more? I suppose this is a very low view of heaven, don't you?" And we
both smiled.

"I think the next dwellers in this house ought to find a
decided atmosphere of contentment," said I. "Have you ever
thought that it took us some time to make it your house instead of Miss Brandon's? It used to seem to me that it was
still under her management, that she was its mistress; but
now it belongs to you, and if I were ever to come back without you I should find you here."

It is bewildering to know that this is the last chapter, and
that it must not be long. I remember so many of our pleasures of which I have hardly said a word. There were our
guests, of whom I have told you nothing, and of whom there
was so much to say. Of course we asked my Aunt Mary to
visit us, and Miss Margaret Tennant, and many of our girl-
friends. All the people we know who have yachts made the
port of Deephaven if they were cruising in the neighboring
waters. Once a most cheerful party of Kate's cousins and
some other young people whom we knew very well came to
visit us in this way, and the yacht was kept in the harbor a
week or more, while we were all as gay as bobolinks and went
frisking about the country, and kept late hours in the sober
old Brandon house. My Aunt Mary, who was with us, and
Kate's aunt, Mrs. Thorniford, who knew the Carews, and was
commander of the yacht-party, tried to keep us in order, and
to make us ornaments to Deephaven society instead of reproaches and stumbling-blocks. Kate's younger brothers were

with us, waiting until it was time for them to go back to college, and I think there never had been such picnics in Deephaven before, and I fear there never will be again.

We are fond of reading, and we meant to do a great deal of it, as every one does who goes away for the summer; but I must confess that our grand plans were not well carried out. Our German dictionaries were on the table in the west parlor until the sight of them mortified us, and finally, to avoid their silent reproach, I put them in the closet, with the excuse that it would be as easy to get them there, and they would be out of the way. We used to have the magazines sent us from town; you would have smiled at the box of books which we carried to Deephaven, and indeed we sent two or three times for others; but I do not remember that we ever carried out that course of study which we had planned with so much interest. We were out of doors so much that there was often little time for anything else.

Kate said one day that she did not care, in reading, to always making new acquaintances, but to be seeing more of old ones; and I think it is a very wise idea. We each have our pet books; Kate carries with her a much-worn copy of "Mr. Rutherford's Children," which has been her delight ever since she can remember. Sibyl and Chryssa are dear old friends, though I suppose now it is not merely what Kate reads, but what she associates with the story. I am not often separated from Jean Ingelow's "Stories told to a Child," that charmingly wise and pleasant little book. It is always new, like Kate's favorite. It is very hard to make a list of the books one likes best, but I remember that we had "The Village on the Cliff," and "Henry Esmond," and "Tom Brown at Rugby," with his more serious ancestor, "Sir Thomas Browne." I am sure we had "Fenelon," for we always have that; and there was "Pet Marjorie," and "Rab," and "Annals of a Parish," and "The Life of the Reverend Sydney Smith"; beside Miss Tytler's "Days of Yore," and "The Holy and Profane State," by Thomas Fuller, from which Kate gets so much entertainment and profit. We read Mr. Emerson's essays together, out of doors, and some stories which had been our dear friends at school, like "Leslie Goldthwaite." There was a very good library in the house, and we both like old books, so we enjoyed that. And we used to read the Spectator, and many old-fashioned stories and essays and sermons, with much more pleasure because they had such quaint old brown leather bindings. You will not doubt that we had some cherished volumes of poetry, or that we used to read them aloud to each other when we sat in our favorite corner of the rocks at the shore, or were in the pine woods of an afternoon.

We used to go out to tea, and do a great deal of social visiting, which was very pleasant. Dinner-parties were not in fashion, though it was a great attention to be asked to spend the day, which courtesy we used to delight in extending to our friends; and we entertained company in that way often. When we first went out we were somewhat interesting on account of our clothes, which were of later pattern than had been adopted generally in Deephaven. We used to take great pleasure in arraying ourselves on high days and holidays, since when we went wandering on shore, or out sailing or rowing, we did not always dress as befitted our position in the town. Fish-scales and blackberry-briers so soon disfigure one's clothes.

We became in the course of time learned in all manner of 'longshore lore, and even profitably employed ourselves one morning in going clam-digging with old Ben Horn, a most fascinating ancient mariner. We both grew so well and brown and strong, and Kate and I did not get tired of each other at all, which I think was wonderful, for few friendships would bear such a test. We were together always, and alone together a great deal; and we became wonderfully well acquainted. We are such good friends that we often were silent for a long time, when mere acquaintances would have felt compelled to talk and try to entertain each other.

Before we left the leaves had fallen off all the trees except the oaks, which make in cold weather one of the dreariest sounds one ever hears: a shivering rustle, which makes one pity the tree and imagine it shelterless and forlorn. The sea had looked rough and cold for many days, and the old house itself had grown chilly,—all the world seemed waiting for the snow to come. There was nobody loitering on the wharves, and when we went down the street we walked fast, arm in arm, to keep warm. The houses were shut up as close as possible, and the old sailors did not seem cheery any longer; they looked forlorn, and it was not a pleasant prospect to be so long weather-bound in port. If they ventured out, they put on ancient great-coats, with huge flaps to the pockets and large horn buttons, and they looked contemptuously at the vane, which always pointed to the north or east. It felt like winter, and the captains rolled more than ever as they walked, as if they were on deck in a heavy sea. The rheumatism claimed many victims, and there was one day, it must be confessed, when a biting, icy fog was blown in-shore, that Kate and I were willing to admit that we could be as comfortable in town, and it was almost time for sealskin jackets.

In the front yards we saw the flower-beds black with frost, except a few brave pansies which had kept green and had bloomed under the tall china-aster stalks, and one day we picked some of these little flowers to put between the leaves of a book and take away with us. I think we loved Deephaven all the more in those last days, with a bit of compassion in our tenderness for the dear old town which had so little to amuse it. So long a winter was coming, but we thought with a sigh how pleasant it would be in the spring.

You would have smiled at the treasures we brought away with us. We had become so fond of even our fishing-lines; and this very day you may see in Kate's room two great bunches of Deephaven cat-o'-nine-tails. They were much in our way on the journey home, but we clung affectionately to these last sheaves of our harvest.

The morning we came away our friends were all looking out from door or window to see us go by, and after we had passed the last house and there was no need to smile any longer, we were very dismal. The sun was shining again bright and warm as if the Indian summer were beginning, and we wished that it had been a rainy day.

The thought of Deephaven will always bring to us our long quiet summer days, and reading aloud on the rocks by the sea, the fresh salt air, and the glory of the sunsets; the wail of the Sunday psalm-singing at church, the yellow lichen that grew over the trees, the houses, and the stone-walls; our boating and wanderings ashore; our importance as members of society, and how kind every one was to us both. By and by the Deephaven warehouses will fall and be used for firewood by the fisher-people, and the wharves will be worn away by the tides. The few old gentlefolks who still linger will be dead then; and I wonder if some day Kate Lancaster and I will go down to Deephaven for the sake of old times, and read the epitaphs in the burying-ground, look out to sea, and talk quietly about the girls who were so happy there one summer long before. I should like to walk along the beach at sunset, and watch the color of the marshes and the sea change as the light of the sky goes out. It would make the old days come back vividly. We should see the roofs and chimneys of the village, and the great Chantrey elms look black against the sky. A little later the marsh fog would show faintly white, and we should feel it deliciously cold and wet against our hands and faces; when we looked up there would be a star; the crickets would chirp loudly; perhaps some late sea-birds would fly inland. Turning, we should see the lighthouse lamp shine out over the water, and the great sea would move and speak to us lazily in its idle, high-tide sleep.

A COUNTRY DOCTOR

Contents

I

THE LAST MILE

I T had been one of the warm and almost sultry days which
sometimes come in November; a maligned month, which
is really an epitome of the other eleven, or a sort of index to
the whole year's changes of storm and sunshine. The afternoon was like spring, the air was soft and damp, and the buds
of the willows had been beguiled into swelling a little, so that
there was a bloom over them, and the grass looked as if it had
been growing green of late instead of fading steadily. It
seemed like a reprieve from the doom of winter, or from even
November itself.

The dense and early darkness which usually follows such
unseasonable mildness had already begun to cut short the
pleasures of this spring-like day, when a young woman, who
carried a child in her arms, turned from a main road of Oldfields into a foot-path which led southward across the fields
and pastures. She seemed sure of her way, and kept the path
without difficulty, though a stranger might easily have lost it
here and there, where it led among the patches of sweet-fern
or bayberry bushes, or through shadowy tracts of small white-
pines. She stopped sometimes to rest, and walked more and
more wearily, with increasing effort; but she kept on her way
desperately, as if it would not do to arrive much later at the
place which she was seeking. The child seemed to be asleep; it
looked too heavy for so slight a woman to carry.

The path led after a while to a more open country, there
was a low hill to be climbed, and at its top the slender figure
stopped and seemed to be panting for breath. A follower
might have noticed that it bent its head over the child's for a
moment as it stood, dark against the darkening sky. There
had formerly been a defense against the Indians on this hill,
which in the daytime commanded a fine view of the sur-
rounding country, and the low earthworks or foundations of
the garrison were still plainly to be seen. The woman seated
herself on the sunken wall in spite of the dampness and increasing chill, still holding the child, and rocking to and fro

like one in despair. The child waked and began to whine and cry a little in that strange, lonely place, and after a few minutes, perhaps to quiet it, they went on their way. Near the foot of the hill was a brook, swollen by the autumn rains; it made a loud noise in the quiet pasture, as if it were crying out against a wrong or some sad memory. The woman went toward it at first, following a slight ridge which was all that remained of a covered path which had led down from the garrison to the spring below at the brookside. If she had meant to quench her thirst here, she changed her mind, and suddenly turned to the right, following the brook a short distance, and then going straight toward the river itself and the high uplands, which by daylight were smooth pastures with here and there a tangled apple-tree or the grassy cellar of a long vanished farm-house.

It was night now; it was too late in the year for the chirp of any insects; the moving air, which could hardly be called wind, swept over in slow waves, and a few dry leaves rustled on an old hawthorn tree which grew beside the hollow where a house had been, and a low sound came from the river. The whole country side seemed asleep in the darkness, but the lonely woman felt no lack of companionship; it was well suited to her own mood that the world slept and said nothing to her,—it seemed as if she were the only creature alive.

A little this side of the river shore there was an old burial place, a primitive spot enough, where the graves were only marked by rough stones, and the short, sheep-cropped grass was spread over departed generations of the farmers and their wives and children. By day it was in sight of the pine woods and the moving water, and nothing hid it from the great sky overhead, but now it was like a prison walled about by the barriers of night. However eagerly the woman had hurried to this place, and with what purpose she may have sought the river bank, when she recognized her surroundings she stopped for a moment, swaying and irresolute. "No, no!" sighed the child plaintively, and she shuddered, and started forward; then, as her feet stumbled among the graves, she turned and fled. It no longer seemed solitary, but as if a legion of ghosts which had been wandering under cover of the dark had discovered this intruder, and were chasing her and flocking around her and oppressing her from every side. And as she caught sight of a light in a far-away farmhouse window, a light which had been shining after her all the way down to the river, she tried to hurry toward it. The unnatural strength of terror urged her on; she retraced her steps like some pursued animal; she remembered, one after another, the fearful stories she had known of that ancient neighborhood; the child cried, but she could not answer it. She fell again and again, and at last all her strength seemed to fail her, her feet refused to carry her farther and she crept painfully, a few yards at a time, slowly along the ground. The fear of her superhuman enemies had forsaken her, and her only desire was to reach the light that shone from the looming shadow of the house.

At last she was close to it; at last she gave one great sigh, and the child fell from her grasp; at last she clutched the edge of the worn doorstep with both hands, and lay still.

II

THE FARM-HOUSE KITCHEN

INDOORS there was a cheerful company; the mildness of the evening had enticed two neighbors of Mrs. Thacher, the mistress of the house, into taking their walks abroad, and so, with their heads well protected by large gingham handkerchiefs, they had stepped along the road and up the lane to spend a social hour or two. John Thacher, their old neighbor's son, was known to be away serving on a jury in the county town, and they thought it likely that his mother would enjoy company. Their own houses stood side by side. Mrs. Jacob Dyer and Mrs. Martin Dyer were their names, and excellent women they were. Their husbands were twin-brothers, curiously alike and amazingly fond of each other, though either would have scorned to make any special outward demonstration of it. They were spending the evening together in brother Martin's house, and were talking over the purchase of a bit of woodland, and the profit of clearing it, when their wives had left them without any apology to visit Mrs. Thacher, as we have already seen.

This was the nearest house and only a quarter of a mile away, and when they opened the door they had found Mrs. Thacher spinning.

"I must own up, I am glad to see you more 'n common," she said. "I don't feel scary at being left sole alone; it ain't that, but I have been getting through with a lonesome spell of another kind. John, he does as well as a man can, but here I be,—here I be," —and the good woman could say no more, while her guests understood readily enough the sorrow that had found no words.

"I suppose you haven't got no news from Ad'line?" asked Mrs. Martin bluntly. "We was speaking of her as we come along, and saying it seemed to be a pity she should'nt feel it was best to come back this winter and help you through; only one daughter, and left alone as you be, with the bad spells you are liable to in winter time—but there, it ain't her way— her ambitions ain't what they should be, that's all I can say."

"If she'd got a gift for anything special, now," continued Mrs. Jake, "we should feel it was different and want her to have a chance, but she's just like other folks for all she felt so much above farming. I don't see as she can do better than come back to the old place, or leastways to the village, and fetch up the little gal to be some use. She might dressmake or do millinery work; she always had a pretty taste, and 't would be better than roving. I 'spose 't would hurt her pride,"—but Mrs. Thacher flushed at this, and Mrs. Martin came to the rescue.

"You'll think we're reg'lar Job's comforters," cried the good soul hastily, "but there, Mis' Thacher, you know we feel as if she was our own. There ain't nothing I wouldn't do for Ad'line, sick or well, and I declare I believe she'll pull through yet and make a piece of luck that 'll set us all to work praising of her. She's like to marry again for all I can see, with her good looks. Folks always has their joys and calamities as they go through the world."

Mrs. Thacher shook her head two or three times with a dismal expression, and made no answer. She had pushed back the droning wool-wheel which she had been using, and had taken her knitting from the shelf by the clock and seated herself contentedly, while Mrs. Jake and Mrs. Martin had each produced a blue yarn stocking from a capacious pocket, and the shining steel needles were presently all clicking together. One knitter after another would sheathe the spare needle under her apron strings, while they asked each other's advice from time to time about the propriety of "narrerin'" or whether it were not best to "widden" according to the progress their respective stockings had made. Mrs. Thacher had lighted an extra candle, and replenished the fire, for the air was chillier since the sun went down. They were all sure of a coming change of weather, and counted various signs, Mrs. Thacher's lowness of spirits among the number, while all three described various minor maladies from which they had suffered during the day, and of which the unseasonable weather was guilty.

"I can't get over the feeling that we are watchin' with somebody," said Mrs. Martin after a while, moved by some strange impulse and looking over her shoulder, at which remark Mrs.

Thacher glanced up anxiously. "Something has been hanging over me all day," said she simply, and at this the needles clicked faster than ever.

"We've been taking rather a low range," suggested Mrs. Jake. "We shall get to telling over ghost stories if we don't look out, and I for one shall be sca't to go home. By the way, I suppose you have heard about old Billy Dow's experience night afore last, Mis' Thacher?"

"John being away, I ain't had nobody to fetch me the news these few days past," said the hostess. "Why what's happened to Billy now?"

The two women looked at each other: "He was getting himself home as best he could,—he owned up to having made a lively evenin' of it,—and I expect he was wandering all over the road and did n't know nothin' except that he was p'inted towards home, an' he stepped off from the high bank this side o' Dunnell's, and rolled down, over and over; and when he come to there was a great white creatur' a-standin' over him, and he thought 't was a ghost. 'T was higher up on the bank than him, and it kind of moved along down 's if 't was coming right on to him, and he got on to his knees and begun to say his Ten Commandments fast 's he could rattle 'em out. He got 'em mixed up, and when the boys heard his teeth a-chattering, they began to laugh and he up an' cleared. Dunnell's boys had been down the road a piece and was just coming home, an' 't was their old white hoss that had got out of the barn, it bein' such a mild night, an' was wandering off. They said to Billy that 't wa'n't everybody could lay a ghost so quick as he could, and they did n't 'spose he had the means so handy."

The three friends laughed, but Mrs. Thacher's face quickly lost its smile and took back its worried look. She evidently was in no mood for joking. "Poor Billy!" said she, "he was called the smartest boy in school; I rec'lect that one of the teachers urged his folks to let him go to college; but 't wa'n't no use; they had n't the money and could n't get it, and 't wa'n't in him to work his way as some do. He's got a master head for figur's. Folks used to get him to post books you know,—but he's past that now. Good-natured creatur' as ever stept; but he always was afeard of the dark,—'seems 's if

I could see him there a-repentin' and the old white hoss shakin' his head,"—and she laughed again, but quickly stopped herself and looked over her shoulder at the window.

"Would ye like the curtain drawed?" asked Mrs. Jake. But Mrs. Thacher shook her head silently, while the gray cat climbed up into her lap and laid down in a round ball to sleep.

"She's a proper cosset, ain't she?" inquired Mrs. Martin approvingly, while Mrs. Jake asked about the candles, which gave a clear light. "Be they the last you run?" she inquired, but was answered to the contrary, and a brisk conversation followed upon the proper proportions of tallow and bayberry wax, and the dangers of the new-fangled oils which the village shop-keepers were attempting to introduce. Sperm oil was growing more and more dear in price and worthless in quality, and the old-fashioned lamps were reported to be past their usefulness.

"I must own I set most by good candle light," said Mrs. Martin. " 'T is no expense to speak of where you raise the taller, and it's cheerful and bright in winter time. In old times when the houses were draftier they was troublesome about flickering, candles was; but land! think how comfortable we live now to what we used to! Stoves is such a convenience; the fire's so much handier. Housekeepin' don't begin to be the trial it was once."

"I must say I like old-fashioned cookin' better than oven cookin'," observed Mrs. Jake. "Seems to me's if the taste of things was all drawed up chimbly. Be you going to do much for Thanksgivin', Mis' Thacher? I 'spose not;" and moved by a sudden kind impulse, she added, "Why can't you and John jine with our folks? 't would n't put us out, and 't will be lonesome for ye."

" 'T won't be no lonesomer than last year was, nor the year before," and Mrs. Thacher's face quivered a little as she rose and took one of the candles, and opened the trap door that covered the cellar stairs. "Now don't ye go to makin' yourself work," cried the guests. "No, don't! we ain't needin' nothin'; we was late about supper." But their hostess stepped carefully down and disappeared for a few minutes, while the cat hovered anxiously at the edge of the black pit.

"I forgot to ask ye if ye'd have some cider?" a sepulchral voice asked presently; "but I don't know now's I can get at it. I told John I shouldn't want any whilst he was away, and so he ain't got the spiggit in yet," to which Mrs. Jake and Mrs. Martin both replied that they were no hands for that drink, unless 't was a drop right from the press, or a taste o' good hard cider towards the spring of the year; and Mrs. Thacher soon returned with some slices of cake in a plate and some apples held in her apron. One of her neighbors took the candle as she reached up to put it on the floor, and when the trap door was closed again all three drew up to the table and had a little feast. The cake was of a kind peculiar to its maker, who prided herself upon never being without it; and there was some trick of her hand or a secret ingredient which was withheld when she responded with apparent cheerfulness to requests for its recipe. As for the apples, they were grown upon an old tree, one of whose limbs had been grafted with some unknown variety of fruit so long ago that the history was forgotten; only that an English gardener, many years before, had brought some cuttings from the old country, and one of them had somehow come into the possession of John Thacher's grandfather when grafted fruit was a thing to be treasured and jealously guarded. It had been told that when the elder Thacher had given away cuttings he had always stolen to the orchards in the night afterward and ruined them. However, when the family had grown more generous in later years it had seemed to be without avail, for, on their neighbors' trees or their own, the English apples had proved worthless. Whether it were some favoring quality in that spot of soil or in the sturdy old native tree itself, the rich golden apples had grown there, year after year, in perfection, but nowhere else.

"There ain't no such apples as these, to my mind," said Mrs. Martin, as she polished a large one with her apron and held it up to the light, and Mrs. Jake murmured assent, having already taken a sufficient first bite.

"There's only one little bough that bears any great," said Mrs. Thacher, "but it's come to that once before, and another branch has shot up and been likely as if it was a young tree."

The good souls sat comfortably in their splint-bottomed, straight-backed chairs, and enjoyed this mild attempt at a festival. Mrs. Thacher even grew cheerful and responsive, for her guests seemed so light-hearted and free from care that the sunshine of their presence warmed her own chilled and fearful heart. They embarked upon a wide sea of neighborhood gossip and parish opinions, and at last some one happened to speak again of Thanksgiving, which at once turned the tide of conversation, and it seemed to ebb suddenly, while the gray, dreary look once more overspread Mrs. Thacher's face.

"I don't see why you won't keep with our folks this year; you and John," once more suggested Mrs. Martin. " 'T ain't wuth while to be making yourselves dismal here to home; the day 'll be lonesome for you at best, and you shall have whatever we've got and welcome."

" 'T won't be lonesomer this year than it was last, nor the year before that, and we've stood it somehow or 'nother," answered Mrs. Thacher for the second time, while she rose to put more wood in the stove. "Seems to me 't is growing cold; I felt a draught acrost my shoulders. These nights is dreadful chill; you feel the damp right through your bones. I never saw it darker than 't was last evenin'. I thought it seemed kind o' stived up here in the kitchen, and I opened the door and looked out, and I declare I couldn't see my hand before me."

"It always kind of scares me these black nights," said Mrs. Jake Dyer. "I expect something to clutch at me every minute, and I feel as if some sort of a creatur' was travelin' right behind me when I am out door in the dark. It makes it bad havin' a wanin' moon just now when the fogs hangs so low. It al'ays seems to me as if 't was darker when she rises late towards mornin' than when she's gone altogether. I do' know why 't is."

"I rec'lect once," Mrs. Thacher resumed, "when Ad'line was a baby and John was just turned four year old, their father had gone down river in the packet, and I was expectin' on him home at supper time, but he didn't come; 't was late in the fall, and a black night as I ever see. Ad'line was taken with something like croup, and I had an end o' candle in the candlestick that I lighted, and 't wa'n't long afore it was burnt down, and I went down cellar to the box where I kep' 'em, and if you will believe it, the rats had got to it, and there wasn't a week o' one left. I was near out anyway. We didn't have this cook-stove then, and I cal'lated I could make up a good lively blaze, so I come up full o' scold as I could be, and then I found I'd burnt up all my dry wood. You see, I thought certain he'd be home and I was tendin' to the child'n, but I started to go out o' the door and found it had come on to rain hard, and I said to myself I would n't go out to the woodpile and get my clothes all damp, 'count o' Ad-'line, and the candle end would last a spell longer, and he'd be home by that time. I had n't a least o' suspicion but what he was dallying round up to the Corners, 'long o' the rest o' the men, bein' 't was Saturday night, and I was some put out about it, for he knew the baby was sick, and I hadn't nobody with me. I set down and waited, but he never come, and it rained hard as I ever see it, and I left his supper standin' right in the floor, and then I begun to be distressed for fear somethin' had happened to Dan'l, and I set to work and cried, and the candle end give a flare and went out, and by 'n' by the fire begun to get low and I took the child'n and went to bed to keep warm; 't was an awful cold night, considerin' 't was such a heavy rain, and there I laid awake and thought I heard things steppin' about the room, and it seemed to me as if 't was a week long before mornin' come, and as if I'd got to be an old woman. I did go through with everything that night. 'T was that time Dan'l broke his leg, you know; they was takin' a deck load of oak knees down by the packet, and one on 'em rolled down from the top of the pile and struck him just below the knee. He was poling, for there wan't a breath o' wind, and he always felt certain there was somethin' mysterious about it. He'd had a good deal worse knocks than that seemed to be, as only left a black and blue spot, and he said he never see a deck load o' timber piled securer. He had some queer notions about the doin's o' sperits, Dan'l had; his old Aunt Parser was to blame for it. She lived with his father's folks, and used to fill him and the rest o' the child'n with all sorts o' ghost stories and stuff. I used to tell him she'd a' be'n hung for a witch if she'd lived in them old Salem days. He always used to be tellin' what everything was the sign of, when we was first married, till I laughed him out of it. It made me kind of notional. There's too much now we can't make sense of without addin' to it out o' our own heads."

Mrs. Jake and Mrs. Martin were quite familiar with the story of the night when there were no candles and Mr. Thacher had broken his leg, having been present themselves early in the morning afterward, but they had listened with none the less interest. These country neighbors knew their friends' affairs as well as they did their own, but such an audience is never impatient. The repetitions of the best stories are signal events, for ordinary circumstances do not inspire them. Affairs must rise to a certain level before a narration of some great crisis is suggested, and exactly as a city audience is well contented with hearing the plays of Shakespeare over and over again, so each man and woman of experience is permitted to deploy their well-known but always interesting stories upon the rustic stage.

"I must say I can't a-bear to hear anything about ghosts after sundown," observed Mrs. Jake, who was at times somewhat troubled by what she and her friends designated as "narves." "Day-times I don't believe in 'em 'less it's something creepy more 'n common, but after dark it scares me to pieces. I do' know but I shall be afeared to go home," and she laughed uneasily. "There! when I get through with this needle I believe I won't knit no more. The back o' my neck is all numb."

"Don't talk o' goin' home yet awhile," said the hostess, looking up quickly as if she hated the thought of being left alone again. " 'T is just on the edge of the evenin'; the nights is so long now we think it's bedtime half an hour after we've got lit up. 'T was a good lift havin' you step over to-night. I was really a-dreadin' to set here by myself," and for some minutes nobody spoke and the needles clicked faster than ever. Suddenly there was a strange sound outside the door, and they stared at each other in terror and held their breath, but nobody stirred. This was no familiar footstep; presently they heard a strange little cry, and still they feared to look, or to know what was waiting outside. Then Mrs. Thacher took a candle in her hand, and, still hesitating, asked once, "Who is there?" and, hearing no answer, slowly opened the door.

III

AT JAKE AND MARTIN'S

In the mean time, the evening had been much enjoyed by the brothers who were spending it together in Martin Dyer's kitchen. The houses stood side by side, but Mr. Jacob Dyer's youngest daughter, the only one now left at home, was receiving a visit from her lover, or, as the family expressed it, the young man who was keeping company with her, and her father, mindful of his own youth, had kindly withdrawn. Martin's children were already established in homes of their own, with the exception of one daughter who was at work in one of the cotton factories at Lowell in company with several of her acquaintances. It has already been said that Jake and Martin liked nobody's company so well as their own. Their wives had a time-honored joke about being comparatively unnecessary to their respective partners, and indeed the two men had a curiously dependent feeling toward each other. It was the close sympathy which twins sometimes have to each, and had become a byword among all their acquaintances. They were seldom individualized in any way, and neither was able to distinguish himself, apparently, for one always heard of the family as Jake and Martin's folks, and of their possessions, from least to greatest, as belonging to both brothers. The only time they had ever been separated was once in their early youth, when Jake had been fired with a desire to go to sea; but he deserted the coastwise schooner in the first port and came home, because he could not bear it any longer without his brother. Martin had no turn for seafaring, so Jake remained ashore and patiently made a farmer of himself for love's sake, and in spite of a great thirst for adventure that had never ceased to fever his blood. It was astonishing how much they found to say to each other when one considers that their experiences were almost constantly the same; but nothing contented them better than an uninterrupted evening spent in each other's society, and as they hoed corn or dug potatoes, or mowed, or as they drove to the Corners, sitting stiffly upright in the old-fashioned thorough-braced wagon, they were always to be seen talking as if it were the first meeting after a long separation. But, having taken these quiet times for the discussion of all possible and impossible problems, they were men of fixed opinions, and were ready at a moment's warning to render exact decisions. They were not fond of society as a rule; they found little occasion for much talk with their neighbors, but used as few words as possible. Nobody was more respected than the brothers. It was often said of them that their word was their bond, and as they passed from youth to middle age, and in these days were growing to look like elderly men, they were free from shame or reproach, though not from much good-natured joking and friendly fun. Their farm had been owned in the family since the settlement of the country, and the house which Martin occupied was very old. Jake's had been built for him when he was married, from timber cut in their own woodlands, and after thirty years of wear it looked scarcely newer than its companion. And when it is explained that they had married sisters, because, as people said, they even went courting together, it will be easy to see that they had found life more harmonious than most people do. Sometimes the wife of one brother would complain that her sister enjoyed undue advantages and profits from the estate, but there was rarely any disagreement, and Mrs. Jake was mistress of the turkeys and Mrs. Martin held sway over the hens, while they divided the spoils amiably at Thanksgiving time when the geese were sold. If it were a bad year for turkeys, and the tender young were chilled in the wet grass, while the hens flourished steadily the season through, Mrs. Jake's spirits drooped and she became envious of the good fortune which flaunted itself before her eyes, but on the whole, they suffered and enjoyed together, and found no fault with their destinies. The two wives, though the affection between them was of an ordinary sort, were apt to form a league against the brothers, and this prevented a more troublesome rivalry which might have existed between the households.

Jake and Martin were particularly enjoying the evening. Some accident had befallen the cooking-stove, which the brothers had never more than half approved, it being one of

the early patterns, and a poor exchange for the ancient meth-
ods of cookery in the wide fireplace. "The women" had had a
natural desire to be equal with their neighbors, and knew better than their husbands did the difference this useful invention had made in their every-day work. However, this one
night the conservative brothers could take a mild revenge;
and when their wives were well on their way to Mrs. Thacher's they had assured each other that, if the plaguey thing
were to be carried to the Corners in the morning to be exchanged or repaired, it would be as well to have it in readiness, and had quickly taken down its pipes and lifted it as if it
were a feather to the neighboring woodshed. Then they hastily pried away a fireboard which closed the great fireplace, and
looked smilingly upon the crane and its pothooks and the
familiar iron dogs which had been imprisoned there in darkness for many months. They brought in the materials for an
old-fashioned fire, backlog, forestick, and crowsticks, and
presently seated themselves before a crackling blaze. Martin
brought a tall, brown pitcher of cider from the cellar and set
two mugs beside it on the small table, and for some little time
they enjoyed themselves in silence, after which Jake remarked
that he did n't know but they'd got full enough of a fire for
such a mild night, but he wished his own stove and the new
one too could be dropped into the river for good and all.

They put the jug of cider between the andirons, and then,
moved by a common impulse, drew their chairs a little farther
from the mounting flames, before they quenched their thirst
from the mugs.

"I call that pretty cider," said Martin; " 't is young yet, but
it has got some weight a'ready, and 't is smooth. There's a
sight o' difference between good upland fruit and the sposhy
apples that grows in wet ground. An' I take it that the bar'l
has an influence: some bar'ls kind of wilt cider and some
smarten it up, and keep it hearty. Lord! what stuff some folks
are willin' to set before ye! 't ain't wuth the name o' cider, nor
no better than the rensin's of a vinegar cask."

"And then there's weather too," agreed Mr. Jacob Dyer,
"had ought to be took into consideration. Git your apples just
in the right time—not too early to taste o' the tree, nor too
late to taste o' the ground, and just in the snap o' time as to

ripeness', on a good sharp day with the sun a-shining; have 'em into the press and what comes out is *cider*. I think if we've had any fault in years past, 'twas puttin' off makin' a little too late. But I don't see as this could be beat. I don't know's you feel like a pipe, but I believe I'll light up," and thereupon a good portion of black-looking tobacco was cut and made fine in each of the hard left hands, and presently the clay pipes were touched off with a live coal, and great clouds of smoke might have been seen to disappear under the edge of the fire-place, drawn quickly up the chimney by the draft of the blazing fire.

Jacob pushed back his chair another foot or two, and Martin soon followed, mentioning that it was getting hot, but it was well to keep out the damp.

"What set the women out to go traipsin' up to Thacher's folks?" inquired Jacob, holding his cider mug with one hand and drumming it with the finger ends of the other.

"I had an idee that they wanted to find out if anything had been heard about Ad'line's getting home for Thanksgiving," answered Martin, turning to look shrewdly at his brother. "Women folks does suffer if there's anything goin' on they can't find out about. 'Liza said she was going to invite Mis' Thacher and John to eat a piece o' our big turkey, but she didn't s'pose they'd want to leave. Curi's about Ad'line, ain't it? I expected when her husband died she'd be right back here with what she'd got; at any rate, till she'd raised the child to some size. There'd be no expense here to what she'd have elsewhere, and here's her ma'am beginnin' to age. She can't do what she used to, John was tellin' of me; and I don't doubt 't'as worn upon her more'n folks thinks."

"I don't lay no great belief that John'll get home from court," said Jacob Dyer. "They say that court's goin' to set till Christmas maybe; there's an awful string o' cases on the docket. Oh, 'twas you told me, wa'n't it? Most like they'll let up for a couple o' days for Thanksgivin', but John mightn't think 'twas wuth his while to travel here and back again 'less he had something to do before winter shets down. Perhaps they'll prevail upon the old lady, I wish they would, I'm sure; but an only daughter forsakin' her so, 'twas most too bad of Ad'line. She al'ays had dreadful high notions when she wa'n't no more 'n a baby; and, good conscience, how she liked to rig up when she first used to come back from Lowell! Better ha' put her money out to interest."

"I believe in young folks makin' all they can o' theirselves," announced Martin, puffing hard at his pipe and drawing a little farther still from the fireplace, because the scorching red coals had begun to drop beneath the forestick. "I've give my child'n the best push forrard I could, an' you've done the same. Ad'line had a dreadful cravin' to be somethin' more 'n common; but it don't look as if she was goin' to make out any great. 'T was unfortunate her losin' of her husband, but I s'pose you've heard hints that they wa'n't none too equal-minded. She'd a done better to have worked on a while to Lowell and got forehanded, and then married some likely young fellow and settled down here, or to the Corners if she did n't want to farm it. There was Jim Hall used to be hang-ing round, and she'd been full as well off to-day if she'd took him, too. 'T ain't no use for folks to marry one that's of an-other kind and belongs different. It's like two fiddles that plays different tunes, — you can't make nothin' on't, no matter if both on em's trying their best, 'less one on 'em beats the other down entirely and has all the say, and ginerally 't is the worst one does it. Ad'line's husband wa'n't nothin' to boast of from all we can gather, but they did n't think alike about nothin'. She could 'a' done well with him if there'd been more of *her*. I don't marvel his folks felt bad: Ad'line did n't act right by 'em."

"Nor they by her," said the twin brother. "I tell ye Ad'line would have done 'em credit if she'd been let. I seem to think how 't was with her; when she was there to work in the shop she thought 't would be smart to marry him and then she'd be a lady for good and all. And all there was of it, she found his folks felt put out and hurt, and instead of pleasing 'em up and doing the best she could, she did n't know no better than to aggravate 'em. She was wrong there, but I hold to it that if they'd pleased her up a little and done well by her, she'd ha' bloomed out, and fell right in with their ways. She's got out-ward ambitions enough, but I view it she was all a part of his foolishness to them; I dare say they give her the blame o' the whole on't. Ad'line ought to had the sense to see they had some right on their side. Folks say he was the smartest fellow in his class to college."

"Good King Agrippy! how hot it does git," said Jake rising indignantly, as if the fire alone were to blame. "I must shove back the cider again or 't will bile over, spite of everything. But 't is called unwholesome to get a house full o' damp in the fall o' the year; 't will freeze an' thaw in the walls all winter. I must git me a new pipe if we go to the Corners to-morrow. I s'pose I 've told ye of a pipe a man had aboard the schooner that time I went to sea?"

Martin gave a little grumble of assent.

" 'T was made o' some sort o' whitish stuff like clay, but 't wa'n't shaped like none else I ever see and it had a silver trimmin' round it; 't was very light to handle and it drawed most excellent. I al'ays kind o' expected he may have stole it; he was a hard lookin' customer, a Dutchman or from some o' them parts o' the earth. I wish while I was about it I 'd gone one trip more."

"Was it you was tellin' me that Ad'line was to work again in Lowell? I should n't think her husband's folks would want the child to be fetched up there in them boardin' houses"—

"Belike they don't," responded Jacob, "but when they get Ad'line to come round to their ways o' thinkin' now, after what 's been and gone, they 'll have cause to thank themselves. She 's just like her gre't grandsir Thacher; you can see she 's made out o' the same stuff. You might ha' burnt him to the stake, and he 'd stick to it he liked it better 'n hanging and al'ays meant to die that way. There 's an awful bad streak in them Thachers, an' you know it as well as I do. I expect there 'll be bad and good Thachers to the end o' time. I 'm glad for the old lady 's sake that John ain't one o' the drinkin' ones. Ad'line 'll give no favors to her husband's folks, nor take none. There 's plenty o' wrongs to both sides, but as I view it, the longer he 'd lived the worse 't would been for him. She was a well made, pretty lookin' girl, but I tell ye 't was like setting a laylock bush to grow beside an ellum tree, and expecting of 'em to keep together. They wa'n't mates. He 'd had a different fetchin' up, and he *was* different, and I wa'n't surprised when I come to see how things had turned out,—I believe I shall have to set the door open a half a minute, 't is gettin' dreadful"—but there was a sudden flurry outside, and the sound of heavy footsteps, the bark of the startled cur, who was growing very old and a little deaf, and Mrs. Martin burst into the room and sank into the nearest chair, to gather a little breath before she could tell her errand. "For God's sake what's happened?" cried the men.

They presented a picture of mingled comfort and misery at which Mrs. Martin would have first laughed and then scolded at any other time. The two honest red faces were well back toward the farther side of the room from the fire, which still held its own; it was growing toward low tide in the cider jug and its attendant mugs, and the pipes were lying idle. The mistress of the old farm-house did not fail to notice that high treason had been committed during her short absence, but she made no comment upon the fireplace nor on anything else, and gasped as soon as she could that one of the men must go right up to the Corners for the doctor and hurry back with him, for 't was a case of life and death.

"Mis' Thacher?" "Was it a shock?" asked the brothers in sorrowful haste, while Mrs. Martin told the sad little story of Adeline's having come from nobody knew where, wet and forlorn, carrying her child in her arms. She looked as if she were in the last stages of a decline. She had fallen just at the doorstep and they had brought her in, believing that she was dead. "But while there's life, there's hope," said Mrs. Martin, "and I'll go back with you if you'll harness up. Jacob must stop to look after this gre't fire or 't will burn the house down," and this was the punishment which befell Jacob, since nothing else would have kept him from also journeying toward the Thacher house.

A little later the bewildered horse had been fully wakened and harnessed; Jacob's daughter and her lover had come eagerly out to hear what had happened; Mrs. Martin had somehow found a chance amidst all the confusion to ascend to her garret in quest of some useful remedies in the shape of herbs, and then she and her husband set forth on their benevolent errands. Martin was very apt to look on the dark side of things, and it was a curious fact that while the two sisters were like the brothers, one being inclined to despondency and one to enthusiasm, the balance was well kept by each of the men having chosen his opposite in temperament. Accordingly, while Martin heaved a great sigh from time to time and groaned softly, "Pore gal—pore gal!" his partner was brimful of zealous eagerness to return to the scene of distress and sorrow which she had lately left. Next to the doctor himself, she was the authority on all medical subjects for that neighborhood, and it was some time since her skill had been needed.

"Does the young one seem likely?" asked Martin with solemn curiosity.

"Fur's I could see," answered his wife promptly, "but nobody took no great notice of it. Pore Ad'line catched hold of it with such a grip as she was comin' to that we couldn't git it away from her and had to fetch 'em in both to once. Come urge the beast along, Martin, I'll give ye the partic'lars tomorrow, I do' know's Ad'line's livin' now. We got her right to bed's I told you, and I set right off considerin' that I could git over the ground fastest of any. Mis' Thacher of course wouldn't leave and Jane's heavier than I be." Martin's smile was happily concealed by the darkness; his wife and her sister had both grown stout steadily as they grew older, but each insisted upon the other's greater magnitude and consequent incapacity for quick movement. A casual observer would not have been persuaded that there was a pound's weight of difference between them.

Martin Dyer meekly suggested that perhaps he'd better go in a minute to see if there was anything Mis' Thacher needed, but Eliza, his wife, promptly said that she didn't want anything but the doctor as quick as she could get him, and disappeared up the short lane while the wagon rattled away up the road. The white mist from the river clung close to the earth, and it was impossible to see even the fences near at hand, though overhead there were a few dim stars. The air had grown somewhat softer, yet there was a sharp chill in it, and the ground was wet and sticky under foot. There were lights in the bedroom and in the kitchen of the Thacher house, but suddenly the bedroom candle flickered away and the window was darkened. Mrs. Martin's heart gave a quick throb, perhaps Adeline had already died. It might have been a shortsighted piece of business that she had gone home for her husband.

IV

LIFE AND DEATH

THE sick woman had refused to stay in the bedroom after she had come to her senses. She had insisted that she could not breathe, and that she was cold and must go back to the kitchen. Her mother and Mrs. Jake had wrapped her in blankets and drawn the high-backed wooden rocking chair close to the stove, and here she was just established when Mrs. Martin opened the outer door. Any one of less reliable nerves would have betrayed the shock which the sight of such desperate illness must have given. The pallor, the suffering, the desperate agony of the eyes, were far worse than the calmness of death, but Mrs. Martin spoke cheerfully, and even when her sister whispered that their patient had been attacked by a hæmorrhage, she manifested no concern.

"How long has this be'n a-goin' on, Ad'line? Why did n't you come home before and get doctored up? You 're all run down." Mrs. Thacher looked frightened when this questioning began, but turned her face toward her daughter, eager to hear the answer.

"I 've been sick off and on all summer," said the young woman, as if it were almost impossible to make the effort of speaking. "See if the baby 's covered up warm, will you, Aunt 'Liza?"

"Yes, dear," said the kind-hearted woman, the tears starting to her eyes at the sound of the familiar affectionate fashion of speech which Adeline had used in her childhood. "Don't you worry one mite; we 're going to take care of you and the little gal too;" and then nobody spoke, while the only sound was the difficult breathing of the poor creature by the fire. She seemed like one dying, there was so little life left in her after her piteous homeward journey. The mother watched her eagerly with a mingled feeling of despair and comfort; it was terrible to have a child return in such sad plight, but it was a blessing to have her safe at home, and to be able to minister to her wants while life lasted.

They all listened eagerly for the sound of wheels, but it

seemed a long time before Martin Dyer returned with the doctor. He had been met just as he was coming in from the other direction, and the two men had only paused while the tired horse was made comfortable, and a sleepy boy dispatched with the medicine for which he had long been waiting. The doctor's housekeeper had besought him to wait long enough to eat the supper which she had kept waiting, but he laughed at her and shook his head gravely, as if he already understood that there should be no delay. When he was fairly inside the Thacher kitchen, the benefaction of his presence was felt by every one. It was most touching to see the patient's face lose its worried look, and grow quiet and comfortable as if here were some one on whom she could entirely depend. The doctor's greeting was an every-day cheerful response to the women's welcome, and he stood for a minute warming his hands at the fire as if he had come upon a commonplace errand. There was something singularly self-reliant and composed about him; one felt that he was the wielder of great powers over the enemies, disease and pain, and that his brave hazel eyes showed a rare thoughtfulness and foresight. The rough driving coat which he had thrown off revealed a slender figure with the bowed shoulders of an untiring scholar. His head was finely set and scholarly, and there was that about him which gave certainty, not only of his sagacity and skill, but of his true manhood, his mastery of himself. Not only in this farm-house kitchen, but wherever one might place him, he instinctively took command, while from his great knowledge of human nature he could understand and help many of his patients whose ailments were not wholly physical. He seemed to read at a glance the shame and sorrow of the young woman who had fled to the home of her childhood, dying and worse than defeated, from the battle-field of life. And in this first moment he recognized with dismay the effects of that passion for strong drink which had been the curse of more than one of her ancestors. Even the pallor and the purifying influence of her mortal illness could not disguise these unmistakable signs.

"You can't do me any good, doctor," she whispered. "I shouldn't have let you come if it had been only that. I don't care how soon I am out of this world. But I want you should

look after my little girl," and the poor soul watched the physician's face with keen anxiety as if she feared to see a shadow
of unwillingness, but none came.

"I will do the best I can," and he still held her wrist, apparently thinking more of the fluttering pulse than of what poor
Adeline was saying.

"That was what made me willing to come back," she continued, "you don't know how close I came to not doing it
either. John will be good to her, but she will need somebody
that knows the world better by and by. I wonder if you
could n't show me how to make out a paper giving you the
right over her till she is of age? She must stay here with
mother, long as she wants her. 'T is what I wish I had kept
sense enough to do; life has n't been all play to me;" and the
tears began to roll quickly down the poor creature's thin
cheeks. "The only thing I care about is leaving the baby well
placed, and I want her to have a good chance to grow up a
useful woman. And most of all to keep her out of *their* hands,
I mean her father's folks. I hate 'em, and he cared more for
'em than he did for me, long at the last of it. . . . I could tell
you stories!"—

"But not to-night, Addy," said the doctor gravely, as if he
were speaking to a child. "We must put you to bed and to
sleep, and you can talk about all these troublesome things in
the morning. You shall see about the papers too, if you think
best. Be a good girl now, and let your mother help you to
bed." For the resolute spirit had summoned the few poor
fragments of vitality that were left, and the sick woman was
growing more and more excited. "You may have all the pil-
lows you wish for, and sit up in bed if you like, but you
must n't stay here any longer," and he gathered her in his
arms and quickly carried her to the next room. She made no
resistance, and took the medicine which Mrs. Martin
brought, without a word. There was a blazing fire now in the
bedroom fire-place, and, as she lay still, her face took on a
satisfied, rested look. Her mother sat beside her, tearful, and
yet contented and glad to have her near, and the others whispered together in the kitchen. It might have been the last
night of a long illness instead of the sudden, startling entrance
of sorrow in human shape. "No," said the doctor, "she cannot

last much longer with such a cough as that, Mrs. Dyer. She has almost reached the end of it. I only hope that she will go quickly."

And sure enough; whether the fatal illness had run its natural course, or whether the excitement and the forced strength of the evening before had exhausted the small portion of strength that was left, when the late dawn lighted again those who watched, it found them sleeping, and one was never to wake again in the world she had found so disappointing to her ambitions, and so untrue to its fancied promises.

The doctor had promised to return early, but it was hardly daylight before there was another visitor in advance of him. Old Mrs. Meeker, a neighbor whom nobody liked, but whose favor everybody for some reason or other was anxious to keep, came knocking at the door, and was let in somewhat reluctantly by Mrs. Jake, who was just preparing to go home in order to send one or both the brothers to the village and to acquaint John Thacher with the sad news of his sister's death. He was older than Adeline, and a silent man, already growing to be elderly in his appearance. The women had told themselves and each other that he would take this sorrow very hard, and Mrs. Thacher had said sorrowfully that she must hide her daughter's poor worn clothes, since it would break John's heart to know she had come home so beggarly. The shock of so much trouble was stunning the mother; she did not understand yet, she kept telling the kind friends who sorrowed with her, as she busied herself with the preparations for the funeral. "It don't seem as if 't was Addy," she said over and over again, "but I feel safe about her now, to what I did," and Mrs. Jake and Mrs. Martin, good helpful souls and brimful of compassion, went to and fro with their usual diligence almost as if this were nothing out of the common course of events.

Mrs. Meeker had heard the wagon go by and had caught the sound of the doctor's voice, her house being close by the road, and she had also watched the unusual lights. It was annoying to the Dyers to have to answer questions, and to be called upon to grieve outwardly just then, and it seemed disloyal to the dead woman in the next room to enter upon any discussion of her affairs. But presently the little child, whom nobody had thought of except to see that she still slept, waked and got down from the old settle where she had spent the night, and walked with unsteady short footsteps toward her grandmother, who caught her quickly and held her fast in her arms. The little thing looked puzzled, and frowned, and seemed for a moment unhappy, and then the sunshine of her good nature drove away the clouds and she clapped her hands and laughed aloud, while Mrs. Meeker began to cry again at the sight of this unconscious orphan.

"I'm sure I'm glad she can laugh," said Mrs. Martin. "She'll find enough to cry about later on; I foresee she'll be a great deal o' company to you, Mis' Thacher."

"Though 't ain't every one that has the strength to fetch up a child after they reach your years," said Mrs. Meeker, mournfully. "It's anxious work, but I don't doubt strength will be given you. I s'pose likely her father's folks will do a good deal for her,"—and the three women looked at each other, but neither took it upon herself to answer.

All that day the neighbors and acquaintances came and went in the lane that led to the farm-house. The brothers Jake and Martin made journeys to and from the village. At night John Thacher came home from court with as little to say as ever, but, as everybody observed, looking years older. Young Mrs. Prince's return and sudden death were the only subjects worth talking about in all the country side, and the doctor had to run the usual gauntlet of questions from all his outlying patients and their families. Old Mrs. Thacher looked pale and excited, and insisted upon seeing every one who came to the house, with evident intention to play her part in this strange drama with exactness and courtesy. A funeral in the country is always an era in a family's life; events date from it and centre in it. There are so few circumstances that have in the least a public nature that these conspicuous days receive all the more attention.

But while death seems far more astonishing and unnatural in a city, where the great tide of life rises and falls with little apparent regard to the sinking wrecks, in the country it is not so. The neighbors themselves are those who dig the grave and

carry the dead, whom they or their friends have made ready,
to the last resting-place. With all nature looking on,—the
leaves that must fall, and the grass of the field that must
wither and be gone when the wind passes over,—living
closer to life and in plainer sight of death, they have a different sense of the mysteries of existence. They pay homage to
Death rather than to the dead; they gather from the lonely
farms by scores because there is a funeral, and not because
their friend is dead; and the day of Adeline Prince's burial, the
marvelous circumstances, with which the whole town was already familiar, brought a great company together to follow
her on her last journey.

The day was warm and the sunshine fell caressingly over
the pastures as if it were trying to call back the flowers. By
afternoon there was a tinge of greenness on the slopes and
under the gnarled apple-trees, that had been lost for days before, and the distant hills and mountains, which could be
seen in a circle from the high land where the Thacher farm-
house stood, were dim and blue through the Indian summer
haze. The old men who came to the funeral wore their faded
winter overcoats and clumsy caps all ready to be pulled
down over their ears if the wind should change; and their
wives were also warmly wrapped, with great shawls over
their rounded, hard-worked shoulders; yet they took the best
warmth and pleasantness into their hearts, and watched the
sad proceedings of the afternoon with deepest interest. The
doctor came hurrying toward home just as the long procession was going down the pasture, and he saw it crossing a
low hill; a dark and slender column with here and there a
child walking beside one of the elder mourners. The bearers
went first with the bier; the track was uneven, and the procession was lost to sight now and then behind the slopes.
It was forever a mystery; these people might have been a
company of Druid worshipers, or of strange northern priests
and their people, and the doctor checked his impatient
horse as he watched the retreating figures at their simple
ceremony. He could not help thinking what strange ways
this child of the old farm had followed, and what a quiet
ending it was to her wandering life. "And I have promised

to look after the little girl," he said to himself as he drove away up the road.

It was a long walk for the elderly people from the house near the main highway to the little burying-ground. In the earliest days of the farm the dwelling-place was nearer the river, which was then the chief thoroughfare; and those of the family who had died then were buried on the level bit of up-land ground high above the river itself. There was a wide outlook over the country, and the young pine trees that fringed the shore sang in the south wind, while some great birds swung to and fro overhead, watching the water and the strange company of people who had come so slowly over the land. A flock of sheep had ventured to the nearest hillock of the next pasture, and stood there fearfully, with upraised heads, as if they looked for danger.

John Thacher had brought his sister's child all the way in his arms, and she had clapped her hands and laughed aloud and tried to talk a great deal with the few words she had learned to say. She was very gay in her baby fashion; she was amused with the little crowd so long as it did not trouble her. She fretted only when the grave, kind man, for whom she had instantly felt a great affection, stayed too long by that deep hole in the ground and wept as he saw a strange thing that the people had carried all the way, put down into it out of sight. When he walked on again, she laughed and played; but after they had reached the empty gray house, which somehow looked that day as if it were a mourner also, she shrank from all the strangers, and seemed dismayed and perplexed, and called her mother eagerly again and again. This touched many a heart. The dead woman had been more or less unfamiliar of late years to all of them; and there were few who had really grieved for her until her little child had reminded them of its own loneliness and loss.

That night, after the house was still, John Thacher wrote to acquaint Miss Prince, of Dunport, with his sister's death and to say that it was her wish that the child should remain with them during its minority. They should formally appoint the guardian whom she had selected; they would do their best by the little girl. And when Mrs. Thacher asked if he had blamed Miss Prince, he replied that he had left that to her own conscience.

In the answer which was quickly returned, there was a plea for the custody of the child, her mother's and her own namesake, but this was indignantly refused. There was no love lost between the town and the country household, and for many years all intercourse was at an end. Before twelve months were past, John Thacher himself was carried down to the pasture burying-ground, and his old mother and the little child were left to comfort and take care of each other as best they could in the lonely farm-house.

V

A SUNDAY VISIT

In the gray house on the hill, one spring went by and another, and it seemed to the busy doctor only a few months from the night he first saw his ward before she was old enough to come soberly to church with her grandmother. He had always seen her from time to time, for he had often been called to the farm or to the Dyers and had watched her at play. Once she had stopped him as he drove by to give him a little handful of blue violets, and this had gone straight to his heart, for he had been made too great a bugbear to most children to look for any favor at their hands. He always liked to see her come into church on Sundays, her steps growing quicker and surer as her good grandmother's became more feeble. The doctor was a lonely man in spite of his many friends, and he found himself watching for the little brown face that, half-way across the old meeting-house, would turn round to look for him more than once during the service. At first there was only the top of little Nan Prince's prim best bonnet or hood to be seen, unless it was when she stood up in prayer-time, but soon the bright eyes rose like stars above the horizon of the pew railing, and next there was the whole well-poised little head, and the tall child was possessed by a sense of propriety, and only ventured one or two discreet glances at her old friend.

The office of guardian was not one of great tasks or of many duties, though the child's aunt had insisted upon making an allowance for her of a hundred dollars a year, and this was duly acknowledged and placed to its owner's credit in the savings bank of the next town. Her grandmother Thacher always refused to spend it, saying proudly that she had never been beholden to Miss Prince and she never meant to be, and while she lived the aunt and niece should be kept apart. She would not say that her daughter had never been at fault, but it was through the Princes all the trouble of her life had come.

Dr. Leslie was mindful of his responsibilities, and knew more of his ward than was ever suspected. He was eager that the best district school teacher who could be found should be procured for the Thacher and Dyer neighborhood, and in many ways he took pains that the little girl should have all good things that were possible. He only laughed when her grandmother complained that Nan would not be driven to school, much less persuaded, and that she was playing in the brook, or scampering over the pastures when she should be doing other things. Mrs. Thacher, perhaps unconsciously, had looked for some trace of the father's good breeding and gentlefolk fashions, but this was not a child who took kindly to needlework and pretty clothes. She was fearlessly friendly with every one; she did not seem confused even when the minister came to make his yearly parochial visitation, and as for the doctor, he might have been her own age, for all humility she thought it necessary to show in the presence of this chief among her elders and betters. Old Mrs. Thacher gave little pulls at her granddaughter's sleeves when she kept turning to see the doctor in sermon-time, but she never knew how glad he was, or how willingly he smiled when he felt the child's eyes watching him as a dog's might have done, forcing him to forget the preaching altogether and to attend to this dumb request for sympathy. One blessed day Dr. Leslie had waited in the church porch and gravely taken the child's hand as she came out; and said that he should like to take her home with him; he was going to the lower part of the town late in the afternoon and would leave her then at the farm-house.

"I was going to ask you for something for her shoulder," said Grandmother Thacher, much pleased, "she'll tell you about it, it was a fall she had out of an apple-tree,"—and Nan looked up with not a little apprehension, but presently tucked her small hand inside the doctor's and was more than ready to go with him. "I thought she looked a little pale," the doctor said, to which Mrs. Thacher answered that it was a merciful Providence who had kept the child from breaking her neck, and then, being at the foot of the church steps, they separated. It had been a great trial to the good woman to give up the afternoon service, but she was growing old, as she told herself often in those days, and felt, as she certainly looked, greatly older than her years.

"I feel as if Anna was sure of one good friend, whether I stay with her or not," said the grandmother sorrowfully, as she drove toward home that Sunday noon with Jacob Dyer and his wife. "I never saw the doctor so taken with a child before. 'T was a pity he had to lose his own, and his wife too; how many years ago was it? I should think he'd be lonesome, though to be sure he is n't in the house much. Marilla Thomas keeps his house as clean as a button and she has been a good stand-by for him, but it always seemed sort o' homesick there ever since the day I was to his wife's funeral. She made an awful sight o' friends considering she was so little while in the place. Well I'm glad I let Nanny wear her best dress; I set out not to, it looked so much like rain."

Whatever Marilla Thomas's other failings might have been, she certainly was kind that day to the doctor's little guest. It would have been a hard-hearted person indeed who did not enter somewhat into the spirit of the child's delight. In spite of its being the first time she had ever sat at any table but her grandmother's, she was not awkward or uncomfortable, and was so hungry that she gave pleasure to her entertainers in that way if no other. The doctor leaned back in his chair and waited while the second portion of pudding slowly disappeared, though Marilla could have told that he usually did not give half time enough to his dinner and was off like an arrow the first possible minute. Before he took his often interrupted afternoon nap, he inquired for the damaged shoulder and requested a detailed account of the accident; and presently they were both laughing heartily at Nan's disaster, for she owned that she had chased and treed a stray young squirrel, and that a mossy branch of one of the old apple-trees in the straggling orchard had failed to bear even so light a weight as hers. Nan had come to the ground because she would not loose her hold of the squirrel, though he had slipped through her hands after all as she carried him towards home. The guest was proud to become a patient, especially as the only remedy that was offered was a very comfortable handful of sugar-plums. Nan had never owned so many at once, and in a transport of gratitude and affection she lifted her face to kiss so dear a benefactor.

Her eyes looked up into his, and her simple nature was so unconscious of the true dangers and perils of this world, that his very heart was touched with compassion, and he leagued himself with the child's good angel to defend her against her enemies.

And Nan took fast hold of the doctor's hand as they went to the study. This was the only room in the house which she had seen before; and was so much larger and pleasanter than any she knew elsewhere that she took great delight in it. It was a rough place now, the doctor thought, but always very comfortable, and he laid himself down on the great sofa with a book in his hand, though after a few minutes he grew sleepy and only opened his eyes once to see that Nan was perched in the largest chair with her small hands folded, and her feet very far from the floor. "You may run out to see Marilla, or go about the house anywhere you like; or there are some picture-papers on the table," the doctor said drowsily, and the visitor slipped down from her throne and went softly away.

She had thought the study a very noble room until she had seen the dining-room, but now she wished for another look at the pictures there and the queer clock, and the strange, grand things on the sideboard. The old-fashioned comfort of the house was perfect splendor to the child, and she went about on tiptoe up stairs and down, looking in at the open doors, while she lingered wistfully before the closed ones. She wondered at the great bedsteads with their high posts and dimity hangings, and at the carpets, and the worthy Marilla watched her for a moment as she stood on the threshold of the doctor's own room. The child's quick ear caught the rustle of the housekeeper's Sunday gown; she whispered with shining eyes that she thought the house was beautiful. Did Marilla live here all the time?

"Bless you, yes!" replied Marilla, not without pride, though she added that nobody knew what a sight of care it was.

"I suppose y'r aunt in Dunport lives a good deal better than this;" but the child only looked puzzled and did not answer, while the housekeeper hurried away to the afternoon meeting, for which the bell was already tolling.

The doctor slept on in the shaded study, and after Nan had grown tired of walking softly about the house, she found her way into the garden. After all, there was nothing better than being out of doors, and the apple-trees seemed most familiar and friendly, though she pitied them for being placed so near each other. She discovered a bench under a trellis where a grape-vine and a clematis were tangled together, and here she sat down to spend a little time before the doctor should call her. She wished she could stay longer than that one short afternoon; perhaps some time or other the doctor would invite her again. But what could Marilla have meant about her aunt? She had no aunts except Mrs. Jake and Mrs. Martin; Marilla must well know that their houses were not like Dr. Leslie's; and little Nan built herself a fine castle in Spain, of which this unknown aunt was queen. Certainly her grandmother had now and then let fall a word about "your father's folks"—by and by they might come to see her!

The grape leaves were waving about in the warm wind, and they made a flickering light and shade upon the ground. The clematis was in bloom, and its soft white plumes fringed the archway of the lattice work. As the child looked down the garden walk it seemed very long and very beautiful to her. Her grandmother's flower-garden had been constantly encroached upon by the turf which surrounded it, until the snowberry bush, the London pride, the tiger-lilies, and the crimson phlox were like a besieged garrison.

Nan had already found plenty of wild flowers in the world; there were no entertainments provided for her except those the fields and pastures kindly spread before her admiring eyes. Old Mrs. Thacher had been brought up to consider the hard work of this life, and though she had taken her share of enjoyment as she went along, it was of a somewhat grim and sober sort. She believed that a certain amount of friskiness was as necessary to young human beings as it is to colts, but later both must be harnessed and made to work. As for pleasure itself she had little notion of that. She liked fair weather, and certain flowers were to her the decorations of certain useful plants, but if she had known that her grand-daughter could lie down beside the anemones and watch them move in the wind and nod their heads, and afterward look up into the blue sky to watch the great gulls above the river, or the sparrows flying low, or the crows who went higher, Mrs. Thacher would have understood almost nothing of such delights, and thought it a very idle way of spending one's time.

But as Nan sat in the old summer-house in the doctor's garden, she thought of many things that she must remember to tell her grandmother about this delightful day. The bees were humming in the vines, and as she looked down the wide garden-walk it seemed like the broad aisle in church, and the congregation of plants and bushes all looked at her as if she were in the pulpit. The church itself was not far away, and the windows were open, and sometimes Nan could hear the preacher's voice, and by and by the people began to sing, and she rose solemnly, as if it were her own parishioners in the garden who lifted up their voices. A cheerful robin began a loud solo in one of Dr. Leslie's cherry-trees, and the little girl laughed aloud in her make-believe meeting-house, and then the gate was opened and shut, and the doctor himself appeared, strolling along, and smiling as he came.

He was looking to the right and left at his flowers and trees, and once he stopped and took out his pocket knife to trim a straying branch of honeysuckle, which had wilted and died. When he came to the summer-house, he found his guest sitting there demurely with her hands folded in her lap. She had gathered some little sprigs of box and a few blossoms of periwinkle and late lilies of the valley, and they lay on the bench beside her. "So you did not go to church with Marilla?" the doctor said. "I dare say one sermon a day is enough for so small a person as you." For Nan's part, no sermon at all would have caused little sorrow, though she liked the excitement of the Sunday drive to the village. She only smiled when the doctor spoke, and gave a little sigh of satisfaction a minute afterward when he seated himself beside her.

"We must be off presently," he told her. "I have a long drive to take before night. I would let you go with me, but I am afraid I should keep you too long past your bedtime."

The little girl looked in his kind face appealingly; she could not bear to have the day come to an end. The doctor spoke to her as if she were grown up and understood everything, and this pleased her. It is very hard to be constantly reminded that one is a child, as if it were a crime against society. Dr. Leslie, unlike many others, did not like children because they were children; he now and then made friends with one, just as he added now and then to his narrow circle of grown friends. He felt a certain responsibility for this little girl, and congratulated himself upon feeling an instinctive fondness for her. The good old minister had said only that morning that love is the great motive power, that it is always easy to do things for those whom we love and wish to please, and for this reason we are taught to pray for love to God, and so conquer the difficulty of holiness. "But I must do my duty by her at any rate," the doctor told himself. "I am afraid I have forgotten the child somewhat in past years, and she is a bright little creature."

"Have you been taking good care of yourself?" he added aloud. "I was very tired, for I was out twice in the night taking care of sick people. But you must come to see me again some day. I dare say you and Marilla have made friends with each other. Now we must go, I suppose," and Nan Prince, still silent,—for the pleasure of this time was almost too great,—took hold of the doctor's outstretched hand, and they went slowly up the garden walk together. As they drove slowly down the street they met the people who were coming from church, and the child sat up very straight in the old gig, with her feet on the doctor's medicine-box, and was sure that everybody must be envying her. She thought it was more pleasant than ever that afternoon, as they passed through the open country outside the village; the fields and the trees were marvelously green, and the distant river was shining in the sun. Nan looked anxiously for the gray farmhouse for two or three minutes before they came in sight of it, but at last it showed itself, standing firm on the hillside. It seemed a long time since she had left home in the morning, but this beautiful day was to be one of the landmarks of her memory. Life had suddenly grown much larger, and her familiar horizon had vanished and she discovered a great distance stretching far beyond the old limits. She went gravely into the familiar kitchen, holding fast the bits of box and the periwinkle flowers, quite ready to answer her grandmother's questions, though she was only too certain that it would be impossible to tell any one the whole dear story of that June Sunday.

A little later, as Marilla came sedately home, she noticed in the driveway some fresh hoofmarks which pointed toward the street, and quickly assured herself that they could not have been made very long before. "I wonder what the two of 'em have been doing all the afternoon?" she said to herself. "She's a little lady, that child is; and it's a burnin' shame she should be left to run wild. I never set so much by her mother's looks as some did, but growin' things has blooms as much as they have roots and prickles—and even them Thachers will flower out once in a while."

VI

IN SUMMER WEATHER

ONE morning Dr. Leslie remembered an old patient whom he liked to go to see now and then, perhaps more from the courtesy and friendliness of the thing than from any hope of giving professional assistance. The old sailor, Captain Finch, had long before been condemned as unseaworthy, having suffered for many years from the effects of a bad fall on shipboard. He was a cheerful and wise person, and the doctor was much attached to him, besides knowing that he had borne his imprisonment with great patience, for his life on one of the most secluded farms of the region, surrounded by his wife's kinsfolk, who were all landsmen, could hardly be called anything else. The doctor had once made a voyage to Fayal and from thence to England in a sailing-vessel, having been somewhat delicate in health in his younger days, and this made him a more intelligent listener to the captain's stories than was often available.

Dr. Leslie had brought his case of medicines from mere force of habit, but by way of special prescription he had taken also a generous handful of his best cigars, and wrapped them somewhat clumsily in one of the large sheets of letter-paper which lay on his study table near by. Also he had stopped before the old sideboard in the carefully darkened dining-room, and taken a bottle of wine from one of its cupboards. "This will do him more good than anything, poor old fellow," he told himself, with a sudden warmth in his own heart and a feeling of grateful pleasure because he had thought of doing the kindness.

Marilla called eagerly from the kitchen window to ask where he was going, putting her hand out hastily to part the morning-glory vines, which had climbed their strings and twisted their stems together until they shut out the world from their planter's sight. But the doctor only answered that he should be back at dinner time, and settled himself comfortably in his carriage, smiling as he thought of Marilla's displeasure. She seldom allowed a secret to escape her, if she were once fairly on the scent of it, though she grumbled now, and told herself that she only cared to know for the sake of the people who might come, or to provide against the accident of his being among the missing in case of sudden need. She found life more interesting when there was even a small mystery to be puzzled over. It was impossible for Dr. Leslie to resist teasing his faithful hand-maiden once in a while, but he did it with proper gravity and respect, and their friendship was cemented by these sober jokes rather than torn apart.

The horse knew as well as his master that nothing of particular importance was in hand, and however well he always caught the spirit of the occasion when there was need for hurry, he now jogged along the road, going slowly where the trees cast a pleasant shade, and paying more attention to the flies than to anything else. The doctor seemed to be in deep thought, and old Major understood that no notice was to be taken of constant slight touches of the whip which his master held carelessly. It had been hot, dusty weather until the day and night before, when heavy showers had fallen; the country was looking fresh, and the fields and trees were washed clean at last from the white dust that had powdered them and given the farms a barren and discouraged look.

They had come in sight of Mrs. Thacher's house on its high hillside, and were just passing the abode of Mrs. Meeker, which was close by the roadside in the low land. This was a small, weather-beaten dwelling, and the pink and red hollyhocks showed themselves in fine array against its gray walls. Its mistress's prosaic nature had one most redeeming quality in her love for flowers and her gift in making them grow, and the doctor forgave her many things for the sake of the bright little garden in the midst of the sandy lands which surrounded her garden with their unshaded barrenness. The road that crossed these was hot in summer and swept by bitter winds in winter. It was like a bit of desert dropped by mistake among the green farms and spring-fed forests that covered the rest of the river uplands.

No sentinel was ever more steadfast to his duty in time of war and disorder than Mrs. Meeker, as she sat by the front window, from which she could see some distance either way along the crooked road. She was often absent from her own house to render assistance of one sort or another among her neighbors, but if she were at home it was impossible for man, woman, or child to go by without her challenge or careful inspection. She made couriers of her neighbors, and sent these errand men and women along the country roads or to the village almost daily. She was well posted in the news from both the village and the country side, and however much her acquaintances scolded about her, they found it impossible to resist the fascination of her conversation, and few declined to share in the banquet of gossip which she was always ready to spread. She was quick witted, and possessed of many resources and much cleverness of a certain sort; but it must be confessed that she had done mischief in her day, having been the murderer of more than one neighbor's peace of mind and the assailant of many a reputation. But if she were a dangerous inmate of one's household, few were so attractive or entertaining for the space of an afternoon visit, and it was usually said, when she was seen approaching, that she would be sure to have something to tell. Out in the country, where so many people can see nothing new from one week's end to the other, it is, after all, a great pleasure to have the latest particulars brought to one's door, as a townsman's newspaper is.

Mrs. Meeker knew better than to stop Dr. Leslie if he were going anywhere in a hurry; she had been taught this lesson years ago; but when she saw him journeying in such a leisurely way some instinct assured her of safety, and she came out of her door like a Jack-in-the-box, while old Major, only too ready for a halt, stood still in spite of a desperate twitch of the reins, which had as much effect as pulling at a fish-hook which has made fast to an anchor. Mrs. Meeker feigned a great excitement.

"I won't keep you but a moment," she said, "but I want to hear what you think about Mis' Thacher's chances."

"Mrs. Thacher's?" repeated the doctor, wonderingly. "She's doing well, is n't she? I don't suppose that she will ever be a young woman again."

"I don't know why, but I took it for granted that you was goin' there," explained Mrs. Meeker, humbly. "She has seemed to me as if she was failing all summer. I was up there last night, and I never said so to her, but she had aged dreadfully. I wonder if it's likely she's had a light shock? Sometimes the fust one's kind o' hidden; comes by night or somethin', and folks don't know till they begins to feel the damage of it."

"She has n't looked very well of late," said the doctor. For once in his life he was willing to have a friendly talk, Mrs. Meeker thought, and she proceeded to make the most of her opportunity.

"I think the care of that girl of Ad'line's has been too much for her all along," she announced, "she's wild as a hawk, and a perfect torment. One day she'll come strollin' in and beseechin' me for a bunch o' flowers, and the next she'll be here after dark scarin' me out o' my seven senses. She rigged a tick-tack here the other night against the window, and my heart was in my mouth. I thought 't was a warnin' much as ever I thought anything in my life; the night before my mother died 't was in that same room and against that same winder there came two or three raps, and my sister Drew and me we looked at each other, and turned cold all over, and mother set right up in bed the next night and looked at that winder and then laid back dead. I was all sole alone the other evenin', — Wednesday it was, — and when I heard them raps I mustered up, and went and put my head out o' the door, and I could n't see nothing, and when I went back, knock — knock, it begun again, and I went to the door and harked. I hoped I should hear somebody or 'nother comin' along the road, and then I heard somethin' a rus'lin' amongst the sunflowers and hollyhocks, and then there was a titterin', and come to find out 't was that young one. I chased her up the road till my wind give out, and I had to go and set on the stone wall, and come to. She won't go to bed till she's a mind to. One night I was up there this spring, and she never come in until after nine o'clock, a dark night, too; and the pore old lady was in distress, and thought she'd got into the river. I says to myself there wa'n't no such good news. She told how she'd be'n up into Jake an' Martin's oaks, trying to catch a little screech owl. She belongs with wild creatur's, I do believe, — just the same natur'. She'd better be kept to school, 'stead o' growin' up this way; but she keeps the rest o' the young ones all in a brile, and this last teacher would n't have her there at all. She 'd toll off half the school into the pasture at recess time, and none of 'em would get back for half an hour."

"What 's a tick-tack? I don't remember," asked the doctor, who had been smiling now and then at this complaint.

"They tie a nail to the end of a string, and run it over a bent pin stuck in the sash, and then they get out o' sight and pull, and it clacks against the winder, don't ye see? Ain't it surprisin' how them devil's tricks gets handed down from gineration to gineration, while so much that 's good is forgot," lamented Mrs. Meeker, but the doctor looked much amused.

"She 's a bright child," he said, "and not over strong. I don't believe in keeping young folks shut up in the schoolhouses all summer long."

Mrs. Meeker sniffed disapprovingly. "She 's tougher than ellum roots. I believe you can't kill them peakèd-looking young ones. She 'll run like a fox all day long and live to see us all buried. I can put up with her pranks; 't is of pore old Mis' Thacher I 'm thinkin'. She 's had trouble enough without adding on this young 'scape-gallows. You had better fetch her up to be a doctor," Mrs. Meeker smilingly continued, "I was up there yisterday, and one of the young turkeys had come hoppin' and quawkin' round the doorsteps with its leg broke, and she 'd caught it and fixed it off with a splint before you could say Jack Robi'son. She told how it was the way you 'd done to Jim Finch that fell from the hay-rigging and broke his arm over to Jake an' Martin's, haying time."

"I remember she was standing close by, watching everything I did," said the doctor, his face shining with interest and pleasure. "I shall have to carry her about for clerk. Her father studied medicine you know. It is the most amazing thing how people inherit"—but he did not finish his sentence and pulled the reins so quickly that the wise horse knew there was no excuse for not moving forward.

Mrs. Meeker had hoped for a longer interview. "Stop as you come back, won't you?" she asked. "I 'm goin' to pick you some of the handsomest poppies I ever raised. I got the seed from my sister-in-law's cousin, she that was 'Miry Gregg, and they do beat everything. They wilt so that it ain't no use to pick 'em now, unless you was calc'latin' to come home by the other road. There's nobody sick about here, is there?" to which the doctor returned a shake of the head and the information that he should be returning that way about noon. As he drove up the hill he assured himself with great satisfaction that he believed he had n't told anything that morning which would be repeated all over town before night, while his hostess returned to her house quite dissatisfied with the interview, though she hoped for better fortune on Dr. Leslie's return.

For his part, he drove on slowly past the Thacher farmhouse, looking carefully about him, and sending a special glance up the lane in search of the invalid turkey. "I should like to see how she managed it," he told himself half aloud. "If she shows a gift for such things I 'll take pains to teach her a lesson or two by and by when she is older. . . . Come Major, don't go to sleep on the road!" and in a few minutes the wagon was out of sight, if the reader had stood in the Thacher lane, instead of following the good man farther on his errand of mercy and good fellowship.

At that time in the morning most housekeepers were busy in their kitchens, but Mrs. Thacher came to stand in her doorway, and shaded her forehead and eyes with her hand from the bright sunlight, as she looked intently across the pastures toward the river. She seemed anxious and glanced to and fro across the fields, and presently she turned quickly at the sound of a footstep, and saw her young grand-daughter coming from the other direction round the corner of the house. The child was wet and a little pale, though she evidently had been running.

"What have you been doin' now?" asked the old lady fretfully. "I won't have you gettin' up in the mornin' before I am awake and stealin' out of the house. I think you are drowned in the river or have broken your neck fallin' out of a tree. Here it is after ten o'clock. I 've a mind to send you to bed, Nanny; who got you out of the water, for in it you 've been sure enough?"

"I got out myself," said the little girl. "It was deep, though," and she began to cry, and when she tried to cover her eyes with her already well-soaked little apron, she felt quite broken-hearted and unnerved, and sat down dismally on the doorstep.

"Come in, and put on a dry dress," said her grandmother, not unkindly; "that is, if there's anything but your Sunday one fit to be seen. I've told you often enough not to go playin' in the river, and I've wanted you more than common to go out to Jake and Martin's to borrow me a little cinnamon. You're a real trial this summer. I believe the bigger you are the worse you are. Now just say what you've been about. I declare I shall have to go and have a talk with the doctor, and he'll scold you well. I'm gettin' old and I can't keep after you; you ought to consider me some. You'll think of it when you see me laying dead, what a misery you've be'n. No schoolin' worth namin';" grumbled Mrs. Thacher, as she stepped heavily to and fro in the kitchen, and the little girl disappeared within the bed-room. In a few minutes, however, her unusual depression was driven away by the comfort of dry garments, and she announced triumphantly that she had found a whole flock of young wild ducks, and that she had made a raft and chased them about up and down the river, until the raft had proved unseaworthy, and she had fallen through into the water. Later in the day somebody came from the Jake and Martin homesteads to say that there must be no more pulling down of the ends of the pasture fences. The nails had easily let go their hold of the old boards, and a stone had served our heroine for a useful shipwright's hammer, but the young cattle had strayed through these broken barriers and might have done great damage if they had been discovered a little later,—having quickly hied themselves to a piece of carefully cultivated land. The Jake and Martin families regarded Nan with a mixture of dread and affection. She was bringing a new element into their prosaic lives, and her pranks afforded them a bit of news almost daily. Her imagination was apt to busy itself in inventing tales of her unknown aunt, with which she entertained a grandchild of Martin Dyer, a little girl of nearly her own age. It seemed possible to Nan that any day a carriage drawn by a pair of prancing black horses might be seen turning up the lane, and that a lovely lady might alight and claim her as her only niece. Why this event had not already taken place the child never troubled herself to think, but ever since Marilla had spoken of this aunt's existence, the dreams of her had been growing longer and more charming, until she seemed fit for a queen, and her unseen house a palace. Nan's playmate took pleasure in repeating these glowing accounts to her family, and many were the head-shakings and evil forebodings over the untruthfulness of the heroine of this story. Little Susan Dyer's only aunt, who was well known to her, lived as other people did in a comparatively plain and humble house, and it was not to be wondered at that she objected to hearing continually of an aunt of such splendid fashion. And yet Nan tried over and over again to be in some degree worthy of the relationship. She must not be too unfit to enter upon more brilliant surroundings whenever the time should come,—she took care that her pet chickens and her one doll should have highsounding names, such as would seem proper to the aunt, and, more than this, she took a careful survey of the house whenever she was coming home from school or from play, lest she might come upon her distinguished relative unawares. She had asked her grandmother more than once to tell her about this mysterious kinswoman, but Mrs. Thacher proved strangely uncommunicative, fearing if she answered one easy question it might involve others that were more difficult.

The good woman grew more and more anxious to fulfil her duty to this troublesome young housemate; the child was strangely dear and companionable in spite of her frequent naughtiness. It seemed, too, as if she could do whatever she undertook, and as if she had a power which made her able to use and unite the best traits of her ancestors, the strong capabilities which had been illy balanced or allowed to run to waste in others. It might be said that the materials for a fine specimen of humanity accumulate through several generations, until a child appears who is the heir of all the family wit and attractiveness and common sense, just as one person may inherit the worldly wealth of his ancestry.

VII

FOR THE YEARS TO COME

LATE one summer afternoon Dr. Leslie was waked from an unusually long after-dinner nap by Marilla's footsteps along the hall. She remained standing in the doorway, looking at him for a provoking length of time, and finally sneezed in her most obtrusive and violent manner. At this he sat up quickly and demanded to be told what was the matter, adding that he had been out half the night before, which was no news to the faithful housekeeper.

"There, I'm sure I didn't mean to wake you up," she said, with an apparent lack of self-reproach. "I never can tell whether you are asleep or only kind of drowsin'. There was a boy here just now from old Mis' Cunningham's over on the b'ilin' spring road. They want you to come over quick as convenient. She don't know nothin', the boy said."

"Never did," grumbled the doctor. "I'll go, toward night, but I can't do her any good."

"An' Mis' Thacher is out here waitin' too, but she says if you're busy she'll go along to the stores and stop as she comes back. She looks to me as if she was breakin' up," confided Marilla in a lower tone.

"Tell her I'm ready now," answered the doctor in a more cordial tone, and though he said half to himself and half to Marilla that here was another person who expected him to cure old age, he spoke compassionately, and as if his heart were heavy with the thought of human sorrow and suffering. But he greeted Mrs. Thacher most cheerfully, and joked about Marilla's fear of a fly, as he threw open the blinds of the study window which was best shaded from the sun.

Mrs. Thacher did indeed look changed, and the physician's quick eyes took note of it, and, as he gathered up some letters and newspapers which had been strewn about just after dinner, he said kindly that he hoped she had no need of a doctor. It was plain that the occasion seemed an uncommon one to her. She wore her best clothes, which would not have been necessary for one of her usual business trips to the village, and it seemed to be difficult for her to begin her story. Dr. Leslie, taking a purely professional view of the case, began to consider what form of tonic would be most suitable, whether she had come to ask for one or not.

"I want to have a good talk with you about the little gell; Nanny, you know;" she said at last, and the doctor nodded, and, explaining that there seemed to be a good deal of draught through the room, crossed the floor and gently shut the door which opened into the hall. He smiled a little as he did it, having heard the long breath outside which was the not unfamiliar signal of Marilla's presence. If she were curious, she was a discreet keeper of secrets, and the doctor had more than once indulged her in her sinful listening by way of friendliness and reward. But this subject promised to concern his own affairs too closely, and he became wary of the presence of another pair of ears. He was naturally a man of uncommon reserve, and most loyal in keeping his patients' secrets. If clergymen knew their congregations as well as physicians do, the sermons would be often more closely related to the parish needs. It was difficult for the world to understand why, when Dr. Leslie was anything but prone to gossip, Marilla should have been possessed of such a wealth of knowledge of her neighbors' affairs. Strange to say this wealth was for her own miserly pleasure and not to be distributed, and while she often proclaimed with exasperating triumph that she had known for months some truth just discovered by others, she was regarded by her acquaintances as if she were a dictionary written in some foreign language; immensely valuable, but of no practical use to themselves. It was sometimes difficult not to make an attempt to borrow from her store of news, but nothing delighted her more than to be so approached, and to present impenetrable barriers of discretion to the enemy.

"How is Nanny getting on?" the doctor asked. "She looks stronger than she did a year ago."

"Dear me, she 's wild as ever," answered Mrs. Thacher, trying to smile; "but I 've been distressed about her lately, night and day. I thought perhaps I might see you going by. She 's gettin' to be a great girl, doctor, and I ain't fit to cope with her. I find my strength 's a-goin', and I 'm old before my time;

all my folks was rugged and sound long past my age, but I've had my troubles,—you don't need I should tell you that! Poor Ad'line always give me a feelin' as if I was a hen that has hatched ducks. I never knew exactly how to do for her, she seemed to see everything so different, and Lord only knows how I worry about her; and al'ays did, thinkin' if I'd seen clearer how to do my duty her life might have come out sort of better. And it's the same with little Anna; not that she's so prone to evil as some; she's a lovin'-hearted child if ever one was born, but she's a piece o' mischief; and it may come from her father's folks and their ways o' livin', but she's made o' different stuff, and I ain't fit to make answer for her, or for fetchin' of her up. I come to ask if you won't kindly advise what's best for her. I do' know's anything's got to be done for a good spell yet. I mind what you say about lettin' her run and git strong, and I don't check her. Only it seemed to me that you might want to speak about her sometimes and not do it for fear o' wronging my judgment. I declare I haven't no judgment about what's reasonable for her, and you're her guardeen, and there's the money her father's sister has sent her; 't would burn my fingers to touch a cent of it, but by and by if you think she ought to have schoolin' or anything else you must just say so."

"I think nothing better could have been done for the child than you have done," said Dr. Leslie warmly. "Don't worry yourself, my good friend. As for books, she will take to them of her own accord quite soon enough, and in such weather as this I think one day in the fields is worth five in the school-house. I'll do the best I can for her."

Mrs. Thacher's errand had not yet been told, though she fumbled in her pocket and walked to the open window to look for the neighbor's wagon by which she was to find conveyance home, before she ventured to say anything more. "I don't know's my time'll come for some years yet," she said at length, falteringly, "but I have had it borne in upon my mind a good many ways this summer that I ain't going to stay here a gre't while. I've been troubled considerable by the same complaints that carried my mother off, and I'm built just like her. I don't feel no concern for myself, but it's goin' to leave the child without anybody of her own to look to. There's plenty will befriend her just so long as she's got means, and the old farm will sell for something besides what she's got already, but that ain't everything, and I can't seem to make up my mind to havin' of her boarded about. If 't was so your wife had lived I should know what I'd go down on my knees to her to do, but I can't ask it of you to be burdened with a young child a-growin' up."

The doctor listened patiently, though just before this he had risen and begun to fill a small bottle at the closet shelves, which were stocked close to their perilous edges with various drugs. Without turning to look at his patient he said, "I wish you would take five or six drops of this three times a day, and let me see you again within a week or two." And while the troubled woman turned to look at him with half-surprise, he added, "Don't give yourself another thought about little Nan. If anything should happen to you, I shall be glad to bring her here, and to take care of her as if she were my own. I always have liked her, and it will be as good for me as for her. I would not promise it for any other child, but if you had not spoken to-day, I should have found a way to arrange with you the first chance that came. But I'm getting to be an old fellow myself," he laughed. "I suppose if I get through first you will be friendly to Marilla?" and Mrs. Thacher let a faint sunbeam of a smile shine out from the depths of the handkerchief with which she was trying to stop a great shower of tears. Marilla was not without her little vanities, and being thought youthful was one of the chief desires of her heart.

So Mrs. Thacher went away lighter hearted than she came. She asked the price of the vial of medicine, and was answered that they would talk about that another time; then there was a little sober joking about certain patients who never paid their doctor's bills at all because of a superstition that they would immediately require his aid again. Dr. Leslie stood in his study doorway and watched her drive down the street with Martin Dyer. It seemed to him only a year or two since both the man and woman had been strong and vigorous; now they both looked shrunken, and there was a wornness and feebleness about the bodies which had done such good service. "Come and go," said the doctor to himself, "one generation after another. Getting old! all the good old-fashioned people

on the farms: I never shall care so much to be at the beck and
call of their grandchildren, but I must mend up these old
folks and do the best I can for them as long as they stay;
they're good friends to me. Dear me, how it used to fret me
when I was younger to hear them always talking about old
Doctor Wayland and what he used to do; and here I am the
old doctor myself!" And then he went down the gravel walk
toward the stable with a quick, firm step, which many a
younger man might have envied, to ask for a horse. "You may
saddle him," he directed. "I am only going to old Mrs. Cunningham's, and it is a cool afternoon."

Dr. Leslie had ridden less and less every year of his practice;
but, for some reason best known to himself, he went down
the village street at a mad pace. Indeed, almost everybody
who saw him felt that it was important to go to the next
house to ask if it were known for what accident or desperate
emergency he had been called away.

VIII

A GREAT CHANGE

UNTIL the autumn of this year, life had seemed to flow in one steady, unchanging current. The thought had not entered little Nan Prince's head that changes might be in store for her, for, ever since she could remember, the events of life had followed each other quietly, and except for the differences in every-day work and play, caused by the succession of the seasons, she was not called upon to accommodate herself to new conditions. It was a gentle change at first: as the days grew shorter and the house and cellar were being made ready for winter, her grandmother seemed to have much more to do than usual, and Nan must stay at home to help. She was growing older at any rate; she knew how to help better than she used; she was anxious to show her grandmother how well she could work, and as the river side and the windy pastures grew less hospitable, she did not notice that she was no longer encouraged to go out to play for hours together to amuse herself as best she might, and at any rate keep out of the way. It seemed natural enough now that she should stay in the house, and be entrusted with some regular part of the business of keeping it. For some time Mrs. Thacher had kept but one cow, and early in November, after a good offer for old Brindle had been accepted, it was announced to Nan's surprise that the young cow which was to be Brindle's successor need not be bought until spring; she would be a great care in winter time, and Nan was to bring a quart of milk a day from Jake and Martin's. This did not seem an unpleasant duty while the mild weather lasted; if there came a rainy day, one of the kind neighbors would leave the little pail on his way to the village before the young messenger had started out.

Nan could not exactly understand at last why Mrs. Jake and Mrs. Martin always asked about her grandmother every morning with so much interest and curiosity, or why they came oftener and oftener to help with the heavy work. Mrs. Thacher had never before minded her occasional illnesses so much, and some time passed before Nan's inexperienced eyes and fearless young heart understood that the whole atmosphere which overhung the landscape of her life had somehow changed, that another winter approached full of mystery and strangeness and discomfort of mind, and at last a great storm was almost ready to break into the shelter and comfort of her simple life. Poor Nan! She could not think what it all meant. She was asked many a distressing question, and openly pitied, and heard her future discussed, as if her world might come to an end any day. The doctor had visited her grandmother from time to time, but always while she was at school, until vacation came, and poor Mrs. Thacher grew too feeble to enter into even a part of the usual business of the farmhouse.

One morning, as Nan was coming back from the Dyer farm with the milk, she met Mrs. Meeker in the highway. This neighbor and our heroine were rarely on good terms with each other, since Nan had usually laid herself under some serious charge of wrong-doing, and had come to believe that she would be disapproved in any event, and so might enjoy life as she chose, and revel in harmless malice.

The child could not have told why she shrank from meeting her enemy so much more than usual, and tried to discover some refuge or chance for escape; but, as it was an open bit of the road, and a straight way to the lane, she could have no excuse for scrambling over the stone wall and cutting short the distance. However, her second thought scorned the idea of running away in such cowardly fashion, and not having any recent misdemeanor on her conscience, she went forward unflinchingly.

Mrs. Meeker's tone was not one of complaint, but of pity, and insinuating friendliness. "How's your grandma to-day?" she asked, and Nan, with an unsympathetic answer of "About the same," stepped bravely forward, resenting with all her young soul the discovery that Mrs. Meeker had turned and was walking alongside.

"She's been a good, kind grandma to you, hain't she?" said this unwelcome companion, and when Nan had returned a wondering but almost inaudible assent, she continued, "She'll be a great loss to you, I can tell you. You'll never find nobody to do for you like her. There, you won't realize nothing about it till you've got older'n you be now; but the time'll come when"—and her sharp voice faltered; for Nan had turned to look full in her face, had stopped still in the frozen road, dropped the pail unconsciously and given a little cry, and in another moment was running as a chased wild creature does toward the refuge of its nest. The doctor's horse was fastened at the head of the lane, and Nan knew at last, what any one in the neighborhood could have told her many days before, that her grandmother was going to die. Mrs. Meeker stared after her with a grieved sense of the abrupt ending of the coveted interview, then she recovered her self-possession, and, picking up the forsaken pail, stepped lightly over the ruts and frozen puddles, following Nan eagerly in the hope of witnessing more of such extraordinary behavior, and with the design of offering her services as watcher or nurse in these last hours. At any rate the pail and the milk, which had not been spilt, could not be left in the road.

So the first chapter of the child's life was ended in the early winter weather. There was a new unsheltered grave on the slope above the river, the farm-house door was shut and locked, and the light was out in the kitchen window. It had been a landmark to those who were used to driving along the road by night, and there were sincere mourners for the kindly woman who had kept a simple faith and uprightness all through her long life of trouble and disappointment. Nan and the cat had gone to live in the village, and both, being young, had taken the change with serenity; though at first a piteous sorrow had been waked in the child's heart, a keen and dreadful fear of the future. The past seemed so secure and pleasant, as she looked back, and now she was in the power of a fateful future which had begun with something like a whirlwind that had swept over her, leaving nothing unchanged. It seemed to her that this was to be incessant, and that being grown up was to be at the mercy of sorrow and uncertainty. She was pale and quiet during her last days in the old home, answering questions and obeying directions mechanically; but usually sitting in the least visited part of the kitchen, watching the neighbors as they examined her grandmother's possessions, and properly disposed of the contents of the house. Sometimes a spark flew from her sad and angry eyes, but she made no trouble, and seemed dull and indifferent. Late in the evening Dr. Leslie carried her home with him through the first heavy snow-storm of the year, and between the excitement of being covered from the fast-falling flakes, and so making a journey in the dark, and of keeping hold of the basket which contained the enraged kitten, the grief at leaving home was not dwelt upon.

When she had been unwound from one of the doctor's great cloaks, and her eyes had grown used to the bright light in the dining-room, and Marilla had said that supper had been waiting half an hour, and she did not know how she should get along with a black cat, and then bustled about talking much faster than usual, because the sight of the lonely child had made her ready to cry, Nan began to feel comforted. It seemed a great while ago that she had cried at her grandmother's funeral. If this were the future it was certainly very welcome and already very dear, and the time of distress was like a night of bad dreams between two pleasant days.

It will easily be understood that no great change was made in Dr. Leslie's house. The doctor himself and Marilla were both well settled in their habits, and while they cordially made room for the little girl who was to be the third member of the household, her coming made little difference to either of her elders. There was a great deal of illness that winter, and the doctor was more than commonly busy; Nan was sent to school, and discovered the delight of reading one stormy day when her guardian had given her leave to stay at home, and she had found his own old copy of Robinson Crusoe looking most friendly and inviting in a corner of one of the study shelves. As for school, she had never liked it, and the village school gave her far greater misery than the weather-beaten building at the cross-roads ever had done. She had known many of the village children by sight, from seeing them in church, but she did not number many friends among them, even after the winter was nearly gone and the days began to grow brighter and less cold, and the out-of-door games were a source of great merriment in the playground. Nan's ideas of life were quite unlike those held by these new acquaintances, and she could not gain the least interest in most of the other children, though she grew fond of one boy who was a famous rover and fisherman, and after one of the elder girls had read a composition which fired our heroine's imagination, she worshiped this superior being from a suitable distance, and was her willing adorer and slave. The composition was upon The Moon, and when the author proclaimed the fact that this was the same moon which had looked down upon Abraham, Isaac, and Jacob, little Nan's eyes had opened wide with reverence and awe, and she opened the doors of her heart and soul to lofty thought and high imagination. The big girl, who sat in the back seat and glibly recited amazing lessons in history, and did sums which entirely covered the one small blackboard, was not unmindful of Nan's admiration, and stolidly accepted and munched the offerings of cracked nuts, or of the treasured English apples which had been brought from the farm and kept like a squirrel's hoard in an archway of the cellar by themselves. Nan cherished an idea of going back to the farm to live by herself as soon as she grew a little older, and she indulged in pleasing day-dreams of a most charming life there, with frequent entertainments for her friends, at which the author of the information about the moon would be the favored guest, and Nan herself, in a most childish and provincial fashion, the reigning queen. What did these new town-acquaintances know of the strawberries which grew in the bit of meadow, or the great high-bush blackberries by one of the pasture walls, and what would their pleasure be when they were taken down the river some moonlight night and caught sight of a fire blazing on a distant bank, and went nearer to find a sumptuous feast which Nan herself had arranged? She had been told that her aunt—that mysterious and beneficent aunt—had already sent her money which was lying idle in the bank until she should need to spend it, and her imaginary riches increased week by week, while her horizon of future happiness constantly grew wider.

The other children were not unwilling at first to enter upon an inquisitive friendship with the new-comer; but Marilla was so uncongenial to the noisy visitors, and so fastidious in the matter of snowy and muddy shoes, that she was soon avoided. Nan herself was a teachable child and gave little trouble, and Marilla sometimes congratulated herself because she had reserved the violent objections which had occurred to her mind when the doctor had announced, just before Mrs. Thacher's death, that his ward would henceforth find a home in his house.

Marilla usually sat in the dining-room in the evening, though she was apt to visit the study occasionally, knitting in hand, to give her opinions, or to acquaint herself with various events of which she thought the doctor would be likely to have knowledge. Sometimes in the colder winter nights, she drew a convenient light-stand close beside the kitchen stove and refused to wander far from such comfortable warmth. Now that she had Nan's busy feet to cover, there was less danger than ever that she should be left without knitting-work, and she deeply enjoyed the child's company, since Nan could give innocent answers to many questions which could never be put to elder members of the Dyer and Thacher neighborhood. Mrs. Meeker was apt to be discussed with great freedom, and Nan told long stories about her own childish experiences, which were listened to and encouraged, and matched with others even longer and more circumstantial by Marilla. The doctor, who was always reading when he could find a quiet hour for himself, often smiled as he heard the steady sound of voices from the wide kitchen, and he more than once took a few careful steps into the dining-room, and stood there shaking with laughter at the character of the conversation. Nan, though eager to learn, and curious about many things in life and nature, at first found her school lessons difficult, and sometimes came appealingly to him for assistance, when circumstances had made a temporary ending of her total indifference to getting the lessons at all. For this and other reasons she sometimes sought the study, and drew a small chair beside the doctor's large one before the blazing fire of the black birch logs; and then Marilla in her turn would venture upon the neutral ground between study and kitchen, and smile with satisfaction at the cheerful companionship of the tired man and the idle little girl who had already found her way to his lonely heart. Nan had come to another home; there was no question about what should be done with her and for her, but she was made free of the silent old house, and went on growing taller, and growing dearer, and growing happier day by day. Whatever the future might bring, she would be sure to look back with love and longing to the first summer of her village life, when, seeing that she looked pale and drooping, the doctor, to her intense gratification, took her away from school. Presently, instead of having a ride out into the country as an occasional favor, she might be seen every day by the doctor's side, as if he could not make his morning rounds without her; and in and out of the farm-houses she went, following him like a little dog, or, as Marilla scornfully expressed it, a briar at his heels; sitting soberly by when he dealt his medicines and gave advice, listening to his wise and merry talk with some, and his helpful advice and consolation to others of the country people. Many of these acquaintances treated Nan with great kindness; she half belonged to them, and was deeply interesting for the sake of her other ties of blood and bonds of fortune, while she took their courtesy with thankfulness, and their lack of notice with composure. If there were a shiny apple offered she was glad, but if not, she did not miss it, since her chief delight was in being the doctor's assistant and attendant, and her eyes were always watching for chances when she might be of use. And one day, coming out from a bedroom, the doctor discovered, to his amusement, that her quick and careful fingers had folded the papers of some powders which he had left unfolded on the table. As they drove home together in the bright noon sunshine, he said, as if the question were asked for the sake of joking a little, "What are you going to do when you grow up, Nan?" to which she answered gravely, as if it were the one great question of her life, "I should like best to be a doctor." Strangely enough there flitted through the doctor's mind a remembrance of the day when he had talked with Mrs. Meeker, and had looked up the lane to see the unlucky turkey whose leg had been put into splints. He had wished more than once that he had taken pains to see how the child had managed it; but old Mrs. Thacher had reported the case to have been at lest partially successful.

Nan had stolen a look at her companion after the answer had been given, but had been pleased and comforted to find that he was not laughing at her, and at once began a lively picture of becoming famous in her chosen profession, and the valued partner of Dr. Leslie, whose skill everybody praised so heartily. He should not go out at night, and she would help him so much that he would wonder how he ever had been able to manage his wide-spread practice alone. It was a matter of no concern to her that Marilla had laughed when she had been told of Nan's intentions, and had spoken disrespectfully of women doctors; and the child's heart was full of pride and hope. The doctor stopped his horse suddenly to show Nan some flowers which grew at the roadside, some brilliant cardinals, and she climbed quickly down to gather them. There was an unwritten law that they should keep watch, one to the right hand, and the other to the left, and such treasures of blossoms or wild fruit seldom escaped Nan's vision. Now she felt as if she had been wrong to let her thoughts go wandering, and her cheeks were almost as bright as the scarlet flowers themselves, as she clambered back to the wagon seat. But the doctor was in deep thought, and had nothing more to say for the next mile or two. It had become like a bad-case day suddenly and without apparent reason; but Nan had no suspicion that she was the patient in charge whose welfare seemed to the doctor to be dependent upon his own decisions.

IX

AT DR. LESLIE'S

THAT evening Dr. Leslie made signs that he was not to be interrupted, and even shut the study doors, to which precaution he seldom resorted. He was evidently disturbed when an hour later a vigorous knocking was heard at the seldom-used front entrance, and Marilla ushered in with anything but triumph an elderly gentleman who had been his college classmate. Marilla's countenance wore a forbidding expression, and as she withdrew she took pains to shut the door between the hall and dining-room with considerable violence. It was almost never closed under ordinary circumstances, but the faithful housekeeper was impelled to express her wrath in some way, and this was the first that offered itself. Nan was sitting peacefully in the kitchen playing with her black cat and telling herself stories no doubt, and was quite unprepared for Marilla's change of temper. The bell for the Friday evening prayer-meeting was tolling its last strokes and it was Marilla's habit to attend that service. She was apt to be kept closely at home, it must be acknowledged, and this was one of her few social indulgences. Since Nan had joined the family and proved that she could be trusted with a message, she had been left in charge of the house during this coveted hour on Friday evenings.

Marilla had descended from her room arrayed for church going, but now her bonnet was pulled off as if that were the prime offender, and when the child looked wonderingly around the kitchen, she saw the bread-box brought out from the closet and put down very hard on a table, while Marilla began directly afterward to rattle at the stove.

"I'd like to say to some folks that we don't keep hotel," grumbled the good woman, "I wish to my heart I'd stepped right out o' the front door and gone straight to meetin' and left them there beholdin' of me. Course he hasn't had no supper, nor dinner neither like's not, and if men are ever going to drop down on a family unexpected it's always Friday night when everything's eat up that ever was in the house. I s'pose, after I bake double quantities to-morrow mornin', he'll be drivin' off before noon-time, and treasure it up that we never have nothin' decent to set before folks. Anna, you've got to stir yourself and help, while I get the fire started up; lay one o' them big dinner napkins over the red cloth, and set a plate an' a tea-cup, for as for laying the whole table over again, I won't and I shan't. There's water to cart upstairs and the bed-room to open, but Heaven be thanked I was up there dustin' to-day, and if ever you set a mug of flowers into one o' the spare-rooms again and leave it there a week or ten days to spile, I'll speak about it to the doctor. Now you step out o' my way like a good girl. I don't know whether you or the cat's the worst for gettin' before me when I'm in a drive. I'll set him out somethin' to eat, and then I'm goin' to meetin' if the skies fall."

Nan meekly obeyed directions, and with a sense of guilt concerning the deserted posies went to hover about the study door after the plates were arranged, instead of braving further the stormy atmosphere of the kitchen. Marilla's lamp had shone in so that there had been light enough in the dining-room, but the study was quite dark except where there was one spark at the end of the doctor's half-finished cigar, which was alternately dim and bright like the revolving lantern of a lighthouse.

At that moment the smoker rose, and with his most consid-erate and conciliatory tone asked Marilla for the study lamp, but Nan heard, and ran on tiptoe and presently brought it in from the kitchen, holding it carefully with both hands and walking slowly. She apparently had no thought beyond her errand, but she was brimful of eagerness to see the unex-pected guest; for guests were by no means frequent, and since she had really become aware of a great outside world beyond the boundaries of Oldfields she welcomed the sight of any messengers.

Dr. Leslie hastily pushed away some books from the lamp's place; and noticing that his visitor looked at Nan with sur-prise, quickly explained that this little girl had come to take care of him, and bade Nan speak to Dr. Ferris. Whereupon her bravery was sorely tried, but not overcome, and afterward she sat down in her own little chair, quite prepared to be hospitable. As she heard a sound of water being poured into a pitcher in the best room upstairs, she was ready to laugh if there had been anybody to laugh with, and presently Marilla appeared at the door with the announcement that there was some tea waiting in the dining-room, after which and before anybody had thought of moving, the side gate clacked resolutely, and Marilla, looking more prim and unruffled than usual, sped forth to the enjoyment of her Friday evening privileges.

Nan followed the gentlemen to the dining-room not knowing whether she were wanted or not, but feeling quite assured when it was ascertained that neither sugar nor teaspoons had been provided. The little feast looked somewhat meagre, and the doctor spoke irreverently of his housekeeper and proceeded to abstract a jar of her best strawberry jam from the convenient store-closet, and to collect other articles of food which seemed to him to be inviting, however inappropriate to the occasion. The guest would have none of the jam, but Dr. Leslie cut a slice of the loaf of bread for himself and one for Nan, though it had already waned beyond its last quarter, and nobody knew what would happen if there were no toast at breakfast time. Marilla would never know what a waste of jam was spread upon these slices either, but she was a miser only with the best preserves, and so our friends reveled in their stolen pleasure, and were as merry together as heart could wish.

Nan thought it very strange when she found that the doctor and his guest had been at school together, for the stranger seemed so old and worn. They were talking about other classmates at first, and she sat still to listen, until the hour of Marilla's return drew near and Dr. Leslie prudently returned to his own uninvaded apartment. Nan was told, to her sorrow, that it was past her bed-time and as she stopped to say goodnight, candle in hand, a few moments afterward, the doctor stooped to kiss her with unusual tenderness, and a little later, when she was safe in her small bedroom and under the coverlet which was Marilla's glory, having been knit the winter before in an intricate pattern, she almost shook with fear at the sound of its maker's vengeful footsteps in the lower room. It is to be hoped that the influence of the meeting had been very good, and that one of its attendants had come home equal to great demands upon her fortitude and patience. Nan could not help wishing she had thought to put away the jam, and she wondered how Marilla would treat them all in the morning. But, to do that worthy woman justice, she was mild and considerate, and outdid herself in the breakfast that was set forth in the guest's honor, and Dr. Ferris thought he could do no less than to add to his morning greeting the question why she was not growing old like the rest of them, which, though not answered, was pleasantly received.

The host and guest talked very late the night before, and told each other many things. Dr. Leslie had somewhat unwillingly undertaken the country practice which had grown dearer to him with every year, but there were family reasons why he had decided to stay in Oldfields for a few months at least, and though it was not long before he was left alone, not only by the father and mother whose only child he was, but by his wife and child, he felt less and less inclination to break the old ties and transplant himself to some more prominent position of the medical world. The leisure he often had at certain seasons of the year was spent in the studies which always delighted him, and little by little he gained great repute among his professional brethren. He was a scholar and a thinker in other than medical philosophies, and most persons who knew anything of him thought it a pity that he should be burying himself alive, as they were pleased to term his devotion to his provincial life. His rare excursions to the cities gave more pleasure to other men than to himself, however, in these later years, and he laughingly proclaimed himself to be growing rusty and behind the times to Dr. Ferris, who smiled indulgently, and did not take the trouble to contradict so untrue and preposterous an assertion.

If one man had been a stayer at home; a vegetable nature, as Dr. Leslie had gone on to say, which has no power to change its locality or to better itself by choosing another and more adequate or stimulating soil; the other had developed the opposite extreme of character, being by nature a rover. From the medical school he had entered at once upon the duties of a naval appointment, and after he had become impatient of its routine of practice and its check upon his freedom, he had gone, always with some sufficient and useful object, to one far country after another. Lately he had spent an unusual number of consecutive months in Japan, which was still unfamiliar even to most professional travelers, and he had come back to America enthusiastic and full of plans for many enterprises which his shrewd, but not very persistent brain had conceived. The two old friends were delighted to see each other, but they took this long-deferred meeting as calmly as if they were always next-door neighbors. It was a most interesting thing that while they led such different lives and took such apparently antagonistic routes of progression, they were pretty sure to arrive at the same conclusion, though it might appear otherwise to a listener who knew them both slightly.

"And who is the little girl?" asked Dr. Ferris, who had refused his entertainer's cigars and produced a pipe from one pocket, after having drawn a handful of curious small jade figures from another and pushed them along the edge of the study table, without comment, for his friend to look at. Some of them were so finely carved that they looked like a heap of grotesque insects struggling together as they lay there, but though Dr. Leslie's eyes brightened as he glanced at them, he gave no other sign of interest at that time, and answered his guest's question instead.

"She is a ward of mine," he said; "she was left quite alone by the death of her grandmother some months ago, and so I brought her here."

"It is n't often that I forget a face," said Dr. Ferris, "but I have been trying to think what association I can possibly have with that child. I remember at last; she looks like a young assistant surgeon who was on the old frigate Fortune with me just before I left the service. I don't think he was from this part of the country though; I never heard what became of him."

"I dare say it was her father; I believe he made a voyage or two," said Dr. Leslie, much interested. "Do you know anything more about him? you always remember everything, Ferris."

"Yes," answered the guest, slowly puffing away at his pipe. "Yes, he was a very bright fellow, with a great gift at doctoring, but he was wilful, full of queer twists and fancies, the marry in haste and repent at his leisure sort of young man."

"Exactly what he did, I suppose," interrupted the host. "Only his leisure was fortunately postponed to the next world, for the most part; he died very young."

"I used to think it a great pity that he had not settled himself ashore in a good city practice," continued Dr. Ferris. "He had a great knack at pleasing people and making friends, and he was always spoiling for want of work. I was ready enough to shirk my part of that, you may be sure, but if you start with a reasonably healthy set of men, crew and officers, and keep good discipline, and have no accidents on the voyage, an old-fashioned ship-master's kit of numbered doses is as good as anything on board a man-of-war in time of peace. You have mild cases that result from over-heating or over-eating, and sometimes a damaged finger to dress, or a tooth to pull. I used to tell young Prince that it was a pity one of the men would n't let himself be chopped to pieces and fitted together again to give us a little amusement."

"That's the name," announced Nan's guardian with great satisfaction. "This is a very small world; we are all within hail of each other. I dare say when we get to Heaven there will not be a stranger to make friends with."

"I could give you more wonderful proofs of that than you would be likely to believe," responded the surgeon. "But tell me how you happened to have anything to do with the child; did Prince wander into this neighborhood?"

"Not exactly, but he fell in love with a young girl who was brought up on one of the farms just out of the village. She was a strange character, a handsome creature, with a touch of foolish ambition, and soon grew impatient of the routine of home life. I believe that she went away at first to work in one of the factories in Lowell, and afterward she drifted to Dunport, where young Prince's people lived, and I dare say it was when he came home from that very voyage you knew of that he saw her and married her. She worked in a dressmaker's shop, and worked very well too, but she had offended his sister to begin with, one day when she was finding fault with some work that had been done for her, and so there was no end of trouble, and the young man had a great battle at home, and the more he was fought the less inclined he was to yield, and at last off he went to be married, and never came home again until he died. It was a wretched story; he only lived two years, and they went from one place to another, and finally the end came in some Western town. He had not been happy with his wife, and they quarreled from time to time, and he asked to be brought back to Dunport and buried. This child was only a baby, and the Princes begged her mother to give her up, and used every means to try to make friends, and to do what was right. But I have always thought there was blame on both sides. At any rate the wife was insolent and unruly, and went flinging out of the house as soon as the funeral was over. I don't know what became of them for a while, but it always seemed to me as if poor Adeline must have had a touch of insanity, which faded away as consumption developed itself. Her mother's people were a fine, honest race, self-reliant and energetic, but there is a very bad streak on the other side. I have heard that she was seen begging somewhere, but I am not sure that it is true; at any rate she would neither come here to her own home nor listen to any plea from her husband's family, and at last came back to the farm one night like a ghost, carrying the child in her arms across the fields; all in rags and tatters, both of them. She confessed to me that she had meant to drown herself and little Nan together. I could never understand why she went down so fast. I know that she had been drinking. Some people might say that it was the scorn of her husband's relatives, but that is all nonsense, and I have no doubt she and the young man might have done very well if this hadn't spoiled all their chances at the outset. She was quite unbalanced and a strange, wild creature, very handsome in her girlhood, but morally undeveloped. It was impossible not to have a liking for her. I remember her when she was a baby."

"And yet people talk about the prosaic New England life!" exclaimed Dr. Ferris. "I wonder where I could match such a story as that, though I dare say that you know a dozen others. I tell you, Leslie, that for intense, self-centred, smouldering volcanoes of humanity, New England cannot be matched the world over. It's like the regions in Iceland that are full of geysers. I don't know whether it is the inheritance from those people who broke away from the old countries, and who ought to be matched to tremendous circumstances of life, but now and then there comes an amazingly explosive and uncontrollable temperament that goes all to pieces from its own conservation and accumulation of force. By and by you will have all blown up,—you quiet descendants of the Pilgrims and Puritans, and have let off your superfluous wickedness like blizzards; and when the blizzards of each family have spent themselves you will grow dull and sober, and all on a level, and be free from the troubles of a transition state. Now, you're neither a new country nor an old one. You ought to see something of the older civilizations to understand what peace of mind is. Unless some importation of explosive material from the westward stirs them up, one century is made the pattern for the next. But it is perfectly wonderful what this climate does for people who come to it,—a south of Ireland fellow, for instance, who has let himself be rained on and then waited for the sun to dry him again, and has grubbed a little in a bit of ground, just enough to hint to it that it had better be making a crop of potatoes for him. I always expect to see the gorse and daisies growing on the old people's heads to match the cabins. But they come over here and forget their idleness, and in a week or two the east winds are making them work, and thrashing them if they are slow, worse than any slave-driver who ever cracked his whip-lash. I wonder how you stand it; I do, indeed! I can't take an afternoon nap or have my coffee in bed of a morning without thinking I must put into port at the next church to be preached at."

Dr. Leslie laughed a little and shook his head gently. "It's very well for you to talk, Ferris," he said, "since you have done more work than any man I know. And I find this neighborhood entirely placid; one bit of news will last us a fortnight. I dare say Marilla will let everybody know that you have come to town, and have explained why she was ten minutes late, even to the minister."

"How about the little girl herself?" asked the guest presently; "she seems well combined, and likely, as they used to say when I was a boy."

Dr. Leslie resumed the subject willingly: "So far as I can see, she has the good qualities of all her ancestors without the bad ones. Her mother's mother was an old fashioned country woman of the best stock. Of course she resented what she believed to be her daughter's wrongs, and refused to have anything to do with her son-in-law's family, and kept the child as carefully as possible from any knowledge of them. Little Nan was not strong at first, but I insisted that she should be allowed to run free out of doors. It seems to me that up to seven or eight years of age children are simply bundles of inheritances, and I can see the traits of one ancestor after another; but a little later than the usual time she began to assert her own individuality, and has grown capitally well in mind and body ever since. There is an amusing trace of the provincial self-reliance and self-respect and farmer-like dignity, added to a quick instinct, and tact and ready courtesy, which must have come from the other side of her ancestry. She is more a child of the soil than any country child I know, and yet she would not put a city household to shame. She has seen nothing of the world of course, but you can see she isn't like the usual village school-girl. There is one thing quite remarkable. I believe she has grown up as naturally as a plant grows, not having been clipped back or forced in any unnatural direction. If ever a human being were untrammeled and left alone to see what will come of it, it is this child. And I will own I am very much interested to see what will appear later."

The navy surgeon's eyes twinkled at this enthusiasm, but he asked soberly what seemed to be our heroine's bent, so far as could be discovered, and laughed outright when he was gravely told that it was a medical bent; a surprising understanding of things pertaining to that most delightful profession.

"But you surely don't mean to let her risk her happiness in following that career?" Dr. Ferris inquired with feigned anxiety for his answer. "You surely aren't going to sacrifice that innocent creature to a theory! I know it's a theory; last time I was here, you could think of nothing but hypnotism or else the action of belladonna in congestion and inflammation of the brain;" and he left his very comfortable chair suddenly, with a burst of laughter, and began to walk up and down the room. "She has no relatives to protect her, and I consider it a shocking case of a guardian's inhumanity. Grown up naturally indeed! I don't doubt that you supplied her with Bell's 'Anatomy' for a picture-book and made her say over the names of the eight little bones of her wrist, instead of 'This little pig went to market.'"

"I only hope that you'll live to grow up yourself, Ferris," said his entertainer, "you'll certainly be an ornament to your generation. What a boy you are! I should think you would feel as old as Methuselah by this time, after having rattled from one place to the next all these years. Don't you begin to get tired?"

"No, I don't believe I do," replied Dr. Ferris, lending himself to this new turn of the conversation, but not half satisfied with the number of his jokes. "I used to be afraid I should, and so I tried to see everything I could of the world before my enthusiasm began to cool. And as for rattling to the next place, as you say, you show yourself to be no traveler by nature, or you wouldn't speak so slightingly. It is extremely dangerous to make long halts. I could cry with homesickness at the thought of the towns I have spent more than a month in; they are like the people one knows; if you see them once, you go away satisfied, and you can bring them to mind afterward, and think how they looked or just where it was you met them,—out of doors or at the club. But if you live with those people, and get fond of them, and have a thousand things to remember, you get more pain than pleasure out of it when you go away. And one can't be everywhere at once, so if you're going to care for things tremendously, you had better stay in one town altogether. No, give me a week or two, and then I've something calling me to the next place; somebody to talk with or a book to see, and off I go. Yet, I've done a good bit of work in my day after all. Did you see that paper of mine in the 'Lancet' about some experiments I made when I was last in India with those tree-growing jugglers? and I worked out some curious things about the mathematics of music on this last voyage home! Why, I thought it would tear my heart in two when I came away. I should have grown to look like the people, and you might have happened to find a likeness of me on a tea plate after another year or two. I made all my plans one day to stay another winter, and next day at eleven o'clock I was steaming down the harbor. But there was a poor young lad I had taken a liking for, an English boy, who was badly off after an accident and needed somebody to look after him. I thought the best thing I could do was to bring him home. Are you going to fit your ward for general practice or for a specialty?"

"I don't know; that'll be for the young person herself to decide," said Dr. Leslie good-humoredly. "But she's showing a real talent for medical matters. It is quite unconscious for the most part, but I find that she understands a good deal already, and she sat here all the afternoon last week with one of my old medical dictionaries. I couldn't help looking over her shoulder as I went by, and she was reading about fevers, if you please, as if it were a story-book. I didn't think it was worth while to tell her we understood things better nowadays, and didn't think it best to bleed as much as old Dr. Rush recommended."

"You're like a hen with one chicken, Leslie," said the friend, still pacing to and fro. "But seriously, I like your notion of her having come to this of her own accord. Most of us are grown in the shapes that society and family preference and prejudice fasten us into, and don't find out until we are well toward middle life that we should have done a great deal better at something else. Our vocations are likely enough to be illy chosen, since few persons are fit to choose them for us, and we are at the most unreasonable stage of life when we choose them for ourselves. And what the Lord made some people for, nobody ever can understand; some of us are for use and more are for waste, like the flowers. I am in such a hurry to know what the next world is like that I can hardly wait to get to it. Good heavens! we live here in our familiar fashion, going at a jog-trot pace round our little circles, with only a friend or two to speak with who understand us, and a pipe and a jack-knife and a few books and some old clothes, and please ourselves by thinking we know the universe! Not a soul of us can tell what it is that sends word to our little fingers to move themselves back and forward."

"We're sure of two things at any rate," said Dr. Leslie, "love to God and love to man. And though I have lived here all my days, I have learned some truths just as well as if I had gone about with you, or even been to the next world and come back. I have seen too many lives go to pieces, and too many dissatisfied faces, and I have heard too many sorrowful confessions from these country death-beds I have watched beside, one after another, for twenty or thirty years. And if I can help one good child to work with nature and not against it, and to follow the lines marked out for her, and she turns out useful and intelligent, and keeps off the rocks of mistaking her duty, I shall be more than glad. I don't care whether it's a man's work or a woman's work; if it is hers I'm going to help her the very best way I can. I don't talk to her of course; she's much too young; but I watch her and mean to put the things in her way that she seems to reach out for and try to find. She is going to be very practical, for her hands can almost always work out her ideas already. I like to see her take hold of things, and I like to see her walk and the way she lifts her feet and puts them down again. I must say, Ferris, there is a great satisfaction in finding a human being once in a while that has some use of itself."

"You're right!" said Dr. Ferris; "but don't be disappointed when she's ten years older if she picks out a handsome young man and thinks there is nothing like housekeeping. Have you taken a look at my pocketful of heathen idols there yet? I don't think you've ever seen their mates."

The stayer at home smiled as if he understood his friend's quiet bit of pleasantry, and reached for one of the treasures, but folded it in his hand without looking at it and seemed to be lost in meditation. The surgeon concluded that he had had enough exercise and laid himself down on the wide sofa at the end of the room, from whence he could watch his companion's face. He clasped his hands under his head and looked eager and interested. He had grown to have something of the appearance of a foreigner, as people often do who have spent much time in eastern countries. The two friends were silent for some minutes, until an impatient voice roused Dr. Leslie from his reflections.

"It always makes me covet my neighbor's wits when I see you!" announced the wanderer. "If I settled myself into a respectable practice I should be obliged to march with the army of doctors who carry a great array of small weapons, and who find out what is the matter with their patients after all sorts of experiment and painstaking analysis, and comparing the results of their thermometers and microscopes with scientific books of reference. After I have done all that, you know, if I have had good luck I shall come to exactly what you can say before you have been with a sick man five minutes. You have the true gift for doctoring, you need no medical dictator, and whatever you study and whatever comes to you in the way of instruction simply ministers to your intuition. It grows to be a wonderful second-sight in such a man as you. I don't believe you investigate a case and treat it as a botanist does a strange flower, once a month. You know without telling yourself what the matter is, and what the special difference is, and the relative dangers of this case and one apparently just like it across the street, and you could do this before you were out of the hospitals. I remember you!" and after a few vigorous puffs of smoke he went on; "It is all very well for the rest of the men to be proud of their book learning, but they don't even try to follow nature, as Sydenham did, who followed no man. I believe such study takes one to more theory and scientific digest rather than to more skill. It is all very well to know how to draw maps when one gets lost on a dark night, or even to begin with astronomical calculations and come down to a chemical analysis of the mud you stand in, but hang me if I would n't rather have the instinct of a dog who can go straight home across a bit of strange country. A man has no right to be a doctor if he does n't simply make everything bend to his work of getting sick people well, and of trying to remedy the failures of strength that come from misuse or inheritance or ignorance. The anatomists and the pathologists have their place, but we must look to the living to learn the laws of life, not to the dead. A wreck shows you where the reef is, perhaps, but not how to manage a ship in the offing. The men who make it their business to write the books and the men who make it their business to follow them are n't the ones for successful practice."

Dr. Leslie smiled, and looked over his shoulder at his beloved library shelves, as if he wished to assure the useful volumes of his continued affection and respect, and said quietly, as if to beg the displeased surgeon's patience with his brethren:

"They go on, poor fellows, studying the symptoms and never taking it in that the life power is at fault. I see more and more plainly that we ought to strengthen and balance the whole system, and aid nature to make the sick man well again. It is nature that does it after all, and diseases are oftener effects of illness than causes. But the young practitioners must follow the text-books a while until they have had enough experience to open their eyes to observe and have learned to think for themselves. I don't know which is worse; too much routine or no study at all. I was trying the other day to count up the different treatments of pneumonia that have been in fashion in our day; there must be seven or eight, and I am only afraid the next thing will be a sort of skepticism and contempt of remedies. Dr. Johnson said long ago that physicians were a class of men who put bodies of which they knew little into bodies of which they knew less, but certainly this isn't the fault of the medicines altogether; you and I know well enough they are often most stupidly used. If we blindly follow the medical dictators, as you call them, and spend our treatment on the effects instead of the causes, what success can we expect? We do want more suggestions from the men at work, but I suppose this is the same with every business. The practical medical men are the juries who settle all the theories of the hour, as they meet emergencies day after day."

"The men who have the true gift for their work," said Dr. Ferris impatiently. "I hadn't the conscience to go on myself, that's why I resigned, you know. I can talk about it, but I am not a good workman. But if there are going to be doctors in the next world, I wish I might be lucky enough to be equal to such a heavenly business. You thought I didn't care enough about the profession to go on, but it wasn't so. Do push your little girl ahead if she has the real fitness. I suppose it is a part of your endowment that you can distinguish the capacities and tendencies of health as well as illness; and there's one thing certain, the world cannot afford to do without the workmen who are masters of their business by divine right."

Dr. Leslie was looking at the jade-stone gods. "I suppose the poor fellows who chipped out these treasures of yours may have thought they were really putting a visible piece of Heaven within their neighbors' reach," he said. "We can't get used to the fact that whatever truly belongs to the next world is not visible in this, and that there is idol-making and worshiping forever going on. When we let ourselves forget to educate our faith and our spiritual intellects, and lose sight of our relation and dependence upon the highest informing strength, we are trying to move our machinery by some inferior motive power. We worship our tools and beg success of them instead of remembering that we are all apprentices to the great Master of our own and every man's craft. It is the great ideas of our work that we need, and the laws of its truths. We shall be more intelligent by and by about making the best of ourselves; our possibilities are infinitely beyond what most people even dream. Spiritual laziness and physical laziness together keep us just this side of sound sleep most of the time. Perhaps you think it is a proper season for one at least?"

"Dear me, no!" said Dr. Ferris, who was evidently quite wide awake. "Do you remember how well Buckle says that the feminine intellect is the higher, and that the great geniuses of the world have possessed it? The gift of intuition reaches directly towards the truth, and it is only reasoning by deduction that can take flight into the upper air of life and certainty. You remember what he says about that?"

"Yes," said Dr. Leslie. "Yes, it isn't a thing one easily forgets. But I have long believed that the powers of Christ were but the higher powers of our common humanity. We recognize them dimly now and then, but few of us dare to say so yet. The world moves very slowly, doesn't it? If Christ were perfect man, He could hardly tell us to follow Him and be like Him, and yet know all the while that it was quite impossible, because a difference in his gifts made his character an unapproachable one to ours. We don't amount to anything, simply because we won't understand that we must receive the strength of Heaven into our souls; that it depends upon our degree of receptivity, and our using the added power that comes in that way; not in our taking our few tools, and our self-esteem and satisfaction with ourselves, and doing our little tricks like dancing dogs; proud because the other dogs can do one less than we, or only bark and walk about on their four legs. It is our souls that make our bodies worth anything, and the life of the soul does n't come from its activity, or any performance of its own. Those things are only the results and the signs of life, not the causes of it."

"Christ in us, the hope of glory," said the other doctor gravely, "and Christ's glory was his usefulness and gift for helping others; I believe there's less quackery in our profession than any other, but it is amazing how we bungle at it. I wonder how you will get on with your little girl? If people did n't have theories of life of their own, or would n't go exactly the wrong way, it would be easier to offer assistance; but where one person takes a right direction of his own accord, there are twenty who wander to and fro."

"I may as well confess to you," he continued presently, "that I have had a *protégé* myself, but I don't look for much future joy in watching the development of my plots. He has taken affairs into his own hands, and I dare say it is much better for him, for if I had caught him young enough, I should have wished him to run the gauntlet of all the professions, not to speak of the arts and sciences. He was a clever young fellow; I saw him married the day before I left England. His wife was the daughter of a curate, and he the younger son of a younger son, and it was a love affair worth two or three story-books. It came to be a question of money alone. I had known the boy the year before in Bombay and chanced to find him one day in the Marine Hospital at Nagasaki. We had been up into the interior together. He was recommended to me as a sort of secretary and assistant and knew more than I did about most things. When he caught sight of me he cried like a baby, and I sat down and heard what the trouble was, for I had let him go off with somebody who could give him a good salary,—a government man of position, and I thought poor Bob would be put in the way of something better. Dear me, the climate was killing him before my eyes, and I took passage for both of us on the next day's steamer. When I got him home I turned my bank account into a cheque and tucked it into his pocket, and told him to marry his wife and settle down and be respectable and forget such a wandering old fellow as I."

The listener made a little sound of mingled admiration and disgust.

"So you're the same piece of improvidence as ever! I wonder if you worked your passage over to Boston, or came as a stowaway? Well, I'm glad to give you house-room, and, to tell the truth, I was wondering how I should get on to-morrow without somebody to help me in a piece of surgery. My neighbors are not very skillful, but they're good men every one of them, unless it's old Jackson, who knows no more about the practice of medicine than a turtle knows about the nearest fixed star. Ferris! I don't wonder at your giving away the last cent you had in the world, I only wonder that you had a cent to give. I hope the young man was grateful, that's all, only I'm not sure I like his taking it."

"He thought I had enough more, I dare say. He said so much I couldn't stand his nonsense. He'll use it better than I could," said the guest briefly. "As I said, I couldn't bring him up; in the first place I haven't the patience, and beside, it wouldn't be just to him. But you must let me know how you get on with your project; I shall make you a day's visit once in six months."

"That'll be good luck," responded the cheerful host. "Now that I am growing old I find I wish for company oftener; just the right man, you know, to come in for an hour or two late in the evening to have a cigar, and not say a word if he doesn't feel like it."

The two friends were very comfortable together; the successive cigars burnt themselves out slowly, and the light of the great lamp was bright in the room. Here and there a tinge of red shone out on the backs of the books that stood close together in the high cases. There was an old engraving or two, and in one corner a solemn bronze figure of Dante, thin and angular, as if he had risen from his coffin to take a last look at this world. Marilla had often spoken of him disrespectfully, and had suggested many other ornaments which might be brought to take his place, but the doctor had never acted upon her suggestions. From the corner of one book-case there hung a huge wasp's nest, and over the mantel-shelf, which was only wide enough for some cigar boxes and a little clock and a few vials of medicines, was a rack where three or four riding whips and a curious silver bit and some long-stemmed pipes found unmolested quarters; and in one corner were some walking sticks and a fishing rod or two which had a very ancient unused look. There was a portrait of Dr. Leslie's grandfather opposite the fire-place; a good-humored looking old gentleman who had been the most famous of the Oldfields ministers. The study-table was wide and long, but it was well covered with a miscellaneous array of its owner's smaller possessions, and the quick-eyed visitor smiled as he caught sight of Nan's new copy of Miss Edgeworth's "Parent's Assistant" lying open and face downward on the top of an instrument case.

Marilla did not hear the doctor and his guest tramp up to bed until very late at night, and though she had tried to keep awake she had been obliged to take a nap first and then wake up again to get the benefit of such an aggravating occasion. "I'm not going to fret myself trying to make one of my baked omelets in the morning," she assured herself, "they'll keep breakfast waiting three quarters of an hour, and it would fall flat sure's the world, and the doctor's got to ride to all p'ints of the compass to-morrow, too."

X

ACROSS THE STREET

It would be difficult to say why the village of Oldfields should have been placed in the least attractive part of the township, if one were not somewhat familiar with the law of growth of country communities. The first settlers, being pious kindred of the Pilgrims, were mindful of the necessity of a meeting-house, and the place for it was chosen with reference to the convenience of most of the worshipers. Then the parson was given a parsonage and a tract of glebe land somewhere in the vicinity of his pulpit, and since this was the centre of social attraction, the blacksmith built his shop at the nearest cross-road. And when some enterprising citizen became possessed of an idea that there were traders enough toiling to and fro on the rough highways to the nearest larger village to make it worth his while to be an interceptor, the first step was taken toward a local centre of commerce, and the village was fairly begun. It had not yet reached a remarkable size, though there was a time-honored joke because an enthusiastic old woman had said once, when four or five houses and a new meeting-house were being built all in one summer, that she expected now that she might live to see Oldfields a seaport town. There had been a great excitement over the second meeting-house, to which the conservative faction had strongly objected, but, after the radicals had once gained the day, other innovations passed without public challenge. The old First Parish Church was very white and held aloft an imposing steeple, and strangers were always commiserated if they had to leave town without the opportunity of seeing its front by moonlight. Behind this, and beyond a green which had been the playground of many generations of boys and girls, was a long row of horse-sheds, where the farmers' horses enjoyed such part of their Sunday rest as was permitted them after bringing heavy loads of rural parishioners to their public devotions. The Sunday church-going was by no means so carefully observed in these days as in former ones, when disinclination was anything but a received excuse.

In Parson Leslie's—the doctor's grandfather's—day, it would have condemned a man or woman to the well-merited reproof of their acquaintances. And indeed most parishioners felt deprived of a great pleasure when, after a week of separation from society, of a routine of prosaic farm-work, they were prevented from seeing their friends parade into church, from hearing the psalm-singing and the sermon, and listening to the news afterward. It was like going to mass and going to the theatre and the opera, and making a round of short calls, and having an outing in one's own best clothes to see other people's, all rolled into one; beside which, there was (and is) a superstitious expectation of good luck in the coming week if the religious obligations were carefully fulfilled. So many of the old ideas of the efficacy of ecclesiasticism still linger, most of them by no means unlawfully. The elder people of New England are as glad to have their clergyman visit them in their last days as if he granted them absolution and extreme unction. The old traditions survive in our instincts, although our present opinions have long since ticketed many thoughts and desires and customs as out of date and quite exploded.

We go so far in our vigorous observance of the first commandment, and our fear of worshiping strange gods, that sometimes we are in danger of forgetting that we must worship God himself. And worship is something different from a certain sort of constant church-going, or from even trying to be conformers and to keep our own laws and our neighbors'.

Because an old-fashioned town like Oldfields grows so slowly and with such extreme deliberation, is the very reason it seems to have such a delightful completeness when it has entered fairly upon its maturity. It is possessed of kindred virtues to a winter pear, which may be unattractive during its preparatory stages, but which takes time to gather from the ground and from the air a pleasant and rewarding individuality and sweetness. The towns which are built in a hurry can be left in a hurry without a bit of regret, and if it is the fate or fortune of the elder villages to find themselves the foundation upon which modern manufacturing communities rear their thinly built houses and workshops, and their quickly disintegrating communities of people, the weaknesses of these are more glaring and hopeless in the contrast. The hurry to make money and do much work, and the ambition to do good work, war with each other, but, as Longfellow has said, the lie is the hurrying second-hand of the clock, and the truth the slower hand that waits and marks the hour. The New England that built itself houses a hundred years ago was far less oppressed by competition and by other questions with which the enormous increase of population is worrying its younger citizens. And the overgrown Oldfields that increase now, street by street, were built then a single steady sound-timbered house at a time, and all the neighbors watched them rise, and knew where the planks were sawn, and where the chimney bricks were burnt.

In these days when Anna Prince was young and had lately come to live in the doctor's square house, with the three peaked windows in the roof, and the tall box borders and lilac bushes in its neat front yard, Oldfields was just beginning to wake from a fifty years' architectural sleep, and rub its eyes, and see what was thought about a smart little house with a sharp gabled roof, and much scalloping of its edges, which a new store-keeper had seen fit to build. There was one long street which had plenty of room on either side for most of the houses, and where it divided, each side of the First Parish Church, it became the East road and the West road, and the rest of the dwellings strayed off somewhat undecidedly toward the world beyond. There were a good many poplars in the front yards, though their former proud ranks were broken in many places, so that surviving veterans stood on guard irregularly before the houses, where usually one or two members of the once busy households were also left alone. Many of the people who lived in the village had outlying land and were farmers of it, but beside the doctor's there were some other households which the land supported indirectly, either through professions or because some kind ancestor had laid by enough money for his children and grandchildren. The ministers were both excellent men; but Dr. Leslie was the only man who looked far ahead or saw much or cared much for true success. In Titian's great Venetian picture of the Presentation of the Virgin, while the little maiden goes soberly up the steps of the temple, in the busy crowd beneath only one man is possessed by the thought that something wonderful is happening, and lifts his head, forgetting the buyers and sellers and gossipers, as his eyes follow the sacred sight. Life goes on everywhere like that fragment of it in the picture, but while the man who knows more than his fellows can be found in every company, and sees the light which beckons him on to the higher meanings and better gifts, his place in society is not always such a comfortable and honored one as Dr. Leslie's. What his friends were apt to call his notions were not of such aggressive nature that he was accused of outlawry, and he was apt to speak his mind uncontradicted and undisturbed. He cared little for the friction and attrition, indeed for the inspiration, which one is sure to have who lives among many people, and which are so dear and so helpful to most of us who fall into ruts if we are too much alone. He loved his friends and his books, though he understood both as few scholars can, and he cared little for social pleasure, though Oldfields was, like all places of its size and dignity, an epitome of the world. One or two people of each class and rank are as good as fifty, and, to use the saying of the doctor's friend, old Captain Finch: "Human nature is the same the world over."

Through the long years of his solitary life, and his busy days as a country practitioner, he had become less and less inclined to take much part in what feeble efforts the rest of the townspeople made to entertain themselves. He was more apt to loiter along the street, stopping here and there to talk with his neighbors at their gates or their front-yard gardening, and not infrequently asked some one who stood in need of such friendliness to take a drive with him out into the country. Nobody was grieved at remembering that he was a repository of many secrets; he was a friend who could be trusted always, though he was one who had been by no means slow to anger or unwilling at times to administer rebuke.

One Sunday afternoon, late in November, while the first snow-storm of the year was beginning, Dr. Leslie threw down a stout French medical work of high renown as if it had failed to fulfil its mission of being instructive first and interesting afterward. He rose from his chair and stood looking at the insulted volume as if he had a mind to apologize and try again, but kept his hands behind him after all. It was thinly dressed in fluttering paper covers, and was so thick and so lightly bound that it had a tendency to divide its material substance into parts, like the seventhlies and eighthlies of an old-fashioned sermon. "Those fellows must be in league with the book-binders over here," grumbled the doctor. "I must send word to that man in New York to have some sort of cover put on these things before they come down." Then he lifted the book again and poised it on one hand, looking at its irregular edges, and reflecting at length that it would be in much better condition if he had not given it a careless crushing in the corner of his carriage the day before. It had been sunshiny, pleasant weather, and he had taken Nan for a long drive in the Saturday half-holiday. He had decided, before starting, that she should manage the reins and he would think over one or two matters and read a while; it had been a great convenience lately that Nan understood the responsibility of a horse and carriage. He was finding her a more and more useful little companion. However, his studies and reflections had been postponed until some other time, for Nan had been very eager to talk about some of her lessons in which it seemed his duty to take an interest. The child seemed stronger and better that autumn than he had ever known her, and her mind had suddenly fastened itself upon certain of her studies. She seemed very quick and very accurate, the doctor thought, and the two traits do not always associate themselves.

He left the table and walked quickly to the west window, and, clasping his hands behind him, stood looking out into the front yard and the street beyond. The ground was already white and he gave a little sigh, for winter weather is rarely a source of happiness to a doctor, although this member of the profession was not made altogether sorrowful by it. He sometimes keenly enjoyed a hard tramp of a mile or two when the roads were so blocked and the snow so blinding that he left his horse in some sheltering barn on his way to an impatient sufferer.

A little way down the street on the other side was a house much like his own, with a row of tall hemlocks beside it, and a front fence higher and more imposing than his, with great posts at the gateway, which held slender urns aloft with funereal solemnity. The doctor's eyesight was not far from perfect, and he looked earnestly at the windows of one of the lower rooms and saw a familiar sight enough; his neighbor Mrs. Graham's face in its accustomed quarter of the sash. Dr. Leslie half smiled as the thought struck him that she always sat so exactly in the same place that her white cap was to be seen through the same lower window-pane. "Most people would have moved their chairs about until they wore holes in the floor," he told himself, and then remembered how many times he had gone to look over at his placid friend, in her favorite afternoon post of observation. He was strongly attached to her, and he reminded himself that she was growing old and that he must try to see her oftener. He valued her companionship, more because he knew it was always ready for him, than because he always availed himself of it, but the sense of mutual dependence made them very familiar to each other when they did meet and had time for a bit of quiet talk.

Dr. Leslie suddenly turned; he had watched long enough to make sure that Mrs. Graham was alone; her head had not moved for many minutes; and at first he was going out of the front door, from some instinct he would hardly have been willing to acknowledge, but he resolutely turned and went out to the dining-room, to tell Marilla, after his usual professional custom of giving notice of his whereabouts, that he was going to Mrs. Graham's. A prompt inquiry came from the kitchen to know if anything ailed her, to which the doctor returned a scornful negative and escaped through the side-door which gave entrance both to the study and the dining-room. There was the usual service at Marilla's meeting-house, but she had not ventured out to attend it, giving the weather and a grumbling toothache for her reasons, though she concealed the fact that the faithless town milliner had disappointed her about finishing her winter bonnet. Marilla had begun life with certain opinions which she had never changed, though time and occasion had lessened the value of some of them. She liked to count herself among those who are persecuted for conscience's sake, and was immensely fond of an argument and of having it known that she was a dissenter from the First Parish Church.

Mrs. Graham looked up with surprise from her book to see the doctor coming in from the street, and, being helplessly lame, sat still, and put out her hand to greet him, with a very pleased look on her face. "Is there anything the matter with me?" she asked. "I have begun to think you don't care to associate with well people; you don't usually go to church in the afternoon either, so you have n't taken refuge here because Mr. Talcot is ill. I must say that I missed hearing the bell; I shall lose myself altogether by the middle of the week. One must have some landmarks."

"Marilla complained yesterday that she was all at sea because her apple pies gave out a day too soon. She put the bread to rise the wrong night, and everything went wrong about the sweeping. It has been a week of great domestic calamity with us, but Nan confided to me this morning that there was some trouble with our bonnet into the bargain. I had forgotten it was time for that," said the doctor, laughing. "We always have a season of great anxiety and disaster until the bonnet question is settled. I keep out of the way as much as I can. Once I tried to be amusing, and said it was a pity the women did not follow their grandmothers' fashion and make a good Leghorn structure last ten years and have no more trouble about it; but I was assured that there was n't a milliner now living who could set such an arrangement going."

"Marilla's taste is not what one might call commonplace," said Mrs. Graham, with a smile. "I think her summer head-covering was a little the most remarkable we have had yet. She dresses so decently otherwise, good soul!"

"It was astonishing," said the doctor gravely, as he stood before the fire thinking how pleasant the room looked; almost as familiar as his own study, with its heavy mahogany furniture and two old portraits and few quaint ornaments. Mrs. Graham's geraniums were all flourishing and green and even in bloom, unlike most treasures of their kind. There was a modern element in the room also,—some pretty cushions and other bits of embroidery; for Mrs. Graham had some grandchildren who were city born and bred, and who made little offerings to her from time to time. On the table near her and between the front windows were many new books and magazines, and though the two neighbors kept up a regular system of exchange, the doctor went nearer to see what might be found. There were a few minutes of silence, and he became conscious that Mrs. Graham was making up her mind to say something, but when she spoke it was only to ask if there were anything serious the matter with the minister.

"Oh, no," said the doctor, "he's a dyspeptic, nervous soul, too conscientious! and when the time arrives for the sacrifice of pigs, and his whole admiring parish vie with each other to offer spare-ribs on that shrine, it goes hard with the poor man."

This was worth hearing, but Mrs. Graham was a little sorry that she had let such a good chance go by for saying something that was near her heart, so presently she added, "I am sorry that poor Marilla hasn't a better gift at personal decoration. It seems a pity to let her disfigure that pretty child with such structures in the way of head-gear. I was so glad when that abominable great summer hat was laid by for the season."

"It was pretty bad," the doctor agreed, in a provokingly indifferent tone, whereupon Mrs. Graham's interest was rekindled, and saying to herself that the poor man did not know the danger and foolishness of such carelessness, she ventured another comment.

"So much depends upon giving a child's taste the right direction."

Dr. Leslie had taken up a magazine, and seemed to have found something that pleased him, but he at once laid it down and glanced once or twice at his hostess, as if he hoped for future instructions. "You see I don't know anything about it, and Nan doesn't think of her clothes at all, so far as I can tell, and so poor Marilla has to do the best she can," he said mildly.

"Oh dear, yes," answered Mrs. Graham, not without impatience. "But the child's appearance is of some importance, and since a dollar or two doesn't make any difference to you, she should be made to look like the little lady that she is. Dear old Mrs. Thacher would turn in her grave, for she certainly had a simple good taste that was better than this. Marilla became the easy prey of that foolish little woman who makes bonnets on the East road. She has done more to deprave the ideas of our townspeople than one would believe, and they tell you with such pleasure that she used to work in New York, as if that settled the question. It is a comfort to see old Sally Turner and Miss Betsy Milman go by in their decent dark silk bonnets that good Susan Martin made for them. If I could go out to-morrow I believe I would rather hunt for a very large velvet specimen of her work, which is somewhere upstairs in a big bandbox, than trust myself to these ignorant hands. It is a great misfortune to a town if it has been disappointed in its milliner. You are quite at her mercy, and, worse than all, liable to entire social misapprehension when you venture far from home."

"So bonnets are not a question of free will and individual responsibility?" asked the doctor soberly. "I must say that I have wondered sometimes if the women do not draw lots for them. But what shall I do about the little girl? I am afraid I do her great injustice in trying to bring her up at all—it needs a woman's eye."

"Your eye is just as good as anybody's," responded Mrs. Graham quickly, lest the doctor should drift into sad thought about his young wife who had been so long dead and yet seemed always a nearer and dearer living presence to him. He was apt to say a word or two about her and not answer the next question which was put to him, and presently go silently away,—but to-day Mrs. Graham had important business in hand.

"My daughter will be here next week," she observed, presently, "and I'm sure that she will do any shopping for you in Boston with great pleasure. We might forestall Marilla's plans. You could easily say when you go home that you have spoken to me about it. I think it would be an excellent opportunity now, while the East Road establishment is in disfavor," and when the doctor smiled and nodded, his friend and hostess settled herself comfortably in her chair, and felt that she had gained a point.

The sunshine itself could hardly have made that south parlor look pleasanter. There was a log in the fire that was wet, and singing gently to itself, as if the sound of the summer rustlings and chirpings had somehow been stored away in its sap, and above it were some pieces of drier white birch, which

were sending up a yellow conflagration to keep the marauding snow-flakes from coming down the chimney. The geraniums looked brighter than by daylight, and seemed to hold
their leaves toward the fireplace as if they were hands; and
were even leaning out a little way themselves and lifting their
blossoms like torches, as if they were a reserve force, a little
garrison of weaker soldiers who were also enemies of the
cold. The gray twilight was gathering out of doors; the trees
looked naked and defenceless, as one saw them through the
windows. Mrs. Graham tapped the arms of her chair gently
with the tips of her fingers, and in a few minutes the doctor
closed the book he was looking over and announced that the
days were growing very short. There was something singularly pleasant to both the friends in their quiet Sunday afternoon companionship.

"You used to pay me a Sunday visit every week," said the
old lady, pleased to find that her guest still lingered. "I don't
know why, but I always have a hope that you will find time to
run over for half an hour. I said to myself yesterday that a
figure of me in wax would do just as well as anything nowadays. I get up and dress myself, and make the journey down-
stairs, and sit here at the window and have my dinner and go
through the same round day after day. If it were n't for a
certain amount of expense it incurs, and occupation to other
people, I think it would be of very little use. However, there
are some people still left who need me. Who is it says—Bé-
ranger perhaps—that to love benefits one's self, and to inspire
love benefits others. I like to think that the children and
grandchildren have the old place to think of and come back
to. I can see that it is a great bond between them all, and that
is very good. I begin to feel like a very old woman; it would
be quite different, you know, if I were active and busy out of
doors, and the bustling sort of person for which nature intended me. As it is, my mind is bustling enough for itself and
its body both."

"Well," said the doctor, laughing a little, "what is it now?"

"The little girl," answered Mrs. Graham, gravely. "I think it
is quite time she knew something of society. Don't tell yourself that I am notional and frivolous; I know you have put a
great deal of hope and faith and affection into that child's

career. It would disappoint you dreadfully if she were not interesting and harmonious to people in general. It seems a familiar fact now that she should have come to live with you, that she should be growing up in your house; but the first thing we know she will be a young lady instead of an amusing child, and I think that you cannot help seeing that a great deal of responsibility belongs to you. She must be equipped and provisioned for the voyage of life; she must have some resources."

"But I think she has more than most children."

"Yes, yes, I dare say. She is a bright little creature, but her brightness begins to need new things to work upon. She does very well at school now, I hear, and she minds very well and is much less lawless than she used to be; but she is like a candle that refuses to burn, and is satisfied with admiring its candlestick. She is quite the queen of the village children in one way, and in another she is quite apart from them. I believe they envy her and look upon her as being of another sort, and yet count her out of half their plans and pleasures, and she runs home, not knowing whether to be pleased or hurt, and pulls down half a dozen of your books and sits proudly at the window. Her poor foolish mother had some gifts, but she went adrift very soon, and I should teach Nan her duty to her neighbor, and make her take in the idea that she owes something to the world beside following out her own most satisfying plans. When I was a young woman it was a most blessed discovery to me—though I was not any quicker at making it than other people, perhaps,—that, beside being happy myself and valuable to myself, I must fit myself into my place in society. We are seldom left to work alone, you know. No, not even you. I know too much about you to believe that. And it is n't enough that we are willing to talk about ourselves. We must learn to understand the subjects of the day that everybody talks about, and to make sure of a right to stand upon the highest common ground wherever we are. Society is a sort of close corporation, and we must know its watchwords, and keep an interest in its interests and affairs. I call a gentleman the man who, either by birth or by nature, belongs to the best society. There may be bad gentlemen and good gentlemen, but one must feel instinctively at home with a certain class, representatives of which are likely to be found everywhere.

"And as for Nan, you will be disappointed if she does not understand a little later your own way of looking at things. She must n't grow up full of whims and indifferences. I am too fond of you to look forward calmly to your being disappointed, and I do believe she will be a most lovely, daughterly, friendly girl, who will keep you from being lonely as you grow older, and be a great blessing in every way. Yet she has a strange history, and is in a strange position. I hope you will find a good school for her before very long."

This was said after a moment's pause, and with considerable hesitation, and Mrs. Graham was grateful for the gathering darkness which sheltered her, and not a little surprised at the doctor's answer.

"I have been thinking of that," he said quickly, "but it is a great puzzle at present and I am thankful to say, I think it is quite safe to wait a year or two yet. You and I live so much apart from society that we idealize it a good deal, though you are a stray-away bit of it. We too seldom see the ideal gentleman or lady; we have to be contented with keeping the ideal in our minds, it seems to me, and saying that this man is gentlemanly, and that woman ladylike. But I do believe in aiming at the best things, and turning this young creature's good instincts and uncommon powers into the proper channels instead of letting her become singular and self-centred because she does not know enough of people of her own sort."

Mrs. Graham gave a little sound of approval that did not stand for any word in particular: "I wonder if her father's people will ever make any claim to her? She said something about her aunt one day; I think it was to hear whatever I might answer. It seemed to me that the poor child had more pleasure in this unknown possession than was worth while; she appeared to think of her as a sort of fairy godmother who might descend in Oldfields at any moment."

"I did not know she thought of her at all," announced the doctor, somewhat dismayed. "She never has talked about her aunt to me. I dare say that she has been entertained with the whole miserable story."

"Oh, no," answered Mrs. Graham, placidly. "I don't think that is likely, but it is quite reasonable that the child should be aware of some part of it by this time. The Dyer neighbors are far from being reticent, good creatures, and they have little to remember that approaches the interest and excitement of that time. Do you know anything about Miss Prince nowadays? I have not heard anything of her in a long while."

"She still sends the yearly remittance, which I acknowledge and put into the savings bank as I always have done. When Nan came to me I advised Miss Prince that I wished to assume all care of her and should be glad if she would give me entire right to the child, but she took no notice of the request. It really makes no practical difference. Only," and the doctor became much embarrassed, "I must confess that I have a notion of letting her study medicine by and by if she shows a fitness for it."

"Dear, dear!" said the hostess, leaning forward so suddenly that she knocked two or three books from the corner of the table, and feeling very much excited. "John Leslie, I can't believe it! but my dear man used to say you thought twice for everybody else's once. What can have decided you upon such a plan?"

"How happened the judge to say that?" asked the doctor, trying to scoff, but not a little pleased. "I'm sure I can't tell you, Mrs. Graham, only the idea has grown of itself in my mind, as all right ideas do, and everything that I can see seems to favor it. You may think that it is too early to decide, but I see plainly that Nan is not the sort of girl who will be likely to marry. When a man or woman has that sort of self-dependence and unnatural self-reliance, it shows itself very early. I believe that it is a mistake for such a woman to marry. Nan's feeling toward her boy-playmates is exactly the same as toward the girls she knows. You have only to look at the rest of the children together to see the difference; and if I make sure by and by, the law of her nature is that she must live alone and work alone, I shall help her to keep it instead of break it, by providing something else than the business of housekeeping and what is called a woman's natural work, for her activity and capacity to spend itself upon."

"But don't you think that a married life is happiest?" urged

the listener, a good deal shocked at such treason, yet somewhat persuaded by its truth.

"Yes," said Dr. Leslie, sadly. "Yes indeed, for most of us.
We could say almost everything for that side, you and I; but a
rule is sometimes very cruel for its exceptions; and there is a
life now and then which is persuaded to put itself in irons by
the force of custom and circumstances, and from the lack of
bringing reason to bear upon the solving of the most important question of its existence. Of course I don't feel sure yet
that I am right about Nan, but looking at her sad inheritance
from her mother, and her good inheritances from other quarters, I cannot help feeling that she might be far more unhappy
than to be made ready to take up my work here in Oldfields
when I have to lay it down. She will need a good anchor now
and then. Only this summer she had a bad day of it that made
me feel at my wits' end. She was angry with one of the
children at school, and afterward with Marilla because she
scolded her for not keeping better account of the family times
and seasons, and ran away in the afternoon, if you please, and
was not heard from until next morning at breakfast time. She
went to the old place and wandered about the fields as she
used, and crept into some shelter or other. I dare say that she
climbed in at one of the windows of the house, though I
could not make quite sure without asking more questions
than I thought worth while. She came stealing in early in the
morning, looking a little pale and wild, but she has n't played
such a prank since. I had a call to the next town and Marilla
had evidently been awake all night. I got home early in the
morning myself, and was told that it was supposed I had
picked up Nan on the road and carried her with me, so the
blame was all ready for my shoulders unless we had both happened to see the young culprit strolling in at the gate. I was
glad she had punished herself, so that there was no need of
my doing it, though I had a talk with her a day or two afterward, when we were both in our right minds. She is a good
child enough."

"I dare say," remarked Mrs. Graham drily, "but it seems to
me that neither of you took Marilla sufficiently into account.
That must have been the evening that the poor soul went to
nearly every house in town to ask if there were any stray com-

pany to tea. Some of us could not help wondering where the young person was finally discovered. She has a great fancy for the society of Miss Betsy Milman and Sally Turner at present, and I quite sympathize with her. I often look over there and see the end of their house with that one little square window in the very peak of it spying up the street, and wish I could pay them a visit myself and hear a bit of their wise gossip. I quite envy Nan her chance of going in and being half forgotten as she sits in one of their short chairs listening and watching. They used to be great friends of her grandmother's. Oh no; if I could go to see them they would insist upon my going into the best room, and we should all be quite uncomfortable. It is much better to sit here and think about them and hear their flat-irons creak away over the little boys' jackets and trousers."

"I must confess that I have my own clothes mended there to this day," said the doctor. "Marilla says their mending is not what it used to be, too, but it is quite good enough. As for that little window, I hardly ever see it without remembering the day of your aunt Margaret's funeral. I was only a boy and not deeply afflicted, but of course I had my place in the procession and was counted among the mourners, and as we passed the Milman place I saw the old lady's face up there just filling the four small panes. You know she was almost helpless, and how she had got up into the little garret I cannot imagine, but she was evidently determined to inspect the procession as it went down the burying-ground lane. It was a pity they did not cut the window beneath it in the lower room in her day. You know what an odd face she had; I suppose it was distorted by disease and out of all shape it ever knew; but I can see it now, framed in with its cap border and the window as if there were no more of her."

"She really was the most curious old creature; it more than accounts for Mrs. Turner's and Miss Betsy's love for a piece of news," said Mrs. Graham, who was much amused. "But I wish we understood the value of these old news-loving people. So much local history and tradition must die with every one of them if we take no pains to save it. I hope you are wise about getting hold of as much as possible. You doctors ought to be our historians, for you alone see the old country folks familiarly and can talk with them without restraint."

"But we have n't time to do any writing," the guest replied. "That is why our books amount to so little for the most part. The active men, who are really to be depended upon as practitioners, are kept so busy that they are too tired to use the separate gift for writing, even if they possess it, which many do not. And the literary doctors, the medical scholars, are a different class, who have not had the experience which alone can make their advice reliable. I mean of course in practical matters, not anatomy and physiology. But we have to work our way and depend upon ourselves, we country doctors, to whom a consultation is more or less a downfall of pride. Whenever I hear that an old doctor is dead I sigh to think what treasures of wisdom are lost instead of being added to the general fund. That was one advantage of putting the young men with the elder practitioners; many valuable suggestions were handed down in that way."

"I am very well contented with my doctor," said Mrs. Graham, with enthusiasm, at this first convenient opportunity. "And it is very wise of you all to keep up our confidence in the face of such facts as these. You can hardly have the heart to scold any more about the malpractice of patients when we believe in you so humbly and so ignorantly. You are always safe though, for our consciences are usually smarting under the remembrance of some transgression which might have hindered you if it did not. Poor humanity," she added in a tone of compassion. "It has to grope its way through a deal of darkness."

The doctor sighed, but he was uncommonly restful and comfortable in the large arm-chair before the fender. It was quite dark out of doors now, and the fire gave all the light that was in the room. Presently he roused himself a little to say " 'Poor humanity,' indeed! And I suppose nobody sees the failures and miseries as members of my profession do. There will be more and more sorrow and defeat as the population increases and competition with it. It seems to me that to excel in one's work becomes more and more a secondary motive; to do a great deal and be well paid for it ranks first. One feels the injury of such purposes even in Oldfields."

"I cannot see that the world changes much. I often wish that I could, though surely not in this way," said the lame woman from her seat by the window, as the doctor rose to go away. "I find my days piteously alike, and you do not know what a pleasure this talk has been. It satisfies my hungry mind and gives me a great deal to think of; you would not believe what an appetite I had. Oh, don't think I need any excuses, it is a great pleasure to see you drive in and out of the gate, and I like to see your lamp coming into the study, and to know that you are there and fond of me. But winter looked very long and life very short before you came in this afternoon. I suppose you have had enough of society for one day, so I shall not tell you what I mean to have for tea, but next Sunday night I shall expect you to come and bring your ward. Will you please ring, so that Martha will bring the lights? I should like to send Nan a nice letter to read which came yesterday from my little grand-daughter in Rome. I shall be so glad when they are all at home again. She is about Nan's age, you know; I must see to it that they make friends with each other. Don't put me on a dusty top shelf again and forget me for five or six weeks," laughed the hostess, as her guest protested and lingered a minute still before he opened the door.

"You won't say anything of my confidences?" at which Mrs. Graham shakes her head with satisfactory gravity, though if Doctor Leslie had known she was inwardly much amused, and assured herself directly that she hoped to hear no more of such plans; how could he tell that the girl herself would agree to them, and whether Oldfields itself would favor Nan as his own successor and its medical adviser? But John Leslie was a wise, far-seeing man, with a great power of holding to his projects. He really must be kept to his promise of a weekly visit; she was of some use in the world after all, so long as these unprotected neighbors were in it, and at any rate she had gained her point about the poor child's clothes.

As for the doctor, he found the outer world much obscured by the storm, and hoped that nobody would need his services that night, as he went stumbling home though the damp and clogging snow underfoot. He felt a strange pleasure in the sight of a small, round head at the front study window between the glass and the curtain, and Nan came to open the

door for him, while Marilla, whose unwonted Sunday afternoon leisure seemed to have been devoted to fragrant experiments in cookery, called in pleased tones from the dining-
room that she had begun to be afraid he was going to stay
out to supper. It was somehow much more homelike than it
used to be, the doctor told himself, as he pushed his feet into
the slippers which had been waiting before the fire until they
were in danger of being scorched. And before Marilla had
announced with considerable ceremony that tea was upon the
table, he had assured himself that it had been a very pleasant
hour or two at Mrs. Graham's, and it was the best thing in
the world for both of them to see something of each other.
For the little girl's sake he must try to keep out of ruts, and
must get hold of somebody outside his own little world.

But while he called himself an old fogy and other impolite
names he was conscious of a grave and sweet desire to make
the child's life a successful one,—to bring out what was in
her own mind and capacity, and so to wisely educate her, to
give her a place to work in, and wisdom to work with, so far
as he could; for he knew better than most men that it is the
people who can do nothing who find nothing to do, and the
secret of happiness in this world is not only to be useful, but
to be forever elevating one's uses. Some one must be intelligent for a child until it is ready to be intelligent for itself, and
he told himself with new decision that he must be wise in his
laws for Nan and make her keep them, else she never would
be under the grace of any of her own.

XI

NEW OUTLOOKS

D r. Leslie held too securely the affection of his towns-people to be in danger of losing their regard or respect, yet he would have been half pained and half amused if he had known how foolishly his plans, which came in time to be his ward's also, were smiled and frowned upon in the Oldfields houses. Conformity is the inspiration of much second-rate virtue. If we keep near a certain humble level of morality and achievement, our neighbors are willing to let us slip through life unchallenged. Those who anticipate the opinions and decisions of society must expect to be found guilty of many sins.

There was not one of the young village people so well known as the doctor's little girl, who drove with him day by day, and with whom he kept such delightful and trustful companionship. If she had been asked in later years what had decided her to study not only her profession, but any profession, it would have been hard for her to answer anything beside the truth that the belief in it had grown with herself. There had been many reasons why it seemed unnecessary. There was every prospect that she would be rich enough to place her beyond the necessity of self-support. She could have found occupation in simply keeping the doctor's house and being a cordial hostess in that home and a welcome guest in other people's. She was already welcome everywhere in Oldfields, but in spite of this, which would have seemed to fill the hearts and lives of other girls, it seemed to her like a fragment of her life and duty; and when she had ordered her housekeeping and her social duties, there was a restless readiness for a more absorbing duty and industry; and, as the years went by, all her desire tended in one direction. The one thing she cared most to learn increased its attraction continually, and though one might think the purpose of her guardian had had its influence and moulded her character by its persistence, the truth was that the wise doctor simply followed as best he could the leadings of the young nature itself, and so the girl grew naturally year by year, reaching out half unconsciously for what belonged to her life and growth; being taught one thing more than all, that her duty must be followed eagerly and reverently in spite of the adverse reasons which tempted and sometimes baffled her. As she grew older she was to understand more clearly that indecision is but another name for cowardice and weakness; a habit of mind that quickly increases its power of hindrance. She had the faults that belonged to her character, but these were the faults of haste and rashness rather than the more hopeless ones of obstinacy or a lack of will and purpose.

The Sunday evening tea-drinking with Mrs. Graham, though somewhat formidable at first to our heroine, became quickly one of her dearest pleasures, and led to a fast friendship between the kind hostess and her young guest. Soon Nan gave herself eagerly to a plan of spending two or three evenings a week across the way for the purpose of reading aloud, sometimes from books she did not understand, but oftener from books of her own choice. It was supposed to be wholly a kindness on the young girl's part, and Mrs. Graham allowed the excuse of a temporary ailment of her own strong and useful eyes to serve until neither she nor Nan had the least thought of giving up their pleasant habit of reading together. And to this willing listener Nan came in time with her youthful dreams and visions of future prosperities in life, so that presently Mrs. Graham knew many things which would have surprised the doctor, who on the other hand was the keeper of equally amazing and treasured confidences of another sort. It was a great pleasure to both these friends, but most especially to the elderly woman, that Nan seemed so entirely satisfied with their friendship. The busy doctor, who often had more than enough to think and worry about, sometimes could spare but little time to Nan for days together, but her other companion was always waiting for her, and the smile was always ready by way of greeting when the child looked eagerly up at the parlor window. What stories of past days and memories of youth and of long-dead friends belonging to the dear lady's own girlhood were poured into Nan's delighted ears! She came in time to know Mrs. Graham's own immediate ancestors, and the various members of her family with their fates and fortunes, as if she were a contemporary,

and was like another grandchild who was a neighbor and beloved crony, which real blessing none of the true grandchildren had ever been lucky enough to possess. She formed a
welcome link with the outer world, did little Nan, and from
being a cheerful errand-runner, came at last to paying friendly
visits in the neighborhood to carry Mrs. Graham's messages
and assurances. And from all these daily suggestions of courtesy and of good taste and high breeding, and helpful fellowship with good books, and the characters in their stories
which were often more real and dear and treasured in her
thoughts than her actual fellow townsfolk, Nan drew much
pleasure and not a little wisdom; at any rate a direction for
which she would all her life be thankful. It would have been
surprising if her presence in the doctor's house had not after
some time made changes in it, but there was no great difference outwardly except that she gathered some trifling possessions which sometimes harmonized, and as often did not,
with the household gods of the doctor and Marilla. There was
a shy sort of intercourse between Nan and Mrs. Graham's
grandchildren, but it was not very valuable to any of the
young people at first, the country child being too old and full
of experience to fellowship with the youngest, and too un-
versed in the familiar machinery of their social life to feel
much kinship with the eldest.

It was during one of these early summer visits, and directly
after a tea-party which Marilla had proudly projected on
Nan's account, that Dr. Leslie suddenly announced that he
meant to go to Boston for a few days and should take Nan
with him. This event had long been promised, but had
seemed at length like the promise of happiness in a future
world, reasonably certain, but a little vague and distant. It
was a more important thing than anybody understood, for a
dear and familiar chapter of life was ended when the expectant pair drove out of the village on their way to the far-off
railway station, as another had been closed when the door of
the Thacher farm-house had been shut and padlocked, and
Nan had gone home one snowy night to live with the doctor.
The weather at any rate was different now, for it was early
June, the time when doctors can best give themselves a holiday; and though Dr. Leslie assured himself that he had little

wish to take the journey, he felt it quite due to his ward that she should see a little more of the world, and happily due also to certain patients and his brother physicians that he should visit the instrument-makers' shops, and some bookstores; in fact there were a good many important errands to which it was just as well to attend in person. But he watched Nan's wide-open, delighted eyes, and observed her lack of surprise at strange sights, and her perfect readiness for the marvelous, with great amusement. He was touched and pleased because she cared most for what had concerned him; to be told where he lived and studied, and to see the places he had known best, roused most enthusiasm. An afternoon in a corner of the reading-room at the Athenæum library, in which he had spent delightful hours when he was a young man, seemed to please the young girl more than anything else. As he sat beside the table where he had gathered enough books and papers to last for many days, in his delight at taking up again his once familiar habit, Nan looked on with sympathetic eyes, or watched the squirrels in the trees of the quiet Granary Burying Ground, which seemed to her like a bit of country which the noisy city had caught and imprisoned. Now that she was fairly out in the world she felt a new, strange interest in her mysterious aunt, for it was this hitherto unknown space outside the borders of Oldfields to which her father and his people belonged. And as a charming old lady went by in a pretty carriage, the child's gaze followed her wistfully as she and the doctor were walking along the street. With a sudden blaze of imagination she had wished those pleasant eyes might have seen the likeness to her father, of which she had been sometimes told, and that the carriage had been hurried back, so that the long estrangement might be ended. It was a strange thing that, just afterward, Dr. Leslie had, with much dismay, caught sight of the true aunt; for Miss Anna Prince of Dunport had also seen fit to make one of her rare visits to Boston. She looked dignified and stately, but a little severe, as she went down the side street away from them. Nan's quick eyes had noticed already the difference between the city people and the country folks, and would have even recognized a certain provincialism in her father's sister. The doctor had only seen Miss Prince once many years before, but he had known her again with instinctive certainty, and Nan did not guess, though she was most grateful for it, why he reached for her hand, and held it fast as they walked together, just as he always used to do when she was a little girl. She was not yet fully grown, and she never suspected the sudden thrill of dread, and consciousness of the great battle of life which she must soon begin to fight, which all at once chilled the doctor's heart. "It's a cold world, a cold world," he had said to himself. "Only one thing will help her through safely, and that is her usefulness. She shall never be either a thief or a beggar of the world's favor if I can have my wish." And Nan, holding his hand with her warm, soft, childish one, looked up in his face, all unconscious that he thought with pity how unaware she was of the years to come, and of their difference to this sunshine holiday. "And yet I never was so happy at her age as I am this summer," the doctor told himself by way of cheer.

They paid some visits together to Dr. Leslie's much-neglected friends, and it was interesting to see how, for the child's sake, he resumed his place among these acquaintances to whom he had long been linked either personally in times past, or by family ties. He was sometimes reproached for his love of seclusion and cordially welcomed back to his old relations, but as often found it impossible to restore anything but a formal intercourse of a most temporary nature. The people for whom he cared most, all seemed attracted to his young ward, and he noted this with pleasure, though he had not recognized the fact that he had been, for the moment, basely uncertain whether his judgment of her worth would be confirmed. He laughed at the insinuation that he had made a hermit or an outlaw of himself; he would have been still more amused to hear one of his old friends say that this was the reason they had seen so little of him in late years, and that it was a shame that a man of his talent and many values to the world should be hiding his light under the Oldfields bushel, and all for the sake of bringing up this child. As for Nan, she had little to say, but kept her eyes and ears wide open, and behaved herself discreetly. She had ceased to belong only to the village she had left; in these days she became a citizen of the world at large. Her horizon had suddenly become larger, and she might have discovered more than one range of mountains which must be crossed as the years led her forward steadily, one by one.

There is nothing so interesting as to be able to watch the change and progress of the mental and moral nature, provided it grows eagerly and steadily. There must be periods of repose and hibernation like the winter of a plant, and in its springtime the living soul will both consciously and unconsciously reach out for new strength and new light. The leaves and flowers of action and achievement are only the signs of the vitality that works within.

XII

AGAINST THE WIND

DURING the next few years, while Nan was growing up, Oldfields itself changed less than many country towns of its size. Though some faces might be missed or altered, Dr. Leslie's household seemed much the same, and Mrs. Graham, a little thinner and older, but more patient and sweet and delightful than ever, sits at her parlor window and reads new books and old ones, and makes herself the centre of much love and happiness. She and the doctor have grown more and more friendly, and they watch the young girl's development with great pride: they look forward to her vacations more than they would care to confess even to each other; and when she comes home eager and gay, she makes both these dear friends feel young again. When Nan is not there to keep him company, Dr. Leslie always drives, and has grown more careful about the comfort of his carriages, though he tells himself with great pleasure that he is really much more youthful in his feelings than he was twenty years before, and does not hesitate to say openly that he should have been an old fogy by this time if it had not been for the blessing of young companionship. When Nan is pleased to command, he is always ready to take long rides and the two saddles are brushed up, and they wonder why the bits are so tarnished, and she holds his horse's bridle while he goes in to see his patients, and is ready with merry talk or serious questions when he reappears. And one dark night she listens from her window to the demand of a messenger, and softly creeps down stairs and is ready to take her place by his side, and drive him across the hills as if it were the best fun in the world, with the frightened country-boy clattering behind on his bare-backed steed. The moon rises late and they come home just before daybreak, and though the doctor tries to be stern as he says he cannot have such a piece of mischief happen again, he wonders how the girl knew that he had dreaded for once in his life the drive in the dark, and had felt a little less strong than usual.

Marilla still reigns in noble state. She has some time ago accepted a colleague after a preliminary show of resentment, and Nan has little by little infused a different spirit into the housekeeping; and when her friends come to pay visits in the vacations they find the old home a very charming place, and fall quite in love with both the doctor and Mrs. Graham before they go away. Marilla always kept the large east parlor for a sacred shrine of society, to be visited chiefly by herself as guardian priestess; but Nan has made it a pleasanter room than anybody ever imagined possible, and uses it with a freedom which appears to the old housekeeper to lack consideration and respect. Nan makes the most of her vacations, while the neighbors are all glad to see her come back, and some of them are much amused because in summer she still clings to her childish impatience at wearing any head covering, and no matter how much Marilla admires the hat which is decorously worn to church every Sunday morning, it is hardly seen again, except by chance, during the week, and the brown hair is sure to be faded a little before the summer sunshine is past. Nan goes about visiting when she feels inclined, and seems surprisingly unchanged as she seats herself in one of the smoke-browned Dyer kitchens, and listens eagerly to whatever information is offered, or answers cordially all sorts of questions, whether they concern her own experiences or the world's in general. She has never yet seen her father's sister, though she still thinks of her, and sometimes with a strange longing for an evidence of kind feeling and kinship which has never been shown. This has been chief among the vague sorrows of her girlhood. Yet once when her guardian had asked if she wished to make some attempt at intercourse or conciliation, he had been answered, with a scorn and decision worthy of grandmother Thacher herself, that it was for Miss Prince to make advances if she ever wished for either the respect or affection of her niece. But the young girl has clung with touching affection to the memory and association of her childhood, and again and again sought in every season of the year the old playgrounds and familiar corners of the farm, which she has grown fonder of as the months go by. The inherited attachment of generations seems to have been centred in her faithful heart.

It must be confessed that the summer which followed the close of her school-life was, for the most part, very unsatisfactory. Her school-days had been more than usually pleasant and rewarding, in spite of the sorrows and disappointments and unsolvable puzzles which are sure to trouble thoughtful girls of her age. But she had grown so used at last to living by rules and bells that she could not help feeling somewhat adrift without them. It had been so hard to put herself under restraint and discipline after her free life in Oldfields that it was equally hard for a while to find herself at liberty; though, this being her natural state, she welcomed it heartily at first, and was very thankful to be at home. It did not take long to discover that she had no longer the same desire for her childish occupations and amusements; they were only incidental now and pertained to certain moods, and could not again be made the chief purposes of her life. She hardly knew what to do with herself, and sometimes wondered what would become of her, and why she was alive at all, as she longed for some sufficient motive of existence to catch her up into its whirlwind. She was filled with energy and a great desire for usefulness, but it was not with her, as with many of her friends, that the natural instinct toward marriage, and the building and keeping of a sweet home-life, ruled all other plans and possibilities. Her best wishes and hopes led her away from all this, and however tenderly she sympathized in other people's happiness, and recognized its inevitableness, for herself she avoided unconsciously all approach or danger of it. She was trying to climb by the help of some other train of experiences to whatever satisfaction and success were possible for her in this world. If she had been older and of a different nature, she might have been told that to climb up any other way toward a shelter from the fear of worthlessness, and mistake, and reproach, would be to prove herself in most people's eyes a thief and a robber. But in these days she was not fit to reason much about her fate; she could only wait for the problems to make themselves understood, and for the whole influence of her character and of the preparatory years to shape and signify themselves into a simple chart and unmistakable command. And until the power was given to "see life steadily and see it whole," she busied herself aimlessly with such details as were evidently her duty, and sometimes following the right road and often wandering from it in willful impatience, she stumbled along more or less unhappily. It seemed as if everybody had forgotten Nan's gift and love for the great profession which was her childish delight and ambition. To be sure she had studied anatomy and physiology with eager devotion in the meagre text-books at school, though the other girls had grumbled angrily at the task. Long ago, when Nan had confided to her dearest cronies that she meant to be a doctor, they were hardly surprised that she should determine upon a career which they would have rejected for themselves. She was not of their mind, and they believed her capable of doing anything she undertook. Yet to most of them the possible and even probable marriage which was waiting somewhere in the future seemed to hover like a cloudy barrier over the realization of any such unnatural plans.

They assured themselves that their school-mate showed no sign of being the sort of girl who tried to be mannish and to forsake her natural vocation for a profession. She did not look strong-minded; besides she had no need to work for her living, this ward of a rich man, who was altogether the most brilliant and beautiful girl in school. Yet everybody knew that she had a strange tenacity of purpose, and there was a lack of pretension, and a simplicity that scorned the deceits of school-girl existence. Everybody knew too that she was not a commonplace girl, and her younger friends made her the heroine of their fondest anticipations and dreams. But after all, it seemed as if everybody, even the girl herself, had lost sight of the once familiar idea. It was a natural thing enough that she should have become expert in rendering various minor services to the patients in Dr. Leslie's absence, and sometimes assist him when no other person was at hand. Marilla became insensible at the sight of the least dangerous of wounds, and could not be trusted to suggest the most familiar household remedy, after all her years of association with the practice of medicine, and it was considered lucky that Nan had some aptness for such services. In her childhood she had been nicknamed "the little doctor," by the household and even a few familiar friends, but this was apparently outgrown, though her guardian had more than once announced in sudden outbursts of enthusiasm that she already knew more than most of the people who tried to practice medicine. They once in a while talked about some suggestion or discovery which was attracting Dr. Leslie's attention, but the girl seemed hardly to have gained much interest even for this, and became a little shy of being found with one of the medical books in her hand, as she tried to fancy herself in sympathy with the conventional world of school and of the every-day ideas of society. And yet her inward sympathy with a doctor's and a surgeon's work grew stronger and stronger, though she dismissed reluctantly the possibility of following her bent in any formal way, since, after all, her world had seemed to forbid it. As the time drew near for her school-days to be ended, she tried to believe that she should be satisfied with her Oldfields life. She was fond of reading, and she had never lacked employment, besides, she wished to prove herself an intelligent companion to Dr. Leslie, whom she loved more and more dearly as the years went by. There had been a long time of reserve between her childish freedom of intercourse with him and the last year or two when they had begun to speak freely to each other as friend to friend. It was a constant surprise and pleasure to the doctor when he discovered that his former plaything was growing into a charming companion who often looked upon life from the same standpoint as himself, and who had her own outlooks upon the world, from whence she was able to give him by no means worthless intelligence; and after the school-days were over he was not amazed to find how restless and dissatisfied the girl was; how impossible it was for her to content herself with following the round of household duties which were supposed to content young women of her age and station. Even if she tried to pay visits or receive them from her friends, or to go on with her studies, or to review some text-book of which she had been fond, there was no motive for it; it all led to nothing; it began for no reason and ended in no use, as she exclaimed one day most dramatically. Poor Nan hurried through her house business, or neglected it, as the case might be, greatly to Marilla's surprise and scorn, for the girl had always proved herself diligent and interested in the home affairs. More and more she puzzled herself and everybody about her, and as the days went by she spent them out of doors at the old farm, or on the river, or in taking long rides on a young horse; a bargain the doctor had somewhat repented before he found that Nan was helped through some of her troubled hours by the creature's wildness and fleetness. It was very plain that his ward was adrift, and at first the doctor suggested farther study of Latin or chemistry, but afterward philosophically resigned himself to patience, feeling certain that some indication of the right course would not be long withheld, and that a wind from the right quarter would presently fill the flapping sails of this idle young craft and send it on its way.

One afternoon Nan went hurrying out of the house just after dinner, and the doctor saw that her face was unusually troubled. He had asked her if she would like to drive with him to a farm just beyond the Dyers' later in the day, but for a wonder she had refused. Dr. Leslie gave a little sigh as he left the table, and presently watched her go down the street as he stood by the window. It would be very sad if the restlessness and discord of her poor mother should begin to show themselves again; he could not bear to think of such an inheritance.

But Nan thought little of anybody else's discomforts as she hurried along the road; she only wished to get to the beloved farm, and to be free there from questions, and from the evidences of her unfitness for the simple duties which life seemed offering her with heartless irony. She was not good for anything after all, it appeared, and she had been cheating herself. This was no life at all, this fretful idleness; if only she had been trained as boys are, to the work of their lives! She had hoped that Dr. Leslie would help her; he used to talk long ago about her studying medicine, but he must have forgotten that, and the girl savagely rebuked society in general for her unhappiness. Of course she could keep the house, but it was kept already; any one with five senses and good health like hers could prove herself able to do any of the ordinary work of existence. For her part it was not enough to be waited upon and made comfortable, she wanted something more, to be really of use in the world, and to do work which the world needed.

Where the main road turned eastward up the hills, a foot-path, already familiar to the reader, shortened the distance to the farm, and the young girl quickly crossed the rude stile and disappeared among the underbrush, walking bareheaded with the swift steps of a creature whose home was in some such place as this. Often the dry twigs, fallen from the gray lower branches of the pines, crackled and snapped under her feet, or the bushes rustled backed again to their places after she pushed against them in passing; she hurried faster and faster, going first through the dense woods and then out into the sunlight. Once or twice in the open ground she stopped and knelt quickly on the soft turf or moss to look at a little plant, while the birds which she startled came back to their places directly, as if they had been quick to feel that this was a friend and not an enemy, though disguised in human shape. At last Nan reached the moss-grown fence of the farm and leaped over it, and fairly ran to the river-shore, where she went straight to one of the low-growing cedars, and threw herself upon it as if it were a couch. While she sat there, breathing fast and glowing with bright color, the river sent a fresh breeze by way of messenger, and the old cedar held its many branches above her and around her most comfortably, and sheltered her as it had done many times before. It need not have envied other trees the satisfaction of climbing straight upward in a single aspiration of growth.

And presently Nan told herself that there was nothing like a good run. She looked to and fro along the river, and listened to the sheep-bell which tinkled lazily in the pasture behind her. She looked over her shoulder to see if a favorite young birch tree had suffered no harm, for it grew close by the straight-edged path in which the cattle came down to drink. So she rested in the old playground, unconscious that she had been following her mother's footsteps, or that fate had again brought her here for a great decision. Years before, the miserable, suffering woman, who had wearily come to this place to end their lives, had turned away that the child might make her own choice between the good and evil things of life. Though Nan told herself that she must make it plain how she could spend her time in Oldfields to good purpose and be of most use at home, and must get a new strength for these duties, a decision suddenly presented itself to her with a force of reason and necessity the old dream of it had never shown. Why should it not be a reality that she studied medicine?

The thought entirely possessed her, and the glow of excitement and enthusiasm made her spring from the cedar boughs and laugh aloud. Her whole heart went out to this work, and she wondered why she had ever lost sight of it. She was sure this was the way in which she could find most happiness. God had directed her at last, and though the opening of her sealed orders had been long delayed, the suspense had only made her surer that she must hold fast this unspeakably great motive: something to work for with all her might as long as she lived. People might laugh or object. Nothing should turn her aside, and a new affection for kind and patient Dr. Leslie filled her mind. How eager he had been to help her in all her projects so far, and yet it was asking a great deal that he should favor this; he had never seemed to show any suspicion that she would not live on quietly at home like other girls; but while Nan told herself that she would give up any plan, even this, if he could convince her that it would be wrong, still her former existence seemed like a fog and uncertainty of death, from which she had turned away, this time of her own accord, toward a great light of satisfaction and certain safety and helpfulness. The doctor would know how to help her; if she only could study with him that would be enough; and away she went, hurrying down the river-shore as if she were filled with a new life and happiness.

She startled a brown rabbit from under a bush, and made him a grave salutation when he stopped and lifted his head to look at her from a convenient distance. Once she would have stopped and seated herself on the grass to amaze him with courteous attempts at friendliness, but now she only laughed again, and went quickly down the steep bank through the junipers and then hurried along the pebbly margin of the stream toward the village. She smiled to see lying side by side a flint arrowhead and a water-logged bobbin that had floated down from one of the mills, and gave one a toss over the water, while she put the other in her pocket. Her thoughts were busy enough, and though some reasons against the carrying out of her plan ventured to assert themselves, they had no hope of carrying the day, being in piteous minority, though she considered them one by one. By and by she came into the path again, and as she reached the stile she was at first glad and then sorry to see the doctor coming along the high road from the Donnell farm. She was a little dismayed at herself because she had a sudden disinclination to tell this good friend her secret.

But Dr. Leslie greeted her most cheerfully, giving her the reins when she had climbed into the wagon, and they talked of the weather and of the next day's plans as they drove home together. The girl felt a sense of guilt and a shameful lack of courage, but she was needlessly afraid that her happiness might be spoiled by a word from that quarter.

That very evening it was raining outside, and the doctor and Nan were sitting in the library opposite each other at the study-table, and as they answered some letters in order to be ready for the early morning post, they stole a look at each other now and then. The doctor laid down his pen first, and presently, as Nan with a little sigh threw hers into the tray beside it, he reached forward to where there was one of the few uncovered spaces of the dark wood of the table and drew his finger across it. They both saw the shining surface much more clearly, and as the dusty finger was held up and examined carefully by its owner, the girl tried to laugh, and then found her voice trembling as she said: "I believe I haven't forgotten to put the table in order before. I have tried to take care of the study at any rate."

"Nan dear, it isn't the least matter in the world!" said Dr. Leslie. "I think we are a little chilly here this damp night; suppose you light the fire? At any rate it will clear away all those envelopes and newspaper wrappers," and he turned his arm-chair so that it faced the fireplace, and watched the young girl as she moved about the room. She lifted one of the large sticks and stood it on one end at the side of the hearth, and the doctor noticed that she did it less easily than usual and without the old strength and alertness. He had sprung up to help her just too late, but she had indignantly refused any assistance with a half pettishness that was not a common mood with her.

"I don't see why Jane or Marilla, or whoever it was, put that heavy log on at this time of the year," said Dr. Leslie, as if it were a matter of solemn consequence. By this time he had lighted a fresh cigar, and Nan had brought her little wooden chair from some corner of the room where it had always lived since it came with her from the farm. It was a dear old-fashioned little thing, but quite too small for its owner, who had grown up tall and straight, but who had felt a sudden longing to be a child again, as she quietly took her place before the fire.

"That log?" she said, "I wonder if you will never learn that we must not burn it? I saw Marilla myself when she climbed the highest wood-pile at the farther end of the wood-house for it. I suppose all the time I have been away you have been remorselessly burning up the show logs. I don't wonder at her telling me this very morning that she was born to suffer, and suffer she supposed she must. We never used to be allowed to put papers in the fireplace, but you have gained ever so many liberties. I wonder if Marilla really thinks she has had a hard life?" the girl said, in a different tone.

"I wonder if you think yours is hard too?" asked the doctor.

And Nan did not know at first what to say. The bright light of the burning papers and the pine-cone kindlings suddenly faded out and the study seemed dark and strange by contrast; but the doctor did not speak either; he only bent towards her presently, and put his hand on the top of the girl's head and stroked the soft hair once or twice, and then gently turned it until he could see Nan's face.

Her eyes met his frankly as ever, but they were full of tears. "Yes," she said; "I wish you would talk to me. I wish you would give me a great scolding. I never needed it so much in my life. I meant to come home and be very good, and do everything I could to make you happy, but it all grows worse every day. I thought at first I was tired with the last days of school, but it is something more than that. I don't wish in the least that I were back at school, but I can't understand anything; there is something in me that wants to be busy, and can't find anything to do. I don't mean to be discontented; I don't want to be anywhere else in the world."

"There is enough to do," answered the doctor, as placidly as possible, for this was almost the first time he had noticed distinctly the mother's nature in her daughter; a restless, impatient, miserable sort of longing for The Great Something Else, as Dr. Ferris had once called it. "Don't fret yourself, Nan, yours is a short-lived sorrow; for if you have any conscience at all about doing your work you will be sure enough to find it."

"I think I have found it at last, but I don't know whether any one else will agree with me," half whispered poor Nan; while the doctor, in spite of himself, of his age, and experience, and sympathy, and self-control, could not resist a smile. "I hate to talk about myself or to be sentimental, but I want to throw my whole love and life into whatever there is waiting for me to do, and—I began to be afraid I had missed it somehow. Once I thought I should like to be a teacher, and come back here when I was through school and look after the village children. I had such splendid ideas about that, but they all faded out. I went into the school-house one day, and I thought I would rather die than be shut up there from one week's end to another."

"No," said Dr. Leslie, with grave composure. "No, I don't feel sure that you would do well to make a teacher of yourself."

"I wish that I had known when school was over that I must take care of myself, as one or two of the girls meant to do, and sometimes it seems as if I ought," said Nan, after a silence of a few minutes, and this time it was very hard to speak. "You have been so kind, and have done so much for me; I supposed at first there was money enough of my own, but I know now."

"Dear child!" the doctor exclaimed, "you will never know, unless you are left alone as I was, what a blessing it is to have somebody to take care of and to love; I have put you in the place of my own little child, and have watched you grow up here, with more thankfulness every year. Don't ever say another word to me about the money part of it. What had I to spend money for? And now I hear you say all these despairing things; but I am an old man, and I take them for what they are worth. You have a few hard months before you, perhaps, but before you know it they will be over with. Don't worry yourself; look after Marilla a little, and that new hand-maid, and drive about with me. To-morrow I must be on the road all day, and, to tell the truth, I must think over one or two of my cases before I go to bed. Won't you hand me my old prescription book? I was trying to remember something as I came home."

Nan, half-comforted, went to find the book, while Dr. Leslie, puffing his cigar-smoke very fast, looked up through the cloud abstractedly at a new ornament which had been placed above the mantel shelf since we first knew the room. Old Captain Finch had solaced his weary and painful last years by making a beautiful little model of a ship, and had left it in his will to the doctor. There never was a more touching gift, this present owner often thought, and he had put it in its place with reverent hands. A comparison of the two lives came stealing into his mind, and he held the worn prescription-book a minute before he opened it. The poor old captain waiting to be released, stranded on the inhospitable shore of this world, and eager Nan, who was sorrowfully longing for the world's war to begin. "Two idle heroes," thought Dr. Leslie, "and I neither wished to give one his discharge nor the other her commission;" but he said aloud, "Nan, we will take a six o'clock start in the morning, and go down through the sandy plains before the heat begins. I am afraid it will be one of the worst of the dog-days."

"Yes," answered Nan eagerly, and then she came close to the doctor, and looked at him a moment before she spoke, while her face shone with delight. "I am going to be a doctor, too! I have thought it would be the best thing in the world ever since I can remember. The little prescription-book was the match that lit the fire! but I have been wishing to tell you all the evening."

"We must ask Marilla," the doctor began to say, and tried to add, "What *will* she think?" but Nan hardly heard him, and did not laugh at his jokes. For she saw by his face that there was no need of teasing. And she assured herself that if he thought it was only a freak of which she would soon tire, she was quite willing to be put to the proof.

Next morning, for a wonder, Nan waked early, even before the birds had quite done singing, and it seemed a little strange that the weather should be clear and bright, and almost like June, since she was a good deal troubled.

She felt at first as if there were some unwelcome duty in her day's work, and then remembered the early drive with great pleasure, but the next minute the great meaning and responsibility of the decision she had announced the evening before burst upon her mind, and a flood of reasons assailed her why she should not keep to so uncommon a purpose. It seemed to her as if the first volume of life was ended, and as if it had been deceitfully easy, since she had been led straight-forward to this point. It amazed her to find the certainty take possession of her mind that her vocation had been made ready for her from the beginning. She had the feeling of a reformer, a radical, and even of a political agitator, as she tried to face her stormy future in that summer morning loneliness. But by the time she had finished her early breakfast, and was driving out of the gate with the doctor, the day seemed so much like other days that her trouble of mind almost disappeared. Though she had known instinctively that all the early part of her life had favored this daring project, and the next few years would hinder it if they could, still there was something within her stronger than any doubts that could possibly assail her. And instead of finding everything changed, as one always expects to do when a great change has happened to one's self, the road was so familiar, and the condition of the outer world so harmonious, that she hardly understood that she had opened a gate and shut it behind her, between that day and its yesterday. She held the reins, and the doctor was apparently in a most commonplace frame of mind. She wished he would say something about their talk of the night before, but he did not. She seemed very old to herself, older than she ever would seem again, perhaps, but the doctor had apparently relapsed into their old relations as guardian and child. Perhaps he thought she would forget her decision, and did not know how much it meant to her. He was quite provoking. He hurried the horse himself as they went up a somewhat steep ascent, and as Nan touched the not very fleet steed with the whip on the next level bit of road, she was reminded that it was a very hot morning and that they had a great way to drive. When she asked what was the matter with the patient they were on their way to see, she was answered abruptly that he suffered from a complication of disorders, which was the more aggravating because Nan had heard this answer laughed at as being much used by old Dr. Jackson, who was usually unwilling or unable to commit himself to a definite opinion. Nan fancied herself at that minute already a member of the profession, and did not like to be joked with in such a fashion, but she tried to be amused, which generosity was appreciated by her companion better than she knew.

Dr. Leslie was not much of a singer, but he presently lifted what little voice he had, and began to favor Nan with a not very successful rendering of "Bonny Doon." Every minute seemed more critical to the girl beside him, and she thought of several good ways to enter upon a discussion of her great subject, but with unusual restraint and reserve let the moments and the miles go by until the doctor had quickly stepped down from the carriage and disappeared within his patient's door. Nan's old custom of following him had been neglected for some time, since she had found that the appearance of a tall young woman had quite a different effect upon a household from that of a little child. She had formed the habit of carrying a book with her on the long drives, though she often left it untouched while she walked up and down the country roads, or even ventured upon excursions as far afield as she dared, while the doctor made his visit, which was apt to be a long one in the lonely country houses. This morning she had possessed herself of a square, thin volume which gave lists and plates of the nerve system of the human body. The doctor had nearly laughed aloud when he caught sight of it, and when Nan opened it with decision and gravity and read the first page slowly, she was conscious of a lack of interest in her subject. She had lost the great enthusiasm of the night before, and felt like the little heap of ashes which such a burning and heroic self might well have left.

Presently she went strolling down the road, gathering some large leaves on her way, and stopped at the brook, where she pulled up some bits of a strange water-weed, and made them into a damp, round bundle with the leaves and a bit of string. This was a rare plant which they had both noticed the day before, and they had taken some specimens then, Nan being at this time an ardent botanist, but these had withered and been lost, also, on the way home.

Dr. Leslie was in even less of a hurry than usual, and when he came out he looked very much pleased. "I never was more thankful in my life," he said eagerly, as soon as he was within convenient distance. "That poor fellow was at death's door yesterday, and when I saw his wife and little children, and thought his life was all that stood between them and miserable destitution, it seemed to me that I *must* save it! This morning he is as bright as a dollar, but I have been dreading to go into that house ever since I left it yesterday noon. They didn't in the least know how narrow a chance he had. And it isn't the first time I have been chief mourner. Poor souls! they don't dread their troubles half so much as I do. He will have a good little farm here in another year or two, it only needs draining to be excellent land, and he knows that." The doctor turned and looked back over the few acres with great pleasure. "Now we'll go and see about old Mrs. Willet, though I don't believe there's any great need of it. She belongs to one of two very bad classes of patients. It makes me so angry to hear her cough twice as much as need be. In your practice," he continued soberly, "you must remember that there is danger of giving too strong doses to such a sufferer, and too light ones to the friends who insist there is nothing the matter with them. I wouldn't give much for a doctor who can't see for himself in most cases, but not always,—not always."

The doctor was in such a hospitable frame of mind that nobody could have helped telling him anything, and happily he made an excellent introduction for Nan's secret by inquiring how she had got on with her studies, but she directed his attention to the wet plants in the bottom of the carriage, which were complimented before she said, a minute afterward, "Oh, I wonder if I shall make a mistake? I was afraid you would laugh at me, and think it was all nonsense."

"Dear me, no," replied the doctor. "You will be the successor of Mrs. Martin Dyer, and the admiration of the neighborhood;" but changing his tone quickly, he said: "I am going to teach you all I can, just as long as you have any wish to learn. It has not done you a bit of harm to know something about medicine, and I believe in your studying it more than you do yourself. I have always thought about it. But you are very young; there's plenty of time, and I don't mean to be hurried; you must remember that,—though I see your fitness and peculiar adaptability a great deal better than you can these twenty years yet. You will be growing happier these next few years at any rate, however impossible life has seemed to you lately."

"I suppose there will be a great many obstacles," reflected Nan, with an absence of her usual spirit.

"Obstacles! Yes," answered Dr. Leslie, vigorously. "Of course there will be; it is climbing a long hill to try to study medicine or to study anything else. And if you are going to fear obstacles you will have a poor chance at success. There are just as many reasons as you will stop to count up why you should not do your plain duty, but if you are going to make anything of yourself you must go straight ahead, taking it for granted that there will be opposition enough, but doing what is right all the same. I suppose I have repeated to you fifty times what old Friend Meadows told me years ago; he was a great success at money-making, and once I asked him to give me some advice about a piece of property. 'Friend Leslie,' says he, 'thy own opinion is the best for thee; if thee asks ten people what to do, they will tell thee ten things, and then thee does n't know as much as when thee set out,' " and Dr. Leslie, growing very much in earnest, reached forward for the whip. "I want you to be a good woman, and I want you to be all the use you can," he said. "It seems to me like stealing, for men and women to live in the world and do nothing to make it better. You have thought a great deal about this, and so have I, and now we will do the best we can at making a good doctor of you. I don't care whether people think it is a proper vocation for women or not. It seems to me that it is more than proper for you, and God has given you a fitness for it which it is a shame to waste. And if you ever hesitate and regret what you have said, you won't have done yourself any harm by learning how to take care of your own health and other people's."

"But I shall never regret it," said Nan stoutly. "I don't believe I should ever be fit for anything else, and you know as well as I that I must have something to do. I used to wish over and over again that I was a boy, when I was a little thing down at the farm, and the only reason I had in the world was that I could be a doctor, like you."

"Better than that, I hope," said Dr. Leslie. "But you must n't think it will be a short piece of work; it will take more patience than you are ready to give just now, and we will go on quietly and let it grow by the way, like your water-weed here. If you don't drive a little faster, Sister Willet may be gathered before we get to her;" and this being a somewhat unwise and hysterical patient, whose recovery was not in the least despaired of, Dr. Leslie and his young companion were heartlessly merry over her case.

The doctor had been unprepared for such an episode; outwardly, life had seemed to flow so easily from one set of circumstances to the next, and the changes had been so gradual and so natural. He had looked forward with such certainty to Nan's future, that it seemed strange that the formal acceptance of such an inevitable idea as her studying medicine should have troubled her so much.

Separated as he was from the groups of men and women who are responsible for what we call the opinion of society, and independent himself of any fettering conventionalities, he had grown careless of what anybody might say. He only hoped, since his ward had found her proper work, that she would hold to it, and of this he had little doubt. The girl herself quickly lost sight of the fancied difficulty of making the great decision, and, as is usually the case, saw all the first objections and hindrances fade away into a dim distance, and grow less and less noticeable. And more than that, it seemed to her as if she had taken every step of her life straight toward this choice of a profession. So many things she had never understood before, now became perfectly clear and evident proofs that, outside her own preferences and choices, a wise purpose had been at work with her and for her. So it all appeared more natural every day, and while she knew that the excitement and formality of the first very uncomfortable day or two had proved her freedom of choice, it seemed the more impossible that she should have shirked this great commission and trust for which nature had fitted her.

XIII

A STRAIGHT COURSE

T HE NEXT YEAR or two was spent in quiet life at home. It was made evident that, beside her inclination and natural fitness for her chosen work, our student was also developing the other most important requisite, a capacity for hard study and patient continuance. There had been as little said as possible about the plan, but it was not long before the propriety of it became a favorite subject of discussion. It is quite unnecessary, perhaps, to state that everybody had his or her own opinion of the wisdom of such a course, and both Dr. Leslie and his ward suffered much reproach and questioning, as the comments ranged from indignation to amusement. But it was as true of Nan's calling, as of all others, that it would be her own failure to make it respected from which any just contempt might come, and she had thrown herself into her chosen career with such zeal, and pride, and affectionate desire to please her teacher, that the small public who had at first jeered or condemned her came at last to accepting the thing as inevitable and a matter of course, even if they did not actually approve. There was such a vigorous determination in the minds of the doctor and his pupil that Nan should not only be a doctor but a good one, that anything less than a decided fitness for the profession would have doomed them both to disappointment, even with such unwearied effort and painstaking. In the earlier years of his practice Dr. Leslie had been much sought as an instructor, but he had long since begun to deny the young men who had wished to be his students, though hardly one had ever gone from the neighborhood of Oldfields who did not owe much to him for his wise suggestions and practical help.

He patiently taught this eager young scholar day by day, and gave her, as fast as he could, the benefit of the wisdom which he had gained through faithful devotion to his business and the persistent study of many years. Nan followed step by step, and, while becoming more conscious of her own ignorance and of the uncertainties and the laws of the practice of medicine with every week's study, knew better and better that it is resource, and bravery, and being able to think for one's self, that make a physician worth anything. There must be an instinct that recognizes a disease and suggests its remedy, as much as an instinct that finds the right notes and harmonies for a composer of music, or the colors for a true artist's picture, or the results of figures for a mathematician. Men and women may learn these callings from others; may practice all the combinations until they can carry them through with a greater or less degree of unconsciousness of brain and fingers; but there is something needed beside even drill and experience; every student of medicine should be fitted by nature with a power of insight, a gift for his business, for knowing what is the right thing to do, and the right time and way to do it; must have this God-given power in his own nature of using and discovering the resources of medicine without constant reliance upon the books or the fashion. Some men use their ability for their own good and renown, and some think first of the good of others, and as the great poet tells the truths of God, and makes other souls wiser and stronger and fitter for action, so the great doctor works for the body's health, and tries to keep human beings free from the failures that come from neglect and ignorance, and ready to be the soul's instrument of action and service in this world. It is not to keep us from death, it is no superstitious avoidance of the next life, that should call loudest for the physician's skill; but the necessity of teaching and remedying the inferior bodies which have come to us through either our ancestors' foolishness or our own. So few people know even what true and complete physical life is, much less anything of the spiritual existence that is already possible, and so few listen to what the best doctors are trying their best to teach. While half-alive people think it no wrong to bring into the world human beings with even less vitality than themselves, and take no pains to keep the simplest laws of health, or to teach their children to do so, just so long there will be plenty of sorrow of an avoidable kind, and thousands of shipwrecked, and failing, and inadequate, and useless lives in the fullest sense of the word. How can those who preach to the soul hope to be heard by those who do not even make the best of their bodies? but alas, the convenience and easiness, or pleasure, of the present moment is allowed to become the cause of an endless series of terrible effects, which go down into the distance of the future, multiplying themselves a thousandfold.

The doctor told Nan many curious things as they drove about together: certain traits of certain families, and how the Dyers were of strong constitution, and lived to a great age in spite of severe illnesses and accidents and all manner of unfavorable conditions; while the Dunnells, who looked a great deal stronger, were sensitive, and deficient in vitality, so that an apparently slight attack of disease quickly proved fatal. And so Nan knew that one thing to be considered was the family, and another the individual variation, and she began to recognize the people who might be treated fearlessly, because they were safe to form a league with against any ailment, being responsive to medicines, and straightforward in their departure from or return to a state of health; others being treacherous and hard to control; full of surprises, and baffling a doctor with their feints and follies of symptoms; while all the time Death himself was making ready for a last, fatal siege; these all being the representatives of types which might be found everywhere. Often Dr. Leslie would be found eagerly praising some useful old-fashioned drugs which had been foolishly neglected by those who liked to experiment with newer remedies and be "up with the times," as they called their not very intelligent dependence upon the treatment in vogue at the moment among the younger men of certain cliques, to some of whom the brilliant operation was more important than its damaging result. There was, even in those days, a haphazard way of doctoring, in which the health of the patient was secondary to the promotion of new theories, and the young scholar who could write a puzzlingly technical paper too often outranked the old practitioner who conquered some malignant disorder single-handed, where even the malpractice of the patient and his friends had stood like a lion in the way.

But Dr. Leslie was always trying to get at the truth, and nobody recognized more clearly the service which the reverent and truly progressive younger men were rendering to the profession. He added many new publications to his subscription list, and gleaned here and there those notes which he knew would be helpful, and which were suited to the degree of knowledge which his apprentice had already gained. It is needless to say what pleasure it gave him, and what evening talks they had together; what histories of former victories and defeats and curious discoveries were combined, like a bit of novel-reading, with Nan's diligent devotion to her course of study. And presently the girl would take a step or two alone, and even make a visit by herself to see if anything chanced to be needed when a case was progressing favorably, and with the excuse of the doctor's business or over-fatigue. And the physicians of the neighboring towns, who came together occasionally for each other's assistance, most of whom had known Nan from her childhood, though at first they had shrunk from speaking of many details of their professional work in her hearing, and covered their meaning, like the ostriches' heads, in the sand of a Latin cognomen, were soon set at their ease by Nan's unconsciousness of either shamefacedness or disgust, and one by one grew interested in her career, and hopeful of her success.

It is impossible to describe the importance of such experiences as these in forming the character of the young girl's power of resource, and wealth of self-reliance and practical experience. Sometimes in houses where she would have felt at least liberty to go only as spectator and scholar of medicine, Dr. Leslie insisted upon establishing her for a few days as chief nurse and overseer, and before Nan had been at work many months her teacher found her of great use, and grew more proud and glad day by day as he watched her determination, her enthusiasm, and her excellent progress. Over and over again he said to himself, or to her, that she was doing the work for which nature had meant her, and when the time came for her to go away from Oldfields, it seemed more impossible than it ever had before that he should get on without her, at home, or as an independent human being, who was following reverently in the path he had chosen so many years before. For her sake he had reached out again toward many acquaintances from whom he had drifted away, and he made many short journeys to Boston or to New York, and was pleased at his hearty welcome back to the medical meetings he had hardly entered during so many years. He missed not a few old friends, but he quickly made new ones. He was vastly pleased when the younger men seemed glad to hear him speak, and it was often proved that either through study or experience he had caught at some fresh knowledge of which his associates were still ignorant. He had laughingly accused himself of being a rusty country doctor and old fogy who had not kept up with the times; but many a letter followed him home, with thanks for some helpful suggestion or advice as to the management of a troublesome case. He was too far away to give room for any danger of professional jealousy, or for the infringement of that ever lengthening code of etiquette so important to the sensitive medical mind. Therefore he had only much pleasure and a fine tribute of recognition and honor, and he smiled more than once as he sat in the quiet Oldfields study before the fire, and looked up at Captain Finch's little ship, and told Nan of his town experiences, not always omitting, though attempting to deprecate, the compliments, in some half-hour when they were on peculiarly good terms with each other. And Nan believed there could be no better doctor in the world, and stoutly told him so, and yet listened only half-convinced when he said that he had a great mind to go to town and open an office, and make a specialty of treating diseases of the heart, since everybody had a specialty nowadays. He never felt so ready for practice as now, but Nan somehow could not bear the thought of his being anywhere but in his home. For herself, she would have been ready to venture anything if it would further her ever-growing purpose; but that Dr. Leslie should begin a new career or contest with the world seemed impossible. He was not so strong as he used to be, and he was already famous among his fellows. She would help him with his work by and by even more than now, and her own chosen calling of a country doctor was the dearer to her, because he had followed it so gallantly before her loving and admiring eyes. But Dr. Leslie built many a castle in the air, with himself and a great city practice for tenants, and said that it would be a capital thing for Nan; she could go on with it alone by and by. It was astonishing how little some of the city doctors knew: they relied upon each other too much; they should all be forced to drive over hill and dale, and be knocked about in a hard country practice for eight or ten years before they went to town. "Plenty of time to read their books in June and January," the doctor would grumble to himself, and turn to look fondly at the long rows of his dear library acquaintances, his Braithwaites and Lancets, and their younger brothers, beside the first new Sydenham Society's books, with their clumsy blot of gilding. And he would stand sometimes with his hands behind him and look at the many familiar rows of brown leather-covered volumes, most of them delightfully worn with his own use and that of the other physicians whose generous friend and constant instructor he had been through years of sometimes stormy but usually friendly intercourse and association.

When people in general had grown tired of discussing this strange freak and purpose of the doctor and his ward, and had become familiar with Nan's persistent interest and occupation in her studies, there came a time of great discontent to the two persons most concerned. For it was impossible to disguise the fact that the time had again come for the girl to go away from home. They had always looked forward to this, and directed much thought and action toward it, and yet they decided with great regret upon setting a new train of things in motion.

While it was well enough and useful enough that Nan should go on with her present mode of life, they both had a wider outlook, and though with the excuse of her youthfulness they had put off her departure as long as possible, still almost without any discussion it was decided that she must enter the medical school to go through with its course of instruction formally, and receive its authority to practice her profession. They both felt that this held a great many unpleasantnesses among its store of benefits. Nan was no longer to be shielded and protected and guided by some one whose wisdom she rarely questioned, but must make her own decisions instead, and give from her own bounty, and stand in her lot and place. Her later school-days were sure to be more trying than her earlier ones, as they carried her into deeper waters of scholarship, and were more important to her future position before the public.

If a young man plans the same course, everything conspires to help him and forward him, and the very fact of his having chosen one of the learned professions gives him a certain social preëminence and dignity. But in the days of Nan's student life it was just the reverse. Though she had been directed toward such a purpose entirely by her singular talent, instead of by the motives of expediency which rule the decisions of a large proportion of the young men who study medicine, she found little encouragement either from the quality of the school or the interest of society in general. There were times when she actually resented the prospect of the many weeks which she must spend in listening to inferior instruction before gaining a diploma, which was only a formal seal of disapproval in most persons' eyes. And yet, when she remembered her perfect certainty that she was doing the right thing, and remembered what renown some women physicians had won, and the avenues of usefulness which lay open to her on every side, there was no real drawing back, but rather a proud certainty of her most womanly and respectable calling, and a reverent desire to make the best use possible of the gifts God had certainly not made a mistake in giving her. "If He meant I should be a doctor," the girl told herself, "the best thing I can do is to try to be a good one."

So Nan packed her boxes and said good-by to Mrs. Graham, who looked wistful and doubtful, but blessed her most heartily, saying she should miss her sadly in the winter. And Marilla, who had unexpectedly reserved her opinion of late, made believe that she was very busy in the pantry, just as she had done when Nan was being launched for boarding-school. She shook her own floury hands vigorously, and offered one at last, muffled in her apron, and wished our friend good luck, with considerable friendliness, mentioning that she should be glad if Nan would say when she wrote home what shapes they seemed to be wearing for bonnets in the city, though she supposed they would be flaunting for Oldfields anyway. The doctor was going too, and they started for the station much too early for the train, since Dr. Leslie always suffered from a nervous dread of having an unavoidable summons to a distant patient at the last moment.

And when the examinations were over, and Nan had been matriculated, and the doctor had somewhat contemptuously overlooked the building and its capabilities, and had compared those students whom he saw with his remembrance of his own class, and triumphantly picked out a face and figure that looked hopeful here and there; he told himself that like all new growths it was feeble yet, and needed girls like his Nan, with high moral purpose and excellent capacity, who would make the college strong and to be respected. Not such doctors as several of whom he reminded himself, who were disgracing their sex, but those whose lives were ruled by a pettiness of detail, a lack of power, and an absence of high aim. Somehow both our friends lost much of the feeling that Nan was doing a peculiar thing, when they saw so many others following the same path. And having seen Nan more than half-settled in her winter quarters, and knowing that one or two of her former school friends had given her a delighted and most friendly welcome, and having made a few visits to the people whom he fancied would help her in one way or another, Dr. Leslie said good-by, and turned his face homeward, feeling more lonely than he had felt in a great many years before. He thought about Nan a great deal on the journey, though he had provided himself with some most desirable new books. He was thankful he had been able to do a kind turn for one of the most influential doctors, who had cheerfully promised to put some special advantages in Nan's way; but when he reached home the house seemed very empty, and he missed his gay companion as he drove along the country roads. After the days began to grow longer, and the sun brighter, such pleasant letters came from the absent scholar, that the doctor took heart more and more, and went over to Mrs. Graham with almost every fresh bit of news. She smiled, and listened, and applauded, and one day said with delightful cordiality that she wished there were more girls who cared whether their lives really amounted to anything.

But not every one had a talent which was such a stimulus as Nan's.

"Nothing succeeds like success," rejoined the doctor cheerfully, "I always knew the child would do the best she could."

XIV

MISS PRINCE OF DUNPORT

WHILE all these years were passing, Miss Anna Prince the elder was living quietly in Dunport, and she had changed so little that her friends frequently complimented her upon such continued youthfulness. She had by no means forgotten the two greatest among the many losses and sorrows of her life, but the first sharp pain of them was long since over with. The lover from whom she had parted for the sake of a petty misunderstanding had married afterward and died early; but he had left a son of whom Miss Prince was very proud and fond; and she had given him the place in her heart which should have belonged to her own niece. When she thought of the other trial, she believed herself, still, more sinned against than sinning, and gave herself frequent assurances that it had been impossible to act otherwise at the time of her brother's death and his wife's strange behavior afterward. And she had persuaded her conscience to be quiet, until at last, with the ideal of a suspicious, uncongenial, disagreeable group of rustics in her mind, she thought it was well ordered by Heaven that she had been spared any closer intercourse.

Miss Prince was a proud and stately woman of the old New England type: more colonial than American perhaps, and quite provincial in her traditions and prejudices. She was highly respected in her native town, where she was a prominent figure in society. Nobody was more generous and kind or public spirited, as her friends often said, and young George Gerry was well-rewarded, though he gave her great pleasure by his evident affection and interest. He liked to pay frequent visits to his old friend, and to talk with her. She had been a very attractive girl long ago, and the best of her charms had not faded yet; the young man was always welcomed warmly, and had more than once been helped in his projects. His mother was a feeble woman, who took little interest in anything outside her own doors; and he liked himself better as he sat in Miss Prince's parlor than anywhere else. We are always fond of the society of our best selves, and though he was popular with the rest of his townspeople, he somehow could not help trying always to be especially agreeable to Miss Prince.

Although she was apparently free from regrets, and very well satisfied with life, even her best friends did not know how lonely her life had seemed to her, or how sadly hurt she had been by the shame and sorrow of her only brother's marriage. The thought of his child and of the impossibility of taking her to her heart and home had been like a nightmare at first, and yet Miss Prince lacked courage to break down the barriers, and to at least know the worst. She kept the two ideas of the actual niece and the ideal one whom she might have loved so much distinct and separate in her mind, and was divided between a longing to see the girl and a fierce dread of her sudden appearance. She had forbidden any allusion to the subject years and years before, and so had prevented herself from hearing good news as well as bad; though she had always been careful that the small yearly remittance should be promptly sent, and was impatient to receive the formal acknowledgment of it, which she instantly took pains to destroy. She sometimes in these days thought about making her will; there was no hurry about it, but it would be only fair to provide for her nearest of kin, while she was always certain that she should not let all her money and the old house with its handsome furnishings go into such unworthy hands. It was a very hard question to settle, and she thought of it as little as possible, and was sure there was nothing to prevent her living a great many years yet. She loved her old home dearly, and was even proud of it, and had always taken great care of the details of its government. She never had been foolish enough to make away with her handsome mahogany furniture, and to replace it with cheaper and less comfortable chairs and tables, as many of her neighbors had done, and had taken an obstinate satisfaction all through the years when it seemed quite out of date, in insisting upon the polishing of the fine wood and the many brass handles, and of late she had been reaping a reward for her constancy. It had been a marvel to certain progressive people that a person of her comfortable estate should be willing to reflect that there was not a marble-topped table in her house, until it slowly dawned upon them

at last that she was mistress of the finest house in town. Outwardly, it was painted white and stood close upon the street,
with a few steep front steps coming abruptly down into the
middle of the narrow sidewalk; its interior was spacious and
very imposing, not only for the time it was built in the last
century, but for any other time. Miss Prince's ancestors had
belonged to some of the most distinguished among the colonial families, which fact she neither appeared to remember
nor consented to forget; and, as often happened in the seaport towns of New England, there had been one or two men
in every generation who had followed the sea. Her own father
had been among the number, and the closets of the old house
were well provided with rare china and fine old English
crockery that would drive an enthusiastic collector to distrac-
tion. The carved woodwork of the railings and wainscotings
and cornices had been devised by ingenious and patient
craftsmen, and the same portraits and old engravings hung
upon the walls that had been there when its mistress could
first remember. She had always been so well suited with her
home that she had never desired to change it in any particular. Her maids were well drilled to their duties, and Priscilla,
who was chief of the staff, had been in that dignified position
for many years. If Miss Prince's grandmother could return to
Dunport from another world, she would hardly believe that
she had left her earthly home for a day, it presented so nearly
the same appearance.

But however conscientiously the effort had been made to
keep up the old reputation for hospitality, it had somehow
been a failure, and Miss Prince had given fewer entertainments every year. Long ago, while she was still a young
woman, she had begun to wear a certain quaint and elderly
manner, which might have come from association with such
antiquated household gods and a desire to match well with
her beloved surroundings. A great many of her early friends
had died, and she was not the sort of person who can easily
form new ties of intimate friendship. She was very loyal to
those who were still left, and, as has been said, her interest in
George Gerry, who was his father's namesake and likeness,
was a very great pleasure to her. Some persons liked to whisper together now and then about the mysterious niece, who

was never mentioned otherwise. But though curiosity had led to a partial knowledge of our heroine's not unfavorable aspect and circumstances, nobody ever dared to give such information to the person who should have been most interested.

This was one of the standard long stories of Dunport with which old residents liked to regale new-comers, and handsome Jack Prince was the hero of a most edifying romance, being represented as a victim of the Prince pride, as his sister had been before him. His life had been ruined, and he had begged his wretched wife at the last to bring him home to Dunport, alive or dead. The woman had treated Miss Prince with shameful impudence and had disappeared afterward. The child had been brought up with her own people, and it was understood that Miss Prince's efforts to have any connection with them were all thwarted. Lately it had become known that the girl's guardian was a very fine man and was taking a great interest in her. But the reader will imagine how this story grew and changed in different people's minds. Some persons insisted that Miss Prince had declined to see her brother's child, and others that it was denied her. It was often said in these days that Nan must be free to do as she chose, but it was more than likely that she had assumed the prejudices against her aunt with which she must have become most familiar.

As for Miss Prince herself, she had long ago become convinced that there was nothing to be done in this matter. After one has followed a certain course for some time, everything seems to persuade one that no other is possible. Sometimes she feared that an excitement and danger lurked in her future, but, after all, her days went by so calmly, and nearer things seemed so much more important than this vague sorrow and dread, that she went to and fro in the Dunport streets, and was courteous and kind in her own house, and read a sensible book now and then, and spent her time as benevolently and respectably as possible. She was indeed an admirable member of society, who had suffered very much in her youth, and those who knew her well could not be too glad that her later years were passing far less unhappily than most people's.

In the days when her niece had lately finished her first winter at the medical school, Miss Prince had just freed herself from the responsibility of some slight repairs which the house had needed. She had been in many ways much more occupied than usual, and had given hardly a thought to more remote affairs. At last there had come an evening when she felt at leisure, and happily Miss Fraley, one of her earliest friends, had come to pay her a visit. The two ladies sat at the front windows of the west parlor looking out upon the street, while the hostess expressed her gratitude that the overturning of her household affairs was at an end, and that she was all in order for summer. They talked about the damage and discomfort inflicted by masons, and the general havoc which follows a small piece of fallen ceiling. Miss Prince, having made a final round of inspection just after tea, had ascertained that the last of the white dimity curtains and coverings were in their places upstairs in the bedrooms, and her love of order was satisfied. She had complimented Priscilla, and made her and the maids the customary spring present, and had returned to her evening post of observation at the parlor window just as Miss Fraley came in. She was not in the mood for receiving guests, being a trifle tired, but Eunice Fraley was a mild little creature, with a gentle, deprecatory manner which had always appealed to Miss Prince's more chivalrous nature. Besides, she knew this to be a most true and affectionate friend, who had also the gift of appearing when everything was ready for her, as the bluebirds come, and the robins, in the early days of spring.

"I wish I could say that our house was all in order but one closet," said the guest, in a more melancholy tone than usual. "I believe we are more behind-hand than ever this year. You know we have Susan's children with us for a fortnight while she goes away for a rest, and they have been a good deal of care. I think mother is getting tired of them now, though she was very eager to have a visit from them at first. She said this morning that the little girl was worse than a kitten in a fit, and she did hope that Susan wouldn't think it best to pass another week away."

Miss Prince laughed a little, and so did Miss Fraley after a moment's hesitation. She seemed to be in a somewhat sentimental and introspective mood as she looked out of the window in the May twilight.

"I so often feel as if I were not accomplishing anything," she said sadly. "It came over me to-day that here I am, really an old woman, and I am just about where I first started,— doing the same things over and over and no better than ever. I haven't the gift of style; anybody else might have done my work just as well, I am afraid; I am sure the world would have got along just as well without me. Mother has been so active, and has reached such a great age, that perhaps it hasn't been much advantage to me. I have only learned to depend upon her instead of myself. I begin to see that I should have amounted to a great deal more if I had had a home of my own. I sometimes wish that I were as free to go and come as you are, Nancy."

But Miss Prince's thoughts were pleased to take a severely practical turn: "I'm not in the least free," she answered cheerfully. "I believe you need something to strengthen you, Eunice. I haven't seen you so out of spirits for a great while. Free! why I'm tied to this house as if I were the knocker on the front door; and I certainly have a great deal of care. I put the utmost confidence in Priscilla, but those nieces of hers would be going wherever they chose, from garret to cellar, before I was ten miles away from Dunport. I have let the cook go away for a week, and Phœbe and Priscilla are alone. Phœbe is a good little creature; I only hope she won't be married within six months, for I don't know when I have liked a young girl so well. Priscilla was anxious I should take that black-eyed daughter of her brother's, and was quite hurt because I refused."

"I dare say you were right," acknowledged Miss Fraley, though she could not exactly see the obstacles to her friend's freedom in such strong light as was expected.

"I know that it must be difficult for you sometimes," resumed the hostess presently, in a more sympathetic tone. "Your mother naturally finds it hard to give up the rule. We can't expect her to look at life as younger persons do."

"I don't expect it," said poor Miss Fraley appealingly, "and I am sure I try to be considerate; but how would you like it, to be treated as if you were sixteen instead of nearly sixty? I know it says in the Bible that children should obey their parents, but there is no such commandment, that I can see, to women who are old enough to be grandmothers themselves. It does make me perfectly miserable to have everything questioned and talked over that I do; but I know I ought not to say such things. I suppose I shall lie awake half the night grieving over it. You know I have the greatest respect for mother's judgment; I'm sure I don't know what in the world I should do without her."

"You are too yielding, Eunice," said Miss Prince kindly. "You try to please everybody, and that's your way of pleasing yourself; but, after all, I believe we give everybody more satisfaction when we hold fast to our own ideas of right and wrong. There have been a great many friends who were more than willing to give me their advice in all these years that I have been living alone; but I have always made up my mind and gone straight ahead. I have no doubt I should be very impatient now of much comment and talking over; and yet there are so many times when I would give anything to see father or mother for a little while. I haven't suffered from living alone as much as some persons do, but I often feel very sad and lonely when I sit here and think about the past. Dear me! here is Phœbe with the lights, and I dare say it is just as well. I am going to ask you to go up stairs and see the fresh paint, and how ship-shape we are at last, as father used to say."

Miss Fraley rose at once, with an expression of pleasure, and the two friends made a leisurely tour of the old house which seemed all ready for a large family, and though its owner apparently enjoyed her freedom and dominion, it all looked deserted and empty to her guest. They lingered together in the wide lower hall, and parted with unusual affection. This was by no means the first hint that had been given of a somewhat fettered and disappointing home life, though Miss Fraley would have shuddered at the thought of any such report's being sent abroad.

"Send the children round to see me," said Miss Prince, by way of parting benediction. "They can play in the garden an hour or two, and it will be a change for them and for you;" which invitation was gratefully accepted, though Miss Eunice smiled at the idea of their needing a change, when they were sure to be on every wharf in town in the course of the day, and already knew more people in Dunport than she did.

The next morning Miss Prince's sense of general well-being seemed to have deserted her altogether. She was overshadowed by a fear of impending disaster and felt strangely tired and dissatisfied. But she did not believe in moping, and only assured herself that she must make the day an easy one. So, being strong against tides, as some old poet says of the whale, Miss Prince descended the stairs calmly, and advised Priscilla to put off the special work that had been planned until still later in the week. "You had better ask your sister to come and spend the day with you and have a good, quiet visit," which permission Priscilla received without comment, being a person of few words; but she looked pleased, and while her mistress went down the garden walk to breathe the fresh morning air, she concocted a small omelet as an unexpected addition to the breakfast. Miss Prince was very fond of an omelet, but Priscilla, in spite of all her good qualities, was liable to occasional fits of offishness and depression, and in those seasons kept her employer, in one way or another, on short commons.

The day began serenely. It was the morning for the Dunport weekly paper, which Miss Prince sat down at once to read, making her invariable reproachful remark that there was nothing in it, after having devoted herself to this duty for an hour or more. Then she mounted to the upper floor of her house to put away a blanket which had been overlooked in the spring packing of the camphor-wood chests which stood in a solemn row in the north corner of the garret. There were three dormer windows in the front of the garret-roof, and one of these had been a favorite abiding-place in her youth. She had played with her prim Dutch dolls there in her childhood, and she could remember spending hour after hour watching for her father's ship when the family had begun to expect him home at the end of a long voyage. She remembered with a smile how grieved she had been because once he came into port late in the night and surprised them all early in the morning, but he had made amends by taking her back with him when he hurried on board again after a hasty greeting. Miss Prince lived that morning over again as she stood there, old and gray and alone in the world. She could see again the great weather-beaten and tar-darkened ship, and even the wizened monkey which belonged to one of the sailors. She lingered at her father's side admiringly, and felt the tears come into her eyes once more when he gave her a taste of the fiery contents of his tumbler. They were all in his cabin; old Captain Dunn and Captain Denny and Captain Peterbeck were sitting round the little table, also provided with tumblers, as they listened eagerly to the story of the voyage. The sailors came now and then for orders; Nancy thought her handsome father, with his bronzed cheeks and white forehead and curly hair, was every inch a king. He was her hero, and nothing could please her so much to the end of her days as to have somebody announce, whether from actual knowledge or hearsay, that Captain Jack Prince was the best shipmaster that ever sailed out of Dunport. . . . She always was sure there were some presents stored away for herself and young Jack, her brother, in one of the lockers of the little cabin. Poor Jack! how he used to frighten her by climbing the shrouds and waving his cap from almost inaccessible heights. Poor Jack! and Miss Prince climbed the step to look down the harbor again, as if the ship were more than thirty days out from Amsterdam, and might be expected at any time if the voyage had been favorable.

The house was at no great distance from the water side, though the crowded buildings obscured the view from the lower stories. There was nothing coming in from sea but a steam-tug, which did not harmonize with these pleasant reminiscences, though as Miss Prince raised the window a fine salt breeze entered, well warmed with the May sunshine. It had the flavor of tar and the spirit of the high seas, and for a wonder there could be heard the knocking of shipwrights' hammers, which in old times were never silent in the town. As she sat there for a few minutes in the window seat, there came to her other recollections of her later girlhood, when she had stolen to this corner for the sake of being alone with her pleasant thoughts, though she had cried there many an hour after Jack's behavior had given them the sorrow they hardly would own to each other. She remembered hearing her father's angry voice down stairs. No! she would not think of that again, why should she? and she shut the window and went back to be sure that she had locked the camphor chest, and hung its key on the flat-headed rusty nail overhead. Miss Prince heard some one open and shut the front door as she went down, and in the small front room she found Captain Walter Parish, who held a high place among her most intimate friends. He was her cousin, and had become her general adviser and counselor. He sometimes called himself laughingly the ship's husband, for it was he who transacted most of Miss Prince's important business, and selected her paint and shingles and her garden seeds beside, and made and mended her pens. He liked to be useful and agreeable, but he had not that satisfaction in his own home, for his wife had been a most efficient person to begin with, and during his absences at sea in early life had grown entirely self-reliant. The captain joked about it merrily, but he nevertheless liked to feel that he was still important, and Miss Prince generously told him, from time to time, that she did not know how she should get on without him, and considerately kept up the fiction of not wishing to take up his time when he must be busy with his own affairs.

"How are you this fine morning, Cousin Nancy?" said the captain gallantly. "I called to say that Jerry Martin will be here to-morrow without fail. It seems he thought you would send him word when you wanted him next, and he has been working for himself. I don't think the garden will suffer, we have had so much cold weather. And here is a letter I took from the office." He handed it to Miss Prince with a questioning look; he knew the handwriting of her few correspondents almost as well as she, and this was a stranger's.

"Perhaps it is a receipt for my subscription to the"— But Miss Prince never finished the sentence, for when she had fairly taken the letter into her hand, the very touch of it seemed to send a tinge of ashen gray like some quick poison over her face. She stood still, looking at it, then flushed crimson, and sat down in the nearest chair, as if it were impossible to hold herself upright. The captain was uncertain what he ought to do.

"I hope you have n't heard bad news," he said presently, for

Miss Prince had leaned back in the arm-chair and covered her eyes with one hand, while the letter was tightly held in the other.

"It is from my niece," she answered, slowly.

"You don't mean it's from Jack's daughter?" inquired the captain, not without eagerness. He never had suspected such a thing; the only explanation which had suggested itself to his mind was that Miss Prince had been investing some of her money without his advice or knowledge, and he had gone so far as to tell himself that it was just like a woman, and quite good enough for her if she had lost it. "I never thought of its being from her," he said, a little bewildered, for the captain was not a man of quick wit; his powers of reflection served him better. "Well, aren't you going to tell me what she has to say for herself?"

"She proposes to make me a visit," answered Miss Prince, trying to smile as she handed him the little sheet of paper which she had unconsciously crumpled together; but she did not give even one glance at his face as he read it, though she thought it a distressingly long time before he spoke.

"I must say that this is a very good letter, very respectful and lady-like," said the captain honestly, though he felt as if he had been expected to condemn it, and proceeded to read it through again, this time aloud: —

MY DEAR AUNT, — I cannot think it is right that we do not know each other. I should like to go to Dunport for a day some time next month; but if you do not wish to see me you have only to tell me so, and I will not trouble you.

Yours sincerely,
ANNA PRINCE.

"A very good handwriting, too," the captain remarked, and then gathered courage to say that he supposed Miss Prince would give her niece the permission for which she asked. "I have been told that she is a very fine girl," he ventured, as if he were poor Nan's ambassador; and at this Miss Prince's patience gave way.

"Yes, I shall ask her to come, but I do not wish anything said about it; it need not be made the talk of the town." She answered her cousin angrily, and then felt as if she had been unjust. "Do not mind me, Walter," she said; "it has been a terrible grief and trouble to me all these years. Perhaps if I had gone to see those people, and told them all I felt, they would have pitied me, and not blamed me, and so everything would have been better, but it is too late now. I don't know what sort of a person my own niece is, and I wish that I need never find out, but I shall try to do my duty."

The captain was tender-hearted, and seemed quite unmanned, but he gave his eyes a sudden stroke with his hand and turned to go away. "You will command me, Nancy, if I can be of service to you?" he inquired, and his cousin bowed her head in assent. It was, indeed, a dismal hour of the family history.

For some time Miss Prince did not move, except as she watched Captain Parish cross the street and take his leisurely way along the uneven pavement. She was almost tempted to call him back, and felt as if he were the last friend she had in the world, and was leaving her forever. But after she had allowed the worst of the miserable shock to spend itself, she summoned the stern energy for which she was famous, and going with slower steps than usual to the next room, she unlocked the desk of the ponderous secretary and seated herself to write. Before many minutes had passed the letter was folded, and sealed, and addressed, and the next evening Nan was reading it at Oldfields. She was grateful for being asked to come on the 5th of June to Dunport, and to stay a few days if it were convenient, and yet her heart fell because there was not a sign of welcome or affection in the stately fashioning of the note. It had been hardly wise to expect it under the circumstances, the girl assured herself later, and at any rate it was kind in her aunt to answer her own short letter so soon.

XV

HOSTESS AND GUEST

Nan had, indeed, resolved to take a most important step. She had always dismissed the idea of having any communication with her aunt most contemptuously when she had first understood their unhappy position toward each other; but during the last year or two she had been forced to look at the relationship from a wider point of view. Dr. Leslie protested that he had always treated Miss Prince in a perfectly fair and friendly manner, and that if she had chosen to show no interest in her only niece, nobody was to blame but herself. But Nan pleaded that her aunt was no longer young; that she might be wishing that a reconciliation could be brought about; the very fact of her having constantly sent the yearly allowance in spite of Mrs. Thacher's and Dr. Leslie's unwillingness to receive it appealed to the young girl, who was glad to believe that her aunt had, after all, more interest in her than others cared to observe. She had no near relatives except Miss Prince. There were some cousins of old Mrs. Thacher's and their descendants settled in the vicinity of Oldfields; but Nan clung more eagerly to this one closer tie of kindred than she cared to confess even to her guardian. It was too late now for any interference in Dr. Leslie's plans, or usurping of his affectionate relationship; so, after he found that Nan's loyal heart was bent upon making so kind a venture, he said one day, with a smile, that she had better write a letter to her aunt, the immediate result of which we already know. Nan had been studying too hard, and suffering not a little from her long-continued city life, and though the doctor had been making a most charming plan that later in the season they should take a journey together to Canada, he said nothing about that, and told himself with a sigh that this would be a more thorough change, and even urged Nan to stay as long as she pleased in Dunport, if she found her aunt's house pleasant and everything went well. For whether Nan liked Miss Prince remained to be proved, though nobody in their senses could doubt that Miss Prince would be proud of her niece.

It was not until after Nan had fairly started that she began to feel at all dismayed. Perhaps she had done a foolish thing after all; Marilla had not approved the adventure, while at the last minute Nan had become suspicious that the doctor had made another plan, though she contented herself with the remembrance of perfect freedom to go home whenever she chose. She told herself grimly that if her aunt died she should be thankful that she had done this duty; yet when, after a journey of several hours, she knew that Dunport was the next station, her heart began to beat in a ridiculous manner. It was unlike any experience that had ever come to her, and she felt strangely unequal to the occasion. Long ago she had laughed at her early romances of her grand Dunport belongings, but the memory of them lingered still, in spite of this commonplace approach to their realities, and she looked eagerly at the groups of people at the railway station with a great hope and almost certainty that she should find her aunt waiting to meet her. There was no such good fortune, which was a chill at the outset to the somewhat tired young traveler, but she beckoned a driver whom she had just ignored, and presently was shut into a somewhat antiquated public carriage and on her way to Miss Prince's house.

So this was Dunport, and in these very streets her father had played, and here her mother had become deeper and deeper involved in the suffering and tragedy which had clouded the end of her short life. It seemed to the young stranger as if she must shrink away from the curious glances that stray passers-by sent into the old carriage; and that she was going to be made very conspicuous by the newly-awakened interest in a sad story which surely could not have been forgotten. Poor Nan! she sent a swift thought homeward to the doctor's house and Mrs. Graham's; even to the deserted little place which had sheltered her good old grandmother and herself in the first years she could remember. And with strange irony came also a picture of the home of one of her schoolmates,—where the father and mother and their children lived together and loved each other. The tears started to her eyes until some good angel whispered the kind "Come back soon, Nan dear," with which Dr. Leslie had let her go away.

The streets were narrow and roughly paved in the old provincial seaport town; the houses looked a good deal alike as they stood close to the street, though here and there the tops of some fruit trees showed themselves over a high garden fence. And presently before a broad-faced and gambrel-roofed house, the driver stopped his horses, and now only the front door with its bull's-eyed top-lights and shining knocker stood between Nan and her aunt. The coachman had given a resounding summons at this somewhat formidable entrance before he turned to open the carriage door, but Nan had already alighted, and stepped quickly into the hall. Priscilla directed her with some ceremony to the south parlor, and a prim figure turned away from one of the windows that overlooked the garden, and came forward a few steps. "I suppose this is Anna," the not very cordial voice began, and faltered; and then Miss Prince led her niece toward the window she had left, and without a thought of the reserve she had decided upon, pushed one of the blinds wide open, and looked again at Nan's appealing face, half eager herself, and half afraid. Then she fumbled for a handkerchief, and betook herself to the end of the sofa and began to cry: "You are so like my mother and Jack," she said. "I did not think I should be so glad to see you."

The driver had deposited Nan's box, and now appeared at the door of the parlor with Priscilla (who had quite lost her wits with excitement) looking over his shoulder. Nan sprang forward, glad of something to do in the midst of her vague discomfort, and at this sight the hostess recovered herself, and, commanding Priscilla to show Miss Prince to her room, assumed the direction of business affairs.

The best bedroom was very pleasant, though somewhat stiff and unused, and Nan was glad to close its door and find herself in such a comfortable haven of rest and refuge from the teasing details of that strange day. The wind had gone to the eastward, and the salt odor was most delightful to her. A vast inheritance of memories and associations was dimly brought to mind by that breath of the sea and freshness of the June day by the harbor side. Her heart leaped at the thought of the neighborhood of the wharves and shipping, and as she looked out at the ancient street, she told herself with a sense of great fun that if she had been a boy she would inevitably have been a surgeon in the navy. So this was the aunt whom Nan had thought about and dreamed about by day and by night, whose acquaintance had always been a waiting pleasure, and the mere fact of whose existence had always given her niece something to look forward to. She had not known until this moment what a reserved pleasure this meeting had been, and now it was over with. Miss Prince was so much like other people, though why she should not have been it would be difficult to suggest, and Nan's taste had been so educated and instructed by her Oldfields' advantages, not to speak of her later social experiences, that she felt at once that her aunt's world was smaller than her own. There was something very lovable about Miss Prince, in spite of the constraint of her greeting, and for the first time Nan understood that her aunt also had dreaded the meeting. Presently she came to the door, and this time kissed Nan affectionately. "I don't know what to say to you, I am sure," she told the girl, "only I am thankful to have you here. You must understand that it is a great event to me;" at which Nan laughed and spoke some cheerful words. Miss Prince seated herself by the other front window, and looked at her young guest with ever-growing satisfaction. This was no copy of that insolent, ill-bred young woman who had so beguiled and ruined poor Jack; she was a little lady, who did honor to the good name of the Princes and Lesters,—a niece whom anybody might be proud to claim, and whom Miss Prince could cordially entreat to make herself quite at home, for she had only been too long in coming to her own. And presently, when tea was served, the careful ordering of it, which had been meant partly to mock and astonish the girl who could not have been used to such ways of living, seemed only a fitting entertainment for so distinguished a guest. "Blood will tell," murmured Miss Prince to herself as she clinked the teacups and looked at the welcome face the other side of the table. But when they talked together in the evening, it was made certain that Nan was neither ashamed of her mother's people nor afraid to say gravely to Miss Prince that she did not know how much injustice was done to grandmother Thacher, if she believed she were right in making a certain statement. Aunt Nancy smiled, and accepted her rebuff without any show of disapproval, and was glad that the next day was Sunday, so that she could take Nan to church for the admiration of all observers. She was even sorry that she had not told young Gerry to come and pay an evening visit to her niece, and spoke of him once or twice. Her niece observed a slight self-consciousness at such times, and wondered a little who Mr. George Gerry might be.

Nan thought of many things before she fell asleep that night. Her ideas of her father had always been vague, and she had somehow associated him with Dr. Leslie, who had shown her all the fatherliness she had ever known. As for the young man who had died so long ago, if she had said that he seemed to her like a younger brother of Dr. Leslie, it would have been nearest the truth, in spite of the details of the short and disappointed life which had come to her ears. Dr. Ferris had told her almost all she knew of him, but now that she was in her own father's old home, among the very same sights he had known best, he suddenly appeared to her in a vision, as one might say, and invested himself in a cloud of attractive romance. His daughter felt a sudden blaze of delight at this first real consciousness of her kinship. Miss Prince had shown her brother's portrait early in the evening, and had even taken the trouble to light a candle and hold it high, so that Nan could see the handsome, boyish face, in which she recognized quickly the likeness to her own. "He was only thirteen then," said Miss Prince, "but he looks several years older. We all thought that the artist had made a great mistake when it was painted, but poor Jack grew to look like it. Yes, you are wonderfully like him," and she held the light near Nan's face and studied it again as she had just studied the picture. Nan's eyes filled with tears as she looked up at her father's face. The other portraits in the room were all of older people, her grandfather and grandmother and two or three ancestors, and Miss Prince repeated proudly some anecdotes of the most distinguished. "I suppose you never heard of them," she added sadly at the close, but Nan made no answer; it was certainly no fault of her own that she was ignorant of many things, and she would not confess that during the last few years she had found out everything that was possible about her father's people. She was so thankful to have grown up in Oldfields that she could not find it in her heart to rail at the fate that had kept her away from Dunport; but the years of silence had been very unlovely in her aunt.

She wondered, before she went to sleep that night, where her father's room had been, and thought she would ask Miss Prince in the morning. The windows were open, and the June air blew softly in, and sometimes swayed the curtains of the bed. There was a scent of the sea and of roses, and presently up the quiet street came the sound of footsteps and young voices. Nan said to herself that some party had been late in breaking up, and felt her heart thrill with sympathy. She had been dwelling altogether in the past that evening, and she liked to hear the revelers go by. But as they came under the windows she heard one say, "I should be afraid of ghosts in that best room of Miss Prince's," and then they suddenly became quiet, as if they had seen that the windows were open, and Nan first felt like a stranger, but next as if this were all part of the evening's strange experiences, and as if these might be her father's young companions, and she must call to them as they went by.

The next morning both the hostess and her guest waked early, and were eager for the time when they should see each other again. The beauty and quiet of the Sunday morning were very pleasant, and Nan stood for some minutes at the dining-room windows, looking out on the small paved court-yard, and the flowers and green leaves beyond the garden gate. Miss Prince's was one of the fine old houses which kept its garden behind it, well-defended from the street, for the family's own pleasure.

"Those are the same old bushes and trees which we used to play among; I have hardly changed it at all," said Miss Prince, as she came in. It must be confessed that she had lost the feeling of patroness with which she had approached her ac-quaintance with Nan. She was proud and grateful now, and as she saw the girl in her pretty white dress, and found her as simple and affectionate and eager to please as she had thought her the night before, she owned to herself that she had not looked for such happiness to fall into her life. And there was something about the younger Anna Prince which others had quickly recognized; a power of direction and of command. There are some natures like the Prussian blue on a painter's palette, which rules all the other colors it is mixed with; natures which quickly make themselves felt in small or great companies.

Nan discovered her father's silver mug beside her plate, and was fired with a fiercer resentment than she had expected to feel again, at the sight of it. The thought of her childhood in good grandmother Thacher's farm-house came quickly to her mind, with the plain living, to her share of which she had been made a thousand times welcome; while by this richer house, of which she was also heir, such rightful trinkets and treasures had been withheld. But at the next minute she could meet Miss Prince's observant eyes without displeasure, and wisely remembered that she herself had not been responsible for the state of affairs, and that possibly her aunt had been as wronged and insulted and beaten back as she complained. So she pushed the newly-brightened cup aside with an almost careless hand, as a sort of compromise with revenge, and Miss Prince at once caught sight of it. "Dear me," she said, not without confusion, "Priscilla must have thought you would be pleased," and then faltered, "I wish with all my heart you had always had it for your own, my dear." And this was a great deal for Miss Prince to say, as any of her acquaintances could have told her nearest relative, who sat, almost a stranger, at the breakfast-table.

The elder woman felt a little light-headed and unfamiliar to herself as she went up the stairway to get ready for church. It seemed as if she had entered upon a new stage of existence, since for so many years she had resented the existence of her brother's child, and had kept up an imaginary war, in which she ardently fought for her own rights. She had brought forward reason after reason why she must maintain her position as representative of a respected family who had been shamed and disgraced and insulted by her brother's wife. Now all aggressors of her peace, real and imaginary, were routed by the appearance of this young girl upon the field of battle, which she traversed with most innocent and fearless footsteps, looking smilingly into her aunt's face, and behaving almost as if neither of them had been concerned in the family unhappiness. Beside, Nan had already added a new interest to Miss Prince's life, and as this defeated warrior took a best dress from the closet without any of the usual reflection upon so important a step, she felt a great consciousness of having been added to and enriched, as the person might who had suddenly fallen heir to an unexpected property. From this first day she separated herself as much as possible from any thought of guilt or complicity in the long estrangement. She seemed to become used to her niece's presence, and with the new relationship's growth there faded away the thought of the past times. If any one dared to hint that it was a pity this visit had been so long delayed, Miss Prince grandly ignored all personality.

Priscilla had come to the guest's room on some undeclared errand, for it had already been put in order, and she viewed with pleasure the simple arrangements for dressing which were in one place and another about the room. Priscilla had scorned the idea of putting this visitor into the best bedroom, and had had secret expectations that Miss Prince's niece would feel more at home with her than with her mistress. But Miss Anna was as much of a lady as Miss Prince, which was both pleasing and disappointing, as Priscilla hoped to solace some disrespectful feelings of her own heart by taking down Miss Nancy's pride. However, her loyalty to the house was greater than her own very small grudges, and as she pretended to have some difficulty with the fastening of the blind, she said in a whisper, "Y'r aunt'll like to have you make yourself look pretty," which was such a reminder of Marilla's affectionate worldliness that Nan had to laugh aloud. "I'm afraid I haven't anything grand enough," she told the departing housekeeper, whose pleasure it was not hard to discern.

It was with a very gratified mind that Miss Prince walked down the street with her niece and bowed to one and another of her acquaintances. She was entirely careless of what any one should say, but she was brimful of excitement, and answered several of Nan's questions entirely wrong. The old town was very pleasant that Sunday morning. The lilacs were in full bloom, and other early summer flowers in the narrow strips of front-yards or the high-fenced gardens were in blossom too, and the air was full of sweetness and delight. The

ancient seaport had gathered for itself quaint names and treasures; it was pleased with its old fashions and noble memories; its ancient bells had not lost their sweet voices, and a
flavor of the past pervaded everything. The comfortable
houses, the elderly citizens, the very names on the shop signs,
and the worn cobblestones of the streets and flagstones of the
pavements, delighted the young stranger, who felt so unreasonably at home in Dunport. The many faces that had been
colored and fashioned by the sea were strangely different
from those which had known an inland life only, and she
seemed to have come a great deal nearer to foreign life and to
the last century. Her heart softened as she wondered if her
father knew that she was following his boyish footsteps, for
the first time in her life, on that Sunday morning. She would
have liked to wander away by herself and find her way about
the town, but such a proposal was not to be thought of, and
all at once Miss Nancy turned up a narrow side street toward
a high-walled brick church, and presently they walked side by
side up the broad aisle so far that it seemed to Nan as if her
aunt were aiming for the chancel itself, and had some public
ceremony in view, of a penitential nature. They were by no
means early, and the girl was disagreeably aware of a little
rustle of eagerness and curiosity as she took her seat, and was
glad to have fairly gained the shelter of the high-backed pew
as she bent her head. But Miss Prince the senior seemed calm;
she said her prayer, settled herself as usual, putting the footstool in its right place and finding the psalms and the collect.
She then laid the prayer-book on the cushion beside her and
folded her hands in her lap, before she turned discreetly to say
good-morning to Miss Fraley, and exchange greetings until
the clergyman made his appearance. Nan had taken the seat
next the pew door, and was looking about her with great
interest, forgetting herself and her aunt as she wondered that
so dear and quaint a place of worship should be still left in her
iconoclastic native country. She had seen nothing even in
Boston like this, there were so many antique splendors about
the chancel, and many mural tablets on the walls, where she
read with sudden delight her own family name and the list of
virtues which had belonged to some of her ancestors. The
dear old place! there never had been and never could be any

church like it; it seemed to have been waiting all her life for her to come to say her prayers where so many of her own people had brought their sins and sorrows in the long years that were gone. She only wished that the doctor were with her, and the same feeling that used to make her watch for him in her childhood until he smiled back again filled all her loving and grateful heart. She knew that he must be thinking of her that morning; he was not in church himself, he had planned a long drive to the next town but one, to see a dying man, who seemed to be helped only by this beloved physician's presence. There had been some talk between Dr. Leslie and Nan about a medicine which might possibly be of use, and she found herself thinking about that again and again. She had reminded the doctor of it and he had seemed very pleased. It must be longer ago than yesterday since she left Oldfields, it already counted for half a lifetime.

One listener at least was not resentful because the sermon was neither wise nor great, for she had so many things to think of; but while she was sometimes lost in her own thoughts, Nan stole a look at the thinly filled galleries now and then, and at one time was pleased with the sight of the red-cheeked cherubs which seemed to have been caught like clumsy insects and pinned as a sort of tawdry decoration above the tablets where the Apostle's Creed and the Ten Commandments were printed in faded gilt letters. The letter s was made long in these copies and the capitals were of an almost forgotten pattern, and after Nan had discovered her grandfather's name in the prayer-book she held, and had tried again to listen to the discourse, she smiled at the discovery of a familiar face in one of the wall pews. It somehow gave her a feeling of security as being a link with her past experiences, and she looked eagerly again and again until this old acquaintance, who also was a stranger and a guest in Dunport, happened to direct a careless glance toward her, and a somewhat dull and gloomy expression was changed for surprised and curious recognition. When church was over at last Miss Prince seemed to have a great deal to say to her neighbor in the next pew, and Nan stood in her place waiting until her aunt was ready. More than one person had lingered to make sure of a distinct impression of the interesting stranger who had made one of the morning congregation, and Nan smiled suddenly as she thought that it might seem proper that she and her aunt should walk down the aisle together as if they had been married, or as if the ceremony were finished which she had anticipated as they came in. And Miss Prince did make an admirable exit from the church, mustering all her self-possession and taking stately steps at her niece's side, while she sometimes politely greeted her acquaintances. There were flickering spots of color in her cheeks when they were again in the sun-shiny street.

"It is really the first day this summer when I have needed my parasol," said Aunt Nancy, as she unfurled the carefully preserved article of her wardrobe and held it primly aloft. "I am so sorry that our rector was absent this morning. I suppose that you have attended an Episcopal church sometimes; I am glad that you seem to be familiar with the service;" to which Nancy replied that she had been confirmed while she was first at boarding-school, and this seemed to give her aunt great satisfaction. "Very natural and proper, my dear," she said. "It is one thing I have always wished when I thought of you at serious moments. But I was persuaded that you were far from such influences, and that there would be nothing in your surroundings to encourage your inherited love of the church."

"I have always liked it best," said Nan, who seemed all at once to grow taller. "But I think one should care more about being a good woman than a good Episcopalian, Aunt Nancy."

"No doubt," said the elder woman, a little confused and dismayed, though she presently rallied her forces and justly observed that the rules of the church were a means to the end of good living, and happily, before any existing differences of opinion could be discovered, they were interrupted by a pleasant-faced young man, who lifted his hat and gracefully accepted his introduction to the younger Miss Prince.

"This is Mr. George Gerry, Anna, one of my young friends," smiled Aunt Nancy, and saying, as she walked more slowly, "You must come to see us soon, for I shall have to depend upon the younger people to make my niece's stay agreeable."

"I was looking forward to my Sunday evening visit," the wayfarer said hesitatingly; "you have not told me yet that I must not come;" which appeal was only answered by a little laugh from all three, as they separated. And Miss Prince had time to be quite eloquent in her favorite's praise before they reached home. Nan thought her first Dunport acquaintance very pleasant, and frankly said so. This seemed to be very gratifying to her aunt, and they walked toward home together by a roundabout way and in excellent spirits. It seemed more and more absurd to Nan that the long feud and almost tragic state of family affairs should have come to so prosaic a conclusion, and that she who had been the skeleton of her aunt's ancestral closet should have dared to emerge and to walk by her side through the town. After all, here was another proof of the wisdom of the old Spanish proverb, that it takes two to make a quarrel, but only one to end it.

XVI

A JUNE SUNDAY

IT WAS Miss Prince's custom to indulge herself by taking a long Sunday afternoon nap in summer, though on this occasion she spoke of it to her niece as only a short rest. She was glad to gain the shelter of her own room, and as she brushed a little dust from her handsome silk gown before putting it away she held it at arm's length and shook it almost indignantly. Then she hesitated a moment and looked around the comfortable apartment with a fierce disdain. "I wonder what gives me such a sense of importance," she whispered. "I have been making mistakes my whole life long, and giving excuses to myself for not doing my duty. I wish I had made her a proper allowance, to say the least. Everybody must be laughing at me!" and Miss Prince actually stamped her foot. It had been difficult to keep up an appearance of self-respect, but her pride had helped her in that laudable effort, and as she lay down on the couch she tried to satisfy herself with the assurance that her niece should have her rights now, and be treated justly at last.

Miss Fraley had come in to pay a brief visit on her way to Sunday-school just as they finished dinner, and had asked Nan to tea the following Wednesday, expressing also a hope that she would come sooner to call, quite without ceremony. Finding the state of affairs so pleasant, Miss Eunice ventured to say that Nan's father had been a favorite of her mother, who was now of uncommon age. Miss Prince became suddenly stern, but it was only a passing cloud, which disturbed nobody.

Nan had accepted willingly the offered apologies and gayly wished her aunt a pleasant dream, but being wide awake she gladly made use of the quiet time to send a letter home, and to stroll down the garden afterward. It all seemed so unlike what she had expected, yet her former thoughts about her aunt were much more difficult to recall as every hour went by and made the impression of actual things more distinct. Her fancied duty to a lonely old lady who mourned over a sad past seemed quite quixotic when she watched this brisk woman come and go without any hindrance of age, or, now that the first meeting was over, any appearance of former melancholy. As our friend went down the garden she told herself that she was glad to have come; it was quite right, and it was very pleasant, though there was no particular use in staying there long, and after a few days she would go away. Somehow her life seemed a great deal larger for this new experience, and she would try to repeat the visit occasionally. She wished to get Dunport itself by heart, but she had become so used to giving the best of herself to her studies, that she was a little shy of the visiting and the tea-parties and the apparently fruitless society life of which she had already learned something. "I suppose the doctor would say it is good for me," said Nan, somewhat grimly, "but I think it is most satisfactory to be with the persons whose interests and purposes are the same as one's own." The feeling of a lack of connection with the people whom she had met made life appear somewhat blank. She had already gained a certain degree of affection for her aunt; to say the least she was puzzled to account for such an implacable hostility as had lasted for years in the breast of a person so apparently friendly and cordial in her relations with her neighbors. Our heroine was slow to recognize in her relative the same strength of will and of determination which made the framework of her own character,—an iron-like firmness of structure which could not be easily shaken by the changes or opinions of other people. Miss Prince's acquaintances called her a very set person, and were shy of intruding into her secret fastnesses. There were all the traits of character which are necessary for the groundwork of an enterprising life, but Miss Prince seemed to have neither inherited nor acquired any high aims or any especial and fruitful single-heartedness, so her gifts of persistence and self-confidence had ranked themselves for the defense of a comparatively unimportant and commonplace existence. As has been said, she forbade, years before, any mention of her family troubles, and had lived on before the world as if they could be annihilated, and not only were not observable, but never had been. In a more thoughtful and active circle of social life the contrast between her rare capacity and her unnoticeable career would have been more striking. She stood as a fine representative of the old school, but it could not be justly said that she was a forward scholar, since, however sure of some of her early lessons, she was most dull and reluctant before new ones of various enlightening and uplifting descriptions.

Nan had observed that her aunt had looked very tired and spent as she went up-stairs after dinner, and understood better than she had before that this visit was moving the waters of Miss Prince's soul more deeply than had been suspected. She gained a new sympathy, and as the hours of the summer afternoon went by she thought of a great many things which had not been quite plain to her, and strolled about the garden until she knew that by heart, and had made friends with the disorderly company of ladies-delights and periwinkles which had cropped up everywhere, as if the earth were capable of turning itself into such small blossoms without anybody's help, after so many years of unvarying tuition. The cherry-trees and pear-trees had a most venerable look, and the plum-trees were in dismal mourning of black knots. There was a damp and shady corner where Nan found a great many lilies of the valley still lingering, though they had some time ago gone out of bloom in the more sunshiny garden at Oldfields. She remembered that there were no flowers in the house and gathered a great handful at last of one sort and another to carry in.

The dining-room was very dark, and Nan wished at first to throw open the blinds which had been carefully closed. It seemed too early in the summer to shut out the sunshine, but it seemed also a little too soon to interfere with the house-keeping, and so she brought two or three tall champagne glasses from a high shelf of the closet and filled them with her posies, and after putting them in their places, went back to the garden. There was a perfect silence in the house, except for the sound of the tall clock in the dining-room, and it seemed very lonely. She had taken another long look at her father's portrait, but as she shut the rusty-hinged garden gate after her, she smiled at the thought of her unusual idleness, and wondered if it need last until Tuesday, which was the day she had fixed upon for her departure. Nan wished that she dared to go away for a long walk; it was a pity she had not told her aunt of a wish to see something of the town and of the harbor-side that afternoon, but it would certainly be a little strange if she were to disappear, and very likely the long nap would soon come to an end. Being well taught in the details of gardening, she took a knife from her pocket and pruned and trained the shrubs and vines, and sang softly to herself as she thought about her next winter's study and her plans for the rest of the summer, and also decided that she would insist upon the doctor's going away with her for a journey when she reached home again.

After a little while she heard her aunt open the blinds of the garden door and call her in most friendly tones, and when she reached the house Miss Prince was in the south parlor entertaining a visitor,—Captain Walter Parish, who had gladly availed himself of some trifling excuse of a business nature, which involved the signing and sending of a paper by the early post of next day. He was going to his daughter's to tea, and it was quite a long drive to her house, so he had not dared to put off his errand, he explained, lest he should be detained in the evening. But he had been also longing to take a look at Miss Prince's guest. His wife went to another church and he dutifully accompanied her, though he had been brought up with Miss Prince at old St. Ann's.

"So this is my young cousin?" said the captain gallantly, and with great simplicity and tenderness held both Nan's hands and looked full in her face a moment before he kissed her; then to Miss Prince's great discomposure and embarrassment he turned to the window and looked out without saying a word, though he drew the back of his hand across his eyes in sailor-fashion, as if he wished to make them clear while he sighted something on the horizon. Miss Prince thought it was all nonsense and would have liked to say so, though she trusted that her silence was eloquent enough.

"She brings back the past," said Captain Walter as he returned presently and seated himself where he could look at Nan as much as he liked. "She brings back the past."

"You were speaking of old Captain Slater," reminded Miss Prince with some dignity.

"I just came from there," said Captain Parish, with his eyes still fixed on his young relative, though it was with such a friendly gaze that Nan was growing fonder of him every minute. "They told me he was about the same as yesterday. I offered to watch with him to-morrow night. And how do you like the looks of Dunport, my dear?"

Nan answered eagerly with brightening face, and added that she was longing to see more of it; the old wharves especially.

"Now that's good," said the captain; "I wonder if you would care anything about taking a stroll with me in the morning. Your aunt here is a famous housekeeper, and will be glad to get you off her hands, I dare say."

Nan eagerly accepted, and though it was suggested that Miss Prince had a plan for showing the town in the afternoon, she was promptly told that there was nothing easier than taking both these pleasant opportunities. "You would lose yourself among the old store-houses, I'm sure, Nancy," laughed the old sailor, "and you must let me have my way. It's a chance one doesn't get every day, to tell the old Dunport stories to a new listener."

Some one had opened the front door, and was heard coming along the hall. "This is very kind, George," said Miss Prince, with much pleasure, while the captain looked a little disconcerted at his young rival; he assured himself that he would make a long morning's cruise of it, next day, with this attractive sight-seer, and for once the young beaux would be at a disadvantage; the girls of his own day used to think him one of the best of their gallants, and at this thought the captain was invincible. Mr. Gerry must take the second chance.

The blinds were open now, and the old room seemed very pleasant. Nan's brown hair had been blown about not a little in the garden, and as she sat at the end of the long, brass-nailed sofa, a ray of sunshine touched the glass of a picture behind her and flew forward again to tangle itself in her stray locks, so that altogether there was a sort of golden halo about her pretty head. And young Gerry thought he had never seen anything so charming. The white frock was a welcome addition to the usually sombre room, and his eyes quickly saw the flowers on the table. He knew instantly that the bouquet was none of Miss Prince's gathering.

"I hope you won't think I mean to stay as much too late as I have come too early," he laughed. "I must go away soon after tea, for I have promised to talk with the captain of a schooner which is to sail in the morning. Mr. Wills luckily found out that he could give some evidence in a case we are working up."

"The collision?" asked Captain Parish, eagerly. "I was wondering to-day when I saw the Highflyer's foremast between the buildings on Fleet Street as I went to meeting, if they were going to let her lie there and dry-rot. I don't think she's being taken proper care of. I must say I hate to see a good vessel go to ruin when there's no need of it."

"The man in charge was recommended very highly, and everything seemed to be all right when I was on board one day this week," said young Gerry, good-naturedly, and turned to explain to Nan that this vessel had been damaged by collision with another, and the process of settling the matter by litigation had been provokingly slow.

The captain listened with impatience. "I dare say she looked very well to your eyes, but I'd rather have an old ship-master's word for it than a young lawyer's. I haven't boarded her for some weeks; I dare say 'twas before the snow was gone; but she certainly needed attention then. I saw some bad-looking places in the sheathing and planking. There ought to be a coat of paint soon, and plenty of tar carried aloft besides, or there'll be a long bill for somebody to pay before she's seaworthy."

"I wish you would make a careful inspection of her," said the young man, with gratifying deference. "I don't doubt that it is necessary; I will see that you are well satisfied for your services. Of course the captain himself should have stayed there and kept charge, but you remember he was sick and had to resign. He looks feeble yet. I hope nothing will happen to him before the matter is settled up, but we are sure of the trial in September."

"She's going to be rigged with some of your red tape, I'm afraid," said Captain Parish, with great friendliness. "I don't see any reason why I can't look her over to-morrow morning, I'm obliged to you, or at least make a beginning," and he gave a most knowing nod at Nan, as if they would divide the pleasure. "I'll make the excuse of showing this young lady the construction of a good-sized merchant vessel, and then the keeper can't feel affronted. She is going to take a stroll with me along the wharves," he concluded triumphantly. While Mr. Gerry looked wistful for a moment, and Miss Prince quickly took advantage of a pause in the conversation to ask if he knew whether anything pleasant was going forward among the young people this week. She did not wish her niece to have too dull a visit.

"Some of us are going up the river very soon," said the young man, with eager pleasure, looking at Nan. "It would be so pleasant if Miss Prince would join us. We think our Dunport supper parties of that sort would be hard to match."

"The young folks will all be flocking here by to-morrow," said the captain; and Miss Prince answered "Surely," in a tone of command, rather than entreaty. She knew very well how the news of Nan's coming must be flying about the town, and she almost regretted the fact of her own previous silence about this great event. In the mean time Nan was talking to the two gentlemen as if she had already been to her room to smooth her hair, which her aunt looked at reproachfully from time to time, though the sunshine had not wholly left it. The girl was quite unconscious of herself, and glad to have the company and sympathy of these kind friends. She thought once that if she had a brother she would like him to be of young Mr. Gerry's fashion. He had none of the manner which constantly insisted upon her remembering that he was a man and she a girl; she could be good friends with him in the same way that she had been with some Oldfields schoolfellows, and after the captain had reluctantly taken his leave, they had a pleasant talk about out-of-door life and their rides and walks, and were soon exchanging experiences in a way that Miss Nancy smiled upon gladly. It was not to be wondered at that she could not get used to so great a change in her life. She could not feel sure yet that she no longer had a secret, and that this was the niece whom she had so many years dreaded and disclaimed. George Gerry had taken the niece's place in her affections, yet here was Anna, her own namesake, who showed plainly in so many ways the same descent as herself, being as much a Prince as herself in spite of her mother's low origin and worse personal traits, and the loutish companions to whom she had always persuaded herself poor Nan was akin. And it was by no means sure that the last of the Princes was not the best of them; she was very proud of her brother's daughter, and was more at a loss to know how to make excuses for being shortsighted and neglectful. Miss Prince hated to think that Nan had any but the pleasantest associations with her nearest relative; she must surely keep the girl's affection now. She meant to insist at any rate upon Dunport's being her niece's home for the future, though undoubtedly it would be hard at first to break with the many associations of Oldfields. She must write that very night to Dr. Leslie to thank him for his care, and to again express her regret that Anna's misguided young mother should have placed such restrictions upon the child's relations with her nearest of kin, and so have broken the natural ties of nature. And she would not stop there; she would blame herself generously and say how sorry she was that she had been governed by her painful recollections of a time she should now strive to forget. Dr. Leslie must be asked to come and join his ward for a few days, and then they would settle her plans for the future. She should give her niece a handsome allowance at any rate, and then, as Miss Prince looked across the room and forgot her own thoughts in listening to the young people's friendly talk, a sudden purpose flashed through her mind. The dream of her heart began to unfold itself slowly: could anything be so suitable, so comforting to her own mind, as that they should marry each other?

Two days before, her pleasure and pride in the manly fellow, who was almost as dear to her as an own son could be, would have been greatly shocked, but Miss Prince's heart began to beat quickly. It would be such a blessed solution of all the puzzles and troubles of her life if she could have both the young people near her through the years that remained, and when she died, or even before, they could live here in the old house, and begin a new and better order of things in the place of her own failures and shortcomings. It was all so distinct and possible in Miss Prince's mind that only time seemed necessary, and even the time could be made short. She would not put any hindrances between them and their blessed decision.

As she went by them to seek Priscilla, she smoothed the cushion which Nan had leaned upon before she moved a little nearer George Gerry in some sudden excitement of the conversation, which had begun while the captain was still there, and there was a needless distance between them. Then Miss Prince let her hand rest for a minute on the girl's soft hair. "You must ask Mr. Gerry to excuse you for a few minutes, my dear, you have been quite blown about in the garden. I meant to join you there."

"It is a dear old garden," said Nan. "I can't help being almost as fond of it already as I am of ours at home;" but though Aunt Nancy's unwonted caress had been so unlike her conduct in general, this reference to Oldfields called her to her senses, and she went quickly away. She did not like to hear Nan speak in such loving fashion of a house where she had no real right.

But when Mr. George Gerry was left alone, he had pleasant thoughts come flocking in to keep him company in the ladies' stead. He had not dreamed of such a pleasure as this; who could have? and what could Aunt Nancy think of herself!

"It is such a holiday," said Nan, when tea was fairly begun, and her new friend was acknowledging an uncommon attack of hunger, and they were all merry in a sedate way to suit Miss Prince's ideas and preferences. "I have been quite the drudge this winter over my studies, and I feel young and idle again, now that I am making all these pleasant plans." For Mr. Gerry had been talking enthusiastically about some excursions he should arrange to certain charming places in the region of Dunport. Both he and Miss Prince smiled when Nan announced that she was young and idle, and a moment afterward the aunt asked doubtfully about her niece's studies; she supposed that Anna was done with schools.

Nan stopped her hand as it reached for the cup which Miss Prince had just filled. "School; yes," she answered, somewhat bewildered; "but you know I am studying medicine." This most important of all facts had been so present to her own mind, even in the excitement and novelty of her new surroundings, that she could not understand that her aunt was still entirely ignorant of the great purpose of her life.

"What do you mean?" demanded Miss Prince, coldly, and quickly explained to their somewhat amused and astonished companion, "My niece has been the ward of a distinguished physician, and it is quite natural she should have become interested in his pursuits."

"But I am really studying medicine; it is to be my profession," persisted Nan fearlessly, though she was sorry that she had spoiled the harmony of the little company. "And my whole heart is in it, Aunt Nancy."

"Nonsense, my dear," returned Miss Prince, who had recovered her self-possession partially. "Your father gave promise of attaining great eminence in a profession that was very proper for him, but I thought better of Dr. Leslie than this. I cannot understand his indulgence of such a silly notion."

George Gerry felt very uncomfortable. He had been a good deal shocked, but he had a strong impulse to rush into the field as Nan's champion, though it were quite against his conscience. She had been too long in a humdrum country-town with no companion but an elderly medical man. And after a little pause he made a trifling joke about their making the best of the holiday, and the talk was changed to other subjects. The tide was strong against our heroine, but she had been assailed before, and had no idea of sorrowing yet over a lost cause. And for once Miss Prince was in a hurry for Mr. Gerry to go away.

XVII

BY THE RIVER

As NAN went down the street next morning with Captain Parish, who had been most prompt in keeping his appointment, they were met by Mr. Gerry and a young girl who proved to be Captain Parish's niece and the bearer of a cordial invitation. It would be just the evening for a boat-party, and it was hoped that Miss Prince the younger would be ready to go up the river at half-past five.

"Dear me, yes," said the captain; "your aunt will be pleased to have you go, I'm sure. These idle young folks mustn't expect us to turn back now, though, to have a visit from you. We have no end of business on hand."

"If Miss Prince will remember that I was really on my way to see her," said Mary Parish pleasantly, while she looked with eager interest at the stranger. The two girls were quite ready to be friends. "We will just stop to tell your aunt, lest she should make some other plan for you," she added, giving Nan a nod that was almost affectionate. "We have hardly used the boats this year, it has been such a cold, late spring, and we hope for a very good evening. George and I will call for you," and George, who had been listening to a suggestion about the ship business, smiled with pleasure as they separated.

"Nice young people," announced the captain, who was in a sympathetic mood. "There has been some reason for thinking that they meant to take up with each other for good and all. I don't know that either of them could do better, though I like the girl best; that's natural; she's my brother's daughter, and I was her guardian; she only came of age last year. Her father and yours were boys together, younger than I am by a dozen years, both gone before me too," sighed the captain, and quickly changed so sad a subject by directing his companion's attention to one of the old houses, and telling the story of it as they walked along. Luckily they had the Highflyer all to themselves when they reached the wharf, for the keeper had gone up into the town, and his wife, who had set up a frugal housekeeping in the captain's cabin, sat in the shade of the house with her sewing, the Monday's washing having been early spread to the breeze in a corner of the main deck. She accepted Captain Parish's explanations of his presence with equanimity, and seemed surprised and amused at the young landswoman's curiosity and eagerness, for a ship was as commonplace to herself as any farm-house ashore.

"Dear me! you wouldn't know it was the same place," said the captain, in the course of his enumeration of the ropes and yards and other mysterious furnishings of the old craft. "With a good crew aboard, this deck is as busy as a town every day. I don't know how I'm going below until the keeper gets back. I suppose you don't want me to show you the road to the main-to'gallant cross-trees; once I knew it as well as anybody, and I could make quicker time now than most of the youngsters," and the captain gave a knowing glance aloft, while at this moment somebody crossed the gangway plank. It was a broken-down old sailor, who was a familiar sight in Dunport.

"Mornin' to you, sir," and the master of the Highflyer, for the time being, returned the salute with a mixture of dignity and friendliness.

"Goin' to take command?" chuckled the bent old fellow. "I'd like to ship under ye; 't wouldn't be the first time," and he gave his hat an unsettling shake with one hand as he looked at Nan for some sign of recognition, which was quickly given.

"You've shipped under better masters than I. Any man who followed the sea with Cap'n Jack Prince had more to teach than to learn. And here's his grand-daughter before you, and does him credit too," said Captain Walter. "Anna, you won't find many of your grandfather's men about the old wharves, but here's one of the smartest that ever had hold of a hawser."

"Goodsoe by name: I thank ye kindly, cap'n, but I ain't much account nowadays," said the pleased old man, trying to get the captain's startling announcement well settled in his mind. "Old Cap'n Jack Prince's grand-darter? Why Miss Nancy's never been brought to change her mind about nothing, has she?"

"It seems so," answered Nan's escort, laughing as if this were a good joke; and Nan herself could not help smiling.

"I don't believe if the old gentleman can look down at ye he begrudges the worst of his voyages nor the blackest night he ever spent on deck, if you're going to have the spending of the money. Not but what Miss Prince has treated me hand-some right straight along," the old sailor explained, while the inspector, thinking this not a safe subject to continue, spoke suddenly about some fault of the galley; and after this was discussed, the eyes of the two practiced men sought the dam-aged mizzen mast, the rigging of which was hanging in snarled and broken lengths. When Nan asked for some ac-count of the accident, she was told with great confidence that the Highflyer had been fouled, and that it was the other ves-sel's fault; at which she was no wiser than before, having known already that there had been a collision. There seemed to be room enough on the high seas, she ventured to say, or might the mischief have been done in port?

"It does seem as if you ought to know the sense of sea talk without any learning, being Cap'n Jack Prince's grand-darter," said old Goodsoe; for Captain Parish had removed himself to a little distance, and was again investigating the condition of the ship's galley, which one might suppose to have been ne-glected in some unforgivable way, judging from his indignant grumble.

"Fouled, we say aboard ship, when two vessels lay near enough so that they drift alongside. You can see what havick 't would make, for ten to one they don't part again till they have tore each other all to shoestrings; the yards will get locked together, and the same wind that starts one craft starts both, and first one and then t' other lifts with a wave, don't ye see, and the rigging's spoilt in a little time. I've sometimes called it to mind when I've known o' married couples that was n't getting on. 'T is easy to drift alongside, but no matter if they was bound to the same port they'd 'a' done best alone;" and the old fellow shook his head solemnly, and was evidently selecting one of his numerous stories for Nan's edi-fication, when his superior officer came bustling toward them.

"You might as well step down here about four o'clock; I shall have the keys then. I may want you to hold a lantern for me; I'm going into the lower hold and mean to do my work thoroughly, if I do it at all," to which Goodsoe responded "ay, ay, sir," in most seamanlike fashion and hobbled off.

"He'd have kept you there all day," whispered Captain Walter. "He always loved to talk, and now he has nothing else to do; but we are all friendly to Goodsoe. Some of us pay a little every year toward his support, but he has always made himself very useful about the wharves until this last year or two; he thought everything of your grandfather, and I knew it would please him to speak to you. It seems unfortunate that you should have grown up anywhere else than here; but I hope you'll stay now?"

"It is not very likely," said Nan coldly. She wished that the captain would go on with his stories of the former grandeur of Dunport, rather than show any desire to talk about personal matters. She had been little troubled at first by her aunt's evident disapproval the evening before of her plans for the future, for she was so intent upon carrying them out and certain that no one had any right to interfere. Still it would have been better to have been violently opposed than to have been treated like a child whose foolish whim would soon be forgotten when anything better offered itself. Nan felt much older than most girls of her years, and as if her decisions were quite as much to be respected as her aunt's. She had dealt already with graver questions than most persons, and her responsibilities had by no means been light ones. She felt sometimes as if she were separated by half a lifetime from the narrow limits of school life. Yet there was an uncommon childlikeness about her which not only misled these new friends, but many others who had known her longer. And when these listened to accounts of her devotion to her present studies and her marked proficiency, they shook their wise heads smilingly, as if they knew that the girl was innocent of certain proper and insurmountable obstacles farther on.

The air was fresh, and it was so pleasant on the wharf that the captain paced to and fro several times, while he pointed out different objects of interest along the harbor-side, and tapped the rusty anchor and the hawsers with his walking-stick as he went by. He had made some very pointed statements to the keeper's wife about the propriety of opening the hatches on such a morning as that, which she had received without comment, and wished her guests good-day with provoking equanimity. The captain did not like to have his authority ignored, but mentioned placidly that he supposed every idler along shore had been giving advice; though he wondered what Nan's grandfather and old Captain Peterbeck would have said if any one had told them this would be the only square-rigged vessel in Dunport harbor for weeks at a time.

"Dear me!" he exclaimed again presently, "there's young Gerry hard at work!" and he directed his companion's attention to one of the upper windows of the buildings whose fronts had two stories on the main street, while there were five or six on the rear, which faced the river. Nan could see the diligent young man and thought it hard that any one must be drudging within doors that beautiful morning.

"He has always been a great favorite of your aunt's," said Captain Parish, confidentially, after the law student had pretended to suddenly catch sight of the saunterers, and waved a greeting which the captain exultantly returned. "We have always thought that she was likely to make him her heir. She was very fond of his father, you see, and some trouble came between them. Nobody ever knew, because if anybody ever had wit enough to keep her own counsel 't was Nancy Prince. I know as much about her affairs as anybody, and what I say to you is between ourselves. I know just how far to sail with her and when to stop, if I don't want to get wrecked on a lee shore. Your aunt has known how to take care of what she had come to her, and I've done the best I could to help her; it's a very handsome property,—very handsome indeed. She helped George Gerry to get his education, and then he had some little money left him by his father's brother,—no great amount, but enough to give him a start; he's a very smart, upright fellow, and I am glad for whatever Nancy did for him; but it did n't seem fair that he should be stepping into your rights. But I never have dared to speak up for you since one day—she would n't hear a word about it, that 's all I have to remark," the captain concluded in a hurry, for wisdom's sake, though he longed to say more. It seemed outrageous to him at this moment that the girl at his side should have been left among strangers, and he was thankful that she seemed at last to have a good chance of making sure of her rightful possessions.

"But I have n't needed anything," she said, giving Captain Walter a grateful glance for his championship. "And Mr. Gerry is very kind and attentive to my aunt, so I am glad she has been generous to him. He seems a fine fellow, as you say," and Nan thought suddenly that it was very hard for him to have had her appear on the scene by way of rival, if he had been led to suppose that he was her aunt's heir. There were so many new things to think of, that Nan had a bewildering sense of being a stranger and a foreigner in this curiously self-centred Dunport, and a most disturbing element to its peace of mind. She wondered if, since she had not grown up here, it would not have been better to have stayed away altogether. Her own life had always been quite unvexed by any sort of social complications, and she thought how good it would be to leave this talkative and staring little world and go back to Oldfields and its familiar interests and associations. But Dunport was a dear old place, and the warm-hearted captain a most entertaining guide, and by the time their walk was over, the day seemed a most prosperous and entertaining one. Aunt Nancy appeared to be much pleased with the plan for the afternoon, and announced that she had asked some of the young people to come to drink tea the next evening, while she greeted Nan so kindly that the home-coming was particularly pleasant. As for the captain, he was unmistakably happy, and went off down the street with a gentle, rolling gait, and a smile upon his face that fairly matched the June weather, though he was more than an hour late for the little refreshment with which he and certain dignified associates commonly provided themselves at eleven o'clock in the forenoon. Life was as regular ashore as on board ship with these idle mariners of high degree. There was no definite business among them except that of occasionally settling an estate, and the forming of decided opinions upon important questions of the past and future.

The shadows had begun to grow long when the merry company of young people went up river with the tide, and Nan thought she had seldom known such a pleasure away from her own home. She begged for the oars, and kept stroke with George Gerry, pulling so well that they quickly passed the other boat. Mary Parish and the friend who made the fourth of that division of the party sat in the stern and steered with fine dexterity, and the two boats kept near each other, so that Nan soon lost all feeling of strangeness, and shared in the good comradeship to which she had been willingly admitted. It was some time since she had been on the water before, and she thought more than once of her paddling about the river in her childhood, and even regaled the company once with a most amusing mishap, at the remembrance of which she had been forced to laugh outright. The river was broad and brim-ful of water; it seemed high tide already, and the boats pulled easily. The fields sloped down to the river-banks, shaded with elms and parted by hedgerows like a bit of English country. The freshest bloom of the June greenness was in every blade of grass and every leaf. The birds were beginning to sing the long day to a close, and the lowing of cattle echoed from the pastures again and again across the water; while the country boats were going home from the town, sometimes with a crew of women, who seemed to have made this their regular conveyance instead of following the more roundabout high-ways ashore. Some of these navigators rowed with a cross-handed stroke that jerked their boats along in a droll fashion, and some were propelled by one groping oar, the sculler standing at the stern as if he were trying to push his craft out of water altogether and take to the air, toward which the lifted bow pointed. And in one of the river reaches half a mile ahead, two heavy packet boats, with high-peaked lateen sails, like a great bird's single wing, were making all the speed they could toward port before the tide should begin to fall two hours later. The young guest of the party was very happy; she had spent so many of her childish days out of doors that a return to such pleasures always filled her with strange delight. The color was bright in her cheeks, and her half-forgotten girlishness came back in the place of the gravity and dignity that had brought of late a sedate young womanliness to her manner. The two new friends in the stern of the boat were greatly attracted to her, and merry laughter rang out now and then. Nan was so brave and handsome, so willing to be pleased, and so grateful to them for this little festivity, that they quickly became interested in each other, as girls will. The commander thought himself a fortunate fellow, and took every chance of turning his head to catch a glimpse of our heroine, though he always had a good excuse of taking his bearings or inspecting for himself some object afloat or ashore which one of the boat's company had pointed out. And Nan must be told the names of the distant hills which stood out clear in the afternoon light, and to what towns up river the packet boats were bound, and so the time seemed short before the light dory was run in among the coarse river grass and pulled up higher than seemed necessary upon the shore.

Their companions had not chosen so fleet a craft, and were five instead of four at any rate, but they were welcomed somewhat derisively, and all chattered together in a little crowd for a few minutes before they started for a bit of woodland which overhung the river on a high point. The wind rustled the oak leaves and roughened the surface of the water, which spread out into a wide inland bay. The clouds began to gather in the west and to take on wonderful colors, as if such a day must be ended with a grand ceremony, and the sun go down through banners and gay parades of all the forces of the sky. Nan had watched such sunsets from her favorite playground at the farm, and somehow the memory of those days touched her heart more tenderly than they had ever done before, and she wished for a moment that she could get away from the noisy little flock who were busy getting the supper ready, though they said eagerly what a beautiful evening it would be to go back to town, and that they must go far up the river first to meet the moonlight.

In a few minutes Nan heard some one say that water must be brought from a farm-house not far away, and quickly insisted that she should make one of the messengers, and after much discussion and remonstrance, she and young Gerry found themselves crossing the open field together. The girl had left her hat swinging from one of the low oak branches; she wondered why Mary Parish had looked at her first as if she were very fond of her, and then almost appealingly, until the remembrance of Captain Walter's bit of gossip came to mind too late to be acted upon. Nan felt a sudden sympathy, and was sorry she had not thought to share with this favorite among her new friends, the companion whom she had joined so carelessly. George Gerry had some very attractive ways. He did not trouble Nan with unnecessary attentions, as some young men had, and she told herself again, how much she liked him. They walked fast, with free, light steps, and talked as they went in a way that was very pleasant to both of them. Nan was wise to a marvel, the good fellow told himself, and yet such an amusing person. He did not know when he had liked anybody so much; he was very glad to stand well in the sight of these sweet, clear eyes, and could not help telling their owner some of the things that lay very near his heart. He had wished to get away from Dunport; he had not room there; everybody knew him as well as they knew the court-house; he somehow wanted to get to deeper water, and out of his depth, and then swim for it with the rest. And Nan listened with deep sympathy, for she also had felt that a great engine of strength and ambition was at work with her in her plans and studies.

She waited until he should have finished his confidence, to say a word from her own experience, but just then they reached the farm-house and stood together at the low door. There was a meagre show of flowers in the little garden, which the dripping eaves had beaten and troubled in the late rains, and one rosebush was loosely caught to the clapboards here and there.

There did not seem to be anybody in the kitchen, into which they could look through the open doorway, though they could hear steps and voices from some part of the house beyond it; and it was not until they had knocked again loudly that a woman came to answer them, looking worried and pale.

"I never was so glad to see folks, though I don't know who you be," she said hurriedly. "I believe I shall have to ask you to go for help. My man's got hurt; he managed to get home, but he's broke his shoulder, or any ways 't is out o' place. He was to the pasture, and we've got some young cattle, and somehow or 'nother one he'd caught and was meaning to lead home give a jump, and John lost his balance; he says he can't see how 't should 'a' happened, but over he went and got jammed against a rock before he could let go o' the rope he'd put round the critter's neck. He's in dreadful pain so 't I couldn't leave him, and there's nobody but me an' the baby. You'll have to go to the next house and ask them to send; Doctor Bent's always attended of us."

"Let me see him," said Nan with decision. "Wait a minute, Mr. Gerry, or perhaps you had better come in too," and she led the way, while the surprised young man and the mistress of the house followed her. The patient was a strong young fellow, who sat on the edge of the bed in the little kitchen-bedroom, pale as ashes, and holding one elbow with a look of complete misery, though he stopped his groans as the strangers came in.

"Lord bless you, young man! don't wait here," he said; "tell the doctor it may only be out o' place, but I feel as if 't was broke."

But Nan had taken a pair of scissors from the high mantel-piece and was making a cut in the coarse, white shirt, which was already torn and stained by its contact with the ground, and with quick fingers and a look of deep interest made herself sure what had happened, when she stood still for a minute and seemed a little anxious, and all at once entirely determined. "Just lie down on the floor a minute," she said, and the patient with some exclamations, but no objections, obeyed.

Nan pushed the spectators into the doorway of the kitchen, and quickly stooped and unbuttoned her right boot, and then planted her foot on the damaged shoulder and caught up the hand and gave a quick pull, the secret of which nobody understood; but there was an unpleasant cluck as the bone went back into its socket, and a yell from the sufferer, who scrambled to his feet.

"I'll be hanged if she ain't set it," he said, looking quite weak and very much astonished. "You're the smartest young woman I ever see. I shall have to lay down just to pull my wits together. Marthy, a drink of water," and by the time this was brought the excitement seemed to be at an end, though the patient was a little faint, and his wife looked at Nan admiringly. Nan herself was fastening her boot again with unwonted composure. George Gerry had not a word to say, and listened to a simple direction of Nan's as if it were meant for him, and acceded to her remark that she was glad for the shoulder's sake that it did not have to wait and grow worse and worse all the while the doctor was being brought from town. And after a few minutes, when the volley of thanks and compliments could be politely cut short, the two members of the picnic party set forth with their pail of water to join their companions.

"Will you be so good as to tell me how you knew enough to do that?" asked Mr. Gerry humbly, and looking at his companion with admiration. "I should not have had the least idea."

"I was very glad it turned out so well," said Nan simply. "It was a great pleasure to be of use, they were so frightened, poor things. We won't say anything about it, will we?"

But the young man did not like to think yet of the noise the returning bone had made. He was stout-hearted enough usually; as brave a fellow as one could wish to see; but he felt weak and womanish, and somehow wished it had been he who could play the doctor. Nan hurried back bareheaded to the oak grove as if nothing had happened, though, if possible, she looked gayer and brighter than ever. And when the waiting party scolded a little at their slow pace, Miss Prince was much amused and made two or three laughing apologies for their laziness, and even ventured to give the information that they had made a pleasant call at the farm-house.

The clouds were fading fast and the twilight began to gather under the trees before they were ready to go away, and then the high tide had floated off one of the boats, which must be chased and brought back. But presently the picnickers embarked, and, as the moon came up, and the river ebbed, the boats went back to the town and overtook others on the way, and then were pulled up stream again in the favoring eddy to make the evening's pleasure longer; at last Nan was left at her door. She had managed that George Gerry should give Mary Parish his arm, and told them, as they came up the street with her from the wharf, that she had heard their voices Saturday night as they passed under her window: it was Mary Parish herself who had talked about the best room and its ghosts.

XVIII

A SERIOUS TEA-DRINKING

IT WAS very good for Nan to find herself cordially welcomed to a company of young people who had little thought of anything but amusement in the pleasant summer weather. Other young guests came to Dunport just then, and the hospitable town seemed to give itself up to their entertainment. Picnics and tea-drinkings followed each other, and the pleasure boats went up river and down river, while there were walks and rides and drives, and all manner of contrivances and excuses for spending much time together on the part of the young men and maidens. It was a good while since Nan had taken such a long holiday, though she had by no means been without the pleasures of society. Not only had she made friends easily during her school-life and her later studies, but Oldfields itself, like all such good old nests, was apt to call back its wandering fledglings when the June weather came. It delighted her more and more to be in Dunport, and though she sometimes grew impatient, wise Dr. Leslie insisted that she must not hurry home. The change was the very best thing in the world for her. Dr. Ferris had alighted for a day or two in the course of one of his wandering flights; and it seemed to the girl that since everything was getting on so well without her in Oldfields, she had better, as the doctor had already expressed it, let her visit run its course like a fever. At any rate she could not come again very soon, and since her aunt seemed so happy, it was a pity to hurry away and end these days sooner than need be. It had been a charming surprise to find herself such a desired companion, and again and again quite the queen of that little court of frolickers, because lately she had felt like one who looks on at such things, and cannot make part of them. Yet all the time that she was playing she thought of her work with growing satisfaction. By other people the knowledge of her having studied medicine was not very well received. It was considered to have been the fault of Miss Prince, who should not have allowed a whimsical country doctor to have beguiled the girl into such silly notions,

319

and many were the shafts sped toward so unwise an aunt for holding out against her niece so many years. To be sure the child had been placed under a most restricted guardianship; but years ago, it was thought, the matter might have been rearranged, and Nan brought to Dunport. It certainly had been much better for her that she had grown up elsewhere; though, for whatever was amiss and willful in her ways, Old-fields was held accountable. It must be confessed that every one who had known her well had discovered sooner or later the untamed wildnesses which seemed like the tangles which one often sees in field-corners, though a most orderly crop is taking up the best part of the room between the fences. Yet she was hard to find fault with, except by very shortsighted persons who resented the least departure by others from the code they themselves had been pleased to authorize, and who could not understand that a nature like Nan's must and could make and keep certain laws of its own.

There seemed to be a sort of inevitableness about the visit; Nan herself hardly knew why she was drifting on day after day without reasonable excuse. Her time had been most care-fully ordered and spent during the last few years, and now she sometimes had an uneasy feeling and a lack of confidence in her own steadfastness. But everybody took it for granted that the visit must not come to an end. The doctor showed no sign of expecting her. Miss Prince would be sure to resent her going away, and the pleasure-makers marked one day after another for their own. It seemed impossible, and perhaps un-wise, to go on with the reading she had planned, and, in fact, she had been urged to attend to her books rather by habit than natural inclination; and when the temptation to drift with the stream first made itself felt, the reasons for opposing it seemed to fade away. It was easier to remember that Dr. Leslie, and even those teachers who knew her best at the med-ical school, had advised a long vacation.

The first formal visits and entertainments were over with for the most part, and many of the Dunport acquaintances began to seem like old friends. There had been a little joking about Nan's profession, and also some serious remonstrance and unwise championship which did not reach this heroine's ears. It all seemed romantic and most unusual when anybody talked about her story at all, and the conclusion was soon reached that all such whims and extravagances were merely incident to the pre-Dunportian existence, and that now the young guest had come to her own, the responsibilities and larger field of activity would have their influence over her plan of life. The girl herself was disposed to talk very little about this singular fancy; it may have been thought that she had grown ashamed of it as seen by a brighter light, but the truth was it kept a place too near her heart to allow her to gossip with people who had no real sympathy, and who would ask questions from curiosity alone. Miss Eunice Fraley had taken more than one opportunity, however, to confess her interest, though she did this with the manner of one who dares to be a conspirator against public opinion, and possibly the permanent welfare of society, and had avowed, beside, her own horror of a doctor's simplest duties. But poor Miss Fraley looked at her young friend as a caged bird at a window might watch a lark's flight, and was strangely glad whenever there was a chance to spend an hour in Nan's company.

The first evening at Mrs. Fraley's had been a great success, and Miss Prince had been vastly pleased because both the hostess and the guest had received each other's commendation. Mrs. Fraley was, perhaps, the one person whom Miss Prince recognized as a superior officer, and she observed Nan's unconscious and suitable good behavior with great pride. The hostess had formerly been an undisputed ruler of the highest social circles of Dunport society, and now in her old age, when she could no longer be present at any public occasions, she was still the queen of a little court that assembled in her own house. It was true that the list of her subjects grew shorter year by year, but the survivors remained loyal, and hardly expected, or even desired, that any of the newcomers to the town should recognize their ruler. Nan had been much interested in the old lady's stories, and had gladly accepted an invitation to come often to renew the first conversation. She was able to give Mrs. Fraley much welcome information of the ways and fashions of other centres of civilization, and it was a good thing to make the hours seem shorter. The poor old lady had few alleviations; even religion had served her rather as a basis for argument than an accepted reliance and guide; and though she still prided herself on her selection of words, those which she used in formal conversations with the clergyman seemed more empty and meaningless than most others. Mrs. Fraley was leaving this world reluctantly; she had been well fitted by nature for social preeminence, and had never been half satisfied with the opportunities provided for the exercise of her powers. It was only lately that she had been forced to acknowledge that Time showed signs of defeating her in the projects of her life, and she had begun to give up the fight altogether, and to mourn bitterly and aggressively to her anxious and resourceless daughter. It was plain enough that the dissatisfactions and infirmities of age were more than usually great, and poor Eunice was only too glad when the younger Miss Prince proved herself capable of interesting the old friend of her family, and Mrs. Fraley took heart and suggested both informal visits and future entertainments. The prudent daughter was careful not to tell her mother of the guest's revolutionary ideas, and for a time all went well, until some unwise person, unaware of Miss Fraley's warning gestures from the other side of the sitting-room, proceeded to give a totally unnecessary opinion of the propriety of women's studying medicine. Poor Eunice expected that a sharp rebuke, followed by a day or two's disdain and general unpleasantness, would descend upon her quaking shoulders; but, to her surprise, nothing was said until the next morning, when she was bidden, at much inconvenience to the household, to invite Miss Prince and her niece to come that afternoon to drink tea quite informally.

There was a pathetic look in the messenger's faded face,—she felt unusually at odds with fortune as she glided along the street, sheltered by the narrow shadows of the high fences. Nan herself came to the door, and when she threw back the closed blinds and discovered the visitor, she drew her in with most cordial welcome, and the two friends entered the darkened south parlor, where it was cool, and sweet with the fragrance of some honeysuckle which Nan had brought in early that morning from the garden.

"Dear me," said the little woman deprecatingly. "I don't know why I came in at all. I can't stop to make a call. Mother was very desirous that you and your aunt should come over to tea this evening. It seems a good deal to ask in such hot weather, but she has so little to amuse her, and I really don't see that the weather makes much difference, she used to feel the heat very much years ago." And Miss Eunice gave a sigh, and fanned herself slowly, letting the fan which had been put into her hand turn itself quite over on her lap before it came up again. There was an air of antique elegance about this which amused Nan, who stood by the table wiping with her handkerchief some water that had dropped from the vase. A great many of the ladies in church the Sunday before had fanned themselves in this same little languishing way; she remembered one or two funny old persons in Oldfields who gave themselves airs after the same fashion.

"I think we shall both be very pleased," she answered directly, with a bit of a smile; while Miss Fraley gazed at her admiringly, and thought she had never seen the girl look so fresh and fair as she did in this plain, cool little dress. There had been more water than was at first suspected; the handkerchief was a limp, white handful, and they both laughed as it was held up. Miss Fraley insisted that she could not stay. She must go to the shops to do some errands, and hoped to meet Miss Prince who had gone that way half an hour before.

"Don't mind anything mother may say to you," she entreated, after lingering a minute, and looking imploringly in Nan's face. "You know we can't expect a person of her age to look at everything just as we do."

"Am I to be scolded?" asked Nan, serenely. "Do you know what it is about?"

"Oh, perhaps nothing," answered Miss Fraley, quickly. "I ought not to have spoken, only I fancied she was a little distressed at the idea of your being interested in medicines. I don't know anything that is more useful myself. I am sure every family needs to have some one who has some knowledge of such things; it saves calling a doctor. My sister Susan knows more than any of us, and it has been very useful to her with her large family."

"But I shouldn't be afraid to come, I think," said Nan, laughing. "Mrs. Fraley told me that she would finish that story of the diamond ring, you know, and we shall get on capitally. Really I think her stories of old times are wonderfully interesting. I wish I had a gift for writing them down whenever I am listening to her."

Miss Eunice was much relieved, and felt sure that Nan was equal to any emergency. The girl had put a strong young arm quickly round her guest's thin shoulders, and had kissed her affectionately, and this had touched the lonely little woman's very heart.

There were signs of storm in Madam Fraley's face that evening, but everybody feigned not to observe them, and Nan behaved with perilous disregard of a lack of encouragement, and made herself and the company uncommonly merry. She described the bad effect her coming had had upon her aunt's orderly house. She confessed to having left her own possessions in such confusion the evening before when she dressed again to go up the river, that Priscilla had called it a monkey's wedding, and had gone away after one scornful look inside the door. Miss Fraley dared to say that no one could mind seeing such pretty things, and even Miss Prince mentioned that her niece was not so careless as she would make them believe; while Nan begged to know if anybody had ever heard of a monkey's wedding before, and seemed very much amused.

"She called such a disarray in the kitchen one morning the monkey's wedding breakfast," said Miss Prince, as if she never had thought it particularly amusing until this minute. "Priscilla has always made use of a great many old-fashioned expressions."

They had seated themselves at the tea-table; it was evident that Miss Fraley had found it a hard day, for she looked tired and worn. The mistress of the house was dressed in her best and most imposing clothes, and sat solemnly in her place. A careful observer might have seen that the best blue teacups with their scalloped edges were not set forth. The occasion wore the air of a tribunal rather than that of a festival, and it was impossible not to feel a difference between it and the former tea-party.

Miss Prince was not particularly sensitive to moods and atmospheres; she happened to be in very good spirits, and talked for some time before she became entirely aware that something had gone wrong, but presently faltered, and fell under the ban, looking questioningly toward poor Eunice, who busied herself with the tea-tray.

"Nancy," said Mrs. Fraley impatiently, "I was amazed to find that there is a story going about town that your niece here is studying to be a doctor. I hope that you don't countenance any such nonsense?"

Miss Prince looked helpless and confounded, and turned her eyes toward her niece. She could only hope at such a mortifying juncture that Nan was ready to explain, or at least to shoulder the responsibility.

"Indeed she does n't give me any encouragement, Mrs. Fraley," said Nan, fearlessly. "Only this morning she saw a work on ventilation in my room and told me it was n't proper reading for a young woman."

"I really did n't look at the title," said Miss Prince, smiling in spite of herself.

"It does n't seem to improve the health of you young folks because you think it necessary to become familiar with such subjects," announced the irate old lady. It was her habit to take a very slight refreshment at the usual tea hour, and supplement it by a substantial lunch at bed-time, and so now she was not only at leisure herself, but demanded the attention of her guests. She had evidently prepared an opinion, and was determined to give it. Miss Eunice grew smaller and thinner than ever, and fairly shivered with shame behind the tea-tray. She looked steadily at the big sugar-bowl, as if she were thinking whether she might creep into it and pull something over her head. She never liked an argument, even if it were a good-natured one, and always had a vague sense of personal guilt and danger.

"In my time," Mrs. Fraley continued, "it was thought proper for young women to show an interest in household affairs. When I was married it was not asked whether I was acquainted with dissecting-rooms."

"But I don't think there is any need of that," replied Nan. "I think such things are the duty of professional men and women only. I am very far from believing that every girl ought to be a surgeon any more than that she ought to be an astronomer. And as for the younger people's being less strong than the old, I am afraid it is their own fault, since we understand the laws of health better than we used. 'Who breaks, pays,' you know."

It was evidently not expected that the young guest should venture to discuss the question, but rather have accepted her rebuke meekly, and acknowledged herself in the wrong. But she had the courage of her opinions, and the eagerness of youth, and could hardly bear to be so easily defeated. So when Mrs. Fraley, mistaking the moment's silence for a final triumph, said again, that a woman's place was at home, and that a strong-minded woman was out of place, and unwelcome everywhere, the girl's cheeks flushed suddenly.

"I think it is a pity that we have fallen into a habit of using strong-mindedness as a term of rebuke," she said. "I am willing to acknowledge that people who are eager for reforms are apt to develop unpleasant traits, but it is only because they have to fight against opposition and ignorance. When they are dead and the world is reaping the reward of their bravery and constancy, it no longer laughs, but makes statues of them, and praises them, and thanks them in every way it can. I think we ought to judge each other by the highest standards, Mrs. Fraley, and by whether we are doing good work."

"My day is past," said the hostess. "I do not belong to the present, and I suppose my judgment is worth nothing to you;" and Nan looked up quickly and affectionately.

"I should like to have all my friends believe that I am doing right," she said. "I do feel very certain that we must educate people properly if we want them to be worth anything. It is no use to treat all the boys and girls as if nature had meant them for the same business and scholarship, and try to put them through the same drill, for that is sure to mislead and confuse all those who are not perfectly sure of what they want. There are plenty of people dragging themselves miserably through the world, because they are clogged and fettered with work for which they have no fitness. I know I haven't had the experience that you have, Mrs. Fraley, but I can't help believing that nothing is better than to find one's work early and hold fast to it, and put all one's heart into it."

"I have done my best to serve God in the station to which it has pleased Him to call me," said Mrs. Fraley, stiffly. "I believe that a young man's position is very different from a girl's. To be sure, I can give my opinion that everything went better when the master workmen took apprentices to their trades, and there wasn't so much schooling. But I warn you, my dear, that your notion about studying to be a doctor has shocked me very much indeed. I could not believe my ears,—a refined girl who bears an honorable and respected name to think of being a woman doctor! If you were five years older you would never have dreamed of such a thing. It lowers the pride of all who have any affection for you. If it were not that your early life had been somewhat peculiar and most unfortunate, I should blame you more; as it is, I can but wonder at the lack of judgment in others. I shall look forward in spite of it all to seeing you happily married." To which Miss Prince assented with several decided nods.

"This is why I made up my mind to be a physician," said the culprit; and though she had been looking down and growing more uncomfortable every moment, she suddenly gave her head a quick upward movement and looked at Mrs. Fraley frankly, with a beautiful light in her clear eyes. "I believe that God has given me a fitness for it, and that I never could do anything else half so well. Nobody persuaded me into following such a plan; I simply grew toward it. And I have everything to learn, and a great many faults to overcome, but I am trying to get on as fast as may be. I can't be too glad that I have spent my childhood in a way that has helped me to use my gift instead of hindering it. But everything helps a young man to follow his bent; he has an honored place in society, and just because he is a student of one of the learned professions, he ranks above the men who follow other pursuits. I don't see why it should be a shame and dishonor to a girl who is trying to do the same thing and to be of equal use in the world. God would not give us the same talents if what were right for men were wrong for women."

"My dear, it is quite unnatural you see," said the antagonist, impatiently. "Here you are less than twenty-five years old, and I shall hear of your being married next thing,—at least I hope I shall,—and you will laugh at all this nonsense. A woman's place is at home. Of course I know that there have been some women physicians who have attained eminence, and some artists, and all that. But I would rather see a daughter of mine take a more retired place. The best service to the public can be done by keeping one's own house in order and one's husband comfortable, and by attending to those social responsibilities which come in our way. The mothers of the nation have rights enough and duties enough already, and need not look farther than their own firesides, or wish for the plaudits of an ignorant public."

"But if I do not wish to be married, and do not think it right that I should be," said poor Nan at last. "If I have good reasons against all that, would you have me bury the talent God has given me, and choke down the wish that makes itself a prayer every morning that I may do this work lovingly and well? It is the best way I can see of making myself useful in the world. People must have good health or they will fail of reaching what success and happiness are possible for them; and so many persons might be better and stronger than they are now, which would make their lives very different. I do think if I can help my neighbors in this way it will be a great kindness. I won't attempt to say that the study of medicine is a proper vocation for women, only that I believe more and more every year that it is the proper study for me. It certainly cannot be the proper vocation of all women to bring up children, so many of them are dead failures at it; and I don't see why all girls should be thought failures who do not marry. I don't believe that half those who do marry have any real right to it, at least until people use common sense as much in that most important decision as in lesser ones. Of course we can't expect to bring about an ideal state of society all at once; but just because we don't really believe in having the best possible conditions, we make no effort at all toward even better ones. People ought to work with the great laws of nature and not against them."

"You don't know anything about it," said Mrs. Fraley, who hardly knew what to think of this ready opposition. "You don't know what you are talking about, Anna. You have neither age nor experience, and it is easy to see you have been associating with very foolish people. I am the last person to say that every marriage is a lucky one; but if you were my daughter I should never consent to your injuring your chances for happiness in this way."

Nan could not help stealing a glance at poor Miss Eunice, behind her fragile battlement of the tea-set, and was deeply touched at the glance of sympathy which dimly flickered in the lonely eyes. "I do think, mother, that Anna is right about single women's having some occupation," was timidly suggested. "Of course, I mean those who have no special home duties; I can see that life would not"—

"Now Eunice," interrupted the commander in chief, "I do wish you could keep an opinion of your own. You are the last person to take up with such ideas. I have no patience with people who don't know their own minds half an hour together."

"There are plenty of foolish women who marry, I'll acknowledge," said Miss Prince, for the sake of coming to the rescue. "I was really angry yesterday, when Mrs. Gerry told me that everybody was so pleased to hear that Hattie Barlow was engaged, because she was incapable of doing anything to support herself. I couldn't help feeling that if there was so little power that it had never visibly turned itself in any practical direction, she wasn't likely to be a good housekeeper. I think that is a most responsible situation, myself."

Nan looked up gratefully. "It isn't so much that people can't do anything, as that they try to do the wrong things, Aunt Nancy. We all are busy enough or ought to be; only the richest people have the most cares and have to work hardest. I used to think that rich city people did nothing but amuse themselves, when I was a little girl; but I often wonder nowadays at the wisdom and talent that are needed to keep a high social position respected in the world's eyes. It must be an orderly and really strong-minded woman who can keep her business from getting into a most melancholy tangle. Yet nobody is afraid when the most foolish girls take such duties upon themselves, and all the world cries out with fear of disaster, if once in a while one makes up her mind to some other plan of life. Of course I know being married isn't a trade: it is a natural condition of life, which permits a man to follow certain public careers, and forbids them to a woman. And since I have not wished to be married, and have wished to study medicine, I don't see what act of Parliament can punish me."

"Wait until Mr. Right comes along," said Mrs. Fraley, who had pushed back her chair from the table and was beating her foot on the floor in a way that betokened great displeasure and impatience. "I am only thankful I had my day when women were content to be stayers at home. I am only speaking for your good, and you'll live to see the truth of it, poor child!"

"I am sure she will get over this," apologized Miss Prince, after they had reached the parlor, for she found that her niece had lingered with Miss Fraley in the dining-room.

"Don't talk to me about the Princes changing their minds," answered the scornful old hostess. "You ought to know them better than that by this time." But just at that moment young Gerry came tapping at the door, and the two ladies quickly softened their excited looks and welcomed him as the most powerful argument for their side of the debate. It seemed quite a thing of the past that he should have fancied Mary Parish, and more than one whisper had been listened to that the young man was likely to have the Prince inheritance, after all. He looked uncommonly well that evening, and the elder women could not imagine that any damsel of his own age would consider him slightingly. Nan had given a little shrug of impatience when she heard his voice join the weaker ones in the parlor, and a sense of discomfort that she never had felt before came over her suddenly. She reminded herself that she must tell her aunt that very night that the visit must come to an end. She had neglected her books and her drives with the doctor altogether too long already.

XIX

FRIEND AND LOVER

IN THESE summer days the young lawyer's thoughts had
often been busy elsewhere while he sat at the shaded office
window and looked out upon the river. The very housekeeping on the damaged ship became more interesting to him
than his law books, and he watched the keeper's wife at her
various employments on deck, or grew excited as he witnessed the good woman's encounters with marauding small
boys, who prowled about hoping for chances of climbing the
rigging or solving the mysteries of the hold. It had come to
be an uncommon event that a square-rigged vessel should
make the harbor of Dunport, and the elder citizens ignored
the deserted wharves, and talked proudly of the days of Dunport's prosperity, convicting the railroad of its decline as
much as was consistent with their possession of profitable
stock. The younger people took the empty warehouses for
granted, and listened to their grandparents' stories with interest, if they did not hear them too often; and the more enterprising among them spread their wings of ambition and flew
away to the larger cities or to the westward. George Gerry
had stayed behind reluctantly. He had neither enough desire
for a more active life, nor so high a purpose that he could
disregard whatever opposition lay in his way. Yet he was honestly dissatisfied with his surroundings, and thought himself
hardly used by a hindering fate. He believed himself to be
most anxious to get away, yet he was like a ship which will
not be started out of port by anything less than a hurricane.
There really were excuses for his staying at home, and since he
had stopped to listen to them they beguiled him more and
more, and his friends one by one commended his devotion to
his mother and sisters, and sometimes forgot to sympathize
with him for his disappointments as they praised him for being such a dutiful son. To be sure, he might be a great lawyer
in Dunport as well as anywhere else; he would not be the
first; but a more inspiring life might have made him more
enthusiastic and energetic, and if he could have been winning

his way faster elsewhere, and sending home good accounts of himself, not to speak of substantial aid, there is no question whether it would not have given his family greater happiness and done himself more good. He was not possessed of the stern determination which wins its way at all hazards, and so was dependent upon his surroundings for an occasional stimulus.

But Dunport was very grateful to him because he had stayed at home, and he was altogether the most prominent young man in the town. It is so easy to be thankful that one's friends are no worse that one sometimes forgets to remember that they might be better; and it would have been only natural if he thought of himself more highly than he ought to think, since he had received a good deal of applause and admiration. It is true that he had avoided vice more noticeably than he had pursued virtue; but the senior member of the firm, Mr. Sergeant, pronounced his young partner to have been a most excellent student, and not only showed the greatest possible confidence in him, but was transferring a good deal of the business to him already. Miss Prince and her old lawyer had one secret which had never been suspected, and the townspeople thought more than ever of young Mr. Gerry's ability when it was known that the most distinguished legal authority of that region had given him a share of a long-established business. George Gerry had been led to think better of himself, though it had caused him no little wonder when the proposal had been made. It was possible that Mr. Sergeant feared that there might be some alliance offered by his rivals in Dunport. To be sure, the younger firm had been making a good deal of money, but it was less respected by the leading business men. Mr. Sergeant had even conferred with his young friend one morning upon the propriety of some new investments; but Mr. Gerry had never even suspected that they were the price of his own new dignity and claim upon the public honor. Captain Walter Parish and Mr. Sergeant had both been aids and advisers of Miss Prince; but neither had ever known the condition of all her financial affairs, and she had made the most of a comfortable sense of liberty. To do young Gerry justice, he had not hesitated to express his amazement; and among his elders and betters, at

any rate, he had laid his good fortune at the door of Mr.
Sergeant's generosity and kindness instead of his own value.

But at certain seasons of the year, like this, there was no
excitement in the office, and after an attendance at court and
the proper adjustment, whether temporary or permanent, of
the subsequent business, the partners had returned to a
humdrum fulfilling of the minor duties of their profession,
and the younger man worked at his law books when there
were no deeds or affidavits to engage his attention. He
thought of many things as he sat by his window; it was a
great relief to the tiresomeness of the dull rooms to look at
the river and at the shores and hills beyond; to notice carelessly whether the tide came in or went out. He was apt to
feel a sense of dissatisfaction in his leisure moments; and
now a new current was bringing all its force to bear upon
him in his quiet anchorage.

He had looked upon Miss Prince as a kind adviser; he was
on more intimate terms with her than with any woman he
knew; and the finer traits in his character were always brought
out by some compelling force in her dignity and simple ad-
herence to her somewhat narrow code of morals and etiquette. He was grateful to her for many kindnesses; and as he
had grown older and come to perceive the sentiment which
had been the first motive of her affection toward him, he had
instinctively responded with a mingling of gallantry and sympathy which made him, as has been already said, appear at his
very best. The gossips of Dunport had whispered that he
knew that it was more than worth his while to be polite to
Miss Prince; but he was too manly a fellow to allow any trace
of subserviency to show itself in his conduct. As often happens, he had come back to Dunport almost a stranger after
his years of college life were over, and he had a mingled love
and impatience for the old place. The last year had been very
pleasant, however: there were a few young men whose good
comrade and leader he was; his relations with his fellow-
citizens were most harmonious; and as for the girls of his own
age and their younger sisters, who were just growing up, he
was immensely popular and admired by them. It had become
a subject of much discussion whether he and Mary Parish
would not presently decide upon becoming engaged to each

other, until Miss Prince's long-banished niece came to put a new suspicion into everybody's mind.

Many times when George Gerry had a new proof that he had somehow fallen into the habit of walking home with the pleasant girl who was his friend and neighbor, he had told himself abruptly that there was no danger in it, and that they never could have any other feeling for each other. But he had begun to think also that she belonged to him in some vague way, and sometimes acknowledged that it might be a thing to consider more deeply by and by. He was only twenty-six, and the world was still before him, but he was not very sympathetic with other people's enthusiasm over their love affairs, and wondered if it were not largely a matter of temperament, though by and by he should like to have a home of his own.

He was somewhat attracted toward Miss Prince, the younger, for her aunt's sake, and had made up his mind that he would be very attentive to her, no matter how displeasing and uninteresting she might be: it was sure to be a time of trial to his old friend, and he would help all he could to make the visit as bearable as possible. Everybody knew of the niece's existence who had known the Prince family at all, and though Miss Prince had never mentioned the unhappy fact until the day or two before her guest was expected, her young cavalier had behaved with most excellent discretion, and feigning neither surprise nor dismay, accepted the announcement in a way that had endeared him still more to his patroness.

But on the first Sunday morning, when a most admirable young lady had walked up the broad aisle of St. Ann's church, and Mr. Gerry had caught a glimpse of her between the rows of heads which all looked commonplace by contrast, it seemed to begin a new era of things. This was a welcome link with the busier world outside Dunport; this was what he had missed since he had ended his college days, a gleam of cosmopolitan sunshine, which made the provincial fog less attractive than ever. He was anxious to claim companionship with this fair citizen of a larger world, and to disclaim any idea of belonging to the humdrum little circle which exaggerated its own importance. He persuaded himself that he must pay Miss Prince's guest an early visit. It was very exciting and interesting

altogether; and as he watched the flicker of light in our heroine's hair as she sat on the straight sofa in her aunt's parlor on
the Sunday evening, a feeling of great delight stole over him.
He had known many nice girls in his lifetime, but there was
something uncommonly interesting about Miss Anna Prince;
besides, who could help being grateful to her for being so
much nicer than anybody had expected?

And so the days went by. Nobody thought there was any
objection when the junior partner of the law firm took holiday after holiday, for there was little business and Mr. Sergeant liked to keep on with his familiar routine. His old
friends came to call frequently, and they had their conferences
in peace, and were not inclined to object if the younger ears
were being used elsewhere. Young people will be young
people, and June weather does not always last; and if George
Gerry were more devoted to social duties than to legal ones, it
was quite natural, and he had just acquitted himself most
honorably at the May term of court, and was his own master
if he decided to take a vacation.

He had been amused when the announcement had been
made so early in their acquaintance that Nan meant to study
medicine. He believed if there were any fault, it was Dr.
Leslie's, and only thought it a pity that her evident practical
talents had not been under the guidance of a more sensible
director. The girl's impetuous defense of her choice was very
charming; he had often heard Mr. Sergeant speak of the rare
insight and understanding of legal matters which his favorite
daughter had possessed, and her early death had left a lonely
place in the good man's heart. Miss Prince's life at Oldfields
must have been very dull, especially since her boarding-school
days were over. For himself he had a great prejudice against
the usurpation of men's duties and prerogatives by women,
and had spoken of all such assumptions with contempt. It
made a difference that this attractive young student had spoken bravely on the wrong side; but if he had thought much
about it he would have made himself surer and surer that only
time was needed to show her the mistake. If he had gone
deeper into the subject he would have said that he thought it
all nonsense about women's having the worst of it in life; he
had known more than one good fellow who had begun to go

down hill from the day he was married, and if girls would only take the trouble to fit themselves for their indoor business the world would be a vastly more comfortable place. And as for their tinkering at the laws, such projects should be bitterly resented.

It only needed a few days to make it plain to this good fellow that the coming of one of the summer guests had made a great difference in his life. It was easy to find a hundred excuses for going to Miss Prince's, who smiled benignantly upon his evident interest in the fair stranger within her gates. The truth must be confessed, however, that the episode of the lamed shoulder at the picnic party had given Mr. George Gerry great unhappiness. There was something so high and serene in Anna Prince's simplicity and directness, and in the way in which she had proved herself adequate to so unusual an occasion, that he could not help mingling a good deal of admiration with his dissatisfaction. It is in human nature to respect power; but all his manliness was at stake, and his natural rights would be degraded and lost, if he could not show his power to be greater than her own. And as the days went by, every one made him more certain that he longed, more than he had ever longed for anything before, to win her love. His heart had never before been deeply touched, but life seemed now like a heap of dry wood, which had only waited for a live coal to make it flame and leap in mysterious light, and transfigure itself from dullness into a bewildering and unaccountable glory. It was no wonder any longer that poets had sung best of love and its joys and sorrows, and that men and women, since the world began, had followed at its call. All life and its history was explained anew, yet this eager lover felt himself to be the first discoverer of the world's great secret.

It was hard to wait and to lack assurance, but while the hours when he had the ideal and the dream seemed to make him certain, he had only to go back to Miss Prince's to become doubtful and miserable again. The world did not consent to second his haste, and the persons most concerned in his affairs were stupidly slow at understanding the true state of them. While every day made the prize look more desirable, every day seemed to put another barrier between himself and Nan; and when she spoke of her visit's end it was amazing to him that she should not understand his misery. He wondered at himself more and more because he seemed to have the power of behaving much as usual when he was with his friends; it seemed impossible that he could always go on without betraying his thoughts. There was no question of any final opposition to his suit, it seemed to him; he could not be more sure than he was already of Miss Prince's willingness to let him plead his cause with her niece, so many vexed questions would be pleasantly answered; and he ventured to hope that the girl herself would be glad to spend her life in dear old Dunport, where her father's people had been honored for so many years. The good Dr. Leslie must be fast growing old, and, though he would miss his adopted child, it was reasonable that he should be glad to see her happily anchored in a home of her own, before he died. If Nan were friendless and penniless it would make no difference; but nevertheless, for her sake, it was good to remember that some one had said that Dr. Leslie, unlike most physicians, was a man of fortune. And nothing remained but to win an affection which should match his own, and this impatient suitor walked and drove and spent the fleeting hours in waiting for a chance to show himself in the lists of love. It seemed years instead of weeks at last, and yet as if he had only been truly alive and free since love had made him captive. He could not fasten himself down to his work without great difficulty, though he built many a castle in Spain with his imagined wealth, and laid deep plans of study and acquirement which should be made evident as time went on.

All things seemed within his reach in these first days of his enlightenment: it had been like the rising of the sun which showed him a new world of which he was lawful master, but the minor events of his blissful existence began to conspire against him in a provoking way, and presently it was sadly forced upon his understanding that Anna Prince was either unconscious or disdainful of his affection. It could hardly be the latter, for she was always friendly and hospitable, and took his courtesies in such an unsuspecting and grateful way. There was something so self-reliant about her and so independent of any one's protection, that this was the most discouraging thing of all, for his own instinct was that of standing between her and all harm,—of making himself responsible for her shelter and happiness. She seemed to get on capitally well without him, but after all he could not help being conqueror in so just and inevitable a war. The old proverb suddenly changed from a pebble to a diamond, and he thanked the philosopher more than once who had first reminded the world that faint heart ne'er won fair lady; presently he grew sad, as lovers will, and became paler and less vigorous, and made his friends wonder a good deal, until they at last suspected his sweet sorrow, and ranged themselves in eager ranks upon his side, with all history and tradition in their favor.

Nan herself was not among the first to suspect that one of her new friends had proved to be a lover; she had been turned away from such suspicions by her very nature; and when she had been forced to believe in one or two other instances that she was unwillingly drawing to herself the devotion which most women unconsciously seek, she had been made most uncomfortable, and had repelled all possibility of its further progress. She had believed herself proof against such assailment, and so indeed she had been; but on the very evening of her battle for her opinions at Mrs. Fraley's she had been suddenly confronted by a new enemy, a strange power, which seemed so dangerous that she was at first overwhelmed by a sense of her own defenselessness.

She had waited with Miss Fraley, who was not quite ready to leave the dining-room with the rest, and had been much touched by her confidence. Poor Eunice had been very fond of one of her school-fellows, who had afterward entered the navy, and who had been fond of her in return. But as everybody had opposed the match, for her sake, and had placed little reliance in the young man, she had meekly given up all hope of being his wife, and he had died of yellow fever at Key West soon after. "We were not even engaged you know, dear," whispered the little lady, "but somehow I have always felt in my heart that I belonged to him. Though I believe every word you said about a girl's having an independence of her own. It is a great blessing to have always had such a person as my mother to lean upon, but I should be quite helpless if she were taken away. . . . Of course I have had what I needed and what we could afford," she went on, after another pause, "but I never can get over hating to ask for money. I do sometimes envy the women who earn what they spend."

Nan's eyes flashed. "I think it is only fair that even those who have to spend their husband's or their father's money should be made to feel it is their own. If one does absolutely nothing in one's home, and is not even able to give pleasure, then I think it is stealing. I have felt so strongly about that since I have grown up, for you know Dr. Leslie, my guardian, has done everything for me. Aunt Nancy gave me money every year, but I never spent any of it until I went away to school, and then I insisted upon taking that and what my grandmother left me. But my later studies have more than used it all. Dr. Leslie is so kind to me, like an own father, and I am looking forward to my life with him most eagerly. After the next year or two I shall be at home all the time, and I am so glad to think I can really help him, and that we are interested in the same things."

Miss Eunice was a little incredulous, though she did not dare to say so. In the first place, she could not be persuaded that a woman could possibly know as much about diseases and their remedies as a man, and she wondered if even the rural inhabitants of Oldfields would cheerfully accept the change from their trusted physician to his young ward, no matter what sails of diplomas she might spread to the breeze. But Nan's perfect faith and confidence were not to be lightly disputed; and if the practice of medicine by women could be made honorable, it certainly was in able hands here, as far as an admiring friend could decide. Nan was anything but self-asserting, and she had no noisy fashion of thrusting herself before the public gaze, but everybody trusted her who knew her; she had the rare and noble faculty of inspiring confidence.

There was no excuse for a longer absence from the parlor, where Mrs. Fraley was throned in state in her high-backed chair, and was already calling the loiterers. She and Miss Prince were smiling indulgently upon the impatient young man, who was describing to them a meeting of the stockholders of the Turnpike Company, of which he had last year been made secretary. A dividend had been declared, and it was larger than had been expected, and the ladies were as grateful as if he had furnished the means from his own pocket. He looked very tall and handsome and business-like as he rose to salute Miss Fraley and Nan, and presently told his real errand. He apologized for interfering with the little festival, but two or three of the young people had suddenly made a plan for going to see a play which was to be given that night in the town hall by a traveling company. Would Miss Anna Prince care to go, and Miss Fraley?

Nan hardly knew why she at once refused, and was filled with regret when she saw a look of childish expectancy on Miss Eunice's face quickly change to disappointment.

"It is too hot to shut one's self into that close place, I am afraid," she said. "And I am enjoying myself very much here, Mr. Gerry." Which was generous on Nan's part, if one considered the premeditated war which had been waged against her. Then the thought flashed through her mind that it might be a bit of good fun for her companion; and without waiting for either approval or opposition from the elder women, she said, in a different tone, "However, if Miss Fraley will go too, I will accept with pleasure; I suppose it is quite time?" and before there could be a formal dissent she had hurried the pleased daughter of the house, who was not quick in her movements, to her room, and in a few minutes, after a good deal of laughter which the presence of the escort kept anybody from even wishing to silence, the three were fairly started down the street. It was of no avail that Mrs. Fraley condemned her own judgment in not having advised Eunice to stay at home and leave the young people free, and that Miss Prince made a feeble protest for politeness' sake,— the pleasure-makers could not be called back.

Nan had really grown into a great liking for George Gerry. She often thought it would have been very good to have such a brother. But more than one person in the audience thought they had never seen a braver young couple; and the few elderly persons of discretion who had gone to the play felt their hearts thrill with sudden sympathy as our friends went far down the room to their seats. Miss Fraley was almost girlish herself, and looked so pleased and bright that everybody who cared anything about her smiled when they caught sight of her, she was so prim and neat; it was impossible for her, under any circumstances, to look anything but discreet and quaint; but as for Nan, she was beautiful with youth and health; as simply dressed as Miss Eunice, but with the gayety of a flower,—some slender, wild thing, that has sprung up fearlessly under the great sky, with only the sunshine and the wind and summer rain to teach it, and help it fulfill its destiny,—a flower that has grown with no painful effort of its own, but because God made it and kept it; that has bloomed because it has come in the course of its growth to the right time. And Miss Eunice, like a hindered little house-plant, took a long breath of delight as she sat close by her kind young friend, and felt as if somebody had set her roots free from their familiar prison.

To let God make us, instead of painfully trying to make ourselves; to follow the path that his love shows us, instead of through conceit or cowardice or mockery choosing another; to trust Him for our strength and fitness as the flowers do, simply giving ourselves back to Him in grateful service,—this is to keep the laws that give us the freedom of the city in which there is no longer any night of bewilderment or ignorance or uncertainty. So the woman who had lived a life of bondage, whose hardest task-master was herself, and the woman who had been both taught and inspired to hold fast her freedom, sat side by side: the one life having been blighted because it lacked its mate, and was but half a life in itself; while the other, fearing to give half its royalty or to share its bounty, was being tempted to cripple itself, and to lose its strait and narrow way where God had left no room for another.

For as the play went on and the easily pleased audience laughed and clapped its hands, and the tired players bowed and smiled from behind the flaring foot-lights, there was one spectator who was conscious of a great crisis in her own life, which the mimicry of that evening seemed to ridicule and counterfeit. And though Nan smiled with the rest, and even talked with her neighbors while the tawdry curtain had fallen, it seemed to her that the coming of Death at her life's end could not be more strange and sudden than this great barrier which had fallen between her and her girlhood, the dear old life which had kept her so unpuzzled and safe. So this was love at last, this fear, this change, this strange relation to another soul. Who could stand now at her right hand and give her grace to hold fast the truth that her soul must ever be her own?

The only desire that possessed her was to be alone again, to make Love show his face as well as make his mysterious presence felt. She was thankful for the shelter of the crowd, and went on, wishing that the short distance to her aunt's home could be made even shorter. She had felt this man's love for her only in a vague way before, and now, as he turned to speak to her from time to time, she could not meet his eyes. The groups of people bade each other good-night merrily, though the entertainment had been a little tiresome to every one at the last, and it seemed the briefest space of time before Miss Fraley and Nan and their cavalier were left by themselves, and at last Nan and George Gerry were alone together.

For his part he had never been so happy as that night. It seemed to him that his wish was coming true, and he spoke gently enough and of the same things they might have talked about the night before, but a splendid chorus of victory was sounding in his ears; and once, as they stopped for a moment to look between two of the old warehouses at the shining river and the masts and rigging of the ship against the moonlighted sky, he was just ready to speak to the girl at his side. But he looked at her first and then was silent. There was something in her face that forbade it,—a whiteness and a strange look in her eyes, that made him lose all feeling of comradeship or even acquaintance. "I wonder if the old Highflyer will ever go out again?" she said slowly. "Captain Parish told me some time ago that he had found her more badly damaged than he supposed. A vessel like that belongs to the high seas, and is like a prisoner when it touches shore. I believe that the stray souls that have no bodies must sometimes make a dwelling in inanimate things and make us think they are alive. I am always sorry for that ship"—

"Its guardian angel must have been asleep the night of the collision," laughed young Gerry, uneasily; he was displeased with himself the moment afterward, but Nan laughed too, and felt a sense of reprieve; and they went on again and said good night quietly on the steps of the old Prince house. It was very late for Dunport, and the door was shut, but through the bull's-eyed panes of glass overhead a faint light was shining, though it could hardly assert itself against the moonlight. Miss Prince was still down-stairs, and her niece upbraided her, and then began to give an account of the play, which was cut short by the mistress of the house; for after one eager, long look at Nan, she became sleepy and disappointed, and they said good-night; but the girl felt certain that her aunt was leagued against her, and grew sick at heart and tired as she climbed the stairs. There was a letter on the long mahogany table in the hall, and Nan stopped and looked over the railing at it wearily. Miss Prince stopped too, and said she was sorry she had forgotten,—it was from Oldfields, and in Dr. Leslie's writing. But though Nan went back for it, and kissed it more than once before she went to bed, and even put it under her pillow as a comfort and defense against she knew not what, for the first time in her life she was afraid to open it and read the kind words. That night she watched the moonlight creep along the floor, and heard the cocks crow at midnight and in the morning; the birds woke with the new day while she tried to understand the day that had gone, wondering what she must do and say when she faced the world again only a few hours later.

Sometimes she felt herself carried along upon a rushing tide, and was amazed that a hundred gifts and conditions to which she had scarcely given a thought seemed dear and necessary. Once she fancied herself in a quiet home; living there, perhaps, in that very house, and being pleased with her ordering and care-taking. And her great profession was all like a fading dream; it seemed now no matter whether she had ever loved the studies of it, or been glad to think that she had it in her power to make suffering less, or prevent it altogether. Her old ambitions were torn away from her one by one, and in their place came the hardly-desired satisfactions of love and marriage, and home-making and housekeeping, the dear, womanly, sheltered fashions of life, toward which she had been thankful to see her friends go hand in hand, making themselves a complete happiness which nothing else could match. But as the night waned, the certainty of her duty grew clearer and clearer. She had long ago made up her mind that she must not marry. She might be happy, it was true, and make other people so, but her duty was not this, and a certainty that satisfaction and the blessing of God would not follow her into these reverenced and honored limits came to her distinctly. One by one the reasons for keeping on her chosen course grew more unanswerable than ever. She had not thought she should be called to resist this temptation, but since it had come she was glad she was strong enough to meet it. It would be no real love for another person, and no justice to herself, to give up her work, even though holding it fast would bring weariness and pain and reproach, and the loss of many things that other women held dearest and best.

In the morning Nan smiled when her aunt noticed her tired look, and said that the play had been a pursuit of pleasure under difficulties. And though Miss Prince looked up in dismay, and was full of objections and almost querulous reproaches because Nan said she must end her visit within a day or two, she hoped that George Gerry would be, after all, a reason for the girl's staying. Until Nan, who had been standing by the window, looking wistfully at the garden, suddenly turned and said, gently and solemnly, "Listen, Aunt Nancy! I must be about my business; you do not know what it means to me, or what I hope to make it mean to other people." And then Miss Prince knew once for all, that it was useless to hope or to plan any longer. But she would not let herself be vanquished so easily, and summoned to her mind many assurances that girls would not be too easily won, and after a short season of disapproving silence, returned to her usual manner as if there had been neither difference nor dispute.

XX

ASHORE AND AFLOAT

"Your cousin Walter Parish is coming to dine with us to-day," said Miss Prince, later that morning. "He came to the Fraleys just after you went out last evening, to speak with me about a business matter, and waited to walk home with me afterward. I have been meaning to invite him here with his wife, but there does n't seem to be much prospect of her leaving her room for some time yet, and this morning I happened to find an uncommonly good pair of young ducks. Old Mr. Brown has kept my liking for them in mind for a great many years. Your grandfather used to say that there was nothing like a duckling to his taste; he used to eat them in England, but people in this country let them get too old. He was willing to pay a great price for ducklings always; but even Mr. Brown seems to think it is a great wrong not to let them grow until Thanksgiving time, and makes a great many apologies every year. It is from his farm that we always get the best lamb too; they are very nice people, the Browns, but the poor old man seems very feeble this summer. Some day I should really like to take a drive out into the country to see them, you know so well how to manage a horse. You can spare a day or two to give time for that, can't you?"

Nan was sorry to hear the pleading tone, it was so unlike her aunt's usually severe manner, and answered quickly that she should be very glad to make the little excursion. Mr. Brown had asked her to come to the farm one day near the beginning of her visit.

"You must say this is home, if you can," said Miss Prince, who was a good deal excited and shaken that morning, "and not think of yourself as a visitor any more. There are a great many things I hope you can understand, even if I have left them unsaid. It has really seemed more like home since you have been here, and less like a lodging. I wonder how I —When did you see Mr. Brown? I did not know you had ever spoken to him."

"It was some time ago," the girl answered. "I was in the kitchen, and he came to the door. He seemed very glad to see me," and Nan hesitated a moment. "He said I was like my father."

"Yes, indeed," responded Miss Prince, drearily; and the thought seized her that it was very strange that the same mistaken persistency should show itself in father and child in exactly opposite ways. If Nan would only care as much for marrying George Gerry, as her father had for marrying his wretched wife! It seemed more and more impossible that this little lady should be the daughter of such a woman; how dismayed the girl would be if she could be shown her mother's nature as Miss Prince remembered it. Alas! this was already a sorrow which no vision of the reality could deepen, and the frank words of the Oldfields country people about the bad Thachers had not been spoken fruitlessly in the ears of their last descendant.

"I am so glad the captain is coming," Nan said presently, to break the painful silence. "I do hope that he and Dr. Leslie will know each other some time, they would be such capital friends. The doctor sent his kind regards to you in last night's letter, and asked me again to say that he hoped that you would come to us before the summer is over. I should like so much to have you know what Oldfields is like." It was hard to save herself from saying "home" again, instead of Oldfields, but the change of words was made quickly.

"He is very courteous and hospitable, but I never pay visits nowadays," said Miss Prince, and thought almost angrily that there was no necessity for her making a target of herself for all those curious country-people's eyes. And then they rose and separated for a time, each being burdened less by care than thought.

The captain came early to dine, and brought with him his own and Miss Prince's letters from the post-office, together with the morning paper, which he proceeded to read. He also seemed to have a weight upon his mind, but by the time they were at table a mild cheerfulness made itself felt, and Nan summoned all her resources and was gayer and brighter than usual. Miss Prince had gone down town early in the day, and her niece was perfectly sure that there had been a consultation with Mr. Gerry. He had passed the house while Nan sat at her upper window writing, and had looked somewhat wistfully at the door as if he had half a mind to enter it. He was like a great magnet: it seemed impossible to resist looking after him, and indeed his ghost-like presence would not forsake her mind, but seemed urging her toward his visible self. The thought of him was so powerful that the sight of the young man was less strange and compelling, and it was almost a relief to have seen his familiar appearance,—the strong figure in its every-day clothes, his unstudent-like vigor, and easy step as he went by. She liked him still, but she hated love, it was making her so miserable,—even when later she told Captain Parish some delightful Oldfields stories, of so humorous a kind that he laughed long and struck the table more than once, which set the glasses jingling, and gave a splendid approval to the time-honored fun. The ducklings were amazingly good; and when Captain Walter had tasted his wine and read the silver label on the decanter, which as usual gave no evidence of the rank and dignity of the contents, his eyes sparkled with satisfaction, and he turned to his cousin's daughter with impressive gravity.

"You may never have tasted such wine as that," he said. "Your grandfather, the luckiest captain who ever sailed out of Dunport, brought it home fifty years ago, and it was well ripened then. I did n't know there was a bottle of it left, Nancy," he laughed. "My dear, your aunt has undertaken to pay one of us a handsome compliment."

"Your health, cousin Walter!" said the girl quickly, lifting her own glass, and making him a little bow over the old Madeira.

"Bless your dear heart!" responded the captain; "the same good wishes to you in return, and now you must join me in my respects to your aunt. Nancy! I beg you not to waste this in pudding-sauces; that 's the way with you ladies."

The toast-drinking had a good effect upon the little company, and it seemed as if the cloud which had hung over it at first had been blown away. When there was no longer any excuse for lingering at the table, the guest seemed again a little ill at ease, and after a glance at his hostess, proposed to

Nan that they should take a look at the garden. The old sailor had become in his later years a devoted tiller of the soil, and pleaded a desire to see some late roses which were just now in bloom. So he and Nan went down the walk together, and he fidgeted and hurried about for a few minutes before he could make up his mind to begin a speech which was weighing heavily on his conscience.

Nan was sure that something unusual was perplexing him, and answered his unnecessary questions patiently, wondering what he was trying to say.

"Dear me!" he grumbled at last, "I shall have to steer a straight course. The truth is, Nancy has been telling me that I ought to advise with you, and see that you understand what you are about with young Gerry. She has set her heart on your fancying him. I dare say you know she has treated him like a son all through his growing up; but now that you have come to your rightful place, she can't bear to have any-body hint at your going back to the other people. 'T is plain enough what he thinks about it, and I must say I believe it would be for your good. Here you are with your father's family, what is left of it; and I take no liberty when I tell you that your aunt desires this to be your home, and means to give you your father's share of the property now and the rest when she is done with it. It is no more than your rights, and I know as much as anybody about it, and can tell you that there's a handsomer fortune than you may have sus-pected. Money grows fast if it is let alone; and though your aunt has done a good deal for others, her expenses have been well held in hand. I must say I should like to keep you here, child," the captain faltered, "but I shall want to do what's for your happiness. I couldn't feel more earnest about that if I were your own father. You must think it over. I'm not going to beseech you: I learned long ago that 't is no use to drive a Prince."

Nan had tried at first to look unconcerned and treat the matter lightly, but this straightforward talk appealed to her much more than the suggestion and general advice which Miss Prince had implored the captain to give the night before. And now her niece could only thank him for his kindness, and tell him that by and by she would make him understand why she put aside these reasons, and went back to the life she had known before.

But a sudden inspiration made her resolution grow stronger, and she looked at Captain Parish with a convincing bravery.

"When you followed the sea," she said quickly, "if you had a good ship with a freight that you had gathered with great care and hopefulness, and had brought it almost to the market that it was suited for, would you have been persuaded to turn about and take it to some place where it would be next to useless?"

"No," said Captain Parish, "no, I shouldn't," and he half smiled at this illustration.

"I can't tell you all my reasons for not wishing to marry," Nan went on, growing very white and determined, "or all my reasons for wishing to go on with my plan of being a doctor; but I know I have no right to the one way of life, and a perfect one, so far as I can see, to the other. And it seems to me that it would be as sensible to ask Mr. Gerry to be a minister since he has just finished his law studies, as to ask me to be a wife instead of a physician. But what I used to dread without reason a few years ago, I must forbid myself now, because I know the wretched inheritance I might have had from my poor mother's people. I can't speak of that to Aunt Nancy, but you must tell her not to try to make me change my mind."

"Good God!" said the captain. "I dare say you have the right points of it; but if I were a young man 't would go hard with me to let you take your life into your own hands. It's against nature."

"No," said Nan. "The law of right and wrong must rule even love, and whatever comes to me, I must not forget that. Three years ago I had not thought about it so much, and I might not have been so sure; but now I have been taught there is only one road to take. And you must tell Aunt Nancy this."

But when they went back to the house, Miss Prince was not to be seen, and the captain hurried away lest she should make her appearance, for he did not wish just then to talk about the matter any more. He told himself that young people were very different in these days; but when he thought of the words he had heard in the garden, and remembered the pale face and the steadfast, clear-toned voice, he brushed away something like a tear. "If more people used judgment in this same decision the world would be better off," he said, and could not help reminding himself that his own niece, little Mary Parish, who was wearing a wistful countenance in these days, might by and by be happy after all. For Nan's part it was a great relief to have spoken to the kind old man; she felt more secure than before; but sometimes the fear assailed her that some unforeseen event or unreckoned influence might give her back to her indecisions, and that the battle of the night before might after all prove not to be final.

The afternoon wore away, and late in the day our heroine heard George Gerry's step coming up the street. She listened as she sat by the upper window, and found that he was giving a message for her. It was perfect weather to go up the river, he was saying; the tide served just right and would bring them home early; and Miss Prince, who was alone in the parlor, answered with pleased assurance that she was sure her niece would like to go. "Yes," said Nan, calling from the window, urged by a sudden impulse. "Yes indeed, I should like it above all things; I will get ready at once; will you carry two pairs of oars?"

There was a ready assent, but the uncertainty of the tone of it struck Anna Prince's quick ear. She seemed to know that the young man and her aunt were exchanging looks of surprise, and that they felt insecure and uncertain. It was not the yielding maiden who had spoken to her lover, but the girl who was his good comrade and cordial friend. The elder woman shook her head doubtfully; she knew well what this foreboded, and was impatient at the overthrow of her plans; yet she had full confidence in the power of Love. She had seen apparent self-reliance before, and she could not believe that her niece was invincible. At any rate nothing could be more persuasive than a twilight row upon the river, and for her part, she hoped more eagerly than ever that Love would return chief in command of the boat's young crew; and when the young man flushed a little, and looked at her appealingly, as he turned to go down the street, his friend and counselor could not resist giving him a hopeful nod. Nan was singularly frank, and free from affectations, and she might have already decided to lower her colors and yield the victory, and it seemed for a moment that it would be much more like her to do so, than to invite further contest when she was already won. Miss Prince was very kind and sympathetic when this explanation had once forced itself upon her mind; she gave the young girl a most affectionate kiss when she appeared, but at this unmistakable suggestion of pleasure and treasured hopes, Nan turned back suddenly into the shaded parlor, though Mr. Gerry was waiting outside with his favorite oars, which he kept carefully in a corner of the office.

"Dear Aunt Nancy," said the girl, with evident effort, "I am so sorry to disappoint you. I wish for your sake that I had been another sort of woman; but I shall never marry. I know you think I am wrong, but there is something which always tells me I am right, and I must follow another way. I should only wreck my life, and other people's. Most girls have an instinct towards marrying, but mine is all against it, and God knew best when He made me care more for another fashion of life. Don't make me seem unkind! I dare say that I can put it all into words better by and by, but I can never be more certain of it in my own heart than now."

"Sit down a minute," said Miss Prince, slowly. "George can wait. But, Anna, I believe that you are in love with him, and that you are doing wrong to the poor lad, and to yourself, and to me. I lost the best happiness of my life for a whim, and you wish to throw away yours for a theory. I hope you will be guided by me. I have come to love you very much, and it seems as if this would be so reasonable."

"It does make a difference to me that he loves me," confessed the girl. "It is not easy to turn away from him," she said, — still standing, and looking taller than ever, and even thin, with a curious tenseness of her whole being. "It is something that I have found it hard to fight against, but it is not my whole self longing for his love and his companionship. If I heard he had gone to the other side of the world for years and years, I should be glad now and not sorry. I know that all the world's sympathy and all tradition fight on his side; but I can look forward and see something a thousand times better than being his wife, and living here in Dunport keeping his house, and trying to forget all that nature fitted me to do. You don't understand, Aunt Nancy. I wish you could! You see it all another way." And the tears started to the eager young eyes. "Don't you know that Cousin Walter said this very day that the wind which sets one vessel on the right course may set another on the wrong?"

"Nonsense, my dear," said the mistress of the house. "I don't think this is the proper time for you to explain yourself at any rate. I dare say the fresh air will do you good and put everything right too. You have worked yourself into a great excitement over nothing. Don't go out looking so desperate to the poor fellow; he will think strangely of it;" and the girl went out through the wide hall, and wished she were far away from all this trouble.

Nan had felt a strange sense of weariness, which did not leave her even when she was quieted by the fresh breeze of the river-shore, and was contented to let her oars be stowed in the bottom of the boat, and to take the comfortable seat in the stern. She pulled the tiller ropes over her shoulders, and watched her lover's first strong strokes, which had quickly sent them out into the stream, beyond the course of a larger craft which was coming toward the wharf. She wished presently that she had chosen to row, because they would not then be face to face; but, strange to say, since this new experience had come to her, she had not felt so sure of herself as now, and the fear of finding herself too weak to oppose the new tendency of her life had lessened since her first recognition of it the night before. But Nan had fought a hard fight, and had grown a great deal older in those hours of the day and night. She believed that time would make her even more certain that she had done right than she could be now in the heat of the battle, but she wished whatever George Gerry meant to say to her might be soon over with.

They went slowly up the river, which was now quite familiar to the girl who had come to it a stranger only a few weeks before. She liked out-of-door life so well that this country-side of Dunport was already more dear to her than to many who had seen it bloom and fade every year since they could remember. At one moment it seemed but yesterday that she had come to the old town, and at the next she felt as if she had spent half a lifetime there, and as if Oldfields might have changed unbearably since she came away.

Sometimes the young oarsman kept in the middle of the great stream, and sometimes it seemed pleasanter to be near the shore. The midsummer flowers were coming into blossom, and the grass and trees had long since lost the brilliance of their greenness, and wore a look of maturity and completion, as if they had already finished their growth. There was a beautiful softness and harmony of color, a repose that one never sees in a spring landscape. The tide was in, the sun was almost down, and a great, cloudless, infinite sky arched itself from horizon to horizon. It had sent all its brilliance to shine backward from the sun, — the glowing sphere from which a single dazzling ray came across the fields and the water to the boat. In a moment more it was gone, and a shadow quickly fell like that of a tropical twilight; but the west grew golden, and one light cloud, like a floating red feather, faded away upward into the sky. A later bright glow touched some high hills in the east, then they grew purple and gray, and so the evening came that way slowly, and the ripple of the water plashed and sobbed against the boat's side; and presently in the midst of the river's inland bay, after a few last eager strokes, the young man drew in his oars, letting them drop with a noise which startled Nan, who had happened to be looking over her shoulder at the shore.

She knew well enough that he meant to put a grave question to her now, and her heart beat faster and she twisted the tiller cords around her hands unconsciously.

"I think I could break any bonds you might use to keep yourself away from me," he said hurriedly, as he watched her. "I am not fit for you, only that I love you. Somebody told me you meant to go away, and I could not wait any longer before I asked you if you would give yourself to me."

"No, no!" cried Nan, "dear friend, I must not do it; it would all be a mistake. You must not think of it any more. I am so sorry, I ought to have understood what was coming to us, and have gone away long ago."

"It would have made no difference," said the young man, almost angrily. He could not bear delay enough even for speech at that moment; he watched her face desperately for a look of assurance; he leaned toward her and wondered why he had not risked everything, and spoken the evening before when they stood watching the ship's mast, and Nan's hands were close enough to be touched. But the miserable knowledge crept over him that she was a great deal farther away from him than half that small boat's length, and as she looked up at him again, and shook her head gently, a great rage of love and shame at his repulse urged him to plead again. "You are spoiling my life," he cried. "You do not care for that, but without you I shall not care for anything."

"I would rather spoil your life in this way than in a far worse fashion," said Nan sadly. "I will always be your friend, but if I married you I might seem by and by to be your enemy. Yes, you will love somebody else some day, and be a great deal happier than I could have made you, and I shall be so glad. It does not belong to me."

But this seemed too scornful and cold-hearted. "Oh, my love is only worth that to you," the lover said. "You shall know better what it means. I don't want you for my friend, but for my own to keep and to have. It makes me laugh to think of your being a doctor and going back to that country town to throw yourself away for the fancies and silly theories of a man who has lived like a hermit. It means a true life for both of us if you will only say you love me, or even let me ask you again when you have thought of it more. Everybody will say I am in the right."

"Yes, there are reasons enough for it, but there is a better reason against it. If you love me you must help me do what is best," said Nan. "I shall miss you and think of you more than you know when I am away. I never shall forget all these pleasant days we have been together. Oh George!" she cried, in a tone that thrilled him through and through, "I hope you will be friends with me again by and by. You will know then I have done right because it is right and will prove itself. If it is wrong for me I couldn't really make you happy; and over all this and beyond it something promises me and calls me for a life that my marrying you would hinder and not help. It isn't that I should n't be so happy that it is not easy to turn away even from the thought of it; but I know that the days would come when I should see, in a way that would make me long to die, that I had lost the true direction of my life and had misled others beside myself. You don't believe me, but I cannot break faith with my duty. There are many reasons that have forbidden me to marry, and I have a certainty as sure as the stars that the only right condition of life for me is to follow the way that everything until now has pointed out. The great gain and purpose of my being alive is there; and I must not mind the blessings that I shall have to do without."

He made a gesture of impatience and tried to interrupt her, but she said quickly, as if to prevent his speaking: "Listen to me. I can't help speaking plainly. I would not have come with you this afternoon, only I wished to make you understand me entirely. I have never since I can remember thought of myself and my life in any way but unmarried,—going on alone to the work I am fit to do. I do care for you. I have been greatly surprised and shaken because I found how strongly something in me has taken your part, and shown me the possibility of happiness in a quiet life that should centre itself in one man's love, and within the walls of his home. But something tells me all the time that I could not marry the whole of myself as most women can; there is a great share of my life which could not have its way, and could only hide itself and be sorry. I know better and better that most women are made for another sort of existence, but by and by I must do my part in my own way to make many homes happy instead of one; to free them from pain, and teach grown people and little children to keep their bodies free from weakness and deformities. I don't know why God should have made me a doctor, so many other things have seemed fitter for women; but I see the blessedness of such a useful life more and more every year, and I am very thankful for such a trust. It is a splendid thing to have the use of any gift of God. It is n't for us to choose again, or wonder and dispute, but just work in our own places, and leave the rest to God."

The boat was being carried downward by the ebbing tide, and George Gerry took the oars again, and rowed quietly and in silence. He took his defeat unkindly and drearily; he was ashamed of himself once, because some evil spirit told him that he was losing much that would content him, in failing to gain this woman's love. It had all been so fair a prospect of worldly success, and she had been the queen of it. He thought of himself growing old in Mr. Sergeant's dusty office, and that this was all that life could hold for him. Yet to be was better than to have. Alas! if he had been more earnest in his growth, it would have been a power which this girl of high ideals could have been held and mastered by. No wonder that she would not give up her dreams of duty and service, since she had found him less strong than such ideals. The fancied dissatisfaction and piteousness of failure which she would be sure to meet filled his heart with dismay; yet, at that very next moment, resent it as he might, the certainty of his own present defeat and powerlessness could not be misunderstood. Perhaps, after all, she knew what was right; her face wore again the look he had feared to disturb the night before, and his whole soul was filled with homage in the midst of its sorrow, because this girl, who had been his merry companion in the summer holidays, so sweet and familiar and unforgetable in the midst of the simple festivals, stood nearer to holier things than himself, and had listened to the call of God's messengers to whom his own doors had been ignorantly shut. And Nan that night was a soul's physician, though she had been made to sorely hurt her patient before the new healthfulness could well begin.

They floated down the river and tried to talk once or twice, but there were many spaces of silence, and as they walked along the paved streets, they thought of many things. An east wind was blowing in from the sea, and the elm branches were moving restlessly overhead. "It will all be better to-morrow," said Nan, as they stood on the steps at last. "You must come to see Aunt Nancy very often after I have gone, for she will be lonely. And do come in the morning as if nothing had been spoken. I am so sorry. Good-night, and God bless you," she whispered; and when she stood inside the wide doorway, in the dark, she listened to his footsteps as he went away down the street. They were slower than usual, but she did not call him back.

XXI

AT HOME AGAIN

In Oldfields Dr. Leslie had outwardly lived the familiar life to which his friends and patients had long since accustomed themselves; he had seemed a little preoccupied, perhaps, but if that were observed, it was easily explained by his having one or two difficult cases to think about. A few persons suspected that he missed Nan, and was, perhaps, a little anxious lest her father's people in Dunport should claim her altogether. Among those who knew best the doctor and his ward there had been an ardent championship of Nan's rights and dignity, and a great curiosity to know the success of the visit. Dr. Leslie had answered all questions with composure, and with a distressing meagreness of details; but at length Mrs. Graham became sure that he was not altogether free from anxiety, and set her own quick wits at work to learn the cause. It seemed a time of great uncertainty, at any rate. The doctor sometimes brought one of Nan's bright, affectionate letters for his neighbor to read, and they agreed that this holiday was an excellent thing for her, but there was a silent recognition of the fact that this was a critical time in the young girl's history; that it either meant a new direction of her life or an increased activity in the old one. Mrs. Graham was less well than usual in these days, and the doctor found time to make more frequent visits than ever, telling himself that she missed Nan's pleasant companionship, but really wishing as much to receive sympathy as to give it. The dear old lady had laughingly disclaimed any desire to summon her children or grandchildren, saying that she was neither ill enough to need them, nor well enough to enjoy them; and so in the beautiful June weather the two old friends became strangely dear to each other, and had many a long talk which the cares of the world or their own reserve had made them save until this favoring season.

The doctor was acknowledged to be an old man at last, though everybody still insisted that he looked younger than his age, and could not doubt that he had half a lifetime of usefulness before him yet. But it makes a great difference when one's ambitions are transferred from one's own life to that of a younger person's; and while Dr. Leslie grew less careful for himself, trusting to the unconscious certainty of his practiced skill, he pondered eagerly over Nan's future, reminding himself of various hints and suggestions, which must be added to her equipment. Sometimes he wished that she were beginning a few years later, when her position could be better recognized and respected, and she would not have to fight against so much of the opposition and petty fault-finding that come from ignorance; and sometimes he rejoiced that his little girl, as he fondly called her, would be one of the earlier proofs and examples of a certain noble advance and new vantage-ground of civilization. This has been anticipated through all ages by the women who, sometimes honored and sometimes persecuted, have been drawn away from home life by a devotion to public and social usefulness. It must be recognized that certain qualities are required for married, and even domestic life, which all women do not possess; but instead of attributing this to the disintegration of society, it must be acknowledged to belong to its progress.

So long as the visit in Dunport seemed to fulfill its anticipated purpose, and the happy guest was throwing aside her cares and enjoying the merry holiday and the excitement of new friendships and of her uncommon position, so long the doctor had been glad, and far from impatient to have the visit end. But when he read the later and shorter letters again and again in the vain hope of finding something in their wording which should explain the vague unhappiness which had come to him as he had read them first, he began to feel troubled and dismayed. There was something which Nan had not explained; something was going wrong. He was sure that if it were anything he could set right, that she would have told him. She had always done so; but it became evident through the strange sympathy which made him conscious of the mood of others that she was bent upon fighting her way alone.

It was a matter of surprise, and almost of dismay to him early one morning, when he received a brief note from her which told him only that she should be at home late that afternoon. It seemed to the wise old doctor a day of most distressing uncertainty. He tried to make up his mind to accept with true philosophy whatever decision she was bringing him. "Nan is a good girl," he told himself over and over again; "she will try to do right." But she was so young and so generous, and whether she had been implored to break the old ties of home life and affection for her aunt's sake, or whether it was a newer and stronger influence still which had prevailed, waited for explanation. Alas, as was written once, it is often the higher nature that yields, because it is the most generous. The doctor knew well enough the young girl's character. He knew what promises of growth and uncommon achievement were all ready to unfold themselves,—for what great uses she was made. He could not bear the thought of her being handicapped in the race she had been set to run. Yet no one recognized more clearly than he the unseen, and too often unconsidered, factor which is peculiar to each soul, which prevents any other intelligence from putting itself exactly in that soul's place, so that our decisions and aids and suggestions are never wholly sufficient or available for those even whom we love most. He went over the question again and again; he followed Nan in his thoughts as she had grown up,—unprejudiced, unconstrained as is possible for any human being to be. He remembered that her heroes were the great doctors, and that her whole heart had been stirred and claimed by the noble duties and needs of the great profession. She had been careless of the social limitations, of the lack of sympathy, even of the ridicule of the public. She had behaved as a bird would behave if it were assured by beasts and fishes that to walk and to swim were the only proper and respectable means of getting from place to place. She had shown such rare insight into the principles of things; she had even seemed to him, as he watched her, to have anticipated experience, and he could not help believing that it was within her power to add much to the too small fund of certainty, by the sure instinct and aim of her experiment. It counted nothing whether God had put this soul into a man's body or a woman's. He had known best, and He meant it to be the teller of new truth, a revealer of laws, and an influence for good in its capacity for teaching, as well as in its example of pure and reasonable life.

But the old doctor sighed, and told himself that the girl was most human, most affectionate; it was not impossible that, in spite of her apparent absence of certain domestic instincts, they had only lain dormant and were now awake. He could not bear that she should lose any happiness which might be hers; and the tender memory of the blessed companionship which had been withdrawn from his mortal sight only to be given back to him more fully as he had lived closer and nearer to spiritual things, made him shrink from forbidding the same sort of fullness and completion of life to one so dear as Nan. He tried to assure himself that while a man's life is strengthened by his domestic happiness, a woman's must either surrender itself wholly, or relinquish entirely the claims of such duties, if she would achieve distinction or satisfaction elsewhere. The two cannot be taken together in a woman's life as in a man's. One must be made of lesser consequence, though the very natures of both domestic and professional life need all the strength which can be brought to them. The decision between them he knew to be a most grave responsibility, and one to be governed by the gravest moral obligations, and the unmistakable leadings of the personal instincts and ambitions. It was seldom, Dr. Leslie was aware, that so typical and evident an example as this could offer itself of the class of women who are a result of natural progression and variation, not for better work, but for different work, and who are designed for certain public and social duties. But he believed this class to be one that must inevitably increase with the higher developments of civilization, and in later years, which he might never see, the love for humanity would be recognized and employed more intelligently; while now almost every popular prejudice was against his ward, then she would need no vindication. The wielder of ideas has always a certain advantage over the depender upon facts; and though the two classes of minds by no means inevitably belong, the one to women, and the other to men, still women have not yet begun to use the best resources of their natures, having been later developed, and in many countries but recently freed from restraining and hindering influences.

The preservation of the race is no longer the only important question; the welfare of the individual will be considered more and more. The simple fact that there is a majority of women in any centre of civilization means that some are set apart by nature for other uses and conditions than marriage. In ancient times men depended entirely upon the women of their households to prepare their food and clothing,—and almost every man in ordinary circumstances of life was forced to marry for this reason; but already there is a great change. The greater proportion of men and women everywhere will still instinctively and gladly accept the high duties and helps of married life; but as society becomes more intelligent it will recognize the fitness of some persons, and the unfitness of others, making it impossible for these to accept such responsibilities and obligations, and so dignify and elevate home life instead of degrading it.

It had been one thing to act from conviction and from the promptings of instinct while no obstacles opposed themselves to his decisions, and quite another thing to be brought face to face with such an emergency. Dr. Leslie wished first to be able to distinctly explain to himself his reasons for the opinions he held; he knew that he must judge for Nan herself in some measure; she would surely appeal to him; she would bring this great question to him, and look for sympathy and relief in the same way she had tearfully shown him a wounded finger in her childhood. He seemed to see again the entreating eyes, made large with the pain which would not show itself in any other way, and he felt the rare tears fill his own eyes at the thought. "Poor little Nan," he said to himself, "she has been hurt in the great battle, but she is no skulking soldier." He would let her tell her story, and then give her the best help he could; and so when the afternoon shadows were very long across the country, and the hot summer day was almost done, the doctor drove down the wide street and along East Road to the railroad station. As he passed a group of small houses he looked at his watch and found that there was more than time for a second visit to a sick child whose illness had been most serious and perplexing at first, though now she was fast recovering. The little thing smiled as her friend came in, and asked if the young lady were coming to-morrow, for Dr. Leslie had promised a visit and a picture-book from Nan, whom he wished to see and understand the case. They had had a long talk upon such ailments as this just before she went away, and nothing had seemed to rouse her ambition so greatly as her experiences at the children's hospitals the winter before. Now, this weak little creature seemed to be pleading in the name of a great army of sick children, that Nan would not desert their cause; that she would go on, as she had promised them, with her search for ways that should restore their vigor and increase their fitness to take up the work of the world. And yet, a home and children of one's very own, — the doctor, who had held and lost this long ago, felt powerless to decide the future of the young heart which was so dear to him.

Nan saw the familiar old horse and carriage waiting behind the station, and did not fail to notice that the doctor had driven to meet her himself. He almost always did, but her very anxiety to see him again had made her doubtful. The train had hardly stopped before she was standing on the platform and had hastily dropped her checks into the hand of the nearest idle boy, who looked at them doubtfully, as if he hardly dared to hope that he had been mistaken for the hackman. She came quickly to the side of the carriage; the doctor could not look at her, for the horse had made believe that some excitement was necessary, and was making it difficult for the welcome passenger to put her foot on the step. It was all over in a minute. Nan sprang to the doctor's side and away they went down the road. He had caught a glimpse of her shining eyes and eager face as she had hurried toward him, and had said, "Well done!" in a most cheerful and every-day fashion, and then for a minute there was silence.

"Oh, it is so good to get home," said the girl, and her companion turned toward her; he could not wait to hear her story.

"Yes," said Nan, "it is just as well to tell you now. Do you remember you used to say to me when I was a little girl, 'If you know your duty, don't mind the best of reasons for not doing it'?" And the doctor nodded. "I never thought that this reason would come to me for not being a doctor," she went on, "and at first I was afraid I should be conquered, though it was myself who fought myself. But it came to me clearer than ever after a while. I think I could have been fonder of some one than most people are of those whom they marry, but the more I cared for him the less I could give him only part of myself; I knew that was not right. Now that I can look back at it all I am so glad to have had those days; I shall work better all my life for having been able to make myself so perfectly sure that I know my way."

The unconsidered factor had asserted itself in the doctor's favor. He gave the reins to Nan and leaned back in the carriage, but as she bent forward to speak to a friend whom they passed she did not see the look that he gave her.

"I am sure you knew what was right," he said, hastily. "God bless you, dear child!"

Was this little Nan, who had been his play-thing? this brave young creature, to whose glorious future all his heart and hopes went out. In his evening it was her morning, and he prayed that God's angels should comfort and strengthen her and help her to carry the burden of the day. It is only those who can do nothing who find nothing to do, and Nan was no idler; she had come to her work as Christ came to his, not to be ministered unto but to minister.

The months went by swiftly, and through hard work and much study, and many sights of pain and sorrow, this young student of the business of healing made her way to the day when some of her companions announced with melancholy truth that they had finished their studies. They were pretty sure to be accused of having had no right to begin them, or to take such trusts and responsibilities into their hands. But Nan and many of her friends had gladly climbed the hill so far, and with every year's ascent had been thankful for the wider horizon which was spread for their eyes to see.

Dr. Leslie in his quiet study almost wished that he were beginning life again, and sometimes in the twilight, or in long and lonely country drives, believed himself ready to go back twenty years so that he could follow Nan into the future and watch her successes. But he always smiled afterward at such a thought. Twenty years would carry him back to the time when his ward was a little child, not long before she came to live with him. It was best as God had planned it. Nobody had watched the child's development as he had done, or her growth of character, of which all the performances of her later years would be to him only the unnecessary proofs and evidences. He knew that she would be faithful in great things, because she had been faithful in little things, and he should be with her a long time yet, perhaps. God only knew.

There was a great change in the village; there were more small factories now which employed large numbers of young women, and though a new doctor had long ago come to Oldfields who had begun by trying to supersede Dr. Leslie, he had ended by longing to show his gratitude some day for so much help and kindness. More than one appointment had been offered the heroine of this story in the city hospitals. She would have little trouble in making her way since she had the requisite qualities, natural and acquired, which secure success. But she decided for herself that she would neither do this, nor carry out yet the other plan of going on with her studies at some school across the sea. Zurich held out a great temptation, but there was time enough yet, and she would spend a year in Oldfields with the doctor, studying again with him, since she knew better than ever before that she could find no wiser teacher. And it was a great pleasure to belong to the dear old town, to come home to it with her new treasures, so much richer than she had gone away that beside medicines and bandages and lessons in general hygiene for the physical ails of her patients, she could often be a tonic to the mind and soul; and since she was trying to be good, go about doing good in Christ's name to the halt and maimed and blind in spiritual things.

Nobody sees people as they are and finds the chance to help poor humanity as a doctor does. The decorations and deceptions of character must fall away before the great realities of pain and death. The secrets of many hearts and homes must be told to this confessor, and sadder ailments than the textbooks name are brought to be healed by the beloved physicians. Teachers of truth and givers of the laws of life, priests and ministers,—all these professions are joined in one with the gift of healing, and are each part of the charge that a good doctor holds in his keeping.

One day in the beginning of her year at Oldfields, Nan, who had been very busy, suddenly thought it would be well to give herself a holiday; and with a sudden return of her old sense of freedom was going out at the door and down toward the gateway, which opened to a pleasantly wide world beyond. Marilla had taken Nan's successes rather reluctantly, and never hesitated to say that she only hoped to see her well married and settled before she died; though she was always ready to defend her course with even virulence to those who would deprecate it. She now heard Nan shut the door, and called at once from an upper window to know if word had been left where she was going, and the young practitioner laughed aloud as she answered, and properly acknowledged the fetter of her calling.

The leaves were just beginning to fall, and she pushed them about with her feet, and sometimes walked and sometimes ran lightly along the road toward the farm. But when she reached it, she passed the lane and went on to the Dyer houses. Mrs. Jake was ailing as usual, and Nan had told the doctor before she came out that she would venture another professional visit in his stead. She was a great help to him in this way, for his calls to distant towns had increased year by year, and he often found it hard to keep his many patients well in hand.

The old houses had not changed much since she first knew them, and neither they nor their inmates were in any danger of being forgotten by her; the old ties of affection and association grew stronger instead of weaker every year. It pleased and amused the old people to be reminded of the days when Nan was a child and lived among them, and it was a great joy to her to be able to make their pain and discomfort less, and be their interpreter of the outside world.

It was a most lovely day of our heroine's favorite weather. It has been said that November is an epitome of all the months of the year, but for all that, no other season can show anything so beautiful as the best and brightest November days. Nan had spent her summer in a great hospital, where she saw few flowers save human ones, and the warmth and inspiration of this clear air seemed most delightful. She had been somewhat tempted by an offer of a fine position in Canada, and even Dr. Leslie had urged her acceptance, and thought it an uncommonly good chance to have the best hospital experience and responsibility, but she had sent the letter of refusal only that morning. She could not tell yet what her later plans might be; but there was no place like Oldfields, and she thought she had never loved it so dearly as that afternoon.

She looked in at Mrs. Martin's wide-open door first, but finding the kitchen empty, went quickly across to the other house, where Mrs. Jake was propped up in her rocking-chair and began to groan loudly when she saw Nan; but the tonic of so gratifying a presence soon had a most favorable effect. Benignant Mrs. Martin was knitting as usual, and the three women sat together in a friendly group and Nan asked and answered questions most cordially.

"I declare I was sort of put out with the doctor for sending you down here day before yesterday instead of coming himself," stated Mrs. Jake immediately, "but I do' know 's I ever had anything do me so much good as that bottle you gave me."

"Of course!" laughed Nan. "Dr. Leslie sent it to you himself. I told you when I gave it to you."

"Well now, how you talk!" said Mrs. Jake, a little crestfallen. "I begin to find my hearing fails me by spells. But I was bound to give you the credit, for all I've stood out against your meddling with a doctor's business."

Nan laughed merrily. "I am going to steal you for my patient," she answered, "and try all the prescriptions on your case first."

"Land, if you cured her up 't would be like stopping the leaks in a basket," announced Mrs. Martin with a beaming smile, and clicking her knitting-needles excitedly. "She can't hear of a complaint anywheres about but she thinks she's got the mate to it."

"I don't seem to have anything fevery about me," said Mrs. Jake, with an air of patient self-denial; and though both her companions were most compassionate at the thought of her real sufferings, they could not resist the least bit of a smile. "I declare you've done one first-rate thing, if you're never going to do any more," said Mrs. Jake, presently. " 'Liza here's been talking for some time past, about your straightening up the little boy's back,—the one that lives down where Mis' Meeker used to live you know,—but I didn't seem to take it in till he come over here yesterday forenoon. Looks as likely as any child, except it may be he's a little stunted. When I think how he used to creep about there, side of the road, like a hopper-toad, it does seem amazin'!"

Nan's eyes brightened. "I have been delighted about that. I saw him running with the other children as I came down the road. It was a long bit of work, though. The doctor did most of it; I didn't see the child for months, you know. But he needs care yet; I'm going to stop and have another talk with his mother as I go home."

"She's a pore shiftless creature," Mrs. Martin hastened to say. "There, I thought o' the doctor, how he'd laugh, the last time I was in to see her; her baby was sick, and she sent up to know if I'd lend her a variety of herbs, and I didn't know but she might p'isen it, so I stepped down with something myself. She begun to flutter about like she always does, and I picked my way acrost the kitchen to the cradle. 'There,' says she, 'I have been laying out all this week to go up to the Corners and git me two new chairs.' 'I should think you had plenty of chairs now,' said I, and she looked at me sort of surprised, and says she, 'There ain't a chair in this house but what's full.' "

And Nan laughed as heartily as could have been desired before she asked Mrs. Jake a few more appreciative questions about her ailments, and then rose to go away. Mrs. Martin followed her out to the gate; she and Nan had always been very fond of each other, and the elder woman pointed to a field not far away where the brothers were watching a stubble-fire, which was sending up a thin blue thread of smoke into the still air. "They were over in your north lot yesterday," said Mrs. Martin. "They're fullest o' business nowadays when there's least to do. They took it pretty hard when they first had to come down to hiring help, but they kind of enjoy it now. We're all old folks together on the farm, and not good for much. It don't seem but a year or two since your poor mother was playing about here, and then you come along, and now you're the last o' your folks out of all the houseful of 'em I knew. I'll own up sometimes I've thought strange of your fancy for doctoring, but I never said a word to nobody against it, so I haven't got anything to take back as most folks have. I couldn't help thinking when you come in this afternoon and sat there along of us, that I'd give a good deal to have Mis' Thacher step in and see you and know what you've made o' yourself. She had it hard for a good many years, but I believe 't is all made up to her; I do certain."

Nan meant to go back to the village by the shorter way of the little foot-path, but first she went up the grass-grown lane toward the old farm-house. She stood for a minute looking about her and across the well-known fields, and then seated herself on the door-step, and stayed there for some time. There were two or three sheep near by, well covered and rounded by their soft new winter wool, and they all came as close as they dared and looked at her wonderingly. The narrow path that used to be worn to the door-step had been overgrown years ago with the short grass, and in it there was a late little dandelion with hardly any stem at all. The sunshine was warm, and all the country was wrapped in a thin, soft haze.

She thought of her grandmother Thacher, and of the words that had just been said; it was beginning to seem a very great while since the days of the old farm-life, and Nan smiled as she remembered with what tones of despair the good old woman used to repeat the well-worn phrase, that her grandchild would make either something or nothing. It seemed to her that she had brought all the success of the past and her hopes for the future to the dear old place that afternoon. Her early life was spreading itself out like a picture, and as she thought it over and looked back from year to year, she was more than ever before surprised to see the connection of one thing with another, and how some slight acts had been the planting of seeds which had grown and flourished long afterward. And as she tried to follow herself back into the cloudy days of her earliest spring, she rose without knowing why, and went down the pastures toward the river. She passed the old English apple-tree, which still held aloft a flourishing bough. Its fruit had been gathered, but there were one or two stray apples left, and Nan skillfully threw a stick at these by way of summons.

Along this path she had hurried or faltered many a time. She remembered her grandmother's funeral, and how she had walked, with an elderly cousin whom she did not know, at the head of the procession, and had seen Martin Dyer's small grandson peeping like a rabbit from among the underbrush near the shore. Poor little Nan! she was very lonely that day. She had been so glad when the doctor had wrapped her up and taken her home.

She saw the neighborly old hawthorn-tree that grew by a cellar, and stopped to listen to its rustling and to lay her hand upon the rough bark. It had been a cause of wonder once, for she knew no other tree of the kind. It was like a snow-drift when it was in bloom, and in the grass-grown cellar she had spent many an hour, for there was a good shelter from the wind and an excellent hiding-place, though it seemed very shallow now when she looked at it as she went by.

The burying-place was shut in by a plain stone wall, which she had long ago asked the Dyers to build for her, and she leaned over it now and looked at the smooth turf of the low graves. She had always thought she would like to lie there too when her work was done. There were some of the graves which she did not know, but one was her poor young mother's, who had left her no inheritance except some traits that had won Nan many friends; all her evil gifts had been buried with her, the neighbors had said, when the girl was out of hearing, that very afternoon.

There was a strange fascination about these river uplands; no place was so dear to Nan, and yet she often thought with a shudder of the story of those footprints which had sought the river's brink, and then turned back. Perhaps, made pure and strong in a better world, in which some lingering love and faith had given her the true direction at last, where even her love for her child had saved her, the mother had been still taking care of little Nan and guiding her. Perhaps she had helped to make sure of the blessings her own life had lost, of truth and whiteness of soul and usefulness; and so had been still bringing her child in her arms toward the great shelter and home, as she had toiled in her fright and weakness that dark and miserable night toward the house on the hill.

And Nan stood on the shore while the warm wind that gently blew her hair felt almost like a hand, and presently she went closer to the river, and looked far across it and beyond it to the hills. The eagles swung to and fro above the water, but she looked beyond them into the sky. The soft air and the sunshine came close to her; the trees stood about and seemed to watch her; and suddenly she reached her hands upward in an ecstasy of life and strength and gladness. "O God," she said, "I thank thee for my future."

THE COUNTRY OF
THE POINTED FIRS

Contents

I

THE RETURN

THERE was something about the coast town of Dunnet which made it seem more attractive than other maritime villages of eastern Maine. Perhaps it was the simple fact of acquaintance with that neighborhood which made it so attaching, and gave such interest to the rocky shore and dark woods, and the few houses which seemed to be securely wedged and tree-nailed in among the ledges by the Landing. These houses made the most of their seaward view, and there was a gayety and determined floweriness in their bits of garden ground; the small-paned high windows in the peaks of their steep gables were like knowing eyes that watched the harbor and the far sea-line beyond, or looked northward all along the shore and its background of spruces and balsam firs. When one really knows a village like this and its surroundings, it is like becoming acquainted with a single person. The process of falling in love at first sight is as final as it is swift in such a case, but the growth of true friendship may be a lifelong affair.

After a first brief visit made two or three summers before in the course of a yachting cruise, a lover of Dunnet Landing returned to find the unchanged shores of the pointed firs, the same quaintness of the village with its elaborate conventionalities; all that mixture of remoteness, and childish certainty of being the centre of civilization of which her affectionate dreams had told. One evening in June, a single passenger landed upon the steamboat wharf. The tide was high, there was a fine crowd of spectators, and the younger portion of the company followed her with subdued excitement up the narrow street of the salt-aired, white-clapboarded little town.

II

MRS. TODD

LATER, there was only one fault to find with this choice of a summer lodging-place, and that was its complete lack of seclusion. At first the tiny house of Mrs. Almira Todd, which stood with its end to the street, appeared to be retired and sheltered enough from the busy world, behind its bushy bit of a green garden, in which all the blooming things, two or three gay hollyhocks and some London-pride, were pushed back against the gray-shingled wall. It was a queer little garden and puzzling to a stranger, the few flowers being put at a disadvantage by so much greenery; but the discovery was soon made that Mrs. Todd was an ardent lover of herbs, both wild and tame, and the sea-breezes blew into the low end-window of the house laden with not only sweet-brier and sweet-mary, but balm and sage and borage and mint, wormwood and southernwood. If Mrs. Todd had occasion to step into the far corner of her herb plot, she trod heavily upon thyme, and made its fragrant presence known with all the rest. Being a very large person, her full skirts brushed and bent almost every slender stalk that her feet missed. You could always tell when she was stepping about there, even when you were half awake in the morning, and learned to know, in the course of a few weeks' experience, in exactly which corner of the garden she might be.

At one side of this herb plot were other growths of a rustic pharmacopœia, great treasures and rarities among the commoner herbs. There were some strange and pungent odors that roused a dim sense and remembrance of something in the forgotten past. Some of these might once have belonged to sacred and mystic rites, and have had some occult knowledge handed with them down the centuries; but now they pertained only to humble compounds brewed at intervals with molasses or vinegar or spirits in a small caldron on Mrs. Todd's kitchen stove. They were dispensed to suffering neighbors, who usually came at night as if by stealth, bringing their own ancient-looking vials to be filled. One nostrum was called

378

the Indian remedy, and its price was but fifteen cents; the whispered directions could be heard as customers passed the windows. With most remedies the purchaser was allowed to depart unadmonished from the kitchen, Mrs. Todd being a wise saver of steps; but with certain vials she gave cautions, standing in the doorway, and there were other doses which had to be accompanied on their healing way as far as the gate, while she muttered long chapters of directions, and kept up an air of secrecy and importance to the last. It may not have been only the common ails of humanity with which she tried to cope; it seemed sometimes as if love and hate and jealousy and adverse winds at sea might also find their proper remedies among the curious wild-looking plants in Mrs. Todd's garden.

The village doctor and this learned herbalist were upon the best of terms. The good man may have counted upon the unfavorable effect of certain potions which he should find his opportunity in counteracting; at any rate, he now and then stopped and exchanged greetings with Mrs. Todd over the picket fence. The conversation became at once professional after the briefest preliminaries, and he would stand twirling a sweet-scented sprig in his fingers, and make suggestive jokes, perhaps about her faith in a too persistent course of thoroughwort elixir, in which my landlady professed such firm belief as sometimes to endanger the life and usefulness of worthy neighbors.

To arrive at this quietest of seaside villages late in June, when the busy herb-gathering season was just beginning, was also to arrive in the early prime of Mrs. Todd's activity in the brewing of old-fashioned spruce beer. This cooling and refreshing drink had been brought to wonderful perfection through a long series of experiments; it had won immense local fame, and the supplies for its manufacture were always giving out and having to be replenished. For various reasons, the seclusion and uninterrupted days which had been looked forward to proved to be very rare in this otherwise delightful corner of the world. My hostess and I had made our shrewd business agreement on the basis of a simple cold luncheon at noon, and liberal restitution in the matter of hot suppers, to provide for which the lodger might sometimes be seen hurrying down the road, late in the day, with cunner line in hand.

It was soon found that this arrangement made large allowance for Mrs. Todd's slow herb-gathering progresses through woods and pastures. The spruce-beer customers were pretty steady in hot weather, and there were many demands for different soothing syrups and elixirs with which the unwise curiosity of my early residence had made me acquainted. Knowing Mrs. Todd to be a widow, who had little beside this slender business and the income from one hungry lodger to maintain her, one's energies and even interest were quickly bestowed, until it became a matter of course that she should go afield every pleasant day, and that the lodger should answer all peremptory knocks at the side door.

In taking an occasional wisdom-giving stroll in Mrs. Todd's company, and in acting as business partner during her frequent absences, I found the July days fly fast, and it was not until I felt myself confronted with too great pride and pleasure in the display, one night, of two dollars and twenty-seven cents which I had taken in during the day, that I remembered a long piece of writing, sadly belated now, which I was bound to do. To have been patted kindly on the shoulder and called "darlin'," to have been offered a surprise of early mushrooms for supper, to have had all the glory of making two dollars and twenty-seven cents in a single day, and then to renounce it all and withdraw from these pleasant successes, needed much resolution. Literary employments are so vexed with uncertainties at best, and it was not until the voice of conscience sounded louder in my ears than the sea on the nearest pebble beach that I said unkind words of withdrawal to Mrs. Todd. She only became more wistfully affectionate than ever in her expressions, and looked as disappointed as I expected when I frankly told her that I could no longer enjoy the pleasure of what we called "seein' folks." I felt that I was cruel to a whole neighborhood in curtailing her liberty in this most important season for harvesting the different wild herbs that were so much counted upon to ease their winter ails.

"Well, dear," she said sorrowfully, "I've took great advantage o' your bein' here. I ain't had such a season for years, but I have never had nobody I could so trust. All you lack is a few qualities, but with time you'd gain judgment an' experience, an' be very able in the business. I 'd stand right here an' say it to anybody."

Mrs. Todd and I were not separated or estranged by the change in our business relations; on the contrary, a deeper intimacy seemed to begin. I do not know what herb of the night it was that used sometimes to send out a penetrating odor late in the evening, after the dew had fallen, and the moon was high, and the cool air came up from the sea. Then Mrs. Todd would feel that she must talk to somebody, and I was only too glad to listen. We both fell under the spell, and she either stood outside the window, or made an errand to my sitting-room, and told, it might be very commonplace news of the day, or, as happened one misty summer night, all that lay deepest in her heart. It was in this way that I came to know that she had loved one who was far above her.

"No, dear, him I speak of could never think of me," she said. "When we was young together his mother did n't favor the match, an' done everything she could to part us; and folks thought we both married well, but 't wa'n't what either one of us wanted most; an' now we 're left alone again, an' might have had each other all the time. He was above bein' a sea-farin' man, an' prospered more than most; he come of a high family, an' my lot was plain an' hard-workin'. I ain't seen him for some years; he 's forgot our youthful feelin's, I expect, but a woman's heart is different; them feelin's comes back when you think you've done with 'em, as sure as spring comes with the year. An' I 've always had ways of hearin' about him."

She stood in the centre of a braided rug, and its rings of black and gray seemed to circle about her feet in the dim light. Her height and massiveness in the low room gave her the look of a huge sibyl, while the strange fragrance of the mysterious herb blew in from the little garden.

III

THE SCHOOLHOUSE

For some days after this, Mrs. Todd's customers came and went past my windows, and, haying-time being nearly over, strangers began to arrive from the inland country, such was her widespread reputation. Sometimes I saw a pale young creature like a white windflower left over into midsummer, upon whose face consumption had set its bright and wistful mark; but oftener two stout, hard-worked women from the farms came together, and detailed their symptoms to Mrs. Todd in loud and cheerful voices, combining the satisfactions of a friendly gossip with the medical opportunity. They seemed to give much from their own store of therapeutic learning. I became aware of the school in which my landlady had strengthened her natural gift; but hers was always the governing mind, and the final command, "Take of hy'sop one handful" (or whatever herb it was), was received in respectful silence. One afternoon, when I had listened, — it was impossible not to listen, with cottonless ears, — and then laughed and listened again, with an idle pen in my hand, during a particularly spirited and personal conversation, I reached for my hat, and, taking blotting-book and all under my arm, I resolutely fled further temptation, and walked out past the fragrant green garden and up the dusty road. The way went straight uphill, and presently I stopped and turned to look back.

The tide was in, the wide harbor was surrounded by its dark woods, and the small wooden houses stood as near as they could get to the landing. Mrs. Todd's was the last house on the way inland. The gray ledges of the rocky shore were well covered with sod in most places, and the pasture bayberry and wild roses grew thick among them. I could see the higher inland country and the scattered farms. On the brink of the hill stood a little white schoolhouse, much wind-blown and weather-beaten, which was a landmark to seagoing folk; from its door there was a most beautiful view of sea and shore. The summer vacation now prevailed, and after finding the door unfastened, and taking a long look through one of the seaward windows, and reflecting afterward for some time in a shady place near by among the bayberry bushes, I returned to the chief place of business in the village, and, to the amusement of two of the selectmen, brothers and autocrats of Dunnet Landing, I hired the schoolhouse for the rest of the vacation for fifty cents a week.

Selfish as it may appear, the retired situation seemed to possess great advantages, and I spent many days there quite undisturbed, with the sea-breeze blowing through the small, high windows and swaying the heavy outside shutters to and fro. I hung my hat and luncheon-basket on an entry nail as if I were a small scholar, but I sat at the teacher's desk as if I were that great authority, with all the timid empty benches in rows before me. Now and then an idle sheep came and stood for a long time looking in at the door. At sundown I went back, feeling most businesslike, down toward the village again, and usually met the flavor, not of the herb garden, but of Mrs. Todd's hot supper, halfway up the hill. On the nights when there were evening meetings or other public exercises that demanded her presence we had tea very early, and I was welcomed back as if from a long absence.

Once or twice I feigned excuses for staying at home, while Mrs. Todd made distant excursions, and came home late, with both hands full and a heavily laden apron. This was in pennyroyal time, and when the rare lobelia was in its prime and the elecampane was coming on. One day she appeared at the schoolhouse itself, partly out of amused curiosity about my industries; but she explained that there was no tansy in the neighborhood with such snap to it as some that grew about the schoolhouse lot. Being scuffed down all the spring made it grow so much the better, like some folks that had it hard in their youth, and were bound to make the most of themselves before they died.

IV

AT THE SCHOOLHOUSE WINDOW

ONE DAY I reached the schoolhouse very late, owing to attendance upon the funeral of an acquaintance and neighbor, with whose sad decline in health I had been familiar, and whose last days both the doctor and Mrs. Todd had tried in vain to ease. The services had taken place at one o'clock, and now, at quarter past two, I stood at the schoolhouse window, looking down at the procession as it went along the lower road close to the shore. It was a walking funeral, and even at that distance I could recognize most of the mourners as they went their solemn way. Mrs. Begg had been very much respected, and there was a large company of friends following to her grave. She had been brought up on one of the neighboring farms, and each of the few times that I had seen her she professed great dissatisfaction with town life. The people lived too close together for her liking, at the Landing, and she could not get used to the constant sound of the sea. She had lived to lament three seafaring husbands, and her house was decorated with West Indian curiosities, specimens of conch shells and fine coral which they had brought home from their voyages in lumber-laden ships. Mrs. Todd had told me all our neighbor's history. They had been girls together, and, to use her own phrase, had "both seen trouble till they knew the best and worst on 't." I could see the sorrowful, large figure of Mrs. Todd as I stood at the window. She made a break in the procession by walking slowly and keeping the after-part of it back. She held a handkerchief to her eyes, and I knew, with a pang of sympathy, that hers was not affected grief.

Beside her, after much difficulty, I recognized the one strange and unrelated person in all the company, an old man who had always been mysterious to me. I could see his thin, bending figure. He wore a narrow, long-tailed coat and walked with a stick, and had the same "cant to leeward" as the wind-bent trees on the height above.

This was Captain Littlepage, whom I had seen only once or

twice before, sitting pale and old behind a closed window; never out of doors until now. Mrs. Todd always shook her head gravely when I asked a question, and said that he was n't what he had been once, and seemed to class him with her other secrets. He might have belonged with a simple which grew in a certain slug-haunted corner of the garden, whose use she could never be betrayed into telling me, though I saw her cutting the tops by moonlight once, as if it were a charm, and not a medicine, like the great fading bloodroot leaves.

I could see that she was trying to keep pace with the old captain's lighter steps. He looked like an aged grasshopper of some strange human variety. Behind this pair was a short, impatient, little person, who kept the captain's house, and gave it what Mrs. Todd and others believed to be no proper sort of care. She was usually called "that Mari' Harris" in sub-dued conversation between intimates, but they treated her with anxious civility when they met her face to face.

The bay-sheltered islands and the great sea beyond stretched away to the far horizon southward and eastward; the little procession in the foreground looked futile and help-less on the edge of the rocky shore. It was a glorious day early in July, with a clear, high sky; there were no clouds, there was no noise of the sea. The song sparrows sang and sang, as if with joyous knowledge of immortality, and contempt for those who could so pettily concern themselves with death. I stood watching until the funeral procession had crept round a shoulder of the slope below and disappeared from the great landscape as if it had gone into a cave.

An hour later I was busy at my work. Now and then a bee blundered in and took me for an enemy; but there was a use-ful stick upon the teacher's desk, and I rapped to call the bees to order as if they were unruly scholars, or waved them away from their riots over the ink, which I had bought at the Land-ing store, and discovered too late to be scented with berga-mot, as if to refresh the labors of anxious scribes. One anxious scribe felt very dull that day; a sheep-bell tinkled near by, and called her wandering wits after it. The sentences failed to catch these lovely summer cadences. For the first time I began to wish for a companion and for news from the outer world, which had been, half unconsciously, forgotten. Watching the funeral gave one a sort of pain. I began to wonder if I ought not to have walked with the rest, instead of hurrying away at the end of the services. Perhaps the Sunday gown I had put on for the occasion was making this disastrous change of feeling, but I had now made myself and my friends remember that I did not really belong to Dunnet Landing.

I sighed, and turned to the half-written page again.

V

CAPTAIN LITTLEPAGE

I T WAS a long time after this; an hour was very long in that coast town where nothing stole away the shortest minute. I had lost myself completely in work, when I heard footsteps outside. There was a steep footpath between the upper and the lower road, which I climbed to shorten the way, as the children had taught me, but I believed that Mrs. Todd would find it inaccessible, unless she had occasion to seek me in great haste. I wrote on, feeling like a besieged miser of time, while the footsteps came nearer, and the sheep-bell tinkled away in haste as if some one had shaken a stick in its wearer's face. Then I looked, and saw Captain Littlepage passing the nearest window; the next moment he tapped politely at the door.

"Come in, sir," I said, rising to meet him; and he entered, bowing with much courtesy. I stepped down from the desk and offered him a chair by the window, where he seated himself at once, being sadly spent by his climb. I returned to my fixed seat behind the teacher's desk, which gave him the lower place of a scholar.

"You ought to have the place of honor, Captain Littlepage," I said.

"A happy, rural seat of various views,"

he quoted, as he gazed out into the sunshine and up the long wooded shore. Then he glanced at me, and looked all about him as pleased as a child.

"My quotation was from Paradise Lost: the greatest of poems, I suppose you know?" and I nodded. "There's nothing that ranks, to my mind, with Paradise Lost; it's all lofty, all lofty," he continued. "Shakespeare was a great poet; he copied life, but you have to put up with a great deal of low talk."

I now remembered that Mrs. Todd had told me one day that Captain Littlepage had overset his mind with too much reading; she had also made dark reference to his having "spells" of some unexplainable nature. I could not help wondering what errand had brought him out in search of me. There was something quite charming in his appearance: it was a face thin and delicate with refinement, but worn into appealing lines, as if he had suffered from loneliness and misapprehension. He looked, with his careful precision of dress, as if he were the object of cherishing care on the part of elderly unmarried sisters, but I knew Mari' Harris to be a very commonplace, inelegant person, who would have no such standards; it was plain that the captain was his own attentive valet. He sat looking at me expectantly. I could not help thinking that, with his queer head and length of thinness, he was made to hop along the road of life rather than to walk. The captain was very grave indeed, and I bade my inward spirit keep close to discretion.

"Poor Mrs. Begg has gone," I ventured to say. I still wore my Sunday gown by way of showing respect.

"She has gone," said the captain,—"very easy at the last, I was informed; she slipped away as if she were glad of the opportunity."

I thought of the Countess of Carberry and felt that history repeated itself.

"She was one of the old stock," continued Captain Littlepage, with touching sincerity. "She was very much looked up to in this town, and will be missed."

I wondered, as I looked at him, if he had sprung from a line of ministers; he had the refinement of look and air of command which are the heritage of the old ecclesiastical families of New England. But as Darwin says in his autobiography, "there is no such king as a sea-captain; he is greater even than a king or a schoolmaster!"

Captain Littlepage moved his chair out of the wake of the sunshine, and still sat looking at me. I began to be very eager to know upon what errand he had come.

"It may be found out some o' these days," he said earnestly. "We may know it all, the next step; where Mrs. Begg is now, for instance. Certainty, not conjecture, is what we all desire."

"I suppose we shall know it all some day," said I.

"We shall know it while yet below," insisted the captain, with a flush of impatience on his thin cheeks. "We have not looked for truth in the right direction. I know what I speak of; those who have laughed at me little know how much reason my ideas are based upon." He waved his hand toward the village below. "In that handful of houses they fancy that they comprehend the universe."

I smiled, and waited for him to go on.

"I am an old man, as you can see," he continued, "and I have been a shipmaster the greater part of my life,—forty-three years in all. You may not think it, but I am above eighty years of age."

He did not look so old, and I hastened to say so.

"You must have left the sea a good many years ago, then, Captain Littlepage?" I said.

"I should have been serviceable at least five or six years more," he answered. "My acquaintance with certain—my experience upon a certain occasion, I might say, gave rise to prejudice. I do not mind telling you that I chanced to learn of one of the greatest discoveries that man has ever made."

Now we were approaching dangerous ground, but a sudden sense of his sufferings at the hands of the ignorant came to my help, and I asked to hear more with all the deference I really felt. A swallow flew into the schoolhouse at this moment as if a kingbird were after it, and beat itself against the walls for a minute, and escaped again to the open air; but Captain Littlepage took no notice whatever of the flurry.

"I had a valuable cargo of general merchandise from the London docks to Fort Churchill, a station of the old company on Hudson's Bay," said the captain earnestly. "We were delayed in lading, and baffled by head winds and a heavy tumbling sea all the way north-about and across. Then the fog kept us off the coast; and when I made port at last, it was too late to delay in those northern waters with such a vessel and such a crew as I had. They cared for nothing, and idled me into a fit of sickness; but my first mate was a good, excellent man, with no more idea of being frozen in there until spring than I had, so we made what speed we could to get clear of Hudson's Bay and off the coast. I owned an eighth of the vessel, and he owned a sixteenth of her. She was a full-rigged ship, called the Minerva, but she was getting old and leaky. I meant it should be my last v'y'ge in her, and so it proved. She had been an excellent vessel in her day. Of the cowards aboard her I can't say so much."

"Then you were wrecked?" I asked, as he made a long pause.

"I wa'n't caught astern o' the lighter by any fault of mine," said the captain gloomily. "We left Fort Churchill and run out into the Bay with a light pair o' heels; but I had been vexed to death with their red-tape rigging at the company's office, and chilled with stayin' on deck an' tryin' to hurry up things, and when we were well out o' sight o' land, headin' for Hudson's Straits, I had a bad turn o' some sort o' fever, and had to stay below. The days were getting short, and we made good runs, all well on board but me, and the crew done their work by dint of hard driving."

I began to find this unexpected narrative a little dull. Captain Littlepage spoke with a kind of slow correctness that lacked the longshore high flavor to which I had grown used; but I listened respectfully while he explained the winds having become contrary, and talked on in a dreary sort of way about his voyage, the bad weather, and the disadvantages he was under in the lightness of his ship, which bounced about like a chip in a bucket, and would not answer the rudder or properly respond to the most careful setting of sails.

"So there we were blowin' along anyways," he complained; but looking at me at this moment, and seeing that my thoughts were unkindly wandering, he ceased to speak.

"It was a hard life at sea in those days, I am sure," said I, with redoubled interest.

"It was a dog's life," said the poor old gentleman, quite reassured, "but it made men of those who followed it. I see a change for the worse even in our own town here; full of loafers now, small and poor as 't is, who once would have followed the sea, every lazy soul of 'em. There is no occupation so fit for just that class o' men who never get beyond the fo'cas'le. I view it, in addition, that a community narrows down and grows dreadful ignorant when it is shut up to its own affairs, and gets no knowledge of the outside world except from a cheap, unprincipled newspaper. In the old days, a good part o' the best men here knew a hundred ports and something of the way folks lived in them. They saw the world for themselves, and like's not their wives and children saw it with them. They may not have had the best of knowledge to carry with 'em sight-seein', but they were some acquainted with foreign lands an' their laws, an' could see outside the battle for town clerk here in Dunnet; they got some sense o' proportion. Yes, they lived more dignified, and their houses were better within an' without. Shipping's a terrible loss to this part o' New England from a social point o' view, ma'am."

"I have thought of that myself," I returned, with my interest quite awakened. "It accounts for the change in a great many things,—the sad disappearance of sea-captains,—doesn't it?"

"A shipmaster was apt to get the habit of reading," said my companion, brightening still more, and taking on a most touching air of unreserve. "A captain is not expected to be familiar with his crew, and for company's sake in dull days and nights he turns to his book. Most of us old shipmasters came to know 'most everything about something; one would take to readin' on farming topics, and some were great on medicine,—but Lord help their poor crews!—or some were all for history, and now and then there'd be one like me that gave his time to the poets. I was well acquainted with a shipmaster that was all for bees an' bee-keepin'; and if you met him in port and went aboard, he'd sit and talk a terrible while about their havin' so much information, and the money that could be made out of keepin' 'em. He was one of the smartest captains that ever sailed the seas, but they used to call the Newcastle, a great bark he commanded for many years, Tuttle's beehive. There was old Cap'n Jameson: he had notions of Solomon's Temple, and made a very handsome little model of the same, right from the Scripture measurements, same's other sailors make little ships and design new tricks of rigging and all that. No, there's nothing to take the place of shipping in a place like ours. These bicycles offend me dreadfully; they don't afford no real opportunities of experience such as a man gained on a voyage. No: when folks left home in the old days they left it to some purpose, and when they got home they stayed there and had some pride in it. There's no large-minded way of thinking now: the worst have got to be best and rule everything; we're all turned upside down and going back year by year."

"Oh no, Captain Littlepage, I hope not," said I, trying to soothe his feelings.

There was a silence in the schoolhouse, but we could hear the noise of the water on a beach below. It sounded like the strange warning wave that gives notice of the turn of the tide. A late golden robin, with the most joyful and eager of voices, was singing close by in a thicket of wild roses.

VI

THE WAITING PLACE

How did you manage with the rest of that rough voyage on the Minerva?" I asked.

"I shall be glad to explain to you," said Captain Littlepage, forgetting his grievances for the moment. "If I had a map at hand I could explain better. We were driven to and fro 'way up toward what we used to call Parry's Discoveries, and lost our bearings. It was thick and foggy, and at last I lost my ship; she drove on a rock, and we managed to get ashore on what I took to be a barren island, the few of us that were left alive. When she first struck, the sea was somewhat calmer than it had been, and most of the crew, against orders, manned the long-boat and put off in a hurry, and were never heard of more. Our own boat upset, but the carpenter kept himself and me above water, and we drifted in. I had no strength to call upon after my recent fever, and laid down to die; but he found the tracks of a man and dog the second day, and got along the shore to one of those far missionary stations that the Moravians support. They were very poor themselves, and in distress; 'twas a useless place. There were but few Esquimaux left in that region. There we remained for some time, and I became acquainted with strange events."

The captain lifted his head and gave me a questioning glance. I could not help noticing that the dulled look in his eyes had gone, and there was instead a clear intentness that made them seem dark and piercing.

"There was a supply ship expected, and the pastor, an excellent Christian man, made no doubt that we should get passage in her. He was hoping that orders would come to break up the station; but everything was uncertain, and we got on the best we could for a while. We fished, and helped the people in other ways; there was no other way of paying our debts. I was taken to the pastor's house until I got better; but they were crowded, and I felt myself in the way, and made excuse to join with an old seaman, a Scotchman, who had built him a warm cabin, and had room in it for another. He was looked upon with regard, and had stood by the pastor in some troubles with the people. He had been on one of those English exploring parties that found one end of the road to the north pole, but never could find the other. We lived like dogs in a kennel, or so you'd thought if you had seen the hut from the outside; but the main thing was to keep warm; there were piles of birdskins to lie on, and he'd made him a good bunk, and there was another for me. 'T was dreadful dreary waitin' there; we begun to think the supply steamer was lost, and my poor ship broke up and strewed herself all along the shore. We got to watching on the headlands; my men and me knew the people were short of supplies and had to pinch themselves. It ought to read in the Bible, 'Man cannot live by fish alone,' if they'd told the truth of things; 't aint bread that wears the worst on you! First part of the time, old Gaffett, that I lived with, seemed speechless, and I did n't know what to make of him, nor he of me, I dare say; but as we got acquainted, I found he'd been through more disasters than I had, and had troubles that wa'n't going to let him live a great while. It used to ease his mind to talk to an understanding person, so we used to sit and talk together all day, if it rained or blew so that we could n't get out. I'd got a bad blow on the back of my head at the time we came ashore, and it pained me at times, and my strength was broken, anyway; I've never been so able since."

Captain Littlepage fell into a reverie.

"Then I had the good of my reading," he explained presently. "I had no books; the pastor spoke but little English, and all his books were foreign; but I used to say over all I could remember. The old poets little knew what comfort they could be to a man. I was well acquainted with the works of Milton, but up there it did seem to me as if Shakespeare was the king; he has his sea terms very accurate, and some beautiful passages were calming to the mind. I could say them over until I shed tears; there was nothing beautiful to me in that place but the stars above and those passages of verse.

"Gaffett was always brooding and brooding, and talking to himself; he was afraid he should never get away, and it preyed upon his mind. He thought when I got home I could interest the scientific men in his discovery: but they're all taken up with their own notions; some didn't even take pains to answer the letters I wrote. You observe that I said this crippled man Gaffett had been shipped on a voyage of discovery. I now tell you that the ship was lost on its return, and only Gaffett and two officers were saved off the Greenland coast, and he had knowledge later that those men never got back to England; the brig they shipped on was run down in the night. So no other living soul had the facts, and he gave them to me. There is a strange sort of a country 'way up north beyond the ice, and strange folks living in it. Gaffett believed it was the next world to this."

"What do you mean, Captain Littlepage?" I exclaimed. The old man was bending forward and whispering; he looked over his shoulder before he spoke the last sentence.

"To hear old Gaffett tell about it was something awful," he said, going on with his story quite steadily after the moment of excitement had passed. " 'T was first a tale of dogs and sledges, and cold and wind and snow. Then they begun to find the ice grow rotten; they had been frozen in, and got into a current flowing north, far up beyond Fox Channel, and they took to their boats when the ship got crushed, and this warm current took them out of sight of the ice, and into a great open sea; and they still followed it due north, just the very way they had planned to go. Then they struck a coast that wasn't laid down or charted, but the cliffs were such that no boat could land until they found a bay and struck across under sail to the other side where the shore looked lower; they were scant of provisions and out of water, but they got sight of something that looked like a great town. 'For God's sake, Gaffett!' said I, the first time he told me. 'You don't mean a town two degrees farther north than ships had ever been?' for he'd got their course marked on an old chart that he'd pieced out at the top; but he insisted upon it, and told it over and over again, to be sure I had it straight to carry to those who would be interested. There was no snow and ice, he said, after they had sailed some days with that warm current, which seemed to come right from under the ice that they'd been pinched up in and had been crossing on foot for weeks."

"But what about the town?" I asked. "Did they get to the town?"

"They did," said the captain, "and found inhabitants; 'twas an awful condition of things. It appeared, as near as Gaffett could express it, like a place where there was neither living nor dead. They could see the place when they were approaching it by sea pretty near like any town, and thick with habitations; but all at once they lost sight of it altogether, and when they got close inshore they could see the shapes of folks, but they never could get near them,—all blowing gray figures that would pass along alone, or sometimes gathered in companies as if they were watching. The men were frightened at first, but the shapes never came near them,—it was as if they blew back; and at last they all got bold and went ashore, and found birds' eggs and sea fowl, like any wild northern spot where creatures were tame and folks had never been, and there was good water. Gaffett said that he and another man came near one o' the fog-shaped men that was going along slow with the look of a pack on his back, among the rocks, an' they chased him; but, Lord! he flittered away out o' sight like a leaf the wind takes with it, or a piece of cobweb. They would make as if they talked together, but there was no sound of voices, and 'they acted as if they didn't see us, but only felt us coming towards them,' says Gaffett one day, trying to tell the particulars. They couldn't see the town when they were ashore. One day the captain and the doctor were gone till night up across the high land where the town had seemed to be, and they came back at night beat out and white as ashes, and wrote and wrote all next day in their notebooks, and whispered together full of excitement, and they were sharp-spoken with the men when they offered to ask any questions.

"Then there came a day," said Captain Littlepage, leaning toward me with a strange look in his eyes, and whispering quickly. "The men all swore they wouldn't stay any longer; the man on watch early in the morning gave the alarm, and they all put off in the boat and got a little way out to sea. Those folks, or whatever they were, come about 'em like bats; all at once they raised incessant armies, and come as if to drive 'em back to sea. They stood thick at the edge o' the water like the ridges o' grim war; no thought o' flight, none of retreat. Sometimes a standing fight, then soaring on main wing tormented all the air. And when they'd got the boat out o' reach o' danger, Gaffett said they looked back, and there was the town again, standing up just as they'd seen it first, comin' on the coast. Say what you might, they all believed 't was a kind of waiting-place between this world an' the next."

The captain had sprung to his feet in his excitement, and made excited gestures, but he still whispered huskily.

"Sit down, sir," I said as quietly as I could, and he sank into his chair quite spent.

"Gaffett thought the officers were hurrying home to report and to fit out a new expedition when they were all lost. At the time, the men got orders not to talk over what they had seen," the old man explained presently in a more natural tone.

"Were n't they all starving, and was n't it a mirage or something of that sort?" I ventured to ask. But he looked at me blankly.

"Gaffett had got so that his mind ran on nothing else," he went on. "The ship's surgeon let fall an opinion to the captain, one day, that 't was some condition o' the light and the magnetic currents that let them see those folks. 'T wa'n't a right-feeling part of the world, anyway; they had to battle with the compass to make it serve, an' everything seemed to go wrong. Gaffett had worked it out in his own mind that they was all common ghosts, but the conditions were unusual favorable for seeing them. He was always talking about the Ge'graphical Society, but he never took proper steps, as I view it now, and stayed right there at the mission. He was a good deal crippled, and thought they'd confine him in some jail of a hospital. He said he was waiting to find the right men to tell, somebody bound north. Once in a while they stopped there to leave a mail or something. He was set in his notions, and let two or three proper explorin' expeditions go by him because he did n't like their looks; but when I was there he had got restless, fearin' he might be taken away or something. He had all his directions written out straight as a string to give the right ones. I wanted him to trust 'em to me, so I might have something to show, but he would n't. I suppose he's dead now. I wrote to him, an' I done all I could. 'T will be a great exploit some o' these days."

I assented absent-mindedly, thinking more just then of my companion's alert, determined look and the seafaring, ready aspect that had come to his face; but at this moment there fell a sudden change, and the old, pathetic, scholarly look returned. Behind me hung a map of North America, and I saw, as I turned a little, that his eyes were fixed upon the northernmost regions and their careful recent outlines with a look of bewilderment.

VII

THE OUTER ISLAND

G AFFETT with his good bunk and the bird-skins, the story of the wreck of the Minerva, the human-shaped creatures of fog and cobweb, the great words of Milton with which he described their onslaught upon the crew, all this moving tale had such an air of truth that I could not argue with Captain Littlepage. The old man looked away from the map as if it had vaguely troubled him, and regarded me appealingly.

"We were just speaking of"—and he stopped. I saw that he had suddenly forgotten his subject.

"There were a great many persons at the funeral," I hastened to say.

"Oh yes," the captain answered, with satisfaction. "All showed respect who could. The sad circumstances had for a moment slipped my mind. Yes, Mrs. Begg will be very much missed. She was a capital manager for her husband when he was at sea. Oh yes, shipping is a very great loss." And he sighed heavily. "There was hardly a man of any standing who didn't interest himself in some way in navigation. It always gave credit to a town. I call it low-water mark now here in Dunnet."

He rose with dignity to take leave, and asked me to stop at his house some day, when he would show me some outlandish things that he had brought home from sea. I was familiar with the subject of the decadence of shipping interests in all its affecting branches, having been already some time in Dunnet, and I felt sure that Captain Littlepage's mind had now returned to a safe level.

As we came down the hill toward the village our ways divided, and when I had seen the old captain well started on a smooth piece of sidewalk which would lead him to his own door, we parted, the best of friends. "Step in some afternoon," he said, as affectionately as if I were a fellow-shipmaster wrecked on the lee shore of age like himself. I turned toward home, and presently met Mrs. Todd coming toward me with an anxious expression.

"I see you sleevin' the old gentleman down the hill," she suggested.

"Yes. I've had a very interesting afternoon with him," I answered; and her face brightened.

"Oh, then he's all right. I was afraid 't was one o' his flighty spells, an' Mari' Harris would n't"—

"Yes," I returned, smiling, "he has been telling me some old stories, but we talked about Mrs. Begg and the funeral beside, and Paradise Lost."

"I expect he got tellin' of you some o' his great narratives," she answered, looking at me shrewdly. "Funerals always sets him goin'. Some o' them tales hangs together toler'ble well," she added, with a sharper look than before. "An' he's been a great reader all his seafarin' days. Some thinks he overdid, and affected his head, but for a man o' his years he's amazin' now when he's at his best. Oh, he used to be a beautiful man!"

We were standing where there was a fine view of the harbor and its long stretches of shore all covered by the great army of the pointed firs, darkly cloaked and standing as if they waited to embark. As we looked far seaward among the outer islands, the trees seemed to march seaward still, going steadily over the heights and down to the water's edge.

It had been growing gray and cloudy, like the first evening of autumn, and a shadow had fallen on the darkening shore. Suddenly, as we looked, a gleam of golden sunshine struck the outer islands, and one of them shone out clear in the light, and revealed itself in a compelling way to our eyes. Mrs. Todd was looking off across the bay with a face full of affection and interest. The sunburst upon that outermost island made it seem like a sudden revelation of the world beyond this which some believe to be so near.

"That's where mother lives," said Mrs. Todd. "Can't we see it plain? I was brought up out there on Green Island. I know every rock an' bush on it."

"Your mother!" I exclaimed, with great interest.

"Yes, dear, cert'in; I've got her yet, old's I be. She's one of them spry, light-footed little women; always was, an' light-hearted, too," answered Mrs. Todd, with satisfaction. "She's seen all the trouble folks can see, without it's her last sickness; an' she's got a word of courage for everybody. Life ain't spoilt her a mite. She's eighty-six an' I'm sixty-seven, and I've seen the time I've felt a good sight the oldest. 'Land sakes alive!' says she, last time I was out to see her. 'How you do lurch about steppin' into a bo't!' I laughed so I liked to have gone right over into the water; an' we pushed off, an' left her laughin' there on the shore."

The light had faded as we watched. Mrs. Todd had mounted a gray rock, and stood there grand and architectural, like a *caryatide*. Presently she stepped down, and we continued our way homeward.

"You an' me, we'll take a bo't an' go out some day and see mother," she promised me. "'T would please her very much, an' there's one or two sca'ce herbs grows better on the island than anywheres else. I ain't seen their like nowheres here on the main."

"Now I'm goin' right down to get us each a mug o' my beer," she announced as we entered the house, "an' I believe I'll sneak in a little mite o' camomile. Goin' to the funeral an' all, I feel to have had a very wearin' afternoon."

I heard her going down into the cool little cellar, and then there was considerable delay. When she returned, mug in hand, I noticed the taste of camomile, in spite of my protest; but its flavor was disguised by some other herb that I did not know, and she stood over me until I drank it all and said that I liked it.

"I don't give that to everybody," said Mrs. Todd kindly; and I felt for a moment as if it were part of a spell and incantation, and as if my enchantress would now begin to look like the cobweb shapes of the arctic town. Nothing happened but a quiet evening and some delightful plans that we made about going to Green Island, and on the morrow there was the clear sunshine and blue sky of another day.

VIII

GREEN ISLAND

ONE MORNING, very early, I heard Mrs. Todd in the garden outside my window. By the unusual loudness of her remarks to a passer-by, and the notes of a familiar hymn which she sang as she worked among the herbs, and which came as if directed purposely to the sleepy ears of my consciousness, I knew that she wished I would wake up and come and speak to her.

In a few minutes she responded to a morning voice from behind the blinds. "I expect you 're goin' up to your schoolhouse to pass all this pleasant day; yes, I expect you 're goin' to be dreadful busy," she said despairingly.

"Perhaps not," said I. "Why, what 's going to be the matter with you, Mrs. Todd?" For I supposed that she was tempted by the fine weather to take one of her favorite expeditions along the shore pastures to gather herbs and simples, and would like to have me keep the house.

"No, I don't want to go nowhere by land," she answered gayly, — "no, not by land; but I don't know 's we shall have a better day all the rest of the summer to go out to Green Island an' see mother. I waked up early thinkin' of her. The wind 's light northeast, — 't will take us right straight out; an' this time o' year it 's liable to change round southwest an' fetch us home pretty, 'long late in the afternoon. Yes, it 's goin' to be a good day."

"Speak to the captain and the Bowden boy, if you see anybody going by toward the landing," said I. "We 'll take the big boat."

"Oh, my sakes! now you let me do things my way," said Mrs. Todd scornfully. "No, dear, we won't take no big bo't. I 'll just git a handy dory, an' Johnny Bowden an' me, we 'll man her ourselves. I don't want no abler bo't than a good dory, an' a nice light breeze ain't goin' to make no sea; an' Johnny 's my cousin's son, — mother 'll like to have him come; an' he 'll be down to the herrin' weirs all the time we 're there, anyway; we don't want to carry no men folks havin' to be considered every minute an' takin' up all our time. No, you let me do; we'll just slip out an' see mother by ourselves. I guess what breakfast you'll want's about ready now."

I had become well acquainted with Mrs. Todd as landlady, herb-gatherer, and rustic philosopher; we had been discreet fellow-passengers once or twice when I had sailed up the coast to a larger town than Dunnet Landing to do some shopping; but I was yet to become acquainted with her as a mariner. An hour later we pushed off from the landing in the desired dory. The tide was just on the turn, beginning to fall, and several friends and acquaintances stood along the side of the dilapidated wharf and cheered us by their words and evident interest. Johnny Bowden and I were both rowing in haste to get out where we could catch the breeze and put up the small sail which lay clumsily furled along the gunwale. Mrs. Todd sat aft, a stern and unbending law-giver.

"You better let her drift; we'll get there 'bout as quick; the tide'll take her right out from under these old buildin's; there's plenty wind outside."

"Your bo't ain't trimmed proper, Mis' Todd!" exclaimed a voice from shore. "You're lo'ded so the bo't'll drag; you can't git her before the wind, ma'am. You set 'midships, Mis' Todd, an' let the boy hold the sheet 'n' steer after he gits the sail up; you won't never git out to Green Island that way. She's lo'ded bad, your bo't is,—she's heavy behind's she is now!"

Mrs. Todd turned with some difficulty and regarded the anxious adviser, my right oar flew out of water, and we seemed about to capsize. "That you, Asa? Good-mornin'," she said politely. "I al'ays liked the starn seat best. When'd you git back from up country?"

This allusion to Asa's origin was not lost upon the rest of the company. We were some little distance from shore, but we could hear a chuckle of laughter, and Asa, a person who was too ready with his criticism and advice on every possible subject, turned and walked indignantly away.

When we caught the wind we were soon on our seaward course, and only stopped to underrun a trawl, for the floats of which Mrs. Todd looked earnestly, explaining that her mother might not be prepared for three extra to dinner; it was her brother's trawl, and she meant to just run her eye along for the right sort of a little haddock. I leaned over the boat's side with great interest and excitement, while she skillfully handled the long line of hooks, and made scornful remarks upon worthless, bait-consuming creatures of the sea as she reviewed them and left them on the trawl or shook them off into the waves. At last we came to what she pronounced a proper haddock, and having taken him on board and ended his life resolutely, we went our way.

As we sailed along I listened to an increasingly delightful commentary upon the islands, some of them barren rocks, or at best giving sparse pasturage for sheep in the early summer. On one of these an eager little flock ran to the water's edge and bleated at us so affectingly that I would willingly have stopped; but Mrs. Todd steered away from the rocks, and scolded at the sheep's mean owner, an acquaintance of hers, who grudged the little salt and still less care which the patient creatures needed. The hot midsummer sun makes prisons of these small islands that are a paradise in early June, with their cool springs and short thick-growing grass. On a larger island, farther out to sea, my entertaining companion showed me with glee the small houses of two farmers who shared the island between them, and declared that for three generations the people had not spoken to each other even in times of sickness or death or birth. "When the news come that the war was over, one of 'em knew it a week, and never stepped across his wall to tell the others," she said. "There, they enjoy it: they've got to have somethin' to interest 'em in such a place; 't is a good deal more tryin' to be tied to folks you don't like than 't is to be alone. Each of 'em tells the neighbors their wrongs; plenty likes to hear and tell again; them as fetch a bone 'll carry one, an' so they keep the fight a-goin'. I must say I like variety myself; some folks washes Monday an' irons Tuesday the whole year round, even if the circus is goin' by!"

A long time before we landed at Green Island we could see the small white house, standing high like a beacon, where Mrs. Todd was born and where her mother lived, on a green slope above the water, with dark spruce woods still higher. There were crops in the fields, which we presently distinguished from one another. Mrs. Todd examined them while we were still far at sea. "Mother's late potatoes looks backward; ain't had rain enough so far," she pronounced her opinion. "They look weedier than what they call Front Street down to Cowper Centre. I expect brother William is so occupied with his herrin' weirs an' servin' out bait to the schooners that he don't think once a day of the land."

"What's the flag for, up above the spruces there behind the house?" I inquired, with eagerness.

"Oh, that's the sign for herrin'," she explained kindly, while Johnny Bowden regarded me with contemptuous surprise. "When they get enough for schooners they raise that flag; an' when 't is a poor catch in the weir pocket they just fly a little signal down by the shore, an' then the small bo'ts comes and get enough an' over for their trawls. There, look! there she is: mother sees us; she's wavin' somethin' out o' the fore door! She'll be to the landin'-place quick's we are."

I looked, and could see a tiny flutter in the doorway, but a quicker signal had made its way from the heart on shore to the heart on the sea.

"How do you suppose she knows it's me?" said Mrs. Todd, with a tender smile on her broad face. "There, you never get over bein' a child long's you have a mother to go to. Look at the chimney, now; she's gone right in an' brightened up the fire. Well, there, I'm glad mother's well; you'll enjoy seein' her very much."

Mrs. Todd leaned back into her proper position, and the boat trimmed again. She took a firmer grasp of the sheet, and gave an impatient look up at the gaff and the leech of the little sail, and twitched the sheet as if she urged the wind like a horse. There came at once a fresh gust, and we seemed to have doubled our speed. Soon we were near enough to see a tiny figure with handkerchiefed head come down across the field and stand waiting for us at the cove above a curve of pebble beach.

Presently the dory grated on the pebbles, and Johnny Bowden, who had been kept in abeyance during the voyage, sprang out and used manful exertions to haul us up with the next wave, so that Mrs. Todd could make a dry landing.

"You done that very well," she said, mounting to her feet, and coming ashore somewhat stiffly, but with great dignity, refusing our outstretched hands, and returning to possess herself of a bag which had lain at her feet.

"Well, mother, here I be!" she announced with indifference; but they stood and beamed in each other's faces.

"Lookin' pretty well for an old lady, ain't she?" said Mrs. Todd's mother, turning away from her daughter to speak to me. She was a delightful little person herself, with bright eyes and an affectionate air of expectation like a child on a holiday. You felt as if Mrs. Blackett were an old and dear friend before you let go her cordial hand. We all started together up the hill.

"Now don't you haste too fast, mother," said Mrs. Todd warningly; " 'tis a far reach o' risin' ground to the fore door, and you won't set an' get your breath when you're once there, but go trotting about. Now don't you go a mite faster than we proceed with this bag an' basket. Johnny, there, 'll fetch up the haddock. I just made one stop to underrun William's trawl till I come to jes' such a fish's I thought you'd want to make one o' your nice chowders of. I've brought an onion with me that was layin' about on the window-sill at home."

"That's just what I was wantin'," said the hostess. "I give a sigh when you spoke o' chowder, knowin' my onions was out. William forgot to replenish us last time he was to the Landin'. Don't you haste so yourself, Almiry, up this risin' ground. I hear you commencin' to wheeze a'ready."

This mild revenge seemed to afford great pleasure to both giver and receiver. They laughed a little, and looked at each other affectionately, and then at me. Mrs. Todd considerately paused, and faced about to regard the wide sea view. I was glad to stop, being more out of breath than either of my companions, and I prolonged the halt by asking the names of the neighboring islands. There was a fine breeze blowing, which we felt more there on the high land than when we were running before it in the dory.

"Why, this ain't that kitten I saw when I was out last, the one that I said did n't appear likely?" exclaimed Mrs. Todd as we went our way.

"That's the one, Almiry," said her mother. "She always had a likely look to me, an' she's right after her business. I never see such a mouser for one of her age. If 't wan't for William, I never should have housed that other dronin' old thing so long; but he sets by her on account of her havin' a bob tail. I don't deem it advisable to maintain cats just on account of their havin' bob tails; they're like all other curiosities, good for them that wants to see 'em twice. This kitten catches mice for both, an' keeps me respectable as I ain't been for a year. She's a real understandin' little help, this kitten is. I picked her from among five Miss Augusta Pennell had over to Burnt Island," said the old woman, trudging along with the kitten close at her skirts. "Augusta, she says to me, 'Why, Mis' Blackett, you've took the homeliest;' an' says I, 'I've got the smartest; I'm satisfied.'"

"I'd trust nobody sooner'n you to pick out a kitten, mother," said the daughter handsomely, and we went on in peace and harmony.

The house was just before us now, on a green level that looked as if a huge hand had scooped it out of the long green field we had been ascending. A little way above, the dark spruce woods began to climb the top of the hill and cover the seaward slopes of the island. There was just room for the small farm and the forest; we looked down at the fish-house and its rough sheds, and the weirs stretching far out into the water. As we looked upward, the tops of the firs came sharp against the blue sky. There was a great stretch of rough pasture-land round the shoulder of the island to the eastward, and here were all the thick-scattered gray rocks that kept their places, and the gray backs of many sheep that forever wandered and fed on the thin sweet pasturage that fringed the ledges and made soft hollows and strips of green turf like growing velvet. I could see the rich green of bayberry bushes here and there, where the rocks made room. The air was very sweet; one could not help wishing to be a citizen of such a complete and tiny continent and home of fisherfolk.

The house was broad and clean, with a roof that looked heavy on its low walls. It was one of the houses that seem firm-rooted in the ground, as if they were two-thirds below the surface, like icebergs. The front door stood hospitably open in expectation of company, and an orderly vine grew at each side; but our path led to the kitchen door at the house-end, and there grew a mass of gay flowers and greenery, as if they had been swept together by some diligent garden broom into a tangled heap: there were portulacas all along under the lower step and straggling off into the grass, and clustering mallows that crept as near as they dared, like poor relations. I saw the bright eyes and brainless little heads of two half-grown chickens who were snuggled down among the mallows as if they had been chased away from the door more than once, and expected to be again.

"It seems kind o' formal comin' in this way," said Mrs. Todd impulsively, as we passed the flowers and came to the front doorstep; but she was mindful of the proprieties, and walked before us into the best room on the left.

"Why, mother, if you have n't gone an' turned the carpet!" she exclaimed, with something in her voice that spoke of awe and admiration. "When 'd you get to it? I s'pose Mis' Addicks come over an' helped you, from White Island Landing?"

"No, she did n't," answered the old woman, standing proudly erect, and making the most of a great moment. "I done it all myself with William's help. He had a spare day, an' took right holt with me; an' 't was all well beat on the grass, an' turned, an' put down again afore we went to bed. I ripped an' sewed over two o' them long breadths. I ain't had such a good night's sleep for two years."

"There, what do you think o' havin' such a mother as that for eighty-six year old?" said Mrs. Todd, standing before us like a large figure of Victory.

As for the mother, she took on a sudden look of youth; you felt as if she promised a great future, and was beginning, not ending, her summers and their happy toils.

"My, my!" exclaimed Mrs. Todd. "I could n't ha' done it myself, I 've got to own it."

"I was much pleased to have it off my mind," said Mrs. Blackett, humbly; "the more so because along at the first of the next week I was n't very well. I suppose it may have been the change of weather."

Mrs. Todd could not resist a significant glance at me, but, with charming sympathy, she forbore to point the lesson or to connect this illness with its apparent cause. She loomed larger than ever in the little old-fashioned best room, with its few pieces of good furniture and pictures of national interest. The green paper curtains were stamped with conventional landscapes of a foreign order,—castles on inaccessible crags, and lovely lakes with steep wooded shores; under-foot the treasured carpet was covered thick with home-made rugs. There were empty glass lamps and crystallized bouquets of grass and some fine shells on the narrow mantelpiece.

"I was married in this room," said Mrs. Todd unexpectedly; and I heard her give a sigh after she had spoken, as if she could not help the touch of regret that would forever come with all her thoughts of happiness.

"We stood right there between the windows," she added, "and the minister stood here. William would n't come in. He was always odd about seein' folks, just 's he is now. I run to meet 'em from a child, an' William, he 'd take an' run away."

"I 've been the gainer," said the old mother cheerfully. "William has been son an' daughter both since you was married off the island. He 's been 'most too satisfied to stop at home 'long o' his old mother, but I always tell 'em I 'm the gainer."

We were all moving toward the kitchen as if by common instinct. The best room was too suggestive of serious occasions, and the shades were all pulled down to shut out the summer light and air. It was indeed a tribute to Society to find a room set apart for her behests out there on so apparently neighborless and remote an island. Afternoon visits and evening festivals must be few in such a bleak situation at certain seasons of the year, but Mrs. Blackett was of those who do not live to themselves, and who have long since passed the line that divides mere self-concern from a valued share in whatever Society can give and take. There were those of her neighbors who never had taken the trouble to furnish a best room, but Mrs. Blackett was one who knew the uses of a parlor.

"Yes, do come right out into the old kitchen; I shan't make any stranger of you," she invited us pleasantly, after we had been properly received in the room appointed to formality. "I expect Almiry, here, 'll be driftin' out 'mongst the pasture-weeds quick 's she can find a good excuse. 'T is hot now. You 'd better content yourselves till you get nice an' rested, an' 'long after dinner the sea-breeze 'll spring up, an' then you can take your walks, an' go up an' see the prospect from the big ledge. Almiry 'll want to show off everything there is. Then I 'll get you a good cup o' tea before you start to go home. The days are plenty long now."

While we were talking in the best room the selected fish had been mysteriously brought up from the shore, and lay all cleaned and ready in an earthen crock on the table.

"I think William might have just stopped an' said a word," remarked Mrs. Todd, pouting with high affront as she caught sight of it. "He 's friendly enough when he comes ashore, an' was remarkable social the last time, for him."

"He ain't disposed to be very social with the ladies," explained William 's mother, with a delightful glance at me, as if she counted upon my friendship and tolerance. "He 's very particular, and he 's all in his old fishin'-clothes to-day. He 'll want me to tell him everything you said and done, after you 've gone. William has very deep affections. He 'll want to see you, Almiry. Yes, I guess he 'll be in by an' by."

"I 'll search for him by 'n' by, if he don't," proclaimed Mrs. Todd, with an air of unalterable resolution. "I know all of his burrows down 'long the shore. I 'll catch him by hand 'fore he knows it. I 've got some business with William, anyway. I brought forty-two cents with me that was due him for them last lobsters he brought in."

"You can leave it with me," suggested the little old mother, who was already stepping about among her pots and pans in the pantry, and preparing to make the chowder.

I became possessed of a sudden unwonted curiosity in regard to William, and felt that half the pleasure of my visit would be lost if I could not make his interesting acquaintance.

IX

WILLIAM

Mrs. Todd had taken the onion out of her basket and laid it down upon the kitchen table. "There's Johnny Bowden come with us, you know," she reminded her mother. "He'll be hungry enough to eat his size."

"I've got new doughnuts, dear," said the little old lady. "You don't often catch William 'n' me out o' provisions. I expect you might have chose a somewhat larger fish, but I'll try an' make it do. I shall have to have a few extra potatoes, but there's a field full out there, an' the hoe's leanin' against the well-house, in 'mongst the climbin'-beans." She smiled, and gave her daughter a commanding nod.

"Land sakes alive! Le''s blow the horn for William," insisted Mrs. Todd, with some excitement. "He needn't break his spirit so far's to come in. He'll know you need him for something particular, an' then we can call to him as he comes up the path. I won't put him to no pain."

Mrs. Blackett's old face, for the first time, wore a look of trouble, and I found it necessary to counteract the teasing spirit of Almira. It was too pleasant to stay indoors altogether, even in such rewarding companionship; besides, I might meet William; and, straying out presently, I found the hoe by the well-house and an old splint basket at the wood-shed door, and also found my way down to the field where there was a great square patch of rough, weedy potato-tops and tall ragweed. One corner was already dug, and I chose a fat-looking hill where the tops were well withered. There is all the pleasure that one can have in gold-digging in finding one's hopes satisfied in the riches of a good hill of potatoes. I longed to go on; but it did not seem frugal to dig any longer after my basket was full, and at last I took my hoe by the middle and lifted the basket to go back up the hill. I was sure that Mrs. Blackett must be waiting impatiently to slice the potatoes into the chowder, layer after layer, with the fish.

"You let me take holt o' that basket, ma'am," said a pleasant, anxious voice behind me.

I turned, startled in the silence of the wide field, and saw an elderly man, bent in the shoulders as fishermen often are, gray-headed and clean-shaven, and with a timid air. It was William. He looked just like his mother, and I had been imagining that he was large and stout like his sister, Almira Todd; and, strange to say, my fancy had led me to picture him not far from thirty and a little loutish. It was necessary instead to pay William the respect due to age.

I accustomed myself to plain facts on the instant, and we said good-morning like old friends. The basket was really heavy, and I put the hoe through its handle and offered him one end; then we moved easily toward the house together, speaking of the fine weather and of mackerel which were reported to be striking in all about the bay. William had been out since three o'clock, and had taken an extra fare of fish. I could feel that Mrs. Todd's eyes were upon us as we approached the house, and although I fell behind in the narrow path, and let William take the basket alone and precede me at some little distance the rest of the way, I could plainly hear her greet him.

"Got round to comin' in, did n't you?" she inquired, with amusement. "Well, now, that 's clever. Did n't know 's I should see you to-day, William, an' I wanted to settle an account."

I felt somewhat disturbed and responsible, but when I joined them they were on most simple and friendly terms. It became evident that, with William, it was the first step that cost, and that, having once joined in social interests, he was able to pursue them with more or less pleasure. He was about sixty, and not young-looking for his years, yet so undying is the spirit of youth, and bashfulness has such a power of survival, that I felt all the time as if one must try to make the occasion easy for some one who was young and new to the affairs of social life. He asked politely if I would like to go up to the great ledge while dinner was getting ready; so, not without a deep sense of pleasure, and a delighted look of surprise from the two hostesses, we started, William and I, as if both of us felt much younger than we looked. Such was the innocence and simplicity of the moment that when I heard Mrs. Todd laughing behind us in the kitchen I laughed too, but William did not even blush. I think he was a little deaf, and he stepped along before me most businesslike and intent upon his errand.

We went from the upper edge of the field above the house into a smooth, brown path among the dark spruces. The hot sun brought out the fragrance of the pitchy bark, and the shade was pleasant as we climbed the hill. William stopped once or twice to show me a great wasps'-nest close by, or some fishhawks'-nests below in a bit of swamp. He picked a few sprigs of late-blooming linnæa as we came out upon an open bit of pasture at the top of the island, and gave them to me without speaking, but he knew as well as I that one could not say half he wished about linnæa. Through this piece of rough pasture ran a huge shape of stone like the great backbone of an enormous creature. At the end, near the woods, we could climb up on it and walk along to the highest point; there above the circle of pointed firs we could look down over all the island, and could see the ocean that circled this and a hundred other bits of island-ground, the mainland shore and all the far horizons. It gave a sudden sense of space, for nothing stopped the eye or hedged one in,—that sense of liberty in space and time which great prospects always give.

"There ain't no such view in the world, I expect," said William proudly, and I hastened to speak my heartfelt tribute of praise; it was impossible not to feel as if an untraveled boy had spoken, and yet one loved to have him value his native heath.

X

WHERE PENNYROYAL GREW

WE WERE a little late to dinner, but Mrs. Blackett and Mrs. Todd were lenient, and we all took our places after William had paused to wash his hands, like a pious Brahmin, at the well, and put on a neat blue coat which he took from a peg behind the kitchen door. Then he resolutely asked a blessing in words that I could not hear, and we ate the chowder and were thankful. The kitten went round and round the table, quite erect, and, holding on by her fierce young claws, she stopped to mew with pathos at each elbow, or darted off to the open door when a song sparrow forgot himself and lit in the grass too near. William did not talk much, but his sister Todd occupied the time and told all the news there was to tell of Dunnet Landing and its coasts, while the old mother listened with delight. Her hospitality was something exquisite; she had the gift which so many women lack, of being able to make themselves and their houses belong entirely to a guest's pleasure,—that charming surrender for the moment of themselves and whatever belongs to them, so that they make a part of one's own life that can never be forgotten. Tact is after all a kind of mind-reading, and my hostess held the golden gift. Sympathy is of the mind as well as the heart, and Mrs. Blackett's world and mine were one from the moment we met. Besides, she had that final, that highest gift of heaven, a perfect self-forgetfulness. Sometimes, as I watched her eager, sweet old face, I wondered why she had been set to shine on this lonely island of the northern coast. It must have been to keep the balance true, and make up to all her scattered and depending neighbors for other things which they may have lacked.

When we had finished clearing away the old blue plates, and the kitten had taken care of her share of the fresh haddock, just as we were putting back the kitchen chairs in their places, Mrs. Todd said briskly that she must go up into the pasture now to gather the desired herbs.

"You can stop here an' rest, or you can accompany me," she announced. "Mother ought to have her nap, and when we come back she an' William 'll sing for you. She admires music," said Mrs. Todd, turning to speak to her mother.

But Mrs. Blackett tried to say that she could n't sing as she used, and perhaps William would n't feel like it. She looked tired, the good old soul, or I should have liked to sit in the peaceful little house while she slept; I had had much pleasant experience of pastures already in her daughter's company. But it seemed best to go with Mrs. Todd, and off we went.

Mrs. Todd carried the gingham bag which she had brought from home, and a small heavy burden in the bottom made it hang straight and slender from her hand. The way was steep, and she soon grew breathless, so that we sat down to rest awhile on a convenient large stone among the bayberry.

"There, I wanted you to see this, — 't is mother's picture," said Mrs. Todd; " 't was taken once when she was up to Portland, soon after she was married. That 's me," she added, opening another worn case, and displaying the full face of the cheerful child she looked like still in spite of being past sixty. "And here 's William an' father together. I take after father, large and heavy, an' William is like mother's folks, short an' thin. He ought to have made something o' himself, bein' a man an' so like mother; but though he 's been very steady to work, an' kept up the farm, an' done his fishin' too right along, he never had mother's snap an' power o' seein' things just as they be. He 's got excellent judgment, too," meditated William's sister, but she could not arrive at any satisfactory decision upon what she evidently thought his failure in life. "I think it is well to see any one so happy an' makin' the most of life just as it falls to hand," she said as she began to put the daguerreotypes away again; but I reached out my hand to see her mother's once more, a most flower-like face of a lovely young woman in quaint dress. There was in the eyes a look of anticipation and joy, a far-off look that sought the horizon; one often sees it in seafaring families, inherited by girls and boys alike from men who spend their lives at sea, and are always watching for distant sails or the first loom of the land. At sea there is nothing to be seen close by, and this has its counterpart in a sailor's character, in the large and brave and patient traits that are developed, the hopeful pleasantness that one loves so in a seafarer.

When the family pictures were wrapped again in a big handkerchief, we set forward in a narrow footpath and made our way to a lonely place that faced northward, where there was more pasturage and fewer bushes, and we went down to the edge of short grass above some rocky cliffs where the deep sea broke with a great noise, though the wind was down and the water looked quiet a little way from shore. Among the grass grew such pennyroyal as the rest of the world could not provide. There was a fine fragrance in the air as we gathered it sprig by sprig and stepped along carefully, and Mrs. Todd pressed her aromatic nosegay between her hands and offered it to me again and again.

"There's nothin' like it," she said; "oh no, there's no such pennyr'yal as this in the State of Maine. It's the right pattern of the plant, and all the rest I ever see is but an imitation. Don't it do you good?" And I answered with enthusiasm.

"There, dear, I never showed nobody else but mother where to find this place; 't is kind of sainted to me. Nathan, my husband, an' I used to love this place when we was court-in', and"—she hesitated, and then spoke softly—"when he was lost, 't was just off shore tryin' to get in by the short channel out there between Squaw Islands, right in sight o' this headland where we'd set an' made our plans all summer long."

I had never heard her speak of her husband before, but I felt that we were friends now since she had brought me to this place.

" 'T was but a dream with us," Mrs. Todd said. "I knew it when he was gone. I knew it"—and she whispered as if she were at confession—"I knew it afore he started to go to sea. My heart was gone out o' my keepin' before I ever saw Nathan; but he loved me well, and he made me real happy, and he died before he ever knew what he'd had to know if we'd lived long together. 'T is very strange about love. No, Nathan never found out, but my heart was troubled when I knew him first. There's more women likes to be loved than there is of those that loves. I spent some happy hours right here. I always liked Nathan, and he never knew. But this pennyr'yal always reminded me, as I'd sit and gather it and hear him talkin'—it always would remind me of—the other one."

She looked away from me, and presently rose and went on by herself. There was something lonely and solitary about her great determined shape. She might have been Antigone alone on the Theban plain. It is not often given in a noisy world to come to the places of great grief and silence. An absolute, archaic grief possessed this country-woman; she seemed like a renewal of some historic soul, with her sorrows and the remoteness of a daily life busied with rustic simplicities and the scents of primeval herbs.

I was not incompetent at herb-gathering, and after a while, when I had sat long enough waking myself to new thoughts, and reading a page of remembrance with new pleasure, I gathered some bunches, as I was bound to do, and at last we met again higher up the shore, in the plain every-day world we had left behind when we went down to the pennyroyal plot. As we walked together along the high edge of the field we saw a hundred sails about the bay and farther seaward; it was mid-afternoon or after, and the day was coming to an end.

"Yes, they're all makin' towards the shore,—the small craft an' the lobster smacks an' all," said my companion. "We must spend a little time with mother now, just to have our tea, an' then put for home."

"No matter if we lose the wind at sun-down; I can row in with Johnny," said I; and Mrs. Todd nodded reassuringly and kept to her steady plod, not quickening her gait even when we saw William come round the corner of the house as if to look for us, and wave his hand and disappear.

"Why, William's right on deck; I didn't know's we should see any more of him!" exclaimed Mrs. Todd. "Now mother'll put the kettle right on; she's got a good fire goin'." I too could see the blue smoke thicken, and then we both walked a little faster, while Mrs. Todd groped in her full bag of herbs to find the daguerreotypes and be ready to put them in their places.

XI

THE OLD SINGERS

WILLIAM was sitting on the side door step, and the old mother was busy making her tea; she gave into my hand an old flowered-glass tea-caddy.

"William thought you'd like to see this, when he was set-tin' the table. My father brought it to my mother from the island of Tobago; an' here's a pair of beautiful mugs that came with it." She opened the glass door of a little cupboard beside the chimney. "These I call my best things, dear," she said. "You'd laugh to see how we enjoy 'em Sunday nights in winter: we have a real company tea 'stead o' livin' right along just the same, an' I make somethin' good for a s'prise an' put on some o' my preserves, an' we get a-talkin' together an' have real pleasant times."

Mrs. Todd laughed indulgently, and looked to see what I thought of such childishness.

"I wish I could be here some Sunday evening," said I.

"William an' me'll be talkin' about you an' thinkin' o' this nice day," said Mrs. Blackett affectionately, and she glanced at William, and he looked up bravely and nodded. I began to discover that he and his sister could not speak their deeper feelings before each other.

"Now I want you an' mother to sing," said Mrs. Todd abruptly, with an air of command, and I gave William much sympathy in his evident distress.

"After I've had my cup o' tea, dear," answered the old hostess cheerfully; and so we sat down and took our cups and made merry while they lasted. It was impossible not to wish to stay on forever at Green Island, and I could not help saying so.

"I'm very happy here, both winter an' summer," said old Mrs. Blackett. "William an' I never wish for any other home, do we, William? I'm glad you find it pleasant; I wish you'd come an' stay, dear, whenever you feel inclined. But here's Almiry; I always think Providence was kind to plot an' have her husband leave her a good house where she really belonged. She'd been very restless if she'd had to continue here on Green Island. You wanted more scope, didn't you, Almiry, an' to live in a large place where more things grew? Sometimes folks wonders that we don't live together; perhaps we shall some time," and a shadow of sadness and apprehension flitted across her face. "The time o' sickness an' failin' has got to come to all. But Almiry's got an herb that's good for everything." She smiled as she spoke, and looked bright again.

"There's some herb that's good for everybody, except for them that thinks they're sick when they ain't," announced Mrs. Todd, with a truly professional air of finality. "Come, William, let's have Sweet Home, an' then mother'll sing Cupid an' the Bee for us."

Then followed a most charming surprise. William mastered his timidity and began to sing. His voice was a little faint and frail, like the family daguerreotypes, but it was a tenor voice, and perfectly true and sweet. I have never heard Home, Sweet Home sung as touchingly and seriously as he sang it; he seemed to make it quite new; and when he paused for a moment at the end of the first line and began the next, the old mother joined him and they sang together, she missing only the higher notes, where he seemed to lend his voice to hers for the moment and carry on her very note and air. It was the silent man's real and only means of expression, and one could have listened forever, and have asked for more and more songs of old Scotch and English inheritance and the best that have lived from the ballad music of the war. Mrs. Todd kept time visibly, and sometimes audibly, with her ample foot. I saw the tears in her eyes sometimes, when I could see beyond the tears in mine. But at last the songs ended and the time came to say good-by; it was the end of a great pleasure.

Mrs. Blackett, the dear old lady, opened the door of her bedroom while Mrs. Todd was tying up the herb bag, and William had gone down to get the boat ready and to blow the horn for Johnny Bowden, who had joined a roving boat party who were off the shore lobstering.

I went to the door of the bedroom, and thought how pleasant it looked, with its pink-and-white patchwork quilt and the brown unpainted paneling of its woodwork.

"Come right in, dear," she said. "I want you to set down in my old quilted rockin'-chair there by the window; you'll say it's the prettiest view in the house. I set there a good deal to rest me and when I want to read."

There was a worn red Bible on the light-stand, and Mrs. Blackett's heavy silver-bowed glasses; her thimble was on the narrow window-ledge, and folded carefully on the table was a thick striped-cotton shirt that she was making for her son. Those dear old fingers and their loving stitches, that heart which had made the most of everything that needed love! Here was the real home, the heart of the old house on Green Island! I sat in the rocking-chair, and felt that it was a place of peace, the little brown bedroom, and the quiet outlook upon field and sea and sky.

I looked up, and we understood each other without speaking. "I shall like to think o' your settin' here to-day," said Mrs. Blackett. "I want you to come again. It has been so pleasant for William."

The wind served us all the way home, and did not fall or let the sail slacken until we were close to the shore. We had a generous freight of lobsters in the boat, and new potatoes which William had put aboard, and what Mrs. Todd proudly called a full "kag" of prime number one salted mackerel; and when we landed we had to make business arrangements to have these conveyed to her house in a wheelbarrow.

I never shall forget the day at Green Island. The town of Dunnet Landing seemed large and noisy and oppressive as we came ashore. Such is the power of contrast; for the village was so still that I could hear the shy whippoorwills singing that night as I lay awake in my downstairs bedroom, and the scent of Mrs. Todd's herb garden under the window blew in again and again with every gentle rising of the sea-breeze.

XII

A STRANGE SAIL

EXCEPT for a few stray guests, islanders or from the inland country, to whom Mrs. Todd offered the hospitalities of a single meal, we were quite by ourselves all summer; and when there were signs of invasion, late in July, and a certain Mrs. Fosdick appeared like a strange sail on the far horizon, I suffered much from apprehension. I had been living in the quaint little house with as much comfort and unconsciousness as if it were a larger body, or a double shell, in whose simple convolutions Mrs. Todd and I had secreted ourselves, until some wandering hermit crab of a visitor marked the little spare room for her own. Perhaps now and then a castaway on a lonely desert island dreads the thought of being rescued. I heard of Mrs. Fosdick for the first time with a selfish sense of objection; but after all, I was still vacation-tenant of the schoolhouse, where I could always be alone, and it was impossible not to sympathize with Mrs. Todd, who, in spite of some preliminary grumbling, was really delighted with the prospect of entertaining an old friend.

For nearly a month we received occasional news of Mrs. Fosdick, who seemed to be making a royal progress from house to house in the inland neighborhood, after the fashion of Queen Elizabeth. One Sunday after another came and went, disappointing Mrs. Todd in the hope of seeing her guest at church and fixing the day for the great visit to begin; but Mrs. Fosdick was not ready to commit herself to a date. An assurance of "some time this week" was not sufficiently definite from a free-footed housekeeper's point of view, and Mrs. Todd put aside all herb-gathering plans, and went through the various stages of expectation, provocation, and despair. At last she was ready to believe that Mrs. Fosdick must have forgotten her promise and returned to her home, which was vaguely said to be over Thomaston way. But one evening, just as the supper-table was cleared and "readied up," and Mrs. Todd had put her large apron over her head and stepped forth for an evening stroll in the garden, the unexpected happened. She heard the sound of wheels, and gave an excited cry to me, as I sat by the window, that Mrs. Fosdick was coming right up the street.

"She may not be considerate, but she's dreadful good company," said Mrs. Todd hastily, coming back a few steps from the neighborhood of the gate. "No, she ain't a mite considerate, but there's a small lobster left over from your tea; yes, it's a real mercy there's a lobster. Susan Fosdick might just as well have passed the compliment o' comin' an hour ago."

"Perhaps she has had her supper," I ventured to suggest, sharing the housekeeper's anxiety, and meekly conscious of an inconsiderate appetite for my own supper after a long expedition up the bay. There were so few emergencies of any sort at Dunnet Landing that this one appeared overwhelming.

"No, she's rode 'way over from Nahum Brayton's place. I expect they were busy on the farm, and couldn't spare the horse in proper season. You just sly out an' set the teakittle on again, dear, an' drop in a good han'ful o' chips; the fire's all alive. I'll take her right up to lay off her things, an' she'll be occupied with explanations an' gettin' her bunnit off, so you'll have plenty o' time. She's one I shouldn't like to have find me unprepared."

Mrs. Fosdick was already at the gate, and Mrs. Todd now turned with an air of complete surprise and delight to welcome her.

"Why, Susan Fosdick," I heard her exclaim in a fine unhindered voice, as if she were calling across a field, "I come near giving of you up! I was afraid you'd gone an' 'portioned out my visit to somebody else. I s'pose you've been to supper?"

"Lor', no, I ain't, Almiry Todd," said Mrs. Fosdick cheerfully, as she turned, laden with bags and bundles, from making her adieux to the boy driver. "I ain't had a mite o' supper, dear. I've been lottin' all the way on a cup o' that best tea o' yourn,—some o' that Oolong you keep in the little chist. I don't want none o' your useful herbs."

"I keep that tea for ministers' folks," gayly responded Mrs. Todd. "Come right along in, Susan Fosdick. I declare if you ain't the same old sixpence!"

As they came up the walk together, laughing like girls, I fled, full of cares, to the kitchen, to brighten the fire and be sure that the lobster, sole dependence of a late supper, was well out of reach of the cat. There proved to be fine reserves of wild raspberries and bread and butter, so that I regained my composure, and waited impatiently for my own share of this illustrious visit to begin. There was an instant sense of high festivity in the evening air from the moment when our guest had so frankly demanded the Oolong tea.

The great moment arrived. I was formally presented at the stair-foot, and the two friends passed on to the kitchen, where I soon heard a hospitable clink of crockery and the brisk stirring of a tea-cup. I sat in my high-backed rocking-chair by the window in the front room with an unreasonable feeling of being left out, like the child who stood at the gate in Hans Andersen's story. Mrs. Fosdick did not look, at first sight, like a person of great social gifts. She was a serious-looking little bit of an old woman, with a birdlike nod of the head. I had often been told that she was the "best hand in the world to make a visit," — as if to visit were the highest of vocations; that everybody wished for her, while few could get her; and I saw that Mrs. Todd felt a comfortable sense of distinction in being favored with the company of this eminent person who "knew just how." It was certainly true that Mrs. Fosdick gave both her hostess and me a warm feeling of enjoyment and expectation, as if she had the power of social suggestion to all neighboring minds.

The two friends did not reappear for at least an hour. I could hear their busy voices, loud and low by turns, as they ranged from public to confidential topics. At last Mrs. Todd kindly remembered me and returned, giving my door a ceremonious knock before she stepped in, with the small visitor in her wake. She reached behind her and took Mrs. Fosdick's hand as if she were young and bashful, and gave her a gentle pull forward.

"There, I don't know whether you 're goin' to take to each other or not; no, nobody can't tell whether you 'll suit each other, but I expect you 'll get along some way, both having seen the world," said our affectionate hostess. "You can inform Mis' Fosdick how we found the folks out to Green Island the other day. She 's always been well acquainted with mother. I 'll slip out now an' put away the supper things an' set my bread to rise, if you'll both excuse me. You can come out an' keep me company when you get ready, either or both." And Mrs. Todd, large and amiable, disappeared and left us.

Being furnished not only with a subject of conversation, but with a safe refuge in the kitchen in case of incompatibility, Mrs. Fosdick and I sat down, prepared to make the best of each other. I soon discovered that she, like many of the elder women of that coast, had spent a part of her life at sea, and was full of a good traveler's curiosity and enlightenment. By the time we thought it discreet to join our hostess we were already sincere friends.

You may speak of a visit's setting in as well as a tide's, and it was impossible, as Mrs. Todd whispered to me, not to be pleased at the way this visit was setting in; a new impulse and refreshing of the social currents and seldom visited bays of memory appeared to have begun. Mrs. Fosdick had been the mother of a large family of sons and daughters, — sailors and sailors' wives, — and most of them had died before her. I soon grew more or less acquainted with the histories of all their fortunes and misfortunes, and subjects of an intimate nature were no more withheld from my ears than if I had been a shell on the mantelpiece. Mrs. Fosdick was not without a touch of dignity and elegance; she was fashionable in her dress, but it was a curiously well-preserved provincial fashion of some years back. In a wider sphere one might have called her a woman of the world, with her unexpected bits of modern knowledge, but Mrs. Todd's wisdom was an intimation of truth itself. She might belong to any age, like an idyl of Theocritus; but while she always understood Mrs. Fosdick, that entertaining pilgrim could not always understand Mrs. Todd.

That very first evening my friends plunged into a borderless sea of reminiscences and personal news. Mrs. Fosdick had been staying with a family who owned the farm where she was born, and she had visited every sunny knoll and shady field corner; but when she said that it might be for the last time, I detected in her tone something expectant of the contradiction which Mrs. Todd promptly offered.

"Almiry," said Mrs. Fosdick, with sadness, "you may say what you like, but I am one of nine brothers and sisters brought up on the old place, and we're all dead but me."

"Your sister Dailey ain't gone, is she? Why, no, Louisa ain't gone!" exclaimed Mrs. Todd, with surprise. "Why, I never heard of that occurrence!"

"Yes 'm; she passed away last October, in Lynn. She had made her distant home in Vermont State, but she was making a visit to her youngest daughter. Louisa was the only one of my family whose funeral I wasn't able to attend, but 't was a mere accident. All the rest of us were settled right about home. I thought it was very slack of 'em in Lynn not to fetch her to the old place; but when I came to hear about it, I learned that they'd recently put up a very elegant monument, and my sister Dailey was always great for show. She'd just been out to see the monument the week before she was taken down, and admired it so much that they felt sure of her wishes."

"So she's really gone, and the funeral was up to Lynn!" repeated Mrs. Todd, as if to impress the sad fact upon her mind. "She was some years younger than we be, too. I recollect the first day she ever came to school; 't was that first year mother sent me inshore to stay with aunt Topham's folks and get my schooling. You fetched little Louisa to school one Monday mornin' in a pink dress an' her long curls, and she set between you an' me, and got cryin' after a while, so the teacher sent us home with her at recess."

"She was scared of seeing so many children about her; there was only her and me and brother John at home then; the older boys were to sea with father, an' the rest of us wa'n't born," explained Mrs. Fosdick. "That next fall we all went to sea together. Mother was uncertain till the last minute, as one may say. The ship was waiting orders, but the baby that then was, was born just in time, and there was a long spell of extra bad weather, so mother got about again before they had to sail, an' we all went. I remember my clothes were all left ashore in the east chamber in a basket where mother'd took them out o' my chist o' drawers an' left 'em ready to carry aboard. She didn't have nothing aboard, of her own, that she wanted to cut up for me, so when my dress wore out she just put me into a spare suit o' John's, jacket and trousers. I was n't but eight years old an' he was most seven and large of his age. Quick as we made a port she went right ashore an' fitted me out pretty, but we was bound for the East Indies and did n't put in anywhere for a good while. So I had quite a spell o' freedom. Mother made my new skirt long because I was growing, and I poked about the deck after that, real discouraged, feeling the hem at my heels every minute, and as if youth was past and gone. I liked the trousers best; I used to climb the riggin' with 'em and frighten mother till she said an' vowed she 'd never take me to sea again.

I thought by the polite absent-minded smile on Mrs. Todd's face this was no new story.

"Little Louisa was a beautiful child; yes, I always thought Louisa was very pretty," Mrs. Todd said. "She was a dear little girl in those days. She favored your mother; the rest of you took after your father's folks."

"We did certain," agreed Mrs. Fosdick, rocking steadily. "There, it does seem so pleasant to talk with an old acquaintance that knows what you know. I see so many of these new folks nowadays, that seem to have neither past nor future. Conversation's got to have some root in the past, or else you 've got to explain every remark you make, an' it wears a person out."

Mrs. Todd gave a funny little laugh. "Yes 'm, old friends is always best, 'less you can catch a new one that's fit to make an old one out of," she said, and we gave an affectionate glance at each other which Mrs. Fosdick could not have understood, being the latest comer to the house.

XIII

POOR JOANNA

ONE EVENING my ears caught a mysterious allusion which Mrs. Todd made to Shell-heap Island. It was a chilly night of cold northeasterly rain, and I made a fire for the first time in the Franklin stove in my room, and begged my two housemates to come in and keep me company. The weather had convinced Mrs. Todd that it was time to make a supply of cough-drops, and she had been bringing forth herbs from dark and dry hiding-places, until now the pungent dust and odor of them had resolved themselves into one mighty flavor of spearmint that came from a simmering caldron of syrup in the kitchen. She called it done, and well done, and had ostentatiously left it to cool, and taken her knitting-work because Mrs. Fosdick was busy with hers. They sat in the two rocking-chairs, the small woman and the large one, but now and then I could see that Mrs. Todd's thoughts remained with the cough-drops. The time of gathering herbs was nearly over, but the time of syrups and cordials had begun.

The heat of the open fire made us a little drowsy, but something in the way Mrs. Todd spoke of Shell-heap Island waked my interest. I waited to see if she would say any more, and then took a roundabout way back to the subject by saying what was first in my mind: that I wished the Green Island family were there to spend the evening with us,—Mrs. Todd's mother and her brother William.

Mrs. Todd smiled, and drummed on the arm of the rocking-chair. "Might scare William to death," she warned me; and Mrs. Fosdick mentioned her intention of going out to Green Island to stay two or three days, if this wind did n't make too much sea.

"Where is Shell-heap Island?" I ventured to ask, seizing the opportunity.

"Bears nor'east somewheres about three miles from Green Island; right off-shore, I should call it about eight miles out," said Mrs. Todd. "You never was there, dear; 't is off the thoroughfares, and a very bad place to land at best."

"I should think 't was," agreed Mrs. Fosdick, smoothing down her black silk apron. " 'T is a place worth visitin' when you once get there. Some o' the old folks was kind o' fearful about it. 'T was 'counted a great place in old Indian times; you can pick up their stone tools 'most any time if you hunt about. There 's a beautiful spring 'o water, too. Yes, I remember when they used to tell queer stories about Shell-heap Island. Some said 't was a great bangeing-place for the Indians, and an old chief resided there once that ruled the winds; and others said they 'd always heard that once the Indians come down from up country an' left a captive there without any bo't, an' 't was too far to swim across to Black Island, so called, an' he lived there till he perished."

"I 've heard say he walked the island after that, and sharp-sighted folks could see him an' lose him like one o' them citizens Cap'n Littlepage was acquainted with up to the north pole," announced Mrs. Todd grimly. "Anyway, there was Indians,—you can see their shell-heap that named the island; and I 've heard myself that 't was one o' their cannibal places, but I never could believe it. There never was no cannibals on the coast o' Maine. All the Indians o' these regions are tame-looking folks."

"Sakes alive, yes!" exclaimed Mrs. Fosdick. "Ought to see them painted savages I 've seen when I was young out in the South Sea Islands! That was the time for folks to travel, 'way back in the old whalin' days!"

"Whalin' must have been dull for a lady, hardly ever makin' a lively port, and not takin' in any mixed cargoes," said Mrs. Todd. "I never desired to go a whalin' v'y'ge myself."

"I used to return feelin' very slack an' behind the times, 't is true," explained Mrs. Fosdick, "but 't was excitin', an' we always done extra well, and felt rich when we did get ashore. I liked the variety. There, how times have changed; how few seafarin' families there are left! What a lot o' queer folks there used to be about here, anyway, when we was young, Almiry. Everybody 's just like everybody else, now; nobody to laugh about, and nobody to cry about."

It seemed to me that there were peculiarities of character in the region of Dunnet Landing yet, but I did not like to interrupt.

"Yes," said Mrs. Todd after a moment of meditation, "there was certain a good many curiosities of human natur' in this neighborhood years ago. There was more energy then, and in some the energy took a singular turn. In these days the young folks is all copy-cats, 'fraid to death they won't be all just alike; as for the old folks, they pray for the advantage o' bein' a little different."

"I ain't heard of a copy-cat this great many years," said Mrs. Fosdick, laughing; " 't was a favorite term o' my grand-mother's. No, I wa'n't thinking o' those things, but of them strange straying creatur's that used to rove the country. You don't see them now, or the ones that used to hive away in their own houses with some strange notion or other."

I thought again of Captain Littlepage, but my companions were not reminded of his name; and there was brother William at Green Island, whom we all three knew.

"I was talking o' poor Joanna the other day. I had n't thought of her for a great while," said Mrs. Fosdick abruptly. "Mis' Brayton an' I recalled her as we sat together sewing. She was one o' your peculiar persons, wa'n't she? Speaking of such persons," she turned to explain to me, "there was a sort of a nun or hermit person lived out there for years all alone on Shell-heap Island. Miss Joanna Todd, her name was, — a cousin o' Almiry's late husband."

I expressed my interest, but as I glanced at Mrs. Todd I saw that she was confused by sudden affectionate feeling and un-mistakable desire for reticence.

"I never want to hear Joanna laughed about," she said anxiously.

"Nor I," answered Mrs. Fosdick reassuringly. "She was crossed in love, — that was all the matter to begin with; but as I look back, I can see that Joanna was one doomed from the first to fall into a melancholy. She retired from the world for good an' all, though she was a well-off woman. All she wanted was to get away from folks; she thought she was n't fit to live with anybody, and wanted to be free. Shell-heap Island come to her from her father, and first thing folks knew she 'd gone off out there to live, and left word she did n't want no company. 'T was a bad place to get to, unless the wind an' tide were just right; 't was hard work to make a landing."

"What time of year was this?" I asked.

"Very late in the summer," said Mrs. Fosdick. "No, I never could laugh at Joanna, as some did. She set everything by the young man, an' they were going to marry in about a month, when he got bewitched with a girl 'way up the bay, and married her, and went off to Massachusetts. He was n't well thought of,—there were those who thought Joanna's money was what had tempted him; but she 'd given him her whole heart, an' she wa'n't so young as she had been. All her hopes were built on marryin', an' havin' a real home and somebody to look to; she acted just like a bird when its nest is spoilt. The day after she heard the news she was in dreadful woe, but the next she came to herself very quiet, and took the horse and wagon, and drove fourteen miles to the lawyer's, and signed a paper givin' her half of the farm to her brother. They never had got along very well together, but he did n't want to sign it, till she acted so distressed that he gave in. Edward Todd's wife was a good woman, who felt very bad indeed, and used every argument with Joanna; but Joanna took a poor old boat that had been her father's and lo'ded in a few things, and off she put all alone, with a good land breeze, right out to sea. Edward Todd ran down to the beach, an' stood there cryin' like a boy to see her go, but she was out o' hearin'. She never stepped foot on the mainland again long as she lived."

"How large an island is it? How did she manage in winter?" I asked.

"Perhaps thirty acres, rocks and all," answered Mrs. Todd, taking up the story gravely. "There can't be much of it that the salt spray don't fly over in storms. No, 't is a dreadful small place to make a world of; it has a different look from any of the other islands, but there's a sheltered cove on the south side, with mud-flats across one end of it at low water where there's excellent clams, and the big shell-heap keeps some o' the wind off a little house her father took the trouble to build when he was a young man. They said there was an old house built o' logs there before that, with a kind of natural cellar in the rock under it. He used to stay out there days to a time, and anchor a little sloop he had, and dig clams to fill it, and sail up to Portland. They said the dealers always gave him an extra price, the clams were so noted. Joanna used to go out and stay with him. They were always great companions, so she knew just what 't was out there. There was a few sheep that belonged to her brother an' her, but she bargained for him to come and get them on the edge o' cold weather. Yes, she desired him to come for the sheep; an' his wife thought perhaps Joanna 'd return, but he said no, an' lo'ded the bo't with warm things an' what he thought she 'd need through the winter. He come home with the sheep an' left the other things by the house, but she never so much as looked out o' the window. She done it for a penance. She must have wanted to see Edward by that time."

Mrs. Fosdick was fidgeting with eagerness to speak.

"Some thought the first cold snap would set her ashore, but she always remained," concluded Mrs. Todd soberly.

"Talk about the men not having any curiosity!" exclaimed Mrs. Fosdick scornfully. "Why, the waters round Shell-heap Island were white with sails all that fall. 'T was never called no great of a fishin'-ground before. Many of 'em made excuse to go ashore to get water at the spring; but at last she spoke to a bo't-load, very dignified and calm, and said that she 'd like it better if they 'd make a practice of getting water to Black Island or somewheres else and leave her alone, except in case of accident or trouble. But there was one man who had always set everything by her from a boy. He 'd have married her if the other had n't come about an' spoilt his chance, and he used to get close to the island, before light, on his way out fishin', and throw a little bundle 'way up the green slope front o' the house. His sister told me she happened to see, the first time, what a pretty choice he made o' useful things that a woman would feel lost without. He stood off fishin', and could see them in the grass all day, though sometimes she 'd come out and walk right by them. There was other bo'ts near, out after mackerel. But early next morning his present was gone. He did n't presume too much, but once he took her a nice firkin o' things he got up to Portland, and when spring come he landed her a hen and chickens in a nice little coop. There was a good many old friends had Joanna on their minds."

"Yes," said Mrs. Todd, losing her sad reserve in the growing sympathy of these reminiscences. "How everybody used to notice whether there was smoke out of the chimney! The Black Island folks could see her with their spy-glass, and if they'd ever missed getting some sign o' life they'd have sent notice to her folks. But after the first year or two Joanna was more and more forgotten as an every-day charge. Folks lived very simple in those days, you know," she continued, as Mrs. Fosdick's knitting was taking much thought at the moment. "I expect there was always plenty of driftwood thrown up, and a poor failin' patch of spruces covered all the north side of the island, so she always had something to burn. She was very fond of workin' in the garden ashore, and that first summer she began to till the little field out there, and raised a nice parcel o' potatoes. She could fish, o' course, and there was all her clams an' lobsters. You can always live well in any wild place by the sea when you'd starve to death up country, except 't was berry time. Joanna had berries out there, blackberries at least, and there was a few herbs in case she needed them. Mullein in great quantities and a plant o' wormwood I remember seeing once when I stayed there, long before she fled out to Shell-heap. Yes, I recall the wormwood, which is always a planted herb, so there must have been folks there before the Todds' day. A growin' bush makes the best gravestone; I expect that wormwood always stood for somebody's solemn monument. Catnip, too, is a very endurin' herb about an old place."

"But what I want to know is what she did for other things," interrupted Mrs. Fosdick. "Almiry, what did she do for clothin' when she needed to replenish, or risin' for her bread, or the piece-bag that no woman can live long without?"

"Or company," suggested Mrs. Todd. "Joanna was one that loved her friends. There must have been a terrible sight o' long winter evenin's that first year."

"There was her hens," suggested Mrs. Fosdick, after reviewing the melancholy situation. "She never wanted the sheep after that first season. There wa'n't no proper pasture for sheep after the June grass was past, and she ascertained the fact and couldn't bear to see them suffer; but the chickens done well. I remember sailin' by one spring afternoon, an' seein' the coops out front o' the house in the sun. How long was it before you went out with the minister? You were the first ones that ever really got ashore to see Joanna."

I had been reflecting upon a state of society which admitted such personal freedom and a voluntary hermitage. There was something mediæval in the behavior of poor Joanna Todd under a disappointment of the heart. The two women had drawn closer together, and were talking on, quite unconscious of a listener.

"Poor Joanna!" said Mrs. Todd again, and sadly shook her head as if there were things one could not speak about.

"I called her a great fool," declared Mrs. Fosdick, with spirit, "but I pitied her then, and I pity her far more now. Some other minister would have been a great help to her, — one that preached self-forgetfulness and doin' for others to cure our own ills; but Parson Dimmick was a vague person, well meanin', but very numb in his feelin's. I don't suppose at that troubled time Joanna could think of any way to mend her troubles except to run off and hide."

"Mother used to say she did n't see how Joanna lived without having nobody to do for, getting her own meals and tending her own poor self day in an' day out," said Mrs. Todd sorrowfully.

"There was the hens," repeated Mrs. Fosdick kindly. "I expect she soon came to makin' folks o' them. No, I never went to work to blame Joanna, as some did. She was full o' feeling, and her troubles hurt her more than she could bear. I see it all now as I could n't when I was young."

"I suppose in old times they had their shut-up convents for just such folks," said Mrs. Todd, as if she and her friend had disagreed about Joanna once, and were now in happy harmony. She seemed to speak with new openness and freedom. "Oh yes, I was only too pleased when the Reverend Mr. Dimmick invited me to go out with him. He had n't been very long in the place when Joanna left home and friends. 'T was one day that next summer after she went, and I had been married early in the spring. He felt that he ought to go out and visit her. She was a member of the church, and might wish to have him consider her spiritual state. I wa'n't so sure o' that, but I always liked Joanna, and I 'd come to be her cousin by marriage. Nathan an' I had conversed about goin' out to pay her a visit, but he got his chance to sail sooner 'n he expected. He always thought everything of her, and last time he come home, knowing nothing of her change, he brought her a beautiful coral pin from a port he'd touched at somewheres up the Mediterranean. So I wrapped the little box in a nice piece of paper and put it in my pocket, and picked her a bunch of fresh lemon balm, and off we started."

Mrs. Fosdick laughed. "I remember hearin' about your trials on the v'y'ge," she said.

"Why, yes," continued Mrs. Todd in her company manner. "I picked her the balm, an' we started. Why, yes, Susan, the minister liked to have cost me my life that day. He would fasten the sheet, though I advised against it. He said the rope was rough an' cut his hand. There was a fresh breeze, an' he went on talking rather high flown, an' I felt some interested. All of a sudden there come up a gust, and he give a screech and stood right up and called for help, 'way out there to sea. I knocked him right over into the bottom o' the bo't, getting by to catch hold of the sheet an' untie it. He wasn't but a little man; I helped him right up after the squall passed, and made a handsome apology to him, but he did act kind o' offended."

"I do think they ought not to settle them landlocked folks in parishes where they're liable to be on the water," insisted Mrs. Fosdick. "Think of the families in our parish that was scattered all about the bay, and what a sight o' sails you used to see, in Mr. Dimmick's day, standing across to the mainland on a pleasant Sunday morning, filled with church-going folks, all sure to want him some time or other! You couldn't find no doctor that would stand up in the boat and screech if a flaw struck her."

"Old Dr. Bennett had a beautiful sailboat, didn't he?" responded Mrs. Todd. "And how well he used to brave the weather! Mother always said that in time o' trouble that tall white sail used to look like an angel's wing comin' over the sea to them that was in pain. Well, there's a difference in gifts. Mr. Dimmick was not without light."

"'T was light o' the moon, then," snapped Mrs. Fosdick; "he was pompous enough, but I never could remember a single word he said. There, go on, Mis' Todd; I forget a great deal about that day you went to see poor Joanna."

"I felt she saw us coming, and knew us a great way off; yes, I seemed to feel it within me," said our friend, laying down her knitting. "I kept my seat, and took the bo't inshore without saying a word; there was a short channel that I was sure Mr. Dimmick wasn't acquainted with, and the tide was very low. She never came out to warn us off nor anything, and I thought, as I hauled the bo't up on a wave and let the Reverend Mr. Dimmick step out, that it was somethin' gained to be safe ashore. There was a little smoke out o' the chimney o' Joanna's house, and it did look sort of homelike and pleasant with wild mornin'-glory vines trained up; an' there was a plot o' flowers under the front window, portulacas and things. I believe she'd made a garden once, when she was stopping there with her father, and some things must have seeded in. It looked as if she might have gone over to the other side of the island. 'T was neat and pretty all about the house, and a lovely day in July. We walked up from the beach together very sedate, and I felt for poor Nathan's little pin to see if 't was safe in my dress pocket. All of a sudden Joanna come right to the fore door and stood there, not sayin' a word."

XIV

THE HERMITAGE

$\mathbf{M}$Y COMPANIONS and I had been so intent upon the subject of the conversation that we had not heard any one open the gate, but at this moment, above the noise of the rain, we heard a loud knocking. We were all startled as we sat by the fire, and Mrs. Todd rose hastily and went to answer the call, leaving her rocking-chair in violent motion. Mrs. Fosdick and I heard an anxious voice at the door speaking of a sick child, and Mrs. Todd's kind, motherly voice inviting the messenger in: then we waited in silence. There was a sound of heavy dropping of rain from the eaves, and the distant roar and undertone of the sea. My thoughts flew back to the lonely woman on her outer island; what separation from humankind she must have felt, what terror and sadness, even in a summer storm like this!

"You send right after the doctor if she ain't better in half an hour," said Mrs. Todd to her worried customer as they parted; and I felt a warm sense of comfort in the evident resources of even so small a neighborhood, but for the poor hermit Joanna there was no neighbor on a winter night.

"How did she look?" demanded Mrs. Fosdick, without preface, as our large hostess returned to the little room with a mist about her from standing long in the wet doorway, and the sudden draught of her coming beat out the smoke and flame from the Franklin stove. "How did poor Joanna look?"

"She was the same as ever, except I thought she looked smaller," answered Mrs. Todd after thinking a moment; perhaps it was only a last considering thought about her patient. "Yes, she was just the same, and looked very nice, Joanna did. I had been married since she left home, an' she treated me like her own folks. I expected she'd look strange, with her hair turned gray in a night or somethin', but she wore a pretty gingham dress I'd often seen her wear before she went away; she must have kept it nice for best in the afternoons. She always had beautiful, quiet manners. I remember she waited till we were close to her, and then kissed me real affectionate, and inquired for Nathan before she shook hands with the minister, and then she invited us both in. 'T was the same little house her father had built him when he was a bachelor, with one livin'-room, and a little mite of a bedroom out of it where she slept, but 't was neat as a ship's cabin. There was some old chairs, an' a seat made of a long box that might have held boat tackle an' things to lock up in his fishin' days, and a good enough stove so anybody could cook and keep warm in cold weather. I went over once from home and stayed 'most a week with Joanna when we was girls, and those young happy days rose up before me. Her father was busy all day fishin' or clammin'; he was one o' the pleasantest men in the world, but Joanna's mother had the grim streak, and never knew what 't was to be happy. The first minute my eyes fell upon Joanna's face that day I saw how she had grown to look like Mis' Todd. 'T was the mother right over again."

"Oh dear me!" said Mrs. Fosdick.

"Joanna had done one thing very pretty. There was a little piece o' swamp on the island where good rushes grew plenty, and she'd gathered 'em, and braided some beautiful mats for the floor and a thick cushion for the long bunk. She'd showed a good deal of invention; you see there was a nice chance to pick up pieces o' wood and boards that drove ashore, and she'd made good use o' what she found. There wasn't no clock, but she had a few dishes on a shelf, and flowers set about in shells fixed to the walls, so it did look sort of homelike, though so lonely and poor. I couldn't keep the tears out o' my eyes, I felt so sad. I said to myself, I must get mother to come over an' see Joanna; the love in mother's heart would warm her, an' she might be able to advise."

"Oh no, Joanna was dreadful stern," said Mrs. Fosdick.

"We were all settin' down very proper, but Joanna would keep stealin' glances at me as if she was glad I come. She had but little to say; she was real polite an' gentle, and yet forbiddin'. The minister found it hard," confessed Mrs. Todd; "he got embarrassed, an' when he put on his authority and asked her if she felt to enjoy religion in her present situation, an' she replied that she must be excused from answerin', I thought I should fly. She might have made it easier for him; after all, he was the minister and had taken some trouble to come out, though 't was kind of cold an' unfeelin' the way he inquired. I thought he might have seen the little old Bible a-layin' on the shelf close by him, an' I wished he knew enough to just lay his hand on it an' read somethin' kind an' fatherly 'stead of accusin' her, an' then given poor Joanna his blessin' with the hope she might be led to comfort. He did offer prayer, but 't was all about hearin' the voice o' God out o' the whirlwind; and I thought while he was goin' on that anybody that had spent the long cold winter all alone out on Shell-heap Island knew a good deal more about those things than he did. I got so provoked I opened my eyes and stared right at him.

"She did n't take no notice, she kep' a nice respectful manner towards him, and when there come a pause she asked if he had any interest about the old Indian remains, and took down some queer stone gouges and hammers off of one of her shelves and showed them to him same 's if he was a boy. He remarked that he 'd like to walk over an' see the shell-heap; so she went right to the door and pointed him the way. I see then that she 'd made her some kind o' sandal-shoes out o' the fine rushes to wear on her feet; she stepped light an' nice in 'em as shoes."

Mrs. Fosdick leaned back in her rocking-chair and gave a heavy sigh.

"I did n't move at first, but I 'd held out just as long as I could," said Mrs. Todd, whose voice trembled a little. "When Joanna returned from the door, an' I could see that man's stupid back departin' among the wild rose bushes, I just ran to her an' caught her in my arms. I was n't so big as I be now, and she was older than me, but I hugged her tight, just as if she was a child. 'Oh, Joanna dear,' I says, 'won't you come ashore an' live 'long o' me at the Landin', or go over to Green Island to mother's when winter comes? Nobody shall trouble you, an' mother finds it hard bein' alone. I can't bear to leave you here'—and I burst right out crying. I 'd had my own trials, young as I was, an' she knew it. Oh, I did entreat her; yes, I entreated Joanna."

"What did she say then?" asked Mrs. Fosdick, much moved.

"She looked the same way, sad an' remote through it all," said Mrs. Todd mournfully. "She took hold of my hand, and we sat down close together; 't was as if she turned round an' made a child of me. 'I have n't got no right to live with folks no more,' she said. 'You must never ask me again, Almiry: I 've done the only thing I could do, and I 've made my choice. I feel a great comfort in your kindness, but I don't deserve it. I have committed the unpardonable sin; you don't understand,' says she humbly. 'I was in great wrath and trouble, and my thoughts was so wicked towards God that I can't expect ever to be forgiven. I have come to know what it is to have patience, but I have lost my hope. You must tell those that ask how 't is with me,' she said, 'an' tell them I want to be alone.' I could n't speak; no, there wa'n't anything I could say, she seemed so above everything common. I was a good deal younger then than I be now, and I got Nathan's little coral pin out o' my pocket and put it into her hand; and when she saw it and I told her where it come from, her face did really light up for a minute, sort of bright an' pleasant. 'Nathan an' I was always good friends; I 'm glad he don't think hard of me,' says she. 'I want you to have it, Almiry, an' wear it for love o' both o' us,' and she handed it back to me. 'You give my love to Nathan,—he 's a dear good man,' she said; 'an' tell your mother, if I should be sick she must n't wish I could get well, but I want her to be the one to come.' Then she seemed to have said all she wanted to, as if she was done with the world, and we sat there a few minutes longer together. It was real sweet and quiet except for a good many birds and the sea rollin' up on the beach; but at last she rose, an' I did too, and she kissed me and held my hand in hers a minute, as if to say good-by; then she turned and went right away out o' the door and disappeared.

"The minister come back pretty soon, and I told him I was all ready, and we started down to the bo't. He had picked up some round stones and things and was carrying them in his pocket-handkerchief; an' he sat down amidships without making any question, and let me take the rudder an' work the bo't, an' made no remarks for some time, until we sort of eased it off speaking of the weather, an' subjects that arose as we skirted Black Island, where two or three families lived belongin' to the parish. He preached next Sabbath as usual, somethin' high soundin' about the creation, and I couldn't help thinkin' he might never get no further; he seemed to know no remedies, but he had a great use of words."

Mrs. Fosdick sighed again. "Hearin' you tell about Joanna brings the time right back as if 'twas yesterday," she said. "Yes, she was one o' them poor things that talked about the great sin; we don't seem to hear nothing about the unpardonable sin now, but you may say 'twas not uncommon then."

"I expect that if it had been in these days, such a person would be plagued to death with idle folks," continued Mrs. Todd, after a long pause. "As it was, nobody trespassed on her; all the folks about the bay respected her an' her feelings; but as time wore on, after you left here, one after another ventured to make occasion to put somethin' ashore for her if they went that way. I know mother used to go to see her sometimes, and send William over now and then with something fresh an' nice from the farm. There is a point on the sheltered side where you can lay a boat close to shore an' land anything safe on the turf out o' reach o' the water. There were one or two others, old folks, that she would see, and now an' then she'd hail a passin' boat an' ask for somethin'; and mother got her to promise that she would make some sign to the Black Island folks if she wanted help. I never saw her myself to speak to after that day."

"I expect nowadays, if such a thing happened, she'd have gone out West to her uncle's folks or up to Massachusetts and had a change, an' come home good as new. The world's bigger an' freer than it used to be," urged Mrs. Fosdick.

"No," said her friend. "'Tis like bad eyesight, the mind of such a person: if your eyes don't see right there may be a remedy, but there's no kind of glasses to remedy the mind. No, Joanna was Joanna, and there she lays on her island where she lived and did her poor penance. She told mother the day she was dyin' that she always used to want to be fetched inshore when it come to the last; but she'd thought it over, and desired to be laid on the island, if 'twas thought right. So the funeral was out there, a Saturday afternoon in September. 'Twas a pretty day, and there wa'n't hardly a boat on the coast within twenty miles that didn't head for Shell-heap cram-full o' folks, an' all real respectful, same 's if she 'd always stayed ashore and held her friends. Some went out o' mere curiosity, I don't doubt,—there 's always such to every funeral; but most had real feelin', and went purpose to show it. She 'd got most o' the wild sparrows as tame as could be, livin' out there so long among 'em, and one flew right in and lit on the coffin an' begun to sing while Mr. Dimmick was speakin'. He was put out by it, an' acted as if he did n't know whether to stop or go on. I may have been prejudiced, but I wa'n't the only one thought the poor little bird done the best of the two."

"What became o' the man that treated her so, did you ever hear?" asked Mrs. Fosdick. "I know he lived up to Massachusetts for a while. Somebody who came from the same place told me that he was in trade there an' doin' very well, but that was years ago."

"I never heard anything more than that; he went to the war in one o' the early rigiments. No, I never heard any more of him," answered Mrs. Todd. "Joanna was another sort of person, and perhaps he showed good judgment in marryin' somebody else, if only he 'd behaved straight-forward and manly. He was a shifty-eyed, coaxin' sort of man, that got what he wanted out o' folks, an' only gave when he wanted to buy, made friends easy and lost 'em without knowin' the difference. She 'd had a piece o' work tryin' to make him walk accordin' to her right ideas, but she 'd have had too much variety ever to fall into a melancholy. Some is meant to be the Joannas in this world, an' 't was her poor lot."

XV

ON SHELL-HEAP ISLAND

SOME TIME after Mrs. Fosdick's visit was over and we had returned to our former quietness, I was out sailing alone with Captain Bowden in his large boat. We were taking the crooked northeasterly channel seaward, and were well out from shore while it was still early in the afternoon. I found myself presently among some unfamiliar islands, and suddenly remembered the story of poor Joanna. There is something in the fact of a hermitage that cannot fail to touch the imagination; the recluses are a sad kindred, but they are never commonplace. Mrs. Todd had truly said that Joanna was like one of the saints in the desert; the loneliness of sorrow will forever keep alive their sad succession.

"Where is Shell-heap Island!" I asked eagerly.

"You see Shell-heap now, layin' 'way out beyond Black Island there," answered the captain, pointing with outstretched arm as he stood, and holding the rudder with his knee.

"I should like very much to go there," said I, and the captain, without comment, changed his course a little more to the eastward and let the reef out of his mainsail.

"I don't know 's we can make an easy landin' for ye," he remarked doubtfully. "May get your feet wet; bad place to land. Trouble is I ought to have brought a tag-boat; but they clutch on to the water so, an' I do love to sail free. This gre't boat gets easy bothered with anything trailin'. 'T ain't breakin' much on the meetin'-house ledges; guess I can fetch in to Shell-heap."

"How long is it since Miss Joanna Todd died?" I asked, partly by way of explanation.

"Twenty-two years come September," answered the captain, after reflection. "She died the same year my oldest boy was born, an' the town house was burnt over to the Port. I did n't know but you merely wanted to hunt for some o' them Indian relics. Long 's you want to see where Joanna lived— No, 't ain't breakin' over the ledges; we'll manage to fetch across the shoals somehow, 't is such a distance to go 'way round, and tide's a-risin'," he ended hopefully, and we sailed steadily on, the captain speechless with intent watching of a difficult course, until the small island with its low whitish promontory lay in full view before us under the bright afternoon sun.

The month was August, and I had seen the color of the islands change from the fresh green of June to a sunburnt brown that made them look like stone, except where the dark green of the spruces and fir balsam kept the tint that even winter storms might deepen, but not fade. The few wind-bent trees on Shell-heap Island were mostly dead and gray, but there were some low-growing bushes, and a stripe of light green ran along just above the shore, which I knew to be wild morning-glories. As we came close I could see the high stone walls of a small square field, though there were no sheep left to assail it; and below, there was a little harbor-like cove where Captain Bowden was boldly running the great boat in to seek a landing-place. There was a crooked channel of deep water which led close up against the shore.

"There, you hold fast for'ard there, an' wait for her to lift on the wave. You'll make a good landin' if you're smart; right on the port-hand side!" the captain called excitedly; and I, standing ready with high ambition, seized my chance and leaped over to the grassy bank.

"I'm beat if I ain't aground after all!" mourned the captain despondently.

But I could reach the bowsprit, and he pushed with the boat-hook, while the wind veered round a little as if on purpose and helped with the sail; so presently the boat was free and began to drift out from shore.

"Used to call this p'int Joanna's wharf privilege, but 't has worn away in the weather since her time. I thought one or two bumps wouldn't hurt us none,—paint's got to be renewed, anyway,—but I never thought she'd tetch. I figured on shyin' by," the captain apologized. "She's too gre't a boat to handle well in here; but I used to sort of shy by in Joanna's day, an' cast a little somethin' ashore—some apples or a couple o' pears if I had 'em—on the grass, where she'd be sure to see."

I stood watching while Captain Bowden cleverly found his

way back to deeper water. "You need n't make no haste," he called to me; "I 'll keep within call. Joanna lays right up there in the far corner o' the field. There used to be a path led to the place. I always knew her well. I was out here to the funeral.

I found the path; it was touching to discover that this lonely spot was not without its pilgrims. Later generations will know less and less of Joanna herself, but there are paths trodden to the shrines of solitude the world over,—the world cannot forget them, try as it may; the feet of the young find them out because of curiosity and dim foreboding, while the old bring hearts full of remembrance. This plain anchorite had been one of those whom sorrow made too lonely to brave the sight of men, too timid to front the simple world she knew, yet valiant enough to live alone with her poor insistent human nature and the calms and passions of the sea and sky.

The birds were flying all about the field; they fluttered up out of the grass at my feet as I walked along, so tame that I liked to think they kept some happy tradition from summer to summer of the safety of nests and good fellowship of mankind. Poor Joanna's house was gone except the stones of its foundations, and there was little trace of her flower garden except a single faded sprig of much-enduring French pinks, which a great bee and a yellow butterfly were befriending together. I drank at the spring, and thought that now and then some one would follow me from the busy, hard-worked, and simple-thoughted countryside of the mainland, which lay dim and dreamlike in the August haze, as Joanna must have watched it many a day. There was the world, and here was she with eternity well begun. In the life of each of us, I said to myself, there is a place remote and islanded, and given to endless regret or secret happiness; we are each the uncompanioned hermit and recluse of an hour or a day; we understand our fellows of the cell to whatever age of history they may belong.

But as I stood alone on the island, in the sea-breeze, suddenly there came a sound of distant voices; gay voices and laughter from a pleasure-boat that was going seaward full of boys and girls. I knew, as if she had told me, that poor Joanna must have heard the like on many and many a summer afternoon, and must have welcomed the good cheer in spite of hopelessness and winter weather, and all the sorrow and disappointment in the world.

XVI

THE GREAT EXPEDITION

MRS. TODD never by any chance gave warning over night of her great projects and adventures by sea and land. She first came to an understanding with the primal forces of nature, and never trusted to any preliminary promise of good weather, but examined the day for herself in its infancy. Then, if the stars were propitious, and the wind blew from a quarter of good inheritance whence no surprises of sea-turns or southwest sultriness might be feared, long before I was fairly awake I used to hear a rustle and knocking like a great mouse in the walls, and an impatient tread on the steep garret stairs that led to Mrs. Todd's chief place of storage. She went and came as if she had already started on her expedition with utmost haste and kept returning for something that was forgotten. When I appeared in quest of my breakfast, she would be absent-minded and sparing of speech, as if I had displeased her, and she was now, by main force of principle, holding herself back from altercation and strife of tongues.

These signs of a change became familiar to me in the course of time, and Mrs. Todd hardly noticed some plain proofs of divination one August morning when I said, without preface, that I had just seen the Beggs' best chaise go by, and that we should have to take the grocery. Mrs. Todd was alert in a moment.

"There! I might have known!" she exclaimed. "It's the 15th of August, when he goes and gets his money. He heired an annuity from an uncle o' his on his mother's side. I understood the uncle said none o' Sam Begg's wife's folks should make free with it, so after Sam's gone it'll all be past an' spent, like last summer. That's what Sam prospers on now, if you can call it prosperin'. Yes, I might have known. 'T is the 15th o' August with him, an' he gener'ly stops to dinner with a cousin's widow on the way home. Feb'uary an' August is the times. Takes him 'bout all day to go an' come."

I heard this explanation with interest. The tone of Mrs. Todd's voice was complaining at the last.

"I like the grocery just as well as the chaise," I hastened to say, referring to a long-bodied high wagon with a canopy-top, like an attenuated four-posted bedstead on wheels, in which we sometimes journeyed. "We can put things in behind—roots and flowers and raspberries, or anything you are going after—much better than if we had the chaise."

Mrs. Todd looked stony and unwilling. "I counted upon the chaise," she said, turning her back to me, and roughly pushing back all the quiet tumblers on the cupboard shelf as if they had been impertinent. "Yes, I desired the chaise for once. I ain't goin' berryin' nor to fetch home no more wilted vegetation this year. Season's about past, except for a poor few o' late things," she added in a milder tone. "I'm goin' up country. No, I ain't intendin' to go berryin'. I've been plottin' for it the past fortnight and hopin' for a good day."

"Would you like to have me go too?" I asked frankly, but not without a humble fear that I might have mistaken the purpose of this latest plan.

"Oh certain, dear!" answered my friend affectionately. "Oh no, I never thought o' any one else for comp'ny, if it's convenient for you, long's poor mother ain't come. I ain't nothin' like so handy with a conveyance as I be with a good bo't. Comes o' my early bringing-up. I expect we've got to make that great high wagon do. The tires want settin' and 't is all loose-jointed, so I can hear it shackle the other side o' the ridge. We'll put the basket in front. I ain't goin' to have it bouncin' an' twirlin' all the way. Why, I've been makin' some nice hearts and rounds to carry."

These were signs of high festivity, and my interest deepened moment by moment.

"I'll go down to the Beggs' and get the horse just as soon as I finish my breakfast," said I. "Then we can start whenever you are ready."

Mrs. Todd looked cloudy again. "I don't know but you look nice enough to go just as you be," she suggested doubtfully. "No, you wouldn't want to wear that pretty blue dress o' yourn 'way up country. 'T ain't dusty now, but it may be comin' home. No, I expect you'd rather not wear that and the other hat."

"Oh yes. I shouldn't think of wearing these clothes," said I, with sudden illumination. "Why, if we're going up country and are likely to see some of your friends, I'll put on my blue dress, and you must wear your watch; I am not going at all if you mean to wear the big hat."

"Now you're behavin' pretty," responded Mrs. Todd, with a gay toss of her head and a cheerful smile, as she came across the room, bringing a saucerful of wild raspberries, a pretty piece of salvage from supper-time. "I was cast down when I see you come to breakfast. I didn't think 't was just what you'd select to wear to the reunion, where you're goin' to meet everybody."

"What reunion do you mean?" I asked, not without amazement. "Not the Bowden Family's? I thought that was going to take place in September."

"To-day's the day. They sent word the middle o' the week. I thought you might have heard of it. Yes, they changed the day. I been thinkin' we'd talk it over, but you never can tell beforehand how it's goin' to be, and 't ain't worth while to wear a day all out before it comes." Mrs. Todd gave no place to the pleasures of anticipation, but she spoke like the oracle that she was. "I wish mother was here to go," she continued sadly. "I did look for her last night, and I couldn't keep back the tears when the dark really fell and she wa'n't here, she does so enjoy a great occasion. If William had a mite o' snap an' ambition, he'd take the lead at such a time. Mother likes variety, and there ain't but a few nice opportunities 'round here, an' them she has to miss 'less she contrives to get ashore to me. I do re'lly hate to go to the reunion without mother, an' 't is a beautiful day; everybody'll be asking where she is. Once she'd have got here anyway. Poor mother's beginnin' to feel her age."

"Why, there's your mother now!" I exclaimed with joy, I was so glad to see the dear old soul again. "I hear her voice at the gate." But Mrs. Todd was out of the door before me.

There, sure enough, stood Mrs. Blackett, who must have left Green Island before daylight. She had climbed the steep road from the water-side so eagerly that she was out of breath, and was standing by the garden fence to rest. She held an old-fashioned brown wicker cap-basket in her hand, as if visiting were a thing of every day, and looked up at us as pleased and triumphant as a child.

"Oh, what a poor, plain garden! Hardly a flower in it except your bush o' balm!" she said. "But you do keep your garden neat, Almiry. Are you both well, an' goin' up country with me?" She came a step or two closer to meet us, with quaint politeness and quite as delightful as if she were at home. She dropped a quick little curtsey before Mrs. Todd.

"There, mother, what a girl you be! I am so pleased! I was just bewailin' you," said the daughter, with unwonted feeling. "I was just bewailin' you, I was so disappointed, an' I kep' myself awake a good piece o' the night scoldin' poor William. I watched for the boat till I was ready to shed tears yisterday, and when 't was comin' dark I kep' making errands out to the gate an' down the road to see if you wa'n't in the doldrums somewhere down the bay."

"There was a head wind, as you know," said Mrs. Blackett, giving me the cap-basket, and holding my hand affectionately as we walked up the clean-swept path to the door. "I was partly ready to come, but dear William said I should be all tired out and might get cold, havin' to beat all the way in. So we give it up, and set down and spent the evenin' together. It was a little rough and windy outside, and I guess 't was better judgment; we went to bed very early and made a good start just at daylight. It's been a lovely mornin' on the water. William thought he'd better fetch across beyond Bird Rocks, rowin' the greater part o' the way; then we sailed from there right over to the Landin', makin' only one tack. William'll be in again for me to-morrow, so I can come back here an' rest me over night, an' go to meetin' to-morrow, and have a nice, good visit."

"She was just havin' her breakfast," said Mrs. Todd, who had listened eagerly to the long explanation without a word of disapproval, while her face shone more and more with joy. "You just sit right down an' have a cup of tea and rest you while we make our preparations. Oh, I am so gratified to think you've come! Yes, she was just havin' her breakfast, and we were speakin' of you. Where's William?"

"He went right back; he said he expected some schooners

in about noon after bait, but he'll come an' have his dinner with us to-morrow, unless it rains; then next day. I laid his best things out all ready," explained Mrs. Blackett, a little anxiously. "This wind will serve him nice all the way home. Yes, I will take a cup of tea, dear,—a cup of tea is always good; and then I'll rest a minute and be all ready to start."

"I do feel condemned for havin' such hard thoughts o' William," openly confessed Mrs. Todd. She stood before us so large and serious that we both laughed and could not find it in our hearts to convict so rueful a culprit. "He shall have a good dinner to-morrow, if it can be got, and I shall be real glad to see William," the confession ended handsomely, while Mrs. Blackett smiled approval and made haste to praise the tea. Then I hurried away to make sure of the grocery wagon. Whatever might be the good of the reunion, I was going to have the pleasure and delight of a day in Mrs. Blackett's company, not to speak of Mrs. Todd's.

The early morning breeze was still blowing, and the warm, sunshiny air was of some ethereal northern sort, with a cool freshness as if it came over new-fallen snow. The world was filled with a fragrance of fir-balsam and the faintest flavor of seaweed from the ledges, bare and brown at low tide in the little harbor. It was so still and so early that the village was but half awake. I could hear no voices but those of the birds, small and great,—the constant song sparrows, the clink of a yellow-hammer over in the woods, and the far conversation of some deliberate crows. I saw William Blackett's escaping sail already far from land, and Captain Littlepage was sitting behind his closed window as I passed by, watching for some one who never came. I tried to speak to him, but he did not see me. There was a patient look on the old man's face, as if the world were a great mistake and he had nobody with whom to speak his own language or find companionship.

XVII

A COUNTRY ROAD

WHATEVER doubts and anxieties I may have had about the inconvenience of the Beggs' high wagon for a person of Mrs. Blackett's age and shortness, they were happily overcome by the aid of a chair and her own valiant spirit. Mrs. Todd bestowed great care upon seating us as if we were taking passage by boat, but she finally pronounced that we were properly trimmed. When we had gone only a little way up the hill she remembered that she had left the house door wide open, though the large key was safe in her pocket. I offered to run back, but my offer was met with lofty scorn, and we lightly dismissed the matter from our minds, until two or three miles further on we met the doctor, and Mrs. Todd asked him to stop and ask her nearest neighbor to step over and close the door if the dust seemed to blow in the afternoon.

"She'll be there in her kitchen; she'll hear you the minute you call; 't won't give you no delay," said Mrs. Todd to the doctor. "Yes, Mis' Dennett's right there, with the windows all open. It isn't as if my fore door opened right on the road, anyway." At which proof of composure Mrs. Blackett smiled wisely at me.

The doctor seemed delighted to see our guest; they were evidently the warmest friends, and I saw a look of affectionate confidence in their eyes. The good man left his carriage to speak to us, but as he took Mrs. Blackett's hand he held it a moment, and, as if merely from force of habit, felt her pulse as they talked; then to my delight he gave the firm old wrist a commending pat.

"You're wearing well: good for another ten years at this rate," he assured her cheerfully, and she smiled back. "I like to keep a strict account of my old stand-bys," and he turned to me. "Don't you let Mrs. Todd overdo to-day,—old folks like her are apt to be thoughtless;" and then we all laughed, and, parting, went our ways gayly.

"I suppose he puts up with your rivalry the same as ever?"

asked Mrs. Blackett. "You and he are as friendly as ever, I see, Almiry," and Almira sagely nodded.

"He's got too many long routes now to stop to 'tend to all his door patients," she said, "especially them that takes pleasure in talkin' themselves over. The doctor and me have got to be kind of partners; he's gone a good deal, far an' wide. Looked tired, did n't he? I shall have to advise with him an' get him off for a good rest. He'll take the big boat from Rockland an' go off up to Boston an' mouse round among the other doctors, once in two or three years, and come home fresh as a boy. I guess they think consider'ble of him up there." Mrs. Todd shook the reins and reached determinedly for the whip, as if she were compelling public opinion.

Whatever energy and spirit the white horse had to begin with were soon exhausted by the steep hills and his discernment of a long expedition ahead. We toiled slowly along. Mrs. Blackett and I sat together, and Mrs. Todd sat alone in front with much majesty and the large basket of provisions. Part of the way the road was shaded by thick woods, but we also passed one farmhouse after another on the high uplands, which we all three regarded with deep interest, the house itself and the barns and garden-spots and poultry all having to suffer an inspection of the shrewdest sort. This was a highway quite new to me; in fact, most of my journeys with Mrs. Todd had been made afoot and between the roads, in open pasture-lands. My friends stopped several times for brief dooryard visits, and made so many promises of stopping again on the way home that I began to wonder how long the expedition would last. I had often noticed how warmly Mrs. Todd was greeted by her friends, but it was hardly to be compared to the feeling now shown toward Mrs. Blackett. A look of delight came to the faces of those who recognized the plain, dear old figure beside me; one revelation after another was made of the constant interest and intercourse that had linked the far island and these scattered farms into a golden chain of love and dependence.

"Now, we must n't stop again if we can help it," insisted Mrs. Todd at last. "You'll get tired, mother, and you'll think the less o' reunions. We can visit along here any day. There, if they ain't frying doughnuts in this next house, too! These are new folks, you know, from over St. George way; they took this old Talcot farm last year. 'T is the best water on the road, and the check-rein's come undone—yes, we'd best delay a little and water the horse."

We stopped, and seeing a party of pleasure-seekers in holiday attire, the thin, anxious mistress of the farmhouse came out with wistful sympathy to hear what news we might have to give. Mrs. Blackett first spied her at the half-closed door, and asked with such cheerful directness if we were trespassing that, after a few words, she went back to her kitchen and reappeared with a plateful of doughnuts.

"Entertainment for man and beast," announced Mrs. Todd with satisfaction. "Why, we've perceived there was new doughnuts all along the road, but you're the first that has treated us."

Our new acquaintance flushed with pleasure, but said nothing.

"They're very nice; you've had good luck with 'em," pronounced Mrs. Todd. "Yes, we've observed there was doughnuts all the way along; if one house is frying all the rest is; 't is so with a great many things."

"I don't suppose likely you're goin' up to the Bowden reunion?" asked the hostess as the white horse lifted his head and we were saying good-by.

"Why, yes," said Mrs. Blackett and Mrs. Todd and I, all together.

"I am connected with the family. Yes, I expect to be there this afternoon. I've been lookin' forward to it," she told us eagerly.

"We shall see you there. Come and sit with us if it's convenient," said dear Mrs. Blackett, and we drove away.

"I wonder who she was before she was married?" said Mrs. Todd, who was usually unerring in matters of genealogy. "She must have been one of that remote branch that lived down beyond Thomaston. We can find out this afternoon. I expect that the families'll march together, or be sorted out some way. I'm willing to own a relation that has such proper ideas of doughnuts."

"I seem to see the family looks," said Mrs. Blackett. "I wish we'd asked her name. She's a stranger, and I want to help make it pleasant for all such."

"She resembles Cousin Pa'lina Bowden about the fore-head," said Mrs. Todd with decision.

We had just passed a piece of woodland that shaded the road, and come out to some open fields beyond, when Mrs. Todd suddenly reined in the horse as if somebody had stood on the roadside and stopped her. She even gave that quick reassuring nod of her head which was usually made to answer for a bow, but I discovered that she was looking eagerly at a tall ash-tree that grew just inside the field fence.

"I thought 't was goin' to do well," she said complacently as we went on again. "Last time I was up this way that tree was kind of drooping and discouraged. Grown trees act that way sometimes, same's folks; then they'll put right to it and strike their roots off into new ground and start all over again with real good courage. Ash-trees is very likely to have poor spells; they ain't got the resolution of other trees."

I listened hopefully for more; it was this peculiar wisdom that made one value Mrs. Todd's pleasant company.

"There's sometimes a good hearty tree growin' right out of the bare rock, out o' some crack that just holds the roots;" she went on to say, "right on the pitch o' one o' them bare stony hills where you can't seem to see a wheel-barrowful o' good earth in a place, but that tree'll keep a green top in the driest summer. You lay your ear down to the ground an' you'll hear a little stream runnin'. Every such tree has got its own livin' spring; there's folks made to match 'em."

I could not help turning to look at Mrs. Blackett, close beside me. Her hands were clasped placidly in their thin black woolen gloves, and she was looking at the flowery wayside as we went slowly along, with a pleased, expectant smile. I do not think she had heard a word about the trees.

"I just saw a nice plant o' elecampane growin' back there," she said presently to her daughter.

"I have n't got my mind on herbs to-day," responded Mrs. Todd, in the most matter-of-fact way. "I'm bent on seeing folks," and she shook the reins again.

I for one had no wish to hurry, it was so pleasant in the shady roads. The woods stood close to the road on the right;

on the left were narrow fields and pastures where there were as many acres of spruces and pines as there were acres of bay and juniper and huckleberry, with a little turf between. When I thought we were in the heart of the inland country, we reached the top of a hill, and suddenly there lay spread out before us a wonderful great view of well-cleared fields that swept down to the wide water of a bay. Beyond this were distant shores like another country in the midday haze which half hid the hills beyond, and the far-away pale blue mountains on the northern horizon. There was a schooner with all sails set coming down the bay from a white village that was sprinkled on the shore, and there were many sailboats flitting about. It was a noble landscape, and my eyes, which had grown used to the narrow inspection of a shaded roadside, could hardly take it in.

"Why, it's the upper bay," said Mrs. Todd. "You can see 'way over into the town of Fessenden. Those farms 'way over there are all in Fessenden. Mother used to have a sister that lived up that shore. If we started as early's we could on a summer mornin', we couldn't get to her place from Green Island till late afternoon, even with a fair, steady breeze, and you had to strike the time just right so as to fetch up 'long o' the tide and land near the flood. 'Twas ticklish business, an' we didn't visit back an' forth as much as mother desired. You have to go 'way down the co'st to Cold Spring Light an' round that long point,—up here's what they call the Back Shore."

"No, we were 'most always separated, my dear sister and me, after the first year she was married," said Mrs. Blackett. "We had our little families an' plenty o' cares. We were always lookin' forward to the time we could see each other more. Now and then she'd get out to the island for a few days while her husband'd go fishin'; and once he stopped with her an' two children, and made him some flakes right there and cured all his fish for winter. We did have a beautiful time together, sister an' me; she used to look back to it long's she lived."

"I do love to look over there where she used to live," Mrs. Blackett went on as we began to go down the hill. "It seems as if she must still be there, though she's long been gone. She loved their farm,—she did n't see how I got so used to our island; but somehow I was always happy from the first."

"Yes, it's very dull to me up among those slow farms," declared Mrs. Todd. "The snow troubles 'em in winter. They're all besieged by winter, as you may say; 't is far better by the shore than up among such places. I never thought I should like to live up country."

"Why, just see the carriages ahead of us on the next rise!" exclaimed Mrs. Blackett. "There's going to be a great gathering, don't you believe there is, Almiry? It has n't seemed up to now as if anybody was going but us. An' 't is such a beautiful day, with yesterday cool and pleasant to work an' get ready, I should n't wonder if everybody was there, even the slow ones like Phebe Ann Brock."

Mrs. Blackett's eyes were bright with excitement, and even Mrs. Todd showed remarkable enthusiasm. She hurried the horse and caught up with the holiday-makers ahead. "There's all the Dep'fords goin', six in the wagon," she told us joyfully; "an' Mis' Alva Tilley's folks are now risin' the hill in their new carryall."

Mrs. Blackett pulled at the neat bow of her black bonnet-strings, and tied them again with careful precision. "I believe your bonnet's on a little bit sideways, dear," she advised Mrs. Todd as if she were a child; but Mrs. Todd was too much occupied to pay proper heed. We began to feel a new sense of gayety and of taking part in the great occasion as we joined the little train.

XVIII

THE BOWDEN REUNION

I T IS very rare in country life, where high days and holidays are few, that any occasion of general interest proves to be less than great. Such is the hidden fire of enthusiasm in the New England nature that, once given an outlet, it shines forth with almost volcanic light and heat. In quiet neighborhoods such inward force does not waste itself upon those petty excitements of every day that belong to cities, but when, at long intervals, the altars to patriotism, to friendship, to the ties of kindred, are reared in our familiar fields, then the fires glow, the flames come up as if from the inexhaustible burning heart of the earth; the primal fires break through the granite dust in which our souls are set. Each heart is warm and every face shines with the ancient light. Such a day as this has transfiguring powers, and easily makes friends of those who have been cold-hearted, and gives to those who are dumb their chance to speak, and lends some beauty to the plainest face.

"Oh, I expect I shall meet friends to-day that I have n't seen in a long while," said Mrs. Blackett with deep satisfaction. "'T will bring out a good many of the old folks, 't is such a lovely day. I 'm always glad not to have them disappointed."

"I guess likely the best of 'em 'll be there," answered Mrs. Todd with gentle humor, stealing a glance at me. "There 's one thing certain: there 's nothing takes in this whole neighborhood like anything related to the Bowdens. Yes, I do feel that when you call upon the Bowdens you may expect most families to rise up between the Landing and the far end of the Back Cove. Those that are n't kin by blood are kin by marriage."

"There used to be an old story goin' about when I was a girl," said Mrs. Blackett, with much amusement. "There was a great many more Bowdens then than there are now, and the folks was all setting in meeting a dreadful hot Sunday afternoon, and a scatter-witted little bound girl came running to the meetin'-house door all out o' breath from somewheres in the neighborhood. 'Mis' Bowden, Mis' Bowden!' says she.

'Your baby's in a fit!' They used to tell that the whole congregation was up on its feet in a minute and right out into the aisles. All the Mis' Bowdens was setting right out for home; the minister stood there in the pulpit tryin' to keep sober, an' all at once he burst right out laughin'. He was a very nice man, they said, and he said he'd better give 'em the benediction, and they could hear the sermon next Sunday, so he kept it over. My mother was there, and she thought certain 't was me."

"None of our family was ever subject to fits," interrupted Mrs. Todd severely. "No, we never had fits, none of us, and 't was lucky we did n't 'way out there to Green Island. Now these folks right in front: dear sakes knows the bunches o' soothing catnip an' yarrow I 've had to favor old Mis' Evins with dryin'! You can see it right in their expressions, all them Evins folks. There, just you look up to the cross-roads, mother," she suddenly exclaimed. "See all the teams ahead of us. And oh, look down on the bay; yes, look down on the bay! See what a sight o' boats, all headin' for the Bowden place cove!"

"Oh, ain't it beautiful!" said Mrs. Blackett, with all the delight of a girl. She stood up in the high wagon to see everything, and when she sat down again she took fast hold of my hand.

"Had n't you better urge the horse a little, Almiry?" she asked. "He's had it easy as we came along, and he can rest when we get there. The others are some little ways ahead, and I don't want to lose a minute."

We watched the boats drop their sails one by one in the cove as we drove along the high land. The old Bowden house stood, low-storied and broad-roofed, in its green fields as if it were a motherly brown hen waiting for the flock that came straying toward it from every direction. The first Bowden settler had made his home there, and it was still the Bowden farm; five generations of sailors and farmers and soldiers had been its children. And presently Mrs. Blackett showed me the stone-walled burying-ground that stood like a little fort on a knoll overlooking the bay, but, as she said, there were plenty of scattered Bowdens who were not laid there, — some lost at sea, and some out West, and some who died in the war; most of the home graves were those of women.

We could see now that there were different footpaths from along shore and across country. In all these there were straggling processions walking in single file, like old illustrations of the Pilgrim's Progress. There was a crowd about the house as if huge bees were swarming in the lilac bushes. Beyond the fields and cove a higher point of land ran out into the bay, covered with woods which must have kept away much of the northwest wind in winter. Now there was a pleasant look of shade and shelter there for the great family meeting.

We hurried on our way, beginning to feel as if we were very late, and it was a great satisfaction at last to turn out of the stony highroad into a green lane shaded with old apple-trees. Mrs. Todd encouraged the horse until he fairly pranced with gayety as we drove round to the front of the house on the soft turf. There was an instant cry of rejoicing, and two or three persons ran toward us from the busy group.

"Why, dear Mis' Blackett!—here's Mis' Blackett!" I heard them say, as if it were pleasure enough for one day to have a sight of her. Mrs. Todd turned to me with a lovely look of triumph and self-forgetfulness. An elderly man who wore the look of a prosperous sea-captain put up both arms and lifted Mrs. Blackett down from the high wagon like a child, and kissed her with hearty affection. "I was master afraid she would n't be here," he said, looking at Mrs. Todd with a face like a happy sunburnt schoolboy, while everybody crowded round to give their welcome.

"Mother's always the queen," said Mrs. Todd. "Yes, they'll all make everything of mother; she'll have a lovely time to-day. I would n't have had her miss it, and there won't be a thing she'll ever regret, except to mourn because William wa'n't here."

Mrs. Blackett having been properly escorted to the house, Mrs. Todd received her own full share of honor, and some of the men, with a simple kindness that was the soul of chivalry, waited upon us and our baskets and led away the white horse. I already knew some of Mrs. Todd's friends and kindred, and felt like an adopted Bowden in this happy moment. It seemed to be enough for any one to have arrived by the same conveyance as Mrs. Blackett, who presently had her court inside the house, while Mrs. Todd, large, hospitable, and preëminent, was the centre of a rapidly increasing crowd about the lilac bushes. Small companies were continually coming up the long green slope from the water, and nearly all the boats had come to shore. I counted three or four that were baffled by the light breeze, but before long all the Bowdens, small and great, seemed to have assembled, and we started to go up to the grove across the field.

Out of the chattering crowd of noisy children, and large-waisted women whose best black dresses fell straight to the ground in generous folds, and sunburnt men who looked as serious as if it were town-meeting day, there suddenly came silence and order. I saw the straight, soldierly little figure of a man who bore a fine resemblance to Mrs. Blackett, and who appeared to marshal us with perfect ease. He was imperative enough, but with a grand military sort of courtesy, and bore himself with solemn dignity of importance. We were sorted out according to some clear design of his own, and stood as speechless as a troop to await his orders. Even the children were ready to march together, a pretty flock, and at the last moment Mrs. Blackett and a few distinguished companions, the ministers and those who were very old, came out of the house together and took their places. We ranked by fours, and even then we made a long procession.

There was a wide path mowed for us across the field, and, as we moved along, the birds flew up out of the thick second crop of clover, and the bees hummed as if it still were June. There was a flashing of white gulls over the water where the fleet of boats rode the low waves together in the cove, swaying their small masts as if they kept time to our steps. The plash of the water could be heard faintly, yet still be heard; we might have been a company of ancient Greeks going to celebrate a victory, or to worship the god of harvests in the grove above. It was strangely moving to see this and to make part of it. The sky, the sea, have watched poor humanity at its rites so long; we were no more a New England family celebrating its own existence and simple progress; we carried the tokens and inheritance of all such households from which this had descended, and were only the latest of our line. We possessed the instincts of a far, forgotten childhood; I found myself thinking that we ought to be carrying green branches and singing as we went. So we came to the thick shaded grove still silent, and were set in our places by the straight trees that swayed together and let sunshine through here and there like a single golden leaf that flickered down, vanishing in the cool shade.

The grove was so large that the great family looked far smaller than it had in the open field; there was a thick growth of dark pines and firs with an occasional maple or oak that gave a gleam of color like a bright window in the great roof. On three sides we could see the water, shining behind the tree-trunks, and feel the cool salt breeze that began to come up with the tide just as the day reached its highest point of heat. We could see the green sunlit field we had just crossed as if we looked out at it from a dark room, and the old house and its lilacs standing placidly in the sun, and the great barn with a stockade of carriages from which two or three care-taking men who had lingered were coming across the field together. Mrs. Todd had taken off her warm gloves and looked the picture of content.

"There!" she exclaimed. "I 've always meant to have you see this place, but I never looked for such a beautiful opportunity—weather an' occasion both made to match. Yes, it suits me: I don't ask no more. I want to know if you saw mother walkin' at the head! It choked me right up to see mother at the head, walkin' with the ministers," and Mrs. Todd turned away to hide the feelings she could not instantly control.

"Who was the marshal?" I hastened to ask. "Was he an old soldier?"

"Don't he do well?" answered Mrs. Todd with satisfaction.

"He don't often have such a chance to show off his gifts," said Mrs. Caplin, a friend from the Landing who had joined us. "That's Sant Bowden; he always takes the lead, such days. Good for nothing else most o' his time; trouble is, he"—

I turned with interest to hear the worst. Mrs. Caplin's tone was both zealous and impressive.

"Stim'lates," she explained scornfully.

"No, Santin never was in the war," said Mrs. Todd with lofty indifference. "It was a cause of real distress to him. He kep' enlistin', and traveled far an' wide about here, an' even took the bo't and went to Boston to volunteer; but he ain't a sound man, an' they wouldn't have him. They say he knows all their tactics, an' can tell all about the battle o' Waterloo well's he can Bunker Hill. I told him once the country'd lost a great general, an' I meant it, too."

"I expect you're near right," said Mrs. Caplin, a little crestfallen and apologetic.

"I be right," insisted Mrs. Todd with much amiability. " 'T was most too bad to cramp him down to his peaceful trade, but he's a most excellent shoemaker at his best, an' he always says it's a trade that gives him time to think an' plan his manœuvres. Over to the Port they always invite him to march Decoration Day, same as the rest, an' he does look noble; he comes of soldier stock."

I had been noticing with great interest the curiously French type of face which prevailed in this rustic company. I had said to myself before that Mrs. Blackett was plainly of French descent, in both her appearance and her charming gifts, but this is not surprising when one has learned how large a proportion of the early settlers on this northern coast of New England were of Huguenot blood, and that it is the Norman Englishman, not the Saxon, who goes adventuring to a new world.

"They used to say in old times," said Mrs. Todd modestly, "that our family came of very high folks in France, and one of 'em was a great general in some o' the old wars. I sometimes think that Santin's ability has come 'way down from then. 'T ain't nothin' he's ever acquired; 't was born in him. I don't know's he ever saw a fine parade, or met with those that studied up such things. He's figured it all out an' got his papers so he knows how to aim a cannon right for William's fish-house five miles out on Green Island, or up there on Burnt Island where the signal is. He had it all over to me one day, an' I tried hard to appear interested. His life's all in it, but he will have those poor gloomy spells come over him now an' then, an' then he has to drink."

Mrs. Caplin gave a heavy sigh.

"There's a great many such strayaway folks, just as there is plants," continued Mrs. Todd, who was nothing if not botanical. "I know of just one sprig of laurel that grows over back here in a wild spot, an' I never could hear of no other on this coast. I had a large bunch brought me once from Massachusetts way, so I know it. This piece grows in an open spot where you'd think 't would do well, but it's sort o' poor-lookin'. I've visited it time an' again, just to notice its poor blooms. 'T is a real Sant Bowden, out of its own place."

Mrs. Caplin looked bewildered and blank. "Well, all I know is, last year he worked out some kind of a plan so's to parade the county conference in platoons, and got 'em all flustered up tryin' to sense his ideas of a holler square," she burst forth, "They was holler enough anyway after ridin' 'way down from up country into the salt air, and they'd been treated to a sermon on faith an' works from old Fayther Harlow that never knows when to cease. 'T wa'n't no time for tactics then,— they wa'n't a-thinkin' of the church military. Sant, he could n't do nothin' with 'em. All he thinks of, when he sees a crowd, is how to march 'em. 'T is all very well when he don't 'tempt too much. He never did act like other folks."

"Ain't I just been maintainin' that he ain't like 'em?" urged Mrs. Todd decidedly. "Strange folks has got to have strange ways, for what I see."

"Somebody observed once that you could pick out the likeness of 'most every sort of a foreigner when you looked about you in our parish," said Sister Caplin, her face brightening with sudden illumination. "I did n't see the bearin' of it then quite so plain. I always did think Mari' Harris resembled a Chinee."

"Mari' Harris was pretty as a child, I remember," said the pleasant voice of Mrs. Blackett, who, after receiving the affectionate greetings of nearly the whole company, came to join us,—to see, as she insisted, that we were out of mischief.

"Yes, Mari' was one o' them pretty little lambs that make dreadful homely old sheep," replied Mrs. Todd with energy. "Cap'n Littlepage never'd look so disconsolate if she was any sort of a proper person to direct things. She might divert him; yes, she might divert the old gentleman, an' let him think he had his own way, 'stead o' arguing everything down to the bare bone. 'T would n't hurt her to sit down an' hear his great stories once in a while."

"The stories are very interesting," I ventured to say.

"Yes, you always catch yourself a-thinkin' what if they was all true, and he had the right of it," answered Mrs. Todd. "He's a good sight better company, though dreamy, than such sordid creatur's as Mari' Harris."

"Live and let live," said dear old Mrs. Blackett gently. "I haven't seen the captain for a good while, now that I ain't so constant to meetin'," she added wistfully. "We always have known each other."

"Why, if it is a good pleasant day to-morrow, I'll get William to call an' invite the capt'in to dinner. William'll be in early so's to pass up the street without meetin' anybody."

"There, they're callin' out it's time to set the tables," said Mrs. Caplin, with great excitement.

"Here's Cousin Sarah Jane Blackett! Well, I am pleased, certain!" exclaimed Mrs. Todd, with unaffected delight; and these kindred spirits met and parted with the promise of a good talk later on. After this there was no more time for conversation until we were seated in order at the long tables.

"I'm one that always dreads seeing some o' the folks that I don't like, at such a time as this," announced Mrs. Todd privately to me after a season of reflection. We were just waiting for the feast to begin. "You wouldn't think such a great creatur' 's I be could feel all over pins an' needles. I remember, the day I promised to Nathan, how it come over me, just 's I was feelin' happy 's I could, that I'd got to have an own cousin o' his for my near relation all the rest o' my life, an' it seemed as if die I should. Poor Nathan saw somethin' had crossed me,—he had very nice feelings,—and when he asked me what 'twas, I told him. 'I never could like her myself,' said he. 'You sha'n't be bothered, dear,' he says; an' 'twas one o' the things that made me set a good deal by Nathan, he didn't make a habit of always opposin', like some men. 'Yes,' says I, 'but think o' Thanksgivin' times an' funerals; she's our relation, an' we've got to own her.' Young folks don't think o' those things. There she goes now, do let's pray her by!" said Mrs. Todd, with an alarming transition from general opinions to particular animosities. "I hate her just the same as I always did; but she's got on a real pretty dress. I do try to remember that she's Nathan's cousin. Oh dear, well; she's gone by after all, an' ain't seen me. I expected she'd come pleasantin' round just to show off an' say afterwards she was acquainted."

This was so different from Mrs. Todd's usual largeness of mind that I had a moment's uneasiness; but the cloud passed quickly over her spirit, and was gone with the offender.

There never was a more generous out-of-door feast along the coast than the Bowden family set forth that day. To call it a picnic would make it seem trivial. The great tables were edged with pretty oak-leaf trimming, which the boys and girls made. We brought flowers from the fence-thickets of the great field; and out of the disorder of flowers and provisions suddenly appeared as orderly a scheme for the feast as the marshal had shaped for the procession. I began to respect the Bowdens for their inheritance of good taste and skill and a certain pleasing gift of formality. Something made them do all these things in a finer way than most country people would have done them. As I looked up and down the tables there was a good cheer, a grave soberness that shone with pleasure, a humble dignity of bearing. There were some who should have sat below the salt for lack of this good breeding; but they were not many. So, I said to myself, their ancestors may have sat in the great hall of some old French house in the Middle Ages, when battles and sieges and processions and feasts were familiar things. The ministers and Mrs. Blackett, with a few of their rank and age, were put in places of honor, and for once that I looked any other way I looked twice at Mrs. Blackett's face, serene and mindful of privilege and responsibility, the mistress by simple fitness of this great day.

Mrs. Todd looked up at the roof of green trees, and then carefully surveyed the company. "I see 'em better now they're all settin' down," she said with satisfaction. "There's old Mr. Gilbraith and his sister. I wish they were settin' with us; they're not among folks they can parley with, an' they look disappointed."

As the feast went on, the spirits of my companion steadily rose. The excitement of an unexpectedly great occasion was a subtle stimulant to her disposition, and I could see that sometimes when Mrs. Todd had seemed limited and heavily domestic, she had simply grown sluggish for lack of proper surroundings. She was not so much reminiscent now as expectant, and as alert and gay as a girl. We who were her neighbors were full of gayety, which was but the reflected light from her beaming countenance. It was not the first time that I was full of wonder at the waste of human ability in this world, as a botanist wonders at the wastefulness of nature, the thousand seeds that die, the unused provision of every sort. The reserve force of society grows more and more amazing to one's thought. More than one face among the Bowdens showed that only opportunity and stimulus were lacking,—a narrow set of circumstances had caged a fine able character and held it captive. One sees exactly the same types in a country gathering as in the most brilliant city company. You are safe to be understood if the spirit of your speech is the same for one neighbor as for the other.

XIX

THE FEAST'S END

THE FEAST was a noble feast, as has already been said. There was an elegant ingenuity displayed in the form of pies which delighted my heart. Once acknowledge that an American pie is far to be preferred to its humble ancestor, the English tart, and it is joyful to be reassured at a Bowden reunion that invention has not yet failed. Beside a delightful variety of material, the decorations went beyond all my former experience; dates and names were wrought in lines of pastry and frosting on the tops. There was even more elaborate reading matter on an excellent early-apple pie which we began to share and eat, precept upon precept. Mrs. Todd helped me generously to the whole word *Bowden*, and consumed *Reunion* herself, save an undecipherable fragment; but the most renowned essay in cookery on the tables was a model of the old Bowden house made of durable gingerbread, with all the windows and doors in the right places, and sprigs of genuine lilac set at the front. It must have been baked in sections, in one of the last of the great brick ovens, and fastened together on the morning of the day. There was a general sigh when this fell into ruin at the feast's end, and it was shared by a great part of the assembly, not without seriousness, and as if it were a pledge and token of loyalty. I met the maker of the gingerbread house, which had called up lively remembrances of a childish story. She had the gleaming eye of an enthusiast and a look of high ideals.

"I could just as well have made it all of frosted cake," she said, "but 't would n't have been the right shade; the old house, as you observe, was never painted, and I concluded that plain gingerbread would represent it best. It was n't all I expected it would be," she said sadly, as many an artist had said before her of his work.

There were speeches by the ministers; and there proved to be a historian among the Bowdens, who gave some fine anecdotes of the family history; and then appeared a poetess, whom Mrs. Todd regarded with wistful compassion and indulgence, and when the long faded garland of verses came to an appealing end, she turned to me with words of praise.

"Sounded pretty," said the generous listener. "Yes, I thought she did very well. We went to school together, an' Mary Anna had a very hard time; trouble was, her mother thought she'd given birth to a genius, an' Mary Anna's come to believe it herself. There, I don't know what we should have done without her; there ain't nobody else that can write poetry between here and 'way up towards Rockland; it adds a great deal at such a time. When she speaks o' those that are gone, she feels it all, and so does everybody else, but she harps too much. I'd laid half of that away for next time, if I was Mary Anna. There comes mother to speak to her, an' old Mr. Gilbraith's sister; now she'll be heartened right up. Mother'll say just the right thing."

The leave-takings were as affecting as the meetings of these old friends had been. There were enough young persons at the reunion, but it is the old who really value such opportunities; as for the young, it is the habit of every day to meet their comrades, — the time of separation has not come. To see the joy with which these elder kinsfolk and acquaintances had looked in one another's faces, and the lingering touch of their friendly hands; to see these affectionate meetings and then the reluctant partings, gave one a new idea of the isolation in which it was possible to live in that after all thinly settled region. They did not expect to see one another again very soon; the steady, hard work on the farms, the difficulty of getting from place to place, especially in winter when boats were laid up, gave double value to any occasion which could bring a large number of families together. Even funerals in this country of the pointed firs were not without their social advantages and satisfactions. I heard the words "next summer" repeated many times, though summer was still ours and all the leaves were green.

The boats began to put out from shore, and the wagons to drive away. Mrs. Blackett took me into the old house when we came back from the grove: it was her father's birthplace and early home, and she had spent much of her own childhood there with her grandmother. She spoke of those days as if they had but lately passed; in fact, I could imagine that the house looked almost exactly the same to her. I could see the brown rafters of the unfinished roof as I looked up the steep staircase, though the best room was as handsome with its good wainscoting and touch of ornament on the cornice as any old room of its day in a town.

Some of the guests who came from a distance were still sitting in the best room when we went in to take leave of the master and mistress of the house. We all said eagerly what a pleasant day it had been, and how swiftly the time had passed. Perhaps it is the great national anniversaries which our country has lately kept, and the soldiers' meetings that take place everywhere, which have made reunions of every sort the fashion. This one, at least, had been very interesting. I fancied that old feuds had been overlooked, and the old saying that blood is thicker than water had again proved itself true, though from the variety of names one argued a certain adulteration of the Bowden traits and belongings. Clannishness is an instinct of the heart,—it is more than a birthright, or a custom; and lesser rights were forgotten in the claim to a common inheritance.

We were among the very last to return to our proper lives and lodgings. I came near to feeling like a true Bowden, and parted from certain new friends as if they were old friends; we were rich with the treasure of a new remembrance.

At last we were in the high wagon again; the old white horse had been well fed in the Bowden barn, and we drove away and soon began to climb the long hill toward the wooded ridge. The road was new to me, as roads always are, going back. Most of our companions had been full of anxious thoughts of home,—of the cows, or of young children likely to fall into disaster,—but we had no reasons for haste, and drove slowly along, talking and resting by the way. Mrs. Todd said once that she really hoped her front door had been shut on account of the dust blowing in, but added that nothing made any weight on her mind except not to forget to turn a few late mullein leaves that were drying on a newspaper in the little loft. Mrs. Blackett and I gave our word of honor that we would remind her of this heavy responsibility. The way seemed short, we had so much to talk about. We climbed hills where we could see the great bay and the islands, and then went down into shady valleys where the air began to feel like evening, cool and damp with a fragrance of wet ferns. Mrs. Todd alighted once or twice, refusing all assistance in securing some boughs of a rare shrub which she valued for its bark, though she proved incommunicative as to her reasons. We passed the house where we had been so kindly entertained with doughnuts earlier in the day, and found it closed and deserted, which was a disappointment.

"They must have stopped to tea somewheres and thought they'd finish up the day," said Mrs. Todd. "Those that enjoyed it best 'll want to get right home so 's to think it over."

"I didn't see the woman there after all, did you?" asked Mrs. Blackett as the horse stopped to drink at the trough.

"Oh yes, I spoke with her," answered Mrs. Todd, with but scant interest or approval. "She ain't a member o' our family."

"I thought you said she resembled Cousin Pa'lina Bowden about the forehead," suggested Mrs. Blackett.

"Well, she don't," answered Mrs. Todd impatiently. "I ain't one that's ord'narily mistaken about family likenesses, and she didn't seem to meet with friends, so I went square up to her. 'I expect you're a Bowden by your looks,' says I. 'Yes, I take it you're one o' the Bowdens.' 'Lor', no,' says she. 'Dennett was my maiden name, but I married a Bowden for my first husband. I thought I'd come an' just see what was a-goin' on'!"

Mrs. Blackett laughed heartily. "I'm goin' to remember to tell William o' that," she said. "There, Almiry, the only thing that's troubled me all this day is to think how William would have enjoyed it. I do so wish William had been there."

"I sort of wish he had, myself," said Mrs. Todd frankly.

"There wa'n't many old folks there, somehow," said Mrs. Blackett, with a touch of sadness in her voice. "There ain't so many to come as there used to be, I'm aware, but I expected to see more."

"I thought they turned out pretty well, when you come to think of it; why, everybody was sayin' so an' feelin' gratified," answered Mrs. Todd hastily with pleasing unconsciousness; then I saw the quick color flash into her cheek, and presently she made some excuse to turn and steal an anxious look at her mother. Mrs. Blackett was smiling and thinking about her happy day, though she began to look a little tired. Neither of my companions was troubled by her burden of years. I hoped in my heart that I might be like them as I lived on into age, and then smiled to think that I too was no longer very young. So we always keep the same hearts, though our outer framework fails and shows the touch of time.

" 'T was pretty when they sang the hymn, was n't it?" asked Mrs. Blackett at suppertime, with real enthusiasm. "There was such a plenty o' men's voices; where I sat it did sound beautiful. I had to stop and listen when they came to the last verse."

I saw that Mrs. Todd's broad shoulders began to shake. "There was good singers there; yes, there was excellent singers," she agreed heartily, putting down her teacup, "but I chanced to drift alongside Mis' Peter Bowden o' Great Bay, an' I could n't help thinkin' if she was as far out o' town as she was out o' tune, she would n't get back in a day."

XX

ALONG SHORE

ONE DAY as I went along the shore beyond the old wharves and the newer, high-stepped fabric of the steamer landing, I saw that all the boats were beached, and the slack water period of the early afternoon prevailed. Nothing was going on, not even the most leisurely of occupations, like baiting trawls or mending nets, or repairing lobster pots; the very boats seemed to be taking an afternoon nap in the sun. I could hardly discover a distant sail as I looked seaward, except a weather-beaten lobster smack, which seemed to have been taken for a plaything by the light airs that blew about the bay. It drifted and turned about so aimlessly in the wide reach off Burnt Island, that I suspected there was nobody at the wheel, or that she might have parted her rusty anchor chain while all the crew were asleep.

I watched her for a minute or two; she was the old Miranda, owned by some of the Caplins, and I knew her by an odd shaped patch of newish duck that was set into the peak of her dingy mainsail. Her vagaries offered such an exciting subject for conversation that my heart rejoiced at the sound of a hoarse voice behind me. At that moment, before I had time to answer, I saw something large and shapeless flung from the Miranda's deck that splashed the water high against her black side, and my companion gave a satisfied chuckle. The old lobster smack's sail caught the breeze again at this moment, and she moved off down the bay. Turning, I found old Elijah Tilley, who had come softly out of his dark fish house, as if it were a burrow.

"Boy got kind o' drowsy steerin' of her; Monroe he hove him right overboard; 'wake now fast enough," explained Mr. Tilley, and we laughed together.

I was delighted, for my part, that the vicissitudes and dangers of the Miranda, in a rocky channel, should have given me this opportunity to make acquaintance with an old fisherman to whom I had never spoken. At first he had seemed to be one of those evasive and uncomfortable persons who are so suspicious of you that they make you almost suspicious of yourself. Mr. Elijah Tilley appeared to regard a stranger with scornful indifference. You might see him standing on the pebble beach or in a fishhouse doorway, but when you came nearer he was gone. He was one of the small company of elderly, gaunt-shaped great fishermen whom I used to like to see leading up a deep-laden boat by the head, as if it were a horse, from the water's edge to the steep slope of the pebble beach. There were four of these large old men at the Landing, who were the survivors of an earlier and more vigorous generation. There was an alliance and understanding between them, so close that it was apparently speechless. They gave much time to watching one another's boats go out or come in; they lent a ready hand at tending one another's lobster traps in rough weather; they helped to clean the fish, or to sliver porgies for the trawls, as if they were in close partnership; and when a boat came in from deep-sea fishing they were never far out of the way, and hastened to help carry it ashore, two by two, splashing alongside, or holding its steady head, as if it were a willful sea colt. As a matter of fact no boat could help being steady and way-wise under their instant direction and companionship. Abel's boat and Jonathan Bowden's boat were as distinct and experienced personalities as the men themselves, and as inexpressive. Arguments and opinions were unknown to the conversation of these ancient friends; you would as soon have expected to hear small talk in a company of elephants as to hear old Mr. Bowden or Elijah Tilley and their two mates waste breath upon any form of trivial gossip. They made brief statements to one another from time to time. As you came to know them you wondered more and more that they should talk at all. Speech seemed to be a light and elegant accomplishment, and their unexpected acquaintance with its arts made them of new value to the listener. You felt almost as if a landmark pine should suddenly address you in regard to the weather, or a lofty-minded old camel make a remark as you stood respectfully near him under the circus tent.

I often wondered a great deal about the inner life and thought of these self-contained old fishermen; their minds seemed to be fixed upon nature and the elements rather than upon any contrivances of man, like politics or theology. My friend, Captain Bowden, who was the nephew of the eldest of this group, regarded them with deference; but he did not belong to their secret companionship, though he was neither young nor talkative.

"They've gone together ever since they were boys, they know most everything about the sea amon'st them," he told me once. "They was always just as you see 'em now since the memory of man."

These ancient seafarers had houses and lands not outwardly different from other Dunnet Landing dwellings, and two of them were fathers of families, but their true dwelling places were the sea, and the stony beach that edged its familiar shore, and the fishhouses, where much salt brine from the mackerel kits had soaked the very timbers into a state of brown permanence and petrifaction. It had also affected the old fishermen's hard complexions, until one fancied that when Death claimed them it could only be with the aid, not of any slender modern dart, but the good serviceable harpoon of a seventeenth century woodcut.

Elijah Tilley was such an evasive, discouraged-looking person, heavy-headed, and stooping so that one could never look him in the face, that even after his friendly exclamation about Monroe Pennell, the lobster smack's skipper, and the sleepy boy, I did not venture at once to speak again. Mr. Tilley was carrying a small haddock in one hand, and presently shifted it to the other hand lest it might touch my skirt. I knew that my company was accepted, and we walked together a little way.

"You mean to have a good supper," I ventured to say, by way of friendliness.

"Goin' to have this 'ere haddock an' some o' my good baked potatoes; must eat to live," responded my companion with great pleasantness and open approval. I found that I had suddenly left the forbidding coast and come into a smooth little harbor of friendship.

"You ain't never been up to my place," said the old man. "Folks don't come now as they used to; no, 't ain't no use to ask folks now. My poor dear she was a great hand to draw young company."

I remembered that Mrs. Todd had once said that this old fisherman had been sore stricken and unconsoled at the death of his wife.

"I should like very much to come," said I. "Perhaps you are going to be at home later on?"

Mr. Tilley agreed, by a sober nod, and went his way bent-shouldered and with a rolling gait. There was a new patch high on the shoulder of his old waistcoat, which corresponded to the renewing of the Miranda's mainsail down the bay, and I wondered if his own fingers, clumsy with much deep-sea fishing, had set it in.

"Was there a good catch to-day?" I asked, stopping a moment. "I didn't happen to be on the shore when the boats came in."

"No; all come in pretty light," answered Mr. Tilley. "Addicks an' Bowden they done the best; Abel an' me we had but a slim fare. We went out 'arly, but not so 'arly as sometimes; looked like a poor mornin'. I got nine haddick, all small, and seven fish; the rest on 'em got more fish than haddick. Well, I don't expect they feel like bitin' every day; we l'arn to humor 'em a little, an' let 'em have their way 'bout it. These plaguey dog-fish kind of worry 'em." Mr. Tilley pronounced the last sentence with much sympathy, as if he looked upon himself as a true friend of all the haddock and codfish that lived on the fishing grounds, and so we parted.

Later in the afternoon I went along the beach again until I came to the foot of Mr. Tilley's land, and found his rough track across the cobble-stones and rocks to the field edge, where there was a heavy piece of old wreck timber, like a ship's bone, full of treenails. From this a little footpath, narrow with one man's treading, led up across the small green field that made Mr. Tilley's whole estate, except a straggling pasture that tilted on edge up the steep hillside beyond the house and road. I could hear the tinkle-tankle of a cow-bell somewhere among the spruces by which the pasture was being walked over and forested from every side; it was likely to be called the wood lot before long, but the field was unmolested. I could not see a bush or a brier anywhere within its walls, and hardly a stray pebble showed itself. This was most surprising in that country of firm ledges, and scattered stones which all the walls that industry could devise had hardly begun to clear away off the land. In the narrow field I noticed some stout stakes, apparently planted at random in the grass and among the hills of potatoes, but carefully painted yellow and white to match the house, a neat sharp-edged little dwelling, which looked strangely modern for its owner. I should have much sooner believed that the smart young wholesale egg merchant of the Landing was its occupant than Mr. Tilley, since a man's house is really but his larger body, and expresses in a way his nature and character.

I went up the field, following the smooth little path to the side door. As for using the front door, that was a matter of great ceremony; the long grass grew close against the high stone step, and a snowberry bush leaned over it, top-heavy with the weight of a morning-glory vine that had managed to take what the fishermen might call a half hitch about the door-knob. Elijah Tilley came to the side door to receive me; he was knitting a blue yarn stocking without looking on, and was warmly dressed for the season in a thick blue flannel shirt with white crockery buttons, a faded waistcoat and trousers heavily patched at the knees. These were not his fishing clothes. There was something delightful in the grasp of his hand, warm and clean, as if it never touched anything but the comfortable woolen yarn, instead of cold sea water and slippery fish.

"What are the painted stakes for, down in the field?" I hastened to ask, and he came out a step or two along the path to see; and looked at the stakes as if his attention were called to them for the first time.

"Folks laughed at me when I first bought this place an' come here to live," he explained. "They said 't wa'n't no kind of a field privilege at all; no place to raise anything, all full o' stones. I was aware 't was good land, an' I worked some on it—odd times when I did n't have nothin' else on hand—till I cleared them loose stones all out. You never see a prettier piece than 't is now; now did ye? Well, as for them painted marks, them 's my buoys. I struck on to some heavy rocks that did n't show none, but a plow 'd be liable to ground on 'em, an' so I ketched holt an' buoyed 'em same's you see. They don't trouble me no more'n if they wa'n't there."

"You haven't been to sea for nothing," I said laughing.

"One trade helps another," said Elijah with an amiable smile. "Come right in an' set down. Come in an' rest ye," he exclaimed, and led the way into his comfortable kitchen. The sunshine poured in at the two further windows, and a cat was curled up sound asleep on the table that stood between them. There was a new-looking light oilcloth of a tiled pattern on the floor, and a crockery teapot, large for a household of only one person, stood on the bright stove. I ventured to say that somebody must be a very good housekeeper.

"That's me," acknowledged the old fisherman with frankness. "There ain't nobody here but me. I try to keep things looking right, same's poor dear left 'em. You set down here in this chair, then you can look off an' see the water. None on 'em thought I was goin' to get along alone, no way, but I wa'n't goin' to have my house turned upsi' down an' all changed about; no, not to please nobody. I was the only one knew just how she liked to have things set, poor dear, an' I said I was goin' to make shift, and I have made shift. I'd rather tough it out alone." And he sighed heavily, as if to sigh were his familiar consolation.

We were both silent for a minute; the old man looked out of the window, as if he had forgotten I was there.

"You must miss her very much?" I said at last.

"I do miss her," he answered, and sighed again. "Folks all kep' repeatin' that time would ease me, but I can't find it does. No, I miss her just the same every day."

"How long is it since she died?" I asked.

"Eight year now, come the first of October. It don't seem near so long. I've got a sister that comes and stops 'long o' me a little spell, spring an' fall, an' odd times if I send after her. I ain't near so good a hand to sew as I be to knit, and she's very quick to set everything to rights. She's a married woman with a family; her son's folks lives at home, an' I can't make no great claim on her time. But it makes me a kind o' good excuse, when I do send, to help her a little; she ain't none too well off. Poor dear always liked her, and we used to contrive our ways together. 'T is full as easy to be alone. I set here an' think it all over, an' think considerable when the weather's bad to go outside. I get so some days it feels as if poor dear might step right back into this kitchen. I keep a watchin' them doors as if she might step in to ary one. Yes, ma'am, I keep a-lookin' off an' droppin' o' my stitches; that's just how it seems. I can't git over losin' of her no way nor no how. Yes, ma'am, that's just how it seems to me."

I did not say anything, and he did not look up.

"I git feelin' so sometimes I have to lay everything by an' go out door. She was a sweet pretty creatur' long's she lived," the old man added mournfully. "There's that little rockin' chair o' her'n, I set an' notice it an' think how strange 't is a creatur' like her should be gone an' that chair be here right in its old place."

"I wish I had known her; Mrs. Todd told me about your wife one day," I said.

"You'd have liked to come and see her; all the folks did," said poor Elijah. "She'd been so pleased to hear everything and see somebody new that took such an int'rest. She had a kind o' gift to make it pleasant for folks. I guess likely Almiry Todd told you she was a pretty woman, especially in her young days; late years, too, she kep' her looks and come to be so pleasant lookin'." There, 't ain't so much matter, I shall be done afore a great while. No; I sha'n't trouble the fish a great sight more."

The old widower sat with his head bowed over his knitting, as if he were hastily shortening the very thread of time. The minutes went slowly by. He stopped his work and clasped his hands firmly together. I saw he had forgotten his guest, and I kept the afternoon watch with him. At last he looked up as if but a moment had passed of his continual loneliness.

"Yes, ma'am, I'm one that has seen trouble," he said, and began to knit again.

The visible tribute of his careful housekeeping, and the clean bright room which had once enshrined his wife, and now enshrined her memory, was very moving to me; he had no thought for any one else or for any other place. I began to see her myself in her home,—a delicate-looking, faded little woman, who leaned upon his rough strength and affectionate heart, who was always watching for his boat out of this very window, and who always opened the door and welcomed him when he came home.

"I used to laugh at her, poor dear," said Elijah, as if he read my thought. "I used to make light of her timid notions. She used to be fearful when I was out in bad weather or baffled about gittin' ashore. She used to say the time seemed long to her, but I 've found out all about it now. I used to be dreadful thoughtless when I was a young man and the fish was bitin' well. I 'd stay out late some o' them days, an' I expect she 'd watch an' watch an' lose heart a-waitin'. My heart alive! what a supper she 'd git, an' be right there watchin' from the door, with somethin' over her head if 't was cold, waitin' to hear all about it as I come up the field. Lord, how I think o' all them little things!"

"This was what she called the best room; in this way," he said presently, laying his knitting on the table, and leading the way across the front entry and unlocking a door, which he threw open with an air of pride. The best room seemed to me a much sadder and more empty place than the kitchen; its conventionalities lacked the simple perfection of the humbler room and failed on the side of poor ambition; it was only when one remembered what patient saving, and what high respect for society in the abstract go to such furnishing that the little parlor was interesting at all. I could imagine the great day of certain purchases, the bewildering shops of the next large town, the aspiring anxious woman, the clumsy sea-tanned man in his best clothes, so eager to be pleased, but at ease only when they were safe back in the sail-boat again, going down the bay with their precious freight, the hoarded money all spent and nothing to think of but tiller and sail. I looked at the unworn carpet, the glass vases on the mantel-piece with their prim bunches of bleached swamp grass and dusty marsh rosemary, and I could read the history of Mrs. Tilley's best room from its very beginning.

"You see for yourself what beautiful rugs she could make; now I 'm going to show you her best tea things she thought so much of," said the master of the house, opening the door of a shallow cupboard. "That 's real chiny, all of it on those two shelves," he told me proudly. "I bought it all myself, when we was first married, in the port of Bordeaux. There never was one single piece of it broke until— Well, I used to say, long as she lived, there never was a piece broke, but long at the last I noticed she'd look kind o' distressed, an' I thought 't was 'count o' me boastin'. When they asked if they should use it when the folks was here to supper, time o' her funeral, I knew she'd want to have everything nice, and I said 'certain.' Some o' the women they come runnin' to me an' called me, while they was takin' of the chiny down, an' showed me there was one o' the cups broke an' the pieces wropped in paper and pushed way back here, corner o' the shelf. They didn't want me to go an' think they done it. Poor dear! I had to put right out o' the house when I see that. I knowed in one minute how 't was. We'd got so used to sayin' 't was all there just's I fetched it home, an' so when she broke that cup somehow or 'nother she couldn't frame no words to come an' tell me. She couldn't think 't would vex me, 't was her own hurt pride. I guess there wa'n't no other secret ever lay between us."

The French cups with their gay sprigs of pink and blue, the best tumblers, an old flowered bowl and tea caddy, and a ja-panned waiter or two adorned the shelves. These, with a few daguerreotypes in a little square pile, had the closet to them-selves, and I was conscious of much pleasure in seeing them. One is shown over many a house in these days where the interest may be more complex, but not more definite.

"Those were her best things, poor dear," said Elijah as he locked the door again. "She told me that last summer before she was taken away that she couldn't think o' anything more she wanted, there was everything in the house, an' all her rooms was furnished pretty. I was goin' over to the Port, an' inquired for errands. I used to ask her to say what she wanted, cost or no cost—she was a very reasonable woman, an' 't was the place where she done all but her extra shopping. It kind o' chilled me up when she spoke so satisfied."

"You don't go out fishing after Christmas?" I asked, as we came back to the bright kitchen.

"No; I take stiddy to my knitting after January sets in," said the old seafarer. " 'T ain't worth while, fish make off into deeper water an' you can't stand no such perishin' for the sake o' what you get. I leave out a few traps in sheltered coves an' do a little lobsterin' on fair days. The young fellows braves it out, some on 'em; but, for me, I lay in my winter's yarn an' set here where 't is warm, an' knit an' take my comfort. Mother learnt me once when I was a lad; she was a beautiful knitter herself. I was laid up with a bad knee, an' she said 't would take up my time an' help her; we was a large family. They 'll buy all the folks can do down here to Addicks' store. They say our Dunnet stockin's is gettin' to be celebrated up to Boston,—good quality o' wool an' even knittin' or somethin'. I 've always been called a pretty hand to do nettin', but seines is master cheap to what they used to be when they was all hand worked. I change off to nettin' long towards spring, and I piece up my trawls and lines and get my fishin' stuff to rights. Lobster pots they require attention, but I make 'em up in spring weather when it 's warm there in the barn. No; I ain't one o' them that likes to set an' do nothin'."

"You see the rugs, poor dear did them; she wa'n't very partial to knittin'," old Elijah went on, after he had counted his stitches. "Our rugs is beginnin' to show wear, but I can't master none o' them womanish tricks. My sister, she tinkers 'em up. She said last time she was here that she guessed they 'd last my time."

"The old ones are always the prettiest," I said.

"You ain't referrin' to the braided ones now?" answered Mr. Tilley. "You see ours is braided for the most part, an' their good looks is all in the beginnin'. Poor dear used to say they made an easier floor. I go shufflin' round the house same 's if 't was a bo't, and I always used to be stubbin' up the corners o' the hooked kind. Her an' me was always havin' our jokes together same 's a boy an' girl. Outsiders never 'd know nothin' about it to see us. She had nice manners with all, but to me there was nobody so entertainin'. She 'd take off anybody's natural talk winter evenin's when we set here alone, so you 'd think 't was them a-speakin'. There, there!"

I saw that he had dropped a stitch again, and was snarling the blue yarn round his clumsy fingers. He handled it and threw it off at arm's length as if it were a cod line; and frowned impatiently, but I saw a tear shining on his cheek.

I said that I must be going, it was growing late, and asked if I might come again, and if he would take me out to the fishing grounds some day.

"Yes, come any time you want to," said my host, " 't ain't so pleasant as when poor dear was here. Oh, I did n't want to lose her an' she did n't want to go, but it had to be. Such things ain't for us to say; there's no yes an' no to it."

"You find Almiry Todd one o' the best o' women?" said Mr. Tilley as we parted. He was standing in the doorway and I had started off down the narrow green field. "No, there ain't a better hearted woman in the State o' Maine. I've known her from a girl. She's had the best o' mothers. You tell her I'm liable to fetch her up a couple or three nice good mackerel early to-morrow," he said. "Now don't let it slip your mind. Poor dear, she always thought a sight o' Almiry, and she used to remind me there was nobody to fish for her; but I don't rec'lect it as I ought to. I see you drop a line yourself very handy now an' then."

We laughed together like the best of friends, and I spoke again about the fishing grounds, and confessed that I had no fancy for a southerly breeze and a ground swell.

"Nor me neither," said the old fisherman. "Nobody likes 'em, say what they may. Poor dear was disobliged by the mere sight of a bo't. Almiry's got the best o' mothers, I expect you know; Mis' Blackett out to Green Island; and we was always plannin' to go out when summer come; but there, I could n't pick no day's weather that seemed to suit her just right. I never set out to worry her neither, 't wa'n't no kind o' use; she was so pleasant we could n't have no fret nor trouble. 'T was never 'you dear an' you darlin'' afore folks, an' 'you divil' behind the door!"

As I looked back from the lower end of the field I saw him still standing, a lonely figure in the doorway. "Poor dear," I repeated to myself half aloud; "I wonder where she is and what she knows of the little world she left. I wonder what she has been doing these eight years!"

I gave the message about the mackerel to Mrs. Todd.

"Been visitin' with 'Lijah?" she asked with interest. "I expect you had kind of a dull session; he ain't the talkin' kind; dwellin' so much long o' fish seems to make 'em lose the gift o' speech." But when I told her that Mr. Tilley had been talking to me that day, she interrupted me quickly.

"Then 't was all about his wife, an' he can't say nothin' too pleasant neither. She was modest with strangers, but there ain't one o' her old friends can ever make up her loss. For me, I don't want to go there no more. There's some folks you miss and some folks you don't, when they're gone, but there ain't hardly a day I don't think o' dear Sarah Tilley. She was always right there; yes, you knew just where to find her like a plain flower. 'Lijah's worthy enough; I do esteem 'Lijah, but he's a ploddin' man."

XXI

THE BACKWARD VIEW

A T LAST it was the time of late summer, when the house was cool and damp in the morning, and all the light seemed to come through green leaves; but at the first step out of doors the sunshine always laid a warm hand on my shoulder, and the clear, high sky seemed to lift quickly as I looked at it. There was no autumnal mist on the coast, nor any August fog; instead of these, the sea, the sky, all the long shore line and the inland hills, with every bush of bay and every fir-top, gained a deeper color and a sharper clearness. There was something shining in the air, and a kind of lustre on the water and the pasture grass,—a northern look that, except at this moment of the year, one must go far to seek. The sunshine of a northern summer was coming to its lovely end.

The days were few then at Dunnet Landing, and I let each of them slip away unwillingly as a miser spends his coins. I wished to have one of my first weeks back again, with those long hours when nothing happened except the growth of herbs and the course of the sun. Once I had not even known where to go for a walk; now there were many delightful things to be done and done again, as if I were in London. I felt hurried and full of pleasant engagements, and the days flew by like a handful of flowers flung to the sea wind.

At last I had to say good-by to all my Dunnet Landing friends, and my homelike place in the little house, and return to the world in which I feared to find myself a foreigner. There may be restrictions to such a summer's happiness, but the ease that belongs to simplicity is charming enough to make up for whatever a simple life may lack, and the gifts of peace are not for those who live in the thick of battle.

I was to take the small unpunctual steamer that went down the bay in the afternoon, and I sat for a while by my window looking out on the green herb garden, with regret for company. Mrs. Todd had hardly spoken all day except in the briefest and most disapproving way; it was as if we were on the edge of a quarrel. It seemed impossible to take my departure with anything like composure. At last I heard a footstep, and looked up to find that Mrs. Todd was standing at the door.

"I've seen to everything now," she told me in an unusually loud and business-like voice. "Your trunks are on the w'arf by this time. Cap'n Bowden he come and took 'em down himself, an' is going to see that they're safe aboard. Yes, I've seen to all your 'rangements," she repeated in a gentler tone. "These things I've left on the kitchen table you'll want to carry by hand; the basket need n't be returned. I guess I shall walk over towards the Port now an' inquire how old Mis' Edward Caplin is."

I glanced at my friend's face, and saw a look that touched me to the heart. I had been sorry enough before to go away.

"I guess you'll excuse me if I ain't down there to stand round on the w'arf and see you go," she said, still trying to be gruff. "Yes, I ought to go over and inquire for Mis' Edward Caplin; it's her third shock, and if mother gets in on Sunday she'll want to know just how the old lady is." With this last word Mrs. Todd turned and left me as if with sudden thought of something she had forgotten, so that I felt sure she was coming back, but presently I heard her go out of the kitchen door and walk down the path toward the gate. I could not part so; I ran after her to say good-by, but she shook her head and waved her hand without looking back when she heard my hurrying steps, and so went away down the street.

When I went in again the little house had suddenly grown lonely, and my room looked empty as it had the day I came. I and all my belongings had died out of it, and I knew how it would seem when Mrs. Todd came back and found her lodger gone. So we die before our own eyes; so we see some chapters of our lives come to their natural end.

I found the little packages on the kitchen table. There was a quaint West Indian basket which I knew its owner had valued, and which I had once admired; there was an affecting provision laid beside it for my seafaring supper, with a neatly tied bunch of southernwood and a twig of bay, and a little old leather box which held the coral pin that Nathan Todd brought home to give to poor Joanna.

There was still an hour to wait, and I went up to the hill just above the schoolhouse and sat there thinking of things, and looking off to sea, and watching for the boat to come in sight. I could see Green Island, small and darkly wooded at that distance; below me were the houses of the village with their apple-trees and bits of garden ground. Presently, as I looked at the pastures beyond, I caught a last glimpse of Mrs. Todd herself, walking slowly in the footpath that led along, following the shore toward the Port. At such a distance one can feel the large, positive qualities that control a character. Close at hand, Mrs. Todd seemed able and warm-hearted and quite absorbed in her bustling industries, but her distant figure looked mateless and appealing, with something about it that was strangely self-possessed and mysterious. Now and then she stooped to pick something, — it might have been her favorite pennyroyal, — and at last I lost sight of her as she slowly crossed an open space on one of the higher points of land, and disappeared again behind a dark clump of juniper and the pointed firs.

As I came away on the little coastwise steamer, there was an old sea running which made the surf leap high on all the rocky shores. I stood on deck, looking back, and watched the busy gulls agree and turn, and sway together down the long slopes of air, then separate hastily and plunge into the waves. The tide was setting in, and plenty of small fish were coming with it, unconscious of the silver flashing of the great birds overhead and the quickness of their fierce beaks. The sea was full of life and spirit, the tops of the waves flew back as if they were winged like the gulls themselves, and like them had the freedom of the wind. Out in the main channel we passed a bent-shouldered old fisherman bound for the evening round among his lobster traps. He was toiling along with short oars, and the dory tossed and sank and tossed again with the steamer's waves. I saw that it was old Elijah Tilley, and though we had so long been strangers we had come to be warm friends, and I wished that he had waited for one of his mates, it was such hard work to row along shore through

rough seas and tend the traps alone. As we passed I waved my hand and tried to call to him, and he looked up and answered my farewells by a solemn nod. The little town, with the tall masts of its disabled schooners in the inner bay, stood high above the flat sea for a few minutes, then it sank back into the uniformity of the coast, and became indistinguishable from the other towns that looked as if they were crumbled on the furzy-green stoniness of the shore.

The small outer islands of the bay were covered among the ledges with turf that looked as fresh as the early grass; there had been some days of rain the week before, and the darker green of the sweet-fern was scattered on all the pasture heights. It looked like the beginning of summer ashore, though the sheep, round and warm in their winter wool, betrayed the season of the year as they went feeding along the slopes in the low afternoon sunshine. Presently the wind began to blow, and we struck out seaward to double the long sheltering headland of the cape, and when I looked back again, the islands and the headland had run together and Dunnet Landing and all its coasts were lost to sight.

DUNNET LANDING
STORIES

Contents

The Queen's Twin

I.

THE COAST of Maine was in former years brought so near to foreign shores by its busy fleet of ships that among the older men and women one still finds a surprising proportion of travelers. Each seaward-stretching headland with its high-set houses, each island of a single farm, has sent its spies to view many a Land of Eshcol; one may see plain, contented old faces at the windows, whose eyes have looked at far-away ports and known the splendors of the Eastern world. They shame the easy voyager of the North Atlantic and the Mediterranean; they have rounded the Cape of Good Hope and braved the angry seas of Cape Horn in small wooden ships; they have brought up their hardy boys and girls on narrow decks; they were among the last of the Northmen's children to go adventuring to unknown shores. More than this one cannot give to a young State for its enlightenment; the sea captains and the captains' wives of Maine knew something of the wide world, and never mistook their native parishes for the whole instead of a part thereof; they knew not only Thomaston and Castine and Portland, but London and Bristol and Bordeaux, and the strange-mannered harbors of the China Sea.

One September day, when I was nearly at the end of a summer spent in a village called Dunnet Landing, on the Maine coast, my friend Mrs. Todd, in whose house I lived, came home from a long, solitary stroll in the wild pastures, with an eager look as if she were just starting on a hopeful quest instead of returning. She brought a little basket with blackberries enough for supper, and held it towards me so that I could see that there were also some late and surprising raspberries sprinkled on top, but she made no comment upon her wayfaring. I could tell plainly that she had something very important to say.

"You have n't brought home a leaf of anything," I ventured to this practiced herb-gatherer. "You were saying yesterday that the witch hazel might be in bloom."

"I dare say, dear," she answered in a lofty manner; "I ain't goin' to say it was n't; I ain't much concerned either way 'bout the facts o' witch hazel. Truth is, I 've been off visitin'; there 's an old Indian footpath leadin' over towards the Back Shore through the great heron swamp that anybody can't travel over all summer. You have to seize your time some day just now, while the low ground 's summer-dried as it is to-day, and before the fall rains set in. I never thought of it till I was out o' sight o' home, and I says to myself, 'To-day 's the day, certain!' and stepped along smart as I could. Yes, I 've been visitin'. I did get into one spot that was wet underfoot before I noticed; you wait till I get me a pair o' dry woolen stockings, in case of cold, and I 'll come an' tell ye."

Mrs. Todd disappeared. I could see that something had deeply interested her. She might have fallen in with either the sea-serpent or the lost tribes of Israel, such was her air of mystery and satisfaction. She had been away since just before mid-morning, and as I sat waiting by my window I saw the last red glow of autumn sunshine flare along the gray rocks of the shore and leave them cold again, and touch the far sails of some coastwise schooners so that they stood like golden houses on the sea.

I was left to wonder longer than I liked. Mrs. Todd was making an evening fire and putting things in train for supper; presently she returned, still looking warm and cheerful after her long walk.

"There 's a beautiful view from a hill over where I 've been," she told me; "yes, there 's a beautiful prospect of land and sea. You would n't discern the hill from any distance, but 't is the pretty situation of it that counts. I sat there a long spell, and I did wish for you. No, I did n't know a word about goin' when I set out this morning" (as if I had openly reproached her!); "I only felt one o' them travelin' fits comin' on, an' I ketched up my little basket; I did n't know but I might turn and come back time for dinner. I thought it wise to set out your luncheon for you in case I did n't. Hope you had all you wanted; yes, I hope you had enough."

"Oh, yes, indeed," said I. My landlady was always pecu-liarly bountiful in her supplies when she left me to fare for myself, as if she made a sort of peace-offering or affectionate apology.

"You know that hill with the old house right on top, over beyond the heron swamp? You'll excuse me for explainin'," Mrs. Todd began, "but you ain't so apt to strike inland as you be to go right along shore. You know that hill; there's a path leadin' right over to it that you have to look sharp to find nowadays; it belonged to the up-country Indians when they had to make a carry to the landing here to get to the out' islands. I've heard the old folks say that there used to be a place across a ledge where they'd worn a deep track with their moccasin feet, but I never could find it. 'T is so over-grown in some places that you keep losin' the path in the bushes and findin' it as you can; but it runs pretty straight considerin' the lay o' the land, and I keep my eye on the sun and the moss that grows one side o' the tree trunks. Some brook's been choked up and the swamp's bigger than it used to be. Yes; I did get in deep enough, one place!"

I showed the solicitude that I felt. Mrs. Todd was no longer young, and in spite of her strong, great frame and spirited behavior, I knew that certain ills were apt to seize upon her, and would end some day by leaving her lame and ailing.

"Don't you go to worryin' about me," she insisted, "settin' still's the only way the Evil One'll ever get the upper hand o' me. Keep me movin' enough, an' I'm twenty year old summer an' winter both. I don't know why 't is, but I've never happened to mention the one I've been to see. I don't know why I never happened to speak the name of Abby Martin, for I often give her a thought, but 't is a dreadful out-o'-the-way place where she lives, and I haven't seen her myself for three or four years. She's a real good interesting woman, and we're well acquainted; she's nigher mother's age than mine, but she's very young feeling. She made me a nice cup o' tea, and I don't know but I should have stopped all night if I could have got word to you not to worry."

Then there was a serious silence before Mrs. Todd spoke again to make a formal announcement.

"She is the Queen's Twin," and Mrs. Todd looked steadily to see how I might bear the great surprise.

"The Queen's Twin?" I repeated.

"Yes, she's come to feel a real interest in the Queen, and anybody can see how natural 't is. They were born the very same day, and you would be astonished to see what a number o' other things have corresponded. She was speaking o' some o' the facts to me to-day, an' you'd think she'd never done nothing but read history. I see how earnest she was about it as I never did before. I've often and often heard her allude to the facts, but now she's got to be old and the hurry's over with her work, she's come to live a good deal in her thoughts, as folks often do, and I tell you 't is a sight o' company for her. If you want to hear about Queen Victoria, why Mis' Abby Martin'll tell you everything. And the prospect from that hill I spoke of is as beautiful as anything in this world; 't is worth while your goin' over to see her just for that."

"When can you go again?" I demanded eagerly.

"I should say to-morrow," answered Mrs. Todd; "yes, I should say to-morrow; but I expect 't would be better to take one day to rest, in between. I considered that question as I was comin' home, but I hurried so that there wa'n't much time to think. It's a dreadful long way to go with a horse; you have to go 'most as far as the old Bowden place an' turn off to the left, a master long, rough road, and then you have to turn right round as soon as you get there if you mean to get home before nine o'clock at night. But to strike across country from here, there's plenty o' time in the shortest day, and you can have a good hour or two's visit beside; 't ain't but a very few miles, and it's pretty all the way along. There used to be a few good families over there, but they've died and scattered, so now she's far from neighbors. There, she really cried, she was so glad to see anybody comin'. You'll be amused to hear her talk about the Queen, but I thought twice or three times as I set there 't was about all the company she'd got."

"Could we go day after to-morrow?" I asked eagerly.

" 'T would suit me exactly," said Mrs. Todd.

II.

One can never be so certain of good New England weather as in the days when a long easterly storm has blown away the warm late-summer mists, and cooled the air so that however bright the sunshine is by day, the nights come nearer and nearer to frostiness. There was a cold freshness in the morning air when Mrs. Todd and I locked the house-door behind us; we took the key of the fields into our own hands that day, and put out across country as one puts out to sea. When we reached the top of the ridge behind the town it seemed as if we had anxiously passed the harbor bar and were comfortably in open sea at last.

"There, now!" proclaimed Mrs. Todd, taking a long breath, "now I do feel safe. It's just the weather that's liable to bring somebody to spend the day; I've had a feeling of Mis' Elder Caplin from North Point bein' close upon me ever since I waked up this mornin', an' I did n't want to be hampered with our present plans. She's a great hand to visit; she'll be spendin' the day somewhere from now till Thanksgivin', but there's plenty o' places at the Landin' where she goes, an' if I ain't there she'll just select another. I thought mother might be in, too, 't is so pleasant; but I run up the road to look off this mornin' before you was awake, and there was no sign o' the boat. If they had n't started by that time they would n't start, just as the tide is now; besides, I see a lot o' mackerel-men headin' Green Island way, and they'll detain William. No, we're safe now, an' if mother should be comin' in to-morrow we'll have all this to tell her. She an' Mis' Abby Martin's very old friends."

We were walking down the long pasture slopes towards the dark woods and thickets of the low ground. They stretched away northward like an unbroken wilderness; the early mists still dulled much of the color and made the uplands beyond look like a very far-off country.

"It ain't so far as it looks from here," said my companion reassuringly, "but we've got no time to spare either," and she hurried on, leading the way with a fine sort of spirit in her step; and presently we struck into the old Indian footpath, which could be plainly seen across the long-unploughed turf of the pastures, and followed it among the thick, low-growing spruces. There the ground was smooth and brown under foot, and the thin-stemmed trees held a dark and shadowy roof overhead. We walked a long way without speaking;

sometimes we had to push aside the branches, and sometimes we walked in a broad aisle where the trees were larger. It was a solitary wood, birdless and beastless; there was not even a rabbit to be seen, or a crow high in air to break the silence.

"I don't believe the Queen ever saw such a lonesome trail as this," said Mrs. Todd, as if she followed the thoughts that were in my mind. Our visit to Mrs. Abby Martin seemed in some strange way to concern the high affairs of royalty. I had just been thinking of English landscapes, and of the solemn hills of Scotland with their lonely cottages and stone-walled sheepfolds, and the wandering flocks on high cloudy pastures. I had often been struck by the quick interest and familiar allusion to certain members of the royal house which one found in distant neighborhoods of New England; whether some old instincts of personal loyalty have survived all changes of time and national vicissitudes, or whether it is only that the Queen's own character and disposition have won friends for her so far away, it is impossible to tell. But to hear of a twin sister was the most surprising proof of intimacy of all, and I must confess that there was something remarkably exciting to the imagination in my morning walk. To think of being presented at Court in the usual way was for the moment quite commonplace.

III.

Mrs. Todd was swinging her basket to and fro like a schoolgirl as she walked, and at this moment it slipped from her hand and rolled lightly along the ground as if there were nothing in it. I picked it up and gave it to her, whereupon she lifted the cover and looked in with anxiety.

" 'T is only a few little things, but I don't want to lose 'em," she explained humbly. " 'T was lucky you took the other basket if I was goin' to roll it round. Mis' Abby Martin complained o' lacking some pretty pink silk to finish one o' her little frames, an' I thought I'd carry her some, and I had a bunch o' gold thread that had been in a box o' mine this twenty year. I never was one to do much fancy work, but we're all liable to be swept away by fashion. And then there's a small packet o' very choice herbs that I gave a good deal of attention to; they'll smarten her up and give her the best of appetites, come spring. She was tellin' me that spring weather is very wiltin' an' tryin' to her, and she was beginnin' to dread it already. Mother's just the same way; if I could prevail on mother to take some o' these remedies in good season 't would make a world o' difference, but she gets all down hill before I have a chance to hear of it, and then William comes in to tell me, sighin' and bewailin', how feeble mother is. 'Why can't you remember 'bout them good herbs that I never let her be without?' I say to him—he does provoke me so; and then off he goes, sulky enough, down to his boat. Next thing I know, she comes in to go to meetin', wantin' to speak to everybody and feelin' like a girl. Mis' Martin's case is very much the same; but she's nobody to watch her. William's kind o' slow-moulded; but there, any William's better than none when you get to be Mis' Martin's age."

"Hadn't she any children?" I asked.

"Quite a number," replied Mrs. Todd grandly, "but some are gone and the rest are married and settled. She never was a great hand to go about visitin'. I don't know but Mis' Martin might be called a little peculiar. Even her own folks has to make company of her; she never slips in and lives right along with the rest as if 't was at home, even in her own children's houses. I heard one o' her sons' wives say once she'd much rather have the Queen to spend the day if she could choose between the two, but I never thought Abby was so difficult as that. I used to love to have her come; she may have been sort o' ceremonious, but very pleasant and sprightly if you had sense enough to treat her her own way. I always think she'd know just how to live with great folks, and feel easier 'long of them an' their ways. Her son's wife's a great driver with farm-work, boards a great tableful o' men in hayin' time, an' feels right in her element. I don't say but she's a good woman an' smart, but sort o' rough. Anybody that's gentle-mannered an' precise like Mis' Martin would be a sort o' restraint.

"There's all sorts o' folks in the country, same's there is in the city," concluded Mrs. Todd gravely, and I as gravely agreed. The thick woods were behind us now, and the sun was shining clear overhead, the morning mists were gone, and a faint blue haze softened the distance; as we climbed the hill where we were to see the view, it seemed like a summer day. There was an old house on the height, facing south-ward,—a mere forsaken shell of an old house, with empty windows that looked like blind eyes. The frost-bitten grass grew close about it like brown fur, and there was a single crooked bough of lilac holding its green leaves close by the door.

"We'll just have a good piece of bread-an'-butter now," said the commander of the expedition, "and then we'll hang up the basket on some peg inside the house out o' the way o' the sheep, and have a han'some entertainment as we're comin' back. She'll be all through her little dinner when we get there, Mis' Martin will; but she'll want to make us some tea, an' we must have our visit an' be startin' back pretty soon after two. I don't want to cross all that low ground again after it's begun to grow chilly. An' it looks to me as if the clouds might begin to gather late in the afternoon."

Before us lay a splendid world of sea and shore. The autumn colors already brightened the landscape; and here and there at the edge of a dark tract of pointed firs stood a row of bright swamp-maples like scarlet flowers. The blue sea and the great tide inlets were untroubled by the lightest winds.

"Poor land, this is!" sighed Mrs. Todd as we sat down to rest on the worn doorstep. "I've known three good hard-workin' families that come here full o' hope an' pride and tried to make something o' this farm, but it beat 'em all. There's one small field that's excellent for potatoes if you let half of it rest every year; but the land's always hungry. Now, you see them little peakéd-topped spruces an' fir balsams comin' up over the hill all green an' hearty; they've got it all their own way! Seems sometimes as if wild Natur' got jealous over a certain spot, and wanted to do just as she'd a mind to. You'll see here; she'll do her own ploughin' an' harrowin' with frost an' wet, an' plant just what she wants and wait for her own crops. Man can't do nothin' with it, try as he may. I tell you those little trees means business!"

I looked down the slope, and felt as if we ourselves were likely to be surrounded and overcome if we lingered too long. There was a vigor of growth, a persistence and savagery about the sturdy little trees that put weak human nature at complete defiance. One felt a sudden pity for the men and women who had been worsted after a long fight in that lonely place; one felt a sudden fear of the unconquerable, immediate forces of Nature, as in the irresistible moment of a thunderstorm.

"I can recollect the time when folks were shy o' these woods we just come through," said Mrs. Todd seriously. "The men-folks themselves never 'd venture into 'em alone; if their cattle got strayed they 'd collect whoever they could get, and start off all together. They said a person was liable to get bewildered in there alone, and in old times folks had been lost. I expect there was considerable fear left over from the old Indian times, and the poor days o' witchcraft; anyway, I 've seen bold men act kind o' timid. Some women o' the Asa Bowden family went out one afternoon berryin' when I was a girl, and got lost and was out all night; they found 'em middle o' the mornin' next day, not half a mile from home, scared most to death, an' sayin' they 'd heard wolves and other beasts sufficient for a caravan. Poor creatur's! they 'd strayed at last into a kind of low place amongst some alders, an' one of 'em was so overset she never got over it, an' went off in a sort o' slow decline. 'T was like them victims that drowns in a foot o' water; but their minds did suffer dreadful. Some folks is born afraid of the woods and all wild places, but I must say they 've always been like home to me."

I glanced at the resolute, confident face of my companion. Life was very strong in her, as if some force of Nature were personified in this simple-hearted woman and gave her cousinship to the ancient deities. She might have walked the primeval fields of Sicily; her strong gingham skirts might at that very moment bend the slender stalks of asphodel and be fragrant with trodden thyme, instead of the brown wind-brushed grass of New England and frost-bitten goldenrod. She was a great soul, was Mrs. Todd, and I her humble follower, as we went our way to visit the Queen's Twin, leaving the bright view of the sea behind us, and descending to a lower country-side through the dry pastures and fields.

The farms all wore a look of gathering age, though the settlement was, after all, so young. The fences were already fragile, and it seemed as if the first impulse of agriculture had soon spent itself without hope of renewal. The better houses

were always those that had some hold upon the riches of the
sea; a house that could not harbor a fishing-boat in some
neighboring inlet was far from being sure of every-day comforts. The land alone was not enough to live upon in that
stony region; it belonged by right to the forest, and to the
forest it fast returned. From the top of the hill where we had
been sitting we had seen prosperity in the dim distance,
where the land was good and the sun shone upon fat barns,
and where warm-looking houses with three or four chimneys
apiece stood high on their solid ridge above the bay.

As we drew nearer to Mrs. Martin's it was sad to see what
poor bushy fields, what thin and empty dwelling-places had
been left by those who had chosen this disappointing part of
the northern country for their home. We crossed the last field
and came into a narrow rain-washed road, and Mrs. Todd
looked eager and expectant and said that we were almost at
our journey's end. "I do hope Mis' Martin'll ask you into her
best room where she keeps all the Queen's pictures. Yes, I
think likely she will ask you; but 't ain't everybody she deems
worthy to visit 'em, I can tell you!" said Mrs. Todd warningly.
"She's been collectin' 'em an' cuttin' 'em out o' newspapers
an' magazines time out o' mind, and if she heard of anybody
sailin' for an English port she'd contrive to get a little money
to 'em and ask to have the last likeness there was. She's most
covered her best-room wall now; she keeps that room shut up
sacred as a meetin'-house! 'I won't say but I have my favorites
amongst 'em,' she told me t' other day, 'but they're all beautiful to me as they can be!' And she's made some kind o'
pretty little frames for 'em all—you know there's always a
new fashion o' frames comin' round; first 't was shell-work,
and then 't was pine-cones, and bead-work's had its day, and
now she's much concerned with perforated cardboard
worked with silk. I tell you that best room's a sight to see!
But you must n't look for anything elegant," continued Mrs.
Todd, after a moment's reflection. "Mis' Martin's always been
in very poor, strugglin' circumstances. She had ambition for
her children, though they took right after their father an' had
little for themselves; she wa'n't over an' above well married,
however kind she may see fit to speak. She's been patient an'
hard-workin' all her life, and always high above makin' mean

complaints of other folks. I expect all this business about the Queen has buoyed her over many a shoal place in life. Yes, you might say that Abby'd been a slave, but there ain't any slave but has some freedom."

IV.

Presently I saw a low gray house standing on a grassy bank close to the road. The door was at the side, facing us, and a tangle of snowberry bushes and cinnamon roses grew to the level of the window-sills. On the doorstep stood a bent-shouldered, little old woman; there was an air of welcome and of unmistakable dignity about her.

"She sees us coming," exclaimed Mrs. Todd in an excited whisper. "There, I told her I might be over this way again if the weather held good, and if I came I'd bring you. She said right off she'd take great pleasure in havin' a visit from you; I was surprised, she's usually so retirin'."

Even this reassurance did not quell a faint apprehension on our part; there was something distinctly formal in the occasion, and one felt that consciousness of inadequacy which is never easy for the humblest pride to bear. On the way I had torn my dress in an unexpected encounter with a little thornbush, and I could now imagine how it felt to be going to Court and forgetting one's feathers or her Court train.

The Queen's Twin was oblivious of such trifles; she stood waiting with a calm look until we came near enough to take her kind hand. She was a beautiful old woman, with clear eyes and a lovely quietness and genuineness of manner; there was not a trace of anything pretentious about her, or high-flown, as Mrs. Todd would say comprehensively. Beauty in age is rare enough in women who have spent their lives in the hard work of a farmhouse; but autumn-like and withered as this woman may have looked, her features had kept, or rather gained, a great refinement. She led us into her old kitchen and gave us seats, and took one of the little straight-backed chairs herself and sat a short distance away, as if she were giving audience to an ambassador. It seemed as if we should all be standing; you could not help feeling that the habits of her life were more ceremonious, but that for the moment she assumed the simplicities of the occasion.

Mrs. Todd was always Mrs. Todd, too great and self-possessed a soul for any occasion to ruffle. I admired her calmness, and presently the slow current of neighborhood talk carried one easily along; we spoke of the weather and the small adventures of the way, and then, as if I were after all not a stranger, our hostess turned almost affectionately to speak to me.

"The weather will be growing dark in London now. I expect that you've been in London, dear?" she said.

"Oh, yes," I answered. "Only last year."

"It is a great many years since I was there, along in the forties," said Mrs. Martin. " 'T was the only voyage I ever made; most of my neighbors have been great travelers. My brother was master of a vessel, and his wife usually sailed with him; but that year she had a young child more frail than the others, and she dreaded the care of it at sea. It happened that my brother got a chance for my husband to go as supercargo, being a good accountant, and came one day to urge him to take it; he was very ill-disposed to the sea, but he had met with losses, and I saw my own opportunity and persuaded them both to let me go too. In those days they didn't object to a woman's being aboard to wash and mend, the voyages were sometimes very long. And that was the way I come to see the Queen."

Mrs. Martin was looking straight in my eyes to see if I showed any genuine interest in the most interesting person in the world.

"Oh, I am very glad you saw the Queen," I hastened to say. "Mrs. Todd has told me that you and she were born the very same day."

"We were indeed, dear!" said Mrs. Martin, and she leaned back comfortably and smiled as she had not smiled before. Mrs. Todd gave a satisfied nod and glance, as if to say that things were going on as well as possible in this anxious moment.

"Yes," said Mrs. Martin again, drawing her chair a little nearer, " 't was a very remarkable thing; we were born the same day, and at exactly the same hour, after you allowed for all the difference in time. My father figured it out sea-fashion. Her Royal Majesty and I opened our eyes upon this world together; say what you may, 't is a bond between us."

Mrs. Todd assented with an air of triumph, and untied her hat-strings and threw them back over her shoulders with a gallant air.

"And I married a man by the name of Albert, just the same as she did, and all by chance, for I did n't get the news that she had an Albert too till a fortnight afterward; news was slower coming then than it is now. My first baby was a girl, and I called her Victoria after my mate; but the next one was a boy, and my husband wanted the right to name him, and took his own name and his brother Edward's, and pretty soon I saw in the paper that the little Prince o' Wales had been christened just the same. After that I made excuse to wait till I knew what she 'd named her children. I did n't want to break the chain, so I had an Alfred, and my darling Alice that I lost long before she lost hers, and there I stopped. If I 'd only had a dear daughter to stay at home with me, same 's her youngest one, I should have been so thankful! But if only one of us could have a little Beatrice, I 'm glad 't was the Queen; we 've both seen trouble, but she 's had the most care."

I asked Mrs. Martin if she lived alone all the year, and was told that she did except for a visit now and then from one of her grandchildren, "the only one that really likes to come an' stay quiet 'long o' grandma. She always says quick as she 's through her schoolin' she 's goin' to live with me all the time, but she 's very pretty an' has taking ways," said Mrs. Martin, looking both proud and wistful, "so I can tell nothing at all about it! Yes, I 've been alone most o' the time since my Albert was taken away, and that 's a great many years; he had a long time o' failing and sickness first." (Mrs. Todd's foot gave an impatient scuff on the floor.) "An' I 've always lived right here. I ain't like the Queen's Majesty, for this is the only palace I 've got," said the dear old thing, smiling again. "I 'm glad of it too, I don't like changing about, an' our stations in life are set very different. I don't require what the Queen does, but sometimes I 've thought 't was left to me to do the plain things she don't have time for. I expect she 's a beautiful housekeeper, nobody could n't have done better in her high place, and she's been as good a mother as she's been a queen."

"I guess she has, Abby," agreed Mrs. Todd instantly. "How was it you happened to get such a good look at her? I meant to ask you again when I was here t' other day."

"Our ship was layin' in the Thames, right there above Wapping. We was dischargin' cargo, and under orders to clear as quick as we could for Bordeaux to take on an excellent freight o' French goods," explained Mrs. Martin eagerly. "I heard that the Queen was goin' to a great review of her army, and would drive out o' her Buckin'ham Palace about ten o'clock in the mornin', and I run aft to Albert, my husband, and brother Horace where they was standin' together by the hatchway, and told 'em they must one of 'em take me. They laughed, I was in such a hurry, and said they couldn't go; and I found they meant it and got sort of impatient when I began to talk, and I was 'most broken-hearted; 't was all the reason I had for makin' that hard voyage. Albert couldn't help often reproachin' me, for he did so resent the sea, an' I'd known how 't would be before we sailed; but I'd minded nothing all the way till then, and I just crep' back to my cabin an' begun to cry. They was disappointed about their ship's cook, an' I'd cooked for fo'c's'le an' cabin myself all the way over; 't was dreadful hard work, specially in rough weather; we'd had head winds an' a six weeks' voyage. They'd acted sort of ashamed o' me when I pled so to go ashore, an' that hurt my feelin's most of all. But Albert come below pretty soon; I'd never given way so in my life, an' he begun to act frightened, and treated me gentle just as he did when we was goin' to be married, an' when I got over sobbin' he went on deck and saw Horace an' talked it over what they could do; they really had their duty to the vessel, and couldn't be spared that day. Horace was real good when he understood everything, and he come an' told me I'd more than worked my passage an' was goin' to do just as I liked now we was in port. He'd engaged a cook, too, that was comin' aboard that mornin', and he was goin' to send the ship's carpenter with me—a nice fellow from up Thomaston way; he'd gone to put on his ashore clothes as quick's he could. So then I got ready, and we started off in the small boat and rowed up river. I was afraid we were too late, but the tide was setting up very strong, and we landed an' left the boat to a keeper, and I run all the way up those great streets and across a park. 'Twas a great day, with sights o' folks everywhere, but 'twas just as if they was nothin' but wax images to me. I kep' askin' my way an' runnin' on, with the carpenter comin' after as best he could, and just as I worked to the front o' the crowd by the palace, the gates was flung open and out she came; all prancin' horses and shinin' gold, and in a beautiful carriage there she sat; 'twas a moment o' heaven to me. I saw her plain, and she looked right at me so pleasant and happy, just as if she knew there was somethin' different between us from other folks."

There was a moment when the Queen's Twin could not go on and neither of her listeners could ask a question.

"Prince Albert was sitting right beside her in the carriage," she continued. "Oh, he was a beautiful man! Yes, dear, I saw 'em both together just as I see you now, and then she was gone out o' sight in another minute, and the common crowd was all spread over the place pushin' an' cheerin'. 'Twas some kind o' holiday, an' the carpenter and I got separated, an' then I found him again after I did n't think I should, an' he was all for makin' a day of it, and goin' to show me all the sights; he'd been in London before, but I did n't want nothin' else, an' we went back through the streets down to the waterside an' took the boat. I remember I mended an old coat o' my Albert's as good as I could, sittin' on the quarter-deck in the sun all that afternoon, and 'twas all as if I was livin' in a lovely dream. I don't know how to explain it, but there has n't been no friend I've felt so near to me ever since."

One could not say much—only listen. Mrs. Todd put in a discerning question now and then, and Mrs. Martin's eyes shone brighter and brighter as she talked. What a lovely gift of imagination and true affection was in this fond old heart! I looked about the plain New England kitchen, with its wood-smoked walls and homely braided rugs on the worn floor, and all its simple furnishings. The loud-ticking clock seemed to encourage us to speak; at the other side of the room was an early newspaper portrait of Her Majesty the

Queen of Great Britain and Ireland. On a shelf below were some flowers in a little glass dish, as if they were put before a shrine.

"If I could have had more to read, I should have known 'most everything about her," said Mrs. Martin wistfully. "I've made the most of what I did have, and thought it over and over till it came clear. I sometimes seem to have her all my own, as if we'd lived right together. I've often walked out into the woods alone and told her what my troubles was, and it always seemed as if she told me 't was all right, an' we must have patience. I've got her beautiful book about the Highlands; 't was dear Mis' Todd here that found out about her printing it and got a copy for me, and it's been a treasure to my heart, just as if 't was written right to me. I always read it Sundays now, for my Sunday treat. Before that I used to have to imagine a good deal, but when I come to read her book, I knew what I expected was all true. We do think alike about so many things," said the Queen's Twin with affectionate certainty. "You see, there is something between us, being born just at the same time; 't is what they call a birthright. She's had great tasks put upon her, being the Queen, an' mine has been the humble lot; but she's done the best she could, nobody can say to the contrary, and there's something between us; she's been the great lesson I've had to live by. She's been everything to me. An' when she had her Jubilee, oh, how my heart was with her!"

"There, 't wouldn't play the part in her life it has in mine," said Mrs. Martin generously, in answer to something one of her listeners had said. "Sometimes I think, now she's older, she might like to know about us. When I think how few old friends anybody has left at our age, I suppose it may be just the same with her as it is with me; perhaps she would like to know how we came into life together. But I've had a great advantage in seeing her, an' I can always fancy her goin' on, while she don't know nothin' yet about me, except she may feel my love stayin' her heart sometimes an' not know just where it comes from. An' I dream about our being together out in some pretty fields, young as ever we was, and holdin' hands as we walk along. I'd like to know if she ever has that dream too. I used to have days when I made believe she did know, an' was comin' to see me," confessed the speaker shyly, with a little flush on her cheeks; "and I'd plan what I could have nice for supper, and I wasn't goin' to let anybody know she was here havin' a good rest, except I'd wish you, Almira Todd, or dear Mis' Blackett would happen in, for you'd know just how to talk with her. You see, she likes to be up in Scotland, right out in the wild country, better than she does anywhere else."

"I'd really love to take her out to see mother at Green Island," said Mrs. Todd with a sudden impulse.

"Oh, yes! I should love to have you," exclaimed Mrs. Martin, and then she began to speak in a lower tone. "One day I got thinkin' so about my dear Queen," she said, "an' livin' so in my thoughts, that I went to work an' got all ready for her, just as if she was really comin'. I never told this to a livin' soul before, but I feel you'll understand. I put my best fine sheets and blankets I spun an' wove myself on the bed, and I picked some pretty flowers and put 'em all round the house, an' I worked as hard an' happy as I could all day, and had as nice a supper ready as I could get, sort of telling myself a story all the time. She was comin' an' I was goin' to see her again, an' I kep' it up until nightfall; an' when I see the dark an' it come to me I was all alone, the dream left me, an' I sat down on the doorstep an' felt all foolish an' tired. An', if you'll believe it, I heard steps comin', an' an old cousin o' mine come wanderin' along, one I was apt to be shy of. She wasn't all there, as folks used to say, but harmless enough and a kind of poor old talking body. And I went right to meet her when I first heard her call, 'stead o' hidin' as I sometimes did, an' she come in dreadful willin', an' we sat down to supper together; 'twas a supper I should have had no heart to eat alone."

"I don't believe she ever had such a splendid time in her life as she did then. I heard her tell all about it afterwards," exclaimed Mrs. Todd compassionately. "There, now I hear all this it seems just as if the Queen might have known and couldn't come herself, so she sent that poor old creatur' that was always in need!"

Mrs. Martin looked timidly at Mrs. Todd and then at me. "'Twas childish o' me to go an' get supper," she confessed.

"I guess you wa'n't the first one to do that," said Mrs.

Todd. "No, I guess you wa'n't the first one who's got supper that way, Abby," and then for a moment she could say no more.

Mrs. Todd and Mrs. Martin had moved their chairs a little so that they faced each other, and I, at one side, could see them both.

"No, you never told me o' that before, Abby," said Mrs. Todd gently. "Don't it show that for folks that have any fancy in 'em, such beautiful dreams is the real part o' life? But to most folks the common things that happens outside 'em is all in all."

Mrs. Martin did not appear to understand at first, strange to say, when the secret of her heart was put into words; then a glow of pleasure and comprehension shone upon her face. "Why, I believe you're right, Almira!" she said, and turned to me.

"Wouldn't you like to look at my pictures of the Queen?" she asked, and we rose and went into the best room.

v.

The mid-day visit seemed very short; September hours are brief to match the shortening days. The great subject was dismissed for a while after our visit to the Queen's pictures, and my companions spoke much of lesser persons until we drank the cup of tea which Mrs. Todd had foreseen. I happily remembered that the Queen herself is said to like a proper cup of tea, and this at once seemed to make her Majesty kindly join so remote and reverent a company. Mrs. Martin's thin cheeks took on a pretty color like a girl's. "Somehow I always have thought of her when I made it extra good," she said. "I've got a real china cup that belonged to my grandmother, and I believe I shall call it hers now."

"Why don't you?" responded Mrs. Todd warmly, with a delightful smile.

Later they spoke of a promised visit which was to be made in the Indian summer to the Landing and Green Island, but I observed that Mrs. Todd presented the little parcel of dried herbs, with full directions, for a cure-all in the spring, as if there were no real chance of their meeting again first. As we looked back from the turn of the road the Queen's Twin was still standing on the doorstep watching us away, and Mrs. Todd stopped, and stood still for a moment before she waved her hand again.

"There's one thing certain, dear," she said to me with great discernment; "it ain't as if we left her all alone!"

Then we set out upon our long way home over the hill, where we lingered in the afternoon sunshine, and through the dark woods across the heron-swamp.

A Dunnet Shepherdess

I.

EARLY one morning at Dunnet Landing, as if it were still night, I waked, suddenly startled by a spirited conversation beneath my window. It was not one of Mrs. Todd's morning soliloquies; she was not addressing her plants and flowers in words of either praise or blame. Her voice was declamatory though perfectly good-humored, while the second voice, a man's, was of lower pitch and somewhat deprecating.

The sun was just above the sea, and struck straight across my room through a crack in the blind. It was a strange hour for the arrival of a guest, and still too soon for the general run of business, even in that tiny eastern haven where daybreak fisheries and early tides must often rule the day.

The man's voice suddenly declared itself to my sleepy ears. It was Mr. William Blackett's.

"Why, sister Almiry," he protested gently, "I don't need none o' your nostrums!"

"Pick me a small han'ful," she commanded. "No, no, a *small* han'ful, I said,—o' them large pennyr'yal sprigs! I go to all the trouble an' cossetin' of 'em just so as to have you ready to meet such occasions, an' last year, you may remember, you never stopped here at all the day you went up country. An' the frost come at last an' blacked it. I never saw any herb that so objected to gardin ground; might as well try to flourish mayflowers in a common front yard. There, you can come in now, an' set and eat what breakfast you've got patience for. I've found everything I want, an' I'll mash 'em up an' be all ready to put 'em on."

I heard such a pleading note of appeal as the speakers went round the corner of the house, and my curiosity was so demanding, that I dressed in haste, and joined my friends a little later, with two unnoticed excuses of the beauty of the morning, and the early mail boat. William's breakfast had been slighted; he had taken his cup of tea and merely pushed back the rest on the kitchen table. He was now sitting in a helpless condition by the side window, with one of his sister's purple calico aprons pinned close about his neck. Poor William was meekly submitting to being smeared, as to his countenance, with a most pungent and unattractive lotion of pennyroyal and other green herbs which had been hastily pounded and mixed with cream in the little white stone mortar.

I had to cast two or three straightforward looks at William to reassure myself that he really looked happy and expectant in spite of his melancholy circumstances, and was not being overtaken by retribution. The brother and sister seemed to be on delightful terms with each other for once, and there was something of cheerful anticipation in their morning talk. I was reminded of Medea's anointing Jason before the great episode of the iron bulls, but to-day William really could not be going up country to see a railroad for the first time. I knew this to be one of his great schemes, but he was not fitted to appear in public, or to front an observing world of strangers. As I appeared he essayed to rise, but Mrs. Todd pushed him back into the chair.

"Set where you be till it dries on," she insisted. "Land sakes, you'd think he'd get over bein' a boy some time or 'nother, gettin' along in years as he is. An' you'd think he'd seen full enough o' fish, but once a year he has to break loose like this, an' travel off way up back o' the Bowden place—far out o' my beat, 't is—an' go a trout fishin'!"

Her tone of amused scorn was so full of challenge that William changed color even under the green streaks.

"I want some change," he said, looking at me and not at her. "'T is the prettiest little shady brook you ever saw."

"If he ever fetched home more 'n a couple o' minnies, 't would seem worth while," Mrs. Todd concluded, putting a last dab of the mysterious compound so perilously near her brother's mouth that William flushed again and was silent.

A little later I witnessed his escape, when Mrs. Todd had taken the foolish risk of going down cellar. There was a horse and wagon outside the garden fence, and presently we stood where we could see him driving up the hill with thoughtless speed. Mrs. Todd said nothing, but watched him affectionately out of sight.

"It serves to keep the mosquitoes off," she said, and a moment later it occurred to my slow mind that she spoke of the pennyroyal lotion. "I don't know sometimes but William's kind of poetical," she continued, in her gentlest voice. "You'd think if anything could cure him of it, 't would be the fish business."

It was only twenty minutes past six on a summer morning, but we both sat down to rest as if the activities of the day were over. Mrs. Todd rocked gently for a time, and seemed to be lost, though not poorly, like Macbeth, in her thoughts. At last she resumed relations with her actual surroundings. "I shall now put my lobsters on. They'll make us a good supper," she announced. "Then I can let the fire out for all day; give it a holiday, same's William. You can have a little one now, nice an' hot, if you ain't got all the breakfast you want. Yes, I'll put the lobsters on. William was very thoughtful to bring 'em over; William *is* thoughtful; if he only had a spark o' ambition, there be few could match him."

This unusual concession was afforded a sympathetic listener from the depths of the kitchen closet. Mrs. Todd was getting out her old iron lobster pot, and began to speak of prosaic affairs. I hoped that I should hear something more about her brother and their island life, and sat idly by the kitchen window looking at the morning glories that shaded it, believing that some flaw of wind might set Mrs. Todd's mind on its former course. Then it occurred to me that she had spoken about our supper rather than our dinner, and I guessed that she might have some great scheme before her for the day.

When I had loitered for some time and there was no further word about William, and at last I was conscious of receiving no attention whatever, I went away. It was something of a disappointment to find that she put no hindrance in the way of my usual morning affairs, of going up to the empty little white schoolhouse on the hill where I did my task of writing. I had been almost sure of a holiday when I discovered that Mrs. Todd was likely to take one herself; we had not been far afield to gather herbs and pleasures for many days now, but a little later she had silently vanished. I found my luncheon ready on the table in the little entry, wrapped in its shining old homespun napkin, and as if by way of special consolation, there was a stone bottle of Mrs. Todd's best spruce beer, with a long piece of cod line wound round it by which it could be lowered for coolness into the deep schoolhouse well.

I walked away with a dull supply of writing-paper and these provisions, feeling like a reluctant child who hopes to be called back at every step. There was no relenting voice to be heard, and when I reached the schoolhouse, I found that I had left an open window and a swinging shutter the day before, and the sea wind that blew at evening had fluttered my poor sheaf of papers all about the room.

So the day did not begin very well, and I began to recognize that it was one of the days when nothing could be done without company. The truth was that my heart had gone trouting with William, but it would have been too selfish to say a word even to one's self about spoiling his day. If there is one way above another of getting so close to nature that one simply is a piece of nature, following a primeval instinct with perfect self-forgetfulness and forgetting everything except the dreamy consciousness of pleasant freedom, it is to take the course of a shady trout brook. The dark pools and the sunny shallows beckon one on; the wedge of sky between the trees on either bank, the speaking, companioning noise of the water, the amazing importance of what one is doing, and the constant sense of life and beauty make a strange transformation of the quick hours. I had a sudden memory of all this, and another, and another. I could not get myself free from "fishing and wishing."

At that moment I heard the unusual sound of wheels, and I looked past the high-growing thicket of wild-roses and straggling sumach to see the white nose and meagre shape of the Caplin horse; then I saw William sitting in the open wagon, with a small expectant smile upon his face.

"I've got two lines," he said. "I was quite a piece up the road. I thought perhaps 't was so you 'd feel like going."

There was enough excitement for most occasions in hearing William speak three sentences at once. Words seemed but vain to me at that bright moment. I stepped back from the schoolhouse window with a beating heart. The spruce-beer bottle was not yet in the well, and with that and my luncheon, and Pleasure at the helm, I went out into the happy world. The land breeze was blowing, and, as we turned away, I saw a flutter of white go past the window as I left the schoolhouse and my morning's work to their neglected fate.

II.

One seldom gave way to a cruel impulse to look at an ancient seafaring William, but one felt as if he were a growing boy; I only hope that he felt much the same about me. He did not wear the fishing clothes that belonged to his seagoing life, but a strangely shaped old suit of tea-colored linen garments that might have been brought home years ago from Canton or Bombay. William had a peculiar way of giving silent assent when one spoke, but of answering your unspoken thoughts as if they reached him better than words. "I find them very easy," he said, frankly referring to the clothes. "Father had them in his old sea-chest."

The antique fashion, a quaint touch of foreign grace and even imagination about the cut were very pleasing; if ever Mr. William Blackett had faintly resembled an old beau, it was upon that day. He now appeared to feel as if everything had been explained between us, as if everything were quite understood; and we drove for some distance without finding it necessary to speak again about anything. At last, when it must have been a little past nine o'clock, he stopped the horse beside a small farmhouse, and nodded when I asked if I should get down from the wagon. "You can steer about northeast right across the pasture," he said, looking from under the eaves of his hat with an expectant smile. "I always leave the team here."

I helped to unfasten the harness, and William led the horse away to the barn. It was a poor-looking little place, and a forlorn woman looked at us through the window before she appeared at the door. I told her that Mr. Blackett and I came up from the Landing to go fishing. "He keeps a-comin', don't he?" she answered, with a funny little laugh, to which I was at a loss to find answer. When he joined us, I could not see that he took notice of her presence in any way, except to take an armful of dried salt fish from a corded stack in the back of the wagon which had been carefully covered with a piece of old sail. We had left a wake of their pungent flavor behind us all the way. I wondered what was going to become of the rest of them and some fresh lobsters which were also disclosed to view, but he laid the present gift on the doorstep without a word, and a few minutes later, when I looked back as we crossed the pasture, the fish were being carried into the house.

I could not see any signs of a trout brook until I came close upon it in the bushy pasture, and presently we struck into the low woods of straggling spruce and fir mixed into a tangle of swamp maples and alders which stretched away on either hand up and down stream. We found an open place in the pasture where some taller trees seemed to have been overlooked rather than spared. The sun was bright and hot by this time, and I sat down in the shade while William produced his lines and cut and trimmed us each a slender rod. I wondered where Mrs. Todd was spending the morning, and if later she would think that pirates had landed and captured me from the schoolhouse.

III.

The brook was giving that live, persistent call to a listener that trout brooks always make; it ran with a free, swift current even here, where it crossed an apparently level piece of land. I saw two unpromising, quick barbel chase each other upstream from bank to bank as we solemnly arranged our hooks and sinkers. I felt that William's glances changed from anxiety to relief when he found that I was used to such gear; perhaps he felt that we must stay together if I could not bait my own hook, but we parted happily, full of a pleasing sense of companionship.

William had pointed me up the brook, but I chose to go down, which was only fair because it was his day, though one likes as well to follow and see where a brook goes as to find one's way to the places it comes from, and its tiny springs and headwaters, and in this case trout were not to be considered. William's only real anxiety was lest I might suffer from mosquitoes. His own complexion was still strangely impaired by its defenses, but I kept forgetting it, and looking to see if we

were treading fresh pennyroyal underfoot, so efficient was
Mrs. Todd's remedy. I was conscious, after we parted, and I
turned to see if he were already fishing, and saw him wave his
hand gallantly as he went away, that our friendship had made
a great gain.

The moment that I began to fish the brook, I had a sense of
its emptiness; when my bait first touched the water and went
lightly down the quick stream, I knew that there was nothing
to lie in wait for it. It is the same certainty that comes when
one knocks at the door of an empty house, a lack of answering consciousness and of possible response; it is quite different if there is any life within. But it was a lovely brook, and I
went a long way through woods and breezy open pastures,
and found a forsaken house and overgrown farm, and laid up
many pleasures for future joy and remembrance. At the end of
the morning I came back to our meeting-place hungry and
without any fish. William was already waiting, and we did not
mention the matter of trout. We ate our luncheons with good
appetites, and William brought our two stone bottles of
spruce beer from the deep place in the brook where he had
left them to cool. Then we sat awhile longer in peace and
quietness on the green banks.

As for William, he looked more boyish than ever, and kept
a more remote and juvenile sort of silence. Once I wondered
how he had come to be so curiously wrinkled, forgetting,
absent-mindedly, to recognize the effects of time. He did not
expect any one else to keep up a vain show of conversation,
and so I was silent as well as he. I glanced at him now and
then, but I watched the leaves tossing against the sky and the
red cattle moving in the pasture. "I don't know's we need
head for home. It's early yet," he said at last, and I was as
startled as if one of the gray firs had spoken.

"I guess I'll go up-along and ask after Thankful Hight's
folks," he continued. "Mother'd like to get word;" and I nodded a pleased assent.

IV.

William led the way across the pasture, and I followed with
a deep sense of pleased anticipation. I do not believe that my

companion had expected me to make any objection, but I knew that he was gratified by the easy way that his plans for the day were being seconded. He gave a look at the sky to see if there were any portents, but the sky was frankly blue; even the doubtful morning haze had disappeared.

We went northward along a rough, clayey road, across a bare-looking, sunburnt country full of tiresome long slopes where the sun was hot and bright, and I could not help observing the forlorn look of the farms. There was a great deal of pasture, but it looked deserted, and I wondered afresh why the people did not raise more sheep when that seemed the only possible use to make of their land. I said so to Mr. Blackett, who gave me a look of pleased surprise.

"That's what She always maintains," he said eagerly. "She's right about it, too; well, you'll see!" I was glad to find myself approved, but I had not the least idea whom he meant, and waited until he felt like speaking again.

A few minutes later we drove down a steep hill and entered a large tract of dark spruce woods. It was delightful to be sheltered from the afternoon sun, and when we had gone some distance in the shade, to my great pleasure William turned the horse's head toward some bars, which he let down, and I drove through into one of those narrow, still, sweet-scented by-ways which seem to be paths rather than roads. Often we had to put aside the heavy drooping branches which barred the way, and once, when a sharp twig struck William in the face, he announced with such spirit that somebody ought to go through there with an axe, that I felt unexpectedly guilty. So far as I now remember, this was William's only remark all the way through the woods to Thankful Hight's folks, but from time to time he pointed or nodded at something which I might have missed: a sleepy little owl snuggled into the bend of a branch, or a tall stalk of cardinal flowers where the sunlight came down at the edge of a small, bright piece of marsh. Many times, being used to the company of Mrs. Todd and other friends who were in the habit of talking, I came near making an idle remark to William, but I was for the most part happily preserved; to be with him only for a short time was to live on a different level, where thoughts served best because they were thoughts in common;

the primary effect upon our minds of the simple things and beauties that we saw. Once when I caught sight of a lovely gay pigeon-woodpecker eyeing us curiously from a dead branch, and instinctively turned toward William, he gave an indulgent, comprehending nod which silenced me all the rest of the way. The wood-road was not a place for common noisy conversation; one would interrupt the birds and all the still little beasts that belonged there. But it was mortifying to find how strong the habit of idle speech may become in one's self. One need not always be saying something in this noisy world. I grew conscious of the difference between William's usual fashion of life and mine; for him there were long days of silence in a sea-going boat, and I could believe that he and his mother usually spoke very little because they so perfectly understood each other. There was something peculiarly unresponding about their quiet island in the sea, solidly fixed into the still foundations of the world, against whose rocky shores the sea beats and calls and is unanswered.

We were quite half an hour going through the woods; the horse's feet made no sound on the brown, soft track under the dark evergreens. I thought that we should come out at last into more pastures, but there was no half-wooded strip of land at the end; the high woods grew squarely against an old stone wall and a sunshiny open field, and we came out suddenly into broad daylight that startled us and even startled the horse, who might have been napping as he walked, like an old soldier. The field sloped up to a low unpainted house that faced the east. Behind it were long, frost-whitened ledges that made the hill, with strips of green turf and bushes between. It was the wildest, most Titanic sort of pasture country up there; there was a sort of daring in putting a frail wooden house before it, though it might have the homely field and honest woods to front against. You thought of the elements and even of possible volcanoes as you looked up the stony heights. Suddenly I saw that a region of what I had thought gray stones was slowly moving, as if the sun was making my eyesight unsteady.

"There's the sheep!" exclaimed William, pointing eagerly. "You see the sheep?" and sure enough, it was a great company of woolly backs, which seemed to have taken a mysterious protective resemblance to the ledges themselves. I could discover but little chance for pasturage on that high sunburnt ridge, but the sheep were moving steadily in a satisfied way as they fed along the slopes and hollows.

"I never have seen half so many sheep as these, all summer long!" I cried with admiration.

"There ain't so many," answered William soberly. "It's a great sight. They do so well because they're shepherded, but you can't beat sense into some folks."

"You mean that somebody stays and watches them?" I asked.

"She observed years ago in her readin' that they don't turn out their flocks without protection anywhere but in the State o' Maine," returned William. "First thing that put it into her mind was a little old book mother's got; she read it one time when she come out to the Island. They call it the 'Shepherd o' Salisbury Plain.' 'T was n't the purpose o' the book to most, but when she read it, 'There, Mis' Blackett!' she said, 'that's where we've all lacked sense; our Bibles ought to have taught us that what sheep need is a shepherd.' You see most folks about here gave up sheep-raisin' years ago 'count o' the dogs. So she gave up school-teachin' and went out to tend her flock, and has shepherded ever since, an' done well."

For William, this approached an oration. He spoke with enthusiasm, and I shared the triumph of the moment. "There she is now!" he exclaimed, in a different tone, as the tall figure of a woman came following the flock and stood still on the ridge, looking toward us as if her eyes had been quick to see a strange object in the familiar emptiness of the field. William stood up in the wagon, and I thought he was going to call or wave his hand to her, but he sat down again more clumsily than if the wagon had made the familiar motion of a boat, and we drove on toward the house.

It was a most solitary place to live,—a place where one might think that a life could hide itself. The thick woods were between the farm and the main road, and as one looked up and down the country, there was no other house in sight.

"Potatoes look well," announced William. "The old folks used to say that there wa'n't no better land outdoors than the Hight field."

I found myself possessed of a surprising interest in the shepherdess, who stood far away in the hill pasture with her great flock, like a figure of Millet's, high against the sky.

v.

Everything about the old farmhouse was clean and orderly, as if the green dooryard were not only swept, but dusted. I saw a flock of turkeys stepping off carefully at a distance, but there was not the usual untidy flock of hens about the place to make everything look in disarray. William helped me out of the wagon as carefully as if I had been his mother, and nodded toward the open door with a reassuring look at me; but I waited until he had tied the horse and could lead the way, himself. He took off his hat just as we were going in, and stopped for a moment to smooth his thin gray hair with his hand, by which I saw that we had an affair of some ceremony. We entered an old-fashioned country kitchen, the floor scrubbed into unevenness, and the doors well polished by the touch of hands. In a large chair facing the window there sat a masterful-looking old woman with the features of a warlike Roman emperor, emphasized by a bonnet-like black cap with a band of green ribbon. Her sceptre was a palm-leaf fan.

William crossed the room toward her, and bent his head close to her ear.

"Feelin' pretty well to-day, Mis' Hight?" he asked, with all the voice his narrow chest could muster.

"No, I ain't, William. Here I have to set," she answered coldly, but she gave an inquiring glance over his shoulder at me.

"This is the young lady who is stopping with Almiry this summer," he explained, and I approached as if to give the countersign. She offered her left hand with considerable dignity, but her expression never seemed to change for the better. A moment later she said that she was pleased to meet me, and I felt as if the worst were over. William must have felt some apprehension, while I was only ignorant, as we had come across the field. Our hostess was more than disapproving, she was forbidding; but I was not long in suspecting that she felt the natural resentment of a strong energy that has been defeated by illness and made the spoil of captivity.

"Mother well as usual since you was up last year?" and William replied by a series of cheerful nods. The mention of dear Mrs. Blackett was a help to any conversation.

"Been fishin', ashore," he explained, in a somewhat conciliatory voice. "Thought you'd like a few for winter," which explained at once the generous freight we had brought in the back of the wagon. I could see that the offering was no surprise, and that Mrs. Hight was interested.

"Well, I expect they're good as the last," she said, but did not even approach a smile. She kept a straight, discerning eye upon me.

"Give the lady a cheer," she admonished William, who hastened to place close by her side one of the straight-backed chairs that stood against the kitchen wall. Then he lingered for a moment like a timid boy. I could see that he wore a look of resolve, but he did not ask the permission for which he evidently waited.

"You can go search for Esther," she said, at the end of a long pause that became anxious for both her guests. "Esther'd like to see her;" and William in his pale nankeens disappeared with one light step and was off.

VI.

"Don't speak too loud, it jars a person's head," directed Mrs. Hight plainly. "Clear an' distinct is what reaches me best. Any news to the Landin'?"

I was happily furnished with the particulars of a sudden death, and an engagement of marriage between a Caplin, a seafaring widower home from his voyage, and one of the younger Harrises; and now Mrs. Hight really smiled and settled herself in her chair. We exhausted one subject completely before we turned to the other. One of the returning turkeys took an unwarrantable liberty, and, mounting the doorstep, came in and walked about the kitchen without being observed by its strict owner; and the tin dipper slipped off its nail behind us and made an astonishing noise, and jar enough to reach Mrs. Hight's inner ear and make her turn her head to look at it; but we talked straight on. We came at last to understand each other upon such terms of friendship that she unbent her majestic port and complained to me as any poor old woman might of the hardships of her illness. She had already fixed various dates upon the sad certainty of the year when she had the shock, which had left her perfectly helpless except for a clumsy left hand which fanned and gestured, and settled and resettled the folds of her dress, but could do no comfortable time-shortening work.

"Yes'm, you can feel sure I use it what I can," she said severely. " 'T was a long spell before I could let Esther go forth in the mornin' till she'd got me up an' dressed me, but now she leaves things ready overnight and I get 'em as I want 'em with my light pair o' tongs, and I feel very able about helpin' myself to what I once did. Then when Esther returns, all she has to do is to push me out here into the kitchen. Some parts o' the year Esther stays out all night, them moonlight nights when the dogs are apt to be after the sheep, but she don't use herself as hard as she once had to. She's well able to hire somebody, Esther is, but there, you can't find no hired man that wants to git up before five o'clock nowadays; 't ain't as 't was in my time. They're liable to fall asleep, too, and them moonlight nights she's so anxious she can't sleep, and out she goes. There's a kind of a fold, she calls it, up there in a sheltered spot, and she sleeps up in a little shed she's got,—built it herself for lambin' time and when the poor foolish creatur's gets hurt or anything. I've never seen it, but she says it's in a lovely spot and always pleasant in any weather. You see off, other side of the ridge, to the south'ard, where there's houses. I used to think some time I'd get up to see it again, and all them spots she lives in, but I sha'n't now. I'm beginnin' to go back; an' 't ain't surprisin'. I've kind of got used to disappointments," and the poor soul drew a deep sigh.

VII.

It was long before we noticed the lapse of time; I not only told every circumstance known to me of recent events among the households of Mrs. Todd's neighborhood at the shore, but Mrs. Hight became more and more communicative on her part, and went carefully into the genealogical descent and personal experience of many acquaintances, until between us we had pretty nearly circumnavigated the globe and reached Dunnet Landing from an opposite direction to that in which we had started. It was long before my own interest began to flag; there was a flavor of the best sort in her definite and descriptive fashion of speech. It may be only a fancy of my own that in the sound and value of many words, with their lengthened vowels and doubled cadences, there is some faint survival on the Maine coast of the sound of English speech of Chaucer's time.

At last Mrs. Thankful Hight gave a suspicious look through the window.

"Where do you suppose they be?" she asked me. "Esther must ha' been off to the far edge o' everything. I doubt William ain't been able to find her; can't he hear their bells? His hearin' all right?"

William had heard some herons that morning which were beyond the reach of my own ears, and almost beyond eyesight in the upper skies, and I told her so. I was luckily preserved by some unconscious instinct from saying that we had seen the shepherdess so near as we crossed the field. Unless she had fled faster than Atalanta, William must have been but a few minutes in reaching her immediate neighborhood. I now discovered with a quick leap of amusement and delight in my heart that I had fallen upon a serious chapter of romance. The old woman looked suspiciously at me, and I made a dash to cover with a new piece of information; but she listened with lofty indifference, and soon interrupted my eager statements.

"Ain't William been gone some considerable time?" she demanded, and then in a milder tone: "The time has re'lly flown; I do enjoy havin' company. I set here alone a sight o' long days. Sheep is dreadful fools; I expect they heard a strange step, and set right off through bush an' brier, spite of all she could do. But William might have the sense to return, 'stead o' searchin' about. I want to inquire of him about his mother. What was you goin' to say? I guess you'll have time to relate it."

My powers of entertainment were on the ebb, but I doubled my diligence and we went on for another half-hour at least with banners flying, but still William did not reappear. Mrs. Hight frankly began to show fatigue.

"Somethin' 's happened, an' he's stopped to help her," groaned the old lady, in the middle of what I had found to tell her about a rumor of disaffection with the minister of a town I merely knew by name in the weekly newspaper to which Mrs. Todd subscribed. "You step to the door, dear, an' look if you can't see 'em." I promptly stepped, and once outside the house I looked anxiously in the direction which William had taken.

To my astonishment I saw all the sheep so near that I wonder we had not been aware in the house of every bleat and tinkle. And there, within a stone's-throw, on the first long gray ledge that showed above the juniper, were William and the shepherdess engaged in pleasant conversation. At first I was provoked and then amused, and a thrill of sympathy warmed my whole heart. They had seen me and risen as if by magic; I had a sense of being the messenger of Fate. One could almost hear their sighs of regret as I appeared; they must have passed a lovely afternoon. I hurried into the house with the reassuring news that they were not only in sight but perfectly safe, with all the sheep.

VIII.

Mrs. Hight, like myself, was spent with conversation, and had ceased even the one activity of fanning herself. I brought a desired drink of water, and happily remembered some fruit that was left from my luncheon. She revived with splendid vigor, and told me the simple history of her later years since she had been smitten in the prime of her life by the stroke of paralysis, and her husband had died and left her alone with Esther and a mortgage on their farm. There was only one field of good land, but they owned a great region of sheep pasture and a little woodland. Esther had always been laughed at for her belief in sheep-raising when one by one their neighbors were giving up their flocks, and when everything had come to the point of despair she had raised all the money and bought all the sheep she could, insisting that Maine lambs were as good as any, and that there was a straight path by sea to Boston market. And by tending her flock herself she had managed to succeed; she had made money enough to pay off the mortgage five years ago, and now what they did not spend was safe in the bank. "It has been stubborn work, day and night, summer and winter, an' now she's beginnin' to get along in years," said the old mother sadly. "She's tended me 'long o' the sheep, an' she's been a good girl right along, but she ought to have been a teacher;" and Mrs. Hight sighed heavily and plied the fan again.

We heard voices, and William and Esther entered; they did not know that it was so late in the afternoon. William looked almost bold, and oddly like a happy young man rather than an ancient boy. As for Esther, she might have been Jeanne d'Arc returned to her sheep, touched with age and gray with the ashes of a great remembrance. She wore the simple look of sainthood and unfeigned devotion. My heart was moved by the sight of her plain sweet face, weatherworn and gentle in its looks, her thin figure in its close dress, and the strong hand that clasped a shepherd's staff, and I could only hold William in new reverence; this silent farmer-fisherman who knew, and he alone, the noble and patient heart that beat within her breast. I am not sure that they acknowledged even to themselves that they had always been lovers; they could not consent to anything so definite or pronounced; but they were happy in being together in the world. Esther was untouched by the fret and fury of life; she had lived in sunshine and rain among her silly sheep, and been refined instead of coarsened, while her touching patience with a ramping old mother, stung by the sense of defeat and mourning her lost activities, had given back a lovely self-possession, and habit of sweet temper. I had seen enough of old Mrs. Hight to know that nothing a sheep might do could vex a person who was used to the uncertainties and severities of her companionship.

IX.

Mrs. Hight told her daughter at once that she had enjoyed a beautiful call, and got a great many new things to think of.

This was said so frankly in my hearing that it gave a consciousness of high reward, and I was indeed recompensed by
the grateful look in Esther's eyes. We did not speak much
together, but we understood each other. For the poor old
woman did not read, and could not sew or knit with her helpless hand, and they were far from any neighbors, while her
spirit was as eager in age as in youth, and expected even more
from a disappointing world. She had lived to see the mortgage paid and money in the bank, and Esther's success acknowledged on every hand, and there were still a few
pleasures left in life. William had his mother, and Esther had
hers, and they had not seen each other for a year, though
Mrs. Hight had spoken of a year's making no change in
William even at his age. She must have been in the far eighties
herself, but of a noble courage and persistence in the world
she ruled from her stiff-backed rocking-chair.

William unloaded his gift of dried fish, each one chosen
with perfect care, and Esther stood by, watching him, and
then she walked across the field with us beside the wagon. I
believed that I was the only one who knew their happy secret,
and she blushed a little as we said good-by.

"I hope you ain't goin' to feel too tired, mother's so deaf;
no, I hope you won't be tired," she said kindly, speaking as
if she well knew what tiredness was. We could hear the
neglected sheep bleating on the hill in the next moment's
silence. Then she smiled at me, a smile of noble patience, of
uncomprehended sacrifice, which I can never forget. There
was all the remembrance of disappointed hopes, the hardships
of winter, the loneliness of single-handedness in her look, but
I understood, and I love to remember her worn face and her
young blue eyes.

"Good-by, William," she said gently, and William said
good-by, and gave her a quick glance, but he did not turn to
look back, though I did, and waved my hand as she was putting up the bars behind us. Nor did he speak again until we
had passed through the dark woods and were on our way
homeward by the main road. The grave yearly visit had been
changed from a hope into a happy memory.

"You can see the sea from the top of her pasture hill," said
William at last.

"Can you?" I asked, with surprise.

"Yes, it's very high land; the ledges up there show very plain in clear weather from the top of our island, and there's a high upstandin' tree that makes a landmark for the fishin' grounds." And William gave a happy sigh.

When we had nearly reached the Landing, my companion looked over into the back of the wagon and saw that the piece of sailcloth was safe, with which he had covered the dried fish. "I wish we had got some trout," he said wistfully. "They always appease Almiry, and make her feel 't was worth while to go."

I stole a glance at William Blackett. We had not seen a solitary mosquito, but there was a dark stripe across his mild face, which might have been an old scar won long ago in battle.

The Foreigner

O NE EVENING, at the end of August, in Dunnet Landing, I heard Mrs. Todd's firm footstep crossing the small front entry outside my door, and her conventional cough which served as a herald's trumpet, or a plain New England knock, in the harmony of our fellowship.

"Oh, please come in!" I cried, for it had been so still in the house that I supposed my friend and hostess had gone to see one of her neighbors. The first cold northeasterly storm of the season was blowing hard outside. Now and then there was a dash of great raindrops and a flick of wet lilac leaves against the window, but I could hear that the sea was already stirred to its dark depths, and the great rollers were coming in heavily against the shore. One might well believe that Summer was coming to a sad end that night, in the darkness and rain and sudden access of autumnal cold. It seemed as if there must be danger offshore among the outer islands.

"Oh, there!" exclaimed Mrs. Todd, as she entered. "I know nothing ain't ever happened out to Green Island since the world began, but I always do worry about mother in these great gales. You know those tidal waves occur sometimes down to the West Indies, and I get dwellin' on 'em so I can't set still in my chair, nor knit a common row to a stocking. William might get mooning, out in his small bo't, and not observe how the sea was making, an' meet with some accident. Yes, I thought I'd come in and set with you if you wa'n't busy. No, I never feel any concern about 'em in winter 'cause then they're prepared, and all ashore and everything snug. William ought to keep help, as I tell him; yes, he ought to keep help."

I hastened to reassure my anxious guest by saying that Elijah Tilley had told me in the afternoon, when I came along the shore past the fish houses, that Johnny Bowden and the Captain were out at Green Island; he had seen them beating up the bay, and thought they must have put into Burnt Island cove, but one of the lobstermen brought word later that he saw them hauling out at Green Island as he came by, and Captain Bowden pointed ashore and shook his head to say that he did not mean to try to get in. "The old Miranda just managed it, but she will have to stay at home a day or two and put new patches in her sail," I ended, not without pride in so much circumstantial evidence.

Mrs. Todd was alert in a moment. "Then they'll all have a very pleasant evening," she assured me, apparently dismissing all fears of tidal waves and other sea-going disasters. "I was urging Alick Bowden to go ashore some day and see mother before cold weather. He's her own nephew; she sets a great deal by him. And Johnny's a great chum o' William's; don't you know the first day we had Johnny out 'long of us, he took an' give William his money to keep for him that he'd been a-savin', and William showed it to me an' was so affected I thought he was goin' to shed tears? 'T was a dollar an' eighty cents; yes, they'll have a beautiful evenin' all together, and like's not the sea'll be flat as a doorstep come morning."

I had drawn a large wooden rocking-chair before the fire, and Mrs. Todd was sitting there jogging herself a little, knitting fast, and wonderfully placid of countenance. There came a fresh gust of wind and rain, and we could feel the small wooden house rock and hear it creak as if it were a ship at sea.

"Lord, hear the great breakers!" exclaimed Mrs. Todd. "How they pound!—there, there! I always run of an idea that the sea knows anger these nights and gets full o' fight. I can hear the rote o' them old black ledges way down the thoroughfare. Calls up all those stormy verses in the Book o' Psalms; David he knew how old sea-goin' folks have to quake at the heart."

I thought as I had never thought before of such anxieties. The families of sailors and coastwise adventurers by sea must always be worrying about somebody, this side of the world or the other. There was hardly one of Mrs. Todd's elder acquaintances, men or women, who had not at some time or other made a sea voyage, and there was often no news until the voyagers themselves came back to bring it.

"There's a roaring high overhead, and a roaring in the deep sea," said Mrs. Todd solemnly, "and they battle together nights like this. No, I could n't sleep; some women folks always goes right to bed an' to sleep, so 's to forget, but 't ain't my way. Well, it 's a blessin' we don't all feel alike; there 's hardly any of our folks at sea to worry about, nowadays, but I can't help my feelin's, an' I got thinking of mother all alone, if William had happened to be out lobsterin' and could n't make the cove gettin' back."

"They will have a pleasant evening," I repeated. "Captain Bowden is the best of good company."

"Mother 'll make him some pancakes for his supper, like 's not," said Mrs. Todd, clicking her knitting needles and giving a pull at her yarn. Just then the old cat pushed open the unlatched door and came straight toward her mistress's lap. She was regarded severely as she stepped about and turned on the broad expanse, and then made herself into a round cushion of fur, but was not openly admonished. There was another great blast of wind overhead, and a puff of smoke came down the chimney.

"This makes me think o' the night Mis' Cap'n Tolland died," said Mrs. Todd, half to herself. "Folks used to say these gales only blew when somebody 's a-dyin', or the devil was a-comin' for his own, but the worst man I ever knew died a real pretty mornin' in June."

"You have never told me any ghost stories," said I; and such was the gloomy weather and the influence of the night that I was instantly filled with reluctance to have this suggestion followed. I had not chosen the best of moments; just before I spoke we had begun to feel as cheerful as possible. Mrs. Todd glanced doubtfully at the cat and then at me, with a strange absent look, and I was really afraid that she was going to tell me something that would haunt my thoughts on every dark stormy night as long as I lived.

"Never mind now; tell me to-morrow by daylight, Mrs. Todd," I hastened to say, but she still looked at me full of doubt and deliberation.

"Ghost stories!" she answered. "Yes, I don't know but I 've heard a plenty of 'em first an' last. I was just sayin' to myself that this is like the night Mis' Cap'n Tolland died. 'T was the great line storm in September all of thirty, or maybe forty, year ago. I ain't one that keeps much account o' time."

"Tolland? That's a name I have never heard in Dunnet," I said.

"Then you have n't looked well about the old part o' the buryin' ground, no'theast corner," replied Mrs. Todd. "All their women folks lies there; the sea's got most o' the men. They were a known family o' shipmasters in early times. Mother had a mate, Ellen Tolland, that she mourns to this day; died right in her bloom with quick consumption, but the rest o' that family was all boys but one, and older than she, an' they lived hard seafarin' lives an' all died hard. They were called very smart seamen. I 've heard that when the youngest went into one o' the old shippin' houses in Boston, the head o' the firm called out to him: 'Did you say Tolland from Dunnet? That's recommendation enough for any vessel!' There was some o' them old shipmasters as tough as iron, an' they had the name o' usin' their crews very severe, but there wa'n't a man that would n't rather sign with 'em an' take his chances, than with the slack ones that did n't know how to meet accidents."

II.

There was so long a pause, and Mrs. Todd still looked so absent-minded, that I was afraid she and the cat were growing drowsy together before the fire, and I should have no reminiscences at all. The wind struck the house again, so that we both started in our chairs and Mrs. Todd gave a curious, startled look at me. The cat lifted her head and listened too, in the silence that followed, while after the wind sank we were more conscious than ever of the awful roar of the sea. The house jarred now and then, in a strange, disturbing way.

"Yes, they'll have a beautiful evening out to the island," said Mrs. Todd again; but she did not say it gayly. I had not seen her before in her weaker moments.

"Who was Mrs. Captain Tolland?" I asked eagerly, to change the current of our thoughts.

"I never knew her maiden name; if I ever heard it, I 've gone an' forgot; 't would mean nothing to me," answered Mrs. Todd.

"She was a foreigner, an' he met with her out in the Island

o' Jamaica. They said she'd been left a widow with property. Land knows what become of it; she was French born, an' her first husband was a Portugee, or somethin'."

I kept silence now, a poor and insufficient question being worse than none.

"Cap'n John Tolland was the least smartest of any of 'em, but he was full smart enough, an' commanded a good brig at the time, in the sugar trade; he'd taken out a cargo o' pine lumber to the islands from somewheres up the river, an' had been loadin' for home in the port o' Kingston, an' had gone ashore that afternoon for his papers, an' remained afterwards 'long of three friends o' his, all shipmasters. They was havin' their suppers together in a tavern; 't was late in the evenin' an' they was more lively than usual, an' felt boyish; and over opposite was another house full o' company, real bright and pleasant lookin', with a lot o' lights, an' they heard somebody singin' very pretty to a guitar. They wa'n't in no go-to-meetin' condition, an' one of 'em, he slapped the table an' said, 'Le''s go over an' hear that lady sing!' an' over they all went, good honest sailors, but three sheets in the wind, and stepped in as if they was invited, an' made their bows inside the door, an' asked if they could hear the music; they were all respectable well-dressed men. They saw the woman that had the guitar, an' there was a company a-listenin', regular highbinders all of 'em; an' there was a long table all spread out with big candlesticks like little trees o' light, and a sight o' glass an' silver ware; an' part o' the men was young officers in uniform, an' the colored folks was steppin' round servin' 'em, an' they had the lady singin'. 'T was a wasteful scene, an' a loud talkin' company, an' though they was three sheets in the wind themselves there wa'n't one o' them cap'ns but had sense to perceive it. The others had pushed back their chairs, an' their decanters an' glasses was standin' thick about, an' they was teasin' the one that was singin' as if they'd just got her in to amuse 'em. But they quieted down; one o' the young officers had beautiful manners, an' invited the four cap'ns to join 'em, very polite; 't was a kind of public house, and after they'd all heard another song, he come to consult with 'em whether they wouldn't git up and dance a hornpipe or somethin' to the lady's music.

"They was all elderly men an' shipmasters, and owned property; two of 'em was church members in good standin'," continued Mrs. Todd loftily, "an' they wouldn't lend theirselves to no such kick-shows as that, an' spite o' bein' three sheets in the wind, as I have once observed; they waved aside the tumblers of wine the young officer was pourin' out for 'em so freehanded, and said they should rather be excused. An' when they all rose, still very dignified, as I've been well informed, and made their partin' bows and was goin' out, them young sports got round 'em an' tried to prevent 'em, and they had to push an' strive considerable, but out they come. There was this Cap'n Tolland and two Cap'n Bowdens, and the fourth was my own father." (Mrs. Todd spoke slowly, as if to impress the value of her authority.) "Two of them was very religious, upright men, but they would have their night off sometimes, all o' them old-fashioned cap'ns, when they was free of business and ready to leave port.

"An' they went back to their tavern an' got their bills paid, an' set down kind o' mad with everybody by the front windows, mistrusting some o' their tavern charges, like 's not, by that time, an' when they got tempered down, they watched the house over across, where the party was.

"There was a kind of a grove o' trees between the house an' the road, an' they heard the guitar a-goin' an' a-stoppin' short by turns, and pretty soon somebody began to screech, an' they saw a white dress come runnin' out through the bushes, an' tumbled over each other in their haste to offer help; an' out she come, with the guitar, cryin' into the street, and they just walked off four square with her amongst 'em, down toward the wharves where they felt more to home. They couldn't make out at first what 'twas she spoke,—Cap'n Lorenzo Bowden was well acquainted in Havre an' Bordeaux, an' spoke a poor quality o' French, an' she knew a little mite o' English, but not much; and they come somehow or other to discern that she was in real distress. Her husband and her children had died o' yellow fever; they'd all come up to Kingston from one o' the far Wind'ard Islands to get passage on a steamer to France, an' a negro had stole their money off her husband while he lay sick o' the fever, an' she had been befriended some, but the folks that knew about her had died too; it had been a dreadful run o' the fever that season, an' she fell at last to playin' an' singin' for hire, and for what money they'd throw to her round them harbor houses.

"'Twas a real hard case, an' when them cap'ns made out about it, there wa'n't one that meant to take leave without helpin' of her. They was pretty mellow, an' whatever they might lack o' prudence they more'n made up with charity: they didn't want to see nobody abused, an' she was sort of a pretty woman, an' they stopped in the street then an' there an' drew lots who should take her aboard, bein' all bound home. An' the lot fell to Cap'n Jonathan Bowden who did act discouraged; his vessel had but small accommodations, though he could stow a big freight, an' she was a dreadful slow sailer through bein' square as a box, an' his first wife, that was livin' then, was a dreadful jealous woman. He threw himself right onto the mercy o' Cap'n Tolland."

Mrs. Todd indulged herself for a short time in a season of calm reflection.

"I always thought they'd have done better, and more reasonable, to give her some money to pay her passage home to France, or wherever she may have wanted to go," she continued.

I nodded and looked for the rest of the story.

"Father told mother," said Mrs. Todd confidentially, "that Cap'n Jonathan Bowden an' Cap'n John Tolland had both taken a little more than usual; I wouldn't have you think, either, that they both wasn't the best o' men, an' they was solemn as owls, and argued the matter between 'em, an' waved aside the other two when they tried to put their oars in. An' spite o' Cap'n Tolland's bein' a settled old bachelor they fixed it that he was to take the prize on his brig; she was a fast sailer, and there was a good spare cabin or two where he'd sometimes carried passengers, but he'd filled 'em with bags o' sugar on his own account an' was loaded very heavy beside. He said he'd shift the sugar an' get along somehow, an' the last the other three cap'ns saw of the party was Cap'n John handing the lady into his bo't, guitar and all, an' off they all set tow'ds their ships with their men rowin' 'em in the bright moonlight down to Port Royal where the anchorage was, an' where they all lay, goin' out with the tide an' mornin' wind at break o' day. An' the others thought they heard music of the guitar, two o' the bo'ts kept well together, but it may have come from another source."

"Well; and then?" I asked eagerly after a pause. Mrs. Todd was almost laughing aloud over her knitting and nodding emphatically. We had forgotten all about the noise of the wind and sea.

"Lord bless you! he come sailing into Portland with his sugar, all in good time, an' they stepped right afore a justice o' the peace, and Cap'n John Tolland come paradin' home to Dunnet Landin' a married man. He owned one o' them thin, narrow-lookin' houses with one room each side o' the front door, and two slim black spruces spindlin' up against the front windows to make it gloomy inside. There was no horse nor cattle of course, though he owned pasture land, an' you could see rifts o' light right through the barn as you drove by. And there was a good excellent kitchen, but his sister reigned over that; she had a right to two rooms, and took the kitchen an' a bedroom that led out of it; an' bein' given no rights in the kitchen had angered the cap'n so they were n't on no kind o' speakin' terms. He preferred his old brig for comfort, but now and then, between voyages, he 'd come home for a few days, just to show he was master over his part o' the house, and show Eliza she could n't commit no trespass.

"They stayed a little while; 't was pretty spring weather, an' I used to see Cap'n John rollin' by with his arms full o' bundles from the store, lookin' as pleased and important as a boy; an' then they went right off to sea again, an' was gone a good many months. Next time he left her to live there alone, after they 'd stopped at home together some weeks, an' they said she suffered from bein' at sea, but some said that the owners would n't have a woman aboard. 'T was before father was lost on that last voyage of his, an' he and mother went up once or twice to see them. Father said there wa'n't a mite o' harm in her, but somehow or other a sight o' prejudice arose; it may have been caused by the remarks of Eliza an' her feelin's tow'ds her brother. Even my mother had no regard for Eliza Tolland. But mother asked the cap'n's wife to come with her one evenin' to a social circle that was down to the meetin'-house vestry, so she 'd get acquainted a little, an' she appeared

very pretty until they started to have some singin' to the me-
lodeon. Mari' Harris an' one o' the younger Caplin girls undertook to sing a duet, an' they sort o' flatted, an' she put her
hands right up to her ears, and give a little squeal, an' went
quick as could be an' give 'em the right notes, for she could
read the music like plain print, an' made 'em try it over again.
She was real willin' an' pleasant, but that did n't suit, an' she
made faces when they got it wrong. An' then there fell a dead
calm, an' we was all settin' round prim as dishes, an' my
mother, that never expects ill feelin', asked her if she would n't
sing somethin', an' up she got,—poor creatur', it all seems so
different to me now,—an' sung a lovely little song standin' in
the floor; it seemed to have something gay about it that kept
a-repeatin', an' nobody could help keepin' time, an' all of a
sudden she looked round at the tables and caught up a tin
plate that somebody 'd fetched a Washin'ton pie in, an' she
begun to drum on it with her fingers like one o' them tam-
bourines, an' went right on singin' faster an' faster, and next
minute she begun to dance a little pretty dance between the
verses, just as light and pleasant as a child. You could n't help
seein' how pretty 't was; we all got to trottin' a foot, an' some
o' the men clapped their hands quite loud, a-keepin' time,
't was so catchin', an' seemed so natural to her. There wa'n't
one of 'em but enjoyed it; she just tried to do her part, an'
some urged her on, till she stopped with a little twirl of her
skirts an' went to her place again by mother. And I can see
mother now, reachin' over an' smilin' an' pattin' her hand.

"But next day there was an awful scandal goin' in the parish, an' Mari' Harris reproached my mother to her face, an' I
never wanted to see her since, but I 've had to a good many
times. I said Mis' Tolland did n't intend no impropriety,—I
reminded her of David's dancin' before the Lord; but she said
such a man as David never would have thought o' dancin'
right there in the Orthodox vestry, and she felt I spoke with
irreverence.

"And next Sunday Mis' Tolland come walkin' into our
meeting, but I must say she acted like a cat in a strange garret,
and went right out down the aisle with her head in air, from
the pew Deacon Caplin had showed her into. 'T was just in
the beginning of the long prayer. I wish she 'd stayed

through, whatever her reasons were. Whether she'd expected somethin' different, or misunderstood some o' the pastor's remarks, or what 't was, I don't really feel able to explain, but she kind o' declared war, at least folks thought so, an' war 't was from that time. I see she was cryin', or had been, as she passed by me; perhaps bein' in meetin' was what had power to make her feel homesick and strange.

"Cap'n John Tolland was away fittin' out; that next week he come home to see her and say farewell. He was lost with his ship in the Straits of Malacca, and she lived there alone in the old house a few months longer till she died. He left her well off; 't was said he hid his money about the house and she knew where 't was. Oh, I expect you've heard that story told over an' over twenty times, since you've been here at the Landin'?"

"Never one word," I insisted.

"It was a good while ago," explained Mrs. Todd, with reassurance. "Yes, it all happened a great while ago."

III.

At this moment, with a sudden flaw of the wind, some wet twigs outside blew against the window panes and made a noise like a distressed creature trying to get in. I started with sudden fear, and so did the cat, but Mrs. Todd knitted away and did not even look over her shoulder.

"She was a good-looking woman; yes, I always thought Mis' Tolland was good-looking, though she had, as was reasonable, a sort of foreign cast, and she spoke very broken English, no better than a child. She was always at work about her house, or settin' at a front window with her sewing; she was a beautiful hand to embroider. Sometimes, summer evenings, when the windows was open, she'd set an' drum on her guitar, but I don't know as I ever heard her sing but once after the cap'n went away. She appeared very happy about havin' him, and took on dreadful at partin' when he was down here on the wharf, going back to Portland by boat to take ship for that last v'y'ge. He acted kind of ashamed, Cap'n John did; folks about here ain't so much accustomed to show their feelings. The whistle had blown an' they was waitin' for him to get aboard, an' he was put to it to know what to do and treated her very affectionate in spite of all impatience; but mother happened to be there and she went an' spoke, and I remember what a comfort she seemed to be. Mis' Tolland clung to her then, and she would n't give a glance after the boat when it had started, though the captain was very eager a-wavin' to her. She wanted mother to come home with her an' would n't let go her hand, and mother had just come in to stop all night with me an' had plenty o' time ashore, which did n't always happen, so they walked off together, an' 't was some considerable time before she got back.

" 'I want you to neighbor with that poor lonesome creatur',' says mother to me, lookin' reproachful. 'She 's a stranger in a strange land,' says mother. 'I want you to make her have a sense that somebody feels kind to her.'

" 'Why, since that time she flaunted out o' meetin', folks have felt she liked other ways better 'n our 'n,' says I. I was provoked, because I 'd had a nice supper ready, an' mother 'd let it wait so long 't was spoiled. 'I hope you 'll like your supper!' I told her. I was dreadful ashamed afterward of speakin' so to mother.

" 'What consequence is my supper?' says she to me; mother can be very stern, — 'or your comfort or mine, beside letting a foreign person an' a stranger feel so desolate; she 's done the best a woman could do in her lonesome place, and she asks nothing of anybody except a little common kindness. Think if 't was you in a foreign land!'

"And mother set down to drink her tea, an' I set down humbled enough over by the wall to wait till she finished. An' I did think it all over, an' next day I never said nothin', but I put on my bonnet, and went to see Mis' Cap'n Tolland, if 't was only for mother 's sake. 'T was about three quarters of a mile up the road here, beyond the schoolhouse. I forgot to tell you that the cap'n had bought out his sister 's right at three or four times what 't was worth, to save trouble, so they 'd got clear o' her, an' I went round into the side yard sort o' friendly an' sociable, rather than stop an' deal with the knocker an' the front door. It looked so pleasant an' pretty I was glad I come; she had set a little table for supper, though 't was still early, with a white cloth on it, right out under an old apple tree close by the house. I noticed 't was same as with me at home, there was only one plate. She was just coming out with a dish; you could n't see the door nor the table from the road.

"In the few weeks she'd been there she'd got some bloomin' pinks an' other flowers next the doorstep. Somehow it looked as if she'd known how to make it homelike for the cap'n. She asked me to set down; she was very polite, but she looked very mournful, and I spoke of mother, an' she put down her dish and caught holt o' me with both hands an' said my mother was an angel. When I see the tears in her eyes 't was all right between us, and we were always friendly after that, and mother had us come out and make a little visit that summer; but she come a foreigner and she went a foreigner, and never was anything but a stranger among our folks. She taught me a sight o' things about herbs I never knew before nor since; she was well acquainted with the virtues o' plants. She'd act awful secret about some things too, an' used to work charms for herself sometimes, an' some o' the neighbors told to an' fro after she died that they knew enough not to provoke her, but 't was all nonsense; 't is the believin' in such things that causes 'em to be any harm, an' so I told 'em," confided Mrs. Todd contemptuously. "That first night I stopped to tea with her she'd cooked some eggs with some herb or other sprinkled all through, and 't was she that first led me to discern mushrooms; an' she went right down on her knees in my garden here when she saw I had my different officious herbs. Yes, 't was she that learned me the proper use o' parsley too; she was a beautiful cook."

Mrs. Todd stopped talking, and rose, putting the cat gently in the chair, while she went away to get another stick of apple-tree wood. It was not an evening when one wished to let the fire go down, and we had a splendid bank of bright coals. I had always wondered where Mrs. Todd had got such an unusual knowledge of cookery, of the varieties of mushrooms, and the use of sorrel as a vegetable, and other blessings of that sort. I had long ago learned that she could vary her omelettes like a child of France, which was indeed a surprise in Dunnet Landing.

IV.

All these revelations were of the deepest interest, and I was ready with a question as soon as Mrs. Todd came in and had well settled the fire and herself and the cat again.

"I wonder why she never went back to France, after she was left alone?"

"She come here from the French islands," explained Mrs. Todd. "I asked her once about her folks, an' she said they were all dead; 't was the fever took 'em. She made this her home, lonesome as 't was; she told me she had n't been in France since she was 'so small,' and measured me off a child o' six. She 'd lived right out in the country before, so that part wa'n't unusual to her. Oh yes, there was something very strange about her, and she had n't been brought up in high circles nor nothing o' that kind. I think she 'd been really pleased to have the cap'n marry her an' give her a good home, after all she 'd passed through, and leave her free with his money an' all that. An' she got over bein' so strange-looking to me after a while, but 't was a very singular expression: she wore a fixed smile that wa'n't a smile; there wa'n't no light behind it, same 's a lamp can't shine if it ain't lit. I don't know just how to express it, 't was a sort of made countenance."

One could not help thinking of Sir Philip Sidney's phrase, "A made countenance, between simpering and smiling."

"She took it hard, havin' the captain go off on that last voyage," Mrs. Todd went on. "She said somethin' told her when they was partin' that he would never come back. He was lucky to speak a home-bound ship this side o' the Cape o' Good Hope, an' got a chance to send her a letter, an' that cheered her up. You often felt as if you was dealin' with a child's mind, for all she had so much information that other folks had n't. I was a sight younger than I be now, and she made me imagine new things, and I got interested watchin' her an' findin' out what she had to say, but you could n't get to no affectionateness with her. I used to blame me sometimes; we used to be real good comrades goin' off for an afternoon, but I never give her a kiss till the day she laid in her coffin and it come to my heart there wa'n't no one else to do it."

"And Captain Tolland died," I suggested after a while.

"Yes, the cap'n was lost," said Mrs. Todd, "and of course word didn't come for a good while after it happened. The letter come from the owners to my uncle, Cap'n Lorenzo Bowden, who was in charge of Cap'n Tolland's affairs at home, and he come right up for me an' said I must go with him to the house. I had known what it was to be a widow, myself, for near a year, an' there was plenty o' widow women along this coast that the sea had made desolate, but I never saw a heart break as I did then.

"'T was this way: we walked together along the road, me an' uncle Lorenzo. You know how it leads straight from just above the schoolhouse to the brook bridge, and their house was just this side o' the brook bridge on the left hand; the cellar's there now, and a couple or three good-sized gray birches growin' in it. And when we come near enough I saw that the best room, this way, where she most never set, was all lighted up, and the curtains up so that the light shone bright down the road, and as we walked, those lights would dazzle and dazzle in my eyes, and I could hear the guitar a-goin', an' she was singin'. She heard our steps with her quick ears and come running to the door with her eyes a-shinin', an' all that set look gone out of her face, an' begun to talk French, gay as a bird, an' shook hands and behaved very pretty an' girlish, sayin' 't was her fête day. I didn't know what she meant then. And she had gone an' put a wreath o' flowers on her hair an' wore a handsome gold chain that the cap'n had given her; an' there she was, poor creatur', makin' believe have a party all alone in her best room; 't was prim enough to discourage a person, with too many chairs set close to the walls, just as the cap'n's mother had left it, but she had put sort o' long garlands on the walls, droopin' very graceful, and a sight of green boughs in the corners, till it looked lovely, and all lit up with a lot o' candles."

"Oh dear!" I sighed. "Oh, Mrs. Todd, what did you do?"

"She beheld our countenances," answered Mrs. Todd solemnly. "I expect they was telling everything plain enough, but Cap'n Lorenzo spoke the sad words to her as if he had been her father; and she wavered a minute and then over she went on the floor before we could catch hold of her, and then we tried to bring her to herself and failed, and at last we carried her upstairs, an' I told uncle to run down and put out the lights, and then go fast as he could for Mrs. Begg, being very experienced in sickness, an' he so did. I got off her clothes and her poor wreath, and I cried as I done it. We both stayed there that night, and the doctor said 't was a shock when he come in the morning; he'd been over to Black Island an' had to stay all night with a very sick child."

"You said that she lived alone some time after the news came," I reminded Mrs. Todd then.

"Oh yes, dear," answered my friend sadly, "but it wa'n't what you'd call livin'; no, it was only dyin', though at a snail's pace. She never went out again those few months, but for a while she could manage to get about the house a little, and do what was needed, an' I never let two days go by without seein' her or hearin' from her. She never took much notice as I came an' went except to answer if I asked her anything. Mother was the one who gave her the only comfort."

"What was that?" I asked softly.

"She said that anybody in such trouble ought to see their minister, mother did, and one day she spoke to Mis' Tolland, and found that the poor soul had been believin' all the time that there were n't any priests here. We'd come to know she was a Catholic by her beads and all, and that had set some narrow minds against her. And mother explained it just as she would to a child; and uncle Lorenzo sent word right off somewheres up river by a packet that was bound up the bay, and the first o' the week a priest come by the boat, an' uncle Lorenzo was on the wharf 'tendin' to some business; so they just come up for me, and I walked with him to show him the house. He was a kind-hearted old man; he looked so benevolent an' fatherly I could ha' stopped an' told him my own troubles; yes, I was satisfied when I first saw his face, an' when poor Mis' Tolland beheld him enter the room, she went right down on her knees and clasped her hands together to him as if he'd come to save her life, and he lifted her up and blessed her, an' I left 'em together, and slipped out into the open field and walked there in sight so if they needed to call me, and I had my own thoughts. At last I saw him at the door; he had to catch the return boat. I meant to walk back with him and offer him some supper, but he said no, and said he was comin' again if needed, and signed me to go into the house to her, and shook his head in a way that meant he understood everything. I can see him now; he walked with a cane, rather tired and feeble; I wished somebody would come along, so 's to carry him down to the shore.

"Mis' Tolland looked up at me with a new look when I went in, an' she even took hold o' my hand and kept it. He had put some oil on her forehead, but nothing anybody could do would keep her alive very long; 't was his medicine for the soul rather 'n the body. I helped her to bed, and next morning she could n't get up to dress her, and that was Monday, and she began to fail, and 't was Friday night she died." (Mrs. Todd spoke with unusual haste and lack of detail.) "Mrs. Begg and I watched with her, and made everything nice and proper, and after all the ill will there was a good number gathered to the funeral. 'T was in Reverend Mr. Bascom's day, and he done very well in his prayer, considering he could n't fill in with mentioning all the near connections by name as was his habit. He spoke very feeling about her being a stranger and twice widowed, and all he said about her being reared among the heathen was to observe that there might be roads leadin' up to the New Jerusalem from various points. I says to myself that I guessed quite a number must ha' reached there that wa'n't able to set out from Dunnet Landin'!"

Mrs. Todd gave an odd little laugh as she bent toward the firelight to pick up a dropped stitch in her knitting, and then I heard a heartfelt sigh.

" 'T was most forty years ago," she said; "most everybody 's gone a'ready that was there that day."

v.

Suddenly Mrs. Todd gave an energetic shrug of her shoulders, and a quick look at me, and I saw that the sails of her narrative were filled with a fresh breeze.

"Uncle Lorenzo, Cap'n Bowden that I have referred to"—

"Certainly!" I agreed with eager expectation.

"He was the one that had been left in charge of Cap'n John Tolland's affairs, and had now come to be of unforeseen importance.

"Mrs. Begg an' I had stayed in the house both before an' after Mis' Tolland's decease, and she was now in haste to be gone, having affairs to call her home; but uncle come to me as the exercises was beginning, and said he thought I'd better remain at the house while they went to the buryin' ground. I couldn't understand his reasons, an' I felt disappointed, bein' as near to her as most anybody; 't was rough weather, so mother couldn't get in, and didn't even hear Mis' Tolland was gone till next day. I just nodded to satisfy him, 't wa'n't no time to discuss anything. Uncle seemed flustered; he'd gone out deep-sea fishin' the day she died, and the storm I told you of rose very sudden, so they got blown off way down the coast beyond Monhegan, and he'd just got back in time to dress himself and come.

"I set there in the house after I'd watched her away down the straight road far's I could see from the door; 't was a little short walkin' funeral an' a cloudy sky, so everything looked dull an' gray, an' it crawled along all in one piece, same's walking funerals do, an' I wondered how it ever come to the Lord's mind to let her begin down among them gay islands all heat and sun, and end up here among the rocks with a north wind blowin'. 'T was a gale that begun the afternoon before she died, and had kept blowin' off an' on ever since. I'd thought more than once how glad I should be to get home an' out o' sound o' them black spruces a-beatin' an' scratchin' at the front windows.

"I set to work pretty soon to put the chairs back, an' set outdoors some that was borrowed, an' I went out in the kitchen, an' I made up a good fire in case somebody come an' wanted a cup o' tea; but I didn't expect any one to travel way back to the house unless 't was uncle Lorenzo. 'T was growin' so chilly that I fetched some kindlin' wood and made fires in both the fore rooms. Then I set down an' begun to feel as usual, and I got my knittin' out of a drawer. You can't be sorry for a poor creatur' that's come to the end o' all her troubles; my only discomfort was I thought I'd ought to feel worse at losin' her than I did; I was younger then than I be now. And as I set there, I begun to hear some long notes o' dronin' music from upstairs that chilled me to the bone."

Mrs. Todd gave a hasty glance at me.

"Quick 's I could gather me, I went right upstairs to see what 't was," she added eagerly, "an' 't was just what I might ha' known. She 'd always kept her guitar hangin' right against the wall in her room; 't was tied by a blue ribbon, and there was a window left wide open; the wind was veerin' a good deal, an' it slanted in and searched the room. The strings was jarrin' yet.

" 'T was growin' pretty late in the afternoon, an' I begun to feel lonesome as I should n't now, and I was disappointed at having to stay there, the more I thought it over, but after a while I saw Cap'n Lorenzo polin' back up the road all alone, and when he come nearer I could see he had a bundle under his arm and had shifted his best black clothes for his every-day ones. I run out and put some tea into the teapot and set it back on the stove to draw, an' when he come in I reached down a little jug o' spirits,—Cap'n Tolland had left his house well provisioned as if his wife was goin' to put to sea same 's himself, an' there she 'd gone an' left it. There was some cake that Mis' Begg an' I had made the day before. I thought that uncle an' me had a good right to the funeral supper, even if there wa'n't any one to join us. I was lookin' forward to my cup o' tea; 't was beautiful tea out of a green lacquered chest that I 've got now."

"You must have felt very tired," said I, eagerly listening.

"I was 'most beat out, with watchin' an' tendin' and all," answered Mrs. Todd, with as much sympathy in her voice as if she were speaking of another person. "But I called out to uncle as he came in, 'Well, I expect it 's all over now, an' we 've all done what we could. I thought we 'd better have some tea or somethin' before we go home. Come right out in the kitchen, sir,' says I, never thinking but we only had to let the fires out and lock up everything safe an' eat our refreshment, an' go home.

" 'I want both of us to stop here to-night,' says uncle, looking at me very important.

" 'Oh, what for?' says I, kind o' fretful.

" 'I 've got my proper reasons,' says uncle. 'I 'll see you well satisfied, Almira. Your tongue ain't so easy-goin' as some o' the women folks, an' there's property here to take charge of that you don't know nothin' at all about.'

" 'What do you mean?' says I.

" 'Cap'n Tolland acquainted me with his affairs; he hadn't no sort o' confidence in nobody but me an' his wife, after he was tricked into signin' that Portland note, an' lost money. An' she didn't know nothin' about business; but what he didn't take to sea to be sunk with him he's hid somewhere in this house. I expect Mis' Tolland may have told you where she kept things?' said uncle.

"I see he was dependin' a good deal on my answer," said Mrs. Todd, "but I had to disappoint him; no, she had never said nothin' to me.

" 'Well, then, we've got to make a search,' says he, with considerable relish; but he was all tired and worked up, and we set down to the table, an' he had somethin', an' I took my desired cup o' tea, and then I begun to feel more interested.

" 'Where you goin' to look first?' says I, but he give me a short look an' made no answer, and begun to mix me a very small portion out of the jug, in another glass. I took it to please him; he said I looked tired, speakin' real fatherly, and I did feel better for it, and we set talkin' a few minutes, an' then he started for the cellar, carrying an old ship's lantern he fetched out o' the stairway an' lit.

" 'What are you lookin' for, some kind of a chist?' I inquired, and he said yes. All of a sudden it come to me to ask who was the heirs; Eliza Tolland, Cap'n John's own sister, had never demeaned herself to come near the funeral, and uncle Lorenzo faced right about and begun to laugh, sort o' pleased. I thought queer of it; 't wa'n't what he'd taken, which would be nothin' to an old weathered sailor like him.

" 'Who's the heir?' says I the second time.

" 'Why, it's *you*, Almiry,' says he; and I was so took aback I set right down on the turn o' the cellar stairs.

" 'Yes 't is,' said uncle Lorenzo. 'I'm glad of it too. Some thought she didn't have no sense but foreign sense, an' a poor stock o' that, but she said you was friendly to her, an' one day after she got news of Tolland's death, an' I had fetched up his will that left everything to her, she said she was goin' to make a writin', so's you could have things after she was gone, an' she give five hundred to me for bein' executor. Square Pease fixed up the paper, an' she signed it; it's all accordin' to law.' There, I begun to cry," said Mrs. Todd; "I couldn't help it. I wished I had her back again to do somethin' for, an' to make her know I felt sisterly to her more'n I'd ever showed, an' it come over me 't was all too late, an' I cried the more, till uncle showed impatience, an' I got up an' stumbled along down cellar with my apern to my eyes the greater part of the time.

"'I'm goin' to have a clean search,' says he; 'you hold the light.' An' I held it, and he rummaged in the arches an' under the stairs, an' over in some old closet where he reached out bottles an' stone jugs an' canted some kags an' one or two casks, an' chuckled well when he heard there was somethin' inside, — but there wa'n't nothin' to find but things usual in a cellar, an' then the old lantern was givin' out an' we come away.

"'He spoke to me of a chist, Cap'n Tolland did,' says uncle in a whisper. 'He said a good sound chist was as safe a bank as there was, an' I beat him out of such nonsense, 'count o' fire an' other risks.' 'There's no chist in the rooms above,' says I; 'no, uncle, there ain't no sea-chist, for I've been here long enough to see what there was to be seen.' Yet he wouldn't feel contented till he'd mounted up into the toploft; 't was one o' them single, hip-roofed houses that don't give proper accommodation for a real garret, like Cap'n Littlepage's down here at the Landin'. There was broken furniture and rubbish, an' he let down a terrible sight o' dust into the front entry, but sure enough there wasn't no chist. I had it all to sweep up next day.

"'He must have took it away to sea,' says I to the cap'n, an' even then he didn't want to agree, but we was both beat out. I told him where I'd always seen Mis' Tolland get her money from, and we found much as a hundred dollars there in an old red morocco wallet. Cap'n John had been gone a good while a'ready, and she had spent what she needed.

'Twas in an old desk o' his in the settin' room that we found the wallet."

"At the last minute he may have taken his money to sea," I suggested.

"Oh yes," agreed Mrs. Todd. "He did take considerable to make his venture to bring home, as was customary, an' that was drowned with him as uncle agreed; but he had other property in shipping, and a thousand dollars invested in Portland in a cordage shop, but 't was about the time shipping begun to decay, and the cordage shop failed, and in the end I wa'n't so rich as I thought I was goin' to be for those few minutes on the cellar stairs. There was an auction that accumulated something. Old Mis' Tolland, the cap'n's mother, had heired some good furniture from a sister: there was above thirty chairs in all, and they're apt to sell well. I got over a thousand dollars when we come to settle up, and I made uncle take his five hundred; he was getting along in years and had met with losses in navigation, and he left it back to me when he died, so I had a real good lift. It all lays in the bank over to Rockland, and I draw my interest fall an' spring, with the little Mr. Todd was able to leave me; but that's kind o' sacred money; 't was earnt and saved with the hope o' youth, an' I'm very particular what I spend it for. Oh yes, what with ownin' my house, I've been enabled to get along very well, with prudence!" said Mrs. Todd contentedly.

"But there was the house and land," I asked,— "what became of that part of the property?"

Mrs. Todd looked into the fire, and a shadow of disapproval flitted over her face.

"Poor old uncle!" she said, "he got childish about the matter. I was hoping to sell at first, and I had an offer, but he always run of an idea that there was more money hid away, and kept wanting me to delay; an' he used to go up there all alone and search, and dig in the cellar, empty an' bleak as 't was in winter weather or any time. An' he'd come and tell me he'd dreamed he found gold behind a stone in the cellar wall, or somethin'. And one night we all see the light o' fire up that way, an' the whole Landin' took the road, and run to look, and the Tolland property was all in a light blaze. I expect the old gentleman had dropped fire about; he said he'd been up there to see if everything was safe in the afternoon. As for the land, 't was so poor that everybody used to have a joke that the Tolland boys preferred to farm the sea instead. It's 'most all grown up to bushes now, where it ain't poor water grass in the low places. There's some upland that has a pretty view, after you cross the brook bridge. Years an' years after she died, there was some o' her flowers used to come up an' bloom in the door garden. I brought two or three that was unusual down here; they always come up and remind me of her, constant as the spring. But I never did want to fetch home that guitar, some way or 'nother; I wouldn't let it go at the auction, either. It was hangin' right there in the house when the fire took place. I've got some o' her other little things scattered about the house: that picture on the mantel-piece belonged to her."

I had often wondered where such a picture had come from, and why Mrs. Todd had chosen it; it was a French print of the statue of the Empress Josephine in the Savane at old Fort Royal, in Martinique.

VI.

Mrs. Todd drew her chair closer to mine; she held the cat and her knitting with one hand as she moved, but the cat was so warm and so sound asleep that she only stretched a lazy paw in spite of what must have felt like a slight earthquake. Mrs. Todd began to speak almost in a whisper.

"I ain't told you all," she continued; "no, I haven't spoken of all to but very few. The way it came was this," she said solemnly, and then stopped to listen to the wind, and sat for a moment in deferential silence, as if she waited for the wind to speak first. The cat suddenly lifted her head with quick excitement and gleaming eyes, and her mistress was leaning forward toward the fire with an arm laid on either knee, as if they were consulting the glowing coals for some augury. Mrs. Todd looked like an old prophetess as she sat there with the firelight shining on her strong face; she was posed for some great painter. The woman with the cat was as unconscious and as mysterious as any sibyl of the Sistine Chapel.

"There, that's the last struggle o' the gale," said Mrs. Todd, nodding her head with impressive certainty and still looking into the bright embers of the fire. "You'll see!" She gave me another quick glance, and spoke in a low tone as if we might be overheard.

" 'T was such a gale as this the night Mis' Tolland died. She appeared more comfortable the first o' the evenin'; and Mrs. Begg was more spent than I, bein' older, and a beautiful nurse that was the first to see and think of everything, but perfectly quiet an' never asked a useless question. You remember her funeral when you first come to the Landing? And she consented to goin' an' havin' a good sleep while she could, and left me one o' those good little pewter lamps that burnt whale oil an' made plenty o' light in the room, but not too bright to be disturbin'.

"Poor Mis' Tolland had been distressed the night before, an' all that day, but as night come on she grew more and more easy, an' was layin' there asleep; 't was like settin' by any sleepin' person, and I had none but usual thoughts. When the wind lulled and the rain, I could hear the seas, though more distant than this, and I don' know's I observed any other sound than what the weather made; 't was a very solemn feelin' night. I set close by the bed; there was times she looked to find somebody when she was awake. The light was on her face, so I could see her plain; there was always times when she wore a look that made her seem a stranger you'd never set eyes on before. I did think what a world it was that her an' me should have come together so, and she have nobody but Dunnet Landin' folks about her in her extremity. 'You're one o' the stray ones, poor creatur',' I said. I remember those very words passin' through my mind, but I saw reason to be glad she had some comforts, and didn't lack friends at the last, though she'd seen misery an' pain. I was glad she was quiet; all day she'd been restless, and we couldn't understand what she wanted from her French speech. We had the window open to give her air, an' now an' then a gust would strike that guitar that was on the wall and set it swinging by the blue ribbon, and soundin' as if somebody begun to play it. I come near takin' it down, but you never know what'll fret a sick person an' put 'em on the rack, an' that guitar was one o' the few things she'd brought with her."

I nodded assent, and Mrs. Todd spoke still lower.

"I set there close by the bed; I'd been through a good deal for some days back, and I thought I might's well be droppin' asleep too, bein' a quick person to wake. She looked to me as if she might last a day longer, certain, now she'd got more comfortable, but I was real tired, an' sort o' cramped as watchers will get, an' a fretful feeling begun to creep over me such as they often do have. If you give way, there ain't no support for the sick person; they can't count on no composure o' their own. Mis' Tolland moved then, a little restless, an' I forgot me quick enough, an' begun to hum out a little part of a hymn tune just to make her feel everything was as usual an' not wake up into a poor uncertainty. All of a sudden she set right up in bed with her eyes wide open, an' I stood an' put my arm behind her; she had n't moved like that for days. And she reached out both her arms toward the door, an' I looked the way she was lookin', an' I see some one was standin' there against the dark. No, 't wa'n't Mis' Begg; 't was somebody a good deal shorter than Mis' Begg. The lamplight struck across the room between us. I could n't tell the shape, but 't was a woman's dark face lookin' right at us; 't wa'n't but an instant I could see. I felt dreadful cold, and my head begun to swim; I thought the light went out; 't wa'n't but an instant, as I say, an' when my sight come back I could n't see nothing there. I was one that did n't know what it was to faint away, no matter what happened; time was I felt above it in others, but 't was somethin' that made poor human natur' quail. I saw very plain while I could see; 't was a pleasant enough face, shaped somethin' like Mis' Tolland's, and a kind of expectin' look.

"No, I don't expect I was asleep," Mrs. Todd assured me quietly, after a moment's pause, though I had not spoken. She gave a heavy sigh before she went on. I could see that the recollection moved her in the deepest way.

"I suppose if I had n't been so spent an' quavery with long watchin', I might have kept my head an' observed much better," she added humbly; "but I see all I could bear. I did try to act calm, an' I laid Mis' Tolland down on her pillow, an' I was a-shakin' as I done it. All she did was to look up to me so satisfied and sort o' questioning, an' I looked back to her.

" 'You saw her, did n't you?' she says to me, speakin' perfectly reasonable. ' 'T is my mother,' she says again, very feeble, but lookin' straight up at me, kind of surprised with the
pleasure, and smiling as if she saw I was overcome, an' would
have said more if she could, but we had hold of hands. I see
then her change was comin', but I did n't call Mis' Begg, nor
make no uproar. I felt calm then, an' lifted to somethin' different as I never was since. She opened her eyes just as she
was goin'—

" 'You saw her, did n't you?' she said the second time, an' I
says, *Yes, dear, I did; you ain't never goin' to feel strange an'
lonesome no more.'* An' then in a few quiet minutes 't was all
over. I felt they 'd gone away together. No, I wa'n't alarmed
afterward; 't was just that one moment I could n't live under,
but I never called it beyond reason I should see the other
watcher. I saw plain enough there was somebody there with
me in the room.

VII.

" 'T was just such a night as this Mis' Tolland died," repeated Mrs. Todd, returning to her usual tone and leaning
back comfortably in her chair as she took up her knitting.
" 'T was just such a night as this. I 've told the circumstances
to but very few; but I don't call it beyond reason. When folks
is goin' 't is all natural, and only common things can jar upon
the mind. You know plain enough there 's somethin' beyond
this world; the doors stand wide open. 'There 's somethin' of
us that must still live on; we 've got to join both worlds together an' live in one but for the other.' The doctor said that
to me one day, an' I never could forget it; he said 't was in
one o' his old doctor 's books."

We sat together in silence in the warm little room; the rain
dropped heavily from the eaves, and the sea still roared, but
the high wind had done blowing. We heard the far complaining fog horn of a steamer up the Bay.

"There goes the Boston boat out, pretty near on time," said
Mrs. Todd with satisfaction. "Sometimes these late August
storms 'll sound a good deal worse than they really be. I do

hate to hear the poor steamers callin' when they're bewildered in thick nights in winter, comin' on the coast. Yes, there goes the boat; they'll find it rough at sea, but the storm's all over."

William's Wedding

I.

THE HURRY of life in a large town, the constant putting aside of preference to yield to a most unsatisfactory activity, began to vex me, and one day I took the train, and only left it for the eastward-bound boat. Carlyle says somewhere that the only happiness a man ought to ask for is happiness enough to get his work done; and against this the complexity and futile ingenuity of social life seems a conspiracy. But the first salt wind from the east, the first sight of a lighthouse set boldly on its outer rock, the flash of a gull, the waiting procession of seaward-bound firs on an island, made me feel solid and definite again, instead of a poor, incoherent being. Life was resumed, and anxious living blew away as if it had not been. I could not breathe deep enough or long enough. It was a return to happiness.

The coast had still a wintry look; it was far on in May, but all the shore looked cold and sterile. One was conscious of going north as well as east, and as the day went on the sea grew colder, and all the warmer air and bracing strength and stimulus of the autumn weather, and storage of the heat of summer, were quite gone. I was very cold and very tired when I came at evening up the lower bay, and saw the white houses of Dunnet Landing climbing the hill. They had a friendly look, these little houses, not as if they were climbing up the shore, but as if they were rather all coming down to meet a fond and weary traveler, and I could hardly wait with patience to step off the boat. It was not the usual eager company on the wharf. The coming-in of the mail-boat was the one large public event of a summer day, and I was disappointed at seeing none of my intimate friends but Johnny Bowden, who had evidently done nothing all winter but grow, so that his short sea-smitten clothes gave him a look of poverty.

Johnny's expression did not change as we greeted each other, but I suddenly felt that I had shown indifference and inconvenient delay by not coming sooner; before I could make an apology he took my small portmanteau, and walking before me in his old fashion he made straight up the hilly road toward Mrs. Todd's. Yes, he was much grown—it had never occurred to me the summer before that Johnny was likely, with the help of time and other forces, to grow into a young man; he was such a well-framed and well-settled chunk of a boy that nature seemed to have set him aside as something finished, quite satisfactory and entirely completed.

The wonderful little green garden had been enchanted away by winter. There were a few frost-bitten twigs and some thin shrubbery against the fence, but it was a most unpromising small piece of ground. My heart was beating like a lover's as I passed it on the way to the door of Mrs. Todd's house, which seemed to have become much smaller under the influence of winter weather.

'She has n't gone away?' I asked Johnny Bowden with a sudden anxiety just as we reached the doorstep.

'Gone away!' he faced me with blank astonishment,—'I see her settin' by Mis' Caplin's window, the one nighest the road, about four o'clock!' And eager with suppressed news of my coming he made his entrance as if the house were a burrow.

Then on my homesick heart fell the voice of Mrs. Todd. She stopped, through what I knew to be excess of feeling, to rebuke Johnny for bringing in so much mud, and I dallied without for one moment during the ceremony; then we met again face to face.

II.

'I dare say you can advise me what shapes they are going to wear. My meetin'-bunnit ain't going to do me again this year; no! I can't expect 't would do me forever,' said Mrs. Todd, as soon as she could say anything. 'There! do set down and tell me how you have been! We 've got a weddin' in the family, I s'pose you know?'

'A wedding!' said I, still full of excitement.

'Yes; I expect if the tide serves and the line-storm don't overtake him they 'll come in and appear out on Sunday. I should n't have concerned me about the bunnit for a month yet, nobody would notice, but havin' an occasion like this I shall show consider'ble. 'T will be an ordeal for William!'

'For *William*!' I exclaimed. 'What do you mean, Mrs. Todd?'

She gave a comfortable little laugh. 'Well, the Lord's seen reason at last an' removed Mis' Cap'n Hight up to the farm, an' I don't know but the weddin's going to be this week. Esther's had a great deal of business disposin' of her flock, but she's done extra well—the folks that owns the next place goin' up country are well off. 'T is elegant land north side o' that bleak ridge, an' one o' the boys has been Esther's right-hand man of late. She instructed him in all matters, and after she markets the early lambs he's goin' to take the farm on halves, an' she's give the refusal to him to buy her out within two years. She's reserved the buryin'-lot, an' the right o' way in, an'—'

I couldn't stop for details. I demanded reassurance of the central fact.

'William going to be married?' I repeated; whereat Mrs. Todd gave me a searching look that was not without scorn.

'Old Mis' Hight's funeral was a week ago Wednesday, and 't was very well attended,' she assured me after a moment's pause.

'Poor thing!' said I, with a sudden vision of her helplessness and angry battle against the fate of illness; 'it was very hard for her.'

'I thought it was hard for Esther!' said Mrs. Todd without sentiment.

III.

I had an odd feeling of strangeness: I missed the garden, and the little rooms, to which I had added a few things of my own the summer before, seemed oddly unfamiliar. It was like the hermit crab in a cold new shell,—and with the windows shut against the raw May air, and a strange silence and gray-ness of the sea all that first night and day of my visit, I felt as if I had after all lost my hold of that quiet life.

Mrs. Todd made the apt suggestion that city persons were prone to run themselves to death, and advised me to stay and get properly rested now that I had taken the trouble to come. She did not know how long I had been homesick for the conditions of life at the Landing the autumn before—it was natural enough to feel a little unsupported by compelling incidents on my return.

Some one has said that one never leaves a place, or arrives at one, until the next day! But on the second morning I woke with the familiar feeling of interest and ease, and the bright May sun was streaming in, while I could hear Mrs. Todd's heavy footsteps pounding about in the other part of the house as if something were going to happen. There was the first golden robin singing somewhere close to the house, and a lovely aspect of spring now, and I looked at the garden to see that in the warm night some of its treasures had grown a hand's breadth; the determined spikes of yellow daffies stood tall against the doorsteps, and the bloodroot was unfolding leaf and flower. The belated spring which I had left behind farther south had overtaken me on this northern coast. I even saw a presumptuous dandelion in the garden border.

It is difficult to report the great events of New England; expression is so slight, and those few words which escape us in moments of deep feeling look but meagre on the printed page. One has to assume too much of the dramatic fervor as one reads; but as I came out of my room at breakfast-time I met Mrs. Todd face to face, and when she said to me, 'This weather'll bring William in after her; 'tis their happy day!' I felt something take possession of me which ought to communicate itself to the least sympathetic reader of this cold page. It is written for those who have a Dunnet Landing of their own: who either kindly share this with its writer, or possess another.

'I ain't seen his comin' sail yet; he'll be likely to dodge round among the islands so he'll be the less observed,' continued Mrs. Todd. 'You can get a dory up the bay, even a clean new painted one, if you know as how, keepin' it against the high land.' She stepped to the door and looked off to sea as she spoke. I could see her eye follow the gray shores to and fro, and then a bright light spread over her calm face. 'There he comes, and he's striking right in across the open bay like a man!' she said with splendid approval. 'See, there he comes! Yes, there's William, and he's bent his new sail.'

I looked too, and saw the fleck of white no larger than a gull's wing yet, but present to her eager vision.

I was going to France for the whole long summer that year, and the more I thought of such an absence from these simple scenes the more dear and delightful they became. Santa Teresa says that the true proficiency of the soul is not in much thinking, but in much loving, and sometimes I believed that I had never found love in its simplicity as I had found it at Dunnet Landing in the various hearts of Mrs. Blackett and Mrs. Todd and William. It is only because one came to know them, these three, loving and wise and true, in their own habitations. Their counterparts are in every village in the world, thank heaven, and the gift to one's life is only in its discernment. I had only lived in Dunnet until the usual distractions and artifices of the world were no longer in control, and I saw these simple natures clear. 'The happiness of life is in its recognitions. It seems that we are not ignorant of these truths, and even that we believe them; but we are so little accustomed to think of them, they are so strange to us—'

'Well now, deary me!' said Mrs. Todd, breaking into exclamation; 'I've got to fly round—I thought he'd have to beat; he can't sail far on that tack, and he won't be in for a good hour yet—I expect he's made every arrangement, but he said he shouldn't go up after Esther unless the weather was good, and I declare it did look doubtful this morning.'

I remembered Esther's weather-worn face. She was like a Frenchwoman who had spent her life in the fields. I remembered her pleasant look, her childlike eyes, and thought of the astonishment of joy she would feel now in being taken care of and tenderly sheltered from wind and weather after all these years. They were going to be young again now, she and William, to forget work and care in the spring weather. I could hardly wait for the boat to come to land, I was so eager to see his happy face.

'Cake an' wine I'm goin' to set 'em out!' said Mrs. Todd. 'They won't stop to set down for an ordered meal, they'll want to get right out home quick's they can. Yes, I'll give 'em

some cake an' wine—I've got a rare plum-cake from my best
receipt, and a bottle o' wine that the old Cap'n Denton of all
give me, one of two, the day I was married, one we had and
one we saved, and I've never touched it till now. He said
there wa'n't none like it in the State o' Maine.'

It was a day of waiting, that day of spring; the May
weather was as expectant as our fond hearts, and one could
see the grass grow green hour by hour. The warm air was full
of birds, there was a glow of light on the sea instead of the
cold shining of chilly weather which had lingered late. There
was a look on Mrs. Todd's face which I saw once and could
not meet again. She was in her highest mood. Then I went
out early for a walk, and when I came back we sat in different
rooms for the most part. There was such a thrill in the air that
our only conversation was in her most abrupt and incisive
manner. She was knitting, I believe, and as for me I dallied
with a book. I heard her walking to and fro, and the door
being wide open now, she went out and paced the front walk
to the gate as if she walked a quarter-deck.

It is very solemn to sit waiting for the great events of life—
most of us have done it again and again—to be expectant of
life or expectant of death gives one the same feeling.

But at the last Mrs. Todd came quickly back from the gate,
and standing in the sunshine at the door, she beckoned me as
if she were a sibyl.

'I thought you comprehended everything the day you was
up there,' she added with a little more patience in her tone,
but I felt that she thought I had lost instead of gained since
we parted the autumn before.

'William's made this pretext o' goin' fishin' for the last
time. 'T would n't done to take notice, 't would scared him to
death! but there never was nobody took less comfort out o'
forty years courtin'. No, he won't have to make no further
pretexts,' said Mrs. Todd, with an air of triumph.

'Did you know where he was going that day?' I asked with
a sudden burst of admiration at such discernment.

'I did!' replied Mrs. Todd grandly.

'Oh! but that pennyroyal lotion,' I indignantly protested,
remembering that under pretext of mosquitoes she had besmeared the poor lover in an awful way—why, it was outra-

geous! Medea could not have been more conscious of high ultimate purposes.

'Darlin',' said Mrs. Todd, in the excitement of my arrival and the great concerns of marriage, 'he's got a beautiful shaped face, and they pison him very unusual—you wouldn't have had him present himself to his lady all lop-sided with a mosquito-bite? Once when we was young I rode up with him, and they set upon him in concert the minute we entered the woods.' She stood before me reproachfully, and I was conscious of deserved rebuke. 'Yes, you've come just in the nick of time to advise me about a bunnit. They say large bows on top is liable to be worn.'

IV.

The period of waiting was one of direct contrast to these high moments of recognition. The very slowness of the morning hours wasted that sense of excitement with which we had begun the day. Mrs. Todd came down from the mount where her face had shone so bright, to the cares of common life, and some acquaintances from Black Island for whom she had little natural preference or liking came, bringing a poor, sickly child to get medical advice. They were noisy women with harsh, clamorous voices, and they stayed a long time. I heard the clink of teacups, however, and could detect no impatience in the tones of Mrs. Todd's voice; but when they were at last going away, she did not linger unduly over her leave-taking, and returned to me to explain that they were people she had never liked, and they had made an excuse of a friendly visit to save their doctor's bill; but she pitied the poor little child, and knew beside that the doctor was away.

'I had to give 'em the remedies right out,' she told me; 'they wouldn't have bought a cent's worth o' drugs down to the store for that dwindlin' thing. She needed feedin' up, and I don't expect she gets milk enough; they're great butter-makers down to Black Island, 'tis excellent pasturage, but they use no milk themselves, and their butter is heavy laden with salt to make weight, so that you'd think all their ideas come down from Sodom.'

She was very indignant and very wistful about the pale little girl. 'I wish they'd let me kept her,' she said. 'I kind of advised it, and her eyes was so wishful in that pinched face when she heard me, so that I could see what was the matter with her, but they said she wa'n't prepared. Prepared!' And Mrs. Todd snuffed like an offended war-horse, and departed; but I could hear her still grumbling and talking to herself in high dudgeon an hour afterward.

At the end of that time her arch enemy, Mari' Harris, appeared at the side-door with a gingham handkerchief over her head. She was always on hand for the news, and made some formal excuse for her presence, — she wished to borrow the weekly paper. Captain Littlepage, whose housekeeper she was, had taken it from the post-office in the morning, but had forgotten, being of failing memory, what he had done with it.

'How is the poor old gentleman?' asked Mrs. Todd with solicitude, ignoring the present errand of Maria and all her concerns.

I had spoken the evening before of intended visits to Captain Littlepage and Elijah Tilley, and I now heard Mrs. Todd repeating my inquiries and intentions, and fending off with unusual volubility of her own the curious questions that were sure to come. But at last Maria Harris secured an opportunity and boldly inquired if she had not seen William ashore early that morning.

'I don't say he wasn't,' replied Mrs. Todd; 'Thu'sday's a very usual day with him to come ashore.'

'He was all dressed up,' insisted Maria—she really had no sense of propriety. 'I didn't know but they was going to be married?'

Mrs. Todd did not reply. I recognized from the sounds that reached me that she had retired to the fastnesses of the kitchen-closet and was clattering the tins.

'I expect they'll marry soon anyway,' continued the visitor.

'I expect they will if they want to,' answered Mrs. Todd. 'I don't know nothin' 't all about it; that's what folks say.' And presently the gingham handkerchief retreated past my window.

'I routed her, horse and foot,' said Mrs. Todd proudly, coming at once to stand at my door. 'Who's coming now?' as two figures passed inward bound to the kitchen.

They were Mrs. Begg and Johnny Bowden's mother, who were favorites, and were received with Mrs. Todd's usual civilities. Then one of the Mrs. Caplins came with a cup in hand to borrow yeast. On one pretext or another nearly all our acquaintances came to satisfy themselves of the facts, and see what Mrs. Todd would impart about the wedding. But she firmly avoided the subject through the length of every call and errand, and answered the final leading question of each curious guest with her non-committal phrase, 'I don't know nothin' 't all about it; that's what folks say!'

She had just repeated this for the fourth or fifth time and shut the door upon the last comers, when we met in the little front entry. Mrs. Todd was not in a bad temper, but highly amused. 'I've been havin' all sorts o' social privileges, you may have observed. They didn't seem to consider that if they could only hold out till afternoon they'd know as much as I did. There wa'n't but one o' the whole sixteen that showed real interest, the rest demeaned themselves to ask out o' cheap curiosity; no, there wa'n't but one showed any real feelin'.'

'Miss Maria Harris you mean?' and Mrs. Todd laughed.

'Certain, dear,' she agreed, 'how you do understand poor human natur'!'

A short distance down the hilly street stood a narrow house that was newly painted white. It blinded one's eyes to catch the reflection of the sun. It was the house of the minister, and a wagon had just stopped before it; a man was helping a woman to alight, and they stood side by side for a moment, while Johnny Bowden appeared as if by magic, and climbed to the wagon-seat. Then they went into the house and shut the door. Mrs. Todd and I stood close together and watched; the tears were running down her cheeks. I watched Johnny Bowden, who made light of so great a moment by so handling the whip that the old white Caplin horse started up from time to time and was inexorably stopped as if he had some idea of running away. There was something in the back of the wagon which now and then claimed the boy's attention;

he leaned over as if there were something very precious left in his charge; perhaps it was only Esther's little trunk going to its new home.

At last the door of the parsonage opened, and two figures came out. The minister followed them and stood in the doorway, delaying them with parting words; he could not have thought it was a time for admonition.

'He's all alone; his wife's up to Portland to her sister's,' said Mrs. Todd aloud, in a matter-of-fact voice. 'She's a nice woman, but she might ha' talked too much. There! see, they're comin' here. I didn't know how 't would be. Yes, they're comin' up to see us before they go home. I declare, if William ain't lookin' just like a king!'

Mrs. Todd took one step forward, and we stood and waited. The happy pair came walking up the street, Johnny Bowden driving ahead. I heard a plaintive little cry from time to time to which in the excitement of the moment I had not stopped to listen; but when William and Esther had come and shaken hands with Mrs. Todd and then with me, all in silence, Esther stepped quickly to the back of the wagon, and unfastening some cords returned to us carrying a little white lamb. She gave a shy glance at William as she fondled it and held it to her heart, and then, still silent, we went into the house together. The lamb had stopped bleating. It was lovely to see Esther carry it in her arms.

When we got into the house, all the repression of Mrs. Todd's usual manner was swept away by her flood of feeling. She took Esther's thin figure, lamb and all, to her heart and held her there, kissing her as she might have kissed a child, and then held out her hand to William and they gave each other the kiss of peace. This was so moving, so tender, so free from their usual fetters of self-consciousness, that Esther and I could not help giving each other a happy glance of comprehension. I never saw a young bride half so touching in her happiness as Esther was that day of her wedding. We took the cake and wine of the marriage feast together, always in silence, like a true sacrament, and then to my astonishment I found that sympathy and public interest in so great an occasion were going to have their way. I shrank from the thought of William's possible sufferings, but he welcomed both the first group of neighbors and the last with heartiness; and when at last they had gone, for there were thoughtless loiterers in Dunnet Landing, I made ready with eager zeal and walked with William and Esther to the water-side. It was only a little way, and kind faces nodded reassuringly from the windows, while kind voices spoke from the doors. Esther carried the lamb on one arm; she had found time to tell me that its mother had died that morning and she could not bring herself to the thought of leaving it behind. She kept the other hand on William's arm until we reached the landing. Then he shook hands with me, and looked me full in the face to be sure I understood how happy he was, and stepping into the boat held out his arms to Esther—at last she was his own.

I watched him make a nest for the lamb out of an old sea-cloak at Esther's feet, and then he wrapped her own shawl round her shoulders, and finding a pin in the lapel of his Sunday coat he pinned it for her. She looked at him fondly while he did this, and then glanced up at us, a pretty, girlish color brightening her cheeks.

We stood there together and watched them go far out into the bay. The sunshine of the May day was low now, but there was a steady breeze, and the boat moved well.

'Mother'll be watching for them,' said Mrs. Todd. 'Yes, mother'll be watching all day, and waiting. She'll be so happy to have Esther come.'

We went home together up the hill, and Mrs. Todd said nothing more; but we held each other's hand all the way.

SELECTED STORIES
AND SKETCHES

Contents

An Autumn Holiday

I HAD started early in the afternoon for a long walk; it was just the weather for walking, and I went across the fields with a delighted heart. The wind came straight in from the sea, and the sky was bright blue; there was a little tinge of red still lingering on the maples, and my dress brushed over the late golden-rods, while my old dog, who seemed to have taken a new lease of youth, jumped about wildly and raced after the little birds that flew up out of the long brown grass — the constant little chickadees, that would soon sing before the coming of snow. But this day brought no thought of winter; it was one of the October days when to breathe the air is like drinking wine, and every touch of the wind against one's face is a caress: like a quick, sweet kiss, that wind is. You have a sense of companionship; it is a day that loves you.

I went strolling along, with this dear idle day for company; it was a pleasure to be alive, and to go through the dry grass, and to spring over the stone walls and the shaky pasture fences. I stopped by each of the stray apple-trees that came in my way, to make friends with it, or to ask after its health, if it were an old friend. These old apple-trees make very charming bits of the world in October; the leaves cling to them later than to the other trees, and the turf keeps short and green underneath; and in this grass, which was frosty in the morning, and has not quite dried yet, you can find some cold little cider apples, with one side knurly, and one shiny bright red or yellow cheek. They are wet with dew, these little apples, and a black ant runs anxiously over them when you turn them round and round to see where the best place is to bite. There will almost always be a bird's nest in the tree, and it is most likely to be a robin's nest. The prehistoric robins must have been cave dwellers, for they still make their nests as much like cellars as they can, though they follow the new fashion and build them aloft. One always has a thought of spring at the sight of a robin's nest. It is so little while ago that it was spring, and we were so glad to have the birds come back, and the life of the new year was just showing itself; we were

571

looking forward to so much growth and to the realization
and perfection of so many things. I think the sadness of autumn, or the pathos of it, is like that of elderly people. We
have seen how the flowers looked when they bloomed and
have eaten the fruit when it was ripe; the questions have had
their answer, the days we waited for have come and gone.
Everything has stopped growing. And so the children have
grown to be men and women, their lives have been lived, the
autumn has come. We have seen what our lives would be like
when we were older; success or disappointment, it is all over
at any rate. Yet it only makes one sad to think it is autumn
with the flowers or with one's own life, when one forgets that
always and always there will be the spring again.

I am very fond of walking between the roads. One grows
so familiar with the highways themselves. But once leap the
fence and there are a hundred roads that you can take, each
with its own scenery and entertainment. Every walk of this
kind proves itself a tour of exploration and discovery, and the
fields of my own town, which I think I know so well, are
always new fields. I find new ways to go, new sights to see,
new friends among the things that grow, and new treasures
and pleasures every summer; and later, when the frosts have
come and the swamps have frozen, I can go everywhere I like
all over my world.

That afternoon I found something I had never seen before—a little grave alone in a wide pasture which had once
been a field. The nearest house was at least two miles away,
but by hunting for it I found a very old cellar, where the
child's home used to be, not very far off, along the slope. It
must have been a great many years ago that the house had
stood there; and the small slate head-stone was worn away by
the rain and wind, so there was nothing to be read, if indeed
there had ever been any letters on it. It had looked many a
storm in the face, and many a red sunset. I suppose the woods
near by had grown and been cut, and grown again, since it
was put there. There was an old sweet-brier bush growing on
the short little grave, and in the grass underneath I found a
ground-sparrow's nest. It was like a little neighborhood, and
I have felt ever since as if I belonged to it; and I wondered
then if one of the young ground-sparrows was not always

sent to take the nest when the old ones were done with it, so they came back in the spring year after year to live there, and there were always the stone and the sweet-brier bush and the birds to remember the child. It was such a lonely place in that wide field under the great sky, and yet it was so comfortable too; but the sight of the little grave at first touched me strangely, and I tried to picture to myself the procession that came out from the house the day of the funeral, and I thought of the mother in the evening after all the people had gone home, and how she missed the baby, and kept seeing the new grave out here in the twilight as she went about her work. I suppose the family moved away, and so all the rest were buried elsewhere.

I often think of this place, and I link it in my thoughts with something I saw once in the water when I was out at sea: a little boat that some child had lost, that had drifted down the river and out to sea; too long a voyage, for it was a sad little wreck, with even its white sail of a hand-breadth half under water, and its twine rigging trailing astern. It was a silly little boat, and no loss, except to its owner, to whom it had seemed as brave and proud a thing as any ship of the line to you and me. It was a shipwreck of his small hopes, I suppose, and I can see it now, the toy of the great winds and waves, as it floated on its way, while I sailed on mine, out of sight of land.

The little grave is forgotten by everybody but me, I think: the mother must have found the child again in heaven a very long time ago: but in the winter I shall wonder if the snow has covered it well, and next year I shall go to see the sweet-brier bush when it is in bloom. God knows what use that life was, the grave is such a short one, and nobody knows whose little child it was; but perhaps a thousand people in the world to-day are better because it brought a little love into the world that was not there before.

I sat so long here in the sun that the dog, after running after all the birds, and even chasing crickets, and going through a great piece of affectation in barking before an empty woodchuck's hole to kill time, came to sit patiently in front of me, as if he wished to ask when I would go on. I had never been in this part of the pasture before. It was at one side of the way I usually took, so presently I went on to find a favorite track of mine, half a mile to the right, along the bank of a brook. There had been heavy rains the week before, and I found more water than usual running, and the brook was apparently in a great hurry. It was very quiet along the shore of it; the frogs had long ago gone into winter-quarters, and there was not one to splash into the water when he saw me coming. I did not see a musk-rat either, though I knew where their holes were by the piles of fresh-water mussel shells that they had untidily thrown out at their front door. I thought it might be well to hunt for mussels myself, and crack them in search of pearls, but it was too serene and beautiful a day. I was not willing to disturb the comfort of even a shell-fish. It was one of the days when one does not think of being tired: the scent of the dry everlasting flowers, and the freshness of the wind, and the cawing of the crows, all come to me as I think of it, and I remember that I went a long way before I began to think of going home again. I knew I could not be far from a cross-road, and when I climbed a low hill I saw a house which I was glad to make the end of my walk—for a time, at any rate. It was some time since I had seen the old woman who lived there, and I liked her dearly, and was sure of a welcome. I went down through the pasture lane, and just then I saw my father drive away up the road, just too far for me to make him hear when I called. That seemed too bad at first, until I remembered that he would come back again over the same road after a while, and in the mean time I could make my call. The house was low and long and unpainted, with a great many frost-bitten flowers about it. Some hollyhocks were bowed down despairingly, and the morning-glory vines were more miserable still. Some of the smaller plants had been covered to keep them from freezing, and were braving out a few more days, but no shelter would avail them much longer. And already nobody minded whether the gate was shut or not, and part of the great flock of hens were marching proudly about among the wilted posies, which they had stretched their necks wistfully through the fence for all summer. I heard the noise of spinning in the house, and my dog scurried off after the cat as I went in the door. I saw Miss Polly Marsh and her sister, Mrs. Snow, stepping back and forward together spinning yarn at a pair of big wheels. The wheels made such a noise with their whir and creak, and my friends were talking so fast as they twisted and turned the yarn, that they did not hear my footstep, and I stood in the doorway watching them, it was such a quaint and pretty sight. They went together like a pair of horses, and kept step with each other to and fro. They were about the same size, and were cheerful old bodies, looking a good deal alike, with their checked handkerchiefs over their smooth gray hair, their dark gowns made short in the skirts, and their broad little feet in gray stockings and low leather shoes without heels. They stood straight, and though they were quick at their work they moved stiffly; they were talking busily about some one.

"I could tell by the way the doctor looked that he did n't think there was much of anything the matter with her," said Miss Polly Marsh. " 'You need n't tell me,' says I, the other day, when I see him at Miss Martin's. 'She 'd be up and about this minute if she only had a mite o' resolution;' and says he, 'Aunt Polly, you 're as near right as usual;' " and the old lady stopped to laugh a little. "I told him that wa'n't saying much," said she, with an evident consciousness of the underlying compliment and the doctor's good opinion. "I never knew one of that tribe that had n't a queer streak and was n't shif'less; but they 're tougher than ellum roots;" and she gave the wheel an emphatic turn, while Mrs. Snow reached for more rolls of wool, and happened to see me.

"Wherever did you come from?" said they, in great surprise. "Why, you was n't anywhere in sight when I was out speaking to the doctor," said Mrs. Snow. "Oh, come over horseback, I suppose. Well, now, we 're pleased to see ye."

"No," said I, "I walked across the fields. It was too pleasant to stay in the house, and I have n't had a long walk for some time before." I begged them not to stop spinning, but they insisted that they should not have turned the wheels a half-dozen times more, even if I had not come, and they pushed them back to the wall before they came to sit down to talk with me over their knitting—for neither of them were ever known to be idle. Mrs. Snow was only there for a visit; she was a widow, and lived during most of the year with her son; and Aunt Polly was at home but seldom herself, as she was a famous nurse, and was often in demand all through that part of the country. I had known her all my days. Everybody was fond of the good soul, and she had been one of the most useful women in the world. One of my pleasantest memories is of a long but not very painful illness one winter, when she came to take care of me. There was no end either to her stories or her kindness. I was delighted to find her at home that afternoon, and Mrs. Snow also.

Aunt Polly brought me some of her gingerbread, which she knew I liked, and a stout little pitcher of milk, and we sat there together for a while, gossiping and enjoying ourselves. I told all the village news that I could think of, and I was just tired enough to know it, and to be contented to sit still for a while in the comfortable three-cornered chair by the little front window. The October sunshine lay along the clean kitchen floor, and Aunt Polly darted from her chair occasionally to catch stray little wisps of wool which the breeze through the door blew along from the wheels. There was a gay string of red peppers hanging over the very high mantelshelf, and the wood-work in the room had never been painted, and had grown dark brown with age and smoke and scouring. The clock ticked solemnly, as if it were a judge giving the laws of time, and felt itself to be the only thing that did not waste it. There was a bouquet of asparagus and some late sprigs of larkspur and white petunias on the table underneath, and a Leavitt's Almanac lay on the county paper, which was itself lying on the big Bible, of which Aunt Polly made a point of reading two chapters every day in course. I remember her saying, despairingly, one night, half to herself, "I don' know but I may skip the Chronicles next time," but I have never to this day believed that she did. They asked me at once to come into the best room, but I liked the old kitchen best. "Who was it that you were talking about as I came in?" said I. "You said you didn't believe there was much the matter with her." And Aunt Polly clicked her knitting-needles faster, and told me that it was Mary Susan Ash, over by Little Creek.

"They're dreadful nervous, all them Ashes," said Mrs. Snow. "You know young Joe Adams's wife, over our way, is a sister to her, and she's forever a-doctorin'. Poor fellow! *he's* got a drag. I'm real sorry for Joe; but, land sakes alive! he might 'a known better. They said she had an old green band-box with a gingham cover, that was stowed full o' vials, that she moved with the rest of her things when she was married, besides some she car'd in her hands. I guess she ain't in no more hurry to go than any of the rest of us. I've lost every mite of patience with her. I was over there last week one day, and she'd had a call from the new supply—you know Adams's folks is Methodists—and he was took in by her. She made out she'd got the consumption, and she told how many complaints she had, and what a sight o' medicine she took, and she groaned and sighed, and her voice was so weak you could n't more than just hear it. I stepped right into the bed-room after he'd been prayin' with her, and was taking leave. You'd thought, by what he said, she was going right off then. She was coughing dreadful hard, and I knew she had n't no more cough than I had. So says I, 'What's the matter, Ada-line? I'll get ye a drink of water. Something in your throat, I s'pose. I hope you won't go and get cold, and have a cough.' She looked as if she could 'a bit me, but I was just as pleasant 's could be. Land! to see her laying there, I suppose the poor young fellow thought she was all gone. He meant well. I wish he had seen her eating apple-dumplings for dinner. She felt better 'long in the first o' the afternoon before he come. I says to her, right before him, that I guessed them dumplings did her good, but she never made no answer. She will have these dyin' spells. I don't know 's she can help it, but she need n't act as if it was a credit to anybody to be sick and laid up. Poor Joe, he come over for me last week another day, and said she'd been havin' spasms, and asked me if there wa'n't something I could think of. 'Yes,' says I; 'you just take a pail o' stone-cold water, and throw it square into her face; that'll bring her out of it;' and he looked at me a minute, and then he burst out a-laughing—he could n't help it. He's too good to her; that's the trouble."

"You never said that to her about the dumplings?" said Aunt Polly, admiringly. "Well, I should n't ha' dared;" and she rocked and knitted away faster than ever, while we all laughed. "Now with Mary Susan it's different. I suppose she does have the neurology, and she's a poor broken-down creature. I do feel for her more than I do for Adaline. She was always a willing girl, and she worked herself to death, and she can't help these notions, nor being an Ash neither."

"I'm the last one to be hard on anybody that's sick, and in trouble," said Mrs. Snow.

"Bless you, she set up with Ad'line herself three nights in one week, to my knowledge. It's more'n I would do," said Aunt Polly, as if there were danger that I should think Mrs. Snow's kind heart to be made of flint.

"It ain't what I call watching," said she, apologetically. "We both doze off, and then when the folks come in in the morning she'll tell what a sufferin' night she's had. She likes to have it said she has to have watchers."

"It's strange what a queer streak there is running through the whole of 'em," said Aunt Polly, presently. "It always was so, far back's you can follow 'em. Did you ever hear about that great-uncle of theirs that lived over to the other side o' Denby, over to what they call the Denby Meadows? We had a cousin o' my father's that kept house for him (he was a single man), and I spent most of a summer and fall with her once when I was growing up. She seemed to want company: it was a lonesome sort of a place."

"There! I don't know when I have thought to' that," said Mrs. Snow, looking much amused. "What stories you did use to tell, after you come home, about the way he used to act! Dear sakes! she used to keep us laughing till we was tired. Do tell her about him, Polly; she'll like to hear."

"Well, I've forgot a good deal about it: you see it was much as fifty years ago. I wasn't more than seventeen or eighteen years old. He was a very respectable man, old Mr. Dan'el Gunn was, and a cap'n in the militia in his day. Cap'n Gunn, they always called him. He was well off, but he got sunstruck, and never was just right in his mind afterward. When he was getting over his sickness after the stroke he was very wandering, and at last he seemed to get it into his head that he was his own sister Patience that died some five or six years before: she was single too, and she always lived with him. They said when he got so's to sit up in his arm-chair of an afternoon, when he was getting better, he fought 'em dreadfully because they fetched him his own clothes to put on; he said they was brother Dan'el's clothes. So, sure enough, they got out an old double gown, and let him put it on, and he was as peaceable as could be. The doctor told 'em to humor him, but they thought it was a fancy he took, and he would forget it; but the next day he made 'em get the double gown again, and a cap too, and there he used to set up alongside of his bed as prim as a dish. When he got round again so he could set up all day, they thought he wanted the dress; but no; he seemed to be himself, and had on his own clothes just as usual in the morning; but when he took his nap after dinner and waked up again, he was in a dreadful frame o' mind, and had the trousers and coat off in no time, and said he was Patience. He used to fuss with some knitting-work he got hold of somehow; he was good-natured as could be, and sometimes he would make 'em fetch him the cat, because Patience used to have a cat that set in her lap while she knit. I wasn't there then, you know, but they used to tell me about it. Folks used to call him Miss Dan'el Gunn.

"He'd been that way some time when I went over. I'd heard about his notions, and I was scared of him at first, but I found out there wasn't no need. Don't you know I was sort o' 'fraid to go, 'Lizabeth, when Cousin Statiry sent for me after she went home from that visit she made here? She'd told us about him, but sometimes, 'long at the first of it, he used to be cross. He never was after I went there. He was a clever, kind-hearted man, if ever there was one," said Aunt Polly, with decision. "He used to go down to the corner to the store sometimes in the morning, and he would see to business. And before he got feeble sometimes he would work out on the farm all the morning, stiddy as any of the men; but after he come in to dinner he would take off his coat, if he had it on, and fall asleep in his arm-chair, or on a l'unge there was in his bedroom, and when he waked up he would be sort of bewildered for a while, and then he'd step round quick's he could, and get his dress out o' the clothes-press, and the cap, and put 'em on right over the rest of his clothes. He was always small-featured and smooth-shaved, and I don' know as, to come in sudden, you would have thought he was a man, except his hair stood up short and straight all on the top of his head, as men-folks had a fashion o' combing their hair then, and I must say he did make a dreadful ordinary-looking woman. The neighbors got used to his ways, and, land! I never thought nothing of it after the first week or two.

"His sister's clothes that he wore first was too small for him, and so my cousin Statiry, that kep' his house, she made him a linsey-woolsey dress with a considerable short skirt, and he was dreadful pleased with it, she said, because the other one never would button over good, and showed his wais'coat, and she and I used to make him caps; he used to wear the kind all the old women did then, with a big crown, and close round the face. I've got some laid away up-stairs now that was my mother's—she wore caps very young, mother did. His nephew that lived with him carried on the farm, and managed the business, but he always treated the cap'n as if he was head of everything there. Everybody pitied the cap'n; folks respected him; but you couldn't help laughing, to save ye. We used to try to keep him in, afternoons, but we couldn't always."

"Tell her about that day he went to meeting," said Mrs. Snow.

"Why, one of us always used to stay to home with him; we took turns; and somehow or 'nother he never offered to go, though by spells he would be constant to meeting in the morning. Why, bless you, you never'd think anything ailed him a good deal of the time, if you saw him before noon, though sometimes he would be freaky, and hide himself in the barn, or go over in the woods, but we always kept an eye on him. But this Sunday there was going to be a great occasion. Old Parson Croden was going to preach; he was thought more of than anybody in this region: you've heard tell of him a good many times, I s'pose. He was getting to be old, and didn't preach much. He had a colleague, they set so much by him in his parish, and I didn't know's I'd ever get another chance to hear him, so I didn't want to stay to home, and neither did Cousin Statiry; and Jacob Gunn, old Mr. Gunn's nephew, he said it might be the last time ever he'd hear Parson Croden, and he set in the seats anyway; so we talked it all over, and we got a young boy to come and set 'long of the cap'n till we got back. He hadn't offered to go anywhere of an afternoon for a long time. I s'pose he thought women ought to be stayers at home according to Scripture.

"Parson Ridley—his wife was a niece to old Dr. Croden—and the old doctor they was up in the pulpit, and the choir was singing the first hymn—it was a fuguing tune, and they was doing their best: seems to me it was 'Canterbury New.' Yes, it was; I remember I thought how splendid it sounded, and Jacob Gunn he was a-leading off; and I happened to look down the aisle, and who should I see but the poor old cap'n in his cap and gown parading right into meeting before all the folks! There! I wanted to go through the floor. Everybody 'most had seen him at home, but, my goodness! to have him come into meeting!"

"What did you do?" said I.

"Why, nothing," said Miss Polly; "there was nothing *to* do. I thought I should faint away; but I called Cousin Statiry's 'tention, and she looked dreadful put to it for a minute; and then says she, 'Open the door for him; I guess he won't make no trouble,' and, poor soul, he didn't. But to see him come up the aisle! He'd fixed himself nice as he could, poor creatur; he'd raked out Miss Patience's old Navarino bonnet with green ribbons and a willow feather, and set it on right over his cap, and he had her bead bag on his arm, and her turkey-tail fan that he'd got out of the best room; and he come with little short steps up to the pew: and I s'posed he'd set by the door; but no, he made to go by us, up into the corner where she used to set, and took her place, and spread his dress out nice, and got his handkerchief out o' his bag, just's he'd seen her do. He took off his bonnet all of a sudden, as if he'd forgot it, and put it under the seat, like he did his hat—that was the only thing he did that any woman wouldn't have done—and the crown of his cap was bent some. I thought die I should. The pew was one of them up aside the pulpit, a square one, you know, right at the end of the right-hand aisle, so I could see the length of it and out of the door, and there stood that poor boy we'd left to keep the cap'n company, looking as pale as ashes. We found he'd tried every way to keep the old gentleman at home, but he said he got f'erce as could be, so he didn't dare to say no more, and Cap'n Gunn drove him back twice to the house, and that's why he got in so late. I didn't know but it was the boy that had set him on to go to meeting when I see him walk in, and I could 'a wrung his neck; but I guess I misjudged him; he was called a stiddy boy. He married a daughter of Ichabod Pinkham's over to Oak Plains, and I saw a son of his when I was taking care of Miss West last spring through that lung fever—looked like his father. I wish I'd thought to tell him about that Sunday. I heard he was waiting on that pretty Becket girl, the orphan one that lives with Nathan Becket. Her father and mother was both lost at sea, but she's got property."

"What did they say in church when the captain came in, Aunt Polly?" said I.

"Well, a good many of them laughed—they couldn't help it, to save them; but the cap'n he was some hard o' hearin', so he never noticed it, and he set there in the corner and fanned him, as pleased and satisfied as could be. The singers they had the worst time, but they had just come to the end of a verse, and they played on the instruments a good while in between, but I could see 'em shake, and I s'pose the tune did stray a little, though they went through it well. And after the first fun of it was over, most of the folks felt bad. You see, the cap'n had been very much looked up to, and it was his misfortune, and he set there quiet, listening to the preaching. I see some tears in some o' the old folks' eyes: they hated to see him so broke in his mind, you know. There was more than usual of 'em out that day; they knew how bad he'd feel if he realized it. A good Christian man he was, and dreadful precise, I've heard 'em say."

"Did he ever go again?" said I.

"I seem to forget," said Aunt Polly. "I dare say. I wasn't there but from the last of June into November, and when I went over again it wasn't for three years, and the cap'n had been dead some time. His mind failed him more and more along at the last. But I'll tell you what he did do, and it was the week after that very Sunday, too. He heard it given out from the pulpit that the Female Missionary Society would meet with Mis' William Sands the Thursday night o' that week—the sewing society, you know; and he looked round to us real knowing; and Cousin Statiry, says she to me, under her bonnet, 'You don't s'pose he'll want to go?' and I like to have laughed right out. But sure enough he did, and what do you suppose but he made us fix over a handsome black watered silk for him to wear, that had been his sister's best dress. He said he'd outgrown it dreadful quick. Cousin Statiry she wished to heaven she'd thought to put it away, for Jacob had given it to her, and she was meaning to make it over for herself; but it didn't do to cross the cap'n and Jacob Gunn gave Statiry another one—the best he could get, but it wasn't near so good a piece, she thought. He set everything by Statiry, and so did the cap'n, and well they might.

"We hoped he'd forget all about it the next day; but he didn't; and I always thought well of those ladies, they treated him so handsome, and tried to make him enjoy himself. He did eat a great supper; they kep' a-piling up his plate with everything. I couldn't help wondering if some of 'em would have put themselves out much if it had been some poor flighty old woman. The cap'n he was as polite as could be, and when Jacob come to walk home with him he kissed 'em all round and asked 'em to meet at his house. But the greatest was—land! I don't know when I've thought so much about those times—one afternoon he was setting at home in the keeping-room, and Statiry was there, and Deacon Abel Pinkham stopped in to see Jacob Gunn about building some fence, and he found he'd gone to mill, so he waited a while, talking friendly, as they expected Jacob might be home; and the cap'n was as pleased as could be, and he urged the deacon to stop to tea. And when he went away, says he to Statiry, in a dreadful knowing way, 'Which of us do you consider the deacon come to see?' You see, the deacon was a widower. Bless you! when I first come home I used to set everybody laughing, but I forget most of the things now. There was one day, though"—

"Here comes your father," said Mrs. Snow. "Now we mustn't let him go by or you'll have to walk 'way home." And Aunt Polly hurried out to speak to him, while I took my great bunch of golden-rod, which already drooped a little, and followed her, with Mrs. Snow, who confided to me that the captain's nephew Jacob had offered to Polly that summer she was over there, and she never could see why she didn't have him: only love goes where it is sent, and Polly wasn't one to marry for what she could get if she did n't like the man. There was plenty that would have said yes, and thank you too, sir, to Jacob Gunn.

That was a pleasant afternoon. I reached home when it was growing dark and chilly, and the early autumn sunset had almost faded in the west. It was a much longer way home around by the road than by the way I had come across the fields.

From a Mournful Villager

LATELY I have been thinking, with much sorrow, of the approaching extinction of front yards, and of the type of New England village character and civilization with which they are associated. Formerly, because I lived in an old-fashioned New England village, it would have been hard for me to imagine that there were parts of the country where the Front yard, as I knew it, was not in fashion, and that Grounds (however small) had taken its place. No matter how large a piece of land lay in front of a house in old times, it was still a front yard, in spite of noble dimension and the skill of practiced gardeners.

There are still a good many examples of the old manner of out-of-door life and customs, as well as a good deal of the old-fashioned provincial society, left in the eastern parts of the New England States; but put side by side with the society that is American rather than provincial, one discovers it to be in a small minority. The representative United States citizen will be, or already is, a Westerner, and his instincts and ways of looking at things have certain characteristics of their own which are steadily growing more noticeable.

For many years New England was simply a bit of Old England transplanted. We all can remember elderly people whose ideas were wholly under the influence of their English ancestry. It is hardly more than a hundred years since we were English colonies, and not independent United States, and the customs and ideas of the mother country were followed from force of habit. Now one begins to see a difference; the old traditions have had time to almost die out even in the most conservative and least changed towns, and a new element has come in. The true characteristics of American society, as I have said, are showing themselves more and more distinctly to the westward of New England, and come back to it in a tide that steadily sweeps away the old traditions. It rises over the heads of the prim and stately idols before which our grandfathers and grandmothers bowed down and worshiped, and which we ourselves were at least taught to walk softly by as they toppled on their thrones.

One cannot help wondering what a lady of the old school will be like a hundred years from now! But at any rate she will not be in heart and thought and fashion of good breeding as truly an Englishwoman as if she had never stepped out of Great Britain. If one of our own elderly ladies were suddenly dropped into the midst of provincial English society, she would be quite at home; but west of her own Hudson River she is lucky if she does not find herself behind the times, and almost a stranger and a foreigner.

And yet from the first there was a little difference, and the colonies were New England and not Old. In some ways more radical, yet in some ways more conservative, than the people across the water, they showed a new sort of flower when they came into bloom in this new climate and soil. In the old days there had not been time for the family ties to be broken and forgotten. Instead of the unknown English men and women who are our sixth and seventh cousins now, they had first and second cousins then; but there was little communication between one country and the other, and the mutual interest in every-day affairs had to fade out quickly. A traveler was a curiosity, and here, even between the villages themselves, there was far less intercourse than we can believe possible. People stayed on their own ground; their horizons were of small circumference, and their whole interest and thought were spent upon their own land, their own neighbors, their own affairs, while they not only were contented with this state of things but encouraged it. One has only to look at the high-walled pews of the old churches, at the high fences of the town gardens, and at even the strong fortifications around some family lots in the burying-grounds, to be sure of this. The interviewer was not besought and encouraged in those days,—he was defied. In that quarter, at least, they had the advantage of us. Their interest was as real and heartfelt in each other's affairs as ours, let us hope; but they never allowed idle curiosity to show itself in the world's market-place, shameless and unblushing.

There is so much to be said in favor of our own day, and the men and women of our own time, that a plea for a recognition of the quaintness and pleasantness of village life in the old days cannot seem unwelcome, or without deference to all that has come with the later years of ease and comfort, or of discovery in the realms of mind or matter. We are beginning to cling to the elderly people who are so different from ourselves, and for this reason: we are paying them instinctively the honor that is due from us to our elders and betters; they have that grand prestige and dignity that only comes with age; they are like old wines, perhaps no better than many others when they were young, but now after many years they have come to be worth nobody knows how many dollars a dozen, and the connoisseurs make treasures of the few bottles of that vintage which are left.

It was a restricted and narrowly limited life in the old days. Religion, or rather sectarianism, was apt to be simply a matter of inheritance, and there was far more bigotry in every cause and question,—a fiercer partisanship; and because there were fewer channels of activity, and those undivided into specialties, there was a whole-souled concentration of energy that was as efficient as it was sometimes narrow and short-sighted. People were more contented in the sphere of life to which it had pleased God to call them, and they do not seem to have been so often sorely tempted by the devil with a sight of the kingdoms of the world and the glory of them. We are more likely to busy ourselves with finding things to do than in doing with our might the work that is in our hands already. The disappearance of many of the village front yards may come to be typical of the altered position of woman, and mark a stronghold on her way from the much talked-of slavery and subjection to a coveted equality. She used to be shut off from the wide acres of the farm, and had no voice in the world's politics; she must stay in the house, or only hold sway out of doors in this prim corner of land where she was queen. No wonder that women clung to their rights in their flower-gardens then, and no wonder that they have grown a little careless of them now, and that lawn mowers find so ready a sale. The whole world is their front yard nowadays!

There might be written a history of front yards in New England which would be very interesting to read. It would end in a treatise upon landscape gardening and its possibilities, and wild flights of imagination about the culture of plants under glass, the application of artificial heat in forcing, and the curious mingling and development of plant life, but it would begin in the simple time of the early colonists. It must have been hard when, after being familiar with the gardens and parks of England and Holland, they found themselves restricted to front yards by way of pleasure grounds. Perhaps they thought such things were wrong, and that having a pleasant place to walk about in out of doors would encourage idle and lawless ways in the young; at any rate, for several years it was more necessary to raise corn and potatoes to keep themselves from starving than to lay out alleys and plant flowers and box borders among the rocks and stumps. There is a great pathos in the fact that in so stern and hard a life there was time or place for any gardens at all. I can picture to myself the little slips and cuttings that had been brought over in the ship, and more carefully guarded than any of the household goods; I can see the women look at them tearfully when they came into bloom, because nothing else could be a better reminder of their old home. What fears there must have been lest the first winter's cold might kill them, and with what love and care they must have been tended! I know a rose-bush, and a little while ago I knew an apple-tree, that were brought over by the first settlers; the rose still blooms, and until it was cut down the old tree bore apples. It is strange to think that civilized New England is no older than the little red roses that bloom in June on that slope above the river in Kittery. Those earliest gardens were very pathetic in the contrast of their extent and their power of suggestion and association. Every seed that came up was thanked for its kindness, and every flower that bloomed was the child of a beloved ancestry.

It would be interesting to watch the growth of the gardens as life became easier and more comfortable in the colonies. As the settlements grew into villages and towns, and the Indians were less dreadful, and the houses were better and more home-like, the busy people began to find a little time now and then when they could enjoy themselves soberly. Beside the fruits of the earth they could have some flowers and a sprig of sage and southernwood and tansy, or lavender that had come from Surrey and could be dried to be put among the linen as it used to be strewn through the chests and cupboards in the old country.

I like to think of the changes as they came slowly; that after a while tender plants could be kept through the winter, because the houses were better built and warmer, and were no longer rough shelters which were only meant to serve until there could be something better. Perhaps the parlor, or best room, and a special separate garden for the flowers were two luxuries of the same date, and they made a noticeable change in the manner of living,—the best room being a formal recognition of the claims of society, and the front yard an appeal for the existence of something that gave pleasure,—beside the merely useful and wholly necessary things of life. When it was thought worth while to put a fence around the flower-garden the respectability of art itself was established and made secure. Whether the house was a fine one, and its inclosure spacious, or whether it was a small house with only a narrow bit of ground in front, this yard was kept with care, and it was different from the rest of the land altogether. The children were not often allowed to play there, and the family did not use the front door except upon occasions of more or less ceremony. I think that many of the old front yards could tell stories of the lovers who found it hard to part under the stars, and lingered over the gate; and who does not remember the solemn group of men who gather there at funerals, and stand with their heads uncovered as the mourners go out and come in, two by two. I have always felt rich in the possession of an ancient York tradition of an old fellow who demanded, as he lay dying, that the grass in his front yard should be cut at once; it was no use to have it trodden down and spoilt by the folks at the funeral. I always hoped it was good hay weather; but he must have been certain of that when he spoke. Let us hope he did not confuse this world with the next, being so close upon the borders of it! It was not man-like to think of the front yard, since it was the special domain of the women,—the men of the family respected but ignored it,—they had to be teased in the spring to dig the flower beds, but it was the busiest time of the year; one should remember that.

I think many people are sorry, without knowing why, to see the fences pulled down; and the disappearance of plain white palings causes almost as deep regret as that of the handsome ornamental fences and their high posts with urns or great white balls on top. A stone coping does not make up for the loss of them; it always looks a good deal like a lot in a cemetery, for one thing; and then in a small town the grass is not smooth, and looks uneven where the flower-beds were not properly smoothed down. The stray cows trample about where they never went before; the bushes and little trees that were once protected grow ragged and scraggly and out at elbows, and a few forlorn flowers come up of themselves and try hard to grow and to bloom. The ungainly red tubs that are perched on little posts have plants in them, but the poor posies look as if they would rather be in the ground, and as if they are held too near the fire of the sun. If everything must be neglected and forlorn so much the more reason there should be a fence, if but to hide it. Americans are too fond of being stared at; they apparently feel as if it were one's duty to one's neighbor. Even if there is nothing really worth looking at about a house it is still exposed to the gaze of the passersby. Foreigners are far more sensible than we, and the out-of-door home life among them is something we might well try to copy; they often have their meals served out of doors, and one can enjoy an afternoon nap in a hammock, or can take one's work out into the shady garden with great satisfaction, unwatched; and even a little piece of ground can be made, if shut in and kept for the use and pleasure of the family alone, a most charming unroofed and trellised summer ante-room to the house. In a large, crowded town it would be selfish to conceal the rare bits of garden, where the sight of anything green is a godsend; but where there is the whole wide country of fields and woods within easy reach I think there should be high walls around our gardens, and that we lose a great deal in not making them entirely separate from the highway; as much as we should lose in making the walls of our parlors and dining-rooms of glass, and building the house as close to the street as possible.

But to go back to the little front yards: we are sorry to miss them and their tangle or orderliness of roses and larkspur and honeysuckle, Canterbury bells and London pride, lilacs and peonies. These may all bloom better than ever in the new beds that are cut in the turf; but with the side fences that used to come from the corners of the house to the front fence, other barriers, as I have said here over and over, have been taken away, and the old-fashioned village life is becoming extinct. People do not know what they lose when they make way with the reserve, the separateness, the sanctity of the front yard of their grandmothers. It is like writing down the family secrets for any one to read; it is like having everybody call you by your first name and sitting in any pew in church, and like having your house in the middle of a road, to take away the fence which, slight as it may be, is a fortification round your home. More things than one may come in without being asked; we Americans had better build more fences than take any away from our lives. There should be gates for charity to go out and in, and kindness and sympathy, too; but his life and his house are together each man's stronghold and castle, to be kept and defended.

I was much amused once at thinking that the fine old solid paneled doors were being unhinged faster than ever nowadays, since so many front gates have disappeared, and the click of the latch can no longer give notice of the approach of a guest. Now the knocker sounds or the bell rings without note or warning, and the village housekeeper cannot see who is coming in until they have already reached the door. Once the guests could be seen on their way up the walk. It must be a satisfaction to look through the clear spots of the figured ground-glass in the new doors, and I believe if there is a covering inside few doors will be found unprovided with a peephole. It was better to hear the gate open and shut, and if it caught and dragged as front gates are very apt to do you could have time always for a good look out of the window at the approaching friend.

There are few of us who cannot remember a front-yard garden which seemed to us a very paradise in childhood. It was like a miracle when the yellow and white daffies came into bloom in the spring, and there was a time when tiger-lilies and the taller rose-bushes were taller than we were, and we could not look over their heads as we do now. There were always a good many lady's-delights that grew under the bushes, and came up anywhere in the chinks of the walk or the door-step, and there was a little green sprig called ambrosia that was a famous stray-away. Outside the fence one was not unlikely to see a company of French pinks, which were forbidden standing-room inside as if they were tiresome poor relations of the other flowers. I always felt a sympathy for French pinks, — they have a fresh, sweet look, as if they resigned themselves to their lot in life and made the best of it, and remembered that they had the sunshine and rain, and could see what was going on in the world, if they were outlaws.

I like to remember being sent on errands, and being asked to wait while the mistress of the house picked some flowers to send back to my mother. They were almost always prim, flat bouquets in those days; the larger flowers were picked first and stood at the back and looked over the heads of those that were shorter of stem and stature, and the givers always sent a message that they had not stopped to arrange them. I remember that I had even then a great dislike to lemon verbena, and that I would have waited patiently outside a gate all the afternoon if I knew that some one would kindly give me a sprig of lavender in the evening. And lilies did not seem to me overdressed, but it was easy for me to believe that Solomon in all his glory was not arrayed like a great yellow marigold, or even the dear little single ones that were yellow and brown, and bloomed until the snow came.

I wish that I had lived for a little while in those days when lilacs were a new fashion, and it was a great distinction to have some growing in a front yard. It always seems as if lilacs and poplars belonged to the same generation with a certain kind of New English gentlemen and ladies, who were ascetic and severe in some of their fashions, while in others they were more given to pleasuring and mild revelry than either their ancestors or the people who have lived in their houses since. Fifty years ago there seems to have been a last tidal wave of Puritanism which swept over the country, and drowned for a time the sober feasting and dancing which before had been considered no impropriety in the larger villages. Whist-playing was clung to only by the most worldly citizens, and, as for dancing, it was made a sin in itself and a reproach, as if every step was taken willfully in seven-leagued boots toward a place which is to be the final destination of all the wicked.

A single poplar may have a severe and uncharitable look, but a row of them suggests the antique and pleasing pomp and ceremony of their early days, before the sideboard cupboards were only used to keep the boxes of strings and nails and the duster; and the best decanters were put on a high shelf, while the plain ones were used for vinegar in the kitchen closet. There is far less social visiting from house to house than there used to be. People in the smaller towns have more acquaintances who live at a distance than was the case before the days of railroads, and there are more guests who come from a distance, which has something to do with making tea-parties and the entertainment of one's neighbors less frequent than in former times. But most of the New England towns have changed their characters in the last twenty years, since the manufactories have come in and brought together large numbers either of foreigners or of a different class of people from those who used to make the most of the population. A certain class of families is rapidly becoming extinct. There will be found in the older villages very few persons left who belong to this class, which was once far more important and powerful; the oldest churches are apt to be most thinly attended simply because a different sort of ideas, even of heavenly things, attract the newer residents. I suppose that elderly people have said, ever since the time of Shem, Ham, and Japhet's wives in the ark, that society is nothing to what it used to be, and we may expect to be always told what unworthy successors we are of our grandmothers. But the fact remains that a certain element of American society is fast dying out, giving place to the new; and with all our glory and pride in modern progress and success we cling to the old associations regretfully. There is nothing to take the place of the pleasure we have in going to see our old friends in the parlors which have changed little since our childhood. No matter how advanced in years we seem to ourselves we are children still to the gracious hostess. Thank Heaven for the friends who have always known us! They may think us unreliable and young still; they may not understand that we have become busy and more or less important people to ourselves and to the world,—we are pretty sure to be without honor in our own country, but they will never forget us, and we belong to each other and always shall.

I have received many kindnesses at my friends' hands, but I do not know that I have ever felt myself to be a more fortunate or honored guest than I used years ago, when I sometimes went to call upon an elderly friend of my mother who lived in most pleasant and stately fashion. I used to put on my very best manner, and I have no doubt that my thoughts were well ordered, and my conversation as proper as I knew how to make it. I can remember that I used to sit on a tall ottoman, with nothing to lean against, and my feet were off soundings, I was so high above the floor. We used to discuss the weather, and I said that I went to school (sometimes), or that it was then vacation, as the case might be, and we tried to make ourselves agreeable to each other. Presently my lady would take her keys out of her pocket, and sometimes a maid would come to serve me, or else she herself would bring me a silver tray with some pound-cakes baked in hearts and rounds, and a small glass of wine, and I proudly felt that I was a guest, though I was such a little thing an attention was being paid me, and a thrill of satisfaction used to go over me for my consequence and importance. A handful of sugar-plums would have seemed nothing beside this entertainment. I used to be careful not to crumble the cake, and I used to eat it with my gloves on, and a pleasant fragrance would cling for some time afterward to the ends of the short Lisle-thread fingers. I have no doubt that my manners as I took leave were almost as distinguished as those of my hostess, though I might have been wild and shy all the rest of the week. It was not many years ago that I went to my old friend's funeral—and saw them carry her down the long, wide walk, between the tall box borders which were her pride; and all the air was heavy and sweet with the perfume of the early summer blossoms; the white lilacs and the flowering currants were still in bloom, and the rows of her dear Dutch tulips stood dismayed in their flaunting colors and watched her go away.

My sketch of the already out-of-date or fast vanishing village fashions perhaps should be ended here, but I cannot resist a wish to add another bit of autobiography of which I have been again and again reminded in writing these pages. The front yard I knew best belonged to my grandfather's house. My grandmother was a proud and solemn woman, and she hated my mischief, and rightly thought my elder sister a much better child than I. I used to be afraid of her when I was in the house, but I shook off even her authority and forgot I was under anybody's rule when I was out of doors. I was first cousin to a caterpillar if they called me to come in, and I was own sister to a giddy-minded bobolink when I ran away across the fields, as I used to do very often. But when I was a very little child indeed my world was bounded by the fences that were around my home; there were wide green yards and tall elm-trees to shade them; there was a long line of barns and sheds, and one of these had a large room in its upper story, with an old ship's foresail spread over the floor, and made a capital play-room in wet weather. Here fruit was spread in the fall, and there were some old chests and pieces of furniture that had been discarded; it was like the garret, only much pleasanter. The children in the village now cannot possibly be so happy as I was then. I used to mount the fence next the street and watch the people go in and out of the quaint-roofed village shops that stood in a row on the other side, and looked as if they belonged to a Dutch or old English town. They were burnt down long ago, but they were charmingly picturesque; the upper stories sometimes projected over the lower, and the chimneys were sometimes clustered together and built of bright red bricks.

And I was too happy when I could smuggle myself into the front yard, with its four lilac bushes and its white fences to shut it in from the rest of the world, beside other railings that went from the porch down each side of the brick walk, which was laid in a pattern, and had H. C., 1818, cut deeply into one of the bricks near the door-step. The H. C. was for Henry Currier, the mason, who had signed this choice bit of work as if it were a picture, and he had been dead so many years that I used to think of his initials as if the corner brick were a little grave-stone for him. The knocker used to be so bright that it shone at you, and caught your eye bewilderingly, as you came in from the street on a sunshiny day. There were very few flowers, for my grandmother was old and feeble when I knew her, and could not take care of them; but I remember that there were blush roses, and white roses, and cinnamon roses all in a tangle in one corner, and I used to pick the crumpled petals of those to make myself a delicious coddle with ground cinnamon and damp brown sugar. In the spring I used to find the first green grass there, for it was warm and sunny, and I used to pick the little French pinks when they dared show their heads in the cracks of the flag-stones that were laid around the house. There were small shoots of lilac, too, and their leaves were brown and had a faint, sweet fragrance, and a little later the dandelions came into bloom; the largest ones I knew grew there, and they have always been to this day my favorite flowers.

I had my trials and sorrows in this paradise, however; I lost a cent there one day which I never have found yet! And one morning, there suddenly appeared in one corner a beautiful, dark-blue *fleur-de-lis*, and I joyfully broke its neck and carried it into the house, but everybody had seen it, and wondered that I could not have left it alone. Besides this, it befell me later to sin more gravely still; my grandmother had kept some plants through the winter on a three-cornered stand built like a flight of steps, and when the warm spring weather came this was put out of doors. She had a cherished tea-rose bush, and what should I find but a bud on it; it was opened just enough to give a hint of its color. I was very pleased; I snapped it off at once, for I had heard so many times that it was hard to make roses bloom; and I ran in through the hall and up the stairs, where I met my grandmother on the square landing. She sat down in the window-seat, and I showed her proudly what was crumpled in my warm little fist. I can see it now!—it had no stem at all, and for many days afterward I was bowed down with a sense of my guilt and shame, for I was made to understand it was an awful thing to have blighted and broken a treasured flower like that.

It must have been the very next winter that my grandmother died. She had a long illness which I do not remember much about; but the night she died might have been yesterday night, it is all so fresh and clear in my mind. I did not live with her in the old house then, but in a new house close by, across the yard. All the family were at the great house, and I could see that lights were carried hurriedly from one room to another. A servant came to fetch me, but I would not go with her; my grandmother was dying, whatever that might be, and she was taking leave of every one—she was ceremonious even then. I did not dare to go with the rest; I had an intense curiosity to see what dying might be like, but I was afraid to be there with her, and I was also afraid to stay at home alone. I was only five years old. It was in December, and the sky seemed to grow darker and darker, and I went out at last to sit on a door-step and cry softly to myself, and while I was there some one came to another door next the street, and rang the bell loudly again and again. I suppose I was afraid to answer the summons—indeed, I do not know that I thought of it; all the world had been still before, and the bell sounded loud and awful through the empty house. It seemed as if the messenger from an unknown world had come to the wrong house to call my poor grandmother away; and that loud ringing is curiously linked in my mind with the knocking at the gate in "Macbeth." I never can think of one without the other, though there was no fierce Lady Macbeth to bid me not be lost so poorly in my thoughts; for when they all came back awed and tearful, and found me waiting in the cold, alone, and afraid more of this world than the next, they were very good to me. But as for the funeral, it gave me vast entertainment; it was the first grand public occasion in which I had taken any share.

An October Ride

IT WAS a fine afternoon, just warm enough and just cool enough, and I started off alone on horseback, though I do not know why I should say alone when I find my horse such good company. She is called Sheila, and she not only gratifies one's sense of beauty, but is very interesting in her character, while her usefulness in this world is beyond question. I grow more fond of her every week; we have had so many capital good times together, and I am certain that she is as much pleased as I when we start out for a run.

I do not say to every one that I always pronounce her name in German fashion because she occasionally shies, but that is the truth. I do not mind her shying, or a certain mysterious and apparently unprovoked jump, with which she sometimes indulges herself, and no one else rides her, so I think she does no harm, but I do not like the principle of allowing her to be wicked, unrebuked and unhindered, and some day I shall give my mind to admonishing this four-footed Princess of Thule, who seems at present to consider herself at the top of royalty in this kingdom or any other. I believe I should not like her half so well if she were tamer and entirely and stupidly reliable; I glory in her good spirits and I think she has a right to be proud and willful if she chooses. I am proud myself of her quick eye and ear, her sure foot, and her slender, handsome chestnut head. I look at her points of high breeding with admiration, and I thank her heartily for all the pleasure she has given me, and for what I am sure is a steadfast friendship between us,—and a mutual understanding that rarely knows a disappointment or a mistake. She is careful when I come home late through the shadowy, twilighted woods, and I can hardly see my way; she forgets then all her little tricks and capers, and is as steady as a clock with her tramp, tramp, over the rough, dark country roads. I feel as if I had suddenly grown a pair of wings when she fairly flies over the ground and the wind whistles in my ears. There never was a time when she could not go a little faster, but she is willing to go step by step through the close woods, pushing her way

598

through the branches, and stopping considerately when a bough that will not bend tries to pull me off the saddle. And she never goes away and leaves me when I dismount to get some flowers or a drink of spring water, though sometimes she thinks what fun it would be. I cannot speak of all her virtues for I have not learned them yet. We are still new friends, for I have only ridden her two years and I feel all the fascination of the first meeting every time I go out with her, she is so unexpected in her ways; so amusing, so sensible, so brave, and in every way so delightful a horse.

It was in October, and it was a fine day to look at, though some of the great clouds that sailed through the sky were a little too heavy-looking to promise good weather on the morrow, and over in the west (where the wind was coming from) they were packed close together and looked gray and wet. It might be cold and cloudy later, but that would not hinder my ride; it is a capital way to keep warm, to come along a smooth bit of road on the run, and I should have time at any rate to go the way I wished, so Sheila trotted quickly through the gate and out of the village. There was a flicker of color left on the oaks and maples, and though it was not Indian-summer weather it was first cousin to it. I took off my cap to let the wind blow through my hair; I had half a mind to go down to the sea, but it was too late for that; there was no moon to light me home. Sheila took the strip of smooth turf just at the side of the road for her own highway, she tossed her head again and again until I had my hand full of her thin, silky mane, and she gave quick pulls at her bit and hurried little jumps ahead as if she expected me already to pull the reins tight and steady her for a hard gallop. I patted her and whistled at her, I was so glad to see her again and to be out riding, and I gave her part of her reward to begin with, because I knew she would earn it, and then we were on better terms than ever. She has such a pretty way of turning her head to take the square lump of sugar, and she never bit my fingers or dropped the sugar in her life.

Down in the lower part of the town on the edge of York, there is a long tract of woodland, covering what is called the Rocky Hills; rough, high land, that stretches along from beyond Agamenticus, near the sea, to the upper part of Eliot, near the Piscataqua River. Standing on Agamenticus, the woods seem to cover nearly the whole of the country as far as one can see, and there is hardly a clearing to break this long reach of forest of which I speak; there must be twenty miles of it in an almost unbroken line. The roads cross it here and there, and one can sometimes see small and lonely farms hiding away in the heart of it. The trees are for the most part young growth of oak or pine, though I could show you yet many a noble company of great pines that once would have been marked with the king's arrow, and many a royal old oak which has been overlooked in the search for ships' knees and plank for the navy yard, and piles for the always shaky, up-hill and down, pleasant old Portsmouth bridge. The part of these woods which I know best lies on either side the already old new road to York on the Rocky Hills, and here I often ride, or even take perilous rough drives through the cart-paths, the wood roads which are busy thoroughfares in the winter, and are silent and shady, narrowed by green branches and carpeted with slender brakes, and seldom traveled over, except by me, all summer long.

It was a great surprise, or a succession of surprises, one summer, when I found that every one of the old uneven tracks led to or at least led by what had once been a clearing, and in old days must have been the secluded home of some of the earliest adventurous farmers of this region. It must have taken great courage, I think, to strike the first blow of one's axe here in the woods, and it must have been a brave certainty of one's perseverance that looked forward to the smooth field which was to succeed the unfruitful wilderness. The farms were far enough apart to be very lonely, and I suppose at first the cry of fierce wild creatures in the forest was an everyday sound, and the Indians stole like snakes through the bushes and crept from tree to tree about the houses watching, begging, and plundering, over and over again. There are some of these farms still occupied, where the land seems to have become thoroughly civilized, but most of them were deserted long ago; the people gave up the fight with such a persistent willfulness and wildness of nature and went away to the village, or to find more tractable soil and kindlier neighborhoods.

I do not know why it is these silent, forgotten places are so delightful to me; there is one which I always call my farm, and it was a long time after I knew it well before I could find out to whom it had once belonged. In some strange way the place has become a part of my world and to belong to my thoughts and my life.

I suppose every one can say, "I have a little kingdom where I give laws." Each of us has truly a kingdom in thought, and a certain spiritual possession. There are some gardens of mine where somebody plants the seeds and pulls the weeds for me every year without my ever taking a bit of trouble. I have trees and fields and woods and seas and houses, I own a great deal of the world to think and plan and dream about. The picture belongs most to the man who loves it best and sees entirely its meaning. We can always have just as much as we can take of things, and we can lay up as much treasure as we please in the higher world of thought that can never be spoiled or hindered by moth or rust, as lower and meaner wealth can be.

As for this farm of mine, I found it one day when I was coming through the woods on horseback trying to strike a shorter way out into the main road. I was pushing through some thick underbrush, and looking ahead I noticed a good deal of clear sky as if there were an open place just beyond, and presently I found myself on the edge of a clearing. There was a straggling orchard of old apple-trees, the grass about them was close and short like the wide door-yard of an old farm-house and into this cleared space the little pines were growing on every side. The old pines stood a little way back watching their children march in upon their inheritance, as if they were ready to interfere and protect and defend, if any trouble came. I could see that it would not be many years, if they were left alone, before the green grass would be covered, and the old apple-trees would grow mossy and die for lack of room and sunlight in the midst of the young woods. It was a perfect acre of turf, only here and there I could already see a cushion of juniper, or a tuft of sweet fern or bayberry. I walked the horse about slowly, picking a hard little yellow apple here and there from the boughs over my head, and at last I found a cellar all grown over with grass, with not even a bit of a crumbling brick to be seen in the hollow of it. No doubt there were some underground. It was a very large cellar, twice as large as any I had ever found before in any of these deserted places, in the woods or out. And that told me at once that there had been a large house above it, an unusual house for those old days; the family was either a large one, or it had made for itself more than a merely sufficient covering and shelter, with no inch of unnecessary room. I knew I was on very high land, but the trees were so tall and close that I could not see beyond them. The wind blew over pleasantly and it was a curiously protected and hidden place, sheltered and quiet, with its one small crop of cider apples dropping ungathered to the ground, and unharvested there, except by hurrying black ants and sticky, witless little snails.

I suppose my feeling toward this place was like that about a ruin, only this seemed older than a ruin. I could not hear my horse's foot-falls, and an apple startled me when it fell with a soft thud, and I watched it roll a foot or two and then stop, as if it knew it never would have anything more to do in the world. I remembered the Enchanted Palace and the Sleeping Beauty in the Wood, and it seemed as if I were on the way to it, and this was a corner of that palace garden. The horse listened and stood still, without a bit of restlessness, and when we heard the far cry of a bird she looked round at me, as if she wished me to notice that we were not alone in the world, after all. It was strange, to be sure, that people had lived there, and had had a home where they were busy, and where the fortunes of life had found them; that they had followed out the law of existence in its succession of growth and flourishing and failure and decay, within that steadily narrowing circle of trees.

The relationship of untamed nature to what is tamed and cultivated is a very curious and subtle thing to me; I do not know if every one feels it so intensely. In the darkness of an early autumn evening I sometimes find myself whistling a queer tune that chimes in with the crickets' piping and the cries of the little creatures around me in the garden. I have no thought of the rest of the world. I wonder what I am; there is a strange self-consciousness, but I am only a part of one great existence which is called nature. The life in me is a bit of all life, and where I am happiest is where I find that which is next of kin to me, in friends, or trees, or hills, or seas, or beside a flower, when I turn back more than once to look into its face.

The world goes on year after year. We can use its forces, and shape and mould them, and perfect this thing or that, but we cannot make new forces; we only use the tools we find to carve the wood we find. There is nothing new; we discover and combine and use. Here is the wild fruit,—the same fruit at heart as that with which the gardener wins his prize. The world is the same world. You find a diamond, but the diamond was there a thousand years ago; you did not make it by finding it. We grow spiritually, until we grasp some new great truth of God; but it was always true, and waited for us until we came. What is there new and strange in the world except ourselves! Our thoughts are our own; God gives our life to us moment by moment, but He gives it to be our own.

> "Ye on your harps must lean to hear
> A secret chord that mine will bear."

As I looked about me that day I saw the difference that men had made slowly fading out of sight. It was like a dam in a river; when it is once swept away the river goes on the same as before. The old patient, sublime forces were there at work in their appointed way, but perhaps by and by, when the apple-trees are gone and the cellar is only a rough hollow in the woods, some one will again set aside these forces that have worked unhindered, and will bring this corner of the world into a new use and shape. What if we could stop or change forever the working of these powers! But Nature repossesses herself surely of what we boldly claim. The pyramids stand yet, it happens, but where are all those cities that used also to stand in old Egypt, proud and strong, and dating back beyond men's memories or traditions,—turned into sand again and dust that is like all the rest of the desert, and blows about in the wind? Yet there cannot be such a thing as life that is lost. The tree falls and decays, in the dampness of the woods, and is part of the earth under foot, but another tree is growing out of it; perhaps it is part of its own life that is springing again from the part of it that died. God must always be putting again to some use the life that is withdrawn; it must live, because it is Life. There can be no confusion to God in this wonderful world, the new birth of the immortal, the new forms of the life that is from everlasting to everlasting, or the new way in which it comes. But it is only God who can plan and order it all,—who is a father to his children, and cares for the least of us. I thought of his unbroken promises; the people who lived and died in that lonely place knew Him, and the chain of events was fitted to their thoughts and lives, for their development and education. The world was made for them, and God keeps them yet; somewhere in his kingdom they are in their places,—they are not lost; while the trees they left grow older, and the young trees spring up, and the fields they cleared are being covered over and turned into wild land again.

I had visited this farm of mine many times since that first day, but since the last time I had been there I had found out, luckily, something about its last tenant. An old lady whom I knew in the village had told me that when she was a child she remembered another very old woman, who used to live here all alone, far from any neighbors, and that one afternoon she had come with her mother to see her. She remembered the house very well; it was larger and better than most houses in the region. Its owner was the last of her family; but why she lived alone, or what became of her at last, or of her money or her goods, or who were her relatives in the town, my friend did not know. She was a thrifty, well-to-do old soul, a famous weaver and spinner, and she used to come to the meeting-house at the Old Fields every Sunday, and sit by herself in a square pew. Since I knew this, the last owner of my farm has become very real to me, and I thought of her that day a great deal, and could almost see her as she sat alone on her doorstep in the twilight of a summer evening, when the thrushes were calling in the woods; or going down the hills to church, dressed in quaint fashion, with a little sadness in her face as she thought of her lost companions and how she did not use to go to church alone. And I pictured her funeral to myself, and watched her carried away at last by the narrow road that wound among the trees; and there was nobody left in the house after the neighbors from the nearest farms had put it to rights, and had looked over her treasures to their hearts' content. She must have been a fearless woman, and one could not stay in such a place as this, year in and year out, through the long days of summer and the long nights of winter, unless she found herself good company.

I do not think I could find a worse avenue than that which leads to my farm, I think sometimes there must have been an easier way out which I have yet failed to discover, but it has its advantages, for the trees are beautiful and stand close together, and I do not know such green brakes anywhere as those which grow in the shadiest places. I came into a well-trodden track after a while, which led into a small granite quarry, and then I could go faster, and at last I reached a pasture wall which was quickly left behind and I was only a little way from the main road. There were a few young cattle scattered about in the pasture, and some of them which were lying down got up in a hurry and stared at me suspiciously as I rode along. It was very uneven ground, and I passed some stiff, straight mullein stalks which stood apart together in a hollow as if they wished to be alone. They always remind me of the rigid old Scotch Covenanters, who used to gather themselves together in companies, against the law, to worship God in some secret hollow of the bleak hill-side. Even the smallest and youngest of the mulleins was a Covenanter at heart; they had all put by their yellow flowers, and they will stand there, gray and unbending, through the fall rains and winter snows, to keep their places and praise God in their own fashion, and they take great credit to themselves for doing it, I have no doubt, and think it is far better to be a stern and respectable mullein than a straying, idle clematis, that clings and wanders, and cannot bear wet weather. I saw members of the congregation scattered through the pasture and felt like telling them to hurry, for the long sermon had already begun! But one ancient worthy, very late on his way to the meeting, happened to stand in our way, and Sheila bit his dry head off, which was a great pity.

After I was once on the high road it was not long before I found myself in another part of the town altogether. It is great fun to ride about the country; one rouses a great deal of interest; there seems to be something exciting in the sight of a girl on horseback, and people who pass you in wagons turn to look after you, though they never would take the trouble if you were only walking. The country horses shy if you go by them fast, and sometimes you stop to apologize. The boys will leave anything to come and throw a stone at your horse. I think Sheila would like to bite a boy, though sometimes she goes through her best paces when she hears them hooting, as if she thought they were admiring her, which I never allow myself to doubt. It is considered a much greater compliment if you make a call on horseback than if you came afoot, but carriage people are nothing in the country to what they are in the city.

I was on a good road and Sheila was trotting steadily, and I did not look at the western sky behind me until I suddenly noticed that the air had grown colder and the sun had been for a long time behind a cloud; then I found there was going to be a shower, in a very little while, too. I was in a thinly settled part of the town, and at first I could not think of any shelter, until I remembered that not very far distant there was an old house, with a long, sloping roof, which had formerly been the parsonage of the north parish; there had once been a church near by, to which most of the people came who lived in this upper part of the town. It had been for many years the house of an old minister, of widespread fame in his day; I had always heard of him from the elderly people, and I had often thought I should like to go into his house, and had looked at it with great interest, but until within a year or two there had been people living there. I had even listened with pleasure to a story of its being haunted, and this was a capital chance to take a look at the old place, so I hurried toward it.

As I went in at the broken gate it seemed to me as if the house might have been shut up and left to itself fifty years before, when the minister died, so soon the grass grows up after men's footsteps have worn it down, and the traces are lost of the daily touch and care of their hands. The home lot was evidently part of a pasture, and the sheep had nibbled close to the door-step, while tags of their long, spring wool, washed clean by summer rains, were caught in the rose-bushes near by.

It had been a very good house in its day, and had a dignity of its own, holding its gray head high, as if it knew itself to be not merely a farm-house, but a Parsonage. The roof looked as if the next winter's weight of snow might break it in, and the window panes had been loosened so much in their shaking frames that many of them had fallen out on the north side of the house, and were lying on the long grass underneath, blurred and thin but still unbroken. That was the last letter of the house's death warrant, for now the rain could get in, and the crumbling timbers must loose their hold of each other quickly. I had found a dry corner of the old shed for the horse and left her there, looking most ruefully over her shoulder after me as I hurried away, for the rain had already begun to spatter down in earnest. I was not sorry when I found that somebody had broken a pane of glass in the sidelight of the front door, near the latch, and I was very pleased when I found that by reaching through I could unfasten a great bolt and let myself in, as perhaps some tramp in search of shelter had done before me. However, I gave the blackened brass knocker a ceremonious rap or two, and I could have told by the sound of it, if in no other way, that there was nobody at home. I looked up to see a robin's nest on the cornice overhead, and I had to push away the lilacs and a withered hop vine which were both trying to cover up the door.

It gives one a strange feeling, I think, to go into an empty house so old as this. It was so still there that the noise my footsteps made startled me, and the floor creaked and cracked as if some one followed me about. There was hardly a straw left or a bit of string or paper, but the rooms were much worn, the bricks in the fire-places were burnt out, rough and crumbling, and the doors were all worn smooth and round at the edges. The best rooms were wainscoted, but up-stairs there was a long, unfinished room with a little square window at each end, under the sloping roof, and as I listened there to the rain I remembered that I had once heard an old man say wistfully, that he had slept in just such a "linter" chamber as this when he was a boy, and that he never could sleep anywhere now so well as he used there while the rain fell on the roof just over his bed.

Down-stairs I found a room which I knew must have been the study. It was handsomely wainscoted, and the finish of it was even better than that of the parlor. It must have been a most comfortable place, and I fear the old parson was luxurious in his tastes and less ascetic, perhaps, than the more puritanical members of his congregation approved. There was a great fire-place with a broad hearth-stone, where I think he may have made a mug of flip sometimes, and there were several curious, narrow, little cupboards built into the wall at either side, and over the fire-place itself two doors opened and there were shelves inside, broader at the top as the chimney sloped back. I saw some writing on one of these doors and went nearer to read it. There was a date at the top, some time in 1802, and his reverence had had a good quill pen and ink which bravely stood the test of time; he must have been a tall man to have written so high. I thought it might be some record of a great storm or other notable event in his house or parish, but I was amused to find that he had written there on the unpainted wood some valuable recipes for the medical treatment of horses. "It is Useful for a Sprain—and For a Cough, Take of Elecampane"—and so on. I hope he was not a hunting parson, but one could hardly expect to find any reference to the early fathers or federal head-ship in Adam on the cupboard door. I thought of the stories I had heard of the old minister and felt very well acquainted with him, though his books had been taken down and his fire was out, and he himself had gone away. I was glad to think what a good, faithful man he was, who spoke comfortable words to his people and lived pleasantly with them in this quiet country place so many years. There are old people living who have told me that nobody preaches nowadays as he used to preach, and that he used to lift his hat to everybody; that he liked a good dinner, and always was kind to the poor.

I thought as I stood in the study, how many times he must have looked out of the small-paned western windows across the fields, and how in his later days he must have had a treasure of memories of the people who had gone out of that room the better for his advice and consolation, the people whom he had helped and taught and ruled. I could not imagine that he ever angrily took his parishioners to task for their errors of doctrine; indeed, it was not of his active youth and middle age that I thought at all, but of the last of his life, when he sat here in the sunshine of a winter afternoon, and the fire flickered and snapped on the hearth, and he sat before it in his arm-chair with a brown old book which he laid on his knee while he thought and dozed, and roused himself presently to greet somebody who came in, a little awed at first, to talk with him. It was a great thing to be a country minister in those old days, and to be such a minister as he was; truly the priest and ruler of his people. The times have changed, and the temporal power certainly is taken away. The divine right of ministers is almost as little believed in as that of kings, by many people; it is not possible for the influence to be so great, the office and the man are both looked at with less reverence. It is a pity that it should be so, but the conservative people who like old-fashioned ways cannot tell where to place all the blame. And it is very odd to think that these iconoclastic and unpleasant new times of ours will, a little later, be called old times, and that the children, when they are elderly people, will sigh to have them back again.

I was very glad to see the old house, and I told myself a great many stories there, as one cannot help doing in such a place. There must have been so many things happen in so many long lives which were lived there; people have come into the world and gone out of it again from those square rooms with their little windows, and I believe if there are ghosts who walk about in daylight I was only half deaf to their voices, and heard much of what they tried to tell me that day. The rooms which had looked empty at first were filled again with the old clergymen, who met together with important looks and complacent dignity, and eager talk about some minor point in theology that is yet unsettled; the awkward, smiling couples, who came to be married; the mistress of the house, who must have been a stately person in her day; the little children who, under all their shyness, remembered the sugar-plums in the old parson's pockets,—all these, and even the tall cane that must have stood in the entry, were visible to my mind's eye. And I even heard a sermon from the old preacher who died so long ago, on the beauty of a life well spent.

The rain fell steadily and there was no prospect of its stopping, though I could see that the clouds were thinner and that it was only a shower. In the kitchen I found an old chair which I pulled into the study, which seemed more cheerful than the rest of the house, and then I remembered that there were some bits of board in the kitchen also, and the thought struck me that it would be good fun to make a fire in the old fire-place. Everything seemed right about the chimney. I even went up into the garret to look at it there, for I had no wish to set the parsonage on fire, and I brought down a pile of old corn husks for kindlings which I found on the garret floor. I built my fire carefully, with two bricks for andirons, and when I lit it it blazed up gayly, I poked it and it crackled, and though I was very well contented there alone I wished for some friend to keep me company, it was selfish to have so much pleasure with no one to share it. The rain came faster than ever against the windows, and the room would have been dark if it had not been for my fire, which threw out a magnificent yellow light over the old brown wood-work. I leaned back and watched the dry sticks fall apart in red coals and thought I might have to spend the night there, for if it were a storm and not a shower I was several miles from home, and a late October rain is not like a warm one in June to fall upon one's shoulders. I could hear the house leaking when it rained less heavily, and the soot dropped down the chimney and great drops of water came down, too, and spluttered in the fire. I thought what a merry thing it would be if a party of young people ever had to take refuge there, and I could almost see their faces and hear them laugh, though until that minute they had been strangers to me.

But the shower was over at last, and my fire was out, and the last pale shining of the sun came into the windows, and I looked out to see the distant fields and woods all clear again in the late afternoon light. I must hurry to get home before dark, so I raked up the ashes and left my chair beside the fire-place, and shut and fastened the front door after me, and went out to see what had become of my horse, shaking the dust and cobwebs off my dress as I crossed the wet grass to the shed. The rain had come through the broken roof and poor Sheila looked anxious and hungry as if she thought I might have meant to leave her there till morning in that dismal place. I offered her my apologies, but she made even a shorter turn than usual when I had mounted, and we scurried off down the road, spattering ourselves as we went. I hope the ghosts who live in the parsonage watched me with friendly eyes, and I looked back myself, to see a thin blue whiff of smoke still coming up from the great chimney. I wondered who it was that had made the first fire there,—but I think I shall have made the last.

Tom's Husband

I SHALL not dwell long upon the circumstances that led to the marriage of my hero and heroine; though their courtship was, to them, the only one that has ever noticeably approached the ideal, it had many aspects in which it was entirely commonplace in other people's eyes. While the world in general smiles at lovers with kindly approval and sympathy, it refuses to be aware of the unprecedented delight which is amazing to the lovers themselves.

But, as has been true in many other cases, when they were at last married, the most ideal of situations was found to have been changed to the most practical. Instead of having shared their original duties, and, as school-boys would say, going halves, they discovered that the cares of life had been doubled. This led to some distressing moments for both our friends; they understood suddenly that instead of dwelling in heaven they were still upon earth, and had made themselves slaves to new laws and limitations. Instead of being freer and happier than ever before, they had assumed new responsibilities; they had established a new household, and must fulfill in some way or another the obligations of it. They looked back with affection to their engagement; they had been longing to have each other to themselves, apart from the world, but it seemed that they never felt so keenly that they were still units in modern society. Since Adam and Eve were in Paradise, before the devil joined them, nobody has had a chance to imitate that unlucky couple. In some respects they told the truth when, twenty times a day, they said that life had never been so pleasant before; but there were mental reservations on either side which might have subjected them to the accusation of lying. Somehow, there was a little feeling of disappointment, and they caught themselves wondering—though they would have died sooner than confess it—whether they were quite so happy as they had expected. The truth was, they were much happier than people usually are, for they had an uncommon capacity for enjoyment. For a little while they were like a sail-boat that is beating and has to drift a few minutes before it can catch the wind and start off on the other tack. And they had the same feeling, too, that any one is likely to have who has been long pursuing some object of his ambition or desire. Whether it is a coin, or a picture, or a stray volume of some old edition of Shakespeare, or whether it is an office under government or a lover, when fairly in one's grasp there is a loss of the eagerness that was felt in pursuit. Satisfaction, even after one has dined well, is not so interesting and eager a feeling as hunger.

My hero and heroine were reasonably well established to begin with: they each had some money, though Mr. Wilson had most. His father had at one time been a rich man, but with the decline, a few years before, of manufacturing interests, he had become, mostly through the fault of others, somewhat involved; and at the time of his death his affairs were in such a condition that it was still a question whether a very large sum or a moderately large one would represent his estate. Mrs. Wilson, Tom's step-mother, was somewhat of an invalid; she suffered severely at times with asthma, but she was almost entirely relieved by living in another part of the country. While her husband lived, she had accepted her illness as inevitable, and rarely left home; but during the last few years she had lived in Philadelphia with her own people, making short and wheezing visits only from time to time, and had not undergone a voluntary period of suffering since the occasion of Tom's marriage, which she had entirely approved. She had a sufficient property of her own, and she and Tom were independent of each other in that way. Her only other step-child was a daughter, who had married a navy officer, and had at this time gone out to spend three years (or less) with her husband, who had been ordered to Japan.

It is not unfrequently noticed that in many marriages one of the persons who choose each other as partners for life is said to have thrown himself or herself away, and the relatives and friends look on with dismal forebodings and ill-concealed submission. In this case it was the wife who might have done so much better, according to public opinion. She did not think so herself, luckily, either before marriage or afterward, and I do not think it occurred to her to picture to herself the sort of career which would have been her alternative. She had been an only child, and had usually taken her own way. Some one once said that it was a great pity that she had not been obliged to work for her living, for she had inherited a most uncommon business talent, and, without being disreputably keen at a bargain, her insight into the practical working of affairs was very clear and far-reaching. Her father, who had also been a manufacturer, like Tom's, had often said it had been a mistake that she was a girl instead of a boy. Such executive ability as hers is often wasted in the more contracted sphere of women, and is apt to be more a disadvantage than a help. She was too independent and self-reliant for a wife; it would seem at first thought that she needed a wife herself more than she did a husband. Most men like best the women whose natures cling and appeal to theirs for protection. But Tom Wilson, while he did not wish to be protected himself, liked these very qualities in his wife which would have displeased some other men; to tell the truth, he was very much in love with his wife just as she was. He was a successful collector of almost everything but money, and during a great part of his life he had been an invalid, and he had grown, as he laughingly confessed, very old-womanish. He had been badly lamed, when a boy, by being caught in some machinery in his father's mill, near which he was idling one afternoon, and though he had almost entirely outgrown the effect of his injury, it had not been until after many years. He had been in college, but his eyes had given out there, and he had been obliged to leave in the middle of his junior year, though he had kept up a pleasant intercourse with the members of his class, with whom he had been a great favorite. He was a good deal of an idler in the world. I do not think his ambition, except in the case of securing Mary Dunn for his wife, had ever been distinct; he seemed to make the most he could of each day as it came, without making all his days' works tend toward some grand result, and go toward the upbuilding of some grand plan and purpose. He consequently gave no promise of being either distinguished or great. When his eyes would allow, he was an indefatigable reader; and although he would have said that he read only for amusement, yet he amused himself with books that were well worth the time he spent over them.

The house where he lived nominally belonged to his step-mother, but she had taken for granted that Tom would bring his wife home to it, and assured him that it should be to all intents and purposes his. Tom was deeply attached to the old place, which was altogether the pleasantest in town. He had kept bachelor's hall there most of the time since his father's death, and he had taken great pleasure, before his marriage, in refitting it to some extent, though it was already comfortable and furnished in remarkably good taste. People said of him that if it had not been for his illnesses, and if he had been a poor boy, he probably would have made something of himself. As it was, he was not very well known by the towns-people, being somewhat reserved, and not taking much interest in their every-day subjects of conversation. Nobody liked him so well as they liked his wife, yet there was no reason why he should be disliked enough to have much said about him.

After our friends had been married for some time, and had outlived the first strangeness of the new order of things, and had done their duty to their neighbors with so much apparent willingness and generosity that even Tom himself was liked a great deal better than he ever had been before, they were sitting together one stormy evening in the library, before the fire. Mrs. Wilson had been reading Tom the letters which had come to him by the night's mail. There was a long one from his sister in Nagasaki, which had been written with a good deal of ill-disguised reproach. She complained of the small-ness of the income of her share in her father's estate, and said that she had been assured by American friends that the smaller mills were starting up everywhere, and beginning to do well again. Since so much of their money was invested in the factory, she had been surprised and sorry to find by Tom's last letters that he had seemed to have no idea of putting in a proper person as superintendent, and going to work again. Four per cent. on her other property, which she had been told she must soon expect instead of eight, would make a great difference to her. A navy captain in a foreign port was obliged to entertain a great deal, and Tom must know that it cost them much more to live than it did him, and ought to think of their interests. She hoped he would talk over what was best to be done with their mother (who had been made executor, with Tom, of his father's will).

Tom laughed a little, but looked disturbed. His wife had said something to the same effect, and his mother had spoken once or twice in her letters of the prospect of starting the mill again. He was not a bit of a business man, and he did not feel certain, with the theories which he had arrived at of the state of the country, that it was safe yet to spend the money which would have to be spent in putting the mill in order. "They think that the minute it is going again we shall be making money hand over hand, just as father did when we were children," he said. "It is going to cost us no end of money before we can make anything. Before father died he meant to put in a good deal of new machinery, I remember. I don't know anything about the business myself, and I would have sold out long ago if I had had an offer that came anywhere near the value. The larger mills are the only ones that are good for anything now, and we should have to bring a crowd of French Canadians here; the day is past for the people who live in this part of the country to go into the factory again. Even the Irish all go West when they come into the country, and don't come to places like this any more."

"But there are a good many of the old work-people down in the village," said Mrs. Wilson. "Jack Towne asked me the other day if you were n't going to start up in the spring."

Tom moved uneasily in his chair. "I'll put you in for superintendent, if you like," he said, half angrily, whereupon Mary threw the newspaper at him; but by the time he had thrown it back he was in good humor again.

"Do you know, Tom," she said, with amazing seriousness, "that I believe I should like nothing in the world so much as to be the head of a large business? I hate keeping house, — I always did; and I never did so much of it in all my life put together as I have since I have been married. I suppose it is n't womanly to say so, but if I could escape from the whole thing I believe I should be perfectly happy. If you get rich when the mill is going again, I shall beg for a housekeeper, and shirk everything. I give you fair warning. I don't believe I keep this house half so well as you did before I came here."

Tom's eyes twinkled. "I am going to have that glory,—I don't think you do, Polly; but you can't say that I have not been forbearing. I certainly have not told you more than twice how we used to have things cooked. I'm not going to be your kitchen-colonel."

"Of course it seemed the proper thing to do," said his wife, meditatively; "but I think we should have been even happier than we have if I had been spared it. I have had some days of wretchedness that I shudder to think of. I never know what to have for breakfast; and I ought not to say it, but I don't mind the sight of dust. I look upon housekeeping as my life's great discipline;" and at this pathetic confession they both laughed heartily.

"I've a great mind to take it off your hands," said Tom. "I always rather liked it, to tell the truth, and I ought to be a better housekeeper,—I have been at it for five years; though housekeeping for one is different from what it is for two, and one of them a woman. You see you have brought a different element into my family. Luckily, the servants are pretty well drilled. I do think you upset them a good deal at first!"

Mary Wilson smiled as if she only half heard what he was saying. She drummed with her foot on the floor and looked intently at the fire, and presently gave it a vigorous poking. "Well?" said Tom, after he had waited patiently as long as he could.

"Tom! I'm going to propose something to you. I wish you would really do as you said, and take all the home affairs under your care, and let me start the mill. I am certain I could manage it. Of course I should get people who understood the thing to teach me. I believe I was made for it; I should like it above all things. And this is what I will do: I will bear the cost of starting it, myself,—I think I have money enough, or can get it; and if I have not put affairs in the right trim at the end of a year I will stop, and you may make some other arrangement. If I have, you and your mother and sister can pay me back."

"So I am going to be the wife, and you the husband," said Tom, a little indignantly; "at least, that is what people will say. It's a regular Darby and Joan affair, and you think you can do more work in a day than I can do in three. Do you know that you must go to town to buy cotton? And do you know there are a thousand things about it that you don't know?"

"And never will?" said Mary, with perfect good humor. "Why, Tom, I can learn as well as you, and a good deal better, for I like business, and you don't. You forget that I was always father's right-hand man after I was a dozen years old, and that you have let me invest my money and some of your own, and I have n't made a blunder yet."

Tom thought that his wife had never looked so handsome or so happy. "I don't care, I should rather like the fun of knowing what people will say. It is a new departure, at any rate. Women think they can do everything better than men in these days, but I 'm the first man, apparently, who has wished he were a woman."

"Of course people will laugh," said Mary, "but they will say that it 's just like me, and think I am fortunate to have married a man who will let me do as I choose. I don't see why it is n't sensible: you will be living exactly as you were before you married, as to home affairs; and since it was a good thing for you to know something about housekeeping then, I can't imagine why you should n't go on with it now, since it makes me miserable, and I am wasting a fine business talent while I do it. What do we care for people's talking about it?"

"It seems to me that it is something like women's smoking: it is n't wicked, but it is n't the custom of the country. And I don't like the idea of your going among business men. Of course I should be above going with you, and having people think I must be an idiot; they would say that you married a manufacturing interest, and I was thrown in. I can foresee that my pride is going to be humbled to the dust in every way," Tom declared in mournful tones, and began to shake with laughter. "It is one of your lovely castles in the air, dear Polly, but an old brick mill needs a better foundation than the clouds. No, I 'll look around, and get an honest, experienced man for agent. I suppose it 's the best thing we can do, for the machinery ought not to lie still any longer; but I mean to sell the factory as soon as I can. I devoutly wish it would take fire, for the insurance would be the best price we are likely to get.

That is a famous letter from Alice! I am afraid the captain has been growling over his pay, or they have been giving too many little dinners on board ship. If we were rid of the mill, you and I might go out there this winter. It would be capital fun."

Mary smiled again in an absent-minded way. Tom had an uneasy feeling that he had not heard the end of it yet, but nothing more was said for a day or two. When Mrs. Tom Wilson announced, with no apparent thought of being contradicted, that she had entirely made up her mind, and she meant to see those men who had been overseers of the different departments, who still lived in the village, and have the mill put in order at once, Tom looked disturbed, but made no opposition; and soon after breakfast his wife formally presented him with a handful of keys, and told him there was some lamb in the house for dinner; and presently he heard the wheels of her little phaeton rattling off down the road. I should be untruthful if I tried to persuade any one that he was not provoked; he thought she would at least have waited for his formal permission, and at first he meant to take another horse, and chase her, and bring her back in disgrace, and put a stop to the whole thing. But something assured him that she knew what she was about, and he determined to let her have her own way. If she failed, it might do no harm, and this was the only ungallant thought he gave her. He was sure that she would do nothing unladylike, or be unmindful of his dignity; and he believed it would be looked upon as one of her odd, independent freaks, which always had won respect in the end, however much they had been laughed at in the beginning. "Susan," said he, as that estimable person went by the door with the dust-pan, "you may tell Catherine to come to me for orders about the house, and you may do so yourself. I am going to take charge again, as I did before I was married. It is no trouble to me, and Mrs. Wilson dislikes it. Besides, she is going into business, and will have a great deal else to think of."

"Yes, sir; very well, sir," said Susan, who was suddenly moved to ask so many questions that she was utterly silent. But her master looked very happy; there was evidently no disapproval of his wife; and she went on up the stairs, and began to sweep them down, knocking the dust-brush about excitedly, as if she were trying to kill a descending colony of insects.

Tom went out to the stable and mounted his horse, which had been waiting for him to take his customary after-breakfast ride to the post-office, and he galloped down the road in quest of the phaeton. He saw Mary talking with Jack Towne, who had been an overseer and a valued workman of his father's. He was looking much surprised and pleased.

"I wasn't caring so much about getting work, myself," he explained; "I've got what will carry me and my wife through; but it'll be better for the young folks about here to work near home. My nephews are wanting something to do; they were going to Lynn next week. I don't say but I should like to be to work in the old place again. I've sort of missed it, since we shut down."

"I'm sorry I was so long in overtaking you," said Tom, politely, to his wife. "Well, Jack, did Mrs. Wilson tell you she's going to start the mill? You must give her all the help you can."

" 'Deed I will," said Mr. Towne, gallantly, without a bit of astonishment.

"I don't know much about the business yet," said Mrs. Wilson, who had been a little overcome at Jack Towne's lingo of the different rooms and machinery, and who felt an overpowering sense of having a great deal before her in the next few weeks. "By the time the mill is ready, I will be ready, too," she said, taking heart a little; and Tom, who was quick to understand her moods, could not help laughing, as he rode alongside. "We want a new barrel of flour, Tom, dear," she said, by way of punishment for his untimely mirth.

If she lost courage in the long delay, or was disheartened at the steady call for funds, she made no sign; and after a while the mill started up, and her cares were lightened, so that she told Tom that before next pay day she would like to go to Boston for a few days, and go to the theatre, and have a frolic and a rest. She really looked pale and thin, and she said she never worked so hard in all her life; but nobody knew how happy she was, and she was so glad she had married Tom, for some men would have laughed at it.

"I laughed at it," said Tom, meekly. "All is, if I don't cry by and by, because I am a beggar, I shall be lucky." But Mary looked fearlessly serene, and said that there was no danger at present.

It would have been ridiculous to expect a dividend the first year, though the Nagasaki people were pacified with difficulty. All the business letters came to Tom's address, and everybody who was not directly concerned thought that he was the motive power of the reawakened enterprise. Sometimes business people came to the mill, and were amazed at having to confer with Mrs. Wilson, but they soon had to respect her talents and her success. She was helped by the old clerk, who had been promptly recalled and reinstated, and she certainly did capitally well. She was laughed at, as she had expected to be, and people said they should think Tom would be ashamed of himself; but it soon appeared that he was not to blame, and what reproach was offered was on the score of his wife's oddity. There was nothing about the mill that she did not understand before very long, and at the end of the second year she declared a small dividend with great pride and triumph. And she was congratulated on her success, and every one thought of her project in a different way from the way they had thought of it in the beginning. She had singularly good fortune: at the end of the third year she was making money for herself and her friends faster than most people were, and approving letters began to come from Nagasaki. The Ashtons had been ordered to stay in that region, and it was evident that they were continually being obliged to entertain more instead of less. Their children were growing fast, too, and constantly becoming more expensive. The captain and his wife had already begun to congratulate themselves secretly that their two sons would in all probability come into possession, one day, of their uncle Tom's handsome property.

For a good while Tom enjoyed life, and went on his quiet way serenely. He was anxious at first, for he thought that Mary was going to make ducks and drakes of his money and her own. And then he did not exactly like the looks of the thing, either; he feared that his wife was growing successful as a business person at the risk of losing her womanliness. But as time went on, and he found there was no fear of that, he accepted the situation philosophically. He gave up his collection of engravings, having become more interested in one of coins and medals, which took up most of his leisure time. He often went to the city in pursuit of such treasures, and gained much renown in certain quarters as a numismatologist of great skill and experience. But at last his house (which had almost kept itself, and had given him little to do beside ordering the dinners, while faithful old Catherine and her niece Susan were his aids) suddenly became a great care to him. Catherine, who had been the main-stay of the family for many years, died after a short illness, and Susan must needs choose that time, of all others, for being married to one of the second hands in the mill. There followed a long and dismal season of experimenting, and for a time there was a procession of incapable creatures going in at one kitchen door and out of the other. His wife would not have liked to say so, but it seemed to her that Tom was growing fussy about the house affairs, and took more notice of those minor details than he used. She wished more than once, when she was tired, that he would not talk so much about the housekeeping; he seemed sometimes to have no other thought.

In the early days of Mrs. Wilson's business life, she had made it a rule to consult her husband on every subject of importance; but it had speedily proved to be a formality. Tom tried manfully to show a deep interest which he did not feel, and his wife gave up, little by little, telling him much about her affairs. She said that she liked to drop business when she came home in the evening; and at last she fell into the habit of taking a nap on the library sofa, while Tom, who could not use his eyes much by lamp-light, sat smoking or in utter idleness before the fire. When they were first married his wife had made it a rule that she should always read him the evening papers, and afterward they had always gone on with some book of history or philosophy, in which they were both interested. These evenings of their early married life had been charming to both of them, and from time to time one would say to the other that they ought to take up again the habit of reading together. Mary was so unaffectedly tired in the evening that Tom never liked to propose a walk; for, though he was not a man of peculiarly social nature, he had always been accustomed to pay an occasional evening visit to his neighbors in the village. And though he had little interest in the business world, and still less knowledge of it, after a while he wished that his wife would have more to say about what she was planning and doing, or how things were getting on. He thought that her chief aid, old Mr. Jackson, was far more in her thoughts than he. She was forever quoting Jackson's opinions. He did not like to find that she took it for granted that he was not interested in the welfare of his own property; it made him feel like a sort of pensioner and dependent, though, when they had guests at the house, which was by no means seldom, there was nothing in her manner that would imply that she thought herself in any way the head of the family. It was hard work to find fault with his wife in any way, though, to give him his due, he rarely tried.

But, this being a wholly unnatural state of things, the reader must expect to hear of its change at last, and the first blow from the enemy was dealt by an old woman, who lived near by, and who called to Tom one morning, as he was driving down to the village in a great hurry (to post a letter, which ordered his agent to secure a long-wished-for ancient copper coin, at any price), to ask him if they had made yeast that week, and if she could borrow a cupful, as her own had met with some misfortune. Tom was instantly in a rage, and he mentally condemned her to some undeserved fate, but told her aloud to go and see the cook. This slight delay, besides being killing to his dignity, caused him to lose the mail, and in the end his much-desired copper coin. It was a hard day for him, altogether; it was Wednesday, and the first days of the week having been stormy the washing was very late. And Mary came home to dinner provokingly good-natured. She had met an old school-mate and her husband driving home from the mountains, and had first taken them over her factory, to their great amusement and delight, and then had brought them home to dinner. Tom greeted them cordially, and manifested his usual graceful hospitality; but the minute he saw his wife alone he said in a plaintive tone of rebuke, "I should think you might have remembered that the servants are unusually busy to-day. I do wish you would take a little interest in things at home. The women have been washing, and I'm sure I don't know what sort of a dinner we can give your friends. I wish you had thought to bring home some steak. I have been busy myself, and couldn't go down to the village. I thought we would only have a lunch."

Mary was hungry, but she said nothing, except that it would be all right,—she didn't mind; and perhaps they could have some canned soup.

She often went to town to buy or look at cotton, or to see some improvement in machinery, and she brought home beautiful bits of furniture and new pictures for the house, and showed a touching thoughtfulness in remembering Tom's fancies; but somehow he had an uneasy suspicion that she could get along pretty well without him when it came to the deeper wishes and hopes of her life, and that her most important concerns were all matters in which he had no share. He seemed to himself to have merged his life in his wife's; he lost his interest in things outside the house and grounds; he felt himself fast growing rusty and behind the times, and to have somehow missed a good deal in life; he had a suspicion that he was a failure. One day the thought rushed over him that his had been almost exactly the experience of most women, and he wondered if it really was any more disappointing and ignominious to him than it was to women themselves. "Some of them may be contented with it," he said to himself, soberly. "People think women are designed for such careers by nature, but I don't know why I ever made such a fool of myself."

Having once seen his situation in life from such a standpoint, he felt it day by day to be more degrading, and he wondered what he should do about it; and once, drawn by a new, strange sympathy, he went to the little family burying-ground. It was one of the mild, dim days that come sometimes in early November, when the pale sunlight is like the pathetic smile of a sad face, and he sat for a long time on the limp, frost-bitten grass beside his mother's grave.

But when he went home in the twilight his step-mother, who just then was making them a little visit, mentioned that she had been looking through some boxes of hers that had been packed long before and stowed away in the garret.

"Everything looks very nice up there," she said, in her wheezing voice (which, worse than usual that day, always made him nervous); and added, without any intentional slight to his feelings, "I do think you have always been a most excellent housekeeper."

"I'm tired of such nonsense!" he exclaimed, with surprising indignation. "Mary, I wish you to arrange your affairs so that you can leave them for six months at least. I am going to spend this winter in Europe."

"Why, Tom, dear!" said his wife, appealingly. "I couldn't leave my business any way in the"—

But she caught sight of a look on his usually placid countenance that was something more than decision, and refrained from saying anything more.

And three weeks from that day they sailed.

Miss Debby's Neighbors

THERE is a class of elderly New England women which is fast dying out:—those good souls who have sprung from a soil full of the true New England instincts; who were used to the old-fashioned ways, and whose minds were stored with quaint country lore and tradition. The fashions of the newer generations do not reach them; they are quite unconscious of the western spirit and enterprise, and belong to the old days, and to a fast-disappearing order of things.

But a shrewder person does not exist than the spokes-woman of the following reminiscences, whose simple history can be quickly told, since she spent her early life on a lonely farm, leaving it only once for any length of time,—one winter when she learned her trade of tailoress. She afterward sewed for her neighbors, and enjoyed a famous reputation for her skill; but year by year, as she grew older, there was less to do, and at last, to use her own expression, "Everybody got into the way of buying cheap, ready-made-up clothes, just to save 'em a little trouble," and she found herself out of business, or nearly so. After her mother's death, and that of her favorite younger brother Jonas, she left the farm and came to a little house in the village, where she lived most comfortably the rest of her life, having a small property which she used most sensibly. She was always ready to render any special service with her needle, and was a most welcome guest in any household, and a most efficient helper. To be in the same room with her for a while was sure to be profitable, and as she grew older she was delighted to recall the people and events of her earlier life, always filling her descriptions with wise reflections and much quaint humor. She always insisted, not without truth, that the railroads were making everybody look and act of a piece, and that the young folks were more alike than people of her own day. It is impossible to give the delightfulness of her talk in any written words, as well as many of its peculiarities, for her way of going round Robin Hood's barn between the beginning of her story and its end can hardly be followed at all, and certainly not in her own dear loitering footsteps.

On an idle day her most devoted listener thought there was nothing better worth doing than to watch this good soul at work. A book was held open for the looks of the thing, but presently it was allowed to flutter its leaves and close, for Miss Debby began without any apparent provocation: —

"They may say whatever they have a mind to, but they can't persuade me that there's no such thing as special providences," and she twitched her strong linen thread so angrily through the carpet she was sewing, that it snapped and the big needle flew into the air. It had to be found before any further remarks could be made, and the listener also knelt down to search for it. After a while it was discovered clinging to Miss Debby's own dress, and after reharnessing it she went to work again at her long seam. It was always significant of a succession of Miss Debby's opinions when she quoted and berated certain imaginary persons whom she designated as "They," who stood for the opposite side of the question, and who merited usually her deepest scorn and fullest antagonism. Her remarks to these offending parties were always prefaced with "I tell 'em," and to the listener's mind "they" always stood rebuked, but not convinced, in spiritual form it may be, but most intense reality; a little group as solemn as Miss Debby herself. Once the listener ventured to ask who "they" were, in her early childhood, but she was only answered by a frown. Miss Debby knew as well as any one the difference between figurative language and a lie. Sometimes they said what was right and proper, and were treated accordingly; but very seldom, and on this occasion it seemed that they had ventured to trifle with sacred things.

"I suppose you're too young to remember John Ashby's grandmother? A good woman she was, and she had a dreadful time with her family. They never could keep the peace, and there was always as many as two of them who didn't speak with each other. It seems to come down from generation to generation like a——*curse!*" And Miss Debby spoke the last word as if she had meant it partly for her thread, which had again knotted and caught, and she snatched the offered scissors without a word, but said peaceably, after a minute or two, that the thread was n't what it used to be. The next needleful proved more successful, and the listener asked if the Ashbys were getting on comfortably at present.

"They always behave as if they thought they needed nothing," was the response. "Not that I mean that they are any ways contented, but they never will give in that other folks holds a candle to 'em. There 's one kind of pride that I do hate,— when folks is satisfied with their selves and don't see no need of improvement. I believe in self-respect, but I believe in respecting other folks's rights as much as your own; but it takes an Ashby to ride right over you. I tell 'em it 's the spirit of the tyrants of old, and it 's the kind of pride that goes before a fall. John Ashby's grandmother was a clever little woman as ever stepped. She came from over Hardwick way, and I think she kep' 'em kind of decent-behaved as long as she was round; but she got wore out a doin' of it, an' went down to her grave in a quick consumption. My mother set up with her the night she died. It was in May, towards the latter part, and an awful rainy night. It was the storm that always comes in apple-blossom time. I remember well that mother come crying home in the morning and told us Mis' Ashby was dead. She brought Marilly with her, that was about my own age, and was taken away within six months afterwards. She pined herself to death for her mother, and when she caught the scarlet fever she went as quick as cherry-bloom when it 's just ready to fall and a wind strikes it. She wa'n't like the rest of 'em. She took after her mother's folks altogether.

"You know our farm was right next to theirs,— the one Asa Hopper owns now, but he 's let it all run out,— and so, as we lived some ways from the stores, we had to be neighborly, for we depended on each other for a good many things. Families in lonesome places get out of one supply and another, and have to borrow until they get a chance to send to the village; or sometimes in a busy season some of the folks would have to leave work and be gone half a day. Land, you don't know nothing about old times, and the life that used to go on about here. You can't step into a house anywheres now that there ain't the county map and they don't fetch out the photograph book; and in every district you 'll find all the folks has got the same chromo picture hung up, and all sorts of luxuries and makeshifts o' splendor that would have made the folks I was fetched up by stare their eyes out o' their heads. It was all we could do to keep along then; and if anybody was called rich, it was only because he had a great sight of land,—and then it was drudge, drudge the harder to pay the taxes. There was hardly any ready money; and I recollect well that old Tommy Simms was reputed wealthy, and it was told over fifty times a year that he'd got a solid four thousand dollars in the bank. He strutted round like a turkey-cock, and thought he ought to have his first say about everything that was going.

"I was talking about the Ashbys, was n't I? I do' know 's I ever told you about the fight they had after their father died about the old house. Joseph was married to a girl he met in camp-meeting time, who had a little property—two or three hundred dollars—from an old great uncle that she'd been keeping house for; and I don't know what other plans she may have had for spending of her means, but she laid most of it out in a husband; for Joseph never cared any great about her that I could see, though he always treated her well enough. She was a poor ignorant sort of thing, seven years older than he was; but she had a pleasant kind of a face, and seemed like an overgrown girl of six or eight years old. I remember just after they was married Joseph was taken down with a quinsy sore throat,—being always subject to them,—and mother was over in the forenoon, and she was one that was always giving right hand and left, and she told Susan Ellen—that was his wife—to step over in the afternoon and she would give her some blackberry preserve for him; she had some that was nice and it was very healing. So along about half-past one o'clock, just as we had got the kitchen cleared, and mother and I had got out the big wheels to spin a few rolls,—we always liked to spin together, and mother was always good company;—my brother Jonas—that was the youngest of us—looked out of the window, and says he: 'Here comes Joe Ashby's wife with a six-quart pail.'

"Mother she began to shake all over with a laugh she tried to swallow down, but I did n't know what it was all about, and in come poor Susan Ellen and lit on the edge of the first chair and set the pail down beside of her. We tried to make her feel welcome, and spoke about everything we could contrive, seein' as it was the first time she'd been over; and she seemed grateful and did the best she could, and lost her strangeness with mother right away, for mother was the best hand to make folks feel to home with her that I ever come across. There ain't many like her now, nor never was, I tell 'em. But there wa'n't nothing said about the six-quart pail, and there it set on the floor, until Susan Ellen said she must be going and mentioned that there was something said about a remedy for Joseph's throat. 'Oh, yes,' says mother, and she brought out the little stone jar she kept the preserve in, and there wa'n't more than the half of it full. Susan Ellen took up the cover off the pail, and I walked off into the bedroom, for I thought I should laugh, certain. Mother put in a big spoonful, and another, and I heard 'em drop, and she went on with one or two more, and then she give up. 'I'd give you the jar and welcome,' she says, 'but I ain't very well off for preserves, and I was kind of counting on this for tea in case my brother's folks are over.' Susan Ellen thanked her, and said Joseph would be obliged, and back she went acrost the pasture. I can see that big tin pail now a-shining in the sun.

"The old man was alive then, and he took a great spite against poor Susan Ellen, though he never would if he hadn't been set on by John; and whether he was mad because Joseph had stepped in to so much good money or what, I don't know,—but he twitted him about her, and at last he and the old man between 'em was too much to bear, and Joe fitted up a couple o' rooms for himself in a building he'd put up for a kind of work-shop. He used to carpenter by spells, and he clapboarded it and made it as comfortable as he could, and he ordered John out of it for good and all; but he and Susan Ellen both treated the old sir the best they knew how, and Joseph kept right on with his farm work same as ever, and meant to lay up a little more money to join with his wife's, and push off as soon as he could for the sake of peace, though if there was anybody set by the farm it was Joseph. He was to blame for some things,—I never saw an Ashby that wasn't,—and I dare say he was aggravating. They were clearing a piece of woodland that winter, and the old man was laid up in the house with the rheumatism, off and on, and that made him fractious, and he and John connived together, till one day Joseph and Susan Ellen had taken the sleigh and gone to Freeport Four Corners to get some flour and one thing and another, and to have the horse shod beside, so they was likely to be gone two or three hours. John Jacobs was going by with his oxen, and John Ashby and the old man hailed him, and said they 'd give him a dollar if he 'd help 'em, and they hitched the two yoke, his and their 'n, to Joseph's house. There wa'n't any foundation to speak of, the sills set right on the ground, and he 'd banked it up with a few old boards and some pine spills and sand and stuff, just to keep the cold out. There wa'n't but a little snow, and the roads was smooth and icy, and they slipped it along as if it had been a hand-sled, and got it down the road a half a mile or so to the fork of the roads, and left it settin' there right on the heater-piece. Jacobs told afterward that he kind of disliked to do it, but he thought as long as their minds were set, he might as well have the dollar as anybody. He said when the house give a slew on a sideling piece in the road, he heard some of the crockery-ware smash down, and a branch of an oak they passed by caught hold of the stove-pipe that come out through one of the walls, and give that a wrench, but he guessed there wa'n't no great damage. Joseph may have given 'em some provoca-tion before he went away in the morning,—I don't know *but* he did, and I don't know *as* he did,—but at any rate when he was coming home late in the afternoon he caught sight of his house (some of our folks was right behind, and they saw him), and he stood right up in the sleigh and shook his fist, he was so mad; but afterwards he bu'st out laughin'. It did look kind of curi's; it wa'n't bigger than a front entry, and it set up so pert right there on the heater-piece, as if he was calc'latin' to farm it. The folks said Susan Ellen covered up her face in her shawl and began to cry. I s'pose the pore thing was discouraged. Joseph was awful mad,—he was kind of laugh-ing and cryin' together. Our folks stopped and asked him if there was anything they could do, and he said no; but Susan Ellen went in to view how things were, and they made up a fire, and then Joe took the horse home, and I guess they had it hot and heavy. Nobody supposed they 'd ever make up 'less there was a funeral in the family to bring 'em together, the fight had gone so far,—but 'long in the winter old Mr.

Ashby, the boys' father, was taken down with a spell o' sickness, and there wa'n't anybody they could get to come and look after the house. The doctor hunted, and they all hunted, but there did n't seem to be anybody—'t wa'n't so thick settled as now, and there was no spare help—so John had to eat humble pie, and go and ask Susan Ellen if she would n't come back and let by-gones be by-gones. She was as good-natured a creatur' as ever stepped, and did the best she knew, and she spoke up as pleasant as could be, and said she'd go right off that afternoon and help 'em through.

"The old Ashby had been a hard drinker in his day and he was all broke down. Nobody ever saw him that he could n't walk straight, but he got a crooked disposition out of it, if nothing else. I s'pose there never was a man loved sperit better. They said one year he was over to Cyrus Parker's to help with the haying, and there was a jug o' New England rum over by the spring with some gingerbread and cheese and stuff; and he went over about every half an hour to take something, and along about half-past ten he got the jug middling low, so he went to fill it up with a little water, and lost holt of it and it sunk, and they said he drunk the spring dry three times!

"Joe and Susan Ellen stayed there at the old place well into the summer, and then after planting they moved down to the Four Corners where they had bought a nice little place. Joe did well there,—he carried on the carpenter trade, and got smoothed down considerable, being amongst folks. John he married a Pecker girl, and got his match too; she was the only living soul he ever was afraid of. They lived on there a spell and—why, they must have lived there all of fifteen or twenty years, now I come to think of it, for the time they moved was after the railroad was built. 'T was along in the winter and his wife she got a notion to buy a place down to the Falls below the Corners after the mills got started and have John work in the spinning-room while she took boarders. She said 't wa'n't no use staying on the farm, they could n't make a living off from it now they'd cut the growth. Joe's folks and she never could get along, and they said she was dreadfully riled up hearing how much Joe was getting in the machine shop.

"They need n't tell me about special providences being all moonshine," said Miss Debby for the second time, "if here wa'n't a plain one, I 'll never say one word more about it. You see, that very time Joe Ashby got a splinter in his eye and they were afraid he was going to lose his sight, and he got a notion that he wanted to go back to farming. He always set everything by the old place, and he had a boy growing up that neither took to his book nor to mill work, and he wanted to farm it too. So Joe got hold of John one day when he come in with some wood, and asked him why he would n't take his place for a year or two, if he wanted to get to the village, and let him go out to the old place. My brother Jonas was standin' right by and heard 'em and said he never heard nobody speak civiller. But John swore and said he wa'n't going to be caught in no such a trap as that. His father left him the place and he was going to do as he 'd a mind to. There 'd be'n trouble about the property, for old Mr. Ashby had given Joe some money he had in the bank. Joe had got to be well off, he could have bought most any farm about here, but he wanted the old place 'count of his attachment. He set everything by his mother, spite of her being dead so long. John had n't done very well spite of his being so sharp, but he let out the best of the farm on shares, and bought a mis'able sham-built little house down close by the mills, — and then some idea or other got into his head to fit that up to let and move it to one side of the lot, and haul down the old house from the farm to live in themselves. There wa'n't no time to lose, else the snow would be gone; so he got a gang o' men up there and put shoes underneath the sills, and then they assembled all the oxen they could call in, and started. Mother was living then, though she 'd got to be very feeble, and when they come for our yoke she would n't have Jonas let 'em go. She said the old house ought to stay in its place. Everybody had been telling John Ashby that the road was too hilly, and besides the house was too old to move, they 'd rack it all to pieces dragging it so fur; but he would n't listen to no reason.

"I never saw mother so stirred up as she was that day, and when she see the old thing a moving she burst right out crying. We could see one end of it looking over the slope of the hill in the pasture between it and our house. There was two windows that looked our way, and I know Mis' Ashby used to hang a piece o' something white out o' one of 'em when she wanted mother to step over for anything. They set a good deal by each other, and Mis' Ashby was a lame woman. I should n't ha' thought John would had 'em haul the house right over the little gardin she thought so much of, and broke down the laylocks and flowering currant she set everything by. I remember when she died I was n't more 'n seven or eight year old, it was all in full bloom and mother she broke off a branch and laid into the coffin. I do' know as I 've ever seen any since or set in a room and had the sweetness of it blow in at the windows without remembering that day,—'t was the first funeral I ever went to, and that may be some reason. Well, the old house started off and mother watched it as long as she could see it. She was sort o' feeble herself then, as I said, and we went on with the work,—'t was a Saturday, and we was baking and churning and getting things to rights generally. Jonas had been over in the swamp getting out some wood he 'd cut earlier in the winter—and along in the afternoon he come in and said he s'posed I would n't want to ride down to the Corners so late, and I said I did feel just like it, so we started off. We went the Birch Ridge road, because he wanted to see somebody over that way,—and when we was going home by the straight road, Jonas laughed and said we had n't seen anything of John Ashby's moving, and he guessed he 'd got stuck somewhere. He was glad he had n't nothing to do with it. We drove along pretty quick, for we were some belated, and we did n't like to leave mother all alone after it come dark. All of a sudden Jonas stood up in the sleigh, and says he, 'I don't believe but the cars is off the track;' and I looked and there did seem to be something the matter with 'em. They had n't been running more than a couple o' years then, and we was prepared for anything.

"Jonas he whipped up the horse and we got there pretty quick, and I 'll be bound if the Ashby house had n't got stuck fast right on the track, and stir it one way or another they could n't. They 'd been there since quarter-past one, pulling and hauling,—and the men was all hoarse with yelling, and the cars had come from both ways and met there,—one each side of the crossing,—and the passengers was walking about, scolding and swearing,—and somebody'd gone and lit up a gre't bonfire. You never see such a sight in all your life! I happened to look up at the old house, and there were them two top windows that used to look over to our place, and they had caught the shine of the firelight, and made the poor old thing look as if it was scared to death. The men was banging at it with axes and crowbars, and it was dreadful distressing. You pitied it as if it was a live creatur'. It come from such a quiet place, and always looked kind of comfortable, though so much war had gone on amongst the Ashbys. I tell you it was a judgment on John, for they got it shoved back after a while, and then wouldn't touch it again,—not one of the men,—nor let their oxen. The plastering was all stove, and the outside walls all wrenched apart,—and John never did anything more about it; but let it set there all summer, till it burnt down, and there was an end, one night in September. They supposed some traveling folks slept in it and set it afire, or else some boys did it for fun. I was glad it was out of the way. One day, I know, I was coming by with mother, and she said it made her feel bad to see the little strips of leather by the fore door, where Mis' Ashby had nailed up a rosebush once. There! there ain't an Ashby alive now of the old stock, except young John. Joe's son went off to sea, and I believe he was lost somewhere in the China seas, or else he died of a fever; I seem to forget. He was called a smart boy, but he never could seem to settle down to anything. Sometimes I wonder folks is as good as they be, when I consider what comes to 'em from their folks before 'em, and how they're misshaped by nature. Them Ashbys never was like other folks, and yet some good streak or other there was in every one of 'em. You can't expect much from such hindered creatur's,— it's just like beratin' a black and white cat for being a poor mouser. It ain't her fault that the mice see her quicker than they can a gray one. If you get one of them masterful dispositions put with a good strong will towards the right, that's what makes the best of men; but all them Ashbys cared about was to grasp and get, and be cap'ns. They liked to see other folks put down, just as if it was going to set them up. And they didn't know nothing. They make me think of some o' them old marauders that used to hive up into their castles, in old times, and then go out a-over-setting and plundering. And I tell you that same sperit was in 'em. They was born a couple o' hundred years too late. Kind of left-over folks, as it were." And Miss Debby indulged in a quiet chuckle as she bent over her work. "John he got captured by his wife,—she carried too many guns for him. I believe he died very poor and her own son would n't support her, so she died over in Freeport poor-house. And Joe got along better; his wife was clever but rather slack, and it took her a good while to see through things. She married again pretty quick after he died. She had as much as seven or eight thousand dollars, and she was taken just as she stood by a roving preacher that was holding meetings here in the winter time. He sold out her place here, and they went up country somewheres that he come from. Her boy was lost before that, so there was nothing to hinder her. There, don't you think I'm always a-fault-finding! When I get hold of the real thing in folks, I stick to 'em,—but there's an awful sight of poor material walking about that ain't worth the ground it steps on. But when I look back a little ways, I can't blame some of 'em; though it does often seem as if people might do better if they only set to work and tried. I must say I always do feel pleased when I think how mad John was,—this John's father,—when he could n't do just as he'd a mind to with the pore old house. I could n't help thinking of Joe's mansion, that he and his father hauled down to the heater piece in the fork of the roads. Sometimes I wonder where them Ashbys all went to. They'd mistake one place for the other in the next world, for 't would make heaven out o' hell, because they could be disagreeing with somebody, and—well, I don't know,—I'm sure they kep' a good row going while they was in this world. Only with mother;—somehow she could get along with anybody, and not always give 'em their way either."

The Dulham Ladies

To be leaders of society in the town of Dulham was as satisfactory to Miss Dobin and Miss Lucinda Dobin as if Dulham were London itself. Of late years, though they would not allow themselves to suspect such treason, the most ill-bred of the younger people in the village made fun of them behind their backs, and laughed at their treasured summer mantillas, their mincing steps, and the shape of their parasols.

They were always conscious of the fact that they were the daughters of a once eminent Dulham minister; but beside this unanswerable claim to the respect of the First Parish, they were aware that their mother's social position was one of superior altitude. Madam Dobin's grandmother was a Greenaple, of Boston. In her younger days she had often visited her relatives, the Greenaples and Hightrees, and in seasons of festivity she could relate to a select and properly excited audience her delightful experiences of town life. Nothing could be finer than her account of having taken tea at Governor Clovenfoot's on Beacon Street in company with an English lord, who was indulging himself in a brief vacation from his arduous duties at the Court of St. James.

"He exclaimed that he had seldom seen in England so beautiful and intelligent a company of ladies," Madam Dobin would always say in conclusion. "He was decorated with the blue ribbon of the Knights of the Garter." Miss Dobin and Miss Lucinda thought for many years that this famous blue ribbon was tied about the noble gentleman's leg. One day they even discussed the question openly; Miss Dobin placing the decoration at his knee, and Miss Lucinda locating it much lower down, according to the length of the short gray socks with which she was familiar.

"You have no imagination, Lucinda," the elder sister replied impatiently. "Of course, those were the days of small-clothes and long silk stockings!"—whereat Miss Lucinda was rebuked, but not persuaded.

"I wish that my dear girls could have the outlook upon society which fell to my portion," Madam Dobin sighed, after she had set these ignorant minds to rights, and enriched them by communicating the final truth about the blue ribbon. "I must not chide you for the absence of opportunities, but if our cousin Harriet Greenaple were only living you would not lack enjoyment or social education."

Madam Dobin had now been dead a great many years. She seemed an elderly woman to her daughters some time before she left them; later they thought that she had really died comparatively young, since their own years had come to equal the record of hers. When they visited her tall white tombstone in the orderly Dulham burying-ground, it was a strange thought to both the daughters that they were older women than their mother had been when she died. To be sure, it was the fashion to appear older in her day,—they could remember the sober effect of really youthful married persons in cap and frisette; but, whether they owed it to the changed times or to their own qualities, they felt no older themselves than ever they had. Beside upholding the ministerial dignity of their father, they were obliged to give a lenient sanction to the ways of the world for their mother's sake; and they combined the two duties with reverence and impartiality.

Madam Dobin was, in her prime, a walking example of refinements and courtesies. If she erred in any way, it was by keeping too strict watch and rule over her small kingdom. She acted with great dignity in all matters of social administration and etiquette, but, while it must be owned that the parishioners felt a sense of freedom for a time after her death, in their later years they praised and valued her more and more, and often lamented her generously and sincerely.

Several of her distinguished relatives attended Madam Dobin's funeral, which was long considered the most dignified and elegant pageant of that sort which had ever taken place in Dulham. It seemed to mark the close of a famous epoch in Dulham history, and it was increasingly difficult forever afterward to keep the tone of society up to the old standard. Somehow, the distinguished relatives had one by one disappeared, though they all had excellent reasons for the discontinuance of their visits. A few had left this world altogether, and the family circle of the Greenaples and Hightrees was greatly reduced in circumference. Sometimes, in summer, a stray connection drifted Dulham-ward, and was displayed to the townspeople (not to say paraded) by the gratified hostesses. It was a disappointment if the guest could not be persuaded to remain over Sunday and appear at church. When household antiquities became fashionable, the ladies remarked a surprising interest in their corner cupboard and best chairs, and some distant relatives revived their almost forgotten custom of paying a summer visit to Dulham. They were not long in finding out with what desperate affection Miss Dobin and Miss Lucinda clung to their mother's wedding china and other inheritances, and were allowed to depart without a single teacup. One graceless descendant of the Hightrees prowled from garret to cellar, and admired the household belongings diligently, but she was not asked to accept even the dislocated cherry-wood footstool that she had discovered in the far corner of the parsonage pew.

Some of the Dulham friends had long suspected that Madam Dobin made a social misstep when she chose the Reverend Edward Dobin for her husband. She was no longer young when she married, and though she had gone through the wood and picked up a crooked stick at last, it made a great difference that her stick possessed an ecclesiastical bark. The Reverend Edward was, moreover, a respectable graduate of Harvard College, and to a woman of her standards a clergyman was by no means insignificant. It was impossible not to respect his office, at any rate, and she must have treated him with proper veneration for the sake of that, if for no other reason, though his early advantages had been insufficient, and he was quite insensible to the claims of the Greenaple pedigree, and preferred an Indian pudding to pie crust that was, without exaggeration, half a quarter high. The delicacy of Madam Dobin's touch and preference in everything, from hymns to cookery, was quite lost upon this respected preacher, yet he was not without pride or complete confidence in his own decisions.

The Reverend Mr. Dobin was never very enlightening in his discourses, and was providentially stopped short by a stroke of paralysis in the middle of his clerical career. He lived on and on through many dreary years, but his children never accepted the fact that he was a tyrant, and served him humbly and patiently. He fell at last into a condition of great incapacity and chronic trembling, but was able for nearly a quarter of a century to be carried to the meeting-house from time to time to pronounce farewell discourses. On high days of the church he was always placed in the pulpit, and held up his shaking hands when the benediction was pronounced, as if the divine gift were exclusively his own, and the other minister did but say empty words. Afterward, he was usually tired and displeased and hard to cope with, but there was always a proper notice taken of these too often recurring events. For old times' and for pity's sake and from natural goodness of heart, the elder parishioners rallied manfully about the Reverend Mr. Dobin; and whoever his successor or colleague might be, the Dobins were always called the minister's folks, while the active laborer in that vineyard was only Mr. Smith or Mr. Jones, as the case might be. At last the poor old man died, to everybody's relief and astonishment; and after he was properly preached about and lamented, his daughters, Miss Dobin and Miss Lucinda, took a good look at life from a new standpoint, and decided that now they were no longer constrained by home duties they must make themselves a great deal more used to the town.

Sometimes there is such a household as this (which has been perhaps too minutely described), where the parents linger until their children are far past middle age, and always keep them in a too childish and unworthy state of subjection. The Misses Dobin's characters were much influenced by such an unnatural prolongation of the filial relationship, and they were amazingly slow to suspect that they were not so young as they used to be. There was nothing to measure themselves by but Dulham people and things. The elm-trees were growing yet, and many of the ladies of the First Parish were older than they, and called them, with pleasant familiarity, the Dobin girls. These elderly persons seemed really to be growing old, and Miss Lucinda frequently lamented the change in society; she thought it a freak of nature and too sudden blighting of earthly hopes that several charming old friends of her mother's were no longer living. They were advanced in age when Miss Lucinda was a young girl, though time and space are but relative, after all.

Their influence upon society would have made a great difference in many ways. Certainly, the new parishioners, who had often enough been instructed to pronounce their pastor's name as if it were spelled with one "b," would not have boldly returned again and again to their obnoxious habit of saying Dobbin. Miss Lucinda might carefully speak to the neighbor and new-comers of "my sister, Miss Do-bin;" only the select company of intimates followed her lead, and at last there was something humiliating about it, even though many persons spoke of them only as "the ladies."

"The name was originally *D'Aubigne*, we think," Miss Lucinda would say coldly and patiently, as if she had already explained this foolish mistake a thousand times too often. It was like the sorrows in many a provincial château in the Reign of Terror. The ladies looked on with increasing dismay at the retrogression in society. They felt as if they were a feeble garrison, to whose lot it had fallen to repulse a noisy, irreverent mob, an increasing band of marauders who would overthrow all land-marks of the past, all etiquette and social rank. The new minister himself was a round-faced, unspiritual-looking young man, whom they would have instinctively ignored if he had not been a minister. The new people who came to Dulham were not like the older residents, and they had no desire to be taught better. Little they cared about the Greenaples or the Hightrees; and once, when Miss Dobin essayed to speak of some detail of her mother's brilliant opportunities in Boston high life, she was interrupted, and the new-comer who sat next her at the parish sewing society began to talk about something else. We cannot believe that it could have been the tea-party at Governor Clovenfoot's which the rude creature so disrespectfully ignored, but some persons are capable of showing any lack of good taste.

The ladies had an unusual and most painful sense of failure, as they went home together that evening. "I have always made it my object to improve and interest the people at such times; it would seem so possible to elevate their thoughts and direct them into higher channels," said Miss Dobin sadly.

"But as for that Woolden woman, there is no use in casting pearls before swine!"

Miss Lucinda murmured an indignant assent. She had a secret suspicion that the Woolden woman had heard the story in question oftener than had pleased her. She was but an ignorant creature; though she had lived in Dulham twelve or thirteen years, she was no better than when she came. The mistake was in treating sister Harriet as if she were on a level with the rest of the company. Miss Lucinda had observed more than once, lately, that her sister sometimes repeated herself, unconsciously, a little oftener than was agreeable. Perhaps they were getting a trifle dull; toward spring it might be well to pass a few days with some of their friends, and have a change.

"If I have tried to do anything," said Miss Dobin in an icy tone, "it has been to stand firm in my lot and place, and to hold the standard of cultivated mind and elegant manners as high as possible. You would think it had been a hundred years since our mother's death, so completely has the effect of her good breeding and exquisite hospitality been lost sight of, here in Dulham. I could wish that our father had chosen to settle in a larger and more appreciative place. They would like to put us on the shelf, too. I can see that plainly."

"I am sure we have our friends," said Miss Lucinda anxiously, but with a choking voice. "We must not let them think we do not mean to keep up with the times, as we always have. I do feel as if perhaps—our hair"—

And the sad secret was out at last. Each of the sisters drew a long breath of relief at this beginning of a confession.

It was certain that they must take some steps to retrieve their lost ascendency. Public attention had that evening been called to their fast-disappearing locks, poor ladies; and Miss Lucinda felt the discomfort most, for she had been the inheritor of the Hightree hair, long and curly, and chestnut in color. There used to be a waviness about it, and sometimes pretty escaping curls, but these were gone long ago. Miss Dobin resembled her father, and her hair had not been luxuriant, so that she was less changed by its absence than one might suppose. The straightness and thinness had increased so gradually that neither sister had quite accepted the thought that other persons would particularly notice their altered appearance.

They had shrunk, with the reticence born of close family association, from speaking of the cause even to each other, when they made themselves pretty little lace and dotted muslin caps. Breakfast caps, they called them, and explained that these were universally worn in town; the young Princess of Wales originated them, or at any rate adopted them. The ladies offered no apology for keeping the breakfast caps on until bedtime, and in spite of them a forward child had just spoken, loud and shrill, an untimely question in the ears of the for once silent sewing society. "Do Miss Dobbinses wear them great caps because their bare heads is cold?" the little beast had said; and everybody was startled and dismayed.

Miss Dobin had never shown better her good breeding and valor, the younger sister thought.

"No, little girl," replied the stately Harriet, with a chilly smile. "I believe that our head-dresses are quite in the fashion for ladies of all ages. And you must remember that it is never polite to make such personal remarks." It was after this that Miss Dobin had been reminded of Madam Somebody's unusual head-gear at the evening entertainment in Boston. Nobody but the Woolden woman could have interrupted her under such trying circumstances.

Miss Lucinda, however, was certain that the time had come for making some effort to replace her lost adornment. The child had told an unwelcome truth, but had paved the way for further action, and now was the time to suggest something that had slowly been taking shape in Miss Lucinda's mind. A young grand-nephew of their mother and his bride had passed a few days with them, two or three summers before, and the sisters had been quite shocked to find that the pretty young woman wore a row of frizzes, not originally her own, over her smooth forehead. At the time, Miss Dobin and Miss Lucinda had spoken severely with each other of such bad taste, but now it made a great difference that the wearer of the frizzes was not only a relative by marriage and used to good society, but also that she came from town, and might be supposed to know what was proper in the way of toilet.

"I really think, sister, that we had better see about having some—arrangements, next time we go anywhere," Miss Dobin said unexpectedly, with a slight tremble in her voice, just as they reached their own door. "There seems to be quite a fashion for them nowadays. For the parish's sake we ought to recognize"—and Miss Lucinda responded with instant satisfaction. She did not like to complain, but she had been troubled with neuralgic pains in her forehead on suddenly meeting the cold air. The sisters felt a new bond of sympathy in keeping this secret with and for each other; they took pains to say to several acquaintances that they were thinking of going to the next large town to do a few errands for Christmas.

A bright, sunny morning seemed to wish the ladies good-fortune. Old Hetty Downs, their faithful maid-servant and protector, looked after them in affectionate foreboding. "Dear sakes, what devil's wiles may be played on them blessed innocents afore they're safe home again!" she murmured, as they vanished round the corner of the street that led to the railway station.

Miss Dobin and Miss Lucinda paced discreetly side by side down the main street of Westbury. It was nothing like Boston, of course, but the noise was slightly confusing, and the passers-by sometimes roughly pushed against them. Westbury was a consequential manufacturing town, but a great convenience at times like this. The trifling Christmas gifts for their old neighbors and Sunday-school scholars were purchased and stowed away in their neat Fayal basket before the serious commission of the day was attended to. Here and there, in the shops, disreputable frizzes were displayed in unblushing effrontery, but no such vulgar shopkeeper merited the patronage of the Misses Dobin. They pretended not to observe the unattractive goods, and went their way to a low, one-storied building on a side street, where an old tradesman lived. He had been useful to the minister while he still remained upon the earth and had need of a wig, sandy in hue and increasingly sprinkled with gray, as if it kept pace with other changes of existence. But old Paley's shutters were up, and a bar of rough wood was nailed firmly across the one that had lost its fastening and would rack its feeble hinges in the wind. Old Paley had always been polite and bland; they really had looked forward to a little chat with him; they had heard a year or two before of his wife's death, and meant to offer sympathy. His business of hair-dressing had been carried on with that of parasol and umbrella mending, and the condemned umbrella which was his sign cracked and swung in the rising wind, a tattered skeleton before the closed door. The ladies sighed and turned away; they were beginning to feel tired; the day was long, and they had not met with any pleasures yet. "We might walk up the street a little farther," suggested Miss Lucinda; "that is, if you are not tired," as they stood hesitating on the corner after they had finished a short discussion of Mr. Paley's disappearance. Happily it was only a few minutes before they came to a stop together in front of a new, shining shop, where smirking waxen heads all in a row were decked with the latest fashions of wigs and frizzes. One smiling fragment of a gentleman stared so straight at Miss Lucinda with his black eyes that she felt quite coy and embarrassed, and was obliged to feign not to be conscious of his admiration. But Miss Dobin, after a brief delay, boldly opened the door and entered; it was better to be sheltered in the shop than exposed to public remark as they gazed in at the windows. Miss Lucinda felt her heart beat and her courage give out; she, coward like, left the transaction of their business to her sister, and turned to contemplate the back of the handsome model. It was a slight shock to find that he was not so attractive from this point of view. The wig he wore was well made all round, but his shoulders were roughly finished in a substance that looked like plain plaster of Paris.

"What can I have ze pleasure of showing you, young ladees?" asked a person who advanced; and Miss Lucinda faced about to discover a smiling, middle-aged Frenchman, who rubbed his hands together and looked at his customers, first one and then the other, with delightful deference. He seemed a very civil, nice person, the young ladies thought.

"My sister and I were thinking of buying some little arrangements to wear above the forehead." Miss Dobin explained, with pathetic dignity; but the Frenchman spared her any further words. He looked with eager interest at the bonnets, as if no lack had attracted his notice before. "Ah, yes. *Je comprends*; ze high foreheads are not now ze mode. Je prefer them, moi, yes, yes, but ze ladies must accept ze fashion; zay must now cover ze forehead with ze frizzes, ze bangs, you say. As you wis', as you wis'!" and the tactful little man, with many shrugs and merry gestures at such girlish fancies, pulled down one box after another.

It was a great relief to find that this was no worse, to say the least, than any other shopping, though the solemnity and secrecy of the occasion were infringed upon by the great supply of "arrangements" and the loud discussion of the color of some crimps a noisy girl was buying from a young saleswoman the other side of the shop.

Miss Dobin waved aside the wares which were being displayed for her approval. "Something—more simple, if you please,"—she did not like to say "older."

"But these are *très simple*," protested the Frenchman. "We have nothing younger;" and Miss Dobin and Miss Lucinda blushed, and said no more. The Frenchman had his own way; he persuaded them that nothing was so suitable as some conspicuous forelocks that matched their hair as it used to be. They would have given anything rather than leave their breakfast caps at home, if they had known that their proper winter bonnets must come off. They hardly listened to the wig merchant's glib voice as Miss Dobin stood revealed before the merciless mirror at the back of the shop.

He made everything as easy as possible, the friendly creature, and the ladies were grateful to him. Beside, now that the bonnet was on again there was a great improvement in Miss Dobin's appearance. She turned to Miss Lucinda, and saw a gleam of delight in her eager countenance. "It really is very becoming. I like the way it parts over your forehead," said the younger sister, "but if it were long enough to go behind the ears"—"*Non, non,*" entreated the Frenchman. "To make her the old woman at once would be cruelty!" And Lucinda who was wondering how well she would look in her turn, succumbed promptly to such protestations. Yes, there was no use in being old before their time. Dulham was not quite keeping pace with the rest of the world in these days, but they need not drag behind everybody else, just because they lived there.

The price of the little arrangements was much less than the sisters expected, and the uncomfortable expense of their reverend father's wigs had been, it was proved, a thing of the past. Miss Dobin treated her polite Frenchman with great courtesy; indeed, Miss Lucinda had more than once whispered to her to talk French, and as they were bowed out of the shop the gracious *Bong-sure* of the elder lady seemed to act like the string of a shower-bath, and bring down an awesome torrent of foreign words upon the two guileless heads. It was impossible to reply; the ladies bowed again, however, and Miss Lucinda caught a last smile from the handsome wax countenance in the window. He appeared to regard her with fresh approval, and she departed down the street with mincing steps.

"I feel as if anybody might look at me now, sister," said gentle Miss Lucinda. "I confess, I have really suffered sometimes, since I knew I looked so distressed."

"Yours is lighter than I thought it was in the shop," remarked Miss Dobin, doubtfully, but she quickly added that perhaps it would change a little. She was so perfectly satisfied with her own appearance that she could not bear to dim the pleasure of any one else. The truth remained that she never would have let Lucinda choose that particular arrangement if she had seen it first in a good light. And Lucinda was thinking exactly the same of her companion.

"I am sure we shall have no more neuralgia," said Miss Dobin. "I am sorry we waited so long, dear," and they tripped down the main street of Westbury, confident that nobody would suspect them of being over thirty. Indeed, they felt quite girlish, and unconsciously looked sideways as they went along, to see their satisfying reflections in the windows. The great panes made excellent mirrors, with not too clear or lasting pictures of these comforted passers-by.

The Frenchman in the shop was making merry with his assistants. The two great frisettes had long been out of fashion; he had been lying in wait with them for two unsuspecting country ladies, who could be cajoled into such a purchase.

"Sister," Miss Lucinda was saying, "you know there is still an hour to wait before our train goes. Suppose we take a little longer walk down the other side of the way;" and they strolled slowly back again. In fact, they nearly missed the train, naughty girls! Hetty would have been so worried, they assured each other, but they reached the station just in time.

"Lutie," said Miss Dobin, "put up your hand and part it from your forehead; it seems to be getting out of place a little;" and Miss Lucinda, who had just got breath enough to speak, returned the information that Miss Dobin's was almost covering her eyebrows. They might have to trim them a little shorter; of course it could be done. The darkness was falling; they had taken an early dinner before they started, and now they were tired and hungry after the exertion of the afternoon, but the spirit of youth flamed afresh in their hearts, and they were very happy. If one's heart remains young, it is a sore trial to have the outward appearance entirely at variance. It was the ladies' nature to be girlish, and they found it impossible not to be grateful to the flimsy, ineffectual disguise which seemed to set them right with the world. The old conductor, who had known them for many years, looked hard at them as he took their tickets, and, being a man of humor and compassion, affected not to notice anything remarkable in their appearance. "You ladies never mean to grow old, like the rest of us," he said gallantly, and the sisters fairly quaked with joy.

"Bless us!" the obnoxious Mrs. Woolden was saying, at the other end of the car. "There's the old maid Dobbinses, and they've bought 'em some bangs. I expect they wanted to get thatched in a little before real cold weather; but don't they look just like a pair o' poodle dogs."

The little ladies descended wearily from the train. Somehow they did not enjoy a day's shopping as much as they used. They were certainly much obliged to Hetty for sending her niece's boy to meet them, with a lantern; also for having a good warm supper ready when they came in. Hetty took a quick look at her mistresses, and returned to the kitchen. "I knew somebody would be foolin' of 'em," she assured herself angrily, but she had to laugh. Their dear, kind faces were wrinkled and pale, and the great frizzes had lost their pretty curliness, and were hanging down, almost straight and very ugly, into the ladies' eyes. They could not tuck them up under their caps, as they were sure might be done.

Then came a succession of rainy days, and nobody visited

the rejuvenated household. The frisettes looked very bright chestnut by the light of day, and it must be confessed that Miss Dobin took the scissors and shortened Miss Lucinda's half an inch, and Miss Lucinda returned the compliment quite secretly, because each thought her sister's forehead lower than her own. Their dear gray eyebrows were honestly displayed, as if it were the fashion not to have them match with wigs. Hetty at last spoke out, and begged her mistresses, as they sat at breakfast, to let her take the frizzes back and change them. Her sister's daughter worked in that very shop, and, though in the work-room, would be able to oblige them, Hetty was sure.

But the ladies looked at each other in pleased assurance, and then turned together to look at Hetty, who stood already a little apprehensive near the table, where she had just put down a plateful of smoking drop-cakes. The good creature really began to look old.

"They are worn very much in town," said Miss Dobin. "We think it was quite fortunate that the fashion came in just as our hair was growing a trifle thin. I dare say we may choose those that are a shade duller in color when these are a little past. Oh, we shall not want tea this evening, you remember, Hetty. I am glad there is likely to be such a good night for the sewing circle." And Miss Dobin and Miss Lucinda nodded and smiled.

"Oh, my sakes alive!" the troubled handmaiden groaned. "Going to the circle, be they, to be snickered at! Well, the Dobbin girls they was born, and the Dobbin girls they will remain till they die; but if they ain't innocent Christian babes to those that knows 'em well, mark me down for an idjit myself! They believe them front-pieces has set the clock back forty year or more, but if they're pleased to think so, let 'em!"

Away paced the Dulham ladies, late in the afternoon, to grace the parish occasion, and face the amused scrutiny of their neighbors. "I think we owe it to society to observe the fashions of the day," said Miss Lucinda. "A lady cannot afford to be unattractive. I feel now as if we were prepared for anything!"

Marsh Rosemary

I.

O NE hot afternoon in August, a single moving figure might have been seen following a straight road that crossed the salt marshes of Walpole. Everybody else had either stayed at home or crept into such shade as could be found near at hand. The thermometer marked at least ninety degrees. There was hardly a fishing-boat to be seen on the glistening sea, only far away on the hazy horizon two or three coasting schooners looked like ghostly flying Dutchmen, becalmed for once and motionless.

Ashore, the flaring light of the sun brought out the fine, clear colors of the level landscape. The marsh grasses were a more vivid green than usual, the brown tops of those that were beginning to go to seed looked almost red, and the soil at the edges of the tide inlets seemed to be melting into a black, pitchy substance like the dark pigments on a painter's palette. Where the land was higher the hot air flickered above it dizzily. This was not an afternoon that one would naturally choose for a long walk, yet Mr. Jerry Lane stepped briskly forward, and appeared to have more than usual energy. His big boots trod down the soft carpet of pussy-clover that bordered the dusty, whitish road. He struck at the stationary procession of thistles with a little stick as he went by. Flight after flight of yellow butterflies fluttered up as he passed, and then settled down again to their thistle flowers, while on the shiny cambric back of Jerry's Sunday waistcoat basked at least eight large green-headed flies in complete security.

It was difficult to decide why the Sunday waistcoat should have been put on that Saturday afternoon. Jerry had not thought it important to wear his best boots or best trousers, and had left his coat at home altogether. He smiled as he walked along, and once when he took off his hat, as a light breeze came that way, he waved it triumphantly before he put it on again. Evidently this was no common errand that led him due west, and made him forget the hot weather, and caused him to shade his eyes with his hand, as he looked eagerly at a clump of trees and the chimney of a small house a little way beyond the boundary of the marshes, where the higher ground began.

Miss Ann Floyd sat by her favorite window, sewing, twitching her thread less decidedly than usual, and casting a wistful glance now and then down the road or at the bees in her gay little garden outside. There was a grim expression overshadowing her firmly-set, angular face, and the frown that always appeared on her forehead when she sewed or read the newspaper was deeper and straighter than usual. She did not look as if she were conscious of the heat, though she had dressed herself in an old-fashioned skirt of sprigged lawn and a loose jacket of thin white dimity with out-of-date flowing sleeves. Her sandy hair was smoothly brushed; one lock betrayed a slight crinkle at its edge, but it owed nothing to any encouragement of Nancy Floyd's. A hard, honest, kindly face this was, of a woman whom everybody trusted, who might be expected to give of whatever she had to give, good measure, pressed down and running over. She was a lonely soul; she had no near relatives in the world. It seemed always as if nature had been mistaken in not planting her somewhere in a large and busy household.

The little square room, kitchen in winter and sitting-room in summer, was as clean and bare and thrifty as one would expect the dwelling-place of such a woman to be. She sat in a straight-backed, splint-bottomed kitchen chair, and always put back her spool with a click on the very same spot on the window-sill. You would think she had done with youth and with love affairs, yet you might as well expect the ancient cherry-tree in the corner of her yard to cease adventuring its white blossoms when the May sun shone! No woman in Walpole had more bravely and patiently borne the burden of loneliness and lack of love. Even now her outward behavior gave no hint of the new excitement and delight that filled her heart.

"Land sakes alive!" she says to herself presently, "there comes Jerry Lane. I expect, if he sees me settin' to the winder, he'll come in an' dawdle round till supper time!" But good Nancy Floyd smooths her hair hastily as she rises and drops her work, and steps back toward the middle of the room, watching the gate anxiously all the time. Now, Jerry, with a crestfallen look at the vacant window, makes believe that he is going by, and takes a loitering step or two onward, and then stops short; with a somewhat sheepish smile he leans over the neat picket fence and examines the blue and white and pink larkspur that covers most of the space in the little garden. He takes off his hat again to cool his forehead, and replaces it, without a grand gesture this time, and looks again at the window hopefully.

There is a pause. The woman knows that the man is sure she is there; a little blush colors her thin cheeks as she comes boldly to the wide-open front door.

"What do you think of this kind of weather?" asks Jerry Lane, complacently, as he leans over the fence, and surrounds himself with an air of self-sacrifice.

"I call it hot," responds the Juliet from her balcony, with deliberate assurance, "but the corn needs sun, everybody says. I shouldn't have wanted to toil up from the shore under such a glare, if I had been you. Better come in and set a while, and cool off," she added, without any apparent enthusiasm. Jerry was sure to come, any way. She would rather make the suggestion than have him.

Mr. Lane sauntered in, and seated himself opposite his hostess, beside the other small window, and watched her admiringly as she took up her sewing and worked at it with great spirit and purpose. He clasped his hands together and leaned forward a little. The shaded kitchen was very comfortable, after the glaring light outside, and the clean orderliness of the few chairs and the braided rugs and the table under the clock, with some larkspur and asparagus in a china vase for decoration, seemed to please him unexpectedly. "Now just see what ways you women folks have of fixing things up smart!" he ventured gallantly.

Nancy's countenance did not forbid further compliment; she looked at the flowers herself, quickly, and explained that she had gathered them a while ago to send to the minister's sister, who kept house for him. "I saw him going by, and

expected he'd be back this same road. Mis' Elton's be'n havin'
another o' her dyin' spells this noon, and the deacon went by
after him hot foot. I'd souse her well with stone-cold water.
She never sent for me to set up with her; she knows better.
Poor man, 'twas likely he was right into the middle of to-
morrow's sermon. 'T ain't considerate of the deacon, and
when he knows he's got a fool for a wife, he need n't go
round persuading other folks she's so suffering as she makes
out. They ain't got no larkspur this year to the parsonage, and
I was going to let the minister take this over to Amandy; but
I see his wagon over on the other road, going towards the
village, about an hour after he went by here."

It seemed to be a relief to tell somebody all these things
after such a season of forced repression, and Jerry listened
with gratifying interest. "How you do see through folks!" he
exclaimed in a mild voice. Jerry could be very soft spoken if he
thought best. "Mis' Elton's a die-away lookin' creatur'. I
heard of her saying last Sunday, comin' out o' meetin', that
she made an effort to git there once more, but she expected
't would be the last time. Looks as if she eat well, don't she?"
he concluded, in a meditative tone.

"Eat!" exclaimed the hostess, with snapping eyes. "There
ain't no woman in town, sick or well, can lay aside the food
that she does. 'T ain't to the table afore folks, but she goes
seeking round in the cupboards half a dozen times a day. An'
I've heard her remark 't was the last time she ever expected to
visit the sanctuary as much as a dozen times within five
years."

"Some places I've sailed to they'd have hit her over the
head with a club long ago," said Jerry, with an utter lack of
sympathy that was startling. "Well, I must be gettin' back
again. Talkin' of eatin' makes us think o' supper time. Must be
past five, ain't it? I thought I'd just step up to see if there
wa'n't anything I could lend a hand about, this hot day."

Sensible Ann Floyd folded her hands over her sewing, as it
lay in her lap, and looked straight before her without seeing
the pleading face of the guest. This moment was a great crisis
in her life. She was conscious of it, and knew well enough
that upon her next words would depend the course of future
events. The man who waited to hear what she had to say was

indeed many years younger than she, was shiftless and vacillating. He had drifted to Walpole from nobody knew where, and possessed many qualities which she had openly rebuked and despised in other men. True enough, he was good-looking, but that did not atone for the lacks of his character and reputation. Yet she knew herself to be the better man of the two, and since she had surmounted many obstacles already she was confident that, with a push here and a pull there to steady him, she could keep him in good trim. The winters were so long and lonely; her life was in many ways hungry and desolate in spite of its thrift and conformity. She had laughed scornfully when he stopped, one day in the spring, and offered to help her weed her garden; she had even joked with one of the neighbors about it. Jerry had been growing more and more friendly and pleasant ever since. His ease-loving careless nature was like a comfortable cushion for hers, with its angles, its melancholy anticipations and self-questionings. But Jerry liked her, and if she liked him and married him, and took him home, it was nobody's business; and in that moment of surrender to Jerry's cause she arrayed herself at his right hand against the rest of the world, ready for warfare with any and all of its opinions.

She was suddenly aware of the sunburnt face and light, curling hair of her undeclared lover, at the other end of the painted table with its folded leaf. She smiled at him vacantly across the larkspur; then she gave a little start, and was afraid that her thoughts had wandered longer than was seemly. The kitchen clock was ticking faster than usual, as if it were trying to attract attention.

"I guess I'll be getting home," repeated the visitor ruefully, and rose from his chair, but hesitated again at an unfamiliar expression upon his companion's face.

"I don't know as I've got anything extra for supper, but you stop," she said, "an' take what there is. I wouldn't go back across them marshes right in this heat."

Jerry Lane had a lively sense of humor, and a queer feeling of merriment stole over him now, as he watched the mistress of the house. She had risen, too; she looked so simple and so frankly sentimental, there was such an incongruous coyness added to her usually straightforward, angular appearance, that his instinctive laughter nearly got the better of him, and might have lost him the prize for which he had been waiting these many months. But Jerry behaved like a man: he stepped forward and kissed Ann Floyd; he held her fast with one arm as he stood beside her, and kissed her again and again. She was a dear good woman. She had a fresh young heart, in spite of the straight wrinkle in her forehead and her work-worn hands. She had waited all her days for this joy of having a lover.

II.

Even Mrs. Elton revived for a day or two under the tonic of such a piece of news. That was what Jerry Lane had hung round for all summer, everybody knew at last. Now he would strike work and live at his ease, the men grumbled to each other; but all the women of Walpole deplored most the weakness and foolishness of the elderly bride. Ann Floyd was comfortably off, and had something laid by for a rainy day; she would have done vastly better to deny herself such an expensive and utterly worthless luxury as the kind of husband Jerry Lane would make. He had idled away his life. He earned a little money now and then in seafaring pursuits, but was too lazy, in the shore parlance, to tend lobster-pots. What was energetic Ann Floyd going to do with him? She was always at work, always equal to emergencies, and entirely opposed to dullness and idleness and even placidity. She liked people who had some snap to them, she often avowed scornfully, and now she had chosen for a husband the laziest man in Walpole. "Dear sakes," one woman said to another, as they heard the news, "there's no fool like an old fool!"

The days went quickly by, while Miss Ann made her plain wedding clothes. If people expected her to put on airs of youth they were disappointed. Her wedding bonnet was the same sort of bonnet she had worn for a dozen years, and one disappointed critic deplored the fact that she had spruced up so little, and kept on dressing old enough to look like Jerry Lane's mother. As her acquaintances met her they looked at her with close scrutiny, expecting to see some outward trace of such a silly, uncharacteristic departure from good sense and discretion. But Miss Floyd, while she was still Miss Floyd, displayed no silliness and behaved with dignity, while on the Sunday after a quiet marriage at the parsonage she and Jerry Lane walked up the side aisle to their pew, the picture of middle-aged sobriety and respectability. Their fellow parishioners, having recovered from their first astonishment and amusement, settled down to the belief that the newly married pair understood their own business best, and that if anybody could make the best of Jerry and get any work out of him, it was his capable wife.

"And if she undertakes to drive him too hard he can slip off to sea, and they'll be rid of each other," commented one of Jerry's 'longshore companions, as if it were only reasonable that some refuge should be afforded to those who make mistakes in matrimony.

There did not seem to be any mistake at first, or for a good many months afterward. The husband liked the comfort that came from such good housekeeping, and enjoyed a deep sense of having made a good anchorage in a well-sheltered harbor, after many years of thriftless improvidence and drifting to and fro. There were some hindrances to perfect happiness: he had to forego long seasons of gossip with his particular friends, and the outdoor work which was expected of him, though by no means heavy for a person of his strength, fettered his freedom not a little. To chop wood, and take care of a cow, and bring a pail of water now and then, did not weary him so much as it made him practically understand the truth of weakly Sister Elton's remark that life was a constant chore. And when poor Jerry, for lack of other interest, fancied that his health was giving way mysteriously, and brought home a bottle of strong liquor to be used in case of sickness, and placed it conveniently in the shed, Mrs. Lane locked it up in the small chimney cupboard where she kept her camphor bottle and her opodeldoc and the other family medicines. She was not harsh with her husband. She cherished him tenderly, and worked diligently at her trade of tailoress, singing her hymns gayly in summer weather; for she never had been so happy as now, when there was somebody to please beside herself, to cook for and sew for, and to live with and love. But

Jerry complained more and more in his inmost heart that his wife expected too much of him. Presently he resumed an old habit of resorting to the least respected of the two country stores of that neighborhood, and sat in the row of loafers on the outer steps. "Sakes alive," said a shrewd observer one day, "the fools set there and talk and talk about what they went through when they follered the sea, till when the women-folks comes tradin' they are obleeged to climb right over 'em."

But things grew worse and worse, until one day Jerry Lane came home a little late to dinner, and found his wife unusually grim-faced and impatient. He took his seat with an amiable smile, and showed in every way his determination not to lose his temper because somebody else had. It was one of the days when he looked almost boyish and entirely irresponsible. His hair was handsome and curly from the dampness of the east wind, and his wife was forced to remember how, in the days of their courtship, she used to wish that she could pull one of the curling locks straight, for the pleasure of seeing it fly back. She felt old and tired, and was hurt in her very soul by the contrast between herself and her husband. "No wonder I am aging, having to lug everything on my shoulders," she thought. Jerry had forgotten to do whatever she had asked him for a day or two. He had started out that morning to go lobstering, but he had returned from the direction of the village.

"Nancy," he said pleasantly, after he had begun his dinner, a silent and solitary meal, while his wife stitched busily by the window, and refused to look at him,—"Nancy, I've been thinking a good deal about a project."

"I hope it ain't going to cost so much and bring in so little as your other notions have, then," she responded, quickly; though somehow a memory of the hot day when Jerry came and stood outside the fence, and kissed her when it was settled he should stay to supper,—a memory of that day would keep fading and brightening in her mind.

"Yes," said Jerry, humbly, "I ain't done right, Nancy. I ain't done my part for our livin'. I've let it sag right on to you, most ever since we was married. There was that spell when I was kind of weakly, and had a pain acrost me. I tell you what it is: I never was good for nothin' ashore, but now I've got my strength up I'm going to show ye what I can do. I'm promised to ship with Cap'n Low's brother, Skipper Nathan, that sails out o' Eastport in the coasting trade, lumber and so on. I shall get good wages, and you shall keep the whole on 't 'cept what I need for clothes."

"You need n't be so plaintive," said Ann, in a sharp voice. "You can go if you want to. I have always been able to take care of myself, but when it comes to maintainin' two, 't ain't so easy. When be you goin'?"

"I expected you would be sorry," mourned Jerry, his face falling at this outbreak. "Nancy, you need n't be so quick. 'T ain't as if I had n't always set everything by ye, if I be wuthless."

Nancy's eyes flashed fire as she turned hastily away. Hardly knowing where she went, she passed through the open doorway, and crossed the clean green turf of the narrow side yard, and leaned over the garden fence. The young cabbages and cucumbers were nearly buried in weeds, and the currant bushes were fast being turned into skeletons by the ravaging worms. Jerry had forgotten to sprinkle them with hellebore, after all, though she had put the watering-pot into his very hand the evening before. She did not like to have the whole town laugh at her for hiring a man to do his work; she was busy from early morning until late night, but she could not do everything herself. She had been a fool to marry this man, she told herself at last, and a sullen discontent and rage that had been of slow but certain growth made her long to free herself from this unprofitable hindrance for a time, at any rate. Go to sea? Yes, that was the best thing that could happen. Perhaps when he had worked hard a while on schooner fare, he would come home and be good for something!

Jerry finished his dinner in the course of time, and then sought his wife. It was not like her to go away in this silent fashion. Of late her gift of speech had been proved sufficiently formidable, and yet she had never looked so resolutely angry as to-day.

"Nancy," he began,—"Nancy, girl! I ain't goin' off to leave you, if your heart's set against it. I'll spudge up and take right holt."

But the wife turned slowly from the fence and faced him. Her eyes looked as if she had been crying. "You need n't stay on my account," she said. "I 'll go right to work an' fit ye out. I 'm sick of your meechin' talk, and I don't want to hear no more of it. Ef *I* was a man"—

Jerry Lane looked crestfallen for a minute or two; but when his stern partner in life had disappeared within the house, he slunk away among the apple-trees of the little orchard, and sat down on the grass in a shady spot. It was getting to be warm weather, but he would go round and hoe the old girl's garden stuff by and by. There would be something goin' on aboard the schooner, and with delicious anticipation of future pleasure this delinquent Jerry struck his knee with his hand, as if he were clapping a crony on the shoulder. He also winked several times at the same fancied companion. Then, with a comfortable chuckle, he laid himself down, and pulled his old hat over his eyes, and went to sleep, while the weeds grew at their own sweet will, and the currant worms went looping and devouring from twig to twig.

III.

Summer went by, and winter began, and Mr. Jerry Lane did not reappear. He had promised to return in September, when he parted from his wife early in June, for Nancy had relented a little at the last, and sorrowed at the prospect of so long a separation. She had already learned the vacillations and uncertainties of her husband's character; but though she accepted the truth that her marriage had been in every way a piece of foolishness, she still clung affectionately to his assumed fondness for her. She could not believe that his marriage was only one of his makeshifts, and that as soon as he grew tired of the constraint he was ready to throw the benefits of respectable home life to the four winds. A little sentimental speech-making and a few kisses the morning he went away, and the gratitude he might well have shown for her generous care-taking and provision for his voyage won her soft heart back again, and made poor, elderly, simple-hearted Nancy watch him cross the marshes with tears and foreboding. If she could have called him back that day, she would have done so and been thankful. And all summer and winter, whenever the wind blew and thrashed the drooping elm boughs against the low roof over her head, she was as full of fears and anxieties as if Jerry were her only son and making his first voyage at sea. The neighbors pitied her for her disappointment. They liked Nancy; but they could not help saying, "I told you so." It would have been impossible not to respect the brave way in which she met the world's eye, and carried herself with innocent unconsciousness of having committed so laughable and unrewarding a folly. The loafers on the store steps had been unwontedly diverted one day, when Jerry, who was their chief wit and spokesman, rose slowly from his place, and said in pious tones, "Boys, I must go this minute. Grandma will keep dinner waiting." Mrs. Ann Lane did not show in her aging face how young her heart was, and after the schooner Susan Barnes had departed she seemed to pass swiftly from middle life and an almost youthful vigor to early age and a look of spent strength and dissatisfaction. "I suppose he did find it dull," she assured herself, with wistful yearning for his rough words of praise, when she sat down alone to her dinner, or looked up sadly from her work, and missed the amusing though unedifying conversation he was wont to offer occasionally on stormy winter nights. How much of his adventuring was true she never cared to ask. He had come and gone, and she forgave him his shortcomings, and longed for his society with a heavy heart.

One spring day there was news in the Boston paper of the loss of the schooner Susan Barnes with all on board, and Nancy Lane's best friends shook their sage heads, and declared that as far as regarded Jerry Lane, that idle vagabond, it was all for the best. Nobody was interested in any other member of the crew, so the misfortune of the Susan Barnes seemed of but slight consequence in Walpole, she having passed out of her former owners' hands the autumn before. Jerry had stuck by the ship; at least, so he had sent word then to his wife by Skipper Nathan Low. The Susan Barnes was to sail regularly between Shediac and Newfoundland, and Jerry sent five dollars to Nancy, and promised to pay her a visit soon. "Tell her I'm layin' up somethin' handsome," he told the skipper with a grin, "and I 've got some folks in Newfoundland I 'll visit with on this voyage, and then I 'll come ashore for good and farm it."

Mrs. Lane took the five dollars from the skipper as proudly as if Jerry had done the same thing so many times before that she hardly noticed it. The skipper gave the messages from Jerry, and felt that he had done the proper thing. When the news came long afterward that the schooner was lost, that was the next thing that Nancy knew about her wandering mate; and after the minister had come solemnly to inform her of her bereavement, and had gone away again, and she sat down and looked her widowhood in the face, there was not a sadder nor a lonelier woman in the town of Walpole.

All the neighbors came to condole with our heroine, and, though nobody was aware of it, from that time she was really happier and better satisfied with life than she had ever been before. Now she had an ideal Jerry Lane to mourn over and think about, to cherish and admire; she was day by day slowly forgetting the trouble he had been and the bitter shame of him, and exalting his memory to something near saintliness. "He meant well," she told herself again and again. She thought nobody could tell so good a story; she felt that with her own bustling, capable ways he had no chance to do much that he might have done. She had been too quick with him, and alas, alas! how much better she would know how to treat him if she only could see him again! A sense of relief at his absence made her continually assure herself of her great loss, and, false even to herself, she mourned her sometime lover diligently, and tried to think herself a broken-hearted woman. It was thought among those who knew Nancy Lane best that she would recover her spirits in time, but Jerry's wildest anticipations of a proper respect to his memory were more than realized in the first two years after the schooner Susan Barnes went to the bottom of the sea. She mourned for the man he ought to have been, not for the real Jerry, but she had loved him in the beginning enough to make her own love a precious possession for all time to come. It did not matter much, after all, what manner of man he was; she had found in him something on which to spend her hoarded affection.

IV.

Nancy Lane was a peaceable woman and a good neighbor, but she never had been able to get on with one fellow towns-woman, and that was Mrs. Deacon Elton. They managed to keep each other provoked and teased from one year's end to the other, and each good soul felt herself under a moral mi-croscope, and understood that she was judged by a not very lenient criticism and discussion. Mrs. Lane clad herself in sim-ple black after the news came of her husband's timely death, and Mrs. Elton made one of her farewell pilgrimages to church to see the new-made widow walk up the aisle.

"She need n't tell me she lays that affliction so much to heart," the deacon's wife sniffed faintly, after her exhaustion had been met by proper treatment of camphor and a glass of currant wine, at the parsonage, where she rested a while after service. "Nancy Floyd knows she 's well over with such a piece of nonsense. If I had had my health, I should have spo-ken with her and urged her not to take the step in the first place. She has n't spoken six beholden words to me since that vagabond come to Walpole. I dare say she may have heard something I said at the time she married. I declare for 't, I never was so outdone as I was when the deacon came home and told me Nancy Floyd was going to be married. She let herself down too low to ever hold the place again that she used to have in folks' minds. And it 's my opinion," said the sharp-eyed little woman, "she ain't got through with her pay yet."

But Mrs. Elton did not know with what unconscious prophecy her words were freighted.

The months passed by: summer and winter came and went, and even those few persons who were misled by Nancy Lane's stern visage and forbidding exterior into forgetting her kind heart were at last won over to friendliness by her renewed devotion to the sick and old people of the rural community. She was so tender to little children that they all loved her dearly. She was ready to go to any household that needed help, and in spite of her ceaseless industry with her needle she found many a chance to do good, and help her neighbors to lift and carry the burdens of their lives. She blossomed out suddenly into a lovely, painstaking eagerness to be of use; it seemed as if her affectionate heart, once made generous, must go on spending its wealth wherever it could find an excuse. Even Mrs. Elton herself was touched by her old enemy's evident wish to be friends, and said nothing more about poor Nancy's looking as savage as a hawk. The only thing to admit was the truth that her affliction had proved a blessing to her. And it was in a truly kind and compassionate spirit that, after hearing an awful piece of news, the deacon's hysterical wife forbore to spread it far and wide through the town first, and went down to the Widow Lane's one September afternoon. Nancy was stitching busily upon the deacon's new coat, and looked up with a friendly smile as her guest came in, in spite of an instinctive shrug as she had seen her coming up the yard. The dislike of the poor souls for each other was deeper than their philosophy could reach.

Mrs. Elton spent some minutes in the unnecessary endeavor to regain her breath, and to her surprise found she must make a real effort before she could tell her unwelcome news. She had been so full of it all the way from home that she had rehearsed the whole interview; now she hardly knew how to begin. Nancy looked serener than usual, but there was something wistful about her face as she glanced across the room, presently, as if to understand the reason of the long pause. The clock ticked loudly; the kitten clattered a spool against the table-leg, and had begun to snarl the thread around her busy paws, and Nancy looked down and saw her; then the instant consciousness of there being some unhappy reason for Mrs. Elton's call made her forget the creature's mischief, and anxiously lay down her work to listen.

"Skipper Nathan Low was to our house to dinner," the guest began. "He's bargaining with the deacon about some hay. He's got a new schooner, Skipper Nathan has, and is going to build up a regular business of freighting hay to Boston by sea. There's no market to speak of about here, unless you haul it way over to Downer, and you can't make but one turn a day."

"'T would be a good thing," replied Nancy, trying to think that this was all, and perhaps the deacon wanted to hire her own field another year. He had underpaid her once, and they had not been on particularly good terms ever since. She would make her own bargains with Skipper Nathan, she thanked him and his wife!

"He's been down to the provinces these two or three years back, you know," the whining voice went on, and straightforward Ann Lane felt the old animosity rising within her. "At dinner time I wasn't able to eat much of anything, and so I was talking with Cap'n Nathan, and asking him some questions about them parts; and I spoke something about the mercy 't was his life should ha' been spared when that schooner, the Susan Barnes, was lost so quick after he sold out his part of her. And I put in a word, bein' 's we were neighbors, about how edifyin' your course had be'n under affliction. I noticed then he'd looked sort o' queer whilst I was talkin', but there was all the folks to the table, and you know he's a very cautious man, so he spoke of somethin' else. 'T wa'n't half an hour after dinner, I was comin' in with some plates and cups, tryin' to help what my stren'th would let me, and says he, 'Step out a little ways into the piece with me, Mis' Elton. I want to have a word with ye.' I went, too, spite o' my neuralgy, for I saw he'd got somethin' on his mind. 'Look here,' says he, 'I gathered from the way you spoke that Jerry Lane's wife expects he's dead.' Certain, says I, his name was in the list o' the Susan Barnes's crew, and we read it in the paper. 'No,' says he to me, 'he ran away the day they sailed; he wasn't aboard, and he's livin' with another woman down to Shediac.' Them was his very words."

Nancy Lane sank back in her chair, and covered her horror-stricken eyes with her hands. "'T ain't pleasant news to have to tell," Sister Elton went on mildly, yet with evident relish and full command of the occasion. "He said he seen Jerry the morning he came away. I thought you ought to know it. I'll tell you one thing, Nancy: I told the skipper to keep still about it, and now I've told you, I won't spread it no further to set folks a-talking. I'll keep it secret till you say the word. There ain't much trafficking betwixt here and there, and he's dead to you, certain, as much as if he laid up here in the burying-ground."

Nancy had bowed her head upon the table; the thin sandy hair was streaked with gray. She did not answer one word; this was the hardest blow of all.

"I'm much obliged to you for being so friendly," she said after a few minutes, looking straight before her now in a dazed sort of way, and lifting the new coat from the floor, where it had fallen. "Yes, he's dead to me,—worse than dead, a good deal," and her lip quivered. "I can't seem to bring my thoughts to bear. I've got so used to thinkin'— No, don't you say nothin' to the folks, yet. I'd do as much for you." And Mrs. Elton knew that the smitten fellow-creature before her spoke the truth, and forebore.

Two or three days came and went, and with every hour the quiet, simple-hearted woman felt more grieved and unsteady in mind and body. Such a shattering thunderbolt of news rarely falls into a human life. She could not sleep; she wandered to and fro in the little house, and cried until she could cry no longer. Then a great rage spurred and excited her. She would go to Shediac, and call Jerry Lane to account. She would accuse him face to face; and the woman whom he was deceiving, as perhaps he had deceived her, should know the baseness and cowardice of this miserable man. So, dressed in her respectable Sunday clothes, in the gray bonnet and shawl that never had known any journeys except to meeting, or to a country funeral or quiet holiday-making, Nancy Lane trusted herself for the first time to the bewildering railway, to the temptations and dangers of the wide world outside the bounds of Walpole.

Two or three days later still, the quaint, thin figure familiar in Walpole highways flitted down the street of a provincial town. In the most primitive region of China this woman could hardly have felt a greater sense of foreign life and strangeness. At another time her native good sense and shrewd observation would have delighted in the experiences of this first week of travel, but she was too sternly angry and aggrieved, too deeply plunged in a survey of her own calamity, to take much notice of what was going on about her. Later she condemned the unworthy folly of the whole errand, but in these days the impulse to seek the culprit and con-front him was irresistible.

The innkeeper's wife, a kindly creature, had urged this puzzling guest to wait and rest and eat some supper, but Nancy refused, and without asking her way left the brightly lighted, flaring little public room, where curious eyes already offended her, and went out into the damp twilight. The voices of the street boys sounded outlandish, and she felt more and more lonely. She longed for Jerry to appear for protection's sake; she forgot why she sought him, and was eager to shelter herself behind the flimsy bulwark of his manhood. She rebuked herself presently with terrible bitter-ness for a womanish wonder whether he would say, "Why, Nancy, girl!" and be glad to see her. Poor woman, it was a work-laden, serious girlhood that had been hers, at any rate. The power of giving her whole self in unselfish, enthusiastic, patient devotion had not belonged to her youth only; it had sprung fresh and blossoming in her heart as every new year came and went.

One might have seen her stealing through the shadows, skirting the edge of a lumber-yard, stepping among the refuse of the harbor side, asking a question timidly now and then of some passer-by. Yes, they knew Jerry Lane,—his house was only a little way off; and one curious and compassionate Scotchman, divining by some inner sense the exciting nature of the errand, turned back, and offered fruitlessly to go with the stranger. "You know the man?" he asked. "He is his own enemy, but doing better now that he is married. He minds his work, I know that well; but he's taken a good wife." Nancy's heart beat faster with honest pride for a moment, until the shadow of the ugly truth and reality made it sink back to heaviness, and the fire of her smouldering rage was again kin-dled. She would speak to Jerry face to face before she slept, and a horrible contempt and scorn were ready for him, as with a glance either way along the road she entered the nar-row yard, and went noiselessly toward the window of a low, poor-looking house, from whence a bright light was shining out into the night.

Yes, there was Jerry, and it seemed as if she must faint and fall at the sight of him. How young he looked still! The thought smote her like a blow. They never were mates for each other, Jerry and she. Her own life was waning; she was an old woman.

He never had been so thrifty and respectable before; the other woman ought to know the savage truth about him, for all that! But at that moment the other woman stooped beside the supper table, and lifted a baby from its cradle, and put the dear, live little thing into its father's arms. The baby was wide awake, and laughed at Jerry, who laughed back again, and it reached up to catch at a handful of the curly hair which had been poor Nancy's delight.

The other woman stood there looking at them, full of pride and love. She was young, and trig, and neat. She looked a brisk, efficient little creature. Perhaps Jerry would make something of himself now; he always had it in him. The tears were running down Nancy's cheeks; the rain, too, had begun to fall. She stood there watching the little household sit down to supper, and noticed with eager envy how well cooked the food was, and how hungrily the master of the house ate what was put before him. All thoughts of ending the new wife's sin and folly vanished away. She could not enter in and break another heart; hers was broken already, and it would not matter. And Nancy Lane, a widow indeed, crept away again, as silently as she had come, to think what was best to be done, to find alternate woe and comfort in the memory of the sight she had seen.

The little house at the edge of the Walpole marshes seemed full of blessed shelter and comfort the evening that its forsaken mistress came back to it. Her strength was spent; she felt much more desolate now that she had seen with her own eyes that Jerry Lane was alive than when he was counted among the dead. An uncharacteristic disregard of the laws of the land filled this good woman's mind. Jerry had his life to live, and she wished him no harm. She wondered often how the baby grew. She fancied sometimes the changes and conditions of the far-away household. Alas! she knew only too well the weakness of the man, and once, in a grim outburst of impatience, she exclaimed, "I'd rather she should have to cope with him than me!"

But that evening, when she came back from Shediac, and sat in the dark for a long time, lest Mrs. Elton should see the light and risk her life in the evening air to bring unwelcome sympathy,—that evening, I say, came the hardest moment of all, when the Ann Floyd, tailoress, of so many virtuous, self-respecting years, whose idol had turned to clay, who was shamed, disgraced, and wronged, sat down alone to supper in the little kitchen.

She had put one cup and saucer on the table; she looked at them through bitter tears. Somehow a consciousness of her solitary age, her uncompanioned future, rushed through her mind; this failure of her best earthly hope was enough to break a stronger woman's heart.

Who can laugh at my Marsh Rosemary, or who can cry, for that matter? The gray primness of the plant is made up of a hundred colors, if you look close enough to find them. This same Marsh Rosemary stands in her own place, and holds her dry leaves and tiny blossoms steadily toward the same sun that the pink lotus blooms for, and the white rose.

A White Heron

I.

THE WOODS were already filled with shadows one June evening, just before eight o'clock, though a bright sunset still glimmered faintly among the trunks of the trees. A little girl was driving home her cow, a plodding, dilatory, provoking creature in her behavior, but a valued companion for all that. They were going away from whatever light there was, and striking deep into the woods, but their feet were familiar with the path, and it was no matter whether their eyes could see it or not.

There was hardly a night the summer through when the old cow could be found waiting at the pasture bars; on the contrary, it was her greatest pleasure to hide herself away among the high huckleberry bushes, and though she wore a loud bell she had made the discovery that if one stood perfectly still it would not ring. So Sylvia had to hunt for her until she found her, and call Co'! Co'! with never an answering Moo, until her childish patience was quite spent. If the creature had not given good milk and plenty of it, the case would have seemed very different to her owners. Besides, Sylvia had all the time there was, and very little use to make of it. Sometimes in pleasant weather it was a consolation to look upon the cow's pranks as an intelligent attempt to play hide and seek, and as the child had no playmates she lent herself to this amusement with a good deal of zest. Though this chase had been so long that the wary animal herself had given an unusual signal of her whereabouts, Sylvia had only laughed when she came upon Mistress Moolly at the swamp-side, and urged her affectionately homeward with a twig of birch leaves. The old cow was not inclined to wander farther, she even turned in the right direction for once as they left the pasture, and stepped along the road at a good pace. She was quite ready to be milked now, and seldom stopped to browse. Sylvia wondered what her grandmother would say because they were so late. It was a great while since she had left home at half-past five o'clock, but everybody knew the difficulty of making this errand a short one. Mrs. Tilley had chased the hornéd torment too many summer evenings herself to blame any one else for lingering, and was only thankful as she waited that she had Sylvia, nowadays, to give such valuable assistance. The good woman suspected that Sylvia loitered occasionally on her own account; there never was such a child for straying about out-of-doors since the world was made! Everybody said that it was a good change for a little maid who had tried to grow for eight years in a crowded manufacturing town, but, as for Sylvia herself, it seemed as if she never had been alive at all before she came to live at the farm. She thought often with wistful compassion of a wretched geranium that belonged to a town neighbor.

" 'Afraid of folks,' " old Mrs. Tilley said to herself, with a smile, after she had made the unlikely choice of Sylvia from her daughter's houseful of children, and was returning to the farm. " 'Afraid of folks,' they said! I guess she won't be troubled no great with 'em up to the old place!" When they reached the door of the lonely house and stopped to unlock it, and the cat came to purr loudly, and rub against them, a deserted pussy, indeed, but fat with young robins, Sylvia whispered that this was a beautiful place to live in, and she never should wish to go home.

The companions followed the shady wood-road, the cow taking slow steps and the child very fast ones. The cow stopped long at the brook to drink, as if the pasture were not half a swamp, and Sylvia stood still and waited, letting her bare feet cool themselves in the shoal water, while the great twilight moths struck softly against her. She waded on through the brook as the cow moved away, and listened to the thrushes with a heart that beat fast with pleasure. There was a stirring in the great boughs overhead. They were full of little birds and beasts that seemed to be wide awake, and going about their world, or else saying good-night to each other in sleepy twitters. Sylvia herself felt sleepy as she walked along. However, it was not much farther to the house, and the air was soft and sweet. She was not often in the woods so late as this, and it made her feel as if she were a part of the gray shadows and the moving leaves. She was just thinking how long it seemed since she first came to the farm a year ago, and wondering if everything went on in the noisy town just the same as when she was there; the thought of the great red-faced boy who used to chase and frighten her made her hurry along the path to escape from the shadow of the trees.

Suddenly this little woods-girl is horror-stricken to hear a clear whistle not very far away. Not a bird's-whistle, which would have a sort of friendliness, but a boy's whistle, determined, and somewhat aggressive. Sylvia left the cow to whatever sad fate might await her, and stepped discreetly aside into the bushes, but she was just too late. The enemy had discovered her, and called out in a very cheerful and persuasive tone, "Halloa, little girl, how far is it to the road?" and trembling Sylvia answered almost inaudibly, "A good ways."

She did not dare to look boldly at the tall young man, who carried a gun over his shoulder, but she came out of her bush and again followed the cow, while he walked alongside.

"I have been hunting for some birds," the stranger said kindly, "and I have lost my way, and need a friend very much. Don't be afraid," he added gallantly. "Speak up and tell me what your name is, and whether you think I can spend the night at your house, and go out gunning early in the morning."

Sylvia was more alarmed than before. Would not her grandmother consider her much to blame? But who could have foreseen such an accident as this? It did not seem to be her fault, and she hung her head as if the stem of it were broken, but managed to answer "Sylvy," with much effort when her companion again asked her name.

Mrs. Tilley was standing in the doorway when the trio came into view. The cow gave a loud moo by way of explanation.

"Yes, you'd better speak up for yourself, you old trial! Where'd she tucked herself away this time, Sylvy?" But Sylvia kept an awed silence; she knew by instinct that her grandmother did not comprehend the gravity of the situation. She must be mistaking the stranger for one of the farmer-lads of the region.

The young man stood his gun beside the door, and dropped a lumpy game-bag beside it; then he bade Mrs. Tilley good-evening, and repeated his wayfarer's story, and asked if he could have a night's lodging.

"Put me anywhere you like," he said. "I must be off early in the morning, before day; but I am very hungry, indeed. You can give me some milk at any rate, that's plain."

"Dear sakes, yes," responded the hostess, whose long slumbering hospitality seemed to be easily awakened. "You might fare better if you went out to the main road a mile or so, but you're welcome to what we've got. I'll milk right off, and you make yourself at home. You can sleep on husks or feathers," she proffered graciously. "I raised them all myself. There's good pasturing for geese just below here towards the ma'sh. Now step round and set a plate for the gentleman, Sylvy!" And Sylvia promptly stepped. She was glad to have something to do, and she was hungry herself.

It was a surprise to find so clean and comfortable a little dwelling in this New England wilderness. The young man had known the horrors of its most primitive housekeeping, and the dreary squalor of that level of society which does not rebel at the companionship of hens. This was the best thrift of an old-fashioned farmstead, though on such a small scale that it seemed like a hermitage. He listened eagerly to the old woman's quaint talk, he watched Sylvia's pale face and shining gray eyes with ever growing enthusiasm, and insisted that this was the best supper he had eaten for a month, and afterward, the new-made friends sat down in the doorway together while the moon came up.

Soon it would be berry-time, and Sylvia was a great help at picking. The cow was a good milker, though a plaguy thing to keep track of, the hostess gossiped frankly, adding presently that she had buried four children, so Sylvia's mother, and a son (who might be dead) in California were all the children she had left. "Dan, my boy, was a great hand to go gunning," she explained sadly. "I never wanted for pa'tridges or gray squer'ls while he was to home. He's been a great wand'rer, I expect, and he's no hand to write letters. There, I don't blame him, I'd ha' seen the world myself if it had been so I could."

"Sylvia takes after him," the grandmother continued affectionately, after a minute's pause. "There ain't a foot o' ground she don't know her way over, and the wild creatur's counts her one o' themselves. Squer'ls she'll tame to come an' feed right out o' her hands, and all sorts o' birds. Last winter she got the jay-birds to bangeing here, and I believe she'd 'a' scanted herself of her own meals to have plenty to throw out amongst 'em, if I had n't kep' watch. Anything but crows, I tell her, I'm willin' to help support—though Dan he had a tamed one o' them that did seem to have reason same as folks. It was round here a good spell after he went away. Dan an' his father they did n't hitch,—but he never held up his head ag'in after Dan had dared him an' gone off."

The guest did not notice this hint of family sorrows in his eager interest in something else.

"So Sylvy knows all about birds, does she?" he exclaimed, as he looked round at the little girl who sat, very demure but increasingly sleepy, in the moonlight. "I am making a collection of birds myself. I have been at it ever since I was a boy." (Mrs. Tilley smiled.) "There are two or three very rare ones I have been hunting for these five years. I mean to get them on my own ground if they can be found."

"Do you cage 'em up?" asked Mrs. Tilley doubtfully, in response to this enthusiastic announcement.

"Oh no, they're stuffed and preserved, dozens and dozens of them," said the ornithologist, "and I have shot or snared every one myself. I caught a glimpse of a white heron a few miles from here on Saturday, and I have followed it in this direction. They have never been found in this district at all. The little white heron, it is," and he turned again to look at Sylvia with the hope of discovering that the rare bird was one of her acquaintances.

But Sylvia was watching a hop-toad in the narrow footpath.

"You would know the heron if you saw it," the stranger continued eagerly. "A queer tall white bird with soft feathers and long thin legs. And it would have a nest perhaps in the top of a high tree, made of sticks, something like a hawk's nest."

Sylvia's heart gave a wild beat; she knew that strange white bird, and had once stolen softly near where it stood in some bright green swamp grass, away over at the other side of the woods. There was an open place where the sunshine always seemed strangely yellow and hot, where tall, nodding rushes grew, and her grandmother had warned her that she might sink in the soft black mud underneath and never be heard of more. Not far beyond were the salt marshes and just this side the sea itself, which Sylvia wondered and dreamed much about, but never had seen, whose great voice could sometimes be heard above the noise of the woods on stormy nights.

"I can't think of anything I should like so much as to find that heron's nest," the handsome stranger was saying. "I would give ten dollars to anybody who could show it to me," he added desperately, "and I mean to spend my whole vacation hunting for it if need be. Perhaps it was only migrating, or had been chased out of its own region by some bird of prey."

Mrs. Tilley gave amazed attention to all this, but Sylvia still watched the toad, not divining, as she might have done at some calmer time, that the creature wished to get to its hole under the door-step, and was much hindered by the unusual spectators at that hour of the evening. No amount of thought, that night, could decide how many wished-for treasures the ten dollars, so lightly spoken of, would buy.

The next day the young sportsman hovered about the woods, and Sylvia kept him company, having lost her first fear of the friendly lad, who proved to be most kind and sympathetic. He told her many things about the birds and what they knew and where they lived and what they did with themselves. And he gave her a jack-knife, which she thought as great a treasure as if she were a desert-islander. All day long he did not once make her troubled or afraid except when he brought down some unsuspecting singing creature from its bough. Sylvia would have liked him vastly better without his gun; she could not understand why he killed the very birds he seemed to like so much. But as the day waned, Sylvia still watched the young man with loving admiration. She had never seen anybody so charming and delightful; the woman's heart, asleep in the child, was vaguely thrilled by a dream of love. Some premonition of that great power stirred and swayed these young creatures who traversed the solemn woodlands with soft-footed silent care. They stopped to listen to a bird's song; they pressed forward again eagerly, parting the branches—speaking to each other rarely and in whispers; the young man going first and Sylvia following, fascinated, a few steps behind, with her gray eyes dark with excitement.

She grieved because the longed-for white heron was elusive, but she did not lead the guest, she only followed, and there was no such thing as speaking first. The sound of her own unquestioned voice would have terrified her—it was hard enough to answer yes or no when there was need of that. At last evening began to fall, and they drove the cow home together, and Sylvia smiled with pleasure when they came to the place where she heard the whistle and was afraid only the night before.

II.

Half a mile from home, at the farther edge of the woods, where the land was highest, a great pine-tree stood, the last of its generation. Whether it was left for a boundary mark, or for what reason, no one could say; the woodchoppers who had felled its mates were dead and gone long ago, and a whole forest of sturdy trees, pines and oaks and maples, had grown again. But the stately head of this old pine towered above them all and made a landmark for sea and shore miles and miles away. Sylvia knew it well. She had always believed that whoever climbed to the top of it could see the ocean; and the little girl had often laid her hand on the great rough trunk and looked up wistfully at those dark boughs that the wind always stirred, no matter how hot and still the air might be below. Now she thought of the tree with a new excitement, for why, if one climbed it at break of day could not one see all the world, and easily discover from whence the white heron flew, and mark the place, and find the hidden nest?

What a spirit of adventure, what wild ambition! What fancied triumph and delight and glory for the later morning when she could make known the secret! It was almost too real and too great for the childish heart to bear.

All night the door of the little house stood open and the whippoorwills came and sang upon the very step. The young sportsman and his old hostess were sound asleep, but Sylvia's great design kept her broad awake and watching. She forgot to think of sleep. The short summer night seemed as long as the winter darkness, and at last when the whippoorwills ceased, and she was afraid the morning would after all come too soon, she stole out of the house and followed the pasture path through the woods, hastening toward the open ground beyond, listening with a sense of comfort and companionship to the drowsy twitter of a half-awakened bird, whose perch she had jarred in passing. Alas, if the great wave of human interest which flooded for the first time this dull little life should sweep away the satisfactions of an existence heart to heart with nature and the dumb life of the forest!

There was the huge tree asleep yet in the paling moonlight, and small and silly Sylvia began with utmost bravery to mount to the top of it, with tingling, eager blood coursing the channels of her whole frame, with her bare feet and fingers, that pinched and held like bird's claws to the monstrous ladder reaching up, up, almost to the sky itself. First she must mount the white oak tree that grew alongside, where she was almost lost among the dark branches and the green leaves heavy and wet with dew; a bird fluttered off its nest, and a red squirrel ran to and fro and scolded pettishly at the harmless housebreaker. Sylvia felt her way easily. She had often climbed there, and knew that higher still one of the oak's upper branches chafed against the pine trunk, just where its lower boughs were set close together. There, when she made the dangerous pass from one tree to the other, the great enterprise would really begin.

She crept out along the swaying oak limb at last, and took the daring step across into the old pine-tree. The way was harder than she thought; she must reach far and hold fast, the sharp dry twigs caught and held her and scratched her like angry talons, the pitch made her thin little fingers clumsy and stiff as she went round and round the tree's great stem, higher and higher upward. The sparrows and robins in the woods below were beginning to wake and twitter to the dawn, yet it seemed much lighter there aloft in the pine-tree, and the child knew she must hurry if her project were to be of any use.

The tree seemed to lengthen itself out as she went up, and to reach farther and farther upward. It was like a great main-mast to the voyaging earth; it must truly have been amazed that morning through all its ponderous frame as it felt this determined spark of human spirit wending its way from higher branch to branch. Who knows how steadily the least twigs held themselves to advantage this light, weak creature on her way! The old pine must have loved his new dependent. More than all the hawks, and bats, and moths, and even the sweet voiced thrushes, was the brave, beating heart of the solitary gray-eyed child. And the tree stood still and frowned away the winds that June morning while the dawn grew bright in the east.

Sylvia's face was like a pale star, if one had seen it from the ground, when the last thorny bough was past, and she stood trembling and tired but wholly triumphant, high in the tree-top. Yes, there was the sea with the dawning sun making a golden dazzle over it, and toward that glorious east flew two hawks with slow-moving pinions. How low they looked in the air from that height when one had only seen them before far up, and dark against the blue sky. Their gray feathers were as soft as moths; they seemed only a little way from the tree, and Sylvia felt as if she too could go flying away among the clouds. Westward, the woodlands and farms reached miles and miles into the distance; here and there were church steeples, and white villages; truly it was a vast and awesome world!

The birds sang louder and louder. At last the sun came up bewilderingly bright. Sylvia could see the white sails of ships out at sea, and the clouds that were purple and rose-colored and yellow at first began to fade away. Where was the white heron's nest in the sea of green branches, and was this wonderful sight and pageant of the world the only reward for having climbed to such a giddy height? Now look down again, Sylvia, where the green marsh is set among the shining birches and dark hemlocks; there where you saw the white heron once you will see him again; look, look! a white spot of him like a single floating feather comes up from the dead hemlock and grows larger, and rises, and comes close at last, and goes by the landmark pine with steady sweep of wing and outstretched slender neck and crested head. And wait! wait! do not move a foot or a finger, little girl, do not send an arrow of light and consciousness from your two eager eyes, for the heron has perched on a pine bough not far beyond yours, and cries back to his mate on the nest and plumes his feathers for the new day!

The child gives a long sigh a minute later when a company of shouting cat-birds comes also to the tree, and vexed by their fluttering and lawlessness the solemn heron goes away. She knows his secret now, the wild, light, slender bird that floats and wavers, and goes back like an arrow presently to his home in the green world beneath. Then Sylvia, well satisfied, makes her perilous way down again, not daring to look far below the branch she stands on, ready to cry sometimes because her fingers ache and her lamed feet slip. Wondering over and over again what the stranger would say to her, and what he would think when she told him how to find his way straight to the heron's nest.

"Sylvy, Sylvy!" called the busy old grandmother again and again, but nobody answered, and the small husk bed was empty and Sylvia had disappeared.

The guest waked from a dream, and remembering his day's pleasure hurried to dress himself that might it sooner begin. He was sure from the way the shy little girl looked once or twice yesterday that she had at least seen the white heron, and now she must really be made to tell. Here she comes now, paler than ever, and her worn old frock is torn and tattered, and smeared with pine pitch. The grandmother and the sportsman stand in the door together and question her, and the splendid moment has come to speak of the dead hemlock-tree by the green marsh.

But Sylvia does not speak after all, though the old grandmother fretfully rebukes her, and the young man's kind, appealing eyes are looking straight in her own. He can make them rich with money; he has promised it, and they are poor now. He is so well worth making happy, and he waits to hear the story she can tell.

No, she must keep silence! What is it that suddenly forbids her and makes her dumb? Has she been nine years growing and now, when the great world for the first time puts out a hand to her, must she thrust it aside for a bird's sake? The murmur of the pine's green branches is in her ears, she remembers how the white heron came flying through the golden air and how they watched the sea and the morning together, and Sylvia cannot speak; she cannot tell the heron's secret and give its life away.

Dear loyalty, that suffered a sharp pang as the guest went away disappointed later in the day, that could have served and followed him and loved him as a dog loves! Many a night Sylvia heard the echo of his whistle haunting the pasture path as she came home with the loitering cow. She forgot even her sorrow at the sharp report of his gun and the sight of thrushes and sparrows dropping silent to the ground, their songs hushed and their pretty feathers stained and wet with blood. Were the birds better friends than their hunter might have been,—who can tell? Whatever treasures were lost to her, woodlands and summer-time, remember! Bring your gifts and graces and tell your secrets to this lonely country child!

Miss Tempy's Watchers

THE TIME of year was April; the place was a small farming town in New Hampshire, remote from any railroad. One by one the lights had been blown out in the scattered houses near Miss Tempy Dent's; but as her neighbors took a last look out-of-doors, their eyes turned with instinctive curiosity toward the old house, where a lamp burned steadily. They gave a little sigh. "Poor Miss Tempy!" said more than one bereft acquaintance; for the good woman lay dead in her north chamber, and the light was a watcher's light. The funeral was set for the next day, at one o'clock.

The watchers were two of the oldest friends, Mrs. Crowe and Sarah Ann Binson. They were sitting in the kitchen, because it seemed less awesome than the unused best room, and they beguiled the long hours by steady conversation. One would think that neither topics nor opinions would hold out, at that rate, all through the long spring night; but there was a certain degree of excitement just then, and the two women had risen to an unusual level of expressiveness and confidence. Each had already told the other more than one fact that she had determined to keep secret; they were again and again tempted into statements that either would have found impossible by daylight. Mrs. Crowe was knitting a blue yarn stocking for her husband; the foot was already so long that it seemed as if she must have forgotten to narrow it at the proper time. Mrs. Crowe knew exactly what she was about, however; she was of a much cooler disposition than Sister Binson, who made futile attempts at some sewing, only to drop her work into her lap whenever the talk was most engaging.

Their faces were interesting,—of the dry, shrewd, quick-witted New England type, with thin hair twisted neatly back out of the way. Mrs. Crowe could look vague and benignant, and Miss Binson was, to quote her neighbors, a little too sharp-set; but the world knew that she had need to be, with the load she must carry of supporting an inefficient widowed sister and six unpromising and unwilling nieces and nephews.

The eldest boy was at last placed with a good man to learn the mason's trade. Sarah Ann Binson, for all her sharp, anxious aspect, never defended herself, when her sister whined and fretted. She was told every week of her life that the poor children never would have had to lift a finger if their father had lived, and yet she had kept her steadfast way with the little farm, and patiently taught the young people many useful things, for which, as everybody said, they would live to thank her. However pleasureless her life appeared to outward view, it was brimful of pleasure to herself.

Mrs. Crowe, on the contrary, was well to do, her husband being a rich farmer and an easy-going man. She was a stingy woman, but for all that she looked kindly; and when she gave away anything, or lifted a finger to help anybody, it was thought a great piece of beneficence, and a compliment, indeed, which the recipient accepted with twice as much gratitude as double the gift that came from a poorer and more generous acquaintance. Everybody liked to be on good terms with Mrs. Crowe. Socially she stood much higher than Sarah Ann Binson. They were both old schoolmates and friends of Temperance Dent, who had asked them, one day, not long before she died, if they would not come together and look after the house, and manage everything, when she was gone. She may have had some hope that they might become closer friends in this period of intimate partnership, and that the richer woman might better understand the burdens of the poorer. They had not kept the house the night before; they were too weary with the care of their old friend, whom they had not left until all was over.

There was a brook which ran down the hillside very near the house, and the sound of it was much louder than usual. When there was silence in the kitchen, the busy stream had a strange insistence in its wild voice, as if it tried to make the watchers understand something that related to the past.

"I declare, I can't begin to sorrow for Tempy yet. I am so glad to have her at rest," whispered Mrs. Crowe. "It is strange to set here without her, but I can't make it clear that she has gone. I feel as if she had got easy and dropped off to sleep, and I'm more scared about waking her up than knowing any other feeling."

"Yes," said Sarah Ann, "it's just like that, ain't it? But I tell you we are goin' to miss her worse than we expect. She's helped me through with many a trial, has Temperance. I ain't the only one who says the same, neither."

These words were spoken as if there were a third person listening; somebody beside Mrs. Crowe. The watchers could not rid their minds of the feeling that they were being watched themselves. The spring wind whistled in the window crack, now and then, and buffeted the little house in a gusty way that had a sort of companionable effect. Yet, on the whole, it was a very still night, and the watchers spoke in a half-whisper.

"She was the freest-handed woman that ever I knew," said Mrs. Crowe, decidedly. "According to her means, she gave away more than anybody. I used to tell her 't wa'n't right. I used really to be afraid that she went without too much, for we have a duty to ourselves."

Sister Binson looked up in a half-amused, unconscious way, and then recollected herself.

Mrs. Crowe met her look with a serious face. "It ain't so easy for me to give as it is for some," she said simply, but with an effort which was made possible only by the occasion. "I should like to say, while Tempy is laying here yet in her own house, that she has been a constant lesson to me. Folks are too kind, and shame me with thanks for what I do. I ain't such a generous woman as poor Tempy was, for all she had nothin' to do with, as one may say."

Sarah Binson was much moved at this confession, and was even pained and touched by the unexpected humility. "You have a good many calls on you"—she began, and then left her kind little compliment half finished.

"Yes, yes, but I've got means enough. My disposition's more of a cross to me as I grow older, and I made up my mind this morning that Tempy's example should be my pattern henceforth." She began to knit faster than ever.

"'T ain't no use to get morbid: that's what Tempy used to say herself," said Sarah Ann, after a minute's silence. "Ain't it strange to say 'used to say'?" and her own voice choked a little. "She never did like to hear folks git goin' about themselves."

"'T was only because they're apt to do it so as other folks will say 't was n't so, an' praise 'em up," humbly replied Mrs. Crowe, "and that ain't my object. There wa'n't a child but what Tempy set herself to work to see what she could do to please it. One time my brother's folks had been stopping here in the summer, from Massachusetts. The children was all little, and they broke up a sight of toys, and left 'em when they were going away. Tempy come right up after they rode by, to see if she could n't help me set the house to rights, and she caught me just as I was going to fling some of the clutter into the stove. I was kind of tired out, starting 'em off in season. 'Oh, give me them!' says she, real pleading; and she wropped 'em up and took 'em home with her when she went, and she mended 'em up and stuck 'em together, and made some young one or other happy with every blessed one. You'd thought I'd done her the biggest favor. 'No thanks to me. I should ha' burnt 'em, Tempy,' says I."

"Some of 'em came to our house, I know," said Miss Binson. "She'd take a lot o' trouble to please a child, 'stead o' shoving of it out o' the way, like the rest of us when we're drove."

"I can tell you the biggest thing she ever gave, and I don't know 's there's anybody left but me to tell it. I don't want it forgot," Sarah Binson went on, looking up at the clock to see how the night was going. "It was that pretty-looking Trevor girl, who taught the Corners school, and married so well afterwards, out in New York State. You remember her, I dare say?"

"Certain," said Mrs. Crowe, with an air of interest.

"She was a splendid scholar, folks said, and give the school a great start; but she'd overdone herself getting her education, and working to pay for it, and she all broke down one spring, and Tempy made her come and stop with her a while,—you remember that? Well, she had an uncle, her mother's brother, out in Chicago, who was well off and friendly, and used to write to Lizzie Trevor, and I dare say make her some presents; but he was a lively, driving man, and did n't take time to stop and think about his folks. He had n't seen her since she was a little girl. Poor Lizzie was so pale and weakly that she just got through the term o' school. She looked as if she was just going straight off in a decline.

Tempy, she cosseted her up a while, and then, next thing folks knew, she was tellin' round how Miss Trevor had gone to see her uncle, and meant to visit Niagary Falls on the way, and stop over night. Now I happened to know, in ways I won't dwell on to explain, that the poor girl was in debt for her schoolin' when she come here, and her last quarter's pay had just squared it off at last, and left her without a cent ahead, hardly; but it had fretted her thinking of it, so she paid it all; they might have dunned her that she owed it to. An' I taxed Tempy about the girl's goin' off on such a journey till she owned up, rather 'n have Lizzie blamed, that she 'd given her sixty dollars, same 's if she was rolling in riches, and sent her off to have a good rest and vacation."

"Sixty dollars!" exclaimed Mrs. Crowe. "Tempy only had ninety dollars a year that came in to her; rest of her livin' she got by helpin' about, with what she raised off this little piece o' ground, sand one side an' clay the other. An' how often I've heard her tell, years ago, that she 'd rather see Niagary than any other sight in the world!"

The women looked at each other in silence; the magnitude of the generous sacrifice was almost too great for their comprehension.

"She was just poor enough to do that!" declared Mrs. Crowe at last, in an abandonment of feeling. "Say what you may, I feel humbled to the dust," and her companion ventured to say nothing. She never had given away sixty dollars at once, but it was simply because she never had it to give. It came to her very lips to say in explanation, "Tempy was so situated;" but she checked herself in time, for she would not break in upon her own loyal guarding of her dependent household.

"Folks say a great deal of generosity, and this one's being public-sperited, and that one free-handed about giving," said Mrs. Crowe, who was a little nervous in the silence. "I suppose we can't tell the sorrow it would be to some folks not to give, same 's 't would be to me not to save. I seem kind of made for that, as if 't was what I'd got to do. I should feel sights better about it if I could make it evident what I was savin' for. If I had a child, now, Sarah Ann," and her voice was a little husky,—"if I had a child, I should think I was heapin' of it up because he was the one trained by the Lord to scatter it again for good. But here's Crowe and me, we can't do anything with money, and both of us like to keep things same's they've always been. Now Priscilla Dance was talking away like a mill-clapper, week before last. She'd think I would go right off and get one o' them new-fashioned gilt-and-white papers for the best room, and some new furniture, an' a marble-top table. And I looked at her, all struck up. 'Why,' says I, 'Priscilla, that nice old velvet paper ain't hurt a mite. I shouldn't feel 't was my best room without it. Dan'el says 't is the first thing he can remember rubbin' his little baby fingers on to it, and how splendid he thought them red roses was.' I maintain," continued Mrs. Crowe stoutly, "that folks wastes sights o' good money doin' just such foolish things. Tearin' out the insides o' meetin'-houses, and fixin' the pews different; 't was good enough as 't was with mendin'; then times come, an' they want to put it all back same's 't was before."

This touched upon an exciting subject to active members of that parish. Miss Binson and Mrs. Crowe belonged to opposite parties, and had at one time come as near hard feelings as they could, and yet escape them. Each hastened to speak of other things and to show her untouched friendliness.

"I do agree with you," said Sister Binson, "that few of us know what use to make of money, beyond every-day necessities. You've seen more o' the world than I have, and know what's expected. When it comes to taste and judgment about such things, I ought to defer to others;" and with this modest avowal the critical moment passed when there might have been an improper discussion.

In the silence that followed, the fact of their presence in a house of death grew more clear than before. There was something disturbing in the noise of a mouse gnawing at the dry boards of a closet wall near by. Both the watchers looked up anxiously at the clock; it was almost the middle of the night, and the whole world seemed to have left them alone with their solemn duty. Only the brook was awake.

"Perhaps we might give a look up-stairs now," whispered Mrs. Crowe, as if she hoped to hear some reason against their going just then to the chamber of death; but Sister Binson rose, with a serious and yet satisfied countenance, and lifted the small lamp from the table. She was much more used to watching than Mrs. Crowe, and much less affected by it. They opened the door into a small entry with a steep stairway; they climbed the creaking stairs, and entered the cold upper room on tiptoe. Mrs. Crowe's heart began to beat very fast as the lamp was put on a high bureau, and made long, fixed shadows about the walls. She went hesitatingly toward the solemn shape under its white drapery, and felt a sense of remonstrance as Sarah Ann gently, but in a business-like way, turned back the thin sheet.

"Seems to me she looks pleasanter and pleasanter," whispered Sarah Ann Binson impulsively, as they gazed at the white face with its wonderful smile. "To-morrow 't will all have faded out. I do believe they kind of wake up a day or two after they die, and it's then they go." She replaced the light covering, and they both turned quickly away; there was a chill in this upper room.

"'T is a great thing for anybody to have got through, ain't it?" said Mrs. Crowe softly, as she began to go down the stairs on tiptoe. The warm air from the kitchen beneath met them with a sense of welcome and shelter.

"I don' know why it is, but I feel as near again to Tempy down here as I do up there," replied Sister Binson. "I feel as if the air was full of her, kind of. I can sense things, now and then, that she seems to say. Now I never was one to take up with no nonsense of sperits and such, but I declare I felt as if she told me just now to put some more wood into the stove."

Mrs. Crowe preserved a gloomy silence. She had suspected before this that her companion was of a weaker and more credulous disposition than herself. "'T is a great thing to have got through," she repeated, ignoring definitely all that had last been said. "I suppose you know as well as I that Tempy was one that always feared death. Well, it's all put behind her now; she knows what 't is." Mrs. Crowe gave a little sigh, and Sister Binson's quick sympathies were stirred toward this other old friend, who also dreaded the great change.

"I'd never like to forgit almost those last words Tempy spoke plain to me," she said gently, like the comforter she truly was. "She looked up at me once or twice, that last afternoon after I come to set by her, and let Mis' Owen go home; and I says, 'Can I do anything to ease you, Tempy?' and the tears come into my eyes so I couldn't see what kind of a nod she give me. 'No, Sarah Ann, you can't, dear,' says she; and then she got her breath again, and says she, looking at me real meanin', 'I'm only a-gettin' sleepier and sleepier; that's all there is,' says she, and smiled up at me kind of wishful, and shut her eyes. I knew well enough all she meant. She'd been lookin' out for a chance to tell me, and I don' know's she ever said much afterwards."

Mrs. Crowe was not knitting; she had been listening too eagerly. "Yes, 't will be a comfort to think of that sometimes," she said, in acknowledgment.

"I know that old Dr. Prince said once, in evenin' meetin', that he'd watched by many a dyin' bed, as we well knew, and enough o' his sick folks had been scared o' dyin' their whole lives through; but when they come to the last, he'd never seen one but was willin', and most were glad, to go. ''T is as natural as bein' born or livin' on,' he said. I don't know what had moved him to speak that night. You know he wa'n't in the habit of it, and 't was the monthly concert of prayer for foreign missions anyways," said Sarah Ann; "but 't was a great stay to the mind to listen to his words of experience."

"There never was a better man," responded Mrs. Crowe, in a really cheerful tone. She had recovered from her feeling of nervous dread, the kitchen was so comfortable with lamplight and firelight; and just then the old clock began to tell the hour of twelve with leisurely whirring strokes.

Sister Binson laid aside her work, and rose quickly and went to the cupboard. "We'd better take a little to eat," she explained. "The night will go fast after this. I want to know if you went and made some o' your nice cupcake, while you was home to-day?" she asked, in a pleased tone; and Mrs. Crowe acknowledged such a gratifying piece of thoughtfulness for this humble friend who denied herself all luxuries. Sarah Ann brewed a generous cup of tea, and the watchers drew their chairs up to the table presently, and quelled their hunger with good country appetites. Sister Binson put a spoon into a small, old-fashioned glass of preserved quince, and passed it to her friend. She was most familiar with the house, and played the part of hostess. "Spread some o' this on your bread and butter," she said to Mrs. Crowe. "Tempy wanted me to use some three or four times, but I never felt to. I know she'd like to have us comfortable now, and would urge us to make a good supper, poor dear."

"What excellent preserves she did make!" mourned Mrs. Crowe. "None of us has got her light hand at doin' things tasty. She made the most o' everything, too. Now, she only had that one old quince-tree down in the far corner of the piece, but she'd go out in the spring and tend to it, and look at it so pleasant, and kind of expect the old thorny thing into bloomin'."

"She was just the same with folks," said Sarah Ann. "And she'd never git more'n a little apernful o' quinces, but she'd have every mite o' goodness out o' those, and set the glasses up onto her best-room closet shelf, *so* pleased. 'T wa'n't but a week ago to-morrow mornin' I fetched her a little taste o' jelly in a teaspoon; and she says 'Thank ye,' and took it, an' the minute she tasted it she looked up at me as worried as could be. 'Oh, I don't want to eat that,' says she. 'I always keep that in case o' sickness.' 'You're goin' to have the good o' one tumbler yourself,' says I. 'I'd just like to know who's sick now, if you ain't!' An' she couldn't help laughin', I spoke up so smart. Oh, dear me, how I shall miss talkin' over things with her! She always sensed things, and got just the p'int you meant."

"She didn't begin to age until two or three years ago, did she?" asked Mrs. Crowe. "I never saw anybody keep her looks as Tempy did. She looked young long after I begun to feel like an old woman. The doctor used to say 't was her young heart, and I don't know but what he was right. How she did do for other folks! There was one spell she wasn't at home a day to a fortnight. She got most of her livin' so, and that made her own potatoes and things last her through. None o' the young folks could get married without her, and all the old ones was disappointed if she wa'n't round when they was down with sickness and had to go. An' cleanin', or tailorin' for boys, or rug-hookin',—there was nothin' but what she could do as handy as most. 'I do love to work,'—ain't you heard her say that twenty times a week?"

Sarah Ann Binson nodded, and began to clear away the empty plates. "We may want a taste o' somethin' more towards mornin'," she said. "There's plenty in the closet here; and in case some comes from a distance to the funeral, we'll have a little table spread after we get back to the house."

"Yes, I was busy all the mornin'. I've cooked up a sight o' things to bring over," said Mrs. Crowe. "I felt 't was the last I could do for her."

They drew their chairs near the stove again, and took up their work. Sister Binson's rocking-chair creaked as she rocked; the brook sounded louder than ever. It was more lonely when nobody spoke, and presently Mrs. Crowe returned to her thoughts of growing old.

"Yes, Tempy aged all of a sudden. I remember I asked her if she felt as well as common, one day, and she laughed at me good. There, when Dan'el begun to look old, I couldn't help feeling as if somethin' ailed him, and like as not 't was somethin' he was goin' to git right over, and I dosed him for it stiddy, half of one summer."

"How many things we shall be wanting to ask Tempy!" exclaimed Sarah Ann Binson, after a long pause. "I can't make up my mind to doin' without her. I wish folks could come back just once, and tell us how 't is where they've gone. Seems then we could do without 'em better."

The brook hurried on, the wind blew about the house now and then; the house itself was a silent place, and the supper, the warm fire, and an absence of any new topics for conversation made the watchers drowsy. Sister Binson closed her eyes first, to rest them for a minute; and Mrs. Crowe glanced at her compassionately, with a new sympathy for the hard-worked little woman. She made up her mind to let Sarah Ann have a good rest, while she kept watch alone; but in a few minutes her own knitting was dropped, and she, too, fell asleep. Overhead, the pale shape of Tempy Dent, the outworn body of that generous, loving-hearted, simple soul, slept on also in its white raiment. Perhaps Tempy herself stood near, and saw her own life and its surroundings with new understanding. Perhaps she herself was the only watcher.

Later, by some hours, Sarah Ann Binson woke with a start.

There was a pale light of dawn outside the small windows. Inside the kitchen, the lamp burned dim. Mrs. Crowe awoke, too.

"I think Tempy'd be the first to say 't was just as well we both had some rest," she said, not without a guilty feeling.

Her companion went to the outer door, and opened it wide. The fresh air was none too cold, and the brook's voice was not nearly so loud as it had been in the midnight darkness. She could see the shapes of the hills, and the great shadows that lay across the lower country. The east was fast growing bright.

"'T will be a beautiful day for the funeral," she said, and turned again, with a sigh, to follow Mrs. Crowe up the stairs. The world seemed more and more empty without the kind face and helpful hands of Tempy Dent.

A Winter Courtship

THE passenger and mail transportation between the towns of North Kilby and Sanscrit Pond was carried on by Mr. Jefferson Briley, whose two-seated covered wagon was usually much too large for the demands of business. Both the Sanscrit Pond and North Kilby people were stayers-at-home, and Mr. Briley often made his seven-mile journey in entire solitude, except for the limp leather mail-bag, which he held firmly to the floor of the carriage with his heavily shod left foot. The mail-bag had almost a personality to him, born of long association. Mr. Briley was a meek and timid-looking body, but he held a warlike soul, and encouraged his fancies by reading awful tales of bloodshed and lawlessness in the far West. Mindful of stage robberies and train thieves, and of express messengers who died at their posts, he was prepared for anything; and although he had trusted to his own strength and bravery these many years, he carried a heavy pistol under his front-seat cushion for better defense. This awful weapon was familiar to all his regular passengers, and was usually shown to strangers by the time two of the seven miles of Mr. Briley's route had been passed. The pistol was not loaded. Nobody (at least not Mr. Briley himself) doubted that the mere sight of such a weapon would turn the boldest adventurer aside.

Protected by such a man and such a piece of armament, one gray Friday morning in the edge of winter, Mrs. Fanny Tobin was traveling from Sanscrit Pond to North Kilby. She was an elderly and feeble-looking woman, but with a shrewd twinkle in her eyes, and she felt very anxious about her numerous pieces of baggage and her own personal safety. She was enveloped in many shawls and smaller wrappings, but they were not securely fastened, and kept getting undone and flying loose, so that the bitter December cold seemed to be picking a lock now and then, and creeping in to steal away the little warmth she had. Mr. Briley was cold, too, and could only cheer himself by remembering the valor of those pony-express drivers of the pre-railroad days, who had to cross the Rocky Mountains on the great California route. He spoke at length

of their perils to the suffering passenger, who felt none the
warmer, and at last gave a groan of weariness.

"How fur did you say 't was now?"

"I do' know's I said, Mis' Tobin," answered the driver,
with a frosty laugh. "You see them big pines, and the side of a
barn just this way, with them yellow circus bills? That's my
three-mile mark."

"Be we got four more to make? Oh, my laws!" mourned
Mrs. Tobin. "Urge the beast, can't ye, Jeff'son? I ain't used to
bein' out in such bleak weather. Seems if I couldn't git my
breath. I'm all pinched up and wigglin' with shivers now.
'T ain't no use lettin' the hoss go step-a-ty-step, this fashion."

"Landy me!" exclaimed the affronted driver. "I don't see
why folks expects me to race with the cars. Everybody that
gits in wants me to run the hoss to death on the road. I make
a good everage o' time, and that's all I *can* do. Ef you was to
go back an' forth every day but Sabbath fur eighteen years,
you'd want to ease it all you could, and let those thrash the
spokes out o' their wheels that wanted to. North Kilby, Mon-
days, Wednesdays, and Fridays; Sanscrit Pond, Tuesdays,
Thu'sdays, an' Saturdays. Me an' the beast's done it eighteen
years together, and the creatur' warn't, so to say, young when
we begun it, nor I neither. I re'lly didn't know's she'd hold
out till this time. There, git up, will ye, old mar'!" as the beast
of burden stopped short in the road.

There was a story that Jefferson gave this faithful creature a
rest three times a mile, and took four hours for the journey by
himself, and longer whenever he had a passenger. But in
pleasant weather the road was delightful, and full of people
who drove their own conveyances, and liked to stop and talk.
There were not many farms, and the third growth of white
pines made a pleasant shade, though Jefferson liked to say that
when he began to carry the mail his way lay through an open
country of stumps and sparse underbrush, where the white
pines nowadays completely arched the road.

They had passed the barn with circus posters, and felt
colder than ever when they caught sight of the weather-
beaten acrobats in their tights.

"My gorry!" exclaimed Widow Tobin, "them pore creatur's
looks as cheerless as little birch-trees in snow-time. I hope

they dresses 'em warmer this time o' year. Now, there! look at that one jumpin' through the little hoop, will ye?"

"He could n't git himself through there with two pair o' pants on," answered Mr. Briley. "I expect they must have to keep limber as eels. I used to think, when I was a boy, that 't was the only thing I could ever be reconciled to do for a livin'. I set out to run away an' follow a rovin' showman once, but mother needed me to home. There warn't nobody but me an' the little gals."

"You ain't the only one that's be'n disapp'inted o' their heart's desire," said Mrs. Tobin sadly. " 'T warn't so that I could be spared from home to learn the dressmaker's trade."

" 'T would a come handy later on, I declare," answered the sympathetic driver, "bein' 's you went an' had such a passel o' gals to clothe an' feed. There, them that's livin' is all well off now, but it must ha' been some inconvenient for ye when they was small."

"Yes, Mr. Briley, but then I've had my mercies, too," said the widow somewhat grudgingly. "I take it master hard now, though, havin' to give up my own home and live round from place to place, if they be my own child'en. There was Ad'line and Susan Ellen fussin' an' bickerin' yesterday about who'd got to have me next; and, Lord be thanked, they both wanted me right off but I hated to hear 'em talkin' of it over. I'd rather live to home, and do for myself."

"I've got consider'ble used to boardin'," said Jefferson, "sence ma'am died, but it made me ache 'long at the fust on 't, I tell ye. Bein' on the road 's I be, I could n't do no ways at keepin' house. I should want to keep right there and see to things."

"Course you would," replied Mrs. Tobin, with a sudden inspiration of opportunity which sent a welcome glow all over her. "Course you would, Jeff'son,"—she leaned toward the front seat; "that is to say, onless you had jest the right one to do it for ye."

And Jefferson felt a strange glow also, and a sense of unexpected interest and enjoyment.

"See here, Sister Tobin," he exclaimed with enthusiasm. "Why can't ye take the trouble to shift seats, and come front here long o' me? We could put one buff'lo top o' the other,—

they're both wearin' thin,—and set close, and I do' know but we sh'd be more protected ag'inst the weather."

"Well, I could n't be no colder if I was froze to death," answered the widow, with an amiable simper. "Don't ye let me delay you, nor put you out, Mr. Briley. I don't know 's I'd set forth to-day if I'd known 't was so cold; but I had all my bundles done up, and I ain't one that puts my hand to the plough an' looks back, 'cordin' to Scriptur'."

"You would n't wanted me to ride all them seven miles alone?" asked the gallant Briley sentimentally, as he lifted her down, and helped her up again to the front seat. She was a few years older than he, but they had been schoolmates, and Mrs. Tobin's youthful freshness was suddenly revived to his mind's eye. She had a little farm; there was nobody left at home now but herself, and so she had broken up housekeeping for the winter. Jefferson himself had savings of no mean amount.

They tucked themselves in, and felt better for the change, but there was a sudden awkwardness between them; they had not had time to prepare for an unexpected crisis.

"They say Elder Bickers, over to East Sanscrit, 's been and got married again to a gal that 's four year younger than his oldest daughter," proclaimed Mrs. Tobin presently. "Seems to me 't was fool's business."

"I view it so," said the stage-driver. "There 's goin' to be a mild open winter for that fam'ly."

"What a joker you be for a man that 's had so much responsibility!" smiled Mrs. Tobin, after they had done laughing. "Ain't you never 'fraid, carryin' mail matter and such valuable stuff, that you 'll be set on an' robbed, 'specially by night?"

Jefferson braced his feet against the dasher under the worn buffalo skin. "It is kind o' scary, or would be for some folks, but I 'd like to see anybody get the better o' me. I go armed, and I don't care who knows it. Some o' them drover men that comes from Canady looks as if they did n't care what they did, but I look 'em right in the eye every time."

"Men folks is brave by natur'," said the widow admiringly. "You know how Tobin would let his fist right out at anybody that ondertook to sass him. Town-meetin' days, if he got disappointed about the way things went, he'd lay 'em out in win'rows; and ef he had n't been a church-member he'd been a real fightin' character. I was always 'fraid to have him roused, for all he was so willin' and meechin' to home, and set round clever as anybody. My Susan Ellen used to boss him same's the kitten, when she was four year old."

"I've got a kind of a sideways cant to my nose, that Tobin give me when we was to school. I don't know 's you ever noticed it," said Mr. Briley. "We was scufflin', as lads will. I never bore him no kind of a grudge. I pitied ye, when he was taken away. I re'lly did, now, Fanny. I liked Tobin first-rate, and I liked you. I used to say you was the han'somest girl to school."

"Lemme see your nose. 'T is all straight, for what I know," said the widow gently, as with a trace of coyness she gave a hasty glance. "I don't know but what 't is warped a little, but nothin' to speak of. You 've got real nice features, like your marm 's folks."

It was becoming a sentimental occasion, and Jefferson Briley felt that he was in for something more than he had bargained. He hurried the faltering sorrel horse, and began to talk of the weather. It certainly did look like snow, and he was tired of bumping over the frozen road.

"I should n't wonder if I hired a hand here another year, and went off out West myself to see the country."

"Why, how you talk!" answered the widow.

"Yes 'm," pursued Jefferson. " 'T is tamer here than I like, and I was tellin' 'em yesterday I've got to know this road most too well. I'd like to go out an' ride in the mountains with some o' them great clipper coaches, where the driver don't know one minute but he'll be shot dead the next. They carry an awful sight o' gold down from the mines, I expect."

"I should be scairt to death," said Mrs. Tobin. "What creatur 's men folks be to like such things! Well, I do declare."

"Yes," explained the mild little man. "There's sights of desp'radoes makes a han'some livin' out o' followin' them coaches, an' stoppin' an' robbin' 'em clean to the bone. Your money *or* your life!" and he flourished his stub of a whip over the sorrel mare.

"Landy me! you make me run all of a cold creep. Do tell somethin' heartenin', this cold day. I shall dream bad dreams all night."

"They put on black crape over their heads," said the driver mysteriously. "Nobody knows who most on 'em be, and like as not some o' them fellows come o' good families. They've got so they stop the cars, and go right through 'em bold as brass. I could make your hair stand on end, Mis' Tobin,—I could *so!*"

"I hope none on 'em'll git round our way, I'm sure," said Fanny Tobin. "I don't want to see none on 'em in their crape bunnits comin' after me."

"I ain't goin' to let nobody touch a hair o' your head," and Mr. Briley moved a little nearer, and tucked in the buffaloes again.

"I feel considerable warm to what I did," observed the widow by way of reward.

"There, I used to have my fears," Mr. Briley resumed, with an inward feeling that he never would get to North Kilby depot a single man. "But you see I hadn't nobody but myself to think of. I've got cousins, as you know, but nothin' nearer, and what I've laid up would soon be parted out; and—well, I suppose some folks would think o' me if anything was to happen."

Mrs. Tobin was holding her cloud over her face,—the wind was sharp on that bit of open road,—but she gave an encouraging sound, between a groan and a chirp.

"'T wouldn't be like nothin' to me not to see you drivin' by," she said, after a minute. "I shouldn't know the days o' the week. I says to Susan Ellen last week I was sure 't was Friday, and she said no, 't was Thursday; but next minute you druv by and headin' toward North Kilby, so we found I was right."

"I've got to be a featur' of the landscape," said Mr. Briley plaintively. "This kind o' weather the old mare and me, we wish we was done with it, and could settle down kind o' comfortable. I've been lookin' this good while, as I drove the road, and I've picked me out a piece o' land two or three times. But I can't abide the thought o' buildin',—'t would plague me to death; and both Sister Peak to North Kilby and

Mis' Deacon Ash to the Pond, they vie with one another to do well by me, fear I'll like the other stoppin'-place best."

"*I* shouldn't covet livin' long o' neither one o' them women," responded the passenger with some spirit. "I see some o' Mis' Peak's cookin' to a farmers' supper once, when I was visitin' Susan Ellen's folks, an' I says 'Deliver me from sech pale-complected baked beans as them!' and she give a kind of a quack. She was settin' jest at my left hand, and couldn't help hearin' of me. I wouldn't have spoken if I had known, but she needn't have let on they was hers an' make everything unpleasant. 'I guess them beans taste just as well as other folks',' says she, and she wouldn't never speak to me afterward."

"Do' know's I blame her," ventured Mr. Briley. "Women folks is dreadful pudjicky about their cookin'. I've always heard you was one o' the best o' cooks, Mis' Tobin. I know them doughnuts an' things you've give me in times past, when I was drivin' by. Wish I had some on 'em now. I never let on, but Mis' Ash's cookin' 's the best by a long chalk. Mis' Peak's handy about some things, and looks after mendin' of me up."

"It doos seem as if a man o' your years and your quiet make ought to have a home you could call your own," suggested the passenger. "I kind of hate to think o' your bangein' here and boardin' there, and one old woman mendin', and the other settin' ye down to meals that like 's not don't agree with ye."

"Lor', now, Mis' Tobin, le's not fuss round no longer," said Mr. Briley impatiently. "You know you covet me same 's I do you."

"I don't nuther. Don't you go an' say fo'lish things you can't stand to."

"I've been tryin' to git a chance to put in a word with you ever sence— Well, I expected you'd want to get your feelin's kind o' calloused after losin' Tobin."

"There's nobody can fill his place," said the widow.

"I do' know but I can fight for ye town-meetin' days, on a pinch," urged Jefferson boldly.

"I never see the beat o' you men fur conceit," and Mrs. Tobin laughed. "I ain't goin' to bother with ye, gone half the

time as you be, an' carryin' on with your Mis' Peaks and Mis'
Ashes. I dare say you've promised yourself to both on 'em
twenty times."

"I hope to gracious if I ever breathed a word to none on
'em!" protested the lover. "'T ain't for lack o' opportunities
set afore me, nuther;" and then Mr. Briley craftily kept silence, as if he had made a fair proposal, and expected a definite reply.

The lady of his choice was, as she might have expressed it,
much beat about. As she soberly thought, she was getting
along in years, and must put up with Jefferson all the rest of
the time. It was not likely she would ever have the chance of
choosing again, though she was one who liked variety.

Jefferson was n't much to look at, but he was pleasant and
appeared boyish and young-feeling. "I do' know 's I should
do better," she said unconsciously and half aloud. "Well, yes,
Jefferson, seein' it 's you. But we 're both on us kind of old to
change our situation." Fanny Tobin gave a gentle sigh.

"Hooray!" said Jefferson. "I was scairt you meant to keep
me sufferin' here a half an hour. I declare, I 'm more pleased
than I calc'lated on. An' I expected till lately to die a single
man!"

"'T would re'lly have been a shame; 't ain't natur'," said
Mrs. Tobin, with confidence. "I don't see how you held out
so long with bein' solitary."

"I 'll hire a hand to drive for me, and we 'll have a good
comfortable winter, me an' you an' the old sorrel. I 've been
promisin' of her a rest this good while."

"Better keep her a steppin'," urged thrifty Mrs. Fanny.
"She 'll stiffen up master, an' disapp'int ye, come spring."

"You 'll have me, now, won't ye, sartin?" pleaded Jefferson,
to make sure. "You ain't one o' them that plays with a man's
feelin's. Say right out you 'll have me."

"I s'pose I shall have to," said Mrs. Tobin somewhat
mournfully. "I feel for Mis' Peak an' Mis' Ash, pore creatur's.
I expect they 'll be hardshipped. They 've always been hard-
worked, an' may have kind o' looked forward to a little ease.
But one on 'em would be left lamentin', anyhow," and she
gave a girlish laugh. An air of victory animated the frame of
Mrs. Tobin. She felt but twenty-five years of age. In that mo-

ment she made plans for cutting her Briley's hair, and making him look smartened-up and ambitious. Then she wished that she knew for certain how much money he had in the bank; not that it would make any difference now. "He need n't bluster none before me," she thought gayly. "He's harmless as a fly."

"Who'd have thought we'd done such a piece of engineerin', when we started out?" inquired the dear one of Mr. Briley's heart, as he tenderly helped her to alight at Susan Ellen's door.

"Both on us, jest the least grain," answered the lover. "Gimme a good smack, now, you clever creatur';" and so they parted. Mr. Bailey had been taken on the road in spite of his pistol.

Going to Shrewsbury

THE TRAIN stopped at a way station with apparent unwillingness, and there was barely time for one elderly passenger to be hurried on board before a sudden jerk threw her
almost off her unsteady old feet and we moved on. At my first
glance I saw only a perturbed old countrywoman, laden with
a large basket and a heavy bundle tied up in an old-fashioned
bundle-handkerchief; then I discovered that she was a friend
of mine, Mrs. Peet, who lived on a small farm, several miles
from the village. She used to be renowned for good butter
and fresh eggs and the earliest cowslip greens; in fact, she
always made the most of her farm's slender resources; but it
was some time since I had seen her drive by from market in
her ancient thorough-braced wagon.

The brakeman followed her into the crowded car, also carrying a number of packages. I leaned forward and asked Mrs.
Peet to sit by me; it was a great pleasure to see her again. The
brakeman seemed relieved, and smiled as he tried to put part
of his burden into the rack overhead; but even the flowered
carpet-bag was much too large, and he explained that he
would take care of everything at the end of the car. Mrs. Peet
was not large herself, but with the big basket, and the bundle-
handkerchief, and some possessions of my own we had very
little spare room.

"So this 'ere is what you call ridin' in the cars! Well, I do
declare!" said my friend, as soon as she had recovered herself
a little. She looked pale and as if she had been in tears, but
there was the familiar gleam of good humor in her tired old
eyes.

"Where in the world are you going, Mrs. Peet?" I asked.

"Can't be you ain't heared about me, dear?" said she. "Well,
the world's bigger than I used to think 't was. I've broke
up,—'t was the only thing *to* do,—and I'm a-movin' to
Shrewsbury."

"To Shrewsbury? Have you sold the farm?" I exclaimed,
with sorrow and surprise. Mrs. Peet was too old and too characteristic to be suddenly transplanted from her native soil.

" 'T wa'n't mine, the place wa'n't." Her pleasant face hard-ened slightly. "He was coaxed an' over-persuaded into signin' off before he was taken away. Is'iah, son of his sister that married old Josh Peet, come it over him about his bein' past work and how he 'd do for him like an own son, an' we owed him a little somethin'. I 'd paid off everythin' but that, an' was fool enough to leave it till the last, on account o' Is'iah's bein' a relation and not needin' his pay much as some others did. It 's hurt me to have the place fall into other hands. Some wanted me to go right to law; but 't would n't be no use. Is'iah 's smarter 'n I be about them matters. You see he 's got my name on the paper, too; he said 't was somethin' 'bout bein' responsible for the taxes. We was scant o' money, an' I was wore out with watchin' an' being broke o' my rest. After my tryin' hard for risin' forty-five year to provide for bein' past work, here I be, dear, here I be! I used to drive things smart, you remember. But we was fools enough in '72 to put about everythin' we had safe in the bank into that spool fac-tory that come to nothin'. But I tell ye I could ha' kept myself long 's I lived, if I could ha' held the place. I 'd parted with most o' the woodland, if Is'iah 'd coveted it. He was welcome to that, 'cept what might keep me in oven-wood. I 've always desired to travel an' see somethin' o' the world, but I 've got the chance now when I don't value it no great."

"Shrewsbury is a busy, pleasant place," I ventured to say by way of comfort, though my heart was filled with rage at the trickery of Isaiah Peet, who had always looked like a fox and behaved like one.

"Shrewsbury 's be'n held up consid'able for me to smile at," said the poor old soul, "but I tell ye, dear, it 's hard to go an' live twenty-two miles from where you 've always had your home and friends. It may divert me, but it won't be home. You might as well set out one o' my old apple-trees on the beach, so 't could see the waves come in, — there would n't be no please to it."

"Where are you going to live in Shrewsbury?" I asked presently.

"I don't expect to stop long, dear creatur'. I 'm 'most seventy-six year old," and Mrs. Peet turned to look at me with pathetic amusement in her honest wrinkled face. "I said right out to Is'iah, before a roomful o' the neighbors, that I expected it of him to git me home an' bury me when my time come, and do it respectable; but I wanted to airn my livin', if 't was so I could, till then. He 'd made sly talk, you see, about my electin' to leave the farm and go 'long some o' my own folks; but"—and she whispered this carefully—"he did n't give me no chance to stay there without hurtin' my pride and dependin' on him. I ain't said that to many folks, but all must have suspected. A good sight on 'em 's had money of Is'iah, though, and they don't like to do nothin' but take his part an' be pretty soft spoken, fear it 'll git to his ears. Well, well, dear, we 'll let it be bygones, and not think of it no more;" but I saw the great tears roll slowly down her cheeks, and she pulled her bonnet forward impatiently, and looked the other way.

"There looks to be plenty o' good farmin' land in this part o' the country," she said, a minute later. "Where be we now? See them handsome farm buildin's; he must be a well-off man." But I had to tell my companion that we were still within the borders of the old town where we had both been born. Mrs. Peet gave a pleased little laugh, like a girl. "I'm expectin' Shrewsbury to pop up any minute. I'm feared to be kerried right by. I wa'n't never aboard of the cars before, but I've so often thought about 'em I don't know but it seems natural. Ain't it jest like flyin' through the air? I can't catch holt to see nothin'. Land! and here's my old cat goin' too, and never mistrustin'. I ain't told you that I'd fetched her."

"Is she in that basket?" I inquired with interest.

"Yis, dear. Truth was, I calc'lated to have her put out o' the misery o' movin', an spoke to one o' the Barnes boys, an' he promised me all fair; but he wa'n't there in season, an' I kind o' made excuse to myself to fetch her along. She 's an' old creatur', like me, an' I can make shift to keep her some way or 'nuther; there 's probably mice where we 're goin', an' she 's a proper mouser that can about keep herself if there 's any sort o' chance. 'T will be somethin' o' home to see her goin' an' comin', but I expect we 're both on us goin' to miss our old haunts. I 'd love to know what kind o' mousin' there 's goin' to be for me."

"You must n't worry," I answered, with all the bravery and assurance that I could muster. "Your niece will be thankful to have you with her. Is she one of Mrs. Winn's daughters?"

"Oh, no, they ain't able; it's Sister Wayland's darter Isabella, that married the overseer of the gre't carriage-shop. I ain't seen her since just after she was married; but I turned to her first because I knew she was best able to have me, and then I can see just how the other girls is situated and make me some kind of a plot. I wrote to Isabella, though she *is* ambitious, and said 't was so I 'd got to ask to come an' make her a visit, an' she wrote back she would be glad to have me; but she did n't write right off, and her letter was scented up dreadful strong with some sort o' essence, and I don't feel heartened about no great of a welcome. But there, I 've got eyes, an' I can see *how* 't is when I git *where* 't is. Sister Winn's gals ain't married, an' they 've always boarded, an' worked in the shop on trimmin's. Isabella's well off; she had some means from her father's sister. I thought it all over by night an' day, an' I recalled that our folks kept Sister Wayland's folks all one winter, when he 'd failed up and got into trouble. I 'm reckonin' on sendin' over to-night an' gittin' the Winn gals to come and see me and advise. Perhaps some on 'em may know of somebody that 'll take me for what help I can give about house, or some clever folks that have been lookin' for a smart cat, any ways; no, I don't know 's I could let her go to strangers.

"There was two or three o' the folks round home that acted real warm-hearted towards me, an' urged me to come an' winter with 'em," continued the exile; "an' this mornin' I wished I 'd agreed to, 't was so hard to break away. But now it 's done I feel more 'n ever it 's best. I could n't bear to live right in sight o' the old place, and come spring I should n't 'prove of nothing Is'iah ondertakes to do with the land. Oh, dear sakes! now it comes hard with me not to have had no child'n. When I was young an' workin' hard and into everything, I felt kind of free an' superior to them that was so blessed, an' their houses cluttered up from mornin' till night, but I tell ye it comes home to me now. I 'd be most willin' to own to even Is'iah, mean 's he is; but I tell ye I 'd took it out of him 'fore he was a grown man, if there 'd be'n any virtue in cow-hidin'

of him. Folks don't look like wild creatur's for nothin'.
Is'iah's got fox blood in him, an' p'r'haps 't is his misfortune.
His own mother always favored the looks of an old fox, true's
the world; she was a poor tool,—a poor tool! I d'know's we
ought to blame him same's we do.

"I've always been a master proud woman, if I was riz
among the pastures," Mrs. Peet added, half to herself. There
was no use in saying much to her; she was conscious of little
beside her own thoughts and the smouldering excitement
caused by this great crisis in her simple existence. Yet the atmosphere of her loneliness, uncertainty, and sorrow was so
touching that after scolding again at her nephew's treachery,
and finding the tears come fast to my eyes as she talked, I
looked intently out of the car window, and tried to think
what could be done for the poor soul. She was one of the
old-time people, and I hated to have her go away; but even if
she could keep her home she would soon be too feeble to live
there alone, and some definite plan must be made for her
comfort. Farms in that neighborhood were not valuable. Perhaps through the agency of the law and quite in secret, Isaiah
Peet could be forced to give up his unrighteous claim. Perhaps, too, the Winn girls, who were really no longer young,
might have saved something, and would come home again.
But it was easy to make such pictures in one's mind, and I
must do what I could through other people, for I was just
leaving home for a long time. I wondered sadly about Mrs.
Peet's future, and the ambitious Isabella, and the favorite Sister Winn's daughters, to whom, with all their kindliness of
heart, the care of so old and perhaps so dependent an aunt
might seem impossible. The truth about life in Shrewsbury
would soon be known; more than half the short journey was
already past.

To my great pleasure, my fellow-traveler now began to forget her own troubles in looking about her. She was an alert,
quickly interested old soul, and this was a bit of neutral
ground between the farm and Shrewsbury, where she was un-
attached and irresponsible. She had lived through the last
tragic moments of her old life, and felt a certain relief, and
Shrewsbury might be as far away as the other side of the
Rocky Mountains for all the consciousness she had of its real

existence. She was simply a traveler for the time being, and began to comment, with delicious phrases and shrewd understanding of human nature, on two or three persons near us who attracted her attention.

"Where do you s'pose they be all goin'?" she asked contemptuously. "There ain't none on 'em but what looks kind o' respectable. I'll warrant they've left work to home they'd ought to be doin'. I knowed, if ever I stopped to think, that cars was hived full o' folks, an' wa'n't run to an' fro for nothin'; but these can't be quite up to the average, be they? Some on 'em's real thrif'less; guess they've be'n shoved out o' the last place, an' goin' to try the next one,—*like me*, I suppose you'll want to say! Jest see that flauntin' old creatur' that looks like a stopped clock. There! everybody can't be o' one goodness, even preachers."

I was glad to have Mrs. Peet amused, and we were as cheerful as we could be for a few minutes. She said earnestly that she hoped to be forgiven for such talk, but there were some kinds of folks in the cars that she never had seen before. But when the conductor came to take her ticket she relapsed into her first state of mind, and was at a loss.

"You'll have to look after me, dear, when we get to Shrewsbury," she said, after we had spent some distracted moments in hunting for the ticket, and the cat had almost escaped from the basket, and the bundle-handkerchief had become untied and all its miscellaneous contents scattered about our laps and the floor. It was a touching collection of the last odds and ends of Mrs. Peet's housekeeping: some battered books, and singed holders for flatirons, and the faded little shoulder shawl that I had seen her wear many a day about her bent shoulders. There were her old tin match-box spilling all its matches, and a goose-wing for brushing up ashes, and her much-thumbed Leavitt's Almanac. It was most pathetic to see these poor trifles out of their places. At last the ticket was found in her left-hand woolen glove, where her stiff, workworn hand had grown used to the feeling of it.

"I shouldn't wonder, now, if I come to like living over to Shrewsbury first-rate," she insisted, turning to me with a hopeful, eager look to see if I differed. "You see 't won't be so tough for me as if I hadn't always felt it lurking within me to go off some day or 'nother an' see how other folks did things. I do' know but what the Winn gals have laid up somethin' sufficient for us to take a house, with the little mite I've got by me. I might keep house for us all, 'stead o' boardin' round in other folks' houses. That I ain't never been demeaned to, but I dare say I should find it pleasant in some ways. Town folks has got the upper hand o' country folks, but with all their work an' pride they can't make a dandelion. I do' know the times when I've set out to wash Monday mornin's, an' tied out the line betwixt the old pucker-pear tree and the corner o' the barn, an' thought, 'Here I be with the same kind o' week's work right over again.' I'd wonder kind o' f'erce if I couldn't git out of it noways; an' now here I be out of it, and an uprooteder creatur' never stood on the airth. Just as I got to feel I had somethin' ahead come that spool-factory business. There! you know he never was a forehanded man; his health was slim, and he got discouraged pretty nigh before ever he begun. I hope he don't know I'm turned out o' the old place. 'Is'iah 's well off; he'll do the right thing by ye,' says he. But my! I turned hot all over when I found out what I'd put my name to,—me that had always be'n counted a smart woman! I did undertake to read it over, but I couldn't sense it. I've told all the folks so when they laid it off on to me some: but hand-writin' is awful tedious readin' and my head felt that day as if the works was gone.

"I ain't goin' to sag on to nobody," she assured me eagerly, as the train rushed along. "I've got more work in me now than folks expects at my age. I may be consid'able use to Isabella. She's got a family, an' I'll take right holt in the kitchen or with the little gals. She had four on 'em, last I heared. Isabella was never one that liked house-work. Little gals! I do' know now but what they must be about grown, time doos slip away so. I expect I shall look outlandish to 'em. But there! everybody knows me to home, an' nobody knows me to Shrewsbury; 't won't make a mite o' difference, if I take holt willin'."

I hoped, as I looked at Mrs. Peet, that she would never be persuaded to cast off the gathered brown silk bonnet and the plain shawl that she had worn so many years; but Isabella might think it best to insist upon more modern fashions. Mrs.

Peet suggested, as if it were a matter of little consequence, that she had kept it in mind to buy some mourning; but there were other things to be thought of first, and so she had let it go until winter, any way, or until she should be fairly settled in Shrewsbury.

"Are your nieces expecting you by this train?" I was moved to ask, though with all the good soul's ready talk and appealing manner I could hardly believe that she was going to Shrewsbury for more than a visit; it seemed as if she must return to the worn old farmhouse over by the sheep-lands. She answered that one of the Barnes boys had written a letter for her the day before, and there was evidently little uneasiness about her first reception.

We drew near the junction where I must leave her within a mile of the town. The cat was clawing indignantly at the basket, and her mistress grew as impatient of the car. She began to look very old and pale, my poor fellow-traveler, and said that she felt dizzy, going so fast. Presently the friendly red-cheeked young brakeman came along, bringing the carpet-bag and other possessions, and insisted upon taking the alarmed cat beside, in spite of an aggressive paw that had worked its way through the wicker prison. Mrs. Peet watched her goods disappear with suspicious eyes, and clutched her bundle-handkerchief as if it might be all that she could save. Then she anxiously got to her feet, much too soon, and when I said good-by to her at the car door she was ready to cry. I pointed to the car which she was to take next on the branch line of railway, and I assured her that it was only a few minutes' ride to Shrewsbury, and that I felt certain she would find somebody waiting. The sight of that worn, thin figure adventuring alone across the platform gave my heart a sharp pang as the train carried me away.

Some of the passengers who sat near asked me about my old friend with great sympathy, after she had gone. There was a look of tragedy about her, and indeed it had been impossible not to get a good deal of her history, as she talked straight on in the same tone, when we stopped at a station, as if the train were going at full speed, and some of her remarks caused pity and amusements by turns. At the last minute she said, with deep self-reproach, "Why, I have n't asked a word about your folks; but you'd ought to excuse such an old stray hen as I be."

In the spring I was driving by on what the old people of my native town call the sheep-lands road, and the sight of Mrs. Peet's former home brought our former journey freshly to my mind. I had last heard from her just after she got to Shrewsbury, when she had sent me a message.

"Have you ever heard how she got on?" I eagerly asked my companion.

"Did n't I tell you that I met her in Shrewsbury High Street one day?" I was answered. "She seemed perfectly delighted with everything. Her nieces have laid up a good bit of money, and are soon to leave the mill, and most thankful to have old Mrs. Peet with them. Somebody told me that they wished to buy the farm here, and come back to live, but she would n't hear of it, and thought they would miss too many privileges. She has been going to concerts and lectures this winter, and insists that Isaiah did her a good turn."

We both laughed. My own heart was filled with joy, for the uncertain, lonely face of this homeless old woman had often haunted me. The rain-blackened little house did certainly look dreary, and a whole lifetime of patient toil had left few traces. The pucker-pear tree was in full bloom, however, and gave a welcome gayety to the deserted door-yard.

A little way beyond we met Isaiah Peet, the prosperous money-lender, who had cheated the old woman of her own. I fancied that he looked somewhat ashamed, as he recognized us. To my surprise, he stopped his horse in most social fashion.

"Old Aunt Peet's passed away," he informed me briskly. "She had a shock, and went right off sudden yesterday forenoon. I'm about now tendin' to the funeral 'rangements. She's be'n extry smart, they say, all winter,—out to meetin' last Sabbath; never enjoyed herself so complete as she has this past month. She'd be'n a very hard-workin' woman. Her folks was glad to have her there, and give her every attention. The place here never was good for nothin'. The old gen'le-man,—uncle, you know,—he wore hisself out tryin' to make a livin' off from it."

There was an ostentatious sympathy and half-suppressed excitement from bad news which were quite lost upon us, and we did not linger to hear much more. It seemed to me as if I had known Mrs. Peet better than any one else had known her. I had counted upon seeing her again, and hearing her own account of Shrewsbury life, its pleasures and its limitations. I wondered what had become of the cat and the contents of the faded bundle-handkerchief.

The White Rose Road

BEING a New Englander, it is natural that I should first speak about the weather. Only the middle of June, the green fields, and blue sky, and bright sun, with a touch of northern mountain wind blowing straight toward the sea, could make such a day, and that is all one can say about it. We were driving seaward through a part of the country which has been least changed in the last thirty years,—among farms which have been won from swampy lowland, and rocky, stump-buttressed hillsides: where the forests wall in the fields, and send their outposts year by year farther into the pastures. There is a year or two in the history of these pastures before they have arrived at the dignity of being called woodland, and yet are too much shaded and overgrown by young trees to give proper pasturage, when they made delightful harbors for the small wild creatures which yet remain, and for wild flowers and berries. Here you send an astonished rabbit scurrying to his burrow, and there you startle yourself with a partridge, who seems to get the best of the encounter. Sometimes you see a hen partridge and her brood of chickens crossing your path with an air of comfortable door-yard security. As you drive along the narrow, grassy road, you see many charming sights and delightful nooks on either hand, where the young trees spring out of a close-cropped turf that carpets the ground like velvet. Toward the east and the quaint fishing village of Ogunquit, I find the most delightful woodland roads. There is little left of the large timber which once filled the region, but much young growth, and there are hundreds of acres of cleared land and pasture-ground where the forests are springing fast and covering the country once more, as if they had no idea of losing in their war with civilization and the intruding white settler. The pine woods and the Indians seem to be next of kin, and the former owners of this corner of New England are the only proper figures to paint into such landscapes. The twilight under tall pines seems to be untenanted and to lack something, at first sight, as if one opened the door of an empty house. A farmer passing through with his axe is but an intruder, and children straying home from school give one a feeling of solicitude at their unprotectedness. The pine woods are the red man's house, and it may be hazardous even yet for the gray farmhouses to stand so near the eaves of the forest. I have noticed a distrust of the deep woods, among elderly people, which was something more than a fear of losing their way. It was a feeling of defenselessness against some unrecognized but malicious influence.

Driving through the long woodland way, shaded and chilly when you are out of the sun; across the Great Works River and its pretty elm-grown intervale; across the short bridges of brown brooks; delayed now and then by the sight of ripe strawberries in sunny spots by the roadside, one comes to a higher open country, where farm joins farm, and the cleared fields lie all along the highway, while the woods are pushed back a good distance on either hand. The wooded hills, bleak here and there with granite ledges, rise beyond. The houses are beside the road, with green door-yards and large barns, almost empty now, and with wide doors standing open, as if they were already expecting the hay crop to be brought in. The tall green grass is waving in the fields as the wind goes over, and there is a fragrance of whiteweed and ripe strawberries and clover blowing through the sunshiny barns, with their lean sides and their festoons of brown, dusty cobwebs; dull, comfortable creatures they appear to imaginative eyes, waiting hungrily for their yearly meal. The eave-swallows are teasing their sleepy shapes, like the birds which flit about great beasts; gay, movable, irreverent, almost derisive, those barn swallows fly to and fro in the still, clear air.

The noise of our wheels brings fewer faces to the windows than usual, and we lose the pleasure of seeing some of our friends who are apt to be looking out, and to whom we like to say good-day. Some funeral must be taking place, or perhaps the women may have gone out into the fields. It is hoeing-time and strawberry-time, and already we have seen some of the younger women at work among the corn and potatoes. One sight will be charming to remember. On a green hillside sloping to the west, near one of the houses, a thin little girl was working away lustily with a big hoe on a patch of land perhaps fifty feet by twenty. There were all sorts of things growing there, as if a child's fancy had made the choice,—straight rows of turnips and carrots and beets, a little of everything, one might say; but the only touch of color was from a long border of useful sage in full bloom of dull blue, on the upper side. I am sure this was called Katy's or Becky's *piece* by the elder members of the family. One can imagine how the young creature had planned it in the spring, and persuaded the men to plough and harrow it, and since then had stoutly done all the work herself, and meant to send the harvest of the piece to market, and pocket her honest gains, as they came in, for some great end. She was as thin as a grasshopper, this busy little gardener, and hardly turned to give us a glance, as we drove slowly up the hill close by. The sun will brown and dry her like a spear of grass on that hot slope, but a spark of fine spirit is in the small body, and I wish her a famous crop. I hate to say that the piece looked backward, all except the sage, and that it was a heavy bit of land for the clumsy hoe to pick at. The only puzzle is, what she proposes to do with so long a row of sage. Yet there may be a large family with a downfall of measles yet ahead, and she does not mean to be caught without sage-tea.

Along this road every one of the old farmhouses has at least one tall bush of white roses by the door,—a most lovely sight, with buds and blossoms, and unvexed green leaves. I wish that I knew the history of them, and whence the first bush was brought. Perhaps from England itself, like a red rose that I know in Kittery, and the new shoots from the root were given to one neighbor after another all through the district. The bushes are slender, but they grow tall without climbing against the wall, and sway to and fro in the wind with a grace of youth and an inexpressible charm of beauty. How many lovers must have picked them on Sunday evenings, in all the bygone years, and carried them along the roads or by the pasture footpaths, hiding them clumsily under their Sunday coats if they caught sight of any one coming. Here, too, where the sea wind nips many a young life before its prime, how often the white roses have been put into paler hands, and withered there!

In spite of the serene and placid look of the old houses, one who has always known them cannot help thinking of the sorrows of these farms and their almost undiverted toil. Near the little gardener's plot, we turned from the main road and drove through lately cleared woodland up to an old farmhouse, high on a ledgy hill, whence there is a fine view of the country seaward and mountainward. There were few of the once large household left there: only the old farmer, who was crippled by war wounds, active, cheerful man that he was once, and two young orphan children. There has been much hard work spent on the place. Every generation has toiled from youth to age without being able to make much beyond a living. The dollars that can be saved are but few, and sickness and death have often brought their bitter cost. The mistress of the farm was helpless for many years; through all the summers and winters she sat in her pillowed rocking-chair in the plain room. She could watch the seldom-visited lane, and beyond it, a little way across the fields, were the woods; besides these, only the clouds in the sky. She could not lift her food to her mouth; she could not be her husband's working partner. She never went into another woman's house to see her works and ways, but sat there, aching and tired, vexed by flies and by heat, and isolated in long storms. Yet the whole countryside neighbored her with true affection. Her spirit grew stronger as her body grew weaker, and the doctors, who grieved because they could do so little with their skill, were never confronted by that malady of the spirit, a desire for ease and laziness, which makes the soundest of bodies useless and complaining. The thought of her blooms in one's mind like the whitest of flowers; it makes one braver and more thankful to remember the simple faith and patience with which she bore her pain and trouble. How often she must have said, "I wish I could do something for you in return," when she was doing a thousand times more than if, like her neighbors, she followed the simple round of daily life! She was doing constant kindness by her example; but nobody can tell the woe of her long days and nights, the solitude of her spirit, as she was being lifted by such hard ways to the knowledge of higher truth and experience. Think of her pain when, one after another, her children fell ill and died, and she could not tend them! And now, in the same worn chair where she lived and slept sat her husband, helpless too, thinking of her, and missing her more than if she had been sometimes away from home, like other women. Even a stranger would miss her in the house.

There sat the old farmer looking down the lane in his turn, bearing his afflictions with a patient sternness that may have been born of watching his wife's serenity. There was a half-withered rose lying within his reach. Some days nobody came up the lane, and the wild birds that ventured near the house and the clouds that blew over were his only entertainment. He had a fine face, of the older New England type, clean-shaven and strong-featured,—a type that is fast passing away. He might have been a Cumberland dalesman, such were his dignity, and self-possession, and English soberness of manner. His large frame was built for hard work, for lifting great weights and pushing his plough through new-cleared land. We felt at home together, and each knew many things that the other did of earlier days, and of losses that had come with time. I remembered coming to the old house often in my childhood; it was in this very farm lane that I first saw anemones, and learned what to call them. After we drove away, this crippled man must have thought a long time about my elders and betters, as if he were reading their story out of a book. I suppose he has hauled many a stick of timber pine down for ship-yards, and gone through the village so early in the winter morning that I, waking in my warm bed, only heard the sleds creak through the frozen snow as the slow oxen plodded by.

Near the house a trout brook comes plashing over the ledges. At one place there is a most exquisite waterfall, to which neither painter's brush nor writer's pen can do justice. The sunlight falls through flickering leaves into the deep glen, and makes the foam whiter and the brook more golden-brown. You can hear the merry noise of it all night, all day, in the house. A little way above the farmstead it comes through marshy ground, which I fear has been the cause of much illness and sorrow to the poor, troubled family. I had a thrill of pain, as it seemed to me that the brook was mocking at all that trouble with all its wild carelessness and loud laughter, as it hurried away down the glen.

When we had said good-by and were turning the horses away, there suddenly appeared in a footpath that led down from one of the green hills the young grandchild, just coming home from school. She was as quick as a bird, and as shy in her little pink gown, and balanced herself on one foot, like a flower. The brother was the elder of the two orphans; he was the old man's delight and dependence by day, while his hired man was afield. The sober country boy had learned to wait and tend, and the young people were indeed a joy in that lonely household. There was no sign that they ever played like other children,—no truckle-cart in the yard, no doll, no bits of broken crockery in order on a rock. They had learned a fashion of life from their elders, and already could lift and carry their share of the burdens of life.

It was a country of wild flowers; the last of the columbines were clinging to the hillsides; down in the small, fenced meadows belonging to the farm were meadow rue just coming in flower, and red and white clover; the golden buttercups were thicker than the grass, while many mulleins were standing straight and slender among the pine stumps, with their first blossoms atop. Rudbeckias had found their way in, and appeared more than ever like bold foreigners. Their names should be translated into country speech, and the children ought to call them "rude-beckies," by way of relating them to bouncing-bets and sweet-williams. The pasture grass was green and thick after the plentiful rains, and the busy cattle took little notice of us as they browsed steadily and tinkled their pleasant bells. Looking off, the smooth, round back of Great Hill caught the sunlight with its fields of young grain, and all the long, wooded slopes and valleys were fresh and fair in the June weather, away toward the blue New Hampshire hills on the northern horizon. Seaward stood Agamenticus, dark with its pitch pines, and the far sea itself, blue and calm, ruled the uneven country with its unchangeable line.

Out on the white rose road again, we saw more of the rose-trees than ever, and now and then a carefully tended flower garden, always delightful to see and think about. These are not made by merely looking through a florist's catalogue, and ordering this or that new seedling and a proper selection of bulbs or shrubs; everything in a country garden has its history and personal association. The old bushes, the perennials, are apt to have most tender relationship with the hands that planted them long ago. There is a constant exchange of such treasures between the neighbors, and in the spring, slips and cuttings may be seen rooting on the window ledges, while the house plants give endless work all winter long, since they need careful protection against frost in long nights of the severe weather. A flower-loving woman brings back from every one of her infrequent journeys some treasure of flower-seeds or a huge miscellaneous nosegay. Time to work in the little plot of pleasure-ground is hardly won by the busy mistress of the farmhouse. The most appealing collection of flowering plants and vines that I ever saw was in Virginia, once, above the exquisite valley spanned by the Natural Bridge, a valley far too little known or praised. I had noticed an old log house, as I learned to know the outlook from the picturesque hotel, and was sure that it must give a charming view from its perch on the summit of a hill.

One day I went there,—one April day, when the whole landscape was full of color from the budding trees,—and before I could look at the view, I caught sight of some rare vines, already in leaf, about the dilapidated walls of the cabin. Then across the low paling I saw the brilliant colors of tulips and daffodils. There were many rose-bushes; in fact, the whole top of the hill was a flower garden, once well cared for and carefully ordered. It was all the work of an old woman of Scotch-Irish descent, who had been busy with the cares of life, and a very hard worker; yet I was told that to gratify her love for flowers she would often go afoot many miles over those rough Virginia roads, with a root or cutting from her own garden, to barter for a new rose or a brighter blossom of some sort, with which she would return in triumph. I fancied that sometimes she had to go by night on these charming quests. I could see her business-like, small figure setting forth down the steep path, when she had a good conscience toward her housekeeping and the children were in order to be left. I am sure that her friends thought of her when they were away from home and could bring her an offering of something rare. Alas, she had grown too old and feeble to care for her dear blossoms any longer, and had been forced to go to live with a married son. I dare say that she was thinking of her garden that very day, and wondering if this plant or that were not in bloom, and perhaps had a heartache at the thought that her tenants, the careless colored children, might tread the young shoots of peony and rose, and make havoc in the herb-bed. It was an uncommon collection, made by years of patient toil and self-sacrifice.

I thought of that deserted Southern garden as I followed my own New England road. The flower-plots were in gay bloom all along the way; almost every house had some flowers before it, sometimes carefully fenced about by stakes and barrel staves from the miscreant hens and chickens which lurked everywhere, and liked a good scratch and fluffing in soft earth this year as well as any other. The world seemed full of young life. There were calves tethered in pleasant shady spots, and puppies and kittens adventuring from the door-ways. The trees were full of birds: bobolinks, and cat-birds, and yellow-hammers, and golden robins, and sometimes a thrush, for the afternoon was wearing late. We passed the spring which once marked the boundary where three towns met,—Berwick, York, and Wells,—a famous spot in the early settlement of the country, but many of its old traditions are now forgotten. One of the omnipresent regicides of Charles the First is believed to have hidden himself for a long time under a great rock close by. The story runs that he made his miserable home in this den for several years, but I believe that there is no record that more than three of the regicides escaped to this country, and their wanderings are otherwise accounted for. There is a firm belief that one of them came to York, and was the ancestor of many persons now living there, but I do not know whether he can have been the hero of the Baker's Spring hermitage beside. We stopped to drink some of the delicious water, which never fails to flow cold and clear under the shade of a great oak, and were amused with the sight of a flock of gay little country children who passed by in deep conversation. What could such atoms of humanity be talking about? "Old times," said John, the master of horse, with instant decision.

We met now and then a man or woman, who stopped to give us hospitable greeting; but there was no staying for visits, lest the daylight might fail us. It was delightful to find this old-established neighborhood so thriving and populous, for a few days before I had driven over three miles of road, and passed only one house that was tenanted, and six cellars or crumbling chimneys where good farmhouses had been, the lilacs blooming in solitude, and the fields, cleared with so much difficulty a century or two ago, all going back to the original woodland from which they were won. What would the old farmers say to see the fate of their worthy bequest to the younger generation? They would wag their heads sorrowfully, with sad foreboding.

After we had passed more woodland and a well-known quarry, where, for a wonder, the derrick was not creaking and not a single hammer was clinking at the stone wedges, we did not see any one hoeing in the fields, as we had seen so many on the white rose road, the other side of the hills. Presently we met two or three people walking sedately, clad in their best clothes. There was a subdued air of public excitement and concern, and one of us remembered that there had been a death in the neighborhood; this was the day of the funeral. The man had been known to us in former years. We had an instinct to hide our unsympathetic pleasuring, but there was nothing to be done except to follow our homeward road straight by the house.

The occasion was nearly ended by this time: the borrowed chairs were being set out in the yard in little groups; even the funeral supper had been eaten, and the brothers and sisters and near relatives of the departed man were just going home. The new grave showed plainly out in the green field near by. He had belonged to one of the ancient families of the region, long settled on this old farm by the narrow river; they had given their name to a bridge, and the bridge had christened the meeting-house which stood close by. We were much struck by the solemn figure of the mother, a very old woman, as she walked toward her old home with some of her remaining children. I had not thought to see her again, knowing her great age and infirmity. She was like a presence out of the last century, tall and still erect, dark-eyed and of striking features, and a firm look not modern, but as if her mind were still set upon an earlier and simpler scheme of life. An air of dominion cloaked her finely. She had long been queen of her surroundings and law-giver to her great family. Royalty is a quality, one of Nature's gifts, and there one might behold it as truly as if Victoria Regina Imperatrix had passed by. The natural instincts common to humanity were there undisguised, unconcealed, simply accepted. We had seen a royal progress; she was the central figure of that rural society; as you looked at the little group, you could see her only. Now that she came abroad so rarely, her presence was not without deep significance, and so she took her homeward way with a primitive kind of majesty.

It was evident that the neighborhood was in great excitement and quite thrown out of its usual placidity. An acquaintance came from a small house farther down the road, and we stopped for a word with him. We spoke of the funeral, and were told something of the man who had died. "Yes, and there's a man layin' very sick here," said our friend in an excited whisper. "*He* won't last but a day or two. There's another man buried yesterday that was struck by lightnin', comin' acrost a field when that great shower begun. The lightnin' stove through his hat and run down all over him, and ploughed a spot in the ground." There was a knot of people about the door; the minister of that scattered parish stood among them, and they all looked at us eagerly, as if we too might be carrying news of a fresh disaster through the countryside.

Somehow the melancholy tales did not touch our sympathies as they ought, and we could not see the pathetic side of them as at another time, the day was so full of cheer and the sky and earth so glorious. The very fields looked busy with their early summer growth, the horses began to think of the clack of the oat-bin cover, and we were hurried along between the silvery willows and the rustling alders, taking time to gather a handful of stray-away conserve roses by the roadside; and where the highway made a long bend eastward among the farms, two of us left the carriage, and followed a footpath along the green river bank and through the pastures, coming out to the road again only a minute later than the horses. I believe that it is an old Indian trail followed from the salmon falls farther down the river, where the up-country Indians came to dry the plentiful fish for their winter supplies. I have traced the greater part of this deep-worn footpath, which goes straight as an arrow across the country, the first day's trail being from the falls (where Mason's settlers came in 1627, and built their Great Works of a saw-mill with a gang of saws, and presently a grist mill beside) to Emery's Bridge. I should like to follow the old footpath still farther. I found part of it by accident a long time ago. Once, as you came close to the river, you were sure to find fishermen scattered along,—sometimes I myself have been discovered; but it is not much use to go fishing any more. If some public-spirited person would kindly be the Frank Buckland of New England, and try to have the laws enforced that protect the inland fisheries, he would do his country great service. Years ago, there were so many salmon that, as an enthusiastic old friend once assured me, "you could walk across on them below the falls;" but now they are unknown, simply because certain substances which would enrich the farms are thrown from factories and tanneries into our clear New England streams. Good river fish are growing very scarce. The smelts, and bass, and shad have all left this upper branch of the Piscataqua, as the salmon left it long ago, and the supply of one necessary sort of good cheap food is lost to a growing community, for the lack of a little thought and care in the factory companies and saw-mills, and the building in some cases of fish-ways over the dams. I think that the need of preaching against this bad economy is very great. The sight of a proud lad with a string of undersized trout will scatter half the idlers in town into the pastures next day, but everybody patiently accepts the depopulation of a fine clear river, where the tide comes fresh from the sea to be tainted by the spoiled stream, which started from its mountain sources as pure as heart could wish. Man has done his best to ruin the world he lives in, one is tempted to say at impulsive first thought; but after all, as I mounted the last hill before reaching the village, the houses took on a new look of comfort and pleasantness; the fields that I knew so well were a fresher green than before, the sun was down, and the provocations of the day seemed very slight compared to the satisfaction. I believed that with a little more time we should grow wiser about our fish and other things beside.

It will be good to remember the white rose road and its quietness in many a busy town day to come. As I think of these slight sketches, I wonder if they will have to others a tinge of sadness; but I have seldom spent an afternoon so full of pleasure and fresh and delighted consciousness of the possibilities of rural life.

The Town Poor

M RS. WILLIAM TRIMBLE and Miss Rebecca Wright were driving along Hampden east road, one afternoon in early spring. Their progress was slow. Mrs. Trimble's sorrel horse was old and stiff, and the wheels were clogged by clay mud. The frost was not yet out of the ground, although the snow was nearly gone, except in a few places on the north side of the woods, or where it had drifted all winter against a length of fence.

"There must be a good deal o' snow to the nor'ard of us yet," said weather-wise Mrs. Trimble. "I feel it in the air; 't is more than the ground-damp. We ain't goin' to have real nice weather till the up-country snow 's all gone."

"I heard say yesterday that there was good sleddin' yet, all up through Parsley," responded Miss Wright. "I shouldn't like to live in them northern places. My cousin Ellen's husband was a Parsley man, an' he was obliged, as you may have heard, to go up north to his father's second wife's funeral; got back day before yesterday. 'T was about twenty-one miles, an' they started on wheels; but when they'd gone nine or ten miles, they found 't was no sort o' use, an' left their wagon an' took a sleigh. The man that owned it charged 'em four an' six, too. I shouldn't have thought he would; they told him they was goin' to a funeral; an' they had their own buffaloes an' everything."

"Well, I expect it's a good deal harder scratchin', up that way; they have to git money where they can; the farms is very poor as you go north," suggested Mrs. Trimble kindly. " 'T ain't none too rich a country where we be, but I 've always been grateful I wa'n't born up to Parsley."

The old horse plodded along, and the sun, coming out from the heavy spring clouds, sent a sudden shine of light along the muddy road. Sister Wright drew her large veil forward over the high brim of her bonnet. She was not used to driving, or to being much in the open air; but Mrs. Trimble was an active business woman, and looked after her own affairs herself, in all weathers. The late Mr. Trimble had left her a good farm, but not much ready money, and it was often said that she was better off in the end than if he had lived. She regretted his loss deeply, however; it was impossible for her to speak of him, even to intimate friends, without emotion, and nobody had ever hinted that this emotion was insincere. She was most warm-hearted and generous, and in her limited way played the part of Lady Bountiful in the town of Hampden.

"Why, there's where the Bray girls lives, ain't it?" she exclaimed, as, beyond a thicket of witch-hazel and scrub-oak, they came in sight of a weather-beaten, solitary farmhouse. The barn was too far away for thrift or comfort, and they could see long lines of light between the shrunken boards as they came nearer. The fields looked both stony and sodden. Somehow, even Parsley itself could be hardly more forlorn.

"Yes'm," said Miss Wright, "that's where they live now, poor things. I know the place, though I ain't been up here for years. You don't suppose, Mis' Trimble—I ain't seen the girls out to meetin' all winter. I've re'lly been covetin'"—

"Why, yes, Rebecca, of course we could stop," answered Mrs. Trimble heartily. "The exercises was over earlier 'n I expected, an' you're goin' to remain over night long o' me, you know. There won't be no tea till we git there, so we can't be late. I'm in the habit o' sendin' a basket to the Bray girls when any o' our folks is comin' this way, but I ain't been to see 'em since they moved up here. Why, it must be a good deal over a year ago. I know 't was in the late winter they had to make the move. 'T was cruel hard, I must say, an' if I hadn't been down with my pleurisy fever I'd have stirred round an' done somethin' about it. There was a good deal o' sickness at the time, an'—well, 't was kind o' rushed through, breakin' of 'em up, an' lots o' folks blamed the selec'*men*; but when 't was done, 't was done, an' nobody took holt to undo it. Ann an' Mandy looked same 's ever when they come to meetin', 'long in the summer,—kind o' wishful, perhaps. They've always sent me word they was gittin' on pretty comfortable."

"That would be their way," said Rebecca Wright. "They never was any hand to complain, though Mandy's less cheerful than Ann. If Mandy'd been spared such poor eyesight, an'

Ann had n't got her lame wrist that wa'n't set right, they'd kep' off the town fast enough. They both shed tears when they talked to me about havin' to break up, when I went to see 'em before I went over to brother Asa's. You see we was brought up neighbors, an' we went to school together, the Brays an' me. 'T was a special Providence brought us home this road, I've been so covetin' a chance to git to see 'em. My lameness hampers me."

"I'm glad we come this way, myself," said Mrs. Trimble.

"I'd like to see just how they fare," Miss Rebecca Wright continued. "They give their consent to goin' on the town because they knew they'd got to be dependent, an' so they felt 't would come easier for all than for a few to help 'em. They acted real dignified an' right-minded, contrary to what most do in such cases, but they was dreadful anxious to see who would bid 'em off, town-meeting day; they did so hope 't would be somebody right in the village. I just sat down an' cried good when I found Abel Janes's folks had got hold of 'em. They always had the name of bein' slack an' poor-spirited, an' they did it just for what they got out o' the town. The selectmen this last year ain't what we have had. I hope they've been considerate about the Bray girls."

"I should have be'n more considerate about fetchin' of you over," apologized Mrs. Trimble. "I've got my horse, an' you're lame-footed; 't is too far for you to come. But time does slip away with busy folks, an' I forgit a good deal I ought to remember."

"There's nobody more considerate than you be," protested Miss Rebecca Wright.

Mrs. Trimble made no answer, but took out her whip and gently touched the sorrel horse, who walked considerably faster, but did not think it worth while to trot. It was a long, round-about way to the house, farther down the road and up a lane.

"I never had any opinion of the Bray girls' father, leavin' 'em as he did," said Mrs. Trimble.

"He was much praised in his time, though there was always some said his early life had n't been up to the mark," explained her companion. "He was a great favorite of our then preacher, the Reverend Daniel Longbrother. They did a good deal for the parish, but they did it their own way. Deacon Bray was one that did his part in the repairs without urging. You know 't was in his time the first repairs was made, when they got out the old soundin'-board an' them handsome square pews. It cost an awful sight o' money, too. They had n't done payin' up that debt when they set to alter it again an' git the walls frescoed. My grandmother was one that always spoke her mind right out, an' she was dreadful opposed to breakin' up the square pews where she'd always set. They was countin' up what 't would cost in parish meetin', an' she riz right up an' said 't would n't cost nothin' to let 'em stay, an' there wa'n't a house carpenter left in the parish that could do such nice work, an' time would come when the great-grandchildren would give their eye-teeth to have the old meetin'-house look just as it did then. But haul the inside to pieces they would and did."

"There come to be a real fight over it, did n't there?" agreed Mrs. Trimble soothingly. "Well, 't wa'n't good taste. I remember the old house well. I come here as a child to visit a cousin o' mother's, an' Mr. Trimble's folks was neighbors, an' we was drawed to each other then, young's we was. Mr. Trimble spoke of it many's the time, — that first time he ever see me, in a leghorn hat with a feather; 't was one that mother had, an' pressed over."

"When I think of them old sermons that used to be preached in that old meetin'-house of all, I'm glad it's altered over, so's not to remind folks," said Miss Rebecca Wright, after a suitable pause. "Them old brimstone discourses, you know, Mis' Trimble. Preachers is far more reasonable, nowadays. Why, I set an' thought, last Sabbath, as I listened, that if old Mr. Longbrother an' Deacon Bray could hear the difference they'd crack the ground over 'em like pole beans, an' come right up 'long side their headstones."

Mrs. Trimble laughed heartily, and shook the reins three or four times by way of emphasis. "There's no gitting round you," she said, much pleased. "I should think Deacon Bray would want to rise, any way, if 't was so he could, an' knew how his poor girls was farin'. A man ought to provide for his folks he's got to leave behind him, specially if they're women. To be sure, they had their little home; but we've seen how, with all their industrious ways, they had n't means to keep it. I s'pose he thought he'd got time enough to lay by, when he give so generous in collections; but he did n't lay by, an' there they be. He might have took lessons from the squirrels: even them little wild creatur's makes them their winter hoards, an' men-folks ought to know enough if squirrels does. 'Be just before you are generous:' that's what was always set for the B's in the copy-books, when I was to school, and it often runs through my mind."

" 'As for man, his days are as grass,'—that was for A; the two go well together," added Miss Rebecca Wright soberly. "My good gracious, ain't this a starved-lookin' place? It makes me ache to think them nice Bray girls has to brook it here."

The sorrel horse, though somewhat puzzled by an unexpected deviation from his homeward way, willingly came to a stand by the gnawed corner of the door-yard fence, which evidently served as hitching-place. Two or three ragged old hens were picking about the yard, and at last a face appeared at the kitchen window, tied up in a handkerchief, as if it were a case of toothache. By the time our friends reached the side door next this window, Mrs. Janes came disconsolately to open it for them, shutting it again as soon as possible, though the air felt more chilly inside the house.

"Take seats," said Mrs. Janes briefly. "You'll have to see me just as I be. I have been suffering these four days with the ague, and everything to do. Mr. Janes is to court, on the jury. 'T was inconvenient to spare him. I should be pleased to have you lay off your things."

Comfortable Mrs. Trimble looked about the cheerless kitchen, and could not think of anything to say; so she smiled blandly and shook her head in answer to the invitation. "We'll just set a few minutes with you, to pass the time o' day, an' then we must go in an' have a word with the Miss Brays, bein' old acquaintance. It ain't been so we could git to call on 'em before. I don't know's you're acquainted with Miss R'becca Wright. She's been out of town a good deal."

"I heard she was stopping over to Plainfields with her brother's folks," replied Mrs. Janes, rocking herself with irregular motion, as she sat close to the stove. "Got back some time in the fall, I believe?"

"Yes 'm," said Miss Rebecca, with an undue sense of guilt and conviction. "We 've been to the installation over to the East Parish, an' thought we 'd stop in; we took this road home to see if 't was any better. How is the Miss Brays gettin' on?"

"They 're well 's common," answered Mrs. Janes grudgingly. "I was put out with Mr. Janes for fetchin' of 'em here, with all I 've got to do, an' I own I was kind o' surly to 'em 'long to the first of it. He gits the money from the town, an' it helps him out; but he bid 'em off for five dollars a month, an' we can't do much for 'em at no such price as that. I went an' dealt with the selec'men, an' made 'em promise to find their firewood an' some other things extra. They was glad to get rid o' the matter the fourth time I went, an' would ha' promised 'most anything. But Mr. Janes don't keep me half the time in oven-wood, he 's off so much, an' we was cramped o' room, any way. I have to store things up garrit a good deal, an' that keeps me trampin' right through their room. I do the best for 'em I can, Mis' Trimble, but 't ain't so easy for me as 't is for you, with all your means to do with."

The poor woman looked pinched and miserable herself, though it was evident that she had no gift at house or home keeping. Mrs. Trimble's heart was wrung with pain, as she thought of the unwelcome inmates of such a place; but she held her peace bravely, while Miss Rebecca again gave some brief information in regard to the installation.

"You go right up them back stairs," the hostess directed at last. "I 'm glad some o' you church folks has seen fit to come an' visit 'em. There ain't been nobody here this long spell, an' they 've aged a sight since they come. They always send down a taste out of your baskets, Mis' Trimble, an' I relish it, I tell you. I 'll shut the door after you, if you don't object. I feel every draught o' cold air."

"I 've always heard she was a great hand to make a poor mouth. Wa'n't she from somewheres up Parsley way?" whispered Miss Rebecca, as they stumbled in the half-light.

"Poor meechin' body, wherever she come from," replied Mrs. Trimble, as she knocked at the door.

There was silence for a moment after this unusual sound; then one of the Bray sisters opened the door. The eager guests stared into a small, low room, brown with age, and gray, too, as if former dust and cobwebs could not be made wholly to disappear. The two elderly women who stood there looked like captives. Their withered faces wore a look of apprehension, and the room itself was more bare and plain than was fitting to their evident refinement of character and self-respect. There was an uncovered small table in the middle of the floor, with some crackers on a plate; and, for some reason or other, this added a great deal to the general desolation.

But Miss Ann Bray, the elder sister, who carried her right arm in a sling, with piteously drooping fingers, gazed at the visitors with radiant joy. She had not seen them arrive.

The one window gave only the view at the back of the house, across the fields, and their coming was indeed a surprise. The next minute she was laughing and crying together. "Oh, sister!" she said, "if here ain't our dear Mis' Trimble!— an' my heart o' goodness, 't is 'Becca Wright, too! What dear good creatur's you be! I've felt all day as if something good was goin' to happen, an' was just sayin' to myself 't was most sundown now, but I would n't let on to Mandany I'd give up hope quite yet. You see, the scissors stuck in the floor this very mornin' an' it's always a reliable sign. There, I've got to kiss ye both again!"

"I don't know where we can all set," lamented sister Mandana. "There ain't but the one chair an' the bed; t' other chair's too rickety; an' we've been promised another these ten days; but first they've forgot it, an' next Mis' Janes can't spare it,—one excuse an' another. I am goin' to git a stump o' wood an' nail a board on to it, when I can git outdoor again," said Mandana, in a plaintive voice. "There, I ain't goin' to complain o' nothin', now you've come," she added; and the guests sat down, Mrs. Trimble, as was proper, in the one chair.

"We've sat on the bed many's the time with you, 'Becca, an' talked over our girl nonsense, ain't we? You know where 't was—in the little back bedroom we had when we was girls, an' used to peek out at our beaux through the strings o' mornin'-glories," laughed Ann Bray delightedly, her thin face shining more and more with joy. "I brought some o' them mornin'-glory seeds along when I come away, we'd raised 'em so many years; an' we got 'em started all right, but the hens found 'em out. I declare I chased them poor hens, foolish as 't was; but the mornin'-glories I 'd counted on a sight to remind me o' home. You see, our debts was so large, after my long sickness an' all, that we did n't feel 't was right to keep back anything we could help from the auction."

It was impossible for any one to speak for a moment or two; the sisters felt their own uprooted condition afresh, and their guests for the first time really comprehended the piteous contrast between that neat little village house, which now seemed a palace of comfort, and this cold, unpainted upper room in the remote Janes farmhouse. It was an unwelcome thought to Mrs. Trimble that the well-to-do town of Hampden could provide no better for its poor than this, and her round face flushed with resentment and the shame of personal responsibility. "The girls shall be well settled in the village before another winter, if I pay their board myself," she made an inward resolution, and took another almost tearful look at the broken stove, the miserable bed, and the sisters' one hair-covered trunk, on which Mandana was sitting. But the poor place was filled with a golden spirit of hospitality.

Rebecca was again discoursing eloquently of the installation; it was so much easier to speak of general subjects, and the sisters had evidently been longing to hear some news. Since the late summer they had not been to church, and presently Mrs. Trimble asked the reason.

"Now, don't you go to pouring out our woes, Mandy!" begged little old Ann, looking shy and almost girlish, and as if she insisted upon playing that life was still all before them and all pleasure. "Don't you go to spoilin' their visit with our complaints! They know well 's we do that changes must come, an' we 'd been so wonted to our home things that this come hard at first; but then they felt for us, I know just as well 's can be. 'T will soon be summer again, an' 't is real pleasant right out in the fields here, when there ain't too hot a spell. I 've got to know a sight o' singin' birds since we come."

"Give me the folks I 've always known," sighed the younger sister, who looked older than Miss Ann, and less even-tempered. "You may have your birds, if you want 'em. I do re'lly long to go to meetin' an' see folks go by up the aisle.

Now, I will speak of it, Ann, whatever you say. We need, each of us, a pair o' good stout shoes an' rubbers,—ours are all wore out; an' we've asked an' asked, an' they never think to bring 'em, an'"—

Poor old Mandana, on the trunk, covered her face with her arms and sobbed aloud. The elder sister stood over her, and patted her on the thin shoulder like a child, and tried to comfort her. It crossed Mrs. Trimble's mind that it was not the first time one had wept and the other had comforted. The sad scene must have been repeated many times in that long, drear winter. She would see them forever after in her mind as fixed as a picture, and her own tears fell fast.

"You didn't see Mis' Janes's cunning little boy, the next one to the baby, did you?" asked Ann Bray, turning round quickly at last, and going cheerfully on with the conversation. "Now, hush, Mandy, dear; they'll think you're childish! He's a dear, friendly little creatur', an' likes to stay with us a good deal, though we feel's if it 't was too cold for him, now we are waitin' to get us more wood."

"When I think of the acres o' woodland in this town!" groaned Rebecca Wright. "I believe I'm goin' to preach next Sunday, 'stead o' the minister, an' I'll make the sparks fly. I've always heard the saying, 'What's everybody's business is nobody's business,' an' I've come to believe it."

"Now, don't you, 'Becca. You've happened on a kind of a poor time with us, but we've got more belongings than you see here, an' a good large cluset, where we can store those things there ain't room to have about. You an' Miss Trimble have happened on a kind of poor day, you know. Soon's I git me some stout shoes an' rubbers, as Mandy says, I can fetch home plenty o' little dry boughs o' pine; you remember I was always a great hand to roam in the woods? If we could only have a front room, so 't we could look out on the road an' see passin', an' was shod for meetin', I don' know's we should complain. Now we're just goin' to give you what we've got, an' make out with a good welcome. We make more tea 'n we want in the mornin', an' then let the fire go down, since 't has been so mild. We've got a *good* cluset" (disappearing as she spoke), "an' I know this to be good tea, 'cause it's some o' yourn, Mis' Trimble. An' here's our sprigged chiny cups that

R'becca knows by sight, if Mis' Trimble don't. We kep' out four of 'em, an' put the even half dozen with the rest of the auction stuff. I've often wondered who'd got 'em, but I never asked, for fear 't would be somebody that would distress us. They was mother's, you know."

The four cups were poured, and the little table pushed to the bed, where Rebecca Wright still sat, and Mandana, wiping her eyes, came and joined her. Mrs. Trimble sat in her chair at the end, and Ann trotted about the room in pleased content for a while, and in and out of the closet, as if she still had much to do; then she came and stood opposite Mrs. Trimble. She was very short and small, and there was no painful sense of her being obliged to stand. The four cups were not quite full of cold tea, but there was a clean old tablecloth folded double, and a plate with three pairs of crackers neatly piled, and a small—it must be owned, a very small—piece of hard white cheese. Then, for a treat, in a glass dish, there was a little preserved peach, the last—Miss Rebecca knew it instinctively—of the household stores brought from their old home. It was very sugary, this bit of peach; and as she helped her guests and sister Mandy, Miss Ann Bray said, half unconsciously, as she often had said with less reason in the old days, "Our preserves ain't so good as usual this year; this is beginning to candy." Both the guests protested, while Rebecca added that the taste of it carried her back, and made her feel young again. The Brays had always managed to keep one or two peach-trees alive in their corner of a garden. "I've been keeping this preserve for a treat," said her friend. "I'm glad to have you eat some, 'Becca. Last summer I often wished you was home an' could come an' see us, 'stead o' being away off to Plainfields."

The crackers did not taste too dry. Miss Ann took the last of the peach on her own cracker; there could not have been quite a small spoonful, after the others were helped, but she asked them first if they would not have some more. Then there was a silence, and in the silence a wave of tender feeling rose high in the hearts of the four elderly women. At this moment the setting sun flooded the poor plain room with light; the unpainted wood was all of a golden-brown, and Ann Bray, with her gray hair and aged face, stood at the head of the table in a kind of aureole. Mrs. Trimble's face was all aquiver as she looked at her; she thought of the text about two or three being gathered together, and was half afraid.

"I believe we ought to 've asked Mis' Janes if she would n't come up," said Ann. "She 's real good feelin', but she 's had it very hard, an' gits discouraged. I can't find that she 's ever had anything real pleasant to look back to, as we have. There, next time we 'll make a good heartenin' time for her too."

The sorrel horse had taken a long nap by the gnawed fence-rail, and the cool air after sundown made him impatient to be gone. The two friends jolted homeward in the gathering darkness, through the stiffening mud, and neither Mrs. Trimble nor Rebecca Wright said a word until they were out of sight as well as out of sound of the Janes house. Time must elapse before they could reach a more familiar part of the road and resume conversation on its natural level.

"I consider myself to blame," insisted Mrs. Trimble at last. "I have n't no words of accusation for nobody else, an' I ain't one to take comfort in calling names to the board o' selec'-*men*. I make no reproaches, an' I take it all on my own shoulders; but I 'm goin' to stir about me, I tell you! I shall begin early to-morrow. They 're goin' back to their own house, — it 's been standin' empty all winter, — an' the town 's goin' to give 'em the rent an' what firewood they need; it won't come to more than the board 's payin' out now. An' you an' me 'll take this same horse an' wagon, an' ride an' go afoot by turns, an' git means enough together to buy back their furniture an' whatever was sold at that plaguey auction; an' then we 'll put it all back, an' tell 'em they 've got to move to a new place, an' just carry 'em right back again where they come from. An' don't you never tell, R'becca, but here I be a widow woman, layin' up what I make from my farm for nobody knows who, an' I 'm goin' to do for them Bray girls all I 'm a mind to. I should be sca't to wake up in heaven, an' hear anybody there ask how the Bray girls was. Don't talk to me about the town o' Hampden, an' don't ever let me hear the name o' town poor! I 'm ashamed to go home an' see what 's set out for supper. I wish I 'd brought 'em right along."

"I was goin' to ask if we could n't git the new doctor to go up an' do somethin' for poor Ann's arm," said Miss Rebecca. "They say he 's very smart. If she could get so 's to braid straw or hook rugs again, she 'd soon be earnin' a little somethin'. An' may be he could do somethin' for Mandy's eyes. They did use to live so neat an' ladylike. Somehow I could n't speak to tell 'em there that 't was I bought them six best cups an' saucers, time of the auction; they went very low, as everything else did, an' I thought I could save it some other way. They shall have 'em back an' welcome. You 're real wholehearted, Mis' Trimble. I expect Ann 'll be sayin' that her father's child'n wa'n't goin' to be left desolate, an' that all the bread he cast on the water 's comin' back through you."

"I don't care what she says, dear creatur'!" exclaimed Mrs. Trimble. "I 'm full o' regrets I took time for that installation, an' set there seepin' in a lot o' talk this whole day long, except for its kind of bringin' us to the Bray girls. I wish to my heart 't was to-morrow mornin' a'ready, an' I a-startin' for the selec'*men*."

A Native of Winby

O N THE teacher's desk, in the little roadside school-house, there was a bunch of Mayflowers, beside a dented and bent brass bell, a small Worcester's Dictionary without any cover, and a worn morocco-covered Bible. These were placed in an orderly row, and behind them was a small wooden box which held some broken pieces of blackboard crayon. The teacher, whom no timid new scholar could look at boldly, wore her accustomed air of authority and importance. She might have been nineteen years old,—not more,—but for the time being she scorned the frivolities of youth.

The hot May sun was shining in at the smoky small-paned windows; sometimes an outside shutter swung to with a creak, and eclipsed the glare. The narrow door stood wide open, to the left as you faced the desk, and an old spotted dog lay asleep on the step, and looked wise and old enough to have gone to school with several generations of children. It was half past three o'clock in the afternoon, and the primer class, settled into the apathy of after-recess fatigue, presented a straggling front, as they stood listlessly on the floor. As for the big boys and girls, they also were longing to be at liberty, but the pretty teacher, Miss Marilla Hender, seemed quite as energetic as when school was begun in the morning.

The spring breeze blew in at the open door, and even fluttered the primer leaves, but the back of the room felt hot and close, as if it were midsummer. The children in the class read their lessons in those high-keyed, droning voices which older teachers learn to associate with faint powers of perception. Only one or two of them had an awakened human look in their eyes, such as Matthew Arnold delighted himself in finding so often in the school-children of France. Most of these poor little students were as inadequate, at that weary moment, to the pursuit of letters as if they had been woolly spring lambs on a sunny hillside. The teacher corrected and admonished with great patience, glancing now and then toward points of danger and insurrection, whence came a suspicious buzz of whispering from behind a desk-lid or a pair of widespread large geographies. Now and then a toiling child would rise and come down the aisle, with his forefinger firm upon a puzzling word as if it were an unclassified insect. It was a lovely beckoning day out-of-doors. The children felt like captives; there was something that provoked rebellion in the droning voices, the buzzing of an early wild bee against the sunlit pane, and even in the stuffy familiar odor of the place,—the odor of apples and crumbs of doughnuts and gingerbread in the dinner pails on the high entry nails, and of all the little gowns and trousers that had brushed through junipers and young pines on their way to school.

The bee left his prisoning pane at last, and came over to the Mayflowers, which were in full bloom, although the season was very late, and deep in the woods there were still some graybacked snowdrifts, speckled with bits of bark and moss from the trees above.

"Come, come, Ezra!" urged the young teacher, rapping her desk sharply. "Stop watchin' that common bee! You know well enough what those letters spell. You won't learn to read at this rate until you are a grown man. Mind your book, now; you ought to remember who went to this school when he was a little boy. You've heard folks tell about the Honorable Joseph K. Laneway? He used to be in primer just as you are now, and 't was n't long before he was out of it, either, and was called the smartest boy in school. He's got to be a general and a Senator, and one of the richest men out West. You don't seem to have the least mite of ambition to-day, any of you!"

The exhortation, entirely personal in the beginning, had swiftly passed to a general rebuke. Ezra looked relieved, and the other children brightened up as they recognized a tale familiar to their ears. Anything was better than trying to study in that dull last hour of afternoon school.

"Yes," continued Miss Hender, pleased that she had at last roused something like proper attention, "you all ought to be proud that you are schoolmates of District Number Four, and can remember that the celebrated General Laneway had the same early advantages as you, and think what he has made of himself by perseverance and ambition."

The pupils were familiar enough with the illustrious history of their noble predecessor. They were sure to be told, in lawless moments, that if Mr. Laneway were to come in and see them he would be mortified to death; and the members of the school committee always referred to him, and said that he had been a poor boy, and was now a self-made man,—as if every man were not self-made as to his character and reputation!

At this point, young Johnny Spencer showed his next neighbor, in the back of his Colburn's Arithmetic, an imaginary portrait of their district hero, which caused them both to chuckle derisively. The Honorable Mr. Laneway figured on the flyleaf as an extremely cross-eyed person, with strangely crooked legs and arms and a terrific expression. He was outlined with red and blue pencils as to coat and trousers, and held a reddened scalp in one hand and a blue tomahawk in the other; being closely associated in the artist's mind with the early settlements of the far West.

There was a noise of wheels in the road near by, and, though Miss Hender had much more to say, everybody ceased to listen to her, and turned toward the windows, leaning far forward over their desks to see who might be passing. They caught a glimpse of a shiny carriage; the old dog bounded out, barking, but nothing passed the open door. The carriage had stopped; some one was coming to the school; somebody was going to be called out! It could not be the committee, whose pompous and uninspiring spring visit had taken place only the week before.

Presently a well-dressed elderly man, with an expectant, masterful look, stood on the doorstep, glanced in with a smile, and knocked. Miss Marilla Hender blushed, smoothed her pretty hair anxiously with both hands, and stepped down from her little platform to answer the summons. There was hardly a shut mouth in the primer class.

"Would it be convenient for you to receive a visitor to the school?" the stranger asked politely, with a fine bow of deference to Miss Hender. He looked much pleased and a little excited, and the teacher said,—

"Certainly; step right in, won't you, sir?" in quite another tone from that in which she had just addressed the school.

The boys and girls were sitting straight and silent in their places, in something like a fit of apprehension and unpreparedness at such a great emergency. The guest represented a type of person previously unknown in District Number Four. Everything about him spoke of wealth and authority. The old dog returned to the doorstep, and after a careful look at the invader approached him, with a funny doggish grin and a desperate wag of the tail, to beg for recognition.

The teacher gave her chair on the platform to the guest, and stood beside him with very red cheeks, smoothing her hair again once or twice, and keeping the hard-wood ruler fast in hand, like a badge of office. "Primer class may now retire!" she said firmly, although the lesson was not more than half through; and the class promptly escaped to their seats, waddling and stumbling, until they all came up behind their desks, face foremost, and added themselves to the number of staring young countenances. After this there was a silence, which grew more and more embarrassing.

"Perhaps you would be pleased to hear our first class in geography, sir?" asked the fair Marilla, recovering her presence of mind; and the guest kindly assented.

The young teacher was by no means willing to give up a certainty for an uncertainty. Yesterday's lesson had been well learned; she turned back to the questions about the State of Kansota, and at the first sentence the mysterious visitor's dignity melted into an unconscious smile. He listened intently for a minute, and then seemed to reoccupy himself with his own thoughts and purposes, looking eagerly about the old school-house, and sometimes gazing steadily at the children. The lesson went on finely, and when it was finished Miss Hender asked the girl at the head of the class to name the States and Territories, which she instantly did, mispronouncing nearly all the names of the latter; then others stated boundaries and capitals, and the resources of the New England States, passing on finally to the names of the Presidents. Miss Hender glowed with pride; she had worked hard over the geography class in the winter term, and it did not fail her on this great occasion. When she turned bravely to see if the gentleman would like to ask any questions, she found that he was apparently lost in a deep reverie, so she repeated her own question more distinctly.

"They have done very well,—very well indeed," he answered kindly; and then, to every one's surprise, he rose, went up the aisle, pushed Johnny Spencer gently along his bench, and sat down beside him. The space was cramped, and the stranger looked huge and uncomfortable, so that everybody laughed, except one of the big girls, who turned pale with fright, and thought he must be crazy. When this girl gave a faint squeak Miss Hender recovered herself, and rapped twice with the ruler to restore order; then became entirely tranquil. There had been talk of replacing the hacked and worn old school-desks with patent desks and chairs; this was probably an agent connected with that business. At once she was resolute and self-reliant, and said, "No whispering!" in a firm tone that showed she did not mean to be trifled with. The geography class was dismissed, but the elderly gentleman, in his handsome overcoat, still sat there wedged in at Johnny Spencer's side.

"I presume, sir, that you are canvassing for new desks," said Miss Hender, with dignity. "You will have to see the supervisor and the selectmen." There did not seem to be any need of his lingering, but she had an ardent desire to be pleasing to a person of such evident distinction. "We always tell strangers—I thought, sir, you might be gratified to know—that this is the school-house where the Honorable Joseph K. Laneway first attended school. All do not know that he was born in this town, and went West very young; it is only about a mile from here where his folks used to live."

At this moment the visitor's eyes fell. He did not look at pretty Marilla any more, but opened Johnny Spencer's arithmetic, and, seeing the imaginary portrait of the great General Laneway, laughed a little,—a very deep-down comfortable laugh it was,—while Johnny himself turned cold with alarm, he could not have told why.

It was very still in the school-room; the bee was buzzing and bumping at the pane again; the moment was one of intense expectation.

The stranger looked at the children right and left. "The fact is this, young people," said he, in a tone that was half pride and half apology, "I am Joseph K. Laneway myself."

He tried to extricate himself from the narrow quarters of the desk, but for an embarrassing moment found that he was stuck fast. Johnny Spencer instinctively gave him an assisting push, and once free the great soldier, statesman, and millionaire took a few steps forward to the open floor; then, after hesitating a moment, he mounted the little platform and stood in the teacher's place. Marilla Hender was as pale as ashes.

"I have thought many times," the great guest began, "that some day I should come back to visit this place, which is so closely interwoven with the memories of my childhood. In my counting-room, on the fields of war, in the halls of Congress, and most of all in my Western home, my thoughts have flown back to the hills and brooks of Winby and to this little old school-house. I could shut my eyes and call back the buzz of voices, and fear my teacher's frown, and feel my boyish ambitions waking and stirring in my breast. On that bench where I just sat I saw some notches that I cut with my first jackknife fifty-eight years ago this very spring. I remember the faces of the boys and girls who went to school with me, and I see their grandchildren before me. I know that one is a Goodsoe and another a Winn by the old family look. One generation goes, and another comes.

"There are many things that I might say to you. I meant, even in those early restricted days, to make my name known, and I dare say that you too have ambition. Be careful what you wish for in this world, for if you wish hard enough you are sure to get it. I once heard a very wise man say this, and the longer I live the more firmly I believe it to be true. But wishing hard means working hard for what you want, and the world's prizes wait for the men and women who are ready to take pains to win them. Be careful and set your minds on the best things. I meant to be a rich man when I was a boy here, and I stand before you a rich man, knowing the care and anxiety and responsibility of wealth. I meant to go to Congress, and I am one of the Senators from Kansota. I say this as humbly as I say it proudly. I used to read of the valor and patriotism of the old Greeks and Romans with my youthful blood leaping along my veins, and it came to pass that my own country was in danger, and that I could help to fight her battles. Perhaps some one of these little lads has before him a more eventful life than I have lived, and is looking forward to activity and honor and the pride of fame. I wish him all the joy that I have had, all the toil that I have had, and all the bitter disappointments even; for adversity leads a man to depend upon that which is above him, and the path of glory is a lonely path, beset by temptations and a bitter sense of the weakness and imperfection of man. I see my life spread out like a great picture, as I stand here in my boyhood's place. I regret my failures. I thank God for what in his kind providence has been honest and right. I am glad to come back, but I feel, as I look in your young faces, that I am an old man, while your lives are just beginning. When you remember, in years to come, that I came here to see the old school-house, remember that I said: Wish for the best things, and work hard to win them; try to be good men and women, for the honor of the school and the town, and the noble young country that gave you birth; be kind at home and generous abroad. Remember that I, an old man who had seen much of life, begged you to be brave and good."

The Honorable Mr. Laneway had rarely felt himself so moved in any of his public speeches, but he was obliged to notice that for once he could not hold his audience. The primer class especially had begun to flag in attention, but one or two faces among the elder scholars fairly shone with vital sympathy and a lovely prescience of their future. Their eyes met his as if they struck a flash of light. There was a sturdy boy who half rose in his place unconsciously, the color coming and going in his cheeks; something in Mr. Laneway's words lit the altar flame in his reverent heart.

Marilla Hender was pleased and a little dazed; she could not have repeated what her illustrious visitor had said, but she longed to tell everybody the news that he was in town, and had come to school to make an address. She had never seen a great man before, and really needed time to reflect upon him and to consider what she ought to say. She was just quivering with the attempt to make a proper reply and thank Mr. Laneway for the honor of his visit to the school, when he asked her which of the boys could be trusted to drive back his hired horse to the Four Corners. Eight boys, large and small, nearly every boy in the school, rose at once and snapped insistent fingers; but Johnny Spencer alone was desirous not to attract attention to himself. The Colburn's Intellectual Arithmetic with the portrait had been well secreted between his tight jacket and his shirt. Miss Hender selected a trustworthy freckled person in long trousers, who was half way to the door in an instant, and was heard almost immediately to shout loudly at the quiet horse.

Then the Hero of District Number Four made his acknowledgments to the teacher. "I fear that I have interrupted you too long," he said, with pleasing deference.

Marilla replied that it was of no consequence; she hoped he would call again. She may have spoken primly, but her pretty eyes said everything that her lips forgot. "My grandmother will want to see you, sir," she ventured to say. "I guess you will remember her,—Mis' Hender, she that was Abby Harran. She has often told me how you used to get your lessons out o' the same book."

"Abby Harran's granddaughter?" Mr. Laneway looked at her again with fresh interest. "Yes, I wish to see her more than any one else. Tell her that I am coming to see her before I go away, and give her my love. Thank you, my dear," as Marilla offered his missing hat. "Good-by, boys and girls." He stopped and looked at them once more from the boys' entry, and turned again to look back from the very doorstep.

"Good-by, sir,—good-by," piped two or three of the young voices; but most of the children only stared, and neither spoke nor moved.

"We will omit the class in Fourth Reader this afternoon. The class in grammar may recite," said Miss Hender in her most contained and official manner.

The grammar class sighed like a single pupil, and obeyed. She was very stern with the grammar class, but every one in school had an inner sense that it was a great day in the history of District Number Four.

II.

The Honorable Mr. Laneway found the outdoor air very fresh and sweet after the closeness of the school-house. It had just that same odor in his boyhood, and as he escaped he had a delightful sense of playing truant or of having an unexpected holiday. It was easier to think of himself as a boy, and to slip back into boyish thoughts, than to bear the familiar burden of his manhood. He climbed the tumble-down stone wall across the road, and went along a narrow path to the spring that bubbled up clear and cold under a great red oak. How many times he had longed for a drink of that water, and now here it was, and the thirst of that warm spring day was hard to quench! Again and again he stopped to fill the birch-bark dipper which the school-children had made, just as his own comrades made theirs years before. The oak-tree was dying at the top. The pine woods beyond had been cut and had grown again since his boyhood, and looked much as he remembered them. Beyond the spring and away from the woods the path led across overgrown pastures to another road, perhaps three quarters of a mile away, and near this road was the small farm which had been his former home. As he walked slowly along, he was met again and again by some reminder of his youthful days. He had always liked to refer to his early life in New England in his political addresses, and had spoken more than once of going to find the cows at nightfall in the autumn evenings, and being glad to warm his bare feet in the places where the sleepy beasts had lain, before he followed their slow steps homeward through bush and brier. The Honorable Mr. Laneway had a touch of true sentiment which added much to his really stirring and effective campaign speeches. He had often been called the "king of the platform" in his adopted State. He had long ago grown used to saying "Go" to one man, and "Come" to another, like the ruler of old; but all his natural power of leadership and habit of authority disappeared at once as he trod the pasture slopes, calling back the remembrance of his childhood. Here was the place where two lads, older than himself, had killed a terrible woodchuck at bay in the angle of a great rock; and just beyond was the sunny spot where he had picked a bunch of pink and white anemones under a prickly barberry thicket, to give to Abby Harran in morning school. She had put them into her desk, and let them wilt there, but she was pleased when she took them. Abby Harran, the little teacher's grandmother, was a year older than he, and had wakened the earliest thought of love in his youthful breast.

It was almost time to catch the first sight of his birthplace. From the knoll just ahead he had often seen the light of his mother's lamp, as he came home from school on winter afternoons; but when he reached the knoll the old house was gone, and so was the great walnut-tree that grew beside it, and a pang of disappointment shot through this devout pilgrim's heart. He never had doubted that the old farm was somebody's home still, and had counted upon the pleasure of spending a night there, and sleeping again in that room under the roof, where the rain sounded loud, and the walnut branches brushed to and fro when the wind blew, as if they were the claws of tigers. He hurried across the worn-out fields, long ago turned into sheep pastures, where the last year's tall grass and golden-rod stood gray and winter-killed; tracing the old walls and fences, and astonished to see how small the fields had been. The prosperous owner of Western farming lands could not help remembering those widespread luxuriant acres, and the broad outlooks of his Western home.

It was difficult at first to find exactly where the house had stood; even the foundations had disappeared. At last in the long, faded grass he discovered the doorstep, and near by was a little mound where the great walnut-tree stump had been. The cellar was a mere dent in the sloping ground; it had been filled in by the growing grass and slow processes of summer and winter weather. But just at the pilgrim's right were some thorny twigs of an old rosebush. A sudden brightening of memory brought to mind the love that his mother—dead since his fifteenth year—had kept for this sweetbrier. How often she had wished that she had brought it to her new home! So much had changed in the world, so many had gone into the world of light, and here the faithful blooming thing was yet alive! There was one slender branch where green buds were starting, and getting ready to flower in the new year.

The afternoon wore late, and still the gray-haired man lingered. He might have laughed at some one else who gave himself up to sad thoughts, and found fault with himself, with no defendant to plead his cause at the bar of conscience. It was an altogether lonely hour. He had dreamed all his life, in a sentimental, self-satisfied fashion, of this return to Winby. It had always appeared to be a grand affair, but so far he was himself the only interested spectator at his poor occasion. There was even a dismal consciousness that he had been undignified, perhaps even a little consequential and silly, in the old school-house. The picture of himself on the war-path, in Johnny Spencer's arithmetic, was the only tribute that this longed-for day had held, but he laughed aloud delightedly at the remembrance and really liked that solemn little boy who sat at his own old desk. There was another older lad, who sat at the back of the room, who reminded Mr. Laneway of himself in his eager youth. There was a spark of light in that fellow's eyes. Once or twice in the earlier afternoon, as he drove along, he had asked people in the road if there were a Laneway family in that neighborhood, but everybody had said no in indifferent fashion. Somehow he had been expecting that every one would know him and greet him, and give him credit for what he had tried to do, but old Winby had her own affairs to look after, and did very well without any of his help.

Mr. Laneway acknowledged to himself at this point that he was weak and unmanly. There must be some old friends who would remember him, and give him as hearty a welcome as the greeting he had brought for them. So he rose and went his way westward toward the sunset. The air was growing damp and cold, and it was time to make sure of shelter. This was hardly like the visit he had meant to pay to his birthplace. He wished with all his heart that he had never come back. But he walked briskly away, intent upon wider thoughts as the fresh evening breeze quickened his steps. He did not consider where he was going, but was for a time the busy man of affairs, stimulated by the unconscious influence of his surroundings. The slender gray birches and pitch pines of that neglected pasture had never before seen a hat and coat exactly in the fashion. They may have been abashed by the presence of a United States Senator and Western millionaire, though a piece of New England ground that had often felt the tread of his bare feet was not likely to quake because a pair of smart shoes stepped hastily along the school-house path.

III.

There was an imperative knock at the side door of the Hender farmhouse, just after dark. The young school-mistress had come home late, because she had stopped all the way along to give people the news of her afternoon's experience. Marilla was not coy and speechless any longer, but sat by the kitchen stove telling her eager grandmother everything she could remember or could imagine.

"Who's that knocking at the door?" interrupted Mrs. Hender. "No, I'll go myself; I'm nearest."

The man outside was cold and foot-weary. He was not used to spending a whole day unrecognized, and, after being first amused, and even enjoying a sense of freedom at escaping his just dues of consideration and respect, he had begun to feel as if he were old and forgotten, and was hardly sure of a friend in the world.

Old Mrs. Hender came to the door, with her eyes shining with delight, in great haste to dismiss whoever had knocked, so that she might hear the rest of Marilla's story. She opened the door wide to whoever might have come on some country errand, and looked the tired and faint-hearted Mr. Laneway full in the face.

"Dear heart, come in!" she exclaimed, reaching out and taking him by the shoulder, as he stood humbly on a lower step. "Come right in, Joe. Why, I should know you anywhere! Why, Joe Laneway, *you same boy!*"

In they went to the warm, bright, country kitchen. The delight and kindness of an old friend's welcome and her instant sympathy seemed the loveliest thing in the world. They sat down in two old straight-backed kitchen chairs. They still held each other by the hand, and looked in each other's face. The plain old room was aglow with heat and cheerfulness; the tea-kettle was singing; a drowsy cat sat on the wood-box with her paws tucked in; and the house dog came forward in a friendly way, wagging his tail, and laid his head on their clasped hands.

"And to think I have n't seen you since your folks moved out West, the next spring after you were thirteen in the winter," said the good woman. "But I s'pose there ain't been anybody that has followed your career closer than I have, accordin' to their opportunities. You 've done a great work for your country, Joe. I 'm proud of you clean through. Sometimes folks has said, 'There, there, Mis' Hender, what be you goin' to say now?' but I 've always told 'em to wait. I knew you saw your reasons. You was always an honest boy." The tears started and shone in her kind eyes. Her face showed that she had waged a bitter war with poverty and sorrow, but the look of affection that it wore, and the warm touch of her hard hand, misshapen and worn with toil, touched her old friend in his inmost heart, and for a minute neither could speak.

"They do say that women folks have got no natural head for politics, but I always could seem to sense what was goin' on in Washington, if there was any sense to it," said grandmother Hender at last.

"Nobody could puzzle you at school, I remember," answered Mr. Laneway, and they both laughed heartily. "But surely this granddaughter does not make your household? You have sons?"

"Two beside her father. He died; but they 're both away, up toward Canada, buying cattle. We are getting along considerable well these last few years, since they got a mite o' capital together; but the old farm was n't really able to maintain us, with the heavy expenses that fell on us unexpected year by year. I 've seen a great sight of trouble, Joe. My boy John, Marilla's father, and his nice wife,—I lost 'em both early, when Marilla was but a child. John was the flower o' my family. He would have made a name for himself. You would have taken to John."

"I was sorry to hear of your loss," said Mr. Laneway. "He was a brave man. I know what he did at Fredericksburg. You remember that I lost my wife and my only son?"

There was a silence between the friends, who had no need for words now; they understood each other's heart only too well. Marilla, who sat near them, rose and went out of the room.

"Yes, yes, daughter," said Mrs. Hender, calling her back, "we ought to be thinkin' about supper."

"I was going to light a little fire in the parlor," explained Marilla, with a slight tone of rebuke in her clear girlish voice.

"Oh, no, you ain't,—not now, at least," protested the elder woman decidedly. "Now, Joseph, what should you like to have for supper? I wish to my heart I had some fried turnovers, like those you used to come after when you was a boy. I can make 'em just about the same as mother did. I'll be bound you've thought of some old-fashioned dish that you'd relish for your supper."

"Rye drop-cakes, then, if they would n't give you too much trouble," answered the Honorable Joseph, with prompt seriousness, "and don't forget some cheese." He looked up at his old playfellow as she stood beside him, eager with affectionate hospitality.

"You've no idea what a comfort Marilla's been," she stopped to whisper. "Always took right hold and helped me when she was a baby. She's as good as made up already to me for my having no daughter. I want you to get acquainted with Marilla."

The granddaughter was still awed and anxious about the entertainment of so distinguished a guest when her grandmother appeared at last in the pantry.

"I ain't goin' to let you do no such a thing, darlin'," said Abby Hender, when Marilla spoke of making something that she called "fairy gems" for tea, after a new and essentially feminine recipe. "You just let me get supper to-night. The Gen'ral has enough kickshaws to eat; he wants a good, hearty, old-fashioned supper,—the same country cooking he remembers when he was a boy. He went so far himself as to speak of rye drop-cakes, an' there ain't one in a hundred, nowadays, knows how to make the kind he means. You go an' lay the table just as we always have it, except you can get out them old big sprigged cups o' my mother's. Don't put on none o' the parlor cluset things."

Marilla went off crestfallen and demurring. She had a noble desire to show Mr. Laneway that they knew how to have things as well as anybody, and was sure that he would consider it more polite to be asked into the best room, and to sit there alone until tea was ready; but the illustrious Mr. Laneway was allowed to stay in the kitchen, in apparent happiness, and to watch the proceedings from beginning to end. The two old friends talked industriously, but he saw his rye drop-cakes go into the oven and come out, and his tea made, and his piece of salt fish broiled and buttered, a broad piece of honeycomb set on to match some delightful thick slices of brown-crusted loaf bread, and all the simple feast prepared. There was a sufficient piece of Abby Hender's best cheese; it must be confessed that there were also some baked beans, and, as one thing after another appeared, the Honorable Joseph K. Laneway grew hungrier and hungrier, until he fairly looked pale with anticipation and delay, and was bidden at that very moment to draw up his chair and make himself a supper if he could. What cups of tea, what uncounted rye drop-cakes, went to the making of that successful supper! How gay the two old friends became, and of what old stories they reminded each other, and how late the dark spring evening grew, before the feast was over and the straight-backed chairs were set against the kitchen wall!

Marilla listened for a time with more or less interest, but at last she took one of her school-books, with slight ostentation, and went over to study by the lamp. Mrs. Hender had brought her knitting-work, a blue woolen stocking, out of a drawer, and sat down serene and unruffled, prepared to keep awake as late as possible. She was a woman who had kept her youthful looks through the difficulties of farm life as few women can, and this added to her guest's sense of home-likeness and pleasure. There was something that he felt to be sisterly and comfortable in her strong figure; he even noticed the little plaid woolen shawl that she wore about her shoulders. Dear, uncomplaining heart of Abby Hender! The appealing friendliness of the good woman made no demands except to be allowed to help and to serve everybody who came in her way.

Now began in good earnest the talk of old times, and what had become of this and that old schoolmate; how one family had come to want and another to wealth. The changes and

losses and windfalls of good fortune in that rural neighborhood were made tragedy and comedy by turns in Abby
Hender's dramatic speech. She grew younger and more entertaining hour by hour, and beguiled the grave Senator into
confidential talk of national affairs. He had much to say, to
which she listened with rare sympathy and intelligence. She
astonished him by her comprehension of difficult questions of
the day, and by her simple good sense. Marilla grew hope-
lessly sleepy, and departed, but neither of them turned to notice her as she lingered a moment at the door to say good-
night. When the immediate subjects of conversation were
fully discussed, however, there was an unexpected interval of
silence, and, after making sure that her knitting stitches
counted exactly right, Abby Hender cast a questioning glance
at the Senator to see if he had it in mind to go to bed. She
was reluctant to end her evening so soon, but determined to
act the part of considerate hostess. The guest was as wide
awake as ever: eleven o'clock was the best part of his evening.

"Cider?" he suggested, with an expectant smile, and Abby
Hender was on her feet in a moment. When she had brought
a pitcher from the pantry, he took a candle from the high
shelf and led the way.

"To think of your remembering our old cellar candlestick
all these years!" laughed the pleased woman, as she followed
him down the steep stairway, and then laughed still more at
his delight in the familiar look of the place.

"Unchanged as the pyramids!" he said. "I suppose those
pound sweetings that used to be in that farthest bin were
eaten up months ago?"

It was plain to see that the household stores were waning
low, as befitted the time of year, but there was still enough in
the old cellar. Care and thrift and gratitude made the poor
farmhouse a rich place. This woman of real ability had spent
her strength from youth to age, and had lavished as much
industry and power of organization in her narrow sphere as
would have made her famous in a wider one. Joseph Laneway
could not help sighing as he thought of it. How many things
this good friend had missed, and yet how much she had been
able to win that makes everywhere the very best of life! Poor
and early widowed, there must have been a constant battle

with poverty on that stony Harran farm, whose owners had been pitied even in his early boyhood, when the best of farming life was none too easy. But Abby Hender had always been one of the leaders of the town.

"Now, before we sit down again, I want you to step into my best room. Perhaps you won't have time in the morning, and I've got something to show you," she said persuasively.

It was a plain, old-fashioned best room, with a look of pleasantness in spite of the spring chill and the stiffness of the best chairs. They lingered before the picture of Mrs. Hender's soldier son, a poor work of a poorer artist in crayons, but the spirit of the young face shone out appealingly. Then they crossed the room and stood before some bookshelves, and Abby Hender's face brightened into a beaming smile of triumph.

"You didn't expect we should have all those books, now, did you, Joe Laneway?" she asked.

He shook his head soberly, and leaned forward to read the titles. There were no very new ones, as if times had been hard of late; almost every volume was either history, or biography, or travel. Their owner had reached out of her own narrow boundaries into other lives and into far countries. He recognized with gratitude two or three congressional books that he had sent her when he first went to Washington, and there was a life of himself, written from a partisan point of view, and issued in one of his most exciting campaigns; the sight of it touched him to the heart, and then she opened it, and showed him the three or four letters that he had written her, — one, in boyish handwriting, describing his adventures on his first Western journey.

"There are a hundred and six volumes now," announced the proud owner of such a library. "I lend 'em all I can, or most of them would look better. I have had to wait a good while for some, and some weren't what I expected 'em to be, but most of 'em's as good books as there is in the world. I've never been so situated that it seemed best for me to indulge in a daily paper, and I don't know but it's just as well; but stories were never any great of a temptation. I know pretty well what's goin' on about me, and I can make that do. Real life's interestin' enough for me."

Mr. Laneway was still looking over the books. His heart smote him for not being thoughtful; he knew well enough that the overflow of his own library would have been delightful to this self-denying, eager-minded soul. "I've been a very busy man all my life, Abby," he said impulsively, as if she waited for some apology for his forgetfulness, "but I'll see to it now that you have what you want to read. I don't mean to lose hold of your advice on state matters." They both laughed, and he added, "I've always thought of you, if I have n't shown it."

"There's more time to read than there used to be; I've had what was best for me," answered the woman gently, with a grateful look on her face, as she turned to glance at her old friend. "Marilla takes hold wonderfully and helps me with the work. In the long winter evenings you can't think what a treat a new book is. I would n't change places with the queen."

They had come back to the kitchen, and she stood before the cupboard, reaching high for two old gayly striped crockery mugs. There were some doughnuts and cheese at hand; their early supper seemed quite forgotten. The kitchen was warm, and they had talked themselves thirsty and hungry; but with what an unexpected tang the cider freshened their throats! Mrs. Hender had picked the apples herself that went to the press; they were all chosen from the old russet tree and the gnarly, red-cheeked, ungrafted fruit that grew along the lane. The flavor made one think of frosty autumn mornings on high hillsides, of north winds and sunny skies. "It 'livens one to the heart," as Mrs. Hender remarked proudly, when the Senator tried to praise it as much as it deserved, and finally gave a cheerful laugh, such as he had not laughed for many a day.

"Why, it seems like drinking the month of October," he told her; and at this the hostess reached over, protesting that the striped mug was too narrow to hold what it ought, and filled it up again.

"Oh, Joe Laneway, to think that I see you at last, after all these years!" she said. "How rich I shall feel with this evening to live over! I've always wanted to see somebody that I'd read about, and now I've got that to remember; but I've always known I should see you again, and I believe 't was the Lord's will."

Early the next morning they said good-by. The early breakfast had to be hurried, and Marilla was to drive Mr. Laneway to the station, three miles away. It was Saturday morning, and she was free from school.

Mr. Laneway strolled down the lane before breakfast was ready, and came back with a little bunch of pink anemones in his hand. Marilla thought that he meant to give them to her, but he laid them beside her grandmother's plate. "You must n't put those in your desk," he said with a smile, and Abby Hender blushed like a girl.

"I 've got those others now, dried and put away somewhere in one of my books," she said quietly, and Marilla wondered what they meant.

The two old friends shook hands warmly at parting. "I wish you could have stayed another day, so I could have had the minister come and see you," urged Mrs. Hender regretfully.

"You could n't have done any more for me. I have had the best visit in the world," he answered, a little shaken, and holding her hand a moment longer, while Marilla sat, young and impatient, in the high wagon. "You 're a dear good woman, Abby. Sometimes when things have gone wrong I 've been sorry that I ever had to leave Winby."

The woman's clear eyes looked straight into his; then fell. "You would n't have done everything you have for the country," she said.

"Give me a kiss; we 're getting to be old folks now," said the General; and they kissed each other gravely.

A moment later Abby Hender stood alone in her dooryard, watching and waving her hand again and again, while the wagon rattled away down the lane and turned into the highroad.

Two hours after Marilla returned from the station, and rushed into the kitchen.

"Grandma!" she exclaimed, "you never did see such a crowd in Winby as there was at the depot! Everybody in town had got word about General Laneway, and they were pushing up to shake hands, and cheering same as at election, and the cars waited much as ten minutes, and all the folks was lookin' out of the windows, and came out on the platforms when they heard who it was. Folks say that he'd been to see the selectmen yesterday before he came to school, and he's goin' to build an elegant town hall, and have the names put up in it of all the Winby men that went to the war." Marilla sank into a chair, flushed with excitement. "Everybody was asking me about his being here last night and what he said to the school. I wished that you'd gone down to the depot instead of me."

"I had the best part of anybody," said Mrs. Hender, smiling and going on with her Saturday morning work. "I'm real glad they showed him proper respect," she added a moment afterward, but her voice faltered.

"Why, you ain't been cryin', grandma?" asked the girl. "I guess you're tired. You had a real good time, now, didn't you?"

"Yes, dear heart!" said Abby Hender. "'T ain't pleasant to be growin' old, that's all. I couldn't help noticin' his age as he rode away. I've always been lookin' forward to seein' him again, an' now it's all over."

Looking Back on Girlhood

IN GIVING this brief account of my childhood, or, to speak exactly, of the surroundings which have affected the course of my work as a writer, my first thought flies back to those who taught me to observe, and to know the deep pleasures of simple things, and to be interested in the lives of people about me.

With its high hills and pine forests, and all its ponds and brooks and distant mountain views, there are few such delightful country towns in New England as the one where I was born. Being one of the oldest colonial settlements, it is full of interesting traditions and relics of the early inhabitants, both Indians and Englishmen. Two large rivers join just below the village at the head of tide-water, and these, with the great inflow from the sea, make a magnificent stream, bordered on its seaward course now by high-wooded banks of dark pines and hemlocks, and again by lovely green fields that slope gently to long lines of willows at the water's edge.

There is never-ending pleasure in making one's self familiar with such a region. One may travel at home in a most literal sense, and be always learning history, geography, botany, or biography—whatever one chooses.

I have had a good deal of journeying in my life, and taken great delight in it, but I have never taken greater delight than in my rides and drives and tramps and voyages within the borders of my native town. There is always something fresh, something to be traced or discovered, something particularly to be remembered. One grows rich in memories and associations.

I believe that we should know our native towns much better than most of us do, and never let ourselves be strangers at home. Particularly when one's native place is so really interesting as my own!

Above tide-water the two rivers are barred by successive falls. You hear the noise of them by night in the village like the sound of the sea, and this fine water power so near the coast, beside a great salmon fishery famous among the Indians, brought the first English settlers to the town in 1627. I know some families who still live upon the lands which their ancestors bought from the Indians, and their single deed bears the queer barbaric signatures.

There are many things to remind one of these early settlers beside the old farms upon which they and their descendants have lived for six or seven generations. One is a quaint fashion of speech which survives among the long-established neighborhoods, in words and phrases common in England in the sixteenth and seventeenth centuries.

One curious thing is the pronunciation of the name of the town: Berwick by the elder people has always been called *Barvik*, after the fashion of Danes and Northmen; never *Berrik*, as the word has so long been pronounced in modern England.

The descendants of the first comers to the town have often been distinguished in the affairs of their time. No village of its size in New England could boast, particularly in the early part of the present century, of a larger number of men and women who kept themselves more closely in touch with "the best that has been thought and said in the world."

As I write this, I keep in mind the truth that I have no inheritance from the ancient worth and dignity of Berwick—or what is now North Berwick—in Maine. My own people are comparatively late comers. I was born in a pleasant old colonial house built near 1750, and bought by my grandfather sixty or seventy years ago, when he brought his household up the river to Berwick from Portsmouth.

He was a sea-captain, and had run away to sea in his boyhood and led a most adventurous life, but was quite ready to forsake seafaring in his early manhood, and at last joined a group of acquaintances who were engaged in the flourishing West India trade of that time.

For many years he kept and extended his interests in shipping, building ships and buying large quantities of timber from the northward and eastward, and sending it down the river and so to sea.

This business was still in existence in my early childhood, and the manner of its conduct was primitive enough, the barter system still prevailing by force of necessity. Those who brought the huge sticks of oak and pine timber for masts and planks were rarely paid in money, which was of comparatively little use in remote and sparsely settled districts. When the sleds and long trains of yoked oxen returned from the river wharves to the stores, they took a lighter load in exchange of flour and rice and barrels of molasses, of sugar and salt and cotton cloth and raisins and spices and tea and coffee; in fact, all the household necessities and luxuries that the northern farms could not supply.

They liked to have a little money with which to pay their taxes and their parish dues, if they were so fortunate as to be parishioners, but they needed very little money besides.

So I came in contact with the up-country people as well as with the sailors and shipmasters of the other side of the business. I used to linger about the busy country stores, and listen to the graphic country talk. I heard the greetings of old friends, and their minute details of neighborhood affairs, their delightful jokes and Munchausen-like reports of tracts of timber-pines ever so many feet through at the butt.

When the great teams came in sight at the head of the village street, I ran to meet them over the creaking snow, if possible to mount and ride into town in triumph; but it was not many years before I began to feel sorry at the sight of every huge lopped stem of oak or pine that came trailing along after the slow-stepping, frosted oxen. Such trees are unreplaceable. I only know of one small group now in all this part of the country of those great timber pines.

My young ears were quick to hear the news of a ship's having come into port, and I delighted in the elderly captains, with their sea-tanned faces, who came to report upon their voyages, dining cheerfully and heartily with my grandfather, who listened eagerly to their exciting tales of great storms on the Atlantic, and winds that blew them north-about, and good bargains in Havana, or Barbadoes, or Havre.

I listened as eagerly as any one; this is the charming way in which I was taught something of a fashion of life already on the wane, and of that subsistence upon sea and forest bounties which is now almost a forgotten thing in my part of New England.

Much freight still came and went by the river gundelows and packets long after the railroad had made such changes, and every village along its line lost its old feeling of self-sufficiency.

In my home the greater part of the minor furnishings had come over in the ships from Bristol and Havre. My grandfather seemed to be a citizen of the whole geography. I was always listening to stories of three wars from older people—the siege of Louisburg, the Revolution, in which my father's ancestors had been honest but mistaken Tories, and in which my mother's, the Gilmans of Exeter, had taken a nobler part.

As for the War of 1812, "the last war," as everybody called it, it was a thing of yesterday in the town. One of the famous privateer crews was gathered along our own river shore, and one member of the crew, in his old age, had been my father's patient.

The Berwick people were great patriots, and were naturally proud of the famous Sullivans, who were born in the upper part of the town, and came to be governors and judge and general.

I often heard about Lafayette, who had made an ever-to-be-remembered visit in order to see again some old friends who lived in the town. The name of a famous Colonel Hamilton, the leader in the last century of the West India trade, and the histories of the old Berwick houses of Chadbourn and Lord were delightfully familiar, and one of the traditions of the latter family is more than good enough to be told again.

There was a Berwick lad who went out on one of the privateers that sailed from Portsmouth in the Revolution. The vessel was taken by a British frigate, and the crew put in irons. One day one of the English midshipmen stood near these prisoners as they took their airing on deck, and spoke contemptuously about "the rebels."

Young Lord heard what he said, and turned himself about to say boldly, "If it were not for your rank, sir, I would make you take that back!"

"No matter about my rank," said the gallant middy. "If you can whip me, you are welcome to."

So they had a "capital good fight," standing over a tea-chest, as proud tradition tells, and the Berwick sailor was the better fighter of the two, and won.

The Englishman shook hands, and asked his name and

promised not to forget him—which was certainly most handsome behavior.

When they reached an English port all the prisoners but one were sent away under guard to join the other American prisoners of war; but the admiral sent for a young man named Nathan Lord, and told him that his Grace the Duke of Clarence, son of his Majesty the King, begged for his pardon, and had left a five-pound note at his disposal.

This was not the first or last Berwick lad who proved himself of good courage in a fight, but there never was another to whip a future King of England, and moreover to be liked the better for it by that fine gentleman.

My grandfather died in my eleventh year, and presently the Civil War began.

From that time the simple village life was at an end. Its provincial character was fading out; shipping was at a disadvantage, and there were no more bronzed sea-captains coming to dine and talk about their voyages, no more bags of filberts or oranges for the children, or great red jars of olives; but in these childish years I had come in contact with many delightful men and women of real individuality and breadth of character, who had fought the battle of life to good advantage, and sometimes against great odds.

In these days I was given to long, childish illnesses, and it must be honestly confessed, to instant drooping if ever I were shut up in school. I had apparently not the slightest desire for learning, but my father was always ready to let me be his companion in long drives about the country.

In my grandfather's business household, my father, unconscious of tonnage and timber measurement, of the markets of the Windward Islands or the Mediterranean ports, had taken to his book, as old people said, and gone to college and begun that devotion to the study of medicine which only ended with his life.

I have tried already to give some idea of my father's character in my story of "The Country Doctor," but all that is inadequate to the gifts and character of the man himself. He gave me my first and best knowledge of books by his own delight and dependence upon them, and ruled my early attempts at writing by the severity and simplicity of his own good taste.

"Don't try to write *about* people and things, tell them just as they are!"

How often my young ears heard these words without comprehending them! But while I was too young and thoughtless to share in an enthusiasm for Sterne or Fielding, and Smollett or Don Quixote, my mother and grandmother were leading me into the pleasant ways of "Pride and Prejudice," and "The Scenes of Clerical Life," and the delightful stories of Mrs. Oliphant.

The old house was well provided with leather-bound books of a deeply serious nature, but in my youthful appetite for knowledge, I could even in the driest find something vital, and in the more entertaining I was completely lost.

My father had inherited from his father an amazing knowledge of human nature, and from his mother's French ancestry, that peculiarly French trait, called *gaieté de cœur*. Through all the heavy responsibilities and anxieties of his busy professional life, this kept him young at heart and cheerful. His visits to his patients were often made perfectly delightful and refreshing to them by his kind heart, and the charm of his personality.

I knew many of the patients whom he used to visit in lonely inland farms, or on the seacoast in York and Wells. I used to follow him about silently, like an undemanding little dog, content to follow at his heels.

I had no consciousness of watching or listening, or indeed of any special interest in the country interiors. In fact, when the time came that my own world of imaginations was more real to me than any other, I was sometimes perplexed at my father's directing my attention to certain points of interest in the character or surroundings of our acquaintances.

I cannot help believing that he recognized, long before I did myself, in what direction the current of purpose in my life was setting. Now, as I write my sketches of country life, I remember again and again the wise things he said, and the sights he made me see. He was only impatient with affectation and insincerity.

I may have inherited something of my father's and grand-father's knowledge of human nature, but my father never lost a chance of trying to teach me to observe. I owe a great deal to his patience with a heedless little girl given far more to dreams than to accuracy, and with perhaps too little natural sympathy for the dreams of others.

The quiet village life, the dull routine of farming or mill life, early became interesting to me. I was taught to find everything that an imaginative child could ask, in the simple scenes close at hand.

I say these things eagerly, because I long to impress upon every boy and girl this truth: that it is not one's surroundings that can help or hinder—it is having a growing purpose in one's life to make the most of whatever is in one's reach.

If you have but a few good books, learn those to the very heart of them. Don't for one moment believe that if you had different surroundings and opportunities you would find the upward path any easier to climb. One condition is like another, if you have not the determination and the power to grow in yourself.

I was still a child when I began to write down the things I was thinking about, but at first I always made rhymes and found prose so difficult that a school composition was a terror to me, and I do not remember ever writing one that was worth anything. But in course of time rhymes themselves became difficult and prose more and more enticing, and I began my work in life, most happy in finding that I was to write of those country characters and rural landscapes to which I myself belonged, and which I had been taught to love with all my heart.

I was between nineteen and twenty when my first sketch was accepted by Mr. Howells for the *Atlantic*. I already counted myself as by no means a new contributor to one or two other magazines—*Young Folks* and *The Riverside*—but I had no literary friends "at court."

I was very shy about speaking of my work at home, and even sent it to the magazine under an assumed name, and then was timid about asking the post-mistress for those mysterious and exciting editorial letters which she announced upon the post-office list as if I were a stranger in the town.

The Passing of Sister Barsett

M<small>RS</small>. M<small>ERCY</small> C<small>RANE</small> was of such firm persuasion that a
house is meant to be lived in, that during many years
she was never known to leave her own neat two-storied
dwelling-place on the Ridge road. Yet being very fond of
company, in pleasant weather she often sat in the side doorway looking out on her green yard, where the grass grew
short and thick and was undisfigured even by a path toward
the steps. All her faded green blinds were securely tied together and knotted on the inside by pieces of white tape;
but now and then, when the sun was not too hot for her
carpets, she opened one window at a time for a few hours,
having pronounced views upon the necessity of light and air.
Although Mrs. Crane was acknowledged by her best friends
to be a peculiar person and very set in her ways, she was
much respected, and one acquaintance vied with another in
making up for her melancholy seclusion by bringing her all
the news they could gather. She had been left alone many
years before by the sudden death of her husband from sun-
stroke, and though she was by no means poor, she had, as
some one said, "such a pretty way of taking a little present
that you couldn't help being pleased when you gave her
anything."

For a lover of society, such a life must have had its difficulties at times, except that the Ridge road was more traveled
than any other in the township, and Mrs. Crane had invented
a system of signals, to which she always resorted in case of
wishing to speak to some one of her neighbors.

The afternoon was wearing late, one day toward the end of
summer, and Mercy Crane sat in her doorway dressed in a
favorite old-fashioned light calico and a small shoulder shawl
figured with large palm leaves. She was making some tatting
of a somewhat intricate pattern; she believed it to be the prettiest and most durable of trimmings, and having decorated
her own wardrobe in the course of unlimited leisure, she was
now making a few yards apiece for each of her more intimate
friends, so that they might have something to remember her

by. She kept glancing up the road as if she expected some one, but the time went slowly by, until at last a woman appeared to view, walking fast, and carrying a large bundle in a checked handkerchief.

Then Mercy Crane worked steadily for a short time without looking up, until the desired friend was crossing the grass between the dusty road and the steps. The visitor was out of breath, and did not respond to the polite greeting of her hostess until she had recovered herself to her satisfaction. Mrs. Crane made her the kind offer of a glass of water or a few peppermints, but was answered only by a shake of the head, so she resumed her work for a time until the silence should be broken.

"I have come from the house of mourning," said Sarah Ellen Dow at last, unexpectedly.

"You don't tell me that Sister Barsett"—

"She's left us this time, she's really gone," and the excited news-bringer burst into tears. The poor soul was completely overwrought; she looked tired and wan, as if she had spent her forces in sympathy as well as hard work. She felt in her great bundle for a pocket handkerchief, but was not successful in the search, and finally produced a faded gingham apron with long, narrow strings, with which she hastily dried her tears. The sad news appealed also to Mercy Crane, who looked across to the apple-trees, and could not see them for a dazzle of tears in her own eyes. The spectacle of Sarah Ellen Dow going home with her humble workaday possessions, from the house where she had gone in haste only a few days before to care for a sick person well known to them both, was a very sad sight.

"You sent word yesterday that you should be returnin' early this afternoon, and would stop. I presume I received the message as you gave it?" asked Mrs. Crane, who was tenacious in such matters; "but I do declare I never looked to hear she was gone."

"She's been failin' right along sence yisterday about this time," said the nurse. "She's taken no notice to speak of, an' been eatin' the vally o' nothin', I may say, sence I went there a-Tuesday. Her sisters both come back yisterday, an' of course

I was expected to give up charge to them. They're used to sickness, an' both havin' such a name for bein' great house-keepers!"

Sarah Ellen spoke with bitterness, but Mrs. Crane was reminded instantly of her own affairs. "I feel condemned that I ain't begun my own fall cleanin' yet," she said, with an ostentatious sigh.

"Plenty o' time to worry about that," her friend hastened to console her.

"I do desire to have everything decent about my house," resumed Mrs. Crane. "There's nobody to do anything but me. If I was to be taken away sudden myself, I shouldn't want to have it said afterwards that there was wisps under my sofy or— There! I can't dwell on my own troubles with Sister Barsett's loss right before me. I can't seem to believe she's really passed away; she always was saying she should go in some o' these spells, but I deemed her to be troubled with narves."

Sarah Ellen Dow shook her head. "I'm all nerved up myself," she said brokenly. "I made light of her sickness when I went there first, I'd seen her what she called dreadful low so many times; but I saw her looks this morning, an' I begun to believe her at last. Them sisters o' hers is the master for unfeelin' hearts. Sister Barsett was a-layin' there yisterday, an' one of 'em was a-settin' right by her tellin' how difficult 't was for her to leave home, her niece was goin' to graduate to the high school, an' they was goin' to have a time in the evening, an' all the exercises promised to be extry interesting. Poor Sister Barsett knew what she said an' looked at her with contempt, an' then she give a glance at me an' closed up her eyes as if 't was for the last time. I know she felt it."

Sarah Ellen Dow was more and more excited by a sense of bitter grievance. Her rule of the afflicted household had evidently been interfered with; she was not accustomed to be ignored and set aside at such times. Her simple nature and uncommon ability found satisfaction in the exercise of authority, but she had now left her post feeling hurt and wronged, besides knowing something of the pain of honest affliction.

"If it hadn't been for esteemin' Sister Barsett as I always

have done, I should have told 'em no, an' held to it, when they asked me to come back an' watch to-night. 'T ain't for none o' their sakes, but Sister Barsett was a good friend to me in her way." Sarah Ellen broke down once more, and felt in her bundle again hastily, but the handkerchief was again elusive, while a small object fell out upon the doorstep with a bounce.

"'T ain't nothin' but a little taste-cake I spared out o' the loaf I baked this mornin'," she explained, with a blush. "I was so shoved out that I seemed to want to turn my hand to somethin' useful an' feel I was still doin' for Sister Barsett. Try a little piece, won't you, Mis' Crane? I thought it seemed light an' good."

They shared the taste-cake with serious enjoyment, and pronounced it very good indeed when they had finished and shaken the crumbs out of their laps. "There's nobody but you shall come an' do for me at the last, if I can have my way about things," said Mercy Crane impulsively. She meant it for a tribute to Miss Dow's character and general ability, and as such it was meekly accepted.

"You're a younger person than I be, an' less wore," said Sarah Ellen, but she felt better now that she had rested, and her conversational powers seemed to be refreshed by her share of the little cake. "Doctor Bangs has behaved real pretty, I can say that," she continued presently in a mournful tone.

"Heretofore, in the sickness of Sister Barsett, I have always felt to hope certain that she would survive; she's recovered from a sight o' things in her day. She has been the first to have all the new diseases that's visited this region. I know she had the spinal mergeetis months before there was any other case about," observed Mrs. Crane with satisfaction.

"An' the new throat troubles, all of 'em," agreed Sarah Ellen; "an' has made trial of all the best patent medicines, an' could tell you their merits as no one else could in this vicinity. She never was one that depended on herbs alone, though she considered 'em extremely useful in some cases. Everybody has their herb, as we know, but I'm free to say that Sister Barsett sometimes done everything she could to kill herself with such rovin' ways o' dosin'. She must see it now she's gone an' can't stuff down no more invigorators." Sarah Ellen Dow burst out suddenly with this, as if she could no longer contain her honest opinion.

"There, there! you're all worked up," answered placid Mercy Crane, looking more interested than ever.

"An' she was dreadful handy to talk religion to other folks, but I've come to a realizin' sense that religion is somethin' besides opinions. She an' Elder French has been mostly of one mind, but I don't know's they've got hold of all the religion there is."

"Why, why, Sarah Ellen!" exclaimed Mrs. Crane, but there was still something in her tone that urged the speaker to further expression of her feelings. The good creature was much excited, her face was clouded with disapproval.

"I ain't forgettin' nothin' about their good points either," she went on in a more subdued tone, and suddenly stopped.

"Preachin' 'll be done away with soon or late,—preachin' o' Elder French's kind," announced Mercy Crane, after waiting to see if her guest did not mean to say anything more. "I should like to read 'em out that verse another fashion: 'Be ye doers o' the word, not preachers only,' would hit it about right; but there, it's easy for all of us to talk. In my early days I used to like to get out to meetin' regular, because sure as I did n't I had bad luck all the week. I did n't feel pacified 'less I'd been half a day, but I was out all day the Sabbath before Mr. Barlow died as he did. So you mean to say that Sister Barsett's really gone?"

Mrs. Crane's tone changed to one of real concern, and her manner indicated that she had put the preceding conversation behind her with decision.

"She was herself to the last," instantly responded Miss Dow. "I see her put out a thumb an' finger from under the spread an' pinch up a fold of her sister Deckett's dress, to try an' see if 't was all wool. I thought 't wa'n't all wool, myself, an' I know it now by the way she looked. She was a very knowin' person about materials; we shall miss poor Mis' Barsett in many ways, she was always the one to consult with about matters o' dress."

"She passed away easy at the last, I hope?" asked Mrs. Crane with interest.

"Why, I wa'n't there, if you'll believe it!" exclaimed Sarah Ellen, flushing, and looking at her friend for sympathy. "Sister Barsett revived up the first o' the afternoon, an' they sent for Elder French. She took notice of him, and he exhorted quite a spell, an' then he spoke o' there being need of air in the room, Mis' Deckett havin' closed every window, an' she asked me of all folks if I hadn't better step out; but Elder French come too, an' he was very reasonable, an' had a word with me about Mis' Deckett an' Mis' Peak an' the way they was workin' things. I told him right out how they never come near when the rest of us was havin' it so hard with her along in the spring, but now they thought she was re'lly goin' to die, they come settlin' down like a pair o' old crows in a field to pick for what they could get. I just made up my mind they should have all the care if they wanted it. It didn't seem as if there was anything more I could do for Sister Barsett, an' I set there in the kitchen within call an' waited, an' when I heard 'em sayin', 'There, she's gone, she's gone!' and Mis' Deckett a-weepin', I put on my bunnit and stepped myself out into the road. I felt to repent after I had gone but a rod, but I was so worked up, an' I thought they'd call me back, an' then I was put out because they didn't, an' so here I be. I can't help it now." Sarah Ellen was crying again; she and Mrs. Crane could not look at each other.

"Well, you set an' rest," said Mrs. Crane kindly, and with the merest shadow of disapproval. "You set an' rest, an' by an' by, if you'd feel better, you could go back an' just make a little stop an' inquire about the arrangements. I wouldn't harbor no feelin's, if they be inconsiderate folks. Sister Barsett has often deplored their actions in my hearing an' wished she had sisters like other folks. With all her faults she was a useful person an' a good neighbor," mourned Mercy Crane sincerely. "She was one that always had somethin' interestin' to tell, an' if it wa'n't for her dyin' spells an' all that sort o' nonsense, she'd make a figger in the world, she would so. She walked with an air always, Mis' Barsett did; you'd ask who she was if you hadn't known, as she passed you by. How quick we forget the outs about anybody that's gone! But I always feel grateful to anybody that's friendly, situated as I be. I shall miss her runnin' over. I can seem to see her now, coming over the rise in the road. But don't you get in a way of takin' things too hard, Sarah Ellen! You've worked yourself all to pieces since I saw you last; you're gettin' to be as lean as a meetin'-house fly. Now, you're comin' in to have a cup o' tea with me, an' then you'll feel better. I've got some new molasses gingerbread that I baked this mornin'."

"I do feel beat out, Mis' Crane," acknowledged the poor little soul, glad of a chance to speak, but touched by this un-expected mark of consideration. "If I could ha' done as I wanted to I should be feelin' well enough, but to be set aside an' ordered about, where I'd taken the lead in sickness so much, an' knew how to deal with Sister Barsett so well! She might be livin' now, perhaps"—

"Come; we'd better go in, 't is gettin' damp," and the mis-tress of the house rose so hurriedly as to seem bustling. "Don't dwell on Sister Barsett an' her foolish folks no more; I would n't, if I was you."

They went into the front room, which was dim with the twilight of the half-closed blinds and two great syringa bushes that grew against them. Sarah Ellen put down her bundle and bestowed herself in the large, cane-seated rocking-chair. Mrs. Crane directed her to stay there awhile and rest, and then come out into the kitchen when she got ready.

A cheerful clatter of dishes was heard at once upon Mrs. Crane's disappearance. "I hope she's goin' to make one o' her nice short-cakes, but I don't know's she'll think it quite worth while," thought the guest humbly. She desired to go out into the kitchen, but it was proper behavior to wait until she should be called. Mercy Crane was not a person with whom one could venture to take liberties. Presently Sarah Ellen began to feel better. She did not often find such a quiet place, or the quarter of an hour of idleness in which to enjoy it, and was glad to make the most of this opportunity. Just now she felt tired and lonely. She was a busy, unselfish, eager-minded creature by nature, but now, while grief was some-times uppermost in her mind and sometimes a sense of wrong, every moment found her more peaceful, and the great excitement little by little faded away.

"What a person poor Sister Barsett was to dread growing old so she could n't get about. I'm sure I shall miss her as much as anybody," said Mrs. Crane, suddenly opening the kitchen door, and letting in an unmistakable and delicious odor of short-cake that revived still more the drooping spirits of her guest. "An' a good deal of knowledge has died with her," she added, coming into the room and seeming to make it lighter.

"There, she knew a good deal, but she did n't know all, especially o' doctorin'," insisted Sarah Ellen from the rocking-chair, with an unexpected little laugh. "She used to lay down the law to me as if I had neither sense nor experience, but when it came to her bad spells she'd always send for me. It takes everybody to know everything, but Sister Barsett was of an opinion that her information was sufficient for the town. She was tellin' me the day I went there how she disliked to have old Mis' Doubleday come an' visit with her, an' re-marked that she called Mis' Doubleday very officious. 'Went right down on her knees an' prayed,' says she. 'Anybody would have thought I was a heathen!' But I kind of pacified her feelin's, an' told her I supposed the old lady meant well."

"Did she give away any of her things?—Mis' Barsett, I mean," inquired Mrs. Crane.

"Not in my hearin'," replied Sarah Ellen Dow. "Except one day, the first of the week, she told her oldest sister, Mis' Deckett,—'t was that first day she rode over,—that she might have her green quilted petticoat; you see it was a rainy day, an' Mis' Deckett had complained o' feelin' thin. She went right up an' got it, and put it on an' wore it off, an' I'm sure I thought no more about it, until I heard Sister Barsett groanin' dreadful in the night. I got right up to see what the matter was, an' what do you think but she was wantin' that petticoat back, and not thinking any too well o' Nancy Deck-ett for takin' it when 't was offered. 'Nancy never showed no sense o' propriety,' says Sister Barsett; I just wish you'd heard her go on!

"If she had felt to remember me," continued Sarah Ellen, after they had laughed a little, "I'd full as soon have some of her nice crockery-ware. She told me once, years ago, when I was stoppin' to tea with her an' we were havin' it real friendly, that she should leave me her Britannia tea-set, but I ain't got it in writin', and I can't say she 's ever referred to the matter since. It ain't as if I had a home o' my own to keep it in, but I should have thought a great deal of it for her sake," and the speaker's voice faltered. "I must say that with all her virtues she never was a first-class housekeeper, but I would n't say it to any but a friend. You never eat no preserves o' hers that wa'n't commencin' to work, an' you know as well as I how little forethought she had about putting away her woolens. I sat behind her once in meetin' when I was stoppin' with the Tremletts and so occupied a seat in their pew, an' I see between ten an' a dozen moth millers come workin' out o' her fitch-fur tippet. They was flutterin' round her bonnet same 's 't was a lamp. I should be mortified to death to have such a thing happen to me."

"Every housekeeper has her weak point; I 've got mine as much as anybody else," acknowledged Mercy Crane with spirit, "but you never see no moth millers come workin' out o' me in a public place."

"Ain't your oven beginning to get overhet?" anxiously inquired Sarah Ellen Dow, who was sitting more in the draught, and could not bear to have any accident happen to the supper. Mrs. Crane flew to a short-cake's rescue, and presently called her guest to the table.

The two women sat down to deep and brimming cups of tea. Sarah Ellen noticed with great gratification that her hostess had put on two of the best tea-cups and some citron-melon preserves. It was not an every-day supper. She was used to hard fare, poor, hard-working Sarah Ellen, and this handsome social attention did her good. Sister Crane rarely entertained a friend, and it would be a pleasure to speak of the tea-drinking for weeks to come.

"You 've put yourself out quite a consid'able for me," she acknowledged. "How pretty these cups is! You ought n't to use 'em so common as for me. I wish I had a home I could really call my own to ask you to, but 't ain't never been so I could. Sometimes I wonder what 's goin' to become o' me when I get so I 'm past work. Takin' care o' sick folks an' bein' in houses where there 's a sight goin' on an' everybody in a hurry kind of wears on me now I 'm most a-gittin' in years. I was wishin' the other day that I could get with some comfortable kind of a sick person, where I could live right along quiet as other folks do, but folks never sends for me 'less they're drove to it. I ain't laid up anything to really depend upon."

The situation appealed to Mercy Crane, well to do as she was and not burdened with responsibilities. She stirred uneasily in her chair, but could not bring herself to the point of offering Sarah Ellen the home she coveted.

"Have some hot tea," she insisted, in a matter of fact tone, and Sarah Ellen's face, which had been lighted by a sudden eager hopefulness, grew dull and narrow again.

"Plenty, plenty, Mis' Crane," she said sadly, " 't is beautiful tea,—you always have good tea;" but she could not turn her thoughts from her own uncertain future. "None of our folks has ever lived to be a burden," she said presently, in a pathetic tone, putting down her cup. "My mother was thought to be doing well until four o'clock an' was dead at ten. My Aunt Nancy came to our house well at twelve o'clock an' died that afternoon; my father was sick but ten days. There was dear sister Betsy, she did go in consumption, but 't wa'n't an expensive sickness."

"I've thought sometimes about you, how you'd get past rovin' from house to house one o' these days. I guess your friends will stand by you." Mrs. Crane spoke with unwonted sympathy, and Sarah Ellen's heart leaped with joy.

"You're real kind," she said simply. "There's nobody I set so much by. But I shall miss Sister Barsett, when all's said an' done. She's asked me many a time to stop with her when I wasn't doin' nothin'. We all have our failin's, but she was a friendly creatur'. I sha'n't want to see her laid away."

"Yes, I was thinkin' a few minutes ago that I shouldn't want to look out an' see the funeral go by. She's one o' the old neighbors. I s'pose I shall have to look, or I shouldn't feel right afterward," said Mrs. Crane mournfully. "If I hadn't got so kind of housebound," she added with touching frankness, "I'd just as soon go over with you an' offer to watch this night."

" 'T would astonish Sister Barsett so I don't know but she'd return." Sarah Ellen's eyes danced with amusement; she could not resist her own joke, and Mercy Crane herself had to smile.

"Now I must be goin', or 't will be dark," said the guest, rising and sighing after she had eaten her last crumb of gingerbread. "Yes, thank ye, you 're real good, I will come back if I find I ain't wanted. Look what a pretty sky there is!" and the two friends went to the side door and stood together in a moment of affectionate silence, looking out toward the sunset across the wide fields. The country was still with that deep rural stillness which seems to mean the absence of humanity. Only the thrushes were singing far away in the walnut woods beyond the orchard, and some crows were flying over and cawed once loudly, as if they were speaking to the women at the door.

Just as the friends were parting, after most grateful acknowledgments from Sarah Ellen Dow, some one came driving along the road in a hurry and stopped.

"Who 's that with you, Mis' Crane?" called one of their near neighbors.

"It 's Sarah Ellen Dow," answered Mrs. Crane. "What 's the matter?"

"I thought so, but I couldn't rightly see. Come, they are in a peck o' trouble up to Sister Barsett's, wonderin' where you be," grumbled the man. "They can't do nothin' with her; she 's drove off everybody an' keeps a-screechin' for you. Come, step along, Sarah Ellen, do!"

"Sister Barsett!" exclaimed both the women. Mercy Crane sank down upon the doorstep, but Sarah Ellen stepped out upon the grass all of a tremble, and went toward the wagon. "They said this afternoon that Sister Barsett was gone," she managed to say. "What did they mean?"

"Gone where?" asked the impatient neighbor. "I expect 't was one of her spells. She 's come to; they say she wants somethin' hearty for her tea. Nobody can't take one step till you get there, neither."

Sarah Ellen was still dazed; she returned to the doorway, where Mercy Crane sat shaking with laughter. "I don't know but we might as well laugh as cry," she said in an aimless sort of way. "I know you too well to think you 're going to repeat a single word. Well, I 'll get my bonnet an' start; I expect I 've got considerable to cope with, but I'm well rested. Good-night, Mis' Crane, I certain did have a beautiful tea, whatever the future may have in store."

She wore a solemn expression as she mounted into the wagon in haste and departed, but she was far out of sight when Mercy Crane stopped laughing and went into the house.

Decoration Day

I.

A WEEK before the thirtieth of May, three friends—John Stover and Henry Merrill and Asa Brown—happened to meet on Saturday evening at Barton's store at the Plains. They were ready to enjoy this idle hour after a busy week. After long easterly rains, the sun had at last come out bright and clear, and all the Barlow farmers had been planting. There was even a good deal of ploughing left to be done, the season was so backward.

The three middle-aged men were old friends. They had been school-fellows, and when they were hardly out of their boyhood the war came on, and they enlisted in the same company, on the same day, and happened to march away elbow to elbow. Then came the great experience of a great war, and the years that followed their return from the South had come to each almost alike. These men might have been members of the same rustic household, they knew each other's history so well.

They were sitting on a low wooden bench at the left of the store door as you went in. People were coming and going on their Saturday night errands,—the post-office was in Barton's store,—but the friends talked on eagerly, without being interrupted, except by an occasional nod of recognition. They appeared to take no notice at all of the neighbors whom they saw oftenest. It was a most beautiful evening; the two great elms were almost half in leaf over the blacksmith's shop which stood across the wide road. Farther along were two small old-fashioned houses and the old white church, with its pretty belfry of four arched sides and a tiny dome at the top. The large cockerel on the vane was pointing a little south of west, and there was still light enough to make it shine bravely against the deep blue eastern sky. On the western side of the road, near the store, were the parsonage and the storekeeper's modern house, which had a French roof and some attempt at decoration, which the long-established Barlow people called gingerbread-work, and regarded with mingled pride and disdain. These buildings made the tiny village called Barlow Plains. They stood in the middle of a long narrow strip of level ground. They were islanded by green fields and pastures. There were hills beyond; the mountains themselves seemed very near. Scattered about on the hill slopes were farmhouses, which stood so far apart, with their clusters of out-buildings, that each looked lonely, and the pine woods above seemed to besiege them all. It was lighter on the uplands than it was in the valley, where the three men sat on their bench, with their backs to the store and the western sky.

"Well, here we be 'most into June, an' I 'ain't got a bush-bean above ground," lamented Henry Merrill.

"Your land's always late, ain't it? But you always catch up with the rest on us," Asa Brown consoled him. "I've often observed that your land, though early planted, was late to sprout. I view it there's a good week's difference betwixt me an' Stover an' your folks, but come first o' July we all even up."

"'T is just so," said John Stover, taking his pipe out of his mouth, as if he had a good deal more to say, and then replacing it, as if he had changed his mind.

"Made it extry hard having that long wet spell. Can't none on us take no day off this season," said Asa Brown; but nobody thought it worth his while to respond to such evident truth.

"Next Saturday'll be the thirtieth o' May—that's Decoration Day, ain't it?—come round again. Lord! how the years slip by after you git to be forty-five an' along there!" said Asa again. "I s'pose some o' our folks'll go over to Alton to see the procession, same's usual. I've got to git one o' them small flags to stick on our Joel's grave, an' Mis' Dexter always counts on havin' some for Harrison's lot. I calculate to get 'em somehow. I must make time to ride over, but I don't know where the time's comin' from out o' next week. I wish the women folks would tend to them things. There's the spot where Eb Munson an' John Tighe lays in the poor-farm lot, an' I did mean certain to buy flags for 'em last year an' year before, but I went an' forgot it. I'd like to have folks that rode by notice 'em for once, if they was town paupers. Eb

Munson was as darin' a man as ever stepped out to tuck o' drum.'"

"So he was," said John Stover, taking his pipe with decision and knocking out the ashes. "Drink was his ruin; but I wan't one that could be harsh with Eb, no matter what he done. He worked hard long 's he could, too; but he wan't like a sound man, an' I think he took somethin' first not so much 'cause he loved it, but to kind of keep his strength up so 's he could work, an' then, all of a sudden, rum clinched with him an' threw him. Eb was talkin' 'long o' me one day when he was about half full, an' says he, right out, 'I would n't have fell to this state,' says he, 'if I 'd had me a home an' a little fam 'ly; but it don't make no difference to nobody, and it 's the best comfort I seem to have, an' I ain't goin' to do without it. I 'm ailin' all the time,' says he, 'an' if I keep middlin' full, I make out to hold my own an' to keep along o' my work.' I pitied Eb. I says to him, 'You ain't goin' to bring no disgrace on us old army boys, be you, Eb?' an' he says no, he wan't. I think if he 'd lived to get one o' them big fat pensions, he 'd had it easier. Eight dollars a month paid his board, while he 'd pick up what cheap work he could, an' then he got so that decent folks did n't seem to want the bother of him, an' so he come on the town."

"There was somethin' else to it," said Henry Merrill soberly. "Drink come natural to him, 't was born in him, I expect, an' there wan't nobody that could turn the divil out same 's they did in Scriptur'. His father an' his gran'father was drinkin' men; but they was kind-hearted an' good neighbors, an' never set out to wrong nobody. 'T was the custom to drink in their day; folks was colder an' lived poorer in early times, an' that 's how most of 'em kept a-goin'. But what stove Eb all up was his disapp'intment with Marthy Peck— her forsakin' of him an' marryin' old John Down whilst Eb was off to war. I 've always laid it up ag'inst her."

"So 've I," said Asa Brown. "She did n't use the poor fellow right. I guess she was full as well off, but it 's one thing to show judgment, an' another thing to have heart."

There was a long pause; the subject was too familiar to need further comment.

"There ain't no public sperit here in Barlow," announced

Asa Brown, with decision. "I don't s'pose we could ever get up anything for Decoration Day. I've felt kind of 'shamed, but it always comes in a busy time; 't wan't no time to have it, anyway, right in late plantin'."

" 'T ain't no use to look for public sperit 'less you've got some yourself," observed John Stover soberly; but something had pleased him in the discouraged suggestion. "Perhaps we could mark the day this year. It comes on a Saturday; that ain't nigh so bad as bein' in the middle of the week."

Nobody made any answer, and presently he went on, —

"There was a time along back when folks was too nigh the war-time to give much thought to the bigness of it. The best fellows was them that had stayed to home an' worked their trades an' laid up money; but I don't know 's it 's so now."

"Yes, the fellows that stayed at home got all the fat places, an' when we come back we felt dreadful behind the times," grumbled Asa Brown. "I remember how 't was."

"They begun to call us heroes an' old stick-in-the-mud just about the same time," resumed Stover, with a chuckle. "We wa'n't no hand for strippin' woodland nor even tradin' hosses them first few years. I don' know why 't was we were so beat out. The best most on us could do was to sag right on to the old folks. Father he never wanted me to go to the war, — 't was partly his Quaker breed, — an' he used to be dreadful mortified with the way I hung round down here to the store an' loafed round a-talkin' about when I was out South, an' arguin' with folks that did n't know nothin', about what the generals done. There! I see me now just as he see me then; but after I had my boy-strut out, I took holt o' the old farm 'long o' father, an' I 've made it bounce. Look at them old meadows an' see the herd's grass that come off of 'em last year! I ain't ashamed o' my place now, if I did go to the war."

"It all looks a sight bigger to me now than it did then," said Henry Merrill. "Our goin' to the war, I refer to. We did n't sense it no more than other folks did. I used to be sick o' hearin' their stuff about patriotism and lovin' your country, an' them pieces o' poetry women folks wrote for the papers

on the old flag, an' our fallen heroes, an' them things; they
did n't seem to strike me in the right place; but I tell ye it kind
o' starts me now every time I come on the flag sudden,—it
does so. A spell ago—'long in the fall, I guess it was—I was
over to Alton, an' there was a fire company paradin'. They 'd
got the prize at a fair, an' had just come home on the cars, an'
I heard the band; so I stepped to the front o' the store where
me an' my woman was tradin', an' the company felt well, an'
was comin' along the street 'most as good as troops. I see the
old flag a-comin', kind of blowin' back, an' it went all over
me. Somethin' worked round in my throat; I vow I come
near cryin'. I was glad nobody see me."

"I 'd go to war again in a minute," declared Stover, after an
expressive pause; "but I expect we should know better what
we was about. I don' know but we 've got too many rooted
opinions now to make us the best o' soldiers."

"Martin Tighe an' John Tighe was considerable older than
the rest, and they done well," answered Henry Merrill
quickly. "We three was the youngest of any, but we did think
at the time we knew the most."

"Well, whatever you may say, that war give the country a
great start," said Asa Brown. "I tell ye we just begin to see
the scope on 't. There was my cousin, you know, Dan'l
Evins, that stopped with us last winter; he was tellin' me
that one o' his coastin' trips he was into the port o' Beaufort
lo'din' with yaller-pine lumber, an' he roved into an old
buryin'-ground there is there, an' he see a stone that had on
it some young Southern fellow's name that was killed in the
war, an' under it was, 'He died for his country.' Dan'l
knowed how I used to feel about them South Car'lina goings on, an' I did feel kind o' red an' ugly for a minute, an'
then somethin' come over me, an' I says, 'Well, I don' know
but what the poor chap did, Dan Evins, when you come to
view it all round.' "

The other men made no answer.

"Le's see what we can do this year. I don't care if we be a
poor han'ful," urged Henry Merrill. "The young folks ought
to have the good of it; I 'd like to have my boys see somethin'
different. Le's get together what men there is. How many 's

left, anyhow? I know there was thirty-seven went from old Barlow, three-months' men an' all."

"There can't be over eight now, countin' out Martin Tighe; he can't march," said Stover. "No, 't ain't worth while." But the others did not notice his disapproval.

"There's nine in all," announced Asa Brown, after pondering and counting two or three times on his fingers. "I can't make us no more. I never could carry figur's in my head."

"I make nine," said Merrill. "We'll have Martin ride, an' Jesse Dean too, if he will. He's awful lively on them canes o' his. An' there's Jo Wade with his crutch; he's amazin' spry for a short distance. But we can't let 'em go far afoot; they're decripped men. We'll make 'em all put on what they've got left o' their uniforms, an' we'll scratch round an' have us a fife an' drum, an' make the best show we can."

"Why, Martin Tighe's boy, the next to the oldest, is an excellent hand to play the fife!" said John Stover, suddenly growing enthusiastic. "If you two are set on it, let's have a word with the minister to-morrow, an' see what he says. Perhaps he'll give out some kind of a notice. You have to have a good many bunches o' flowers. I guess we'd better call a meetin', some few on us, an' talk it over first o' the week. 'T would n't be no great of a range for us to take to march from the old buryin'-ground at the meetin'-house here up to the poor-farm an' round by Deacon Elwell's lane, so's to notice them two stones he set up for his boys that was sunk on the man-o'-war. I expect they notice stones same's if the folks laid there, don't they?"

He spoke wistfully. The others knew that Stover was thinking of the stone he had set up to the memory of his only brother, whose nameless grave had been made somewhere in the Wilderness.

"I don't know but what they'll be mad if we don't go by every house in town," he added anxiously, as they rose to go home. "'T is a terrible scattered population in Barlow to favor with a procession."

It was a mild starlit night. The three friends took their separate ways presently, leaving the Plains road and crossing the fields by foot-paths toward their farms.

II.

The week went by, and the next Saturday morning brought fair weather. It was a busy morning on the farms—like any other; but long before noon the teams of horses and oxen were seen going home from work in the fields, and everybody got ready in haste for the great event of the afternoon. It was so seldom that any occasion roused public interest in Barlow that there was an unexpected response, and the green before the old white meeting-house was covered with country wagons and groups of people, whole families together, who had come on foot. The old soldiers were to meet in the church; at half past one the procession was to start, and on its return the minister was to make an address in the old burying-ground. John Stover had been first lieutenant in the war, so he was made captain of the day. A man from the next town had offered to drum for them, and Martin Tighe's proud boy was present with his fife. He had a great longing—strange enough in that peaceful, sheep-raising neighborhood—to go into the army; but he and his elder brother were the mainstay of their crippled father, and he could not be spared from the large household until a younger brother could take his place; so that all his fire and military zeal went for the present into martial tunes, and the fife was a safety-valve for his enthusiasm.

The army men were used to seeing each other; everybody knew everybody in the little country town of Barlow; but when one comrade after another appeared in what remained of his accoutrements, they felt the day to be greater than they had planned, and the simple ceremony proved more solemn than any one expected. They could make no use of their every-day jokes and friendly greetings. Their old blue coats and tarnished army caps looked faded and antiquated enough. One of the men had nothing left but his rusty canteen and rifle; but these he carried like sacred emblems. He had worn out all his army clothes long ago, because he was too poor when he was discharged to buy any others.

When the door of the church opened, the veterans were not abashed by the size and silence of the crowd. They came walking two by two down the steps, and took their places in line as if there were nobody looking on. Their brief evolutions were like a mystic rite. The two lame men refused to do anything but march as best they could; but poor Martin Tighe, more disabled than they, was brought out and lifted into Henry Merrill's best wagon, where he sat up, straight and soldierly, with his boy for driver. There was a little flag in the whip-socket before him, which flapped gayly in the breeze. It was such a long time since he had been seen out-of-doors that everybody found him a great object of interest, and paid him much attention. Even those who were tired of being asked to contribute to his support, who resented the fact of his having a helpless wife and great family; who always insisted that with his little pension and hopeless lameness, his fingerless left hand and failing sight, he could support himself and his household if he chose,—even those persons came forward now to greet him handsomely and with large approval. To be sure, he enjoyed the conversation of idlers, and his wife had a complaining way that was the same as begging, especially since her boys began to grow up and be of some use; and there were one or two near neighbors who never let them really want; so other people, who had cares enough of their own, could excuse themselves for forgetting him the year round, and even call him shiftless. But there were none to look askance at Martin Tighe on Decoration Day, as he sat in the wagon, with his bleached face like a captive's, and his thin, afflicted body. He stretched out his whole hand impartially to those who had remembered and those who had forgotten both his courage at Fredericksburg and his sorry need in Barlow.

Henry Merrill had secured the engine company's large flag in Alton, and now carried it proudly. There were eight men in line, two by two, and marching a good bit apart, to make their line the longer. The fife and drum struck up gallantly together, and the little procession moved away slowly along the country road. It gave an unwonted touch of color to the landscape,—the scarlet, the blue, between the new-ploughed fields and budding roadside thickets, between the wide dim ranges of the mountains, under the great white clouds of the spring sky. Such processions grow more pathetic year by year;

it will not be so long now before wondering children will have seen the last. The aging faces of the men, the renewed comradeship, the quick beat of the hearts that remember, the tenderness of those who think upon old sorrows,—all these make the day a lovelier and a sadder festival. So men's hearts were stirred, they knew not why, when they heard the shrill fife and the incessant drum along the quiet Barlow road, and saw the handful of old soldiers marching by. Nobody thought of them as familiar men and neighbors alone,—they were a part of that army which had saved its country. They had taken their lives in their hands and gone out to fight for their country, plain John Stover and Jesse Dean and the rest. No matter if every other day in the year they counted for little or much, whether they were lame-footed and lagging, whether their farms were of poor soil or rich.

The little troop went in slender line along the road; the crowded country wagons and all the people who went afoot followed Martin Tighe's wagon as if it were a great gathering at a country funeral. The route was short, and the long, straggling line marched slowly; it could go no faster than the lame men could walk.

In one of the houses by the roadside an old woman sat by a window, in an old-fashioned black gown, and clean white cap with a prim border which bound her thin, sharp features closely. She had been for a long time looking out eagerly over the snowberry and cinnamon-rose bushes; her face was pressed close to the pane, and presently she caught sight of the great flag as it came down the road.

"Let me see 'em! I've got to see 'em go by!" she pleaded, trying to rise from her chair alone when she heard the fife, and the women helped her to the door, and held her so that she could stand and wait. She had been an old woman when the war began; she had sent sons and grandsons to the field; they were all gone now. As the men came by, she straightened her bent figure with all the vigor of youth. The fife and drum stopped suddenly; the colors lowered. She did not heed that, but her old eyes flashed and then filled with tears to see the flag going to salute the soldiers' graves. "Thank ye, boys; thank ye!" she cried, in her quavering voice, and they all cheered her. The cheer went back along the straggling line for old Grandmother Dexter, standing there in her front door between the lilacs. It was one of the great moments of the day.

The few old people at the poor-house, too, were waiting to see the show. The keeper's young son, knowing that it was a day of festivity, and not understanding exactly why, had put his toy flag out of the gable window, and there it showed against the gray clapboards like a gay flower. It was the only bit of decoration along the veterans' way, and they stopped and saluted it before they broke ranks and went out to the field corner beyond the poor-farm barn to the bit of ground that held the paupers' unmarked graves. There was a solemn silence while Asa Brown went to the back of Tighe's wagon, where such light freight was carried, and brought two flags, and he and John Stover planted them straight in the green sod. They knew well enough where the right graves were, for these had been made in a corner by themselves, with unwonted sentiment. And so Eben Munson and John Tighe were honored like the rest, both by their flags and by great and unexpected nosegays of spring flowers, daffies and flowering currant and red tulips, which lay on the graves already. John Stover and his comrade glanced at each other curiously while they stood singing, and then laid their own bunches of lilacs down and came away.

Then something happened that almost none of the people in the wagons understood. Martin Tighe's boy, who played the fife, had studied well his part, and on his poor short-winded instrument now sounded taps as well as he could. He had heard it done once in Alton at a soldier's funeral. The plaintive notes called sadly over the fields, and echoed back from the hills. The few veterans could not look at each other; their eyes brimmed up with tears; they could not have spoken. Nothing called back old army days like that. They had a sudden vision of the Virginian camp, the hillside dotted white with tents, the twinkling lights in other camps, and far away the glow of smouldering fires. They heard the bugle call from post to post; they remembered the chilly winter night, the wind in the pines, the laughter of the men. Lights out! Martin Tighe's boy sounded it again sharply. It seemed as if poor Eb Munson and John Tighe must hear it too in their narrow graves.

The procession went on, and stopped here and there at the little graveyards on the farms, leaving their bright flags to flutter through summer and winter rains and snows, and to bleach in the wind and sunshine. When they returned to the church, the minister made an address about the war, and every one listened with new ears. Most of what he said was familiar enough to his listeners; they were used to reading those phrases about the results of the war, the glorious future of the South, in their weekly newspapers; but there never had been such a spirit of patriotism and loyalty waked in Barlow as was waked that day by the poor parade of the remnant of the Barlow soldiers. They sent flags to all the distant graves, and proud were those households who claimed kinship with valor, and could drive or walk away with their flags held up so that others could see that they, too, were of the elect.

III.

It is well that the days are long in the last of May, but John Stover had to hurry more than usual with his evening work, and then, having the longest distance to walk, he was much the latest comer to the Plains store, where his two triumphant friends were waiting for him impatiently on the bench. They also had made excuse of going to the post-office and doing an unnecessary errand for their wives, and were talking together so busily that they had gathered a group about them before the store. When they saw Stover coming, they rose hastily and crossed the road to meet him, as if they were a committee in special session. They leaned against the post-and-board fence, after they had shaken hands with each other solemnly.

"Well, we've had a great day, ain't we, John?" asked Henry Merrill. "You did lead off splendid. We've done a grand thing, now, I tell you. All the folks say we've got to keep it up every year. Everybody had to have a talk about it as I went home. They say they had no idea we should make such a show. Lord! I wish we'd begun while there was more of us!"

"That han'some flag was the great feature," said Asa Brown generously. "I want to pay my part for hirin' it. An' then folks was glad to see poor old Martin made o' some consequence."

"There was half a dozen said to me that another year they

was goin' to have flags out, and trim up their places somehow or 'nother. Folks has feelin' enough, but you 've got to rouse it," said Merrill.

"I have thought o' joinin' the Grand Army over to Alton time an' again, but it 's a good ways to go, an' then the expense has been o' some consideration," Asa continued. "I don't know but two or three over there. You know, most o' the Alton men nat'rally went out in the rigiments t' other side o' the State line, an' they was in other battles, an' never camped nowheres nigh us. Seems to me we ought to have home feelin' enough to do what we can right here."

"The minister says to me this afternoon that he was goin' to arrange an' have some talks in the meetin'-house next winter, an' have some of us tell where we was in the South; an' one night 't will be about camp life, an' one about the long marches, an' then about the battles,—that would take some time,—an' tell all we could about the boys that was killed, an' their record, so they would n't be forgot. He said some of the folks must have the letters we wrote home from the front, an' we could make out quite a history of us. I call Elder Dallas a very smart man; he 'd planned it all out a'ready, for the benefit o' the young folks, he said," announced Henry Merrill, in a tone of approval.

"I s'pose there ain't none of us but could add a little somethin'," answered John Stover modestly. " 'T would re'lly learn the young folks a good deal. I should be scared numb to try an' speak from the pulpit. That ain't what the Elder means, is it? Now I was one that had a good chance to see somethin' o' Washin'ton. I shook hands with President Lincoln, an' I always think I 'm worth lookin' at for that, if I ain't for nothin' else. 'T was that time I was just out o' hospit'l, an' able to crawl about some. I 've often told you how 't was I met him, an' he stopped an' shook hands an' asked where I 'd been at the front an' how I was gettin' along with my hurts. Well, we 'll see how 't is when winter comes. I never thought I had no gift for public speakin', 'less 't was for drivin' cattle or pollin' the house town-meetin' days. Here! I 've got somethin' in mind. You need n't speak about it if I tell it to ye," he added suddenly. "You know all them han'some flowers that was laid on to Eb Munson's grave an' Tighe's? I mistrusted you thought the same thing I did by the way you looked. They come from Marthy Down's front yard. My woman told me when we got home that she knew 'em in a minute; there wa'n't nobody in town had that kind o' red flowers but her. She must ha' kind o' harked back to the days when she was Marthy Peck. She must have come over with 'em after dark, or else dreadful early in the mornin'."

Henry Merrill cleared his throat. "There ain't nothin' half-way 'bout Mis' Down," he said. "I would n't ha' spoken 'bout this 'less you had led right on to it; but I overtook her when I was gittin' towards home this afternoon, an' I see by her looks she was worked up a good deal; but we talked about how well things had gone off, an' she wanted to know what expenses we'd been put to, an' I told her; and she said she'd give five dollars any day I'd stop in for it. An' then she spoke right out. 'I'm alone in the world,' says she, 'and I've got somethin' to do with, an' I'd like to have a plain stone put up to Eb Munson's grave, with the number of his rigiment on it, an' I'll pay the bill. 'T ain't out o' Mr. Down's money,' she says; ''t is mine, an' I want you to see to it.' I said I would, but we'd made a plot to git some o' them soldiers' headstones that's provided by the government. 'T was a shame it had been overlooked so long. 'No,' says she; 'I'm goin' to pay for Eb's myself.' An' I told her there would n't be no objection. Don't ary one o' you speak about it. 'T would n't be fair. She was real well-appearin'. I never felt to respect Marthy so before."

"We was kind o' hard on her sometimes, but folks could n't help it. I've seen her pass Eb right by in the road an' never look at him when he first come home," said John Stover.

"If she had n't felt bad, she would n't have cared one way or t' other," insisted Henry Merrill. "'T ain't for us to judge. Sometimes folks has to get along in years before they see things fair. Come; I must be goin' home. I'm tired as an old dog."

"It seemed kind o' natural to be steppin' out together again. Strange we three got through with so little damage, an' so many dropped round us," said Asa Brown. "I've never been one mite sorry I went out in old A Company. I was thinkin' when I was marchin' to-day, though, that we should all have to take to the wagons before long an' do our marchin' on wheels, so many of us felt kind o' stiff. There's one thing,—folks won't never say again that we can't show no public sperit here in old Barlow."

The Flight of Betsey Lane

ONE windy morning in May, three old women sat together near an open window in the shed chamber of Byfleet Poor-house. The wind was from the northwest, but their window faced the southeast, and they were only visited by an occasional pleasant waft of fresh air. They were close together, knee to knee, picking over a bushel of beans, and commanding a view of the dandelion-starred, green yard below, and of the winding, sandy road that led to the village, two miles away. Some captive bees were scolding among the cobwebs of the rafters overhead, or thumping against the upper panes of glass; two calves were bawling from the barnyard, where some of the men were at work loading a dumpcart and shouting as if every one were deaf. There was a cheerful feeling of activity, and even an air of comfort, about the Byfleet Poor-house. Almost every one was possessed of a most interesting past, though there was less to be said about the future. The inmates were by no means distressed or unhappy; many of them retired to this shelter only for the winter season, and would go out presently, some to begin such work as they could still do, others to live in their own small houses; old age had impoverished most of them by limiting their power of endurance; but far from lamenting the fact that they were town charges, they rather liked the change and excitement of a winter residence on the poor-farm. There was a sharp-faced, hard-worked young widow with seven children, who was an exception to the general level of society, because she deplored the change in her fortunes. The older women regarded her with suspicion, and were apt to talk about her in moments like this, when they happened to sit together at their work.

The three bean-pickers were dressed alike in stout brown ginghams, checked by a white line, and all wore great faded aprons of blue drilling, with sufficient pockets convenient to the right hand. Miss Peggy Bond was a very small, belligerent-

looking person, who wore a huge pair of steel-bowed spectacles, holding her sharp chin well up in air, as if to supplement an inadequate nose. She was more than half blind, but
the spectacles seemed to face upward instead of square
ahead, as if their wearer were always on the sharp lookout
for birds. Miss Bond had suffered much personal damage
from time to time, because she never took heed where she
planted her feet, and so was always tripping and stubbing
her bruised way through the world. She had fallen down
hatchways and cellarways, and stepped composedly into deep
ditches and pasture brooks; but she was proud of stating
that she was upsighted, and so was her father before her. At
the poor-house, where an unusual malady was considered a
distinction, upsightedness was looked upon as a most honorable infirmity. Plain rheumatism, such as afflicted Aunt Lavina Dow, whose twisted hands found even this light work
difficult and tiresome,—plain rheumatism was something of
every-day occurrence, and nobody cared to hear about it.
Poor Peggy was a meek and friendly soul, who never put
herself forward; she was just like other folks, as she always
loved to say, but Mrs. Lavina Dow was a different sort of
person altogether, of great dignity and, occasionally, almost
aggressive behavior. The time had been when she could do a
good day's work with anybody: but for many years now she
had not left the town-farm, being too badly crippled to
work; she had no relations or friends to visit, but from an
innate love of authority she could not submit to being one
of those who are forgotten by the world. Mrs. Dow was the
hostess and social lawgiver here, where she remembered every inmate and every item of interest for nearly forty years,
besides an immense amount of town history and biography
for three or four generations back.

She was the dear friend of the third woman, Betsey Lane;
together they led thought and opinion—chiefly opinion—
and held sway, not only over Byfleet Poor-farm, but also the
selectmen and all others in authority. Betsey Lane had spent
most of her life as aid-in-general to the respected household
of old General Thornton. She had been much trusted and
valued, and, at the breaking up of that once large and flourishing family, she had been left in good circumstances, what

with legacies and her own comfortable savings; but by sad misfortune and lavish generosity everything had been scattered, and after much illness, which ended in a stiffened arm and more uncertainty, the good soul had sensibly decided that it was easier for the whole town to support her than for a part of it. She had always hoped to see something of the world before she died; she came of an adventurous, seafaring stock, but had never made a longer journey than to the towns of Danby and Northville, thirty miles away.

They were all old women; but Betsey Lane, who was sixty-nine, and looked much older, was the youngest. Peggy Bond was far on in the seventies, and Mrs. Dow was at least ten years older. She made a great secret of her years; and as she sometimes spoke of events prior to the Revolution with the assertion of having been an eye-witness, she naturally wore an air of vast antiquity. Her tales were an inexpressible delight to Betsey Lane, who felt younger by twenty years because her friend and comrade was so unconscious of chronological limitations.

The bushel basket of cranberry beans was within easy reach, and each of the pickers had filled her lap from it again and again. The shed chamber was not an unpleasant place in which to sit at work, with its traces of seed corn hanging from the brown cross-beams, its spare churns, and dusty loom, and rickety wool-wheels, and a few bits of old furniture. In one far corner was a wide board of dismal use and suggestion, and close beside it an old cradle. There was a battered chest of drawers where the keeper of the poor-house kept his garden-seeds, with the withered remains of three seed cucumbers ornamenting the top. Nothing beautiful could be discovered, nothing interesting, but there was something usable and homely about the place. It was the favorite and untroubled bower of the bean-pickers, to which they might retreat unmolested from the public apartments of this rustic institution.

Betsey Lane blew away the chaff from her handful of beans. The spring breeze blew the chaff back again, and sifted it over her face and shoulders. She rubbed it out of her eyes impatiently, and happened to notice old Peggy holding her own handful high, as if it were an oblation, and turning her queer, up-tilted head this way and that, to look at the beans sharply, as if she were first cousin to a hen.

"There, Miss Bond, 't is kind of botherin' work for you, ain't it?" Betsey inquired compassionately.

"I feel to enjoy it, anything that I can do my own way so," responded Peggy. "I like to do my part. Ain't that old Mis' Fales comin' up the road? It sounds like her step."

The others looked, but they were not far-sighted, and for a moment Peggy had the advantage. Mrs. Fales was not a favorite.

"I hope she ain't comin' here to put up this spring. I guess she won't now, it 's gettin' so late," said Betsey Lane. "She likes to go rovin' soon as the roads is settled."

" 'T is Mis' Fales!" said Peggy Bond, listening with solemn anxiety. "There, do let 's pray her by!"

"I guess she 's headin' for her cousin's folks up Beech Hill way," said Betsey presently. "If she 'd left her daughter's this mornin', she 'd have got just about as far as this. I kind o' wish she had stepped in just to pass the time o' day, long 's she wa'n't going to make no stop."

There was a silence as to further speech in the shed chamber; and even the calves were quiet in the barnyard. The men had all gone away to the field where corn-planting was going on. The beans clicked steadily into the wooden measure at the pickers' feet. Betsey Lane began to sing a hymn, and the others joined in as best they might, like autumnal crickets; their voices were sharp and cracked, with now and then a few low notes of plaintive tone. Betsey herself could sing pretty well, but the others could only make a kind of accompaniment. Their voices ceased altogether at the higher notes.

"Oh my! I wish I had the means to go to the Centennial," mourned Betsey Lane, stopping so suddenly that the others had to go on croaking and shrilling without her for a moment before they could stop. "It seems to me as if I can't die happy 'less I do," she added; "I ain't never seen nothin' of the world, an' here I be."

"What if you was as old as I be?" suggested Mrs. Dow pompously. "You 've got time enough yet, Betsey; don't you go an' despair. I knowed of a woman that went clean round the world four times when she was past eighty, an' enjoyed herself real well. Her folks followed the sea; she had three sons an' a daughter married,—all shipmasters, and she'd been with her own husband when they was young. She was left a widder early, and fetched up her family herself,—a real stirrin', smart woman. After they'd got married off, an' settled, an' was doing well, she come to be lonesome; and first she tried to stick it out alone, but she wa'n't one that could; an' she got a notion she hadn't nothin' before her but her last sickness, and she wa'n't a person that enjoyed havin' other folks do for her. So one on her boys—I guess 't was the oldest—said he was going to take her to sea; there was ample room, an' he was sailin' a good time o' year for the Cape o' Good Hope an' way up to some o' them tea-ports in the Chiny Seas. She was all high to go, but it made a sight o' talk at her age; an' the minister made it a subject o' prayer the last Sunday, and all the folks took a last leave; but she said to some she'd fetch 'em home something real pritty, and so did. An' then they come home t' other way, round the Horn, an' she done so well, an' was such a sight o' company, the other child'n was jealous, an' she promised she'd go a v'y'ge long o' each on 'em. She was as sprightly a person as ever I see; an' could speak well o' what she'd seen."

"Did she die to sea?" asked Peggy, with interest.

"No, she died to home between v'y'ges, or she'd gone to sea again. I was to her funeral. She liked her son George's ship the best; 't was the one she was going on to Callao. They said the men aboard all called her 'gran'ma'am,' an' she kep' 'em mended up, an' would go below and tend to 'em if they was sick. She might 'a' been alive an' enjoyin' of herself a good many years but for the kick of a cow; 't was a new cow out of a drove, a dreadful unruly beast."

Mrs. Dow stopped for breath, and reached down for a new supply of beans; her empty apron was gray with soft chaff. Betsey Lane, still pondering on the Centennial, began to sing another verse of her hymn, and again the old women joined her. At this moment some strangers came driving round into the yard from the front of the house. The turf was soft, and our friends did not hear the horses' steps. Their voices cracked and quavered; it was a funny little concert, and a lady in an open carriage just below listened with sympathy and amusement.

II.

"Betsey! Betsey! Miss Lane!" a voice called eagerly at the foot of the stairs that led up from the shed. "Betsey! There's a lady here wants to see you right away."

Betsey was dazed with excitement, like a country child who knows the rare pleasure of being called out of school. "Lor', I ain't fit to go down, be I?" she faltered, looking anxiously at her friends; but Peggy was gazing even nearer to the zenith than usual, in her excited effort to see down into the yard, and Mrs. Dow only nodded somewhat jealously, and said that she guessed 't was nobody would do her any harm. She rose ponderously, while Betsey hesitated, being, as they would have said, all of a twitter. "It is a lady, certain," Mrs. Dow assured her; " 't ain't often there's a lady comes here."

"While there was any of Mis' Gen'ral Thornton's folks left, I wa'n't without visits from the gentry," said Betsey Lane, turning back proudly at the head of the stairs, with a touch of old-world pride and sense of high station. Then she disappeared, and closed the door behind her at the stair-foot with a decision quite unwelcome to the friends above.

"She need n't 'a' been so dreadful 'fraid anybody was goin' to listen. I guess we've got folks to ride an' see us, or had once, if we hain't now," said Miss Peggy Bond, plaintively.

"I expect 't was only the wind shoved it to," said Aunt Lavina. "Betsey is one that gits flustered easier than some. I wish 't was somebody to take her off an' give her a kind of a good time; she's young to settle down 'long of old folks like us. Betsey's got a notion o' rovin' such as ain't my natur', but I should like to see her satisfied. She'd been a very understandin' person, if she had the advantages that some does."

" 'T is so," said Peggy Bond, tilting her chin high. "I suppose you can't hear nothin' they're saying? I feel my hearin' ain't up to whar it was. I can hear things close to me well as ever; but there, hearin' ain't everything; 't ain't as if we lived where there was more goin' on to hear. Seems to me them folks is stoppin' a good while."

"They surely be," agreed Lavina Dow.

"I expect it's somethin' particular. There ain't none of the Thornton folks left, except one o' the gran'darters, an' I've often heard Betsey remark that she should never see her more, for she lives to London. Strange how folks feels contented in them strayaway places off to the ends of the airth."

The flies and bees were buzzing against the hot window-panes; the handfuls of beans were clicking into the brown wooden measure. A bird came and perched on the window-sill, and then flitted away toward the blue sky. Below, in the yard, Betsey Lane stood talking with the lady. She had put her blue drilling apron over her head, and her face was shining with delight.

"Lor', dear," she said, for at least the third time, "I remember ye when I first see ye; an awful pritty baby you was, an' they all said you looked just like the old gen'ral. Be you goin' back to foreign parts right away?"

"Yes, I'm going back; you know that all my children are there. I wish I could take you with me for a visit," said the charming young guest. "I'm going to carry over some of the pictures and furniture from the old house; I didn't care half so much for them when I was younger as I do now. Perhaps next summer we shall all come over for a while. I should like to see my girls and boys playing under the pines."

"I wish you re'lly was livin' to the old place," said Betsey Lane. Her imagination was not swift; she needed time to think over all that was being told her, and she could not fancy the two strange houses across the sea. The old Thornton house was to her mind the most delightful and elegant in the world.

"Is there anything I can do for you?" asked Mrs. Strafford kindly,—"anything that I can do for you myself, before I go away? I shall be writing to you, and sending some pictures of the children, and you must let me know how you are getting on."

"Yes, there is one thing, darlin'. If you could stop in the village an' pick me out a pritty, little, small lookin'-glass, that I can keep for my own an' have to remember you by. 'T ain't that I want to set me above the rest o' the folks, but I was always used to havin' my own when I was to your grandma's.

There's very nice folks here, some on 'em, and I'm better off than if I was able to keep house; but sence you ask me, that's the only thing I feel cropin' about. What be you goin' right back for? ain't you goin' to see the great fair to Pheladelphy, that everybody talks about?"

"No," said Mrs. Strafford, laughing at this eager and almost convicting question. "No; I'm going back next week. If I were, I believe that I should take you with me. Good-by, dear old Betsey; you make me feel as if I were a little girl again; you look just the same."

For full five minutes the old woman stood out in the sunshine, dazed with delight, and majestic with a sense of her own consequence. She held something tight in her hand, without thinking what it might be; but just as the friendly mistress of the poor-farm came out to hear the news, she tucked the roll of money into the bosom of her brown gingham dress. " 'T was my dear Mis' Katy Strafford," she turned to say proudly. "She come way over from London; she's been sick; they thought the voyage would do her good. She said most the first thing she had on her mind was to come an' find me, and see how I was, an' if I was comfortable; an' now she's goin' right back. She's got two splendid houses; an' said how she wished I was there to look after things,—she remembered I was always her gran'ma's right hand. Oh, it does so carry me back, to see her! Seems if all the rest on 'em must be there together to the old house. There, I must go right up an' tell Mis' Dow an' Peggy."

"Dinner's all ready; I was just goin' to blow the horn for the men-folks," said the keeper's wife. "They'll be right down. I expect you've got along smart with them beans,—all three of you together;" but Betsey's mind roved so high and so far at that moment that no achievements of bean-picking could lure it back.

III.

The long table in the great kitchen soon gathered its company of waifs and strays,—creatures of improvidence and misfortune, and the irreparable victims of old age. The dinner was satisfactory, and there was not much delay for conversation. Peggy Bond and Mrs. Dow and Betsey Lane always sat together at one end, with an air of putting the rest of the company below the salt. Betsey was still flushed with excitement; in fact, she could not eat as much as usual, and she looked up from time to time expectantly, as if she were likely to be asked to speak of her guest; but everybody was hungry, and even Mrs. Dow broke in upon some attempted confidences by asking inopportunely for a second potato. There were nearly twenty at the table, counting the keeper and his wife and two children, noisy little persons who had come from school with the small flock belonging to the poor widow, who sat just opposite our friends. She finished her dinner before any one else, and pushed her chair back; she always helped with the housework,—a thin, sorry, bad-tempered-looking poor soul, whom grief had sharpened instead of softening. "I expect you feel too fine to set with common folks," she said enviously to Betsey.

"Here I be a-settin'," responded Betsey calmly. "I don' know 's I behave more unbecomin' than usual." Betsey prided herself upon her good and proper manners; but the rest of the company, who would have liked to hear the bit of morning news, were now defrauded of that pleasure. The wrong note had been struck; there was a silence after the clatter of knives and plates, and one by one the cheerful town charges disappeared. The bean-picking had been finished, and there was a call for any of the women who felt like planting corn; so Peggy Bond, who could follow the line of hills pretty fairly, and Betsey herself, who was still equal to anybody at that work, and Mrs. Dow, all went out to the field together. Aunt Lavina labored slowly up the yard, carrying a light splint-bottomed kitchen chair and her knitting-work, and sat near the stone wall on a gentle rise, where she could see the pond and the green country, and exchange a word with her friends as they came and went up and down the rows. Betsey vouchsafed a word now and then about Mrs. Strafford, but you would have thought that she had been suddenly elevated to Mrs. Strafford's own cares and the responsibilities attending them, and had little in common with her old associates. Mrs. Dow and Peggy knew well that these high-feeling times never lasted long, and so they waited with as much patience as they could muster. They were by no means without that true tact which is only another word for unselfish sympathy.

The strip of corn land ran along the side of a great field; at the upper end of it was a field-corner thicket of young maples and walnut saplings, the children of a great nut-tree that marked the boundary. Once, when Betsey Lane found herself alone near this shelter at the end of her row, the other planters having lagged behind beyond the rising ground, she looked stealthily about, and then put her hand inside her gown, and for the first time took out the money that Mrs. Strafford had given her. She turned it over and over with an astonished look: there were new bank-bills for a hundred dollars. Betsey gave a funny little shrug of her shoulders, came out of the bushes, and took a step or two on the narrow edge of turf, as if she were going to dance; then she hastily tucked away her treasure, and stepped discreetly down into the soft harrowed and hoed land, and began to drop corn again, five kernels to a hill. She had seen the top of Peggy Bond's head over the knoll, and now Peggy herself came entirely into view, gazing upward to the skies, and stumbling more or less, but counting the corn by touch and twisting her head about anxiously to gain advantage over her uncertain vision. Betsey made a friendly, inarticulate little sound as they passed; she was thinking that somebody said once that Peggy's eyesight might be remedied if she could go to Boston to the hospital; but that was so remote and impossible an undertaking that no one had ever taken the first step. Betsey Lane's brown old face suddenly worked with excitement, but in a moment more she regained her usual firm expression, and spoke carelessly to Peggy as she turned and came alongside.

The high spring wind of the morning had quite fallen; it was a lovely May afternoon. The woods about the field to the northward were full of birds, and the young leaves scarcely hid the solemn shapes of a company of crows that patiently attended the corn-planting. Two of the men had finished their hoeing, and were busy with the construction of a scarecrow; they knelt in the furrows, chuckling, and looking over some forlorn, discarded garments. It was a time-honored custom to make the scarecrow resemble one of the poor-house family; and this year they intended to have Mrs. Lavina Dow protect the field in effigy; last year it was the counterfeit of Betsey Lane who stood on guard, with an easily recognized quilted hood and the remains of a valued shawl that one of the calves had found airing on a fence and chewed to pieces. Behind the men was the foundation for this rustic attempt at statuary,—an upright stake and bar in the form of a cross. This stood on the highest part of the field; and as the men knelt near it, and the quaint figures of the corn-planters went and came, the scene gave a curious suggestion of foreign life. It was not like New England; the presence of the rude cross appealed strangely to the imagination.

IV.

Life flowed so smoothly, for the most part, at the Byfleet Poor-farm, that nobody knew what to make, later in the summer, of a strange disappearance. All the elder inmates were familiar with illness and death, and the poor pomp of a town-pauper's funeral. The comings and goings and the various misfortunes of those who composed this strange family, related only through its disasters, hardly served for the excitement and talk of a single day. Now that the June days were at their longest, the old people were sure to wake earlier than ever; but one morning, to the astonishment of every one, Betsey Lane's bed was empty; the sheets and blankets, which were her own, and guarded with jealous care, were carefully folded and placed on a chair not too near the window, and Betsey had flown. Nobody had heard her go down the creaking stairs. The kitchen door was unlocked, and the old watch-dog lay on the step outside in the early sunshine, wagging his tail and looking wise, as if he were left on guard and meant to keep the fugitive's secret.

"Never knowed her to do nothin' afore 'thout talking it over a fortnight, and paradin' off when we could all see her," ventured a spiteful voice. "Guess we can wait till night to hear 'bout it."

Mrs. Dow looked sorrowful and shook her head. "Betsey had an aunt on her mother's side that went and drownded of herself; she was a pritty-appearing woman as ever you see."

"Perhaps she's gone to spend the day with Decker's folks," suggested Peggy Bond. "She always takes an extra early start; she was speakin' lately o' going up their way;" but Mrs. Dow shook her head with a most melancholy look. "I'm impressed that something's befell her," she insisted. "I heard her a-groanin' in her sleep. I was wakeful the forepart o' the night,—'t is very unusual with me, too."

"'T wa'n't like Betsey not to leave us any word," said the other old friend, with more resentment than melancholy. They sat together almost in silence that morning in the shed chamber. Mrs. Dow was sorting and cutting rags, and Peggy braided them into long ropes, to be made into mats at a later date. If they had only known where Betsey Lane had gone, they might have talked about it until dinner-time at noon; but failing this new subject, they could take no interest in any of their old ones. Out in the field the corn was well up, and the men were hoeing. It was a hot morning in the shed chamber, and the woolen rags were dusty and hot to handle.

v.

Byfleet people knew each other well, and when this mysteriously absent person did not return to the town-farm at the end of a week, public interest became much excited; and presently it was ascertained that Betsey Lane was neither making a visit to her friends the Deckers on Birch Hill, nor to any nearer acquaintances; in fact, she had disappeared altogether from her wonted haunts. Nobody remembered to have seen her pass, hers had been such an early flitting; and when somebody thought of her having gone away by train, he was laughed at for forgetting that the earliest morning train from South Byfleet, the nearest station, did not start until long after eight o'clock; and if Betsey had designed to be one of the passengers, she would have started along the road at seven, and been seen and known of all women. There was not a kitchen in that part of Byfleet that did not have windows toward the road. Conversation rarely left the level of the neighborhood gossip: to see Betsey Lane, in her best clothes, at that hour in the morning, would have been the signal for much exercise of imagination; but as day after day went by without news, the curiosity of those who knew her best turned slowly into fear, and at last Peggy Bond again gave utterance to the belief that Betsey had either gone out in the early morning and put an end to her life, or that she had gone to the Centennial. Some of the people at table were moved to loud laughter,—it was at supper-time on a Sunday night,—but others listened with great interest.

"She never'd put on her good clothes to drownd herself," said the widow. "She might have thought 't was good as takin' 'em with her, though. Old folks has wandered off an' got lost in the woods afore now."

Mrs. Dow and Peggy resented this impertinent remark, but deigned to take no notice of the speaker. "She wouldn't have wore her best clothes to the Centennial, would she?" mildly inquired Peggy, bobbing her head toward the ceiling. "'T would be a shame to spoil your best things in such a place. An' I don't know of her havin' any money; there's the end o' that."

"You're bad as old Mis' Bland, that used to live neighbor to our folks," said one of the old men. "She was dreadful precise; an' she so begretched to wear a good alapaca dress that was left to her, that it hung in a press forty year, an' baited the moths at last."

"I often seen Mis' Bland a-goin' in to meetin' when I was a young girl," said Peggy Bond approvingly. "She was a good-appearin' woman, an' she left property."

"Wish she'd left it to me, then," said the poor soul opposite, glancing at her pathetic row of children: but it was not good manners at the farm to deplore one's situation, and Mrs. Dow and Peggy only frowned. "Where do you suppose Betsey can be?" said Mrs. Dow, for the twentieth time. "She didn't have no money. I know she ain't gone far, if it's so that she's yet alive. She's b'en real pinched all the spring."

"Perhaps that lady that come one day give her some," the keeper's wife suggested mildly.

"Then Betsey would have told me," said Mrs. Dow, with injured dignity.

VI.

On the morning of her disappearance, Betsey rose even before the pewee and the English sparrow, and dressed herself quietly, though with trembling hands, and stole out of the kitchen door like a plunderless thief. The old dog licked her hand and looked at her anxiously; the tortoise-shell cat rubbed against her best gown, and trotted away up the yard, then she turned anxiously and came after the old woman, following faithfully until she had to be driven back. Betsey was used to long country excursions afoot. She dearly loved the early morning; and finding that there was no dew to trouble her, she began to follow pasture paths and short cuts across the fields, surprising here and there a flock of sleepy sheep, or a startled calf that rustled out from the bushes. The birds were pecking their breakfast from bush and turf; and hardly any of the wild inhabitants of that rural world were enough alarmed by her presence to do more than flutter away if they chanced to be in her path. She stepped along, light-footed and eager as a girl, dressed in her neat old straw bonnet and black gown, and carrying a few belongings in her best bundle-handkerchief, one that her only brother had brought home from the East Indies fifty years before. There was an old crow perched as sentinel on a small, dead pine-tree, where he could warn friends who were pulling up the sprouted corn in a field close by; but he only gave a contemptuous caw as the adventurer appeared, and she shook her bundle at him in revenge, and laughed to see him so clumsy as he tried to keep his footing on the twigs.

"Yes, I be," she assured him. "I'm a-goin' to Pheladelphy, to the Centennial, same's other folks. I'd jest as soon tell ye's not, old crow;" and Betsey laughed aloud in pleased content with herself and her daring, as she walked along. She had only two miles to go to the station at South Byfleet, and she felt for the money now and then, and found it safe enough. She took great pride in the success of her escape, and especially in the long concealment of her wealth. Not a night had passed since Mrs. Strafford's visit that she had not slept with the roll of money under her pillow by night, and buttoned safe inside her dress by day. She knew that everybody would offer advice and even commands about the spending or saving of it; and she brooked no interference.

The last mile of the foot-path to South Byfleet was along the railway track; and Betsey began to feel in haste, though it was still nearly two hours to train time. She looked anxiously forward and back along the rails every few minutes, for fear of being run over; and at last she caught sight of an engine that was apparently coming toward her, and took flight into the woods before she could gather courage to follow the path again. The freight train proved to be at a standstill, waiting at a turnout; and some of the men were straying about, eating their early breakfast comfortably in this time of leisure. As the old woman came up to them, she stopped too, for a moment of rest and conversation.

"Where be ye goin'?" she asked pleasantly; and they told her. It was to the town where she had to change cars and take the great through train; a point of geography which she had learned from evening talks between the men at the farm.

"What'll ye carry me there for?"

"We don't run no passenger cars," said one of the young fellows, laughing. "What makes you in such a hurry?"

"I'm startin' for Pheladelphy, an' it's a gre't ways to go."

"So 't is; but you're consid'able early, if you're makin' for the eight-forty train. See here! you haven't got a needle an' thread 'long of you in that bundle, have you? If you'll sew me on a couple o' buttons, I'll give ye a free ride. I'm in a sight o' distress, an' none o' the fellows is provided with as much as a bent pin."

"You poor boy! I'll have you seen to, in half a minute. I'm troubled with a stiff arm, but I'll do the best I can."

The obliging Betsey seated herself stiffly on the slope of the embankment, and found her thread and needle with utmost haste. Two of the train-men stood by and watched the careful stitches, and even offered her a place as spare brakeman, so that they might keep her near; and Betsey took the offer with considerable seriousness, only thinking it necessary to assure them that she was getting most too old to be out in all weathers. An express went by like an earthquake, and she was presently hoisted on board an empty box-car by two of her new and flattering acquaintances, and found herself before noon at the end of the first stage of her journey, without having spent a cent, and furnished with any amount of thrifty advice. One of the young men, being compassionate of her unprotected state as a traveler, advised her to find out the widow of an uncle of his in Philadelphia, saying despairingly that he could n't tell her just how to find the house; but Miss Betsey Lane said that she had an English tongue in her head, and should be sure to find whatever she was looking for. This unexpected incident of the freight train was the reason why everybody about the South Byfleet station insisted that no such person had taken passage by the regular train that same morning, and why there were those who persuaded themselves that Miss Betsey Lane was probably lying at the bottom of the poor-farm pond.

VII.

"Land sakes!" said Miss Betsey Lane, as she watched a Turkish person parading by in his red fez, "I call the Centennial somethin' like the day o' judgment! I wish I was goin' to stop a month, but I dare say 't would be the death o' my poor old bones."

She was leaning against the barrier of a patent pop-corn establishment, which had given her a sudden reminder of home, and of the winter nights when the sharp-kerneled little red and yellow ears were brought out, and Old Uncle Eph Flanders sat by the kitchen stove, and solemnly filled a great wooden chopping-tray for the refreshment of the company. She had wandered and loitered and looked until her eyes and head had grown numb and unreceptive; but it is only unimaginative persons who can be really astonished. The imagination can always outrun the possible and actual sights and sounds of the world; and this plain old body from Byfleet rarely found anything rich and splendid enough to surprise her. She saw the wonders of the West and the splendors of the East with equal calmness and satisfaction; she had always known that there was an amazing world outside the boundaries of Byfleet. There was a piece of paper in her pocket on which was marked, in her clumsy handwriting, "If Betsey Lane should meet with accident, notify the selectmen of Byfleet;" but having made this slight provision for the future, she had thrown herself boldly into the sea of strangers, and then had made the joyful discovery that friends were to be found at every turn.

There was something delightfully companionable about Betsey; she had a way of suddenly looking up over her big spectacles with a reassuring and expectant smile, as if you were going to speak to her, and you generally did. She must have found out where hundreds of people came from, and whom they had left at home, and what they thought of the great show, as she sat on a bench to rest, or leaned over the railings where free luncheons were afforded by the makers of hot waffles and molasses candy and fried potatoes; and there was not a night when she did not return to her lodgings with a pocket crammed with samples of spool cotton and nobody knows what. She had already collected small presents for almost everybody she knew at home, and she was such a pleasant, beaming old country body, so unmistakably appreciative and interested, that nobody ever thought of wishing that she would move on. Nearly all the busy people of the Exhibition called her either Aunty or Grandma at once, and made little pleasures for her as best they could. She was a delightful contrast to the indifferent, stupid crowd that drifted along, with eyes fixed at the same level, and seeing, even on that level, nothing for fifty feet at a time. "What be you making here, dear?" Betsey Lane would ask joyfully, and the most perfunctory guardian hastened to explain. She squandered money as she had never had the pleasure of doing before, and this hastened the day when she must return to Byfleet. She was always inquiring if there were any spectacle-sellers at hand, and received occasional directions; but it was a difficult place for her to find her way about in, and the very last day of her stay arrived before she found an exhibitor of the desired sort, an oculist and instrument-maker.

"I called to get some specs for a friend that's upsighted," she gravely informed the salesman, to his extreme amusement. "She's dreadful troubled, and jerks her head up like a hen a-drinkin'. She's got a blur a-growin' an' spreadin', an' sometimes she can see out to one side on 't, and more times she can't."

"Cataracts," said a middle-aged gentleman at her side; and Betsey Lane turned to regard him with approval and curiosity.

" 'T is Miss Peggy Bond I was mentioning, of Byfleet Poorfarm," she explained. "I count on gettin' some glasses to relieve her trouble, if there's any to be found."

"Glasses won't do her any good," said the stranger. "Suppose you come and sit down on this bench, and tell me all about it. First, where is Byfleet?" and Betsey gave the directions at length.

"I thought so," said the surgeon. "How old is this friend of yours?"

Betsey cleared her throat decisively, and smoothed her gown over her knees as if it were an apron; then she turned to take a good look at her new acquaintance as they sat on the rustic bench together. "Who be you, sir, I should like to know?" she asked, in a friendly tone.

"My name's Dunster."

"I take it you're a doctor," continued Betsey, as if they had overtaken each other walking from Byfleet to South Byfleet on a summer morning.

"I'm a doctor; part of one at least," said he. "I know more or less about eyes; and I spend my summers down on the shore at the mouth of your river; some day I'll come up and look at this person. How old is she?"

"Peggy Bond is one that never tells her age; 't ain't come quite up to where she'll begin to brag of it, you see," explained Betsey reluctantly; "but I know her to be nigh to seventy-six, one way or t'other. Her an' Mrs. Mary Ann Chick was same year's child'n, and Peggy knows I know it, an' two or three times when we've be'n in the buryin'-ground where Mary Ann lays an' has her dates right on her headstone, I couldn't bring Peggy to take no sort o' notice. I will say she makes, at times, a convenience of being upsighted. But there, I feel for her,—everybody does; it keeps her stubbin' an' trippin' against everything, beakin' and gazin' up the way she has to."

"Yes, yes," said the doctor, whose eyes were twinkling. "I'll

come and look after her, with your town doctor, this summer,—some time in the last of July or first of August."

"You'll find occupation," said Betsey, not without an air of
patronage. "Most of us to the Byfleet Farm has got our ails,
now I tell ye. You ain't got no bitters that'll take a dozen
years right off an ol' lady's shoulders?"

The busy man smiled pleasantly, and shook his head as he
went away. "Dunster," said Betsey to herself, soberly commit-
ting the new name to her sound memory. "Yes, I mustn't
forget to speak of him to the doctor, as he directed. I do'
know now as Peggy would vally herself quite so much accordin' to, if she had her eyes fixed same as other folks. I
expect there wouldn't been a smarter woman in town,
though, if she'd had a proper chance. Now I've done what I
set to do for her, I do believe, an' 't wa'n't glasses, neither. I'll
git her a pritty little shawl with that money I laid aside. Peggy
Bond ain't got a pritty shawl. I always wanted to have a real
good time, an' now I'm havin' it."

VIII.

Two or three days later, two pathetic figures might have
been seen crossing the slopes of the poor-farm field, toward
the low shores of Byfield pond. It was early in the morning,
and the stubble of the lately mown grass was wet with rain
and hindering to old feet. Peggy Bond was more blundering
and liable to stray in the wrong direction than usual; it was
one of the days when she could hardly see at all. Aunt Lavina
Dow was unusually clumsy of movement, and stiff in the
joints; she had not been so far from the house for three years.
The morning breeze filled the gathers of her wide gingham
skirt, and aggravated the size of her unwieldy figure. She
supported herself with a stick, and trusted beside to the
fragile support of Peggy's arm. They were talking together in
whispers.

"Oh, my sakes!" exclaimed Peggy, moving her small head
from side to side. "Hear you wheeze, Mis' Dow! This may be
the death o' you; there, do go slow! You set here on the side-
hill, an' le' me go try if I can see."

"It needs more eyesight than you've got," said Mrs. Dow,

panting between the words. "Oh! to think how spry I was in my young days, an' here I be now, the full of a door, an' all my complaints so aggravated by my size. 'T is hard! 't is hard! but I'm a-doin' of all this for pore Betsey's sake. I know they've all laughed, but I look to see her ris' to the top o' the pond this day, — 't is just nine days since she departed; an' say what they may, I know she hove herself in. It run in her family; Betsey had an aunt that done just so, an' she ain't be'n like herself, a-broodin' an' hivin' away alone, an' nothin' to say to you an' me that was always sich good company all together. Somethin' sprung her mind, now I tell ye, Mis' Bond."

"I feel to hope we sha'n't find her, I must say," faltered Peggy. It was plain that Mrs. Dow was the captain of this doleful expedition. "I guess she ain't never thought o' drownd-in' of herself, Mis' Dow; she's gone off a-visitin' way over to the other side o' South Byfleet; some thinks she's gone to the Centennial even now!"

"She hadn't no proper means, I tell ye," wheezed Mrs. Dow indignantly; "an' if you prefer that others should find her floatin' to the top this day, instid of us that's her best friends, you can step back to the house."

They walked on in aggrieved silence. Peggy Bond trembled with excitement, but her companion's firm grasp never wavered, and so they came to the narrow, gravelly margin and stood still. Peggy tried in vain to see the glittering water and the pond-lilies that starred it; she knew that they must be there; once, years ago, she had caught fleeting glimpses of them, and she never forgot what she had once seen. The clear blue sky overhead, the dark pine-woods beyond the pond, were all clearly pictured in her mind. "Can't you see nothin'?" she faltered; "I believe I'm wuss 'n upsighted this day. I'm going to be blind."

"No," said Lavina Dow solemnly; "no, there ain't nothin' whatever, Peggy. I hope to mercy she ain't"—

"Why, whoever'd expected to find you 'way out here!" exclaimed a brisk and cheerful voice. There stood Betsey Lane herself, close behind them, having just emerged from a thicket of alders that grew close by. She was following the short way homeward from the railroad.

"Why, what's the matter, Mis' Dow? You ain't overdoin', be ye? an' Peggy's all of a flutter. What in the name o' natur' ails ye?"

"There ain't nothin' the matter, as I knows on," responded the leader of this fruitless expedition. "We only thought we'd take a stroll this pleasant mornin'," she added, with sublime self-possession. "Where've you be'n, Betsey Lane?"

"To Pheladelphy, ma'am," said Betsey, looking quite young and gay, and wearing a townish and unfamiliar air that upheld her words. "All ought to go that can; why, you feel's if you'd be'n all round the world. I guess I've got enough to think of and tell ye for the rest o' my days. I've always wanted to go somewheres. I wish you'd be'n there, I do so. I've talked with folks from Chiny an' the back o' Pennsylvany; and I see folks way from Australy that 'peared as well as anybody; an' I see how they made spool cotton, an' sights o' other things; an' I spoke with a doctor that lives down to the beach in the summer, an' he offered to come up 'long in the first of August, an' see what he can do for Peggy's eyesight. There was di'monds there as big as pigeon's eggs; an' I met with Mis' Abby Fletcher from South Byfleet depot; an' there was hogs there that weighed risin' thirteen hunderd"—

"I want to know," said Mrs. Lavina Dow and Peggy Bond, together.

"Well, 'twas a great exper'ence for a person," added Lavina, turning ponderously, in spite of herself, to give a last wistful look at the smiling waters of the pond.

"I don't know how soon I be goin' to settle down," proclaimed the rustic sister of Sindbad. "What's for the good o' one's for the good of all. You just wait till we're setting together up in the old shed chamber! You know, my dear Mis' Katy Strafford give me a han'some present o' money that day she come to see me; and I'd be'n a-dreamin' by night an' day o' seein' that Centennial; and when I come to think on 't I felt sure somebody ought to go from this neighborhood, if 'twas only for the good o' the rest; and I thought I'd better be the one. I wa'n't goin' to ask the selec'men neither. I've come back with one-thirty-five in money, and I see everything there, an' I fetched ye all a little somethin'; but I'm full o' dust now, an' pretty nigh beat out. I never see a place more friendly than Pheladelphy; but 't ain't natural to a Byfleet person to be always walkin' on a level. There, now, Peggy, you take my bundle-handkercher and the basket, and let Mis' Dow sag on to me. I 'll git her along twice as easy."

With this the small elderly company set forth triumphant toward the poor-house, across the wide green field.

The Hiltons' Holiday

THERE was a bright, full moon in the clear sky, and the sunset was still shining faintly in the west. Dark woods stood all about the old Hilton farmhouse, save down the hill, westward, where lay the shadowy fields which John Hilton, and his father before him, had cleared and tilled with much toil,—the small fields to which they had given the industry and even affection of their honest lives.

John Hilton was sitting on the doorstep of his house. As he moved his head in and out of the shadows, turning now and then to speak to his wife, who sat just within the doorway, one could see his good face, rough and somewhat unkempt, as if he were indeed a creature of the shady woods and brown earth, instead of the noisy town. It was late in the long spring evening, and he had just come from the lower field as cheerful as a boy, proud of having finished the planting of his potatoes.

"I had to do my last row mostly by feelin'," he said to his wife. "I'm proper glad I pushed through, an' went back an' ended off after supper. 'T would have taken me a good part o' to-morrow mornin', an' broke my day."

" 'T ain't no use for ye to work yourself all to pieces, John," answered the woman quickly. "I declare it does seem harder than ever that we couldn't have kep' our boy; he'd been comin' fourteen years old this fall, most a grown man, and he'd work right 'longside of ye now the whole time."

" 'T was hard to lose him; I do seem to miss little John," said the father sadly. "I expect there was reasons why 't was best. I feel able an' smart to work; my father was a girt strong man, an' a monstrous worker afore me. 'T ain't that; but I was thinkin' by myself to-day what a sight o' company the boy would ha' been. You know, small 's he was, how I could trust to leave him anywheres with the team, and how he'd beseech to go with me wherever I was goin'; always right in my tracks I used to tell 'em. Poor little John, for all he was so young he had a great deal o' judgment; he'd ha' made a likely man."

The mother sighed heavily as she sat within the shadow.

"But then there's the little girls, a sight o' help an' company," urged the father eagerly, as if it were wrong to dwell upon sorrow and loss. "Katy, she's most as good as a boy, except that she ain't very rugged. She's a real little farmer, she's helped me a sight this spring; an' you've got Susan Ellen, that makes a complete little housekeeper for ye as far as she's learnt. I don't see but we're better off than most folks, each on us having a work-mate."

"That's so, John," acknowledged Mrs. Hilton wistfully, beginning to rock steadily in her straight, splint-bottomed chair. It was always a good sign when she rocked.

"Where be the little girls so late?" asked their father. " 'T is gettin' long past eight o'clock. I don't know when we've all set up so late, but it's so kind o' summer-like an' pleasant. Why, where be they gone?"

"I've told ye; only over to Becker's folks," answered the mother. "I don't see myself what keeps 'em so late; they beseeched me after supper till I let 'em go. They're all in a dazzle with the new teacher; she asked 'em to come over. They say she's unusual smart with 'rethmetic, but she has a kind of a gorpen look to me. She's goin' to give Katy some pieces for her doll, but I told Katy she ought to be ashamed wantin' dolls' pieces, big as she's gettin' to be. I don't know's she ought, though; she ain't but nine this summer."

"Let her take her comfort," said the kind-hearted man. "Them things draws her to the teacher, an' makes them acquainted. Katy's shy with new folks, more so'n Susan Ellen, who's of the business kind. Katy's shy-feelin' and wishful."

"I don't know but she is," agreed the mother slowly. "Ain't it sing'lar how well acquainted you be with that one, an' I with Susan Ellen? 'T was always so from the first. I'm doubtful sometimes our Katy ain't one that'll be like to get married—anyways not about here. She lives right with herself, but Susan Ellen ain't nothin' when she's alone, she's always after company; all the boys is waitin' on her a'ready. I ain't afraid but she'll take her pick when the time comes. I expect

to see Susan Ellen well settled,—she feels grown up now,—
but Katy don't care one mite 'bout none o' them things. She
wants to be rovin' out o' doors. I do believe she'd stand an'
hark to a bird the whole forenoon."

"Perhaps she'll grow up to be a teacher," suggested John
Hilton. "She takes to her book more'n the other one. I
should like one on 'em to be a teacher same's my mother was.
They're good girls as anybody's got."

"So they be," said the mother, with unusual gentleness, and
the creak of her rocking-chair was heard, regular as the ticking of a clock. The night breeze stirred in the great woods,
and the sound of a brook that went falling down the hillside
grew louder and louder. Now and then one could hear the
plaintive chirp of a bird. The moon glittered with whiteness
like a winter moon, and shone upon the low-roofed house
until its small window-panes gleamed like silver, and one
could almost see the colors of a blooming bush of lilac that
grew in a sheltered angle by the kitchen door. There was an
incessant sound of frogs in the lowlands.

"Be you sound asleep, John?" asked the wife presently.

"I don't know but what I was a'most," said the tired man,
starting a little. "I should laugh if I was to fall sound asleep
right here on the step; 't is the bright night, I expect, makes
my eyes feel heavy, an' 't is so peaceful. I was up an' dressed a
little past four an' out to work. Well, well!" and he laughed
sleepily and rubbed his eyes. "Where's the little girls? I'd better step along an' meet 'em."

"I wouldn't just yet; they'll get home all right, but 't is
late for 'em certain. I don't want 'em keepin' Mis' Becker's
folks up neither. There, le''s wait a few minutes," urged Mrs.
Hilton.

"I've be'n a-thinkin' all day I'd like to give the child'n
some kind of a treat," said the father, wide awake now. "I
hurried up my work 'cause I had it so in mind. They don't
have the opportunities some do, an' I want 'em to know the
world, an' not stay right here on the farm like a couple o'
bushes."

"They're a sight better off not to be so full o' notions as
some is," protested the mother suspiciously.

"Certain," answered the farmer; "but they're good, bright child'n, an' commencin' to take a sight o' notice. I want 'em to have all we can give 'em. I want 'em to see how other folks does things."

"Why, so do I,"—here the rocking-chair stopped ominously,—"but so long 's they're contented"—

"Contented ain't all in this world; hopper-toads may have that quality an' spend all their time a-blinkin'. I don't know 's bein' contented is all there is to look for in a child. Ambition 's somethin' to me."

"Now you've got your mind on to some plot or other." (The rocking-chair began to move again.) "Why can't you talk right out?"

" 'T ain't nothin' special," answered the good man, a little ruffled; he was never prepared for his wife's mysterious powers of divination. "Well there, you do find things out the master! I only thought perhaps I'd take 'em to-morrow, an' go off somewhere if 't was a good day. I've been promisin' for a good while I'd take 'em to Topham Corners; they've never been there since they was very small."

"I believe you want a good time yourself. You ain't never got over bein' a boy." Mrs. Hilton seemed much amused. "There, go if you want to an' take 'em; they've got their summer hats an' new dresses. I don't know o' nothin' that stands in the way. I should sense it better if there was a circus or anythin' to go to. Why don't you wait an' let the girls pick 'em some strawberries or nice ros'berries, and then they could take an' sell 'em to the stores?"

John Hilton reflected deeply. "I should like to get me some good yellow-turnip seed to plant late. I ain't more 'n satisfied with what I've been gettin' o' late years o' Ira Speed. An' I'm goin' to provide me with a good hoe; mine 's gettin' wore out an' all shackly. I can't seem to fix it good."

"Them 's excuses," observed Mrs. Hilton, with friendly tolerance. "You just cover up the hoe with somethin', if you get it—I would. Ira Speed 's so jealous he 'll remember it of you this twenty year, your goin' an' buyin' a new hoe o' anybody but him."

"I've always thought 't was a free country," said John Hilton soberly. "I don't want to vex Ira neither; he favors us all he can in trade. 'T is difficult for him to spare a cent, but he 's as honest as daylight."

At this moment there was a sudden sound of young voices, and a pair of young figures came out from the shadow of the woods into the moonlighted open space. An old cock crowed loudly from his perch in the shed, as if he were a herald of royalty. The little girls were hand in hand, and a brisk young dog capered about them as they came.

"Wa'n't it dark gittin' home through the woods this time o' night?" asked the mother hastily, and not without reproach.

"I don't love to have you gone so late; mother an' me was timid about ye, and you 've kep' Mis' Becker's folks up, I expect," said their father regretfully. "I don't want to have it said that my little girls ain't got good manners."

"The teacher had a party," chirped Susan Ellen, the elder of the two children. "Goin' home from school she asked the Grover boys, an' Mary an' Sarah Speed. An' Mis' Becker was real pleasant to us: she passed round some cake, an' handed us sap sugar on one of her best plates, an' we played games an' sung some pieces too. Mis' Becker thought we did real well. I can pick out most of a tune on the cabinet organ; teacher says she 'll give me lessons."

"I want to know, dear!" exclaimed John Hilton.

"Yes, an' we played Copenhagen, an' took sides spellin', an' Katy beat everybody spellin' there was there."

Katy had not spoken; she was not so strong as her sister, and while Susan Ellen stood a step or two away addressing her eager little audience, Katy had seated herself close to her father on the doorstep. He put his arm around her shoulders, and drew her close to his side, where she stayed.

"Ain't you got nothin' to tell, daughter?" he asked, looking down fondly; and Katy gave a pleased little sigh for answer.

"Tell 'em what 's goin' to be the last day o' school, and about our trimmin' the schoolhouse," she said; and Susan Ellen gave the programme in most spirited fashion.

"'T will be a great time," said the mother, when she had finished. "I don't see why folks wants to go trapesin' off to strange places when such things is happenin' right about 'em." But the children did not observe her mysterious air. "Come, you must step yourselves right to bed!"

They all went into the dark, warm house; the bright moon shone upon it steadily all night, and the lilac flowers were shaken by no breath of wind until the early dawn.

II.

The Hiltons always waked early. So did their neighbors, the crows and song-sparrows and robins, the light-footed foxes and squirrels in the woods. When John Hilton waked, before five o'clock, an hour later than usual because he had sat up so late, he opened the house door and came out into the yard, crossing the short green turf hurriedly as if the day were too far spent for any loitering. The magnitude of the plan for taking a whole day of pleasure confronted him seriously, but the weather was fair, and his wife, whose disapproval could not have been set aside, had accepted and even smiled upon the great project. It was inevitable now, that he and the children should go to Topham Corners. Mrs. Hilton had the pleasure of waking them, and telling the news.

In a few minutes they came frisking out to talk over the great plans. The cattle were already fed, and their father was milking. The only sign of high festivity was the wagon pulled out into the yard, with both seats put in as if it were Sunday; but Mr. Hilton still wore his every-day clothes, and Susan Ellen suffered instantly from disappointment.

"Ain't we goin', father?" she asked complainingly; but he nodded and smiled at her, even though the cow, impatient to get to pasture, kept whisking her rough tail across his face. He held his head down and spoke cheerfully, in spite of this vexation.

"Yes, sister, we're goin' certain', an' goin' to have a great time too." Susan Ellen thought that he seemed like a boy at that delightful moment, and felt new sympathy and pleasure at once. "You go an' help mother about breakfast an' them things; we want to get off quick 's we can. You coax mother now, both on ye, an' see if she won't go with us."

"She said she wouldn't be hired to," responded Susan Ellen. "She says it's goin' to be hot, an' she's laid out to go over an' see how her aunt Tamsen Brooks is this afternoon."

The father gave a little sigh; then he took heart again. The

truth was that his wife made light of the contemplated pleasure, and, much as he usually valued her companionship and
approval, he was sure that they should have a better time
without her. It was impossible, however, not to feel guilty of
disloyalty at the thought. Even though she might be completely unconscious of his best ideals, he only loved her and
the ideals the more, and bent his energies to satisfying her
indefinite expectations. His wife still kept much of that youthful beauty which Susan Ellen seemed likely to reproduce.

An hour later the best wagon was ready, and the great expedition set forth. The little dog sat apart, and barked as if it
fell entirely upon him to voice the general excitement. Both
seats were in the wagon, but the empty place testified to Mrs.
Hilton's unyielding disposition. She had wondered why one
broad seat would not do, but John Hilton meekly suggested
that the wagon looked better with both. The little girls sat
on the back seat dressed alike in their Sunday hats of straw
with blue ribbons, and their little plaid shawls pinned neatly
about their small shoulders. They wore gray thread gloves,
and sat very straight. Susan Ellen was half a head the taller,
but otherwise, from behind, they looked much alike. As
for their father, he was in his Sunday best,—a plain black
coat, and a winter hat of felt, which was heavy and rusty-
looking for that warm early summer day. He had it in
mind to buy a new straw hat at Topham, so that this with the
turnip seed and the hoe made three important reasons for
going.

"Remember an' lay off your shawls when you get there, an'
carry them over your arms," said the mother, clucking like an
excited hen to her chickens. "They'll do to keep the dust off
your new dresses goin' an' comin'. An' when you eat your
dinners don't get spots on you, an' don't point at folks as you
ride by, an' stare, or they'll know you come from the country.
An' John, you call into Cousin Ad'line Marlow's an' see how
they all be, an' tell her I expect her over certain to stop awhile
before hayin'. It always eases her phthisic to git up here on
the high land, an' I've got a new notion about doin' over her
best-room carpet sence I see her that'll save rippin' one
breadth. An' don't come home all wore out; an', John, don't
you go an' buy me no kickshaws to fetch home. I ain't a child,

an' you ain't got no money to waste. I expect you'll go, like's not, an' buy you some kind of a foolish boy's hat; do look an' see if it's reasonable good straw, an' won't splinter all off round the edge. An' you mind, John"—

"Yes, yes, hold on!" cried John impatiently; then he cast a last affectionate, reassuring look at her face, flushed with the hurry and responsibility of starting them off in proper shape. "I wish you was goin' too," he said, smiling. "I do so!" Then the old horse started, and they went out at the bars, and began the careful long descent of the hill. The young dog, tethered to the lilac-bush, was frantic with piteous appeals; the little girls piped their eager good-bys again and again, and their father turned many times to look back and wave his hand. As for their mother, she stood alone and watched them out of sight.

There was one place far out on the high-road where she could catch a last glimpse of the wagon, and she waited what seemed a very long time until it appeared and then was lost to sight again behind a low hill. "They're nothin' but a pack o' child'n together," she said aloud; and then felt lonelier than she expected. She even stooped and patted the unresigned little dog as she passed him, going into the house.

The occasion was so much more important than any one had foreseen that both the little girls were speechless. It seemed at first like going to church in new clothes, or to a funeral; they hardly knew how to behave at the beginning of a whole day of pleasure. They made grave bows at such persons of their acquaintance as happened to be straying in the road. Once or twice they stopped before a farmhouse, while their father talked an inconsiderately long time with some one about the crops and the weather, and even dwelt upon town business and the doings of the selectmen, which might be talked of at any time. The explanations that he gave of their excursion seemed quite unnecessary. It was made entirely clear that he had a little business to do at Topham Corners, and thought he had better give the little girls a ride; they had been very steady at school, and he had finished planting, and could take the day as well as not. Soon, however, they all felt as if such an excursion were an every-day affair, and Susan Ellen began to ask eager questions, while Katy silently sat apart enjoying herself as she never had done before. She liked to see the strange houses, and the children who belonged to them; it was delightful to find flowers that she knew growing all along the road, no matter how far she went from home. Each small homestead looked its best and pleasantest, and shared the exquisite beauty that early summer made,—shared the luxury of greenness and floweriness that decked the rural world. There was an early peony or a late lilac in almost every dooryard.

It was seventeen miles to Topham. After a while they seemed very far from home, having left the hills far behind, and descended to a great level country with fewer tracts of woodland, and wider fields where the crops were much more forward. The houses were all painted, and the roads were smoother and wider. It had been so pleasant driving along that Katy dreaded going into the strange town when she first caught sight of it, though Susan Ellen kept asking with bold fretfulness if they were not almost there. They counted the steeples of four churches, and their father presently showed them the Topham Academy, where their grandmother once went to school, and told them that perhaps some day they would go there too. Katy's heart gave a strange leap; it was such a tremendous thing to think of, but instantly the suggestion was transformed for her into one of the certainties of life. She looked with solemn awe at the tall belfry, and the long rows of windows in the front of the academy, there where it stood high and white among the clustering trees. She hoped that they were going to drive by, but something forbade her taking the responsibility of saying so.

Soon the children found themselves among the crowded village houses. Their father turned to look at them with affectionate solicitude.

"Now sit up straight and appear pretty," he whispered to them. "We're among the best people now, an' I want folks to think well of you."

"I guess we're as good as they be," remarked Susan Ellen, looking at some innocent passers-by with dark suspicion, but Katy tried indeed to sit straight, and folded her hands prettily in her lap, and wished with all her heart to be pleasing for her father's sake. Just then an elderly woman saw the wagon and the sedate party it carried, and smiled so kindly that it seemed to Katy as if Topham Corners had welcomed and received them. She smiled back again as if this hospitable person were an old friend, and entirely forgot that the eyes of all Topham had been upon her.

"There, now we 're coming to an elegant house that I want you to see; you 'll never forget it," said John Hilton. "It 's where Judge Masterson lives, the great lawyer; the handsomest house in the county, everybody says."

"Do you know him, father?" asked Susan Ellen.

"I do," answered John Hilton proudly. "Him and my mother went to school together in their young days, and were always called the two best scholars of their time. The judge called to see her once; he stopped to our house to see her when I was a boy. An' then, some years ago—you 've heard me tell how I was on the jury, an' when he heard my name spoken he looked at me sharp, and asked if I wa'n't the son of Catharine Winn, an' spoke most beautiful of your grandmother, an' how well he remembered their young days together."

"I like to hear about that," said Katy.

"She had it pretty hard, I 'm afraid, up on the old farm. She was keepin' school in our district when father married her—that 's the main reason I backed 'em down when they wanted to tear the old schoolhouse all to pieces," confided John Hilton, turning eagerly. "They all say she lived longer up here on the hill than she could anywhere, but she never had her health. I wa'n't but a boy when she died. Father an' me lived alone afterward till the time your mother come; 't was a good while, too; I wa'n't married so young as some. 'T was lonesome, I tell you; father was plumb discouraged losin' of his wife, an' her long sickness an' all set him back, an' we 'd work all day on the land an' never say a word. I s'pose 't is bein' so lonesome early in life that makes me so pleased to have some nice girls growin' up round me now."

There was a tone in her father's voice that drew Katy's heart toward him with new affection. She dimly understood, but Susan Ellen was less interested. They had often heard this story before, but to one child it was always new and to the other old. Susan Ellen was apt to think it tiresome to hear about her grandmother, who, being dead, was hardly worth talking about.

"There's Judge Masterson's place," said their father in an every-day manner, as they turned a corner, and came into full view of the beautiful old white house standing behind its green trees and terraces and lawns. The children had never imagined anything so stately and fine, and even Susan Ellen exclaimed with pleasure. At that moment they saw an old gentleman, who carried himself with great dignity, coming slowly down the wide box-bordered path toward the gate.

"There he is now, there's the judge!" whispered John Hilton excitedly, reining his horse quickly to the green roadside. "He's goin' down-town to his office; we can wait right here an' see him. I can't expect him to remember me; it's been a good many years. Now you are goin' to see the great Judge Masterson!"

There was a quiver of expectation in their hearts. The judge stopped at his gate, hesitating a moment before he lifted the latch, and glanced up the street at the country wagon with its two prim little girls on the back seat, and the eager man who drove. They seemed to be waiting for something; the old horse was nibbling at the fresh roadside grass. The judge was used to being looked at with interest, and responded now with a smile as he came out to the sidewalk, and unexpectedly turned their way. Then he suddenly lifted his hat with grave politeness, and came directly toward them.

"Good-morning, Mr. Hilton," he said. "I am very glad to see you, sir;" and Mr. Hilton, the little girls' own father, took off his hat with equal courtesy, and bent forward to shake hands.

Susan Ellen cowered and wished herself away, but little Katy sat straighter than ever, with joy in her father's pride and pleasure shining in her pale, flower-like little face.

"These are your daughters, I am sure," said the old gentleman kindly, taking Susan Ellen's limp and reluctant hand; but when he looked at Katy, his face brightened. "How she recalls your mother!" he said with great feeling. "I am glad to see this dear child. You must come to see me with your father, my dear," he added, still looking at her. "Bring both the little girls, and let them run about the old garden; the cherries are just getting ripe," said Judge Masterson hospitably. "Perhaps you will have time to stop this afternoon as you go home?"

"I should call it a great pleasure if you would come and see us again some time. You may be driving our way, sir," said John Hilton.

"Not very often in these days," answered the old judge. "I thank you for the kind invitation. I should like to see the fine view again from your hill westward. Can I serve you in any way while you are in town? Good-by, my little friends!"

Then they parted, but not before Katy, the shy Katy, whose hand the judge still held unconsciously while he spoke, had reached forward as he said good-by, and lifted her face to kiss him. She could not have told why, except that she felt drawn to something in the serious, worn face. For the first time in her life the child had felt the charm of manners; perhaps she owned a kinship between that which made him what he was, and the spark of nobleness and purity in her own simple soul. She turned again and again to look back at him as they drove away.

"Now you have seen one of the first gentlemen in the country," said their father. "It was worth comin' twice as far"— but he did not say any more, nor turn as usual to look in the children's faces.

In the chief business street of Topham a great many country wagons like the Hiltons' were fastened to the posts, and there seemed to our holiday-makers to be a great deal of noise and excitement.

"Now I've got to do my errands, and we can let the horse rest and feed," said John Hilton. "I'll slip his headstall right off, an' put on his halter. I'm goin' to buy him a real good treat o' oats. First we'll go an' buy me my straw hat; I feel as if this one looked a little past to wear in Topham. We'll buy the things we want, an' then we'll walk all along the street, so you can look in the windows an' see the han'some things, same's your mother likes to. What was it mother told you about your shawls?"

"To take 'em off an' carry 'em over our arms," piped Susan Ellen, without comment, but in the interest of alighting and finding themselves afoot upon the pavement the shawls were forgotten. The children stood at the doorway of a shop while their father went inside, and they tried to see what the Topham shapes of bonnets were like, as their mother had advised them; but everything was exciting and confusing, and they could arrive at no decision. When Mr. Hilton came out with a hat in his hand to be seen in a better light, Katy whispered that she wished he would buy a shiny one like Judge Masterson's; but her father only smiled and shook his head, and said that they were plain folks, he and Katy. There were dry-goods for sale in the same shop, and a young clerk who was measuring linen kindly pulled off some pretty labels with gilded edges and gay pictures, and gave them to the little girls, to their exceeding joy. He may have had small sisters at home, this friendly lad, for he took pains to find two pretty blue boxes besides, and was rewarded by their beaming gratitude.

It was a famous day; they even became used to seeing so many people pass. The village was full of its morning activity, and Susan Ellen gained a new respect for her father, and an increased sense of her own consequence, because even in Topham several persons knew him and called him familiarly by name. The meeting with an old man who had once been a neighbor seemed to give Mr. Hilton the greatest pleasure. The old man called to them from a house doorway as they were passing, and they all went in. The children seated themselves wearily on the wooden step, but their father shook his old friend eagerly by the hand, and declared that he was delighted to see him so well and enjoying the fine weather.

"Oh, yes," said the old man, in a feeble, quavering voice, "I 'm astonishin' well for my age. I don't complain, John, I don't complain."

They talked long together of people whom they had known in the past, and Katy, being a little tired, was glad to rest, and sat still with her hands folded, looking about the front yard. There were some kinds of flowers that she never had seen before.

"This is the one that looks like my mother," her father said, and touched Katy's shoulder to remind her to stand up and let herself be seen. "Judge Masterson saw the resemblance; we met him at his gate this morning."

"Yes, she certain does look like your mother, John," said the old man, looking pleasantly at Katy, who found that she liked him better than at first. "She does, certain; the best of young folks is, they remind us of the old ones. 'T is nateral to cling to life, folks say, but for me, I git impatient at times. Most everybody 's gone now, an' I want to be goin'. 'T is somethin' before me, an' I want to have it over with. I want to be there 'long o' the rest o' the folks. I expect to last quite a while though; I may see ye couple o' times more, John."

John Hilton responded cheerfully, and the children were urged to pick some flowers. The old man awed them with his impatience to be gone. There was such a townful of people about him, and he seemed as lonely as if he were the last survivor of a former world. Until that moment they had felt as if everything were just beginning.

"Now I want to buy somethin' pretty for your mother," said Mr. Hilton, as they went soberly away down the street, the children keeping fast hold of his hands. "By now the old horse will have eat his dinner and had a good rest, so pretty soon we can jog along home. I 'm goin' to take you round by the academy, and the old North Meeting-house where Dr. Barstow used to preach. Can't you think o' somethin' that your mother 'd want?" he asked suddenly, confronted by a man's difficulty of choice.

"She was talkin' about wantin' a new pepper-box, one day; the top o' the old one won't stay on," suggested Susan Ellen, with delightful readiness. "Can't we have some candy, father?"

"Yes, ma'am," said John Hilton, smiling and swinging her hand to and fro as they walked. "I feel as if some would be good myself. What 's all this?" They were passing a photographer's doorway with its enticing array of portraits. "I do declare!" he exclaimed excitedly, "I 'm goin' to have our pictures taken; 't will please your mother more 'n a little."

This was, perhaps, the greatest triumph of the day, except the delightful meeting with the judge; they sat in a row, with the father in the middle, and there was no doubt as to the excellence of the likeness. The best hats had to be taken off because they cast a shadow, but they were not missed, as their owners had feared. Both Susan Ellen and Katy looked their brightest and best; their eager young faces would forever shine there; the joy of the holiday was mirrored in the little picture. They did not know why their father was so pleased with it; they would not know until age had dowered them with the riches of association and remembrance.

Just at nightfall the Hiltons reached home again, tired out and happy. Katy had climbed over into the front seat beside her father, because that was always her place when they went to church on Sundays. It was a cool evening, there was a fresh sea wind that brought a light mist with it, and the sky was fast growing cloudy. Somehow the children looked different; it seemed to their mother as if they had grown older and taller since they went away in the morning, and as if they belonged to the town now as much as to the country. The greatness of their day's experience had left her far behind; the day had been silent and lonely without them, and she had had their supper ready, and been watching anxiously, ever since five o'clock. As for the children themselves they had little to say at first—they had eaten their luncheon early on the way to Topham. Susan Ellen was childishly cross, but Katy was pathetic and wan. They could hardly wait to show the picture, and their mother was as much pleased as everybody had expected.

"There, what did make you wear your shawls?" she exclaimed a moment afterward, reproachfully. "You ain't been an' wore 'em all day long? I wanted folks to see how pretty your new dresses was, if I did make 'em. Well, well! I wish more 'n ever now I'd gone an' seen to ye!"

"An' here's the pepper-box!" said Katy, in a pleased, unconscious tone.

"That really is what I call beautiful," said Mrs. Hilton, after a long and doubtful look. "Our other one was only tin. I never did look so high as a chiny one with flowers, but I can get us another any time for every day. That's a proper hat, as good as you could have got, John. Where's your new hoe?" she asked as he came toward her from the barn, smiling with satisfaction.

"I declare to Moses if I did n't forget all about it," meekly acknowledged the leader of the great excursion. "That an' my yellow turnip seed, too; they went clean out o' my head, there was so many other things to think of. But 't ain't no sort o' matter; I can get a hoe just as well to Ira Speed's."

His wife could not help laughing. "You an' the little girls have had a great time. They was full o' wonder to me about everything, and I expect they'll talk about it for a week. I guess we was right about havin' 'em see somethin' more o' the world."

"Yes," answered John Hilton, with humility, "yes, we did have a beautiful day. I didn't expect so much. They looked as nice as anybody, and appeared so modest an' pretty. The little girls will remember it perhaps by an' by. I guess they won't never forget this day they had 'long o' father."

It was evening again, the frogs were piping in the lower meadows, and in the woods, higher up the great hill, a little owl began to hoot. The sea air, salt and heavy, was blowing in over the country at the end of the hot bright day. A lamp was lighted in the house, the happy children were talking together, and supper was waiting. The father and mother lingered for a moment outside and looked down over the shadowy fields; then they went in, without speaking. The great day was over, and they shut the door.

The Only Rose

I.

J UST where the village abruptly ended, and the green mow-
ing fields began, stood Mrs. Bickford's house, looking
down the road with all its windows, and topped by two prim
chimneys that stood up like ears. It was placed with an end to
the road, and fronted southward; you could follow a straight
path from the gate past the front door and find Mrs. Bickford
sitting by the last window of all in the kitchen, unless she
were solemnly stepping about, prolonging the stern duties of
her solitary housekeeping.

One day in early summer, when almost every one else in
Fairfield had put her house plants out of doors, there were
still three flower pots on a kitchen window sill. Mrs. Bickford
spent but little time over her rose and geranium and Jerusalem
cherry-tree, although they had gained a kind of personality
born of long association. They rarely undertook to bloom,
but had most courageously maintained life in spite of their
owner's unsympathetic but conscientious care. Later in the
season she would carry them out of doors, and leave them,
until the time of frosts, under the shade of a great apple-tree,
where they might make the best of what the summer had to
give.

The afternoon sun was pouring in, the Jerusalem cherry-
tree drooped its leaves in the heat and looked pale, when a
neighbor, Miss Pendexter, came in from the next house but
one to make a friendly call. As she passed the parlor with its
shut blinds, and the sitting-room, also shaded carefully from
the light, she wished, as she had done many times before, that
somebody beside the owner might have the pleasure of living
in and using so good and pleasant a house. Mrs. Bickford
always complained of having so much care, even while she
valued herself intelligently upon having the right to do as she
pleased with one of the best houses in Fairfield. Miss Pendexter was a cheerful, even gay little person, who always brought
a pleasant flurry of excitement, and usually had a genuine

though small piece of news to tell, or some new aspect of already received information.

Mrs. Bickford smiled as she looked up to see this sprightly neighbor coming. She had no gift at entertaining herself, and was always glad, as one might say, to be taken off her own hands.

Miss Pendexter smiled back, as if she felt herself to be equal to the occasion.

"How be you to-day?" the guest asked kindly, as she entered the kitchen. "Why, what a sight o' flowers, Mis' Bickford! What be you goin' to do with 'em all?"

Mrs. Bickford wore a grave expression as she glanced over her spectacles. "My sister's boy fetched 'em over," she answered. "You know my sister Parsons's a great hand to raise flowers, an' this boy takes after her. He said his mother thought the gardin never looked handsomer, and she picked me these to send over. They was sendin' a team to Westbury for some fertilizer to put on the land, an' he come with the men, an' stopped to eat his dinner 'long o' me. He's been growin' fast, and looks peakëd. I expect sister 'Liza thought the ride, this pleasant day, would do him good. 'Liza sent word for me to come over and pass some days next week, but it ain't so that I can."

"Why, it's a pretty time of year to go off and make a little visit," suggested the neighbor encouragingly.

"I ain't got my sitting-room chamber carpet taken up yet," sighed Mrs. Bickford. "I do feel condemned. I might have done it to-day, but 't was all at end when I saw Tommy coming. There, he's a likely boy, an' so relished his dinner; I happened to be well prepared. I don't know but he's my favorite o' that family. Only I've been sittin' here thinkin', since he went, an' I can't remember that I ever was so belated with my spring cleaning."

" 'T was owin' to the weather," explained Miss Pendexter. "None of us could be so smart as common this year, not even the lazy ones that always get one room done the first o' March, and brag of it to others' shame, and then never let on when they do the rest."

The two women laughed together cheerfully. Mrs. Bickford had put up the wide leaf of her large table between the windows and spread out the flowers. She was sorting them slowly into three heaps.

"Why, I do declare if you have n't got a rose in bloom yourself!" exclaimed Miss Pendexter abruptly, as if the bud had not been announced weeks before, and its progress regularly commented upon. "Ain't it a lovely rose? Why, Mis' Bickford!"

"Yes 'm, it 's out to-day," said Mrs. Bickford, with a somewhat plaintive air. "I 'm glad you come in so as to see it."

The bright flower was like a face. Somehow, the beauty and life of it were surprising in the plain room, like a gay little child who might suddenly appear in a doorway. Miss Pendexter forgot herself and her hostess and the tangled mass of garden flowers in looking at the red rose. She even forgot that it was incumbent upon her to carry forward the conversation. Mrs. Bickford was subject to fits of untimely silence which made her friends anxiously sweep the corners of their minds in search of something to say, but any one who looked at her now could easily see that it was not poverty of thought that made her speechless, but an overburdening sense of the inexpressible.

"Goin' to make up all your flowers into bo'quets? I think the short-stemmed kinds is often pretty in a dish," suggested Miss Pendexter compassionately.

"I thought I should make them into three bo'quets. I wish there wa'n't quite so many. Sister Eliza 's very lavish with her flowers; she 's always been a kind sister, too," said Mrs. Bickford vaguely. She was not apt to speak with so much sentiment, and as her neighbor looked at her narrowly she detected unusual signs of emotion. It suddenly became evident that the three nosegays were connected in her mind with her bereavement of three husbands, and Miss Pendexter's easily roused curiosity was quieted by the discovery that her friend was bent upon a visit to the burying-ground. It was the time of year when she was pretty sure to spend an afternoon there, and sometimes they had taken the walk in company. Miss Pendexter expected to receive the usual invitation, but there was nothing further said at the moment, and she looked again at the pretty rose.

Mrs. Bickford aimlessly handled the syringas and flowering

almond sprays, choosing them out of the fragrant heap only
to lay them down again. She glanced out of the window; then
gave Miss Pendexter a long expressive look.

"I expect you're going to carry 'em over to the burying-
ground?" inquired the guest, in a sympathetic tone.

"Yes'm," said the hostess, now well started in conversation
and in quite her every-day manner. "You see I was goin' over
to my brother's folks to-morrow in South Fairfield, to pass
the day; they said they were goin' to send over to-morrow to
leave a wagon at the blacksmith's, and they'd hitch that to
their best chaise, so I could ride back very comfortable. You
know I have to avoid bein' out in the mornin' sun?"

Miss Pendexter smiled to herself at this moment; she was
obliged to move from her chair at the window, the May sun
was so hot on her back, for Mrs. Bickford always kept the
curtains rolled high up, out of the way, for fear of fading
and dust. The kitchen was a blaze of light. As for the Sunday chaise being sent, it was well known that Mrs. Bickford's married brothers and sisters comprehended the truth
that she was a woman of property, and had neither chick
nor child.

"So I thought 't was a good opportunity to just stop an' see
if the lot was in good order,—last spring Mr. Wallis's stone
hove with the frost; an' so I could take these flowers." She
gave a sigh. "I ain't one that can bear flowers in a close
room,—they bring on a headache; but I enjoy 'em as much as
anybody to look at, only you never know what to put 'em in.
If I could be out in the mornin' sun, as some do, and keep
flowers in the house, I should have me a gardin, certain," and
she sighed again.

"A garden's a sight o' care, but I don't begrudge none o'
the care I give to mine. I have to scant on flowers so's to
make room for pole beans," said Miss Pendexter gayly. She
had only a tiny strip of land behind her house, but she always
had something to give away, and made riches out of her narrow poverty. "A few flowers gives me just as much pleasure as
more would," she added. "You get acquainted with things
when you've only got one or two roots. My sweet-williams is
just like folks."

"Mr. Bickford was partial to sweet-williams," said Mrs. Bickford. "I never knew him to take notice of no other sort of flowers. When we'd be over to Eliza's, he'd walk down her gardin, an' he'd never make no comments until he come to them, and then he'd say, 'Those is sweet-williams.' How many times I've heard him!"

"You ought to have a sprig of 'em for his bo'quet," suggested Miss Pendexter.

"Yes, I've put a sprig in," said her companion.

At this moment Miss Pendexter took a good look at the bouquets, and found that they were as nearly alike as careful hands could make them. Mrs. Bickford was evidently trying to reach absolute impartiality.

"I don't know but you think it's foolish to tie 'em up this afternoon," she said presently, as she wound the first with a stout string. "I thought I could put 'em in a bucket o' water out in the shed, where there's a draught o' air, and then I should have all my time in the morning. I shall have a good deal to do before I go. I always sweep the setting-room and front entry Wednesdays. I want to leave everything nice, goin' away for all day so. So I meant to get the flowers out o' the way this afternoon. Why, it's 'most half past four, ain't it? But I sha'n't pick the rose till mornin'; 't will be blowed out better then."

"The rose?" questioned Miss Pendexter. "Why, are you goin' to pick that, too?"

"Yes, I be. I never like to let 'em fade on the bush. There, that's just what's a-troublin' me," and she turned to give a long, imploring look at the friend who sat beside her. Miss Pendexter had moved her chair before the table in order to be out of the way of the sun. "I don't seem to know which of 'em ought to have it," said Mrs. Bickford despondently. "I do so hate to make a choice between 'em; they all had their good points, especially Mr. Bickford, and I respected 'em all. I don't know but what I think of one on 'em 'most as much as I do of the other."

"Why, 't is difficult for you, ain't it?" responded Miss Pendexter. "I don't know's I can offer advice."

"No, I s'pose not," answered her friend slowly, with a

shadow of disappointment coming over her calm face. "I feel sure you would if you could, Abby."

Both of the women felt as if they were powerless before a great emergency.

"There's one thing,—they're all in a better world now," said Miss Pendexter, in a self-conscious and constrained voice; "they can't feel such little things or take note o' slights same's we can."

"No; I suppose 't is myself that wants to be just," answered Mrs. Bickford. "I feel under obligations to my last husband when I look about and see how comfortable he left me. Poor Mr. Wallis had his great projects, an' perhaps if he'd lived longer he'd have made a record; but when he died he'd failed all up, owing to that patent corn-sheller he'd put everything into, and, as you know, I had to get along 'most any way I could for the next few years. Life was very disappointing with Mr. Wallis, but he meant well, an' used to be an amiable person to dwell with, until his temper got spoilt makin' so many hopes an' havin' 'em turn out failures. He had consider'ble of an air, an' dressed very handsome when I was first acquainted with him, Mr. Wallis did. I don't know's you ever knew Mr. Wallis in his prime?"

"He died the year I moved over here from North Denfield," said Miss Pendexter, in a tone of sympathy. "I just knew him by sight. I was to his funeral. You know you lived in what we call the Wells house then, and I felt it would n't be an intrusion, we was such near neighbors. The first time I ever was in your house was just before that, when he was sick, an' Mary 'Becca Wade an' I called to see if there was anything we could do."

"They used to say about town that Mr. Wallis went to an' fro like a mail-coach an' brought nothin' to pass," announced Mrs. Bickford without bitterness. "He ought to have had a better chance than he did in this little neighborhood. You see, he had excellent ideas, but he never'd learned the machinist's trade, and there was somethin' the matter with every model he contrived. I used to be real narrow-minded when he talked about moving 'way up to Lowell, or some o' them places; I hated to think of leaving my folks; and now I see that I never done right by him. His ideas was good. I know once he was

on a jury, and there was a man stopping to the tavern where
he was, near the court house, a man that traveled for a firm to
Lowell; and they engaged in talk, an' Mr. Wallis let out some
o' his notions an' contrivances, an' he said that man would n't
hardly stop to eat, he was so interested, an' said he 'd look for
a chance for him up to Lowell. It all sounded so well that I
kind of begun to think about goin' myself. Mr. Wallis said
we 'd close the house here, and go an' board through the winter. But he never heard a word from him, and the disappointment was one he never got over. I think of it now different
from what I did then. I often used to be kind of disapproving
to Mr. Wallis; but there, he used to be always tellin' over his
great projects. Somebody told me once that a man by the
same name of the one he met while he was to court had got
some patents for the very things Mr. Wallis used to be workin'
over; but 't was after he died, an' I don't know 's 't was in him
to ever really set things up so other folks could ha' seen their
value. His machines always used to work kind of rickety, but
folks used to come from all round to see 'em; they was curiosities if they wa'n't nothin' else, an' gave him a name."

Mrs. Bickford paused a moment, with some geranium
leaves in her hand, and seemed to suppress with difficulty a
desire to speak even more freely.

"He was a dreadful notional man," she said at last, regretfully, and as if this fact were a poor substitute for what had
just been in her mind. "I recollect one time he worked all
through the early winter over my churn, an' got it so it would
go three quarters of an hour all of itself if you wound it up;
an' if you 'll believe it, he went an' spent all that time for
nothin' when the cow was dry, an' we was with difficulty bor-
rowin' a pint o' milk a day somewheres in the neighborhood
just to get along with." Mrs. Bickford flushed with displeasure, and turned to look at her visitor. "Now what do you
think of such a man as that, Miss Pendexter?" she asked.

"Why, I don't know but 't was just as good for an invention," answered Miss Pendexter timidly; but her friend looked
doubtful, and did not appear to understand.

"Then I asked him where it was, one day that spring when
I 'd got tired to death churnin', an' the butter would n't come
in a churn I 'd had to borrow, and he 'd gone an' took ours all

to pieces to get the works to make some other useless contrivance with. He had no sort of a business turn, but he was well meanin', Mr. Wallis was, an' full o' divertin' talk; they used to call him very good company. I see now that he never had no proper chance. I've always regretted Mr. Wallis," said she who was now the widow Bickford.

"I'm sure you always speak well of him," said Miss Pendexter. "'T was a pity he hadn't got among good business men, who could push his inventions an' do all the business part."

"I was left very poor an' needy for them next few years," said Mrs. Bickford mournfully; "but he never'd give up but what he should die worth his fifty thousand dollars. I don't see now how I ever did get along them next few years without him; but there, I always managed to keep a pig, an' sister Eliza gave me my potatoes, and I made out somehow. I could dig me a few greens, you know, in spring, and then 't would come strawberry-time, and other berries a-followin' on. I was always decent to go to meetin' till within the last six months, an' then I went in bad weather, when folks wouldn't notice; but 't was a rainy summer, an' I managed to get considerable preachin' after all. My clothes looked proper enough when 't was a wet Sabbath. I often think o' them pinched days now, when I'm left so comfortable by Mr. Bickford."

"Yes'm, you've everything to be thankful for," said Miss Pendexter, who was as poor herself at that moment as her friend had ever been, and who could never dream of venturing upon the support and companionship of a pig. "Mr. Bickford was a very personable man," she hastened to say, the confidences were so intimate and interesting.

"Oh, very," replied Mrs. Bickford; "there was something about him that was very marked. Strangers would always ask who he was as he come into meetin'. His words counted; he never spoke except he had to. 'T was a relief at first after Mr. Wallis's being so fluent; but Mr. Wallis was splendid company for winter evenings,—'t would be eight o'clock before you knew it. I didn't use to listen to it all, but he had a great deal of information. Mr. Bickford was dreadful dignified; I used to be sort of meechin' with him along at the first, for fear he'd disapprove of me; but I found out 't wa'n't no need; he was always just that way, an' done everything by rule an' measure.

He had n't the mind of my other husbands, but he was a very dignified appearing man; he used 'most always to sleep in the evenin's, Mr. Bickford did."

"Them is lovely bo'quets, certain!" exclaimed Miss Pendexter. "Why, I could n't tell 'em apart; the flowers are comin' out just right, are n't they?"

Mrs. Bickford nodded assent, and then, startled by sudden recollection, she cast a quick glance at the rose in the window.

"I always seem to forget about your first husband, Mr. Fraley," Miss Pendexter suggested bravely. "I've often heard you speak of him, too, but he'd passed away long before I ever knew you."

"He was but a boy," said Mrs. Bickford. "I thought the world was done for me when he died, but I've often thought since 't was a mercy for him. He come of a very melancholy family, and all his brothers an' sisters enjoyed poor health; it might have been his lot. Folks said we was as pretty a couple as ever come into church; we was both dark, with black eyes an' a good deal o' color,—you would n't expect it to see me now. Albert was one that held up his head, and looked as if he meant to own the town, an' he had a good word for everybody. I don't know what the years might have brought."

There was a long pause. Mrs. Bickford leaned over to pick up a heavy-headed Guelder-rose that had dropped on the floor.

"I expect 't was what they call fallin' in love," she added, in a different tone; "he wa'n't nothin' but a boy, an' I wa'n't nothin' but a girl, but we was dreadful happy. He did n't favor his folks,—they all had hay-colored hair and was faded-looking, except his mother; they was alike, and looked alike, an' set everything by each other. He was just the kind of strong, hearty young man that goes right off if they get a fever. We was just settled on a little farm, an' he'd have done well if he'd had time; as it was, he left debts. He had a hasty temper, that was his great fault, but Albert had a lovely voice to sing; they said there wa'n't no such tenor voice in this part o' the State. I could hear him singin' to himself right out in the field a-ploughin' or hoein', an' he did n't know it half o' the time, no more 'n a common bird would. I don't know 's I valued his gift as I ought to, but there was nothin' ever sounded so sweet to me. I ain't one that ever had much fancy, but I knowed Albert had a pretty voice."

Mrs. Bickford's own voice trembled a little, but she held up the last bouquet and examined it critically. "I must hurry now an' put these in water," she said, in a matter of fact tone. Little Miss Pendexter was so quiet and sympathetic that her hostess felt no more embarrassed than if she had been talking only to herself.

"Yes, they do seem to droop some; 't is a little warm for them here in the sun," said Miss Pendexter; "but you 'll find they 'll all come up if you give them their fill o' water. They 'll look very handsome to-morrow; folks 'll notice them from the road. You 've arranged them very tasty, Mis' Bickford."

"They do look pretty, don't they?" Mrs. Bickford regarded the three in turn. "I want to have them all pretty. You may deem it strange, Abby."

"Why, no, Mis' Bickford," said the guest sincerely, although a little perplexed by the solemnity of the occasion. "I know how 't is with friends,—that having one don't keep you from wantin' another; 't is just like havin' somethin' to eat, and then wantin' somethin' to drink just the same. I expect all friends find their places."

But Mrs. Bickford was not interested in this figure, and still looked vague and anxious as she began to brush the broken stems and wilted leaves into her wide calico apron. "I done the best I could while they was alive," she said, "and mourned 'em when I lost 'em, an' I feel grateful to be left so comfortable now when all is over. It seems foolish, but I 'm still at a loss about that rose."

"Perhaps you 'll feel sure when you first wake up in the morning," answered Miss Pendexter solicitously. "It 's a case where I don't deem myself qualified to offer you any advice. But I 'll say one thing, seeing 's you 've been so friendly spoken and confiding with me. I never was married myself, Mis' Bickford, because it wa'n't so that I could have the one I liked."

"I suppose he ain't livin', then? Why, I wa'n't never aware you had met with a disappointment, Abby," said Mrs. Bickford instantly. None of her neighbors had ever suspected little Miss Pendexter of a romance.

"Yes 'm, he 's livin'," replied Miss Pendexter humbly. "No 'm, I never have heard that he died."

"I want to know!" exclaimed the woman of experience. "Well, I 'll tell you this, Abby: you may have regretted your lot, and felt lonesome and hardshipped, but they all have their faults, and a single woman 's got her liberty, if she ain't got other blessin's."

" 'T would n't have been my choice to live alone," said Abby, meeker than before. "I feel very thankful for my blessin's, all the same. You 've always been a kind neighbor, Mis' Bickford."

"Why can't you stop to tea?" asked the elder woman, with unusual cordiality; but Miss Pendexter remembered that her hostess often expressed a dislike for unexpected company, and promptly took her departure after she had risen to go, glancing up at the bright flower as she passed outside the window. It seemed to belong most to Albert, but she had not liked to say so. The sun was low; the green fields stretched away southward into the misty distance.

II.

Mrs. Bickford's house appeared to watch her out of sight down the road, the next morning. She had lost all spirit for her holiday. Perhaps it was the unusual excitement of the afternoon's reminiscences, or it might have been simply the bright moonlight night which had kept her broad awake until dawn, thinking of the past, and more and more concerned about the rose. By this time it had ceased to be merely a flower, and had become a definite symbol and assertion of personal choice. She found it very difficult to decide. So much of her present comfort and well-being was due to Mr. Bickford; still, it was Mr. Wallis who had been most unfortunate, and to whom she had done least justice. If she owed recognition to Mr. Bickford, she certainly owed amends to Mr. Wallis. If she gave him the rose, it would be for the sake of affectionate apology. And then there was Albert, to whom she had no thought of being either indebted or forgiving. But she could not escape from the terrible feeling of indecision.

It was a beautiful morning for a drive, but Mrs. Bickford was kept waiting some time for the chaise. Her nephew, who was to be her escort, had found much social advantage at the blacksmith's shop, so that it was after ten when she finally started with the three large flat-backed bouquets, covered with a newspaper to protect them from the sun. The petals of the almond flowers were beginning to scatter, and now and then little streams of water leaked out of the newspaper and trickled down the steep slope of her best dress to the bottom of the chaise. Even yet she had not made up her mind; she had stopped trying to deal with such an evasive thing as decision, and leaned back and rested as best she could.

"What an old fool I be!" she rebuked herself from time to time, in so loud a whisper that her companion ventured a respectful "What, ma'am?" and was astonished that she made no reply. John was a handsome young man, but Mrs. Bickford could never cease thinking of him as a boy. He had always been her favorite among the younger members of the family, and now returned this affectionate feeling, being possessed of an instinctive confidence in the sincerities of his prosaic aunt.

As they drove along, there had seemed at first to be something unsympathetic and garish about the beauty of the summer day. After the shade and shelter of the house, Mrs. Bickford suffered even more from a contracted and assailed feeling out of doors. The very trees by the roadside had a curiously fateful, trying way of standing back to watch her, as she passed in the acute agony of indecision, and she was annoyed and startled by a bird that flew too near the chaise in a moment of surprise. She was conscious of a strange reluctance to the movement of the Sunday chaise, as if she were being conveyed against her will; but the companionship of her nephew John grew every moment to be more and more a reliance. It was very comfortable to sit by his side, even though he had nothing to say; he was manly and cheerful, and she began to feel protected.

"Aunt Bickford," he suddenly announced, "I may 's well out with it! I 've got a piece o' news to tell you, if you won't let on to nobody. I expect you'll laugh, but you know I've set everything by Mary Lizzie Gifford ever since I was a boy. Well, sir!"

"Well, sir!" exclaimed aunt Bickford in her turn, quickly roused into most comfortable self-forgetfulness. "I am really pleased. She'll make you a good, smart wife, John. Ain't all the folks pleased, both sides?"

"Yes, they be," answered John soberly, with a happy, important look that became him well.

"I guess I can make out to do something for you to help along, when the right time comes," said aunt Bickford impulsively, after a moment's reflection. "I've known what it is to be starting out in life with plenty o' hope. You ain't calculatin' on gettin' married before fall,—or be ye?"

"'Long in the fall," said John regretfully. "I wish t' we could set up for ourselves right away this summer. I ain't got much ahead, but I can work well as anybody, an' now I'm out o' my time."

"She's a nice, modest, pretty girl. I thought she liked you, John," said the old aunt. "I saw her over to your mother's, last day I was there. Well, I expect you'll be happy."

"Certain," said John, turning to look at her affectionately, surprised by this outspokenness and lack of embarrassment between them. "Thank you, aunt," he said simply; "you're a real good friend to me;" and he looked away again hastily, and blushed a fine scarlet over his sun-browned face. "She's coming over to spend the day with the girls," he added. "Mother thought of it. You don't get over to see us very often."

Mrs. Bickford smiled approvingly. John's mother looked for her good opinion, no doubt, but it was very proper for John to have told his prospects himself, and in such a pretty way. There was no shilly-shallying about the boy.

"My gracious!" said John suddenly. "I'd like to have drove right by the burying-ground. I forgot we wanted to stop."

Strange as it may appear, Mrs. Bickford herself had not noticed the burying-ground, either, in her excitement and pleasure; now she felt distressed and responsible again, and showed it in her face at once. The young man leaped lightly to the ground, and reached for the flowers.

"Here, you just let me run up with 'em," he said kindly. "'T is hot in the sun to-day, an' you'll mind it risin' the hill. We'll stop as I fetch you back to-night, and you can go up comfortable an' walk the yard after sundown when it's cool, an' stay as long as you're a mind to. You seem sort of tired, aunt."

"I don't know but what I will let you carry 'em," said Mrs. Bickford slowly.

To leave the matter of the rose in the hands of fate seemed weakness and cowardice, but there was not a moment for consideration. John was a smiling fate, and his proposition was a great relief. She watched him go away with a terrible inward shaking, and sinking of pride. She had held the flowers with so firm a grasp that her hands felt weak and numb, and as she leaned back and shut her eyes she was afraid to open them again at first for fear of knowing the bouquets apart even at that distance, and giving instructions which she might regret. With a sudden impulse she called John once or twice eagerly; but her voice had a thin and piping sound, and the meditative early crickets that chirped in the fresh summer grass probably sounded louder in John's ears. The bright light on the white stones dazzled Mrs. Bickford's eyes; and then all at once she felt light-hearted, and the sky seemed to lift itself higher and wider from the earth, and she gave a sigh of relief as her messenger came back along the path. "I know who I do hope's got the right one," she said to herself. "There, what a touse I be in! I don't see what I had to go and pick the old rose for, anyway."

"I declare, they did look real handsome, aunt," said John's hearty voice as he approached the chaise. "I set 'em up just as you told me. This one fell out, an' I kept it. I don't know's you'll care. I can give it to Lizzie."

He faced her now with a bright, boyish look. There was something gay in his buttonhole, — it was the red rose.

Aunt Bickford blushed like a girl. "Your choice is easy made," she faltered mysteriously, and then burst out laughing, there in front of the burying-ground. "Come, get right in, dear," she said. "Well, well! I guess the rose was made for you; it looks very pretty in your coat, John."

She thought of Albert, and the next moment the tears came into her old eyes. John was a lover, too.

"My first husband was just such a tall, straight young man as you be," she said as they drove along. "The flower he first give me was a rose."

The Guests of Mrs. Timms

I.

MRS. PERSIS FLAGG stood in her front doorway taking leave of Miss Cynthia Pickett, who had been making a long call. They were not intimate friends. Miss Pickett always came formally to the front door and rang when she paid her visits, but, the week before, they had met at the county conference, and happened to be sent to the same house for entertainment, and so had deepened and renewed the pleasures of acquaintance.

It was an afternoon in early June; the syringa-bushes were tall and green on each side of the stone doorsteps, and were covered with their lovely white and golden flowers. Miss Pickett broke off the nearest twig, and held it before her prim face as she talked. She had a pretty childlike smile that came and went suddenly, but her face was not one that bore the marks of many pleasures. Mrs. Flagg was a tall, commanding sort of person, with an air of satisfaction and authority.

"Oh, yes, gather all you want," she said stiffly, as Miss Pickett took the syringa without having asked beforehand; but she had an amiable expression, and just now her large countenance was lighted up by pleasant anticipation.

"We can tell early what sort of a day it's goin' to be," she said eagerly. "There ain't a cloud in the sky now. I'll stop for you as I come along, or if there should be anything unforeseen to detain me, I'll send you word. I don't expect you'd want to go if it wa'n't so that I could?"

"Oh my sakes, no!" answered Miss Pickett discreetly, with a timid flush. "You feel certain that Mis' Timms won't be put out? I shouldn't feel free to go unless I went 'long o' you."

"Why, nothin' could be plainer than her words," said Mrs. Flagg in a tone of reproval. "You saw how she urged me, an' had over all that talk about how we used to see each other often when we both lived to Longport, and told how she'd been thinkin' of writin', and askin' if it wa'n't so I should be able to come over and stop three or four days as soon as settled weather come, because she could n't make no fire in her best chamber on account of the chimbley smokin' if the wind wa'n't just right. You see how she felt toward me, kissin' of me comin' and goin'? Why, she even asked me who I employed to do over my bonnet, Miss Pickett, just as interested as if she was a sister; an' she remarked she should look for us any pleasant day after we all got home, an' were settled after the conference."

Miss Pickett smiled, but did not speak, as if she expected more arguments still.

"An' she seemed just about as much gratified to meet with you again. She seemed to desire to meet you again very particular," continued Mrs. Flagg. "She really urged us to come together an' have a real good day talkin' over old times—there, don't le' 's go all over it again! I 've always heard she 'd made that old house of her aunt Bascoms' where she lives look real handsome. I once heard her best parlor carpet described as being an elegant carpet, different from any there was round here. Why, nobody could n't be more cordial, Miss Pickett; you ain't goin' to give out just at the last?"

"Oh, no!" answered the visitor hastily; "no, 'm! I want to go full as much as you do, Mis' Flagg, but you see I never was so well acquainted with Mis' Cap'n Timms, an' I always seem to dread putting myself for 'ard. She certain was very urgent, an' she said plain enough to come any day next week, an' here 't is Wednesday, though of course she would n't look for us either Monday or Tuesday. 'T will be a real pleasant occasion, an' now we 've been to the conference it don't seem near so much effort to start."

"Why, I don't think nothin' of it," said Mrs. Flagg proudly. "We shall have a grand good time, goin' together an' all, I feel sure."

Miss Pickett still played with her syringa flower, tapping her thin cheek, and twirling the stem with her fingers. She looked as if she were going to say something more, but after a moment's hesitation she turned away.

"Good-afternoon, Mis' Flagg," she said formally, looking up with a quick little smile; "I enjoyed my call; I hope I ain't kep' you too late; I don't know but what it 's 'most tea-time. Well, I shall look for you in the mornin'."

"Good-afternoon, Miss Pickett; I'm glad I was in when you came. Call again, won't you?" said Mrs. Flagg. "Yes; you may expect me in good season," and so they parted. Miss Pickett went out at the neat clicking gate in the white fence, and Mrs. Flagg a moment later looked out of her sitting-room window to see if the gate were latched, and felt the least bit disappointed to find that it was. She sometimes went out after the departure of a guest, and fastened the gate herself with a loud, rebuking sound. Both of these Woodville women lived alone, and were very precise in their way of doing things.

II.

The next morning dawned clear and bright, and Miss Pickett rose even earlier than usual. She found it most difficult to decide which of her dresses would be best to wear. Summer was still so young that the day had all the freshness of spring, but when the two friends walked away together along the shady street, with a chorus of golden robins singing high overhead in the elms, Miss Pickett decided that she had made a wise choice of her second-best black silk gown, which she had just turned again and freshened. It was neither too warm for the season nor too cool, nor did it look overdressed. She wore her large cameo pin, and this, with a long watch-chain, gave an air of proper mural decoration. She was a straight, flat little person, as if, when not in use, she kept herself, silk dress and all, between the leaves of a book. She carried a noticeable parasol with a fringe, and a small shawl, with a pretty border, neatly folded over her left arm. Mrs. Flagg always dressed in black cashmere, and looked, to hasty observers, much the same one day as another; but her companion recognized the fact that this was the best black cashmere of all, and for a moment quailed at the thought that Mrs. Flagg was paying such extreme deference to their prospective hostess. The visit turned for a moment into an unexpectedly solemn formality, and pleasure seemed to wane before Cynthia Pickett's eyes, yet with great courage she never slackened a single step. Mrs. Flagg carried a somewhat worn black leather hand-bag, which Miss Pickett regretted; it did not give the visit that casual and unpremeditated air which she felt to be more elegant.

"Sha'n't I carry your bag for you?" she asked timidly. Mrs. Flagg was the older and more important person.

"Oh, dear me, no," answered Mrs. Flagg. "My pocket's so remote, in case I should desire to sneeze or anything, that I thought 't would be convenient for carrying my handkerchief and pocket-book; an' then I just tucked in a couple o' glasses o' my crab-apple jelly for Mis' Timms. She used to be a great hand for preserves of every sort, an' I thought 't would be a kind of an attention, an' give rise to conversation. I know she used to make excellent drop-cakes when we was both residin' to Longport; folks used to say she never would give the right receipt, but if I get a real good chance, I mean to ask her. Or why can't you, if I start talkin' about receipts—why can't you say, sort of innocent, that I have always spoken frequently of her drop-cakes, an' ask for the rule? She would be very sensible to the compliment, and could pass it off if she did n't feel to indulge us. There, I do so wish you would!"

"Yes, 'm," said Miss Pickett doubtfully; "I'll try to make the opportunity. I'm very partial to drop-cakes. Was they flour or rye, Mis' Flagg?"

"They was flour, dear," replied Mrs. Flagg approvingly; "crisp an' light as any you ever see."

"I wish I had thought to carry somethin' to make it pleasant," said Miss Pickett, after they had walked a little farther; "but there, I don't know 's 't would look just right, this first visit, to offer anything to such a person as Mis' Timms. In case I ever go over to Baxter again I won't forget to make her some little present, as nice as I've got. 'T was certain very polite of her to urge me to come with you. I did feel very doubtful at first. I did n't know but she thought it behooved her, because I was in your company at the conference, and she wanted to save my feelin's, and yet expected I would decline. I never was well acquainted with her; our folks was n't well off when I first knew her; 't was before uncle Cap'n Dyer passed away an' remembered mother an' me in his will. We could n't make no han'some companies in them days, so we did n't go to none, an' kep' to ourselves; but in my grand-mother's time, mother always said, the families was very friendly. I should n't feel like goin' over to pass the day with Mis' Timms if I did n't mean to ask her to return the visit. Some don't think o' these things, but mother was very set about not bein' done for when she could n't make no return."

" 'When it rains porridge hold up your dish,' " said Mrs. Flagg; but Miss Pickett made no response beyond a feeble "Yes, 'm," which somehow got caught in her pale-green bonnet-strings.

"There, 't ain't no use to fuss too much over all them things," proclaimed Mrs. Flagg, walking along at a good pace with a fine sway of her skirts, and carrying her head high. "Folks walks right by an' forgits all about you; folks can't always be going through with just so much. You 'd had a good deal better time, you an' your ma, if you 'd been freer in your ways; now don't you s'pose you would? 'T ain't what you give folks to eat so much as 't is makin' 'em feel welcome. Now, there 's Mis' Timms; when we was to Longport she was dreadful methodical. She would n't let Cap'n Timms fetch nobody home to dinner without lettin' of her know, same 's other cap'ns' wives had to submit to. I was thinkin', when she was so cordial over to Danby, how she 'd softened with time. Years do learn folks somethin'! She did seem very pleasant an' desirous. There, I am so glad we got started; if she 'd gone an' got up a real good dinner to-day, an' then not had us come till to-morrow, 't would have been real too bad. Where anybody lives alone such a thing is very tryin'."

"Oh, so 't is!" said Miss Pickett. "There, I 'd like to tell you what I went through with year before last. They come an' asked me one Saturday night to entertain the minister, that time we was having candidates"—

"I guess we 'd better step along faster," said Mrs. Flagg suddenly. "Why, Miss Pickett, there 's the stage comin' now! It 's dreadful prompt, seems to me. Quick! there 's folks awaitin', an' I sha'n't get to Baxter in no state to visit Mis' Cap'n Timms if I have to ride all the way there backward!"

III.

The stage was not full inside. The group before the store proved to be made up of spectators, except one man, who climbed at once to a vacant seat by the driver. Inside there was only one person, after two passengers got out, and she preferred to sit with her back to the horses, so that Mrs. Flagg and Miss Pickett settled themselves comfortably in the coveted corners of the back seat. At first they took no notice of their companion, and spoke to each other in low tones, but presently something attracted the attention of all three and engaged them in conversation.

"I never was over this road before," said the stranger. "I s'pose you ladies are well acquainted all along."

"We have often traveled it in past years. We was over this part of it last week goin' and comin' from the county conference," said Mrs. Flagg in a dignified manner.

"What persuasion?" inquired the fellow-traveler, with interest.

"Orthodox," said Miss Pickett quickly, before Mrs. Flagg could speak. "It was a very interestin' occasion; this other lady an' me stayed through all the meetin's."

"I ain't Orthodox," announced the stranger, waiving any interest in personalities. "I was brought up amongst the Freewill Baptists."

"We're well acquainted with several of that denomination in our place," said Mrs. Flagg, not without an air of patronage. "They've never built 'em no church; there ain't but a scattered few."

"They prevail where I come from," said the traveler. "I'm goin' now to visit with a Freewill lady. We was to a conference together once, same's you an' your friend, but 'twas a state conference. She asked me to come some time an' make her a good visit, and I'm on my way now. I didn't seem to have nothin' to keep me to home."

"We're all goin' visitin' to-day, ain't we?" said Mrs. Flagg sociably; but no one carried on the conversation.

The day was growing very warm; there was dust in the sandy road, but the fields of grass and young growing crops looked fresh and fair. There was a light haze over the hills, and birds were thick in the air. When the stage-horses stopped to walk, you could hear the crows caw, and the bobolinks singing, in the meadows. All the farmers were busy in their fields.

"It don't seem but little ways to Baxter, does it?" said Miss Pickett, after a while. "I felt we should pass a good deal o' time on the road, but we must be pretty near half-way there a'ready."

"Why, more'n half!" exclaimed Mrs. Flagg. "Yes; there's Beckett's Corner right ahead, an' the old Beckett house. I haven't been on this part of the road for so long that I feel kind of strange. I used to visit over here when I was a girl. There's a nephew's widow owns the place now. Old Miss Susan Beckett willed it to him, an' he died; but she resides there an' carries on the farm, an unusual smart woman, everybody says. Ain't it pleasant here, right out among the farms!"

"Mis' Beckett's place, did you observe?" said the stranger, leaning forward to listen to what her companions said. "I expect that's where I'm goin'—Mis' Ezra Beckett's?"

"That's the one," said Miss Pickett and Mrs. Flagg together, and they both looked out eagerly as the coach drew up to the front door of a large old yellow house that stood close upon the green turf of the roadside.

The passenger looked pleased and eager, and made haste to leave the stage with her many bundles and bags. While she stood impatiently tapping at the brass knocker, the stagedriver landed a large trunk, and dragged it toward the door across the grass. Just then a busy-looking middle-aged woman made her appearance, with floury hands and a look as if she were prepared to be somewhat on the defensive.

"Why, how do you do, Mis' Beckett?" exclaimed the guest. "Well, here I be at last. I didn't know's you thought I was ever comin'. Why, I do declare, I believe you don't recognize me, Mis' Beckett."

"I believe I don't," said the self-possessed hostess. "Ain't you made some mistake, ma'am?"

"Why, don't you recollect we was together that time to the state conference, an' you said you should be pleased to have me come an' make you a visit some time, an' I said I would certain. There, I expect I look more natural to you now."

Mrs. Beckett appeared to be making the best possible effort, and gave a bewildered glance, first at her unexpected visitor, and then at the trunk. The stage-driver, who watched this encounter with evident delight, turned away with reluctance. "I can't wait all day to see how they settle it," he said, and mounted briskly to the box, and the stage rolled on.

"He might have waited just a minute to see," said Miss Pickett indignantly, but Mrs. Flagg's head and shoulders were already far out of the stage window—the house was on her side. "She ain't got in yet," she told Miss Pickett triumphantly. "I could see 'em quite a spell. With that trunk, too! I do declare, how inconsiderate some folks is!"

" 'T was pushin' an acquaintance most too far, wa'n't it?" agreed Miss Pickett. "There, 't will be somethin' laughable to tell Mis' Timms. I never see anything more divertin'. I shall kind of pity that woman if we have to stop an' git her as we go back this afternoon."

"Oh, don't let 's forget to watch for her," exclaimed Mrs. Flagg, beginning to brush off the dust of travel. "There, I feel an excellent appetite, don't you? And we ain't got more 'n three or four miles to go, if we have that. I wonder what Mis' Timms is likely to give us for dinner; she spoke of makin' a good many chicken-pies, an' I happened to remark how partial I was to 'em. She felt above most of the things we had provided for us over to the conference. I know she was always counted the best o' cooks when I knew her so well to Longport. Now, don't you forget, if there 's a suitable opportunity, to inquire about the drop-cakes;" and Miss Pickett, a little less doubtful than before, renewed her promise.

IV.

"My gracious, won't Mis' Timms be pleased to see us! It 's just exactly the day to have company. And ain't Baxter a sweet pretty place?" said Mrs. Flagg, as they walked up the main street. "Cynthy Pickett, now ain't you proper glad you come? I felt sort o' calm about it part o' the time yesterday, but I ain't felt so like a girl for a good while. I do believe I 'm goin' to have a splendid time."

Miss Pickett glowed with equal pleasure as she paced along. She was less expansive and enthusiastic than her companion, but now that they were fairly in Baxter, she lent herself generously to the occasion. The social distinction of going away to spend a day in company with Mrs. Flagg was by no means small. She arranged the folds of her shawl more carefully over her arm so as to show the pretty palm-leaf border, and then looked up with great approval to the row of great maples that shaded the broad sidewalk. "I wonder if we can't contrive to make time to go an' see old Miss Nancy Fell?" she ventured to ask Mrs. Flagg. "There ain't a great deal o' time before the stage goes at four o'clock; 't will pass quickly, but I should hate to have her feel hurt. If she was one we had visited often at home, I should n't care so much, but such folks feel any little slight. She was a member of our church; I think a good deal of that."

"Well, I hardly know what to say," faltered Mrs. Flagg coldly. "We might just look in a minute; I should n't want her to feel hurt."

"She was one that always did her part, too," said Miss Pickett, more boldly. "Mr. Cronin used to say that she was more generous with her little than many was with their much. If she had n't lived in a poor part of the town, and so been occupied with a different kind of people from us, 't would have made a difference. They say she 's got a comfortable little home over here, an' keeps house for a nephew. You know she was to our meeting one Sunday last winter, and 'peared dreadful glad to get back; folks seemed glad to see her, too. I don't know as you were out."

"She always wore a friendly look," said Mrs. Flagg indulgently. "There, now, there 's Mis' Timms's residence; it 's handsome, ain't it, with them big spruce-trees? I expect she may be at the window now, an' see us as we come along. Is my bonnet on straight, an' everything? The blinds looks open in the room this way; I guess she 's to home fast enough."

The friends quickened their steps, and with shining eyes and beating hearts hastened forward. The slightest mists of uncertainty were now cleared away; they gazed at the house with deepest pleasure; the visit was about to begin.

They opened the front gate and went up the short walk, noticing the pretty herring-bone pattern of the bricks, and as they stood on the high steps Cynthia Pickett wondered whether she ought not to have worn her best dress, even though there was lace at the neck and sleeves, and she usually kept it for the most formal of tea-parties and exceptional parish festivals. In her heart she commended Mrs. Flagg for that familiarity with the ways of a wider social world which had led her to wear the very best among her black cashmeres.

"She's a good while coming to the door," whispered Mrs. Flagg presently. "Either she did n't see us, or else she's slipped upstairs to make some change, an' is just goin' to let us ring again. I've done it myself sometimes. I'm glad we come right over after her urgin' us so; it seems more cordial than to keep her expectin' us. I expect she'll urge us terribly to remain with her over-night."

"Oh, I ain't prepared," began Miss Pickett, but she looked pleased. At that moment there was a slow withdrawal of the bolt inside, and a key was turned, the front door opened, and Mrs. Timms stood before them with a smile. Nobody stopped to think at that moment what kind of smile it was.

"Why, if it ain't Mis' Flagg," she exclaimed politely, "an' Miss Pickett too! I am surprised!"

The front entry behind her looked well furnished, but not exactly hospitable; the stairs with their brass rods looked so clean and bright that it did not seem as if anybody had ever gone up or come down. A cat came purring out, but Mrs. Timms pushed her back with a determined foot, and hastily closed the sitting-room door. Then Miss Pickett let Mrs. Flagg precede her, as was becoming, and they went into a darkened parlor, and found their way to some chairs, and seated themselves solemnly.

"'T is a beautiful day, ain't it?" said Mrs. Flagg, speaking first. "I don't know's I ever enjoyed the ride more. We've been having a good deal of rain since we saw you at the conference, and the country looks beautiful."

"Did you leave Woodville this morning? I thought I had n't heard you was in town," replied Mrs. Timms formally. She was seated just a little too far away to make things seem exactly pleasant. The darkness of the best room seemed to retreat somewhat, and Miss Pickett looked over by the door, where there was a pale gleam from the side-lights in the hall, to try to see the pattern of the carpet; but her effort failed.

"Yes, 'm," replied Mrs. Flagg to the question. "We left Woodville about half past eight, but it is quite a ways from where we live to where you take the stage. The stage does come slow, but you don't seem to mind it such a beautiful day."

"Why, you must have come right to see me first!" said Mrs. Timms, warming a little as the visit went on. "I hope you're going to make some stop in town. I'm sure it was very polite of you to come right an' see me; well, it's very pleasant, I declare. I wish you'd been in Baxter last Sabbath; our minister did give us an elegant sermon on faith an' works. He spoke of the conference, and gave his views on some o' the questions that came up, at Friday evenin' meetin'; but I felt tired after getting home, an' so I wasn't out. We feel very much favored to have such a man amon'st us. He's building up the parish very considerable. I understand the pew-rents come to thirty-six dollars more this quarter than they did last."

"We also feel grateful in Woodville for our pastor's efforts," said Miss Pickett; but Mrs. Timms turned her head away sharply, as if the speech had been untimely, and trembling Miss Pickett had interrupted.

"They're thinking here of raisin' Mr. Barlow's salary another year," the hostess added; "a good many of the old parishioners have died off, but every one feels to do what they can. Is there much interest among the young people in Woodville, Mis' Flagg?"

"Considerable at this time, ma'am," answered Mrs. Flagg, without enthusiasm, and she listened with unusual silence to the subsequent fluent remarks of Mrs. Timms.

The parlor seemed to be undergoing the slow processes of a winter dawn. After a while the three women could begin to see one another's faces, which aided them somewhat in carrying on a serious and impersonal conversation. There were a good many subjects to be touched upon, and Mrs. Timms said everything that she should have said, except to invite her visitors to walk upstairs and take off their bonnets. Mrs. Flagg sat her parlor-chair as if it were a throne, and carried her banner of self-possession as high as she knew how, but toward the end of the call even she began to feel hurried.

"Won't you ladies take a glass of wine an' a piece of cake after your ride?" inquired Mrs. Timms, with an air of hospitality that almost concealed the fact that neither cake nor wine was anywhere to be seen; but the ladies bowed and declined with particular elegance. Altogether it was a visit of extreme propriety on both sides, and Mrs. Timms was very pressing in her invitation that her guests should stay longer.

"Thank you, but we ought to be going," answered Mrs. Flagg, with a little show of ostentation, and looking over her shoulder to be sure that Miss Pickett had risen too. "We've got some little ways to go," she added with dignity. "We should be pleased to have you call an' see us in case you have occasion to come to Woodville," and Miss Pickett faintly seconded the invitation. It was in her heart to add, "Come any day next week," but her courage did not rise so high as to make the words audible. She looked as if she were ready to cry; her usual smile had burnt itself out into gray ashes; there was a white, appealing look about her mouth. As they emerged from the dim parlor and stood at the open front door, the bright June day, the golden-green trees, almost blinded their eyes. Mrs. Timms was more smiling and cordial than ever.

"There, I ought to have thought to offer you fans; I am afraid you was warm after walking," she exclaimed, as if to leave no stone of courtesy unturned. "I have so enjoyed meeting you again, I wish it was so you could stop longer. Why, Mis' Flagg, we haven't said one word about old times when we lived to Longport. I've had news from there, too, since I saw you; my brother's daughter-in-law was here to pass the Sabbath after I returned."

Mrs. Flagg did not turn back to ask any questions as she stepped stiffly away down the brick walk. Miss Pickett followed her, raising the fringed parasol; they both made ceremonious little bows as they shut the high white gate behind them. "Good-by," said Mrs. Timms finally, as she stood in the door with her set smile; and as they departed she came out and began to fasten up a rose-bush that climbed a narrow white ladder by the steps.

"Oh, my goodness alive!" exclaimed Mrs. Flagg, after they had gone some distance in aggrieved silence, "if I haven't gone and forgotten my bag! I ain't goin' back, whatever happens. I expect she'll trip over it in that dark room and break her neck!"

"I brought it; I noticed you'd forgotten it," said Miss Pickett timidly, as if she hated to deprive her companion of even that slight consolation.

"There, I'll tell you what we'd better do," said Mrs. Flagg gallantly; "we'll go right over an' see poor old Miss Nancy Fell; 't will please her about to death. We can say we felt like goin' somewhere to-day, an' 't was a good many years since either one of us had seen Baxter, so we come just for the ride, an' to make a few calls. She'll like to hear all about the conference; Miss Fell was always one that took a real interest in religious matters."

Miss Pickett brightened, and they quickened their step. It was nearly twelve o'clock, they had breakfasted early, and now felt as if they had eaten nothing since they were grown up. An awful feeling of tiredness and uncertainty settled down upon their once buoyant spirits.

"I can forgive a person," said Mrs. Flagg, once, as if she were speaking to herself; "I can forgive a person, but when I'm done with 'em, I'm done."

v.

"I do declare, 't was like a scene in Scriptur' to see that poor good-hearted Nancy Fell run down her walk to open the gate for us!" said Mrs. Persis Flagg later that afternoon, when she and Miss Pickett were going home in the stage. Miss Pickett nodded her head approvingly.

"I had a good sight better time with her than I should have had at the other place," she said with fearless honesty. "If I'd been Mis' Cap'n Timms, I'd made some apology or just passed us the compliment. If it wa'n't convenient, why couldn't she just tell us so after all her urgin' and sayin' how she should expect us?"

"I thought then she'd altered from what she used to be," said Mrs. Flagg. "She seemed real sincere an' open away from home. If she wa'n't prepared to-day, 't was easy enough to say so; we was reasonable folks, an' should have gone away with none but friendly feelin's. We did have a grand good time with Nancy. She was as happy to see us as if we'd been queens."

"'Twas a real nice little dinner," said Miss Pickett gratefully. "I thought I was goin' to faint away just before we got to the house, and I didn't know how I should hold out if she undertook to do anything extra, and keep us a-waitin'; but there, she just made us welcome, simple-hearted, to what she had. I never tasted such dandelion greens; an' that nice little piece o' pork and new biscuit, why, they was just splendid. She must have an excellent good cellar, if 't is such a small house. Her potatoes was truly remarkable for this time o' year. I myself don't deem it necessary to cook potatoes when I'm goin' to have dandelion greens. Now, didn't it put you in mind of that verse in the Bible that says, 'Better is a dinner of herbs where love is'? An' how desirous she'd been to see somebody that could tell her some particulars about the conference!"

"She'll enjoy tellin' folks about our comin' over to see her. Yes, I'm glad we went; 't will be of advantage every way, an' our bein' of the same church an' all, to Woodville. If Mis' Timms hears of our bein' there, she'll see we had reason, an' knew of a place to go. Well, I needn't have brought this old bag!"

Miss Pickett gave her companion a quick resentful glance, which was followed by one of triumph directed at the dust that was collecting on the shoulders of the best black cashmere; then she looked at the bag on the front seat, and suddenly felt illuminated with the suspicion that Mrs. Flagg had secretly made preparations to pass the night in Baxter. The bag looked plump, as if it held much more than the pocketbook and the jelly.

Mrs. Flagg looked up with unusual humility. "I did think about that jelly," she said, as if Miss Pickett had openly reproached her. "I was afraid it might look as if I was tryin' to pay Nancy for her kindness."

"Well, I don't know," said Cynthia; "I guess she'd been pleased. She'd thought you just brought her over a little present: but I do' know as 't would been any good to her after all; she'd thought so much of it, comin' from you, that she'd kep' it till 't was all candied." But Mrs. Flagg didn't look exactly pleased by this unexpected compliment, and her fellow-traveler colored with confusion and a sudden feeling that she had shown undue forwardness.

Presently they remembered the Beckett house, to their great relief, and, as they approached, Mrs. Flagg reached over and moved her hand-bag from the front seat to make room for another passenger. But nobody came out to stop the stage, and they saw the unexpected guest sitting by one of the front windows comfortably swaying a palm-leaf fan, and rocking to and fro in calm content. They shrank back into their corners, and tried not to be seen. Mrs. Flagg's face grew very red.

"She got in, didn't she?" said Miss Pickett, snipping her words angrily, as if her lips were scissors. Then she heard a call, and bent forward to see Mrs. Beckett herself appear in the front doorway, very smiling and eager to stop the stage.

The driver was only too ready to stop his horses. "Got a passenger for me to carry back, ain't ye?" said he facetiously. "Them's the kind I like; carry both ways, make somethin' on a double trip," and he gave Mrs. Flagg and Miss Pickett a friendly wink as he stepped down over the wheel. Then he hurried toward the house, evidently in a hurry to put the baggage on; but the expected passenger still sat rocking and fanning at the window.

"No, sir; I ain't got any passengers," exclaimed Mrs. Beckett, advancing a step or two to meet him, and speaking very loud in her pleasant excitement. "This lady that come this morning wants her large trunk with her summer things that she left to the depot in Woodville. She's very desirous to git into it, so don't you go an' forgit; ain't you got a book or somethin', Mr. Ma'sh? Don't you forgit to make a note of it; here's her check, an' we've kep' the number in case you should mislay it or anything. There's things in the trunk she needs; you know how you overlooked stoppin' to the milliner's for my bunnit last week."

"Other folks disremembers things as well's me," grumbled Mr. Marsh. He turned to give the passengers another wink more familiar than the first, but they wore an offended air, and were looking the other way. The horses had backed a few steps, and the guest at the front window had ceased the steady motion of her fan to make them a handsome bow, and been puzzled at the lofty manner of their acknowledgment.

"Go 'long with your foolish jokes, John Ma'sh!" Mrs. Beckett said cheerfully, as she turned away. She was a comfortable, hearty person, whose appearance adjusted the beauties of hospitality. The driver climbed to his seat, chuckling, and drove away with the dust flying after the wheels.

"Now, she's a friendly sort of a woman, that Mis' Beckett," said Mrs. Flagg unexpectedly, after a few moments of silence, when she and her friend had been unable to look at each other. "I really ought to call over an' see her some o' these days, knowing her husband's folks as well as I used to, an' visitin' of 'em when I was a girl." But Miss Pickett made no answer.

"I expect it was all for the best, that woman's comin'," suggested Mrs. Flagg again hopefully. "She looked like a willing person who would take right hold. I guess Mis' Beckett knows what she's about, and must have had her reasons. Perhaps she thought she'd chance it for a couple o' weeks anyway, after the lady'd come so fur, an' bein' one o' her own denomination. Hayin'-time'll be here before we know it. I think myself, gen'rally speakin', 't is just as well to let anybody know you're comin'."

"Them seemed to be Mis' Cap'n Timms's views," said Miss Pickett in a low tone; but the stage rattled a good deal, and Mrs. Flagg looked up inquiringly, as if she had not heard.

Aunt Cynthy Dallett

I.

"No," said Mrs. Hand, speaking wistfully,—"no, we never were in the habit of keeping Christmas at our house. Mother died when we were all young; she would have been the one to keep up with all new ideas, but father and grandmother were old-fashioned folks, and—well, you know how 't was then, Miss Pendexter: nobody took much notice of the day except to wish you a Merry Christmas."

"They did n't do much to make it merry, certain," answered Miss Pendexter. "Sometimes nowadays I hear folks complainin' o' bein' overtaxed with all the Christmas work they have to do."

"Well, others think that it makes a lovely chance for all that really enjoys givin'; you get an opportunity to speak your kind feelin' right out," answered Mrs. Hand, with a bright smile. "But there! I shall always keep New Year's Day, too; it won't do no hurt to have an extra day kept an' made pleasant. And there's many of the real old folks have got pretty things to remember about New Year's Day."

"Aunt Cynthy Dallett's just one of 'em," said Miss Pendexter. "She's always very reproachful if I don't get up to see her. Last year I missed it, on account of a light fall o' snow that seemed to make the walkin' too bad, an' she sent a neighbor's boy 'way down from the mount'in to see if I was sick. Her lameness confines her to the house altogether now, an' I have her on my mind a good deal. How anybody does get thinkin' of those that lives alone, as they get older! I waked up only last night with a start, thinkin' if Aunt Cynthy's house should get afire or anything, what she would do, 'way up there all alone. I was half dreamin', I s'pose, but I could n't seem to settle down until I got up an' went upstairs to the north garret window to see if I could see any light; but the mountains was all dark an' safe, same's usual. I remember noticin' last time I was there that her chimney needed pointin', and I spoke to her about it,—the bricks looked poor in some places."

"Can you see the house from your north gable window?" asked Mrs. Hand, a little absently.

"Yes 'm; it 's a great comfort that I can," answered her companion. "I have often wished we were near enough to have her make me some sort o' signal in case she needed help. I used to plead with her to come down and spend the winters with me, but she told me one day I might as well try to fetch down one o' the old hemlocks, an' I believe 't was true."

"Your aunt Dallett is a very self-contained person," observed Mrs. Hand.

"Oh, very!" exclaimed the elderly niece, with a pleased look. "Aunt Cynthy laughs, an' says she expects the time will come when age 'll compel her to have me move up an' take care of her; and last time I was there she looked up real funny, an' says, 'I do' know, Abby; I 'm most afeard sometimes that I feel myself beginnin' to look for 'ard to it!' 'T was a good deal, comin' from Aunt Cynthy, an' I so esteemed it."

"She ought to have you there now," said Mrs. Hand. "You 'd both make a savin' by doin' it; but I don't expect she needs to save as much as some. There! I know just how you both feel. I like to have my own home an' do everything just my way too." And the friends laughed, and looked at each other affectionately.

"There was old Mr. Nathan Dunn,—left no debts an' no money when he died," said Mrs. Hand. "'T was over to his niece's last summer. He had a little money in his wallet, an' when the bill for funeral expenses come in there was just exactly enough; some item or other made it come to so many dollars an' eighty-four cents, and, lo an' behold! there was eighty-four cents in a little separate pocket beside the neat fold o' bills, as if the old gentleman had known beforehand. His niece could n't help laughin', to save her; she said the old gentleman died as methodical as he lived. She did n't expect he had any money, an' was prepared to pay for everything herself; she 's very well off."

"'T was funny, certain," said Miss Pendexter. "I expect he felt comfortable, knowin' he had that money by him. 'T is a comfort, when all's said and done, 'specially to folks that's gettin' old."

A sad look shadowed her face for an instant, and then she smiled and rose to take leave, looking expectantly at her hostess to see if there were anything more to be said.

"I hope to come out square myself," she said, by way of farewell pleasantry; "but there are times when I feel doubtful."

Mrs. Hand was evidently considering something, and waited a moment or two before she spoke. "Suppose we both walk up to see your aunt Dallett, New Year's Day, if it ain't too windy and the snow keeps off?" she proposed. "I could n't rise the hill if 't was a windy day. We could take a hearty breakfast an' start in good season; I 'd rather walk than ride, the road's so rough this time o' year."

"Oh, what a person you are to think o' things! I did so dread goin' 'way up there all alone," said Abby Pendexter. "I 'm no hand to go off alone, an' I had it before me, so I really got to dread it. I do so enjoy it after I get there, seein' Aunt Cynthy, an' she 's always so much better than I expect to find her."

"Well, we 'll start early," said Mrs. Hand cheerfully; and so they parted. As Miss Pendexter went down the foot-path to the gate, she sent grateful thoughts back to the little sitting-room she had just left.

"How doors are opened!" she exclaimed to herself. "Here I 've been so poor an' distressed at beginnin' the year with nothin', as it were, that I could n't think o' even goin' to make poor old Aunt Cynthy a friendly call. I 'll manage to make some kind of a little pleasure too, an' somethin' for dear Mis' Hand. 'Use what you 've got,' mother always used to say when every sort of an emergency come up, an' I may only have wishes to give, but I 'll make 'em good ones!"

II.

The first day of the year was clear and bright, as if it were a New Year's pattern of what winter can be at its very best. The two friends were prepared for changes of weather, and met each other well wrapped in their winter cloaks and shawls, with sufficient brown barége veils tied securely over their bonnets. They ignored for some time the plain truth that each carried something under her arm; the shawls were rounded out suspiciously, especially Miss Pendexter's, but each respected the other's air of secrecy. The narrow road was frozen in deep ruts, but a smooth-trodden little foot-path that ran along its edge was very inviting to the wayfarers. Mrs. Hand walked first and Miss Pendexter followed, and they were talking busily nearly all the way, so that they had to stop for breath now and then at the tops of the little hills. It was not a hard walk; there were a good many almost level stretches through the woods, in spite of the fact that they should be a very great deal higher when they reached Mrs. Dallett's door.

"I do declare, what a nice day 't is, an' such pretty footin'!" said Mrs. Hand, with satisfaction. "Seems to me as if my feet went o' themselves; gener'lly I have to toil so when I walk that I can't enjoy nothin' when I get to a place."

"It 's partly this beautiful bracin' air," said Abby Pendexter. "Sometimes such nice air comes just before a fall of snow. Don't it seem to make anybody feel young again and to take all your troubles away?"

Mrs. Hand was a comfortable, well-to-do soul, who seldom worried about anything, but something in her companion's tone touched her heart, and she glanced sidewise and saw a pained look in Abby Pendexter's thin face. It was a moment for confidence.

"Why, you speak as if something distressed your mind, Abby," said the elder woman kindly.

"I ain't one that has myself on my mind as a usual thing, but it does seem now as if I was goin' to have it very hard," said Abby. "Well, I've been anxious before."

"Is it anything wrong about your property?" Mrs. Hand ventured to ask.

"Only that I ain't got any," answered Abby, trying to speak gayly. " 'T was all I could do to pay my last quarter's rent, twelve dollars. I sold my hens, all but this one that had run away at the time, an' now I'm carryin' her up to Aunt Cynthy, roasted just as nice as I know how."

"I thought you was carrying somethin'," said Mrs. Hand, in her usual tone. "For me, I've got a couple o' my mince pies. I thought the old lady might like 'em; one we can eat for our dinner, and one she shall have to keep. But were n't you unwise to sacrifice your poultry, Abby? You always need eggs, and hens don't cost much to keep."

"Why, yes, I shall miss 'em," said Abby; "but, you see, I had to do every way to get my rent-money. Now the shop's shut down I have n't got any way of earnin' anything, and I spent what little I 've saved through the summer."

"Your aunt Cynthy ought to know it an' ought to help you," said Mrs. Hand. "You 're a real foolish person, I must say. I expect you do for her when she ought to do for you."

"She 's old, an' she 's all the near relation I 've got," said the little woman. "I 've always felt the time would come when she 'd need me, but it 's been her great pleasure to live alone an' feel free. I shall get along somehow, but I shall have it hard. Somebody may want help for a spell this winter, but I 'm afraid I shall have to give up my house. 'T ain't as if I owned it. I don't know just what to do, but there 'll be a way."

Mrs. Hand shifted her two pies to the other arm, and stepped across to the other side of the road where the ground looked a little smoother.

"No, I would n't worry if I was you, Abby," she said. "There, I suppose if 't was me I should worry a good deal more! I expect I should lay awake nights." But Abby answered nothing, and they came to a steep place in the road and found another subject for conversation at the top.

"Your aunt don't know we 're coming?" asked the chief guest of the occasion.

"Oh, no, I never send her word," said Miss Pendexter. "She 'd be so desirous to get everything ready, just as she used to."

"She never seemed to make any trouble o' havin' company; she always appeared so easy and pleasant, and let you set with her while she made her preparations," said Mrs. Hand, with great approval. "Some has such a dreadful way of making you feel inopportune, and you can't always send word you 're comin'. I did have a visit once that 's always been a lesson to me; 't was years ago; I don't know 's I ever told you?"

"I don't believe you ever did," responded the listener to this somewhat indefinite prelude.

"Well, 't was one hot summer afternoon. I set forth an' took a great long walk 'way over to Mis' Eben Fulham's, on the crossroad between the cranberry ma'sh and Staples's Corner. The doctor was drivin' that way, an' he give me a lift that shortened it some at the last; but I never should have started, if I'd known 't was so far. I had been promisin' all summer to go, and every time I saw Mis' Fulham, Sundays, she'd say somethin' about it. We wa'n't very well acquainted, but always friendly. She moved here from Bedford Hill."

"Oh, yes; I used to know her," said Abby, with interest.

"Well, now, she did give me a beautiful welcome when I got there," continued Mrs. Hand. " 'T was about four o'clock in the afternoon, an' I told her I'd come to accept her invitation if 't was convenient, an' the doctor had been called several miles beyond and expected to be detained, but he was goin' to pick me up as he returned about seven; 't was very kind of him. She took me right in, and she did appear so pleased, an' I must go right into the best room where 't was cool, and then she said she'd have tea early, and I should have to excuse her a short time. I asked her not to make any difference, and if I could n't assist her; but she said no, I must just take her as I found her; and she give me a large fan, and off she went.

"There. I was glad to be still and rest where 't was cool, an' I set there in the rockin'-chair an' enjoyed it for a while, an' I heard her clacking at the oven door out beyond, an' gittin' out some dishes. She was a brisk-actin' little woman, an' I thought I'd caution her when she come back not to make up a great fire, only for a cup o' tea, perhaps. I started to go right out in the kitchen, an' then somethin' told me I'd better not, we never'd been so free together as that; I did n't know how she'd take it, an' there I set an' set. 'T was sort of a greenish light in the best room, an' it begun to feel a little damp to me,—the s'rubs outside grew close up to the windows. Oh, it did seem dreadful long! I could hear her busy with the dishes an' beatin' eggs an' stirrin', an' I knew she was puttin' herself out to get up a great supper, and I kind o' fidgeted about a little an' even stepped to the door, but I thought she'd expect me to remain where I was. I saw everything in that room forty times over, an' I did divert myself killin' off a brood o' moths that was in a worsted-work mat on the table. It all fell to pieces. I never saw such a sight o' moths to once. But occupation failed after that, an' I begun to feel sort o' tired an' numb. There was one o' them late crickets got into the room an' begun to chirp, an' it sounded kind o' fallish. I couldn't help sayin' to myself that Mis' Fulham had forgot all about my bein' there. I thought of all the beauties of hospitality that ever I see!"—

"Didn't she ever come back at all, not whilst things was in the oven, nor nothin'?" inquired Miss Pendexter, with awe.

"I never see her again till she come beamin' to the parlor door an' invited me to walk out to tea," said Mrs. Hand. "'T was 'most a quarter past six by the clock; I thought 't was seven. I'd thought o' everything, an' I'd counted, an' I'd trotted my foot, an' I'd looked more 'n twenty times to see if there was any more moth-millers."

"I s'pose you did have a very nice tea?" suggested Abby, with interest.

"Oh, a beautiful tea! She couldn't have done more if I'd been the Queen," said Mrs. Hand. "I don't know how she could ever have done it all in the time, I'm sure. The table was loaded down; there was cup-custards and custard pie, an' cream pie, an' two kinds o' hot biscuits, an' black tea as well as green, an' elegant cake,—one kind she'd just made new, and called it quick cake; I've often made it since—an' she'd opened her best preserves, two kinds. We set down together, an' I'm sure I appreciated what she'd done; but 't wa'n't no time for real conversation whilst we was to the table, and before we got quite through the doctor come hurryin' along, an' I had to leave. He asked us if we'd had a good talk, as we come out, an' I couldn't help laughing to myself; but she said quite hearty that she'd had a nice visit from me. She appeared well satisfied, Mis' Fulham did; but for me, I was disappointed; an' early that fall she died."

Abby Pendexter was laughing like a girl; the speaker's tone had grown more and more complaining. "I do call that a funny experience," she said. " 'Better a dinner o' herbs.' I guess that text must ha' risen to your mind in connection. You must tell that to Aunt Cynthy, if conversation seems to fail."

And she laughed again, but Mrs. Hand still looked solemn and reproachful.

"Here we are; there's Aunt Cynthy's lane right ahead, there by the great yellow birch," said Abby. "I must say, you've made the way seem very short, Mis' Hand."

III.

Old Aunt Cynthia Dallett sat in her high-backed rocking-chair by the little north window, which was her favorite dwelling-place.

"New Year's Day again," she said, aloud,—"New Year's Day again!" And she folded her old bent hands, and looked out at the great woodland view and the hills without really seeing them, she was lost in so deep a reverie. "I'm gittin' to be very old," she added, after a little while.

It was perfectly still in the small gray house. Outside in the apple-trees there were some blue-jays flitting about and calling noisily, like schoolboys fighting at their games. The kitchen was full of pale winter sunshine. It was more like late October than the first of January, and the plain little room seemed to smile back into the sun's face. The outer door was standing open into the green dooryard, and a fat small dog lay asleep on the step. A capacious cupboard stood behind Mrs. Dallett's chair and kept the wind away from her corner. Its doors and drawers were painted a clean lead-color, and there were places round the knobs and buttons where the touch of hands had worn deep into the wood. Every braided rug was straight on the floor. The square clock on its shelf between the front windows looked as if it had just had its face washed and been wound up for a whole year to come. If Mrs. Dallett turned her head she could look into the bedroom, where her plump feather bed was covered with its dark blue homespun winter quilt. It was all very peaceful and comfortable, but it was very lonely. By her side, on a light-stand, lay the religious newspaper of her denomination, and a pair of spectacles whose jointed silver bows looked like a funny two-legged beetle cast helplessly upon its back.

"New Year's Day again," said old Cynthia Dallett. Time had left nobody in her house to wish her a Happy New Year,—she was the last one left in the old nest. "I'm gittin' to be very old," she said for the second time; it seemed to be all there was to say.

She was keeping a careful eye on her friendly clock, but it was hardly past the middle of the morning, and there was no excuse for moving; it was the long hour between the end of her slow morning work and the appointed time for beginning to get dinner. She was so stiff and lame that this hour's rest was usually most welcome, but to-day she sat as if it were Sunday, and did not take up her old shallow splint basket of braiding-rags from the side of her footstool.

"I do hope Abby Pendexter'll make out to git up to see me this afternoon as usual," she continued. "I know 't ain't so easy for her to get up the hill as it used to be, but I do seem to want to see some o' my own folks. I wish 't I'd thought to send her word I expected her when Jabez Hooper went back after he came up here with the flour. I'd like to have had her come prepared to stop two or three days."

A little chickadee perched on the window-sill outside and bobbed his head sideways to look in, and then pecked impatiently at the glass. The old woman laughed at him with childish pleasure and felt companioned; it was pleasant at that moment to see the life in even a bird's bright eye.

"Sign of a stranger," she said, as he whisked his wings and flew away in a hurry. "I must throw out some crumbs for 'em; it's getting to be hard pickin' for the stayin'-birds." She looked past the trees of her little orchard now with seeing eyes, and followed the long forest slopes that led downward to the lowland country. She could see the two white steeples of Fairfield Village, and the map of fields and pastures along the valley beyond, and the great hills across the valley to the westward. The scattered houses looked like toys that had been scattered by children. She knew their lights by night, and watched the smoke of their chimneys by day. Far to the northward were higher mountains, and these were already white with snow. Winter was already in sight, but to-day the wind was in the south, and the snow seemed only part of a great picture.

"I do hope the cold'll keep off a while longer," thought Mrs. Dallett. "I don't know how I'm going to get along after the deep snow comes."

The little dog suddenly waked, as if he had had a bad dream, and after giving a few anxious whines he began to bark outrageously. His mistress tried, as usual, to appeal to his better feelings.

"'Tain't nobody, Tiger," she said. "Can't you have some patience? Maybe it's some foolish boys that's rangin' about with their guns." But Tiger kept on, and even took the trouble to waddle in on his short legs, barking all the way. He looked warningly at her, and then turned and ran out again. Then she saw him go hurrying down to the bars, as if it were an occasion of unusual interest.

"I guess somebody is comin'; he don't act as if 'twere a vagrant kind o' noise; must really be somebody in our lane." And Mrs. Dallett smoothed her apron and gave an anxious housekeeper's glance round the kitchen. None of her state visitors, the minister or the deacons, ever came in the morning. Country people are usually too busy to go visiting in the forenoons.

Presently two figures appeared where the road came out of the woods,—the two women already known to the story, but very surprising to Mrs. Dallett; the short, thin one was easily recognized as Abby Pendexter, and the taller, stout one was soon discovered to be Mrs. Hand. Their old friend's heart was in a glow. As the guests approached they could see her pale face with its thin white hair framed under the close black silk handkerchief.

"There she is at her window smilin' away!" exclaimed Mrs. Hand; but by the time they reached the doorstep she stood waiting to meet them.

"Why, you two dear creatur's!" she said, with a beaming smile. "I don't know when I've ever been so glad to see folks comin'. I had a kind of left-all-alone feelin' this mornin', an' I didn't even make bold to be certain o' you, Abby, though it looked so pleasant. Come right in an' set down. You're all out o' breath, ain't you, Mis' Hand?"

Mrs. Dallett led the way with eager hospitality. She was the tiniest little bent old creature, her handkerchiefed head was quick and alert, and her eyes were bright with excitement and feeling, but the rest of her was much the worse for age; she could hardly move, poor soul, as if she had only a make-believe framework of a body under a shoulder-shawl and thick petticoats. She got back to her chair again, and the guests took off their bonnets in the bedroom, and returned discreet and sedate in their black woolen dresses. The lonely kitchen was blest with society at last, to its mistress's heart's content. They talked as fast as possible about the weather, and how warm it had been walking up the mountain, and how cold it had been a year ago, that day when Abby Pendexter had been kept at home by a snowstorm and missed her visit. "And I ain't seen you now, aunt, since the twenty-eighth of September, but I've thought of you a great deal, and looked forward to comin' more 'n usual," she ended, with an affectionate glance at the pleased old face by the window.

"I've been wantin' to see you, dear, and wonderin' how you was gettin' on," said Aunt Cynthy kindly. "And I take it as a great attention to have you come to-day, Mis' Hand," she added, turning again towards the more distinguished guest. "We have to put one thing against another. I should hate dreadfully to live anywhere except on a high hill farm, 'cordin' as I was born an' raised. But there ain't the chance to neighbor that townfolks has, an' I do seem to have more lonely hours than I used to when I was younger. I don't know but I shall soon be gittin' too old to live alone." And she turned to her niece with an expectant, lovely look, and Abby smiled back.

"I often wish I could run in an' see you every day, aunt," she answered. "I have been sayin' so to Mrs. Hand."

"There, how anybody does relish company when they don't have but a little of it!" exclaimed Aunt Cynthia. "I am all alone to-day; there is going to be a shootin'-match some-where the other side o' the mountain, an' Johnny Foss, that does my chores, begged off to go when he brought the milk unusual early this mornin'. Gener'lly he's about here all the fore part of the day; but he don't go off with the boys very often, and I like to have him have a little sport; 't was New Year's Day, anyway; he's a good, stiddy boy for my wants."

"Why, I wish you Happy New Year, aunt!" said Abby, springing up with unusual spirit. "Why, that's just what we come to say, and we like to have forgot all about it!" She kissed her aunt, and stood a minute holding her hand with a soft, affectionate touch. Mrs. Hand rose and kissed Mrs. Dallett too, and it was a moment of ceremony and deep feeling.

"I always like to keep the day," said the old hostess, as they seated themselves and drew their splint-bottomed chairs a little nearer together than before. "You see, I was brought up to it, and father made a good deal of it; he said he liked to make it pleasant and give the year a fair start. I can see him now, how he used to be standing there by the fireplace when we came out o' the two bedrooms early in the morning, an' he always made out, poor's he was, to give us some little present, and he'd heap 'em up on the corner o' the mantelpiece, an' we'd stand front of him in a row, and mother be bustling about gettin' breakfast. One year he give me a beautiful copy o' the 'Life o' General Lafayette,' in a green cover,—I've got it now, but we child'n 'bout read it to pieces,—an' one year a nice piece o' blue ribbon, an' Abby— that was your mother, Abby—had a pink one. Father was real kind to his child'n. I thought o' them early days when I first waked up this mornin', and I couldn't help lookin' up then to the corner o' the shelf just as I used to look."

"There's nothin' so beautiful as to have a bright childhood to look back to," said Mrs. Hand. "Sometimes I think child'n has too hard a time now,—all the responsibility is put on to 'em, since they take the lead o' what to do an' what they want, and get to be so toppin' an' knowin'. 'T was happier in the old days, when the fathers an' mothers done the rulin'."

"They say things have changed," said Aunt Cynthy; "but staying right here, I don't know much of any world but my own world."

Abby Pendexter did not join in this conversation, but sat in her straight-backed chair with folded hands and the air of a good child. The little old dog had followed her in, and now lay sound asleep again at her feet. The front breadth of her black dress looked rusty and old in the sunshine that slanted across it, and the aunt's sharp eyes saw this and saw the careful darns. Abby was as neat as wax, but she looked as if the frost had struck her. "I declare, she's gittin' along in years," thought Aunt Cynthia compassionately. "She begins to look sort o' set and dried up, Abby does. She ought n't to live all alone; she's one that needs company."

At this moment Abby looked up with new interest. "Now, aunt," she said, in her pleasant voice, "I don't want you to forget to tell me if there ain't some sewin' or mendin' I can do whilst I'm here. I know your hands trouble you some, an' I may's well tell you we're bent on stayin' all day an' makin' a good visit, Mis' Hand an' me."

"Thank ye kindly," said the old woman; "I do want a little sewin' done before long, but 't ain't no use to spile a good holiday." Her face took a resolved expression. "I'm goin' to make other arrangements," she said. "No, you need n't come up here to pass New Year's Day an' be put right down to sewin'. I make out to do what mendin' I need, an' to sew on my hooks an' eyes. I get Johnny Ross to thread me up a good lot o' needles every little while, an' that helps me a good deal. Abby, why can't you step into the best room an' bring out the rockin'-chair? I seem to want Mis' Hand to have it."

"I opened the window to let the sun in awhile," said the niece, as she returned. "It felt cool in there an' shut up."

"I thought of doin' it not long before you come," said Mrs. Dallett, looking gratified. Once the taking of such a liberty would have been very provoking to her. "Why, it does seem good to have somebody think o' things an' take right hold like that!"

"I'm sure you would, if you were down at my house," said Abby, blushing. "Aunt Cynthy, I don't suppose you could feel as if 't would be best to come down an' pass the winter with me,—just durin' the cold weather, I mean. You'd see more folks to amuse you, an'—I do think of you so anxious these long winter nights."

There was a terrible silence in the room, and Miss Pendexter felt her heart begin to beat very fast. She did not dare to look at her aunt at first.

Presently the silence was broken. Aunt Cynthia had been gazing out of the window, and she turned towards them a little paler and older than before, and smiling sadly.

"Well, dear, I'll do just as you say," she answered. "I'm beat by age at last, but I've had my own way for eighty-five years, come the month o' March, an' last winter I did use to lay awake an' worry in the long storms. I'm kind o' humble now about livin' alone to what I was once." At this moment a new light shone in her face. "I don't expect you'd be willin' to come up here an' stay till spring,—not if I had Foss's folks stop for you to ride to meetin' every pleasant Sunday, an' take you down to the Corners plenty o' other times besides?" she said beseechingly. "No, Abby, I'm too old to move now; I should be homesick down to the village. If you'll come an' stay with me, all I have shall be yours. Mis' Hand hears me say it."

"Oh, don't you think o' that; you're all I've got near to me in the world, an' I'll come an' welcome," said Abby, though the thought of her own little home gave a hard tug at her heart. "Yes, Aunt Cynthy, I'll come, an' we'll be real comfortable together. I've been lonesome sometimes"—

"'T will be best for both," said Mrs. Hand judicially. And so the great question was settled, and suddenly, without too much excitement, it became a thing of the past.

"We must be thinkin' o' dinner," said Aunt Cynthia gayly. "I wish I was better prepared; but there's nice eggs an' pork an' potatoes, an' you girls can take hold an' help." At this moment the roast chicken and the best mince pies were offered and kindly accepted, and before another hour had gone they were sitting at their New Year feast, which Mrs. Dallett decided to be quite proper for the Queen.

Before the guests departed, when the sun was getting low, Aunt Cynthia called her niece to her side and took hold of her hand.

"Don't you make it too long now, Abby," said she. "I shall be wantin' ye every day till you come; but you mustn't forget what a set old thing I be."

Abby had the kindest of hearts, and was always longing for somebody to love and care for; her aunt's very age and helplessness seemed to beg for pity.

"This is Saturday; you may expect me the early part of the week; and thank you, too, aunt," said Abby.

Mrs. Hand stood by with deep sympathy. "It's the proper

thing," she announced calmly. "You'd both of you be a sight happier; and truth is, Abby's wild an' reckless, an' needs somebody to stand right over her, Mis' Dallett. I guess she'll try an' behave, but there—there's no knowin'!" And they all laughed. Then the New Year guests said farewell and started off down the mountain road. They looked back more than once to see Aunt Cynthia's face at the window as she watched them out of sight. Miss Abby Pendexter was full of excitement; she looked as happy as a child.

"I feel as if we'd gained the battle of Waterloo," said Mrs. Hand. "I've really had a most beautiful time. You an' your aunt mustn't forgit to invite me up some time again to spend another day."

Martha's Lady

I.

ONE DAY, many years ago, the old Judge Pyne house wore an unwonted look of gayety and youthfulness. The high-fenced green garden was bright with June flowers. Under the elms in the large shady front yard you might see some chairs placed near together, as they often used to be when the family were all at home and life was going on gayly with eager talk and pleasure-making; when the elder judge, the grandfather, used to quote that great author, Dr. Johnson, and say to his girls, "Be brisk, be splendid, and be public."

One of the chairs had a crimson silk shawl thrown carelessly over its straight back, and a passer-by, who looked in through the latticed gate between the tall gate-posts with their white urns, might think that this piece of shining East Indian color was a huge red lily that had suddenly bloomed against the syringa bush. There were certain windows thrown wide open that were usually shut, and their curtains were blowing free in the light wind of a summer afternoon; it looked as if a large household had returned to the old house to fill the prim best rooms and find them full of cheer.

It was evident to every one in town that Miss Harriet Pyne, to use the village phrase, had company. She was the last of her family, and was by no means old; but being the last, and wonted to live with people much older than herself, she had formed all the habits of a serious elderly person. Ladies of her age, something past thirty, often wore discreet caps in those days, especially if they were married, but being single, Miss Harriet clung to youth in this respect, making the one concession of keeping her waving chestnut hair as smooth and stiffly arranged as possible. She had been the dutiful companion of her father and mother in their latest years, all her elder brothers and sisters having married and gone, or died and gone, out of the old house. Now that she was left alone it seemed quite the best thing frankly to accept the fact of age, and to turn more resolutely than ever to the companionship of duty and serious books. She was more serious and given to routine than her elders themselves, as sometimes happened when the daughters of New England gentlefolks were brought up wholly in the society of their elders. At thirty-five she had more reluctance than her mother to face an unforeseen occasion, certainly more than her grandmother, who had preserved some cheerful inheritance of gayety and worldliness from colonial times.

There was something about the look of the crimson silk shawl in the front yard to make one suspect that the sober customs of the best house in a quiet New England village were all being set at defiance, and once when the mistress of the house came to stand in her own doorway, she wore the pleased but somewhat apprehensive look of a guest. In these days New England life held the necessity of much dignity and discretion of behavior; there was the truest hospitality and good cheer in all occasional festivities, but it was sometimes a self-conscious hospitality, followed by an inexorable return to asceticism both of diet and of behavior. Miss Harriet Pyne belonged to the very dullest days of New England, those which perhaps held the most priggishness for the learned professions, the most limited interpretation of the word "evangelical," and the pettiest indifference to large things. The outbreak of a desire for larger religious freedom caused at first a most determined reaction toward formalism, especially in small and quiet villages like Ashford, intently busy with their own concerns. It was high time for a little leaven to begin its work, in this moment when the great impulses of the war for liberty had died away and those of the coming war for patriotism and a new freedom had hardly yet begun.

The dull interior, the changed life of the old house, whose former activities seemed to have fallen sound asleep, really typified these larger conditions, and a little leaven had made its easily recognized appearance in the shape of a light-hearted girl. She was Miss Harriet's young Boston cousin, Helena Vernon, who, half-amused and half-impatient at the unnecessary sober-mindedness of her hostess and of Ashford in general, had set herself to the difficult task of gayety. Cousin Harriet looked on at a succession of ingenious and, on the whole, innocent attempts at pleasure, as she might have looked on at the frolics of a kitten who easily substitutes a ball of yarn for the uncertainties of a bird or a wind-blown leaf, and who may at any moment ravel the fringe of a sacred curtain-tassel in preference to either.

Helena, with her mischievous appealing eyes, with her enchanting old songs and her guitar, seemed the more delightful and even reasonable because she was so kind to everybody, and because she was a beauty. She had the gift of most charming manners. There was all the unconscious lovely ease and grace that had come with the good breeding of her city home, where many pleasant people came and went; she had no fear, one had almost said no respect, of the individual, and she did not need to think of herself. Cousin Harriet turned cold with apprehension when she saw the minister coming in at the front gate, and wondered in agony if Martha were properly attired to go to the door, and would by any chance hear the knocker; it was Helena who, delighted to have anything happen, ran to the door to welcome the Reverend Mr. Crofton as if he were a congenial friend of her own age. She could behave with more or less propriety during the stately first visit, and even contrive to lighten it with modest mirth, and to extort the confession that the guest had a tenor voice, though sadly out of practice; but when the minister departed a little flattered, and hoping that he had not expressed himself too strongly for a pastor upon the poems of Emerson, and feeling the unusual stir of gallantry in his proper heart, it was Helena who caught the honored hat of the late Judge Pyne from its last resting-place in the hall, and holding it securely in both hands, mimicked the minister's self-conscious entrance. She copied his pompous and anxious expression in the dim parlor in such delicious fashion that Miss Harriet, who could not always extinguish a ready spark of the original sin of humor, laughed aloud.

"My dear!" she exclaimed severely the next moment, "I am ashamed of your being so disrespectful!" and then laughed again, and took the affecting old hat and carried it back to its place.

"I would not have had any one else see you for the world," she said sorrowfully as she returned, feeling quite self-possessed again, to the parlor doorway; but Helena still sat in the minister's chair, with her small feet placed as his stiff boots had been, and a copy of his solemn expression before they came to speaking of Emerson and of the guitar. "I wish I had asked him if he would be so kind as to climb the cherry-tree," said Helena, unbending a little at the discovery that her cousin would consent to laugh no more. "There are all those ripe cherries on the top branches. I can climb as high as he, but I can't reach far enough from the last branch that will bear me. The minister is so long and thin"—

"I don't know what Mr. Crofton would have thought of you; he is a very serious young man," said cousin Harriet, still ashamed of her laughter. "Martha will get the cherries for you, or one of the men. I should not like to have Mr. Crofton think you were frivolous, a young lady of your opportunities"—but Helena had escaped through the hall and out at the garden door at the mention of Martha's name. Miss Harriet Pyne sighed anxiously, and then smiled, in spite of her deep convictions, as she shut the blinds and tried to make the house look solemn again.

The front door might be shut, but the garden door at the other end of the broad hall was wide open upon the large sunshiny garden, where the last of the red and white peonies and the golden lilies, and the first of the tall blue larkspurs lent their colors in generous fashion. The straight box borders were all in fresh and shining green of their new leaves, and there was a fragrance of the old garden's inmost life and soul blowing from the honeysuckle blossoms on a long trellis. It was now late in the afternoon, and the sun was low behind great apple-trees at the garden's end, which threw their shadows over the short turf of the bleaching-green. The cherry-trees stood at one side in full sunshine, and Miss Harriet, who presently came to the garden steps to watch like a hen at the water's edge, saw her cousin's pretty figure in its white dress of India muslin hurrying across the grass. She was accompanied by the tall, ungainly shape of Martha the new maid, who, dull and indifferent to every one else, showed a surprising willingness and allegiance to the young guest.

"Martha ought to be in the dining-room, already, slow as she is; it wants but half an hour of tea-time," said Miss

Harriet, as she turned and went into the shaded house. It was Martha's duty to wait at table, and there had been many try-ing scenes and defeated efforts toward her education. Martha was certainly very clumsy, and she seemed the clumsier be-cause she had replaced her aunt, a most skillful person, who had but lately married a thriving farm and its prosperous owner. It must be confessed that Miss Harriet was a most bewildering instructor, and that her pupil's brain was easily confused and prone to blunders. The coming of Helena had been somewhat dreaded by reason of this incompetent ser-vice, but the guest took no notice of frowns or futile gestures at the first tea-table, except to establish friendly relations with Martha on her own account by a reassuring smile. They were about the same age, and next morning, before cousin Harriet came down, Helena showed by a word and a quick touch the right way to do something that had gone wrong and been impossible to understand the night before. A moment later the anxious mistress came in without suspicion, but Martha's eyes were as affectionate as a dog's, and there was a new look of hopefulness on her face; this dreaded guest was a friend after all, and not a foe come from proud Boston to confound her ignorance and patient efforts.

The two young creatures, mistress and maid, were hurrying across the bleaching-green.

"I can't reach the ripest cherries," explained Helena po-litely, "and I think that Miss Pyne ought to send some to the minister. He has just made us a call. Why, Martha, you have n't been crying again!"

"Yes 'm," said Martha sadly. "Miss Pyne always loves to send something to the minister," she acknowledged with in-terest, as if she did not wish to be asked to explain these latest tears.

"We'll arrange some of the best cherries in a pretty dish. I'll show you how, and you shall carry them over to the par-sonage after tea," said Helena cheerfully, and Martha accepted the embassy with pleasure. Life was beginning to hold mo-ments of something like delight in the last few days.

"You'll spoil your pretty dress, Miss Helena," Martha gave shy warning, and Miss Helena stood back and held up her skirts with unusual care while the country girl, in her heavy blue checked gingham, began to climb the cherry-tree like a boy.

Down came the scarlet fruit like bright rain into the green grass.

"Break some nice twigs with the cherries and leaves together; oh, you're a duck, Martha!" and Martha, flushed with delight, and looking far more like a thin and solemn blue heron, came rustling down to earth again, and gathered the spoils into her clean apron.

That night at tea, during her hand-maiden's temporary absence, Miss Harriet announced, as if by way of apology, that she thought Martha was beginning to understand something about her work. "Her aunt was a treasure, she never had to be told anything twice; but Martha has been as clumsy as a calf," said the precise mistress of the house. "I have been afraid sometimes that I never could teach her anything. I was quite ashamed to have you come just now, and find me so unprepared to entertain a visitor."

"Oh, Martha will learn fast enough because she cares so much," said the visitor eagerly. "I think she is a dear good girl. I do hope that she will never go away. I think she does things better every day, cousin Harriet," added Helena pleadingly, with all her kind young heart. The china-closet door was open a little way, and Martha heard every word. From that moment, she not only knew what love was like, but she knew love's dear ambitions. To have come from a stony hill-farm and a bare small wooden house, was like a cave-dweller's coming to make a permanent home in an art museum, such had seemed the elaborateness and elegance of Miss Pyne's fashion of life; and Martha's simple brain was slow enough in its processes and recognitions. But with this sympathetic ally and defender, this exquisite Miss Helena who believed in her, all difficulties appeared to vanish.

Later that evening, no longer homesick or hopeless, Martha returned from her polite errand to the minister, and stood with a sort of triumph before the two ladies, who were sitting in the front doorway, as if they were waiting for visitors, Helena still in her white muslin and red ribbons, and Miss Harriet in a thin black silk. Being happily self-forgetful in the greatness of the moment, Martha's manners were perfect, and she looked for once almost pretty and quite as young as she was.

"The minister came to the door himself, and returned his thanks. He said that cherries were always his favorite fruit, and he was much obliged to both Miss Pyne and Miss Vernon. He kept me waiting a few minutes, while he got this book ready to send to you, Miss Helena."

"What are you saying, Martha? I have sent him nothing!" exclaimed Miss Pyne, much astonished. "What does she mean, Helena?"

"Only a few cherries," explained Helena. "I thought Mr. Crofton would like them after his afternoon of parish calls. Martha and I arranged them before tea, and I sent them with our compliments."

"Oh, I am very glad you did," said Miss Harriet, wondering, but much relieved. "I was afraid"—

"No, it was none of my mischief," answered Helena daringly. "I did not think that Martha would be ready to go so soon. I should have shown you how pretty they looked among their green leaves. We put them in one of your best white dishes with the openwork edge. Martha shall show you to-morrow; mamma always likes to have them so." Helena's fingers were busy with the hard knot of a parcel.

"See this, cousin Harriet!" she announced proudly, as Martha disappeared round the corner of the house, beaming with the pleasures of adventure and success. "Look! the minister has sent me a book: Sermons on *what*? Sermons—it is so dark that I can't quite see."

"It must be his 'Sermons on the Seriousness of Life;' they are the only ones he has printed, I believe," said Miss Harriet, with much pleasure. "They are considered very fine discourses. He pays you a great compliment, my dear. I feared that he noticed your girlish levity."

"I behaved beautifully while he stayed," insisted Helena. "Ministers are only men," but she blushed with pleasure. It was certainly something to receive a book from its author, and such a tribute made her of more value to the whole reverent household. The minister was not only a man, but a bachelor, and Helena was at the age that best loves conquest; it was at any rate comfortable to be reinstated in cousin Harriet's good graces.

"Do ask the kind gentleman to tea! He needs a little cheering up," begged the siren in India muslin, as she laid the shiny black volume of sermons on the stone doorstep with an air of approval, but as if they had quite finished their mission.

"Perhaps I shall, if Martha improves as much as she has within the last day or two," Miss Harriet promised hopefully. "It is something I always dread a little when I am all alone, but I think Mr. Crofton likes to come. He converses so elegantly."

II.

These were the days of long visits, before affectionate friends thought it quite worth while to take a hundred miles' journey merely to dine or to pass a night in one another's houses. Helena lingered through the pleasant weeks of early summer, and departed unwillingly at last to join her family at the White Hills, where they had gone, like other households of high social station, to pass the month of August out of town. The happy-hearted young guest left many lamenting friends behind her, and promised each that she would come back again next year. She left the minister a rejected lover, as well as the preceptor of the academy, but with their pride unwounded, and it may have been with wider outlooks upon the world and a less narrow sympathy both for their own work in life and for their neighbors' work and hindrances. Even Miss Harriet Pyne herself had lost some of the unnecessary provincialism and prejudice which had begun to harden a naturally good and open mind and affectionate heart. She was conscious of feeling younger and more free, and not so lonely. Nobody had ever been so gay, so fascinating, or so kind as Helena, so full of social resource, so simple and undemanding in her friendliness. The light of her young life cast no shadow on either young or old companions, her pretty clothes never seemed to make other girls look dull or out of fashion. When she went away up the street in Miss Harriet's carriage to take the slow train toward Boston and the gayeties of the new Profile House, where her mother waited impatiently with a group of Southern friends, it seemed as if there would never be any more picnics or parties in Ashford, and as if society had nothing left to do but to grow old and get ready for winter.

Martha came into Miss Helena's bedroom that last morning, and it was easy to see that she had been crying; she looked just as she did in that first sad week of homesickness and despair. All for love's sake she had been learning to do many things, and to do them exactly right; her eyes had grown quick to see the smallest chance for personal service. Nobody could be more humble and devoted; she looked years older than Helena, and wore already a touching air of caretaking.

"You spoil me, you dear Martha!" said Helena from the bed. "I don't know what they will say at home, I am so spoiled."

Martha went on opening the blinds to let in the brightness of the summer morning, but she did not speak.

"You are getting on splendidly, are n't you?" continued the little mistress. "You have tried so hard that you make me ashamed of myself. At first you crammed all the flowers together, and now you make them look beautiful. Last night cousin Harriet was so pleased when the table was so charming, and I told her that you did everything yourself, every bit. Won't you keep the flowers fresh and pretty in the house until I come back? It's so much pleasanter for Miss Pyne, and you'll feed my little sparrows, won't you? They're growing so tame."

"Oh, yes, Miss Helena!" and Martha looked almost angry for a moment, then she burst into tears and covered her face with her apron. "I could n't understand a single thing when I first came. I never had been anywhere to see anything, and Miss Pyne frightened me when she talked. It was you made me think I could ever learn. I wanted to keep the place, 'count of mother and the little boys; we're dreadful hard pushed. Hepsy has been good in the kitchen; she said she ought to have patience with me, for she was awkward herself when she first came."

Helena laughed; she looked so pretty under the tasseled white curtains.

"I dare say Hepsy tells the truth," she said. "I wish you had told me about your mother. When I come again, some day we'll drive up country, as you call it, to see her. Martha! I wish you would think of me sometimes after I go away. Won't you promise?" and the bright young face suddenly grew grave. "I have hard times myself; I don't always learn things that I ought to learn, I don't always put things straight. I wish you wouldn't forget me ever, and would just believe in me. I think it does more than anything."

"I won't forget," said Martha slowly. "I shall think of you every day." She spoke almost with indifference, as if she had been asked to dust a room, but she turned aside quickly and pulled the little mat under the hot water jug quite out of its former straightness; then she hastened away down the long white entry, weeping as she went.

III.

To lose out of sight the friend whom one has loved and lived to please is to lose joy out of life. But if love is true, there comes presently a higher joy of pleasing the ideal, that is to say, the perfect friend. The same old happiness is lifted to a higher level. As for Martha, the girl who stayed behind in Ashford, nobody's life could seem duller to those who could not understand; she was slow of step, and her eyes were almost always downcast as if intent upon incessant toil; but they startled you when she looked up, with their shining light. She was capable of the happiness of holding fast to a great sentiment, the ineffable satisfaction of trying to please one whom she truly loved. She never thought of trying to make other people pleased with herself; all she lived for was to do the best she could for others, and to conform to an ideal, which grew at last to be like a saint's vision, a heavenly figure painted upon the sky.

On Sunday afternoons in summer, Martha sat by the window of her chamber, a low-storied little room, which looked into the side yard and the great branches of an elm-tree. She never sat in the old wooden rocking-chair except on Sundays like this; it belonged to the day of rest and to happy meditation. She wore her plain black dress and a clean white apron, and held in her lap a little wooden box, with a brass ring on top for a handle. She was past sixty years of age and looked even older, but there was the same look on her face that it had sometimes worn in girlhood. She was the same Martha; her hands were old-looking and work-worn, but her face still shone. It seemed like yesterday that Helena Vernon had gone away, and it was more than forty years.

War and peace had brought their changes and great anxieties, the face of the earth was furrowed by floods and fire, the faces of mistress and maid were furrowed by smiles and tears, and in the sky the stars shone on as if nothing had happened. The village of Ashford added a few pages to its unexciting history, the minister preached, the people listened; now and then a funeral crept along the street, and now and then the bright face of a little child rose above the horizon of a family pew. Miss Harriet Pyne lived on in the large white house, which gained more and more distinction because it suffered no changes, save successive repaintings and a new railing about its stately roof. Miss Harriet herself had moved far beyond the uncertainties of an anxious youth. She had long ago made all her decisions, and settled all necessary questions; her scheme of life was as faultless as the miniature landscape of a Japanese garden, and as easily kept in order. The only important change she would ever be capable of making was the final change to another and a better world; and for that nature itself would gently provide, and her own innocent life.

Hardly any great social event had ruffled the easy current of life since Helena Vernon's marriage. To this Miss Pyne had gone, stately in appearance and carrying gifts of some old family silver which bore the Vernon crest, but not without some protest in her heart against the uncertainties of married life. Helena was so equal to a happy independence and even to the assistance of other lives grown strangely dependent upon her quick sympathies and instinctive decisions, that it was hard to let her sink her personality in the affairs of another. Yet a brilliant English match was not without its attractions to an old-fashioned gentlewoman like Miss Pyne, and Helena herself was amazingly happy; one day there had come a letter to Ashford, in which her very heart seemed to beat with love and self-forgetfulness, to tell cousin Harriet of such new happiness and high hope. "Tell Martha all that I say about my dear Jack," wrote the eager girl; "please show my letter to Martha, and tell her that I shall come home next summer and bring the handsomest and best man in the world to Ashford. I have told him all about the dear house and the dear garden; there never was such a lad to reach for cherries with his six-foot-two." Miss Pyne, wondering a little, gave the letter to Martha, who took it deliberately and as if she wondered too, and went away to read it slowly by herself. Martha cried over it, and felt a strange sense of loss and pain; it hurt her heart a little to read about the cherry-picking. Her idol seemed to be less her own since she had become the idol of a stranger. She never had taken such a letter in her hands before, but love at last prevailed, since Miss Helena was happy, and she kissed the last page where her name was written, feeling overbold, and laid the envelope on Miss Pyne's secretary without a word.

The most generous love cannot but long for reassurance, and Martha had the joy of being remembered. She was not forgotten when the day of the wedding drew near, but she never knew that Miss Helena had asked if cousin Harriet would not bring Martha to town; she should like to have Martha there to see her married. "She would help about the flowers," wrote the happy girl; "I know she will like to come, and I'll ask mamma to plan to have some one take her all about Boston and make her have a pleasant time after the hurry of the great day is over."

Cousin Harriet thought it was very kind and exactly like Helena, but Martha would be out of her element; it was most imprudent and girlish to have thought of such a thing. Helena's mother would be far from wishing for any unnecessary guest just then, in the busiest part of her household, and it was best not to speak of the invitation. Some day Martha should go to Boston if she did well, but not now. Helena did not forget to ask if Martha had come, and was astonished by the indifference of the answer. It was the first thing which reminded her that she was not a fairy princess having everything her own way in that last day before the wedding. She knew that Martha would have loved to be near, for she could not help understanding in that moment of her own happiness the love that was hidden in another heart. Next day this happy young princess, the bride, cut a piece of a great cake and put it into a pretty box that had held one of her wedding presents. With eager voices calling her, and all her friends about her, and her mother's face growing more and more wistful at the thought of parting, she still lingered and ran to take one or two trifles from her dressing-table, a little mirror and some tiny scissors that Martha would remember, and one of the pretty handkerchiefs marked with her maiden name. These she put in the box too; it was half a girlish freak and fancy, but she could not help trying to share her happiness, and Martha's life was so plain and dull. She whispered a message, and put the little package into cousin Harriet's hand for Martha as she said good-by. She was very fond of cousin Harriet. She smiled with a gleam of her old fun; Martha's puzzled look and tall awkward figure seemed to stand suddenly before her eyes, as she promised to come again to Ashford. Impatient voices called to Helena, her lover was at the door, and she hurried away, leaving her old home and her girlhood gladly. If she had only known it, as she kissed cousin Harriet good-by, they were never going to see each other again until they were old women. The first step that she took out of her father's house that day, married, and full of hope and joy, was a step that led her away from the green elms of Boston Common and away from her own country and those she loved best, to a brilliant, much-varied foreign life, and to nearly all the sorrows and nearly all the joys that the heart of one woman could hold or know.

On Sunday afternoons Martha used to sit by the window in Ashford and hold the wooden box which a favorite young brother, who afterward died at sea, had made for her, and she used to take out of it the pretty little box with a gilded cover that had held the piece of wedding-cake, and the small scissors, and the blurred bit of a mirror in its silver case; as for the handkerchief with the narrow lace edge, once in two or three years she sprinkled it as if it were a flower, and spread it out in the sun on the old bleaching-green, and sat near by in the shrubbery to watch lest some bold robin or cherry-bird should seize it and fly away.

IV.

Miss Harriet Pyne was often congratulated upon the good fortune of having such a helper and friend as Martha. As time went on this tall, gaunt woman, always thin, always slow, gained a dignity of behavior and simple affectionateness of look which suited the charm and dignity of the ancient house. She was unconsciously beautiful like a saint, like the picturesqueness of a lonely tree which lives to shelter unnumbered lives and to stand quietly in its place. There was such rustic homeliness and constancy belonging to her, such beautiful powers of apprehension, such reticence, such gentleness for those who were troubled or sick; all these gifts and graces Martha hid in her heart. She never joined the church because she thought she was not good enough, but life was such a passion and happiness of service that it was impossible not to be devout, and she was always in her humble place on Sundays, in the back pew next the door. She had been educated by a remembrance; Helena's young eyes forever looked at her reassuringly from a gay girlish face. Helena's sweet patience in teaching her own awkwardness could never be forgotten.

"I owe everything to Miss Helena," said Martha, half aloud, as she sat alone by the window; she had said it to herself a thousand times. When she looked in the little keepsake mirror she always hoped to see some faint reflection of Helena Vernon, but there was only her own brown old New England face to look back at her wonderingly.

Miss Pyne went less and less often to pay visits to her friends in Boston; there were very few friends left to come to Ashford and make long visits in the summer, and life grew more and more monotonous. Now and then there came news from across the sea and messages of remembrance, letters that were closely written on thin sheets of paper, and that spoke of lords and ladies, of great journeys, of the death of little children and the proud successes of boys at school, of the wedding of Helena Dysart's only daughter; but even that had happened years ago. These things seemed far away and vague, as if they belonged to a story and not to life itself; the true links with the past were quite different. There was the unvarying flock of ground-sparrows that Helena had begun to feed; every morning Martha scattered crumbs for them from the side doorsteps while Miss Pyne watched from the dining-room window, and they were counted and cherished year by year.

Miss Pyne herself had many fixed habits, but little ideality or imagination, and so at last it was Martha who took thought for her mistress, and gave freedom to her own good taste. After a while, without any one's observing the change, the every-day ways of doing things in the house came to be the stately ways that had once belonged only to the entertainment of guests. Happily both mistress and maid seized all possible chances for hospitality, yet Miss Harriet nearly always sat alone at her exquisitely served table with its fresh flowers, and the beautiful old china which Martha handled so lovingly that there was no good excuse for keeping it hidden on closet shelves. Every year when the old cherry-trees were in fruit, Martha carried the round white old English dish with a fretwork edge, full of pointed green leaves and scarlet cherries, to the minister, and his wife never quite understood why every year he blushed and looked so conscious of the pleasure, and thanked Martha as if he had received a very particular attention. There was no pretty suggestion toward the pursuit of the fine art of housekeeping in Martha's limited acquaintance with newspapers that she did not adopt; there was no refined old custom of the Pyne housekeeping that she consented to let go. And every day, as she had promised, she thought of Miss Helena,—oh, many times in every day: whether this thing would please her, or that be likely to fall in with her fancy or ideas of fitness. As far as was possible the rare news that reached Ashford through an occasional letter or the talk of guests was made part of Martha's own life, the history of her own heart. A worn old geography often stood open at the map of Europe on the light-stand in her room, and a little old-fashioned gilt button, set with a bit of glass like a ruby, that had broken and fallen from the trimming of one of Helena's dresses, was used to mark the city of her dwelling-place. In the changes of a diplomatic life Martha followed her lady all about the map. Sometimes the button was at Paris, and sometimes at Madrid; once, to her great anxiety, it remained long at St. Petersburg. For such a slow scholar Martha was not unlearned at last, since everything about life in these foreign towns was of interest to her faithful heart. She satisfied her own mind as she threw crumbs to the tame sparrows; it was all part of the same thing and for the same affectionate reasons.

v.

One Sunday afternoon in early summer Miss Harriet Pyne came hurrying along the entry that led to Martha's room and called two or three times before its inhabitant could reach the door. Miss Harriet looked unusually cheerful and excited, and she held something in her hand. "Where are you, Martha?" she called again. "Come quick, I have something to tell you!"

"Here I am, Miss Pyne," said Martha, who had only stopped to put her precious box in the drawer, and to shut the geography.

"Who do you think is coming this very night at half-past six? We must have everything as nice as we can; I must see Hannah at once. Do you remember my cousin Helena who has lived abroad so long? Miss Helena Vernon,—the Honorable Mrs. Dysart, she is now."

"Yes, I remember her," answered Martha, turning a little pale.

"I knew that she was in this country, and I had written to ask her to come for a long visit," continued Miss Harriet, who did not often explain things, even to Martha, though she was always conscientious about the kind messages that were sent back by grateful guests. "She telegraphs that she means to anticipate her visit by a few days and come to me at once. The heat is beginning in town, I suppose. I daresay, having been a foreigner so long, she does not mind traveling on Sunday. Do you think Hannah will be prepared? We must have tea a little later."

"Yes, Miss Harriet," said Martha. She wondered that she could speak as usual, there was such a ringing in her ears. "I shall have time to pick some fresh strawberries; Miss Helena is so fond of our strawberries."

"Why, I had forgotten," said Miss Pyne, a little puzzled by something quite unusual in Martha's face. "We must expect to find Mrs. Dysart a good deal changed, Martha; it is a great many years since she was here; I have not seen her since her wedding, and she has had a great deal of trouble, poor girl. You had better open the parlor chamber, and make it ready before you go down."

"It is all ready," said Martha. "I can carry some of those little sweet-brier roses upstairs before she comes."

"Yes, you are always thoughtful," said Miss Pyne, with unwonted feeling.

Martha did not answer. She glanced at the telegram wistfully. She had never really suspected before that Miss Pyne knew nothing of the love that had been in her heart all these years; it was half a pain and half a golden joy to keep such a secret; she could hardly bear this moment of surprise.

Presently the news gave wings to her willing feet. When Hannah, the cook, who never had known Miss Helena, went to the parlor an hour later on some errand to her old mistress, she discovered that this stranger guest must be a very important person. She had never seen the tea-table look exactly as it did that night, and in the parlor itself there were fresh blossoming boughs in the old East India jars, and lilies in the paneled hall, and flowers everywhere, as if there were some high festivity.

Miss Pyne sat by the window watching, in her best dress, looking stately and calm; she seldom went out now, and it was almost time for the carriage. Martha was just coming in from the garden with the strawberries, and with more flowers in her apron. It was a bright cool evening in June, the golden robins sang in the elms, and the sun was going down behind the apple-trees at the foot of the garden. The beautiful old house stood wide open to the long-expected guest.

"I think that I shall go down to the gate," said Miss Pyne, looking at Martha for approval, and Martha nodded and they went together slowly down the broad front walk.

There was a sound of horses and wheels on the roadside turf: Martha could not see at first; she stood back inside the gate behind the white lilac-bushes as the carriage came. Miss Pyne was there; she was holding out both arms and taking a tired, bent little figure in black to her heart. "Oh, my Miss Helena is an old woman like me!" and Martha gave a pitiful sob; she had never dreamed it would be like this; this was the one thing she could not bear.

"Where are you, Martha?" called Miss Pyne. "Martha will bring these in; you have not forgotten my good Martha, Helena?" Then Mrs. Dysart looked up and smiled just as she used to smile in the old days. The young eyes were there still in the changed face, and Miss Helena had come.

That night Martha waited in her lady's room just as she used, humble and silent, and went through with the old unforgotten loving services. The long years seemed like days. At last she lingered a moment trying to think of something else that might be done, then she was going silently away, but Helena called her back. She suddenly knew the whole story and could hardly speak.

"Oh, my dear Martha!" she cried, "won't you kiss me good-night? Oh, Martha, have you remembered like this, all these long years!"

The Gray Mills of Farley

THE MILLS of Farley were close together by the river, and the gray houses that belonged to them stood, tall and bare, alongside. They had no room for gardens or even for little green side-yards where one might spend a summer evening. The Corporation, as this compact village was called by those who lived in it, was small but solid; you fancied yourself in the heart of a large town when you stood midway of one of its short streets, but from the street's end you faced a wide green farming country. On spring and summer Sundays, groups of the young folks of the Corporation would stray out along the country roads, but it was very seldom that any of the older people went. On the whole, it seemed as if the closer you lived to the mill-yard gate, the better. You had more time to loiter on a summer morning, and there was less distance to plod through the winter snows and rains. The last stroke of the bell saw almost everybody within the mill doors.

There were always fluffs of cotton in the air like great white bees drifting down out of the picker chimney. They lodged in the cramped and dingy elms and horse-chestnuts which a former agent had planted along the streets, and the English sparrows squabbled over them in eaves-corners and made warm, untidy great nests that would have contented an Arctic explorer. Somehow the Corporation homes looked like make-believe houses or huge stage-properties, they had so little individuality or likeness to the old-fashioned buildings that made homes for people out on the farms. There was more homelikeness in the sparrows' nests, or even the toylike railroad station at the end of the main street, for that was warmed by steam, and the station-master's wife, thriftily taking advantage of the steady heat, brought her house-plants there and kept them all winter on the broad window-sills.

The Corporation had followed the usual fortunes of New England manufacturing villages. Its operatives were at first eager young men and women from the farms near by, these being joined quickly by pale English weavers and spinners, with their hearty-looking wives and rosy children; then came the flock of Irish families, poorer and simpler than the others but learning the work sooner, and gayer-hearted; now the Canadian-French contingent furnished all the new help, and stood in long rows before the noisy looms and chattered in their odd, excited fashion. They were quicker-fingered, and were willing to work cheaper than any other workpeople yet.

There were remnants of each of these human tides to be found as one looked about the mills. Old Henry Dow, the overseer of the cloth-hall, was a Lancashire man and some of his grandchildren had risen to wealth and prominence in another part of the country, while he kept steadily on with his familiar work and authority. A good many elderly Irishmen and women still kept their places; everybody knew the two old sweepers, Mary Cassidy and Mrs. Kilpatrick, who were looked upon as pillars of the Corporation. They and their compatriots always held loyally together and openly resented the incoming of so many French.

You would never have thought that the French were for a moment conscious of being in the least unwelcome. They came gayly into church and crowded the old parishioners of St. Michael's out of their pews, as on week-days they took their places at the looms. Hardly one of the old parishioners had not taken occasion to speak of such aggressions to Father Daley, the priest, but Father Daley continued to look upon them all as souls to be saved and took continual pains to rub up the rusty French which he had nearly forgotten, in order to preach a special sermon every other Sunday. This caused old Mary Cassidy to shake her head gravely.

"Mis' Kilpatrick, ma'am," she said one morning. "Faix, they ain't folks at all, 'tis but a pack of images they do be, with all their chatter like birds in a hedge."

"Sure then, the holy Saint Francis himself was after saying that the little birrds was his sisters," answered Mrs. Kilpatrick, a godly old woman who made the stations every morning, and was often seen reading a much-handled book of devotion. She was moreover always ready with a friendly joke.

"They ain't the same at all was in them innocent times, when there was plinty saints living in the world," insisted Mary Cassidy. "Look at them thrash, now!"

The old sweeping-women were going downstairs with their brooms. It was almost twelve o'clock, and like the old dray-horses in the mill yard they slackened work in good season for the noonday bell. Three gay young French girls ran down-stairs past them; they were let out for the afternoon and were hurrying home to dress and catch the 12:40 train to the next large town.

"That little one is Meshell's daughter; she's a nice child too, very quiet, and has got more Christian tark than most," said Mrs. Kilpatrick. "They live overhead o' me. There's nine o' themselves in the two rooms; two does be boarders."

"Those upper rooms bees very large entirely at Fitzgib-bon's," said Mary Cassidy with unusual indulgence.

" 'Tis all the company cares about is to get a good rent out of the pay. They're asked every little while by honest folks 'on't they build a trifle o' small houses beyond the church up there, but no, they'd rather the money and kape us like bees in them old hives. Sure in winter we're better for having the more fires, but summer is the pinance!"

"They all says 'why don't folks build their own houses'; they does always be talking about Mike Callahan and how well he saved up and owns a pritty place for himself conva-nient to his work. You might tell them he'd money left him by a brother in California till you'd be black in the face, they'd stick to it 'twas in the picker he earnt it from themselves," grumbled Mary Cassidy.

"Them French spinds all their money on their backs, don't they?" suggested Mrs. Kilpatrick, as if to divert the conversa-tion from dangerous channels. "Look at them three girls now, off to Spincer with their fortnight's pay in their pocket!"

"A couple o' onions and a bag o' crackers is all they want and a pinch o' lard to their butter," pronounced Mary Cassidy with scorn. "The whole town of 'em 'on't be the worse of a dollar for steak the week round. They all go back and buy land in Canada, they spend no money here. See how well they forget their pocketbooks every Sunday for the collection. They do be very light too, they've more laugh than ourselves. 'Tis myself's getting old anyway, I don't laugh much now."

"I like to see a pritty girl look fine," said Mrs. Kilpatrick. "No, they don't be young but once——"

The mill bell rang, and there was a moment's hush of the jarring, racketing machinery and a sudden noise of many feet trampling across the dry, hard pine floors. First came an early flight of boys bursting out of the different doors, and chasing one another down the winding stairs two steps at a time. The old sweepers, who had not quite reached the bottom, stood back against the wall for safety's sake until all these had passed, then they kept on their careful way, the crowd passing them by as if they were caught in an eddy of the stream. Last of all they kept sober company with two or three lame persons and a cheerful delayed little group of new doffers, the children who minded bobbins in the weave-room and who were young enough to be tired and even timid. One of these doffers, a pale, pleasant-looking child, was all fluffy with cotton that had clung to her little dark plaid dress. When Mrs. Kilpatrick spoke to her she answered in a hoarse voice that appealed to one's sympathy. You felt that the hot room and dry cotton were to blame for such hoarseness; it had nothing to do with the weather.

"Where are you living now, Maggie, dear?" the old woman asked.

"I'm in Callahan's yet, but they won't keep me after to-day," said the child. "There's a man wants to get board there, they're changing round in the rooms and they've no place for me. Mis' Callahan couldn't keep me 'less I'd get my pay raised."

Mrs. Kilpatrick gave a quick glance at Mary Cassidy. "Come home with me then, till yez get a bite o' dinner, and we'll talk about it," she said kindly to the child. "I'd a wish for company the day."

The two old companions had locked their brooms into a three-cornered closet at the stair-foot and were crossing the mill yard together. They were so much slower than the rest that they could only see the very last of the crowd of mill people disappearing along the streets and into the boarding-house doors. It was late autumn, the elms were bare, one could see the whole village of Farley, all its poverty and lack of beauty, at one glance. The large houses looked as if they belonged to a toy village, and had been carefully put in rows by a childish hand; it was easy to lose all sense of size in looking at them. A cold wind was blowing bits of waste and paper high into the air; now and then a snowflake went swiftly by like a courier of winter. Mary Cassidy and Mrs. Kilpatrick hugged their old woolen shawls closer about their round shoulders, and the little girl followed with short steps alongside.

II.

The agent of the mills was a single man, keen and business-like, but quietly kind to the people under his charge. Some-times, in times of peace, when one looks among one's neighbors wondering who would make the great soldiers and leaders if there came a sudden call to war, one knows with a flash of recognition the presence of military genius in such a man as he. The agent spent his days in following what seemed to many observers to be only a dull routine, but all his steadi-ness of purpose, all his simple intentness, all his gifts of strat-egy and powers of foresight, and of turning an interruption into an opportunity, were brought to bear upon this dull rou-tine with a keen pleasure. A man in his place must know not only how to lead men, but how to make the combination of their force with the machinery take its place as a factor in the business of manufacturing. To master workmen and keep the mills in running order and to sell the goods successfully in open market is as easy to do badly as it is difficult to do well.

The agent's father and mother, young people who lived for a short time in the village, had both died when he was only three years old, and between that time and his ninth year he had learned almost everything that poverty could teach, being left like little Maggie to the mercy of his neighbors. He re-membered with a grateful heart those who were good to him, and told him of his mother, who had married for love but unwisely. Mrs. Kilpatrick was one of these old friends, who said that his mother was a lady, but even Mrs. Kilpatrick, who was a walking history of the Corporation, had never known his mother's maiden name, much less the place of her birth. The first great revelation of life had come when the nine-years-old boy had money in his hand to pay his board. He was conscious of being looked at with a difference; the very woman who had been hardest to him and let him mind her babies all the morning when he, careful little soul, was hardly more than a baby himself, and then pushed him out into the hungry street at dinner time, was the first one who beckoned him now, willing to make the most of his dollar and a quarter a week. It seemed easy enough to rise from uttermost poverty and dependence to where one could set his mind upon the highest honor in sight, that of being agent of the mills, or to work one's way steadily to where such an honor was grasped at thirty-two. Every year the horizon had set its bounds wider and wider, until the mills of Farley held but a small place in the manufacturing world. There were offers enough of more salary and higher position from those who came to know the agent, but he was part of Farley itself, and had come to care deeply about his neighbors, while a larger mill and salary were not exactly the things that could tempt his ambition. It was but a lonely life for a man in the old agent's quarters where one of the widows of the Corporation, a woman who had been brought up in a gentleman's house in the old country, kept house for him with a certain show of propriety. Ever since he was a boy his room was never without its late evening light, and books and hard study made his chief companionship.

As Mrs. Kilpatrick went home holding little Maggie by the hand that windy noon, the agent was sitting in the company's counting-room with one of the directors and largest stockholders, and they were just ending a long talk about the mill affairs. The agent was about forty years old now and looked fifty. He had a pleasant smile, but one saw it rarely enough, and just now he looked more serious than usual.

"I am very glad to have had this long talk with you," said the old director. "You do not think of any other recommendations to be made at the meeting next week?"

The agent grew a trifle paler and glanced behind him to be sure that the clerks had gone to dinner.

"Not in regard to details," he answered gravely. "There is one thing which I see to be very important. You have seen the books, and are clear that nine per cent. dividend can easily be declared?"

"Very creditable, very creditable," agreed the director; he had recognized the agent's ability from the first and always upheld him generously. "I mean to propose a special vote of thanks for your management. There isn't a minor corporation in New England that stands so well to-day."

The agent listened. "We had some advantages, partly by accident and partly by lucky foresight," he acknowledged. "I am going to ask your backing in something that seems to me not only just but important. I hope that you will not declare above a six per cent. dividend at that directors' meeting; at the most, seven per cent.," he said.

"What, what!" exclaimed the listener. "No, sir!"

The agent left his desk-chair and stood before the old director as if he were pleading for himself. A look of protest and disappointment changed the elder man's face and hardened it a little, and the agent saw it.

"You know the general condition of the people here," he explained humbly. "I have taken great pains to keep hold of the best that have come here; we can depend upon them now and upon the quality of their work. They made no resistance when we had to cut down wages two years ago; on the contrary, they were surprisingly reasonable, and you know that we shut down for several weeks at the time of the alterations. We have never put their wages back as we might easily have done, and I happen to know that a good many families have been able to save little or nothing. Some of them have been working here for three generations. They know as well as you and I and the books do when the mills are making money. Now I wish that we could give them the ten per cent. back again, but in view of the general depression perhaps we can't do that except in the way I mean. I think that next year we're going to have a very hard pull to get along, but if we can keep back three per cent., or even two, of this dividend we can not only manage to get on without a shut-down or touching our surplus, which is quite small enough, but I can have some painting and repairing done in the tenements. They've needed it for a long time——"

The old director sprang to his feet. "Aren't the stockholders going to have any rights then?" he demanded. "Within fifteen years we have had three years when we have passed our dividends, but the operatives never can lose a single day's pay!"

"That was before my time," said the agent, quietly. "We have averaged nearly six and a half per cent. a year taking the last twenty years together, and if you go back farther the average is even larger. This has always been a paying property; we've got our new machinery now, and everything in the mills themselves is just where we want it. I look for far better times after this next year, but the market is glutted with goods of our kind, and nothing is going to be gained by cut-downs and forcing lower-cost goods into it. Still, I can keep things going one way and another, making yarn and so on," he said pleadingly. "I should like to feel that we had this extra surplus. I believe that we owe it to our operatives."

The director had walked heavily to the window and put his hands deep into his side-pockets. He had an angry sense that the agent's hands were in his pockets too.

"I've got some pride about that nine per cent., sir," he said loftily to the agent.

"So have I," said the agent, and the two men looked each other in the face.

"I acknowledge my duty to the stockholders," said the younger man presently. "I have tried to remember that duty ever since I took the mills eight years ago, but we've got an excellent body of operatives, and we ought to keep them. I want to show them this next year that we value their help. If times aren't as bad as we fear we shall still have the money——"

"Nonsense. They think they own the mills now," said the director, but he was uncomfortable, in spite of believing he was right. "Where's my hat? I must have my luncheon now, and afterward there'll hardly be time to go down and look at the new power-house with you—I must be off on the quarter-to-two train."

The agent sighed and led the way. There was no use in saying anything more and he knew it. As they walked along they met old Mrs. Kilpatrick returning from her brief noonday meal with little Maggie, whose childish face was radiant. The old woman recognized one of the directors and dropped him a decent curtsey as she had been taught to salute the gentry sixty years before.

The director returned the salutation with much politeness. This was really a pleasant incident, and he took a silver half dollar from his pocket and gave it to the little girl before he went on.

"Kape it safe, darlin'," said the old woman; "you'll need it yet. Don't be spending all your money in sweeties; 'tis a very cold world to them that haves no pince in their pocket."

The child looked up at Mrs. Kilpatrick apprehensively; then the sunshine of hope broke out again through the cloud.

"I am going to save fine till I buy a house, and you and me'll live there together, Mrs. Kilpatrick, and have a lovely coal fire all the time."

"Faix, Maggie, I have always thought some day I'd kape a pig and live pritty in me own house," said Mrs. Kilpatrick. "But I'm the old sweeper yet in Number Two. 'Tis a worrld where some has and more wants," she added with a sigh. "I got the manes for a good buryin', the Lord be praised, and a bitteen more beside. I wouldn't have that if Father Daley was as croping as some."

"Mis' Mullin does always be scolding 'bout Father Daley having all the collections," ventured Maggie, somewhat adrift in so great a subject.

"She's no right then!" exclaimed the old woman angrily; "she'll get no luck to be grudging her pince that way. 'Tis hard work anny priest would have to kape the likes of hersilf from being haythens altogether."

There was a nine per cent. annual dividend declared at the directors' meeting the next week, with considerable applause from the board and sincere congratulations to the agent. He looked thinner and more sober than usual, and several persons present, whose aid he had asked in private, knew very well the reason. After the meeting was over the senior director, and largest stockholder, shook hands with him warmly.

"About that matter you suggested to me the other day," he said, and the agent looked up eagerly. "I consulted several of our board in regard to the propriety of it before we came down, but they all agreed with me that it was no use to cross a bridge until you come to it. Times look a little better, and the operatives will share in the accession of credit to a mill that declares nine per cent. this year. I hope that we shall be able to run the mills with at worst only a moderate cut-down, and they may think themselves very fortunate when so many hands are being turned off everywhere."

The agent's face grew dark. "I hope that times will take a better turn," he managed to say.

"Yes, yes," answered the director. "Good-bye to you, Mr. Agent! I am not sure of seeing you again for some time," he added with unusual kindliness. "I am an old man now to be hurrying round to board meetings and having anything to do with responsibilities like these. My sons must take their turn."

There was an eager protest from the listeners, and presently the busy group of men disappeared on their way to the train. A nine per cent. dividend naturally made the Farley Manufacturing Company's stock go up a good many points, and word came presently that the largest stockholder and one or two other men had sold out. Then the stock ceased to rise, and winter came on apace, and the hard times which the agent had foreseen came also.

III.

One noon in early March there were groups of men and women gathering in the Farley streets. For a wonder, nobody was hurrying toward home and dinner was growing cold on some of the long boarding-house tables.

"They might have carried us through the cold weather; there's but a month more of it," said one middle-aged man sorrowfully.

"They'll be talking to us about economy now, some o' them big thinkers; they'll say we ought to learn how to save; they always begin about that quick as the work stops," said a youngish woman angrily. She was better dressed than most of the group about her and had the keen, impatient look of a leader. "They'll say that manufacturing is going to the dogs, and capital's in worse distress than labor——"

"How is it those big railroads get along? They can't shut down, there's none o' them stops; they cut down sometimes when they have to, but they don't turn off their help this way," complained somebody else.

"Faith then! they don't know what justice is. They talk about their justice all so fine," said a pale-faced young Irishman—"justice is nine per cent. last year for the men that had the money and no rise at all for the men that did the work."

"They say the shut-down's going to last all summer anyway. I'm going to pack my kit to-night," said a young fellow who had just married and undertaken with unusual pride and ambition to keep house. "The likes of me can't be idle. But where to look for any work for a mule spinner, the Lord only knows!"

Even the French were sobered for once and talked eagerly among themselves. Halfway down the street, in front of the French grocery, a man was haranguing his compatriots from the top of a packing-box. Everybody was anxious and excited by the sudden news. No work after a week from to-morrow until times were better. There had already been a cut-down, the mills had not been earning anything all winter. The agent had hoped to keep on for at least two months longer, and then to make some scheme about running at half time in the summer, setting aside the present work for simple yarn-making. He knew well enough that the large families were scattered through the mill rooms and that any pay would be a help. Some of the young men could be put to other work for the company; there was a huge tract of woodland farther back among the hills where some timber could be got ready for shipping. His mind was full of plans and anxieties and the telegram that morning struck him like a blow. He had asked that he might keep the card-room prices up to where the best men could make at least six dollars and a half a week and was hoping for a straight answer, but the words on the yellow paper seemed to dance about and make him dizzy. "Shut down Saturday 9th until times are better!" he repeated to himself. "Shut down until times are worse here in Farley!"

The agent stood at the counting-room window looking out at the piteous, defenseless groups that passed by. He wished bitterly that his own pay stopped with the rest; it did not seem fair that he was not thrown out upon the world too.

"I don't know what they're going to do. They shall have the last cent I've saved before anybody suffers," he said in his heart. But there were tears in his eyes when he saw Mrs. Kilpatrick go limping out of the gate. She waited a moment for her constant companion, poor little Maggie the doffer, and they went away up the street toward their poor lodging holding each other fast by the hand. Maggie's father and grandfather and great-grandfather had all worked in the Farley mills; they had left no heritage but work behind them for this orphan child; they had never been able to save so much that a long illness, a prolonged old age, could not waste their slender hoards away.

<h3 style="text-align:center">IV.</h3>

It would have been difficult for an outsider to understand the sudden plunge from decent comfort to actual poverty in this small mill town. Strange to say, it was upon the smaller families that the strain fell the worst in Farley, and upon men and women who had nobody to look to but themselves. Where a man had a large household of children and several of these were old enough to be at work, and to put aside their wages or pay for their board; where such a man was of a thrifty and saving turn and a ruler of his household like old James Dow in the cloth-hall, he might feel sure of a comfortable hoard and be fearless of a rainy day. But with a young man who worked single-handed for his wife and a little flock, or one who had an invalid to work for, that heaviest of burdens to the poor, the door seemed to be shut and barred against prosperity, and life became a test of one's power of endurance.

The agent went home late that noon from the counting-room. The street was nearly empty, but he had no friendly look or word for anyone whom he passed. Those who knew him well only pitied him, but it seemed to the tired man as if every eye must look at him with reproach. The long mill buildings of gray stone with their rows of deep-set windows wore a repellent look of strength and solidity. More than one man felt bitterly his own personal weakness as he turned to look at them. The ocean of fate seemed to be dashing him against their gray walls—what use was it to fight against the Corporation? Two great forces were in opposition now, and happiness could come only from their serving each other in harmony.

The stronger force of capital had withdrawn from the league; the weaker one, labor, was turned into an utter help-lessness of idleness. There was nothing to be done; you can-not rebel against a shut-down, you can only submit.

A week later the great wheel stopped early on the last day of work. Almost everyone left his special charge of machinery in good order, oiled and cleaned and slackened with a kind of affectionate lingering care, for one person loves his machine as another loves his horse. Even little Maggie pushed her bobbin-box into a safe place near the overseer's desk and tipped it up and dusted it out with a handful of waste. At the foot of the long winding stairs Mrs. Kilpatrick was putting away her broom, and she sighed as she locked the closet door; she had known hard times before. "They'll be wanting me with odd jobs; we'll be after getting along some way," she said with satisfaction.

"March is a long month, so it is—there'll be plinty time for change before the ind of it," said Mary Cassidy hopefully. "The agent will be thinking whatever can he do; sure he's very ingenious. Look at him how well he persuaded the direc-tors to l'ave off wit' making cotton cloth like everybody else, and catch a chance wit' all these new linings and things! He's done very well, too. There bees no sinse in a shut-down anny way, the looms and cards all suffers and the bands all slacks if they don't get stiff. I'd sooner pay folks to tind their work whatever it cost."

" 'Tis true for you," agreed Mrs. Kilpatrick.

"What'll ye do wit' the shild, now she's no chance of pay, any more?" asked Mary relentlessly, and poor Maggie's eyes grew dark with fright as the conversation abruptly pointed her way. She sometimes waked up in misery in Mrs. Kilpatrick's warm bed, crying for fear that she was going to be sent back to the poorhouse.

"Maggie an' me's going to kape together awhile yet," said the good old woman fondly. "She's very handy for me, so she is. We 'on't part with 'ach other whativer befalls, so we 'on't," and Maggie looked up with a wistful smile, only half reassured. To her the shut-down seemed like the end of the world.

Some of the French people took time by the forelock and boarded the midnight train that very Saturday with all their possessions. A little later two or three families departed by the same train, under cover of the darkness between two days, without stopping to pay even their house rent. These mysterious flittings, like that of the famous Tartar tribe, roused a suspicion against their fellow countrymen, but after a succession of such departures almost everybody else thought it far cheaper to stay among friends. It seemed as if at any moment the great mill wheels might begin to turn, and the bell begin to ring, but day after day the little town was still and the bell tolled the hours one after another as if it were Sunday. The mild spring weather came on and the women sat mending or knitting on the doorsteps. More people moved away; there were but few men and girls left now in the quiet boarding-houses, and the spare tables were stacked one upon another at the end of the rooms. When planting-time came, word was passed about the Corporation that the agent was going to portion out a field that belonged to him a little way out of town on the South road, and let every man who had a family take a good-sized piece to plant. He also offered seed potatoes and garden seeds free to anyone who would come and ask for them at his house. The poor are very generous to each other, as a rule, and there was much borrowing and lending from house to house, and it was wonderful how long the people seemed to continue their usual fashions of life without distress. Almost everybody had saved a little bit of money and some had saved more; if one could no longer buy beefsteak he could still buy flour and potatoes, and a bit of pork lent a pleasing flavor, to content an idle man who had nothing to do but to stroll about town.

v.

One night the agent was sitting alone in his large, half-furnished house. Mary Moynahan, his housekeeper, had gone up to the church. There was a timid knock at the door.

There were two persons waiting, a short, thick-set man and a pale woman with dark, bright eyes who was nearly a head taller than her companion.

"Come in, Ellen; I'm glad to see you," said the agent. "Have you got your wheel-barrow, Mike?" Almost all the would-be planters of the field had come under cover of darkness and contrived if possible to avoid each other.

"'Tisn't the potatoes we're after asking, sir," said Ellen. She was always spokeswoman, for Mike had an impediment in his speech. "The childher come up yisterday and got them while you'd be down at the counting-room. 'Twas Mary Moynahan saw to them. We do be very thankful to you, sir, for your kindness."

"Come in," said the agent, seeing there was something of consequence to be said. Ellen Carroll and he had worked side by side many a long day when they were young. She had been a noble wife to Mike, whose poor fortunes she had gladly shared for sake of his good heart, though Mike now and then paid too much respect to his often infirmities. There was a slight flavor of whisky now on the evening air, but it was a serious thing to put on your Sunday coat and go up with your wife to see the agent.

"We've come wanting to talk about any chances there might be with the mill," ventured Ellen timidly, as she stood in the lighted room; then she looked at Mike for reassurance. "We're very bad off, you see," she went on. "Yes, sir, I got them potaties, but I had to bake a little of them for supper and more again the day, for our breakfast. I don't know whatever we'll do whin they're gone. The poor children does be entreating me for them, Dan!"

The mother's eyes were full of tears. It was very seldom now that anybody called the agent by his christian name; there was a natural reserve and dignity about him, and there had come a definite separation between him and most of his old friends in the two years while he had managed to go to the School of Technology in Boston.

"Why didn't you let me know it was bad as that?" he asked. "I don't mean that anybody here should suffer while I've got a cent."

"The folks don't like to be begging, sir," said Ellen sorrowfully, "but there's lots of them does be in trouble. They'd ought to go away when the mills shut down, but for nobody knows where to go. Farley ain't like them big towns where a man'd pick up something else to do. I says to Mike: 'Come, Mike, let's go up after dark and tark to Dan; he'll help us out if he can,' says I——"

"Sit down, Ellen," said the agent kindly, as the poor woman began to cry. He made her take the armchair which the weave-room girls had given him at Christmas two years before. She sat there covering her face with her hands, and trying to keep back her sobs and go quietly on with what she had to say. Mike was sitting across the room with his back to the wall anxiously twirling his hat round and round. "Yis, we're very bad off," he contrived to say after much futile stammering. "All the folks in the Corporation, but Mr. Dow, has got great bills run up now at the stores, and thim that had money saved has lint to thim that hadn't—'twill be long enough before anybody's free. Whin the mills starts up we'll have to spind for everything at once. The children is very hard on their clothes and they're all dropping to pieces. I thought I'd have everything new for them this spring, they do be growing so. I minds them and patches them the best I can." And again Ellen was overcome by tears. "Mike an' me's always been conthrivin' how would we get something laid up, so if anny one would die or be long sick we'd be equal to it, but we've had great pride to see the little gerrls go looking as well as anny, and we've worked very steady, but there's so manny of us we've had to pay rint for a large tenement and we'd only seventeen dollars and a little more when the shutdown was. Sure the likes of us has a right to earn more than our living, ourselves being so willing-hearted. 'Tis a long time now that Mike's been steady. We always had the pride to hope we'd own a house ourselves, and a pieceen o' land, but

I'm thankful now—'tis as well for us; we've no chances to pay taxes now."

Mike made a desperate effort to speak as his wife faltered and began to cry again, and seeing his distress forgot her own, and supplied the halting words. "He wants to know if there's anny work he could get, some place else than Farley. Himself's been sixteen years now in the picker, first he was one of six and now he is one of the four since you got the new machines, yourself knows it well."

The agent knew about Mike; he looked compassionate as he shook his head. "Stay where you are, for a while at any rate. Things may look a little better, it seems to me. We will start up as soon as anyone does. I'll allow you twenty dollars a month after this; here are ten to start with. No, no, I've got no one depending on me and my pay is going on. I'm glad to share it with my friends. Tell the folks to come up and see me, Ahern and Sullivan and Michel and your brother Con; tell anybody you know who is really in distress. You've all stood by me!"

" 'Tis all the lazy ones 'ould be coming if we told on the poor boy," said Ellen gratefully, as they hurried home. "Ain't he got the good heart? We'd ought to be very discrate, Mike!" and Mike agreed by a most impatient gesture, but by the time summer had begun to wane the agent was a far poorer man than when it had begun. Mike and Ellen Carroll were only the leaders of a sorrowful procession that sought his door evening after evening. Some asked for help who might have done without it, but others were saved from actual want. There were a few men who got work among the farms, but there was little steady work. The agent made the most of odd jobs about the mill yards and contrived somehow or other to give almost every household a lift. The village looked more and more dull and forlorn, but in August, when a traveling show ventured to give a performance in Farley, the Corporation hall was filled as it seldom was filled in prosperous times. This made the agent wonder, until he followed the crowd of workless, sadly idle men and women into the place of entertainment and looked at them with a sudden comprehension that they were spending their last cent for a little cheerfulness.

VI.

The agent was going into the counting-room one day when he met old Father Daley and they stopped for a bit of friendly talk.

"Could you come in for a few minutes, sir?" asked the younger man. "There's nobody in the counting-room."

The busy priest looked up at the weather-beaten clock in the mill tower.

"I can," he said. " 'Tis not so late as I thought. We'll soon be having the mail."

The agent led the way and brought one of the directors' comfortable chairs from their committee-room. Then he spun his own chair face-about from before his desk and they sat down. It was a warm day in the middle of September. The windows were wide open on the side toward the river and there was a flicker of light on the ceiling from the sunny water. The noise of the fall was loud and incessant in the room. Somehow one never noticed it very much when the mills were running.

"How are the Duffys?" asked the agent.

"Very bad," answered the old priest gravely. "The doctor sent for me—he couldn't get them to take any medicine. He says that it isn't typhoid; only a low fever among them from bad food and want of care. That tenement is very old and bad, the drains from the upper tenement have leaked and spoiled the whole west side of the building. I suppose they never told you of it?"

"I did the best I could about it last spring," said the agent. "They were afraid of being turned out and they hid it for that reason. The company allowed me something for repairs as usual and I tried to get more; you see I spent it all before I knew what a summer was before us. Whatever I have done since I have paid for, except what they call legitimate work and care of property. Last year I put all Maple Street into first-rate order—and meant to go right through the Corporation. I've done the best I could," he protested with a bright spot of color in his cheeks. "Some of the men have tinkered up their tenements and I have counted it toward the rent, but they don't all know how to drive a nail."

"'Tis true for you; you have done the best you could," said the priest heartily, and both the men were silent, while the river, which was older than they and had seen a whole race of men disappear before they came—the river took this opportunity to speak louder than ever.

"I think that manufacturing prospects look a little brighter," said the agent, wishing to be cheerful. "There are some good orders out, but of course the buyers can take advantage of our condition. The treasurer writes me that we must be firm about not starting up until we are sure of business on a good paying margin."

"Like last year's?" asked the priest, who was resting himself in the armchair. There was a friendly twinkle in his eyes.

"Like last year's," answered the agent. "I worked like two men, and I pushed the mills hard to make that large profit. I saw there was trouble coming, and I told the directors and asked for a special surplus, but I had no idea of anything like this."

"Nine per cent. in these times was too good a prize," said Father Daley, but the twinkle in his eyes had suddenly disappeared.

"You won't get your new church for a long time yet," said the agent.

"No, no," said the old man impatiently. "I have kept the foundations going as well as I could, and the talk, for their own sakes. It gives them something to think about. I took the money they gave me in collections and let them have it back again for work. 'Tis well to lead their minds," and he gave a quick glance at the agent. "'Tis no pride of mine for church-building and no good credit with the bishop I'm after. Young men can be satisfied with those things, not an old priest like me that prays to be a father to his people."

Father Daley spoke as man speaks to man, straight out of an honest heart.

"I see many things now that I used to be blind about long ago," he said. "You may take a man who comes over, him and his wife. They fall upon good wages and their heads are turned with joy. They've been hungry for generations back and they've always seen those above them who dressed fine and lived soft, and they want a taste of luxury too; they're bound to satisfy themselves. So they'll spend and spend and have beefsteak for dinner every day just because they never had enough before, but they'd turn into wild beasts of selfishness, most of 'em, if they had no check. 'Tis there the church steps in. 'Remember your Maker and do Him honor in His house of prayer,' says she. 'Be self-denying, be thinking of eternity and of what's sure to come!' And you will join with me in believing that it's never those who have given most to the church who come first to the ground in a hard time like this. Show me a good church and I'll show you a thrifty people." Father Daley looked eagerly at the agent for sympathy.

"You speak the truth, sir," said the agent. "Those that give most are always the last to hold out with honest independence and the first to do for others."

"Some priests may have plundered their parishes for pride's sake; there's no saying what is in poor human nature," repeated Father Daley earnestly. "God forgive us all for unprofitable servants of Him and His church. I believe in saying more about prayer and right living, and less about collections, in God's house, but it's the giving hand that's the rich hand all the world over."

"I don't think Ireland has ever sent us over many misers; Saint Patrick must have banished them all with the snakes," suggested the agent with a grim smile. The priest shook his head and laughed a little and then both men were silent again in the counting-room.

The mail train whistled noisily up the road and came into the station at the end of the empty street, then it rang its loud bell and puffed and whistled away again.

"I'll bring your mail over, sir," said the agent, presently. "Sit here and rest yourself until I come back and we'll walk home together."

The leather mail-bag looked thin and flat and the leisurely postmaster had nearly distributed its contents by the time the agent had crossed the street and reached the office. His clerks were both off on a long holiday; they were brothers and were glad of the chance to take their vacations together. They had been on lower pay; there was little to do in the counting-room—hardly anybody's time to keep or even a letter to write.

Two or three loiterers stopped the agent to ask him the usual question if there were any signs of starting up; an old farmer who sat in his long wagon before the post-office asked for news too, and touched his hat with an awkward sort of military salute.

"Come out to our place and stop a few days," he said kindly. "You look kind of pinched up and bleached out, Mr. Agent; you can't be needed much here."

"I wish I could come," said the agent, stopping again and looking up at the old man with a boyish, expectant face. Nobody had happened to think about him in just that way, and he was far from thinking about himself. "I've got to keep an eye on the people that are left here; you see they've had a pretty hard summer."

"Not so hard as you have!" said the old man, as the agent went along the street. "You've never had a day of rest more than once or twice since you were born!"

There were two letters and a pamphlet for Father Daley and a thin handful of circulars for the company. In busy times there was often all the mail matter that a clerk could bring. The agent sat down at his desk in the counting-room and the priest opened a thick foreign letter with evident pleasure. "'Tis from an old friend of mine; he's in a monastery in France," he said. "I only hear from him once a year," and Father Daley settled himself in his armchair to read the close-written pages. As for the agent of the mills, he had quickly opened a letter from the treasurer and was not listening to anything that was said.

Suddenly he whirled round in his desk chair and held out the letter to the priest. His hand shook and his face was as pale as ashes.

"What is it? What's the matter?" cried the startled old man, who had hardly followed the first pious salutations of his own letter to their end. "Read it to me yourself, Dan; is there any trouble?"

"Orders—I've got orders to start up; we're going to start—I wrote them last week——"

But the agent had to spring up from his chair and go to the window next the river before he could steady his voice to speak. He thought it was the look of the moving water that made him dizzy. "We're going to start up the mills as soon as I can get things ready." He turned to look up at the thermometer as if it were the most important thing in the world; then the color rushed to his face and he leaned a moment against the wall.

"Thank God!" said the old priest devoutly. "Here, come and sit down, my boy. "Faith, but it's good news, and I'm the first to get it from you."

They shook hands and were cheerful together; the foreign letter was crammed into Father Daley's pocket, and he reached for his big cane.

"Tell everybody as you go up the street, sir," said Dan. "I've got a hurricane of things to see to; I must go the other way down to the storehouses. Tell them to pass the good news about town as fast as they can; 'twill hearten up the women." All the anxious look had gone as if by magic from the agent's face.

Two weeks from that time the old mill bell stopped tolling for the slow hours of idleness and rang out loud and clear for the housekeepers to get up, and rang for breakfast, and later still for all the people to go in to work. Some of the old hands were gone for good and new ones must be broken in in their places, but there were many familiar faces to pass the counting-room windows into the mill yard. There were French families which had reappeared with surprising promptness, Michel and his pretty daughter were there, and a household of cousins who had come to the next tenement. The agent stood with his hands in his pockets and nodded soberly to one group after another. It seemed to him that he had never felt so happy in his life.

"Jolly-looking set this morning," said one of the clerks whose desk was close beside the window; he was a son of one of the directors, who had sent him to the agent to learn something about manufacturing.

"They've had a bitter hard summer that you know nothing about," said the agent slowly.

Just then Mrs. Kilpatrick and old Mary Cassidy came along, and little Maggie was with them. She had got back her old chance at doffing and the hard times were over. They all smiled with such blissful satisfaction that the agent smiled too, and even waved his hand.

CHRONOLOGY

NOTE ON THE TEXTS

NOTES

Chronology

<table>
<tr><td>1849</td><td>Born September 3 in South Berwick, Maine, second daughter of Caroline F. Perry and Dr. Theodore Herman Jewett and named Theodora Sarah Orne Jewett. (Father, b. 1815, was the son of Sarah Orne Jewett, 1794–1819, and Captain Theodore Furber Jewett, b. 1787, a prosperous South Berwick merchant. Father was educated at Bowdoin and Dartmouth, and in Boston and Philadelphia; he then studied and practiced medicine with Dr. William F. Perry, b. 1788, in Exeter, New Hampshire, and married Caroline Frances Perry, b. 1820, the daughter of Dr. Perry and Abigail Gilman Perry, b. 1789. Their first daughter, Mary Rice Jewett, was born in Exeter on June 18, 1847. The family then moved to South Berwick, where father established a rural medical practice; he will also serve as professor of obstetrics at Bowdoin and publish in national medical journals.) Lives with family in the "great house" of grandfather Jewett, along with her great-grandfather Jewett; Mary, grandfather's third wife; and her uncle, William Durham Jewett (b. 1813).</td></tr>
<tr><td>1850–53</td><td>Use of first name Theodora is soon dropped. Father builds smaller house for family in garden of the "great house."</td></tr>
<tr><td>1854</td><td>Great-grandfather Jewett dies, and in December grandfather's wife, Mary, dies.</td></tr>
<tr><td>1855</td><td>Uncle William Jewett marries Augusta Maria Willard Rice, of Kittery, Maine, in April. Jewett begins to attend local school run by Olive and Mary Esther Raynes. Though sister Mary excels at school, Jewett's grades are average. Enjoys playing marbles and hopscotch, flying kites, and rolling hoops; collects white mice, woodchucks, turtles, insects, and other wild specimens. Sister Caroline Augusta born December 13.</td></tr>
<tr><td>1856</td><td>Grandfather Jewett marries fourth wife, Eliza Sewall.</td></tr>
<tr><td>1857</td><td>Enjoys skating and sledding, despite being ill often in winter. Father encourages outdoor activities, hoping they will improve her health. Aunt Augusta dies.</td></tr>
</table>

1858   Spends summer with Perry grandparents in Exeter, New
            Hampshire, and attends local school. Enjoys listening to
            sea stories told by old captains who visit with grandfather
            Jewett at home and in the large general store he owns.

1860   Grandfather Jewett dies January 23; uncle William Jewett
            inherits the "great house" and continues to live there.
            Grandmother Perry dies February 11.

1861–65   Enters Berwick Academy in fall 1861, where sister Mary is
            already enrolled. Class consists of eight boys and four
            girls. Begins to experience severe attacks of rheumatism
            which will plague her for the rest of her life. In order to
            give her some healthy outdoor exercise, her father fre-
            quently takes her out of school to join him on the rounds
            of his rural practice. He teaches her the names of plants
            and animals, and talks to her about her reading, which
            includes Sterne's *Sentimental Journey*, Milton's "L'Alle-
            gro," Tennyson's *Poems*, and Matthew Arnold's "The
            Scholar-Gipsy." On her mother's and grandmother's ad-
            vice reads Jane Austen's *Pride and Prejudice*, George Eliot's
            Scenes of Clerical Life, books by Margaret Oliphant, and
            Harriet Beecher Stowe's Maine novel, *The Pearl of Orr's
            Island* (Jewett will later remember "the exquisite flavor
            and reality of delight that it gave me"). With family, visits
            Exeter relatives often, and during summers goes to the
            shore at Wells, Portsmouth, and Kittery, Maine. Enjoys
            horseback riding in the country.

1866–67   Graduates from Berwick Academy in 1866 and considers
            becoming a doctor, but decides against it because of her
            health; grandfather's wealth frees her from financial pres-
            sure either to support herself or to marry. Visits growing
            number of friends in Newport, Rhode Island, New York
            City, and especially in Boston.

1868   First published story, "Jenny Garrow's Lovers," appears in
            The Flag of Our Union, a Boston periodical, in January,
            signed "A. C. Eliot." Submits two stories in June and
            August to the *Atlantic Monthly*, but both are rejected.
            During winter visits family of maternal uncle John Taylor
            Perry, in Cincinnati, Ohio, where Perry is an editorial
            writer and part-owner of the *Cincinnati Gazette*; takes

classes in painting and dancing and participates in local social activities.

1869   Returns home from Cincinnati in April, accompanied by grandfather Perry. Third story submitted to the *Atlantic*, "Mr. Bruce," is accepted by assistant editor William Dean Howells, and appears in the December number under the name A. C. Eliot; Jewett is paid $50. Enjoys reading Louisa May Alcott's *Little Women* and Hans Christian Andersen's fairy tales. Writes stories for children under the names Alice Eliot and A. C. Eliot that soon appear regularly in a variety of national magazines. Reads George Sand, Dickens, Elizabeth Barrett Browning, Goethe, and Elizabeth Stuart Phelps (author of *The Gates Ajar*). Writes in her diary: "So ends 1869 the happiest year I think I ever had . . . "

1870   Jewett and her sister Mary are baptized and confirmed in St. John's Episcopal Church in Portsmouth, New Hampshire, in November; continues to attend Congregational First Parish Church in South Berwick. Teaches Sunday school for more than a year.

1871   Meets William Dean Howells, now the chief editor of the *Atlantic Monthly*, and he invites her to his home in Cambridge; may have also met at this time James T. Fields, the *Atlantic*'s influential publisher and former editor, and his wife, Annie Adams Fields (b. 1834).

1872   Reads histories of England and other countries. Tries translating a French novel. Pleased that Howells has accepted "The Shore House" (first story set in fictional Maine seaport town of "Deephaven"), but is disappointed that publication is delayed (appears in the *Atlantic* September 1873). While at Wells, Maine, meets and becomes friends with Theophilus Parsons, retired Harvard law professor and leader of the New Church in Boston; they become frequent correspondents and Parsons interests her in writings by and about the Swedish theologian Emmanuel Swedenborg. Continues to exchange visits with a growing number of women, many of whom remain lifelong friends; goes to Boston and Cambridge, to see Ellen Mason, Grace Gordon, Cora Clark (who later marries John Rice), and Lilian and Cornelia Horsford, and to Newport, where through Ellen Mason, who has a summer home there, she has met Sarah Chauncey Woolsey, Susan Travers, and Kate Birckhead (who becomes a particularly close friend at this time).

1873   Takes lessons in music and German. Writes to Horace Scudder, who had earlier accepted some of her stories as editor of the short-lived *Riverside Magazine for Young People* (1867–70): "I am getting quite ambitious and really feel that writing is my work—my business perhaps; and it is so much better than making a mere amusement of it as I used." Often asks Scudder for advice and criticism on her work. Occasionally writes poems, publishing a few in journals.

1874–75   Visits Chicago and the Oneida Indian Reservation in Wisconsin. "Deephaven Cronies" published in *Atlantic*, September 1875.

1876   Visits the Centennial Exposition in Philadelphia in early summer. Enjoys country walks and drives, rowing on the Piscataqua River, and occasional visits to the shore. Meets and begins close two-year friendship with Harriet Waters Preston of Newburyport, Massachusetts, author, translator, and critic for the *Atlantic* (friendship is disrupted for unknown reasons). "Deephaven Excursions" published in September *Atlantic*. With Howells' advice and encouragement, works on expanding and revising Deephaven stories for book publication.

1877   Pleased with the design of first book, *Deephaven*, published by James R. Osgood and Company in April. Receives letter from John Greenleaf Whittier in July highly praising it (their friendship continues until his death in 1892). Visits relatives in Brunswick, Maine, and takes trip to Orrs Island. With part of proceeds from sales of *Deephaven*, buys a horse, which she names Sheila; goes by carriage as far as Exeter, New Hampshire, to visit aunts and grandfather, and Amesbury, Massachusetts, to see Whittier.

1878   Goes to Washington, D.C., in February for two-month visit with Mary Bucklin Davenport Claflin and her husband, Massachusetts congressman (and former governor)

William Claflin. Goes to many social functions, meets Abraham Lincoln's son Robert, and attends reception given by President Rutherford B. Hayes. *Play Days; A Book of Stories for Children*, published by Houghton, Osgood and Company (successor to James R. Osgood and Company), collects pieces that appeared between 1870 and 1878 in the journals *St. Nicholas*, *The Independent*, *The Riverside Magazine*, and *Sunday Afternoon*. Father dies of a sudden heart attack on September 20 during a visit to White Mountains of New Hampshire with mother and sister Mary.

1879   Collection of seven stories for adults, *Old Friends and New*, published by Houghton, Osgood and Company; except for "Lady Ferry," which was rejected by Howells when Jewett submitted it to the *Atlantic*, the stories had all previously appeared in periodicals from 1869 to 1879. Attends in December belated "Breakfast" party given by the *Atlantic* in honor of Oliver Wendell Holmes' 70th birthday; guests include Howells, Whittier, Charles Dudley Warner (co-author with Mark Twain of *The Gilded Age*), Mark Twain, Ralph Waldo Emerson, Julia Ward Howe, and Harriet Beecher Stowe.

1880   Suffers increasingly during winter from rheumatic pain in joints and head. Attempts, unsuccessfully, to persuade Henry Mills Alden, editor of *Harper's Magazine*, to reconsider accepting "An October Ride," one of her favorite stories, saying that it belongs with the already accepted story "An Autumn Holiday." Visits James and Annie Fields in September at their summer home, Gambrel Cottage, on Thunderbolt Hill in Manchester, Massachusetts, on the north shore of Massachusetts Bay. During stay goes with Annie Fields to visit poet Celia Thaxter, a good friend of Whittier, at her home on Appledore Island in the Isles of Shoals off Portsmouth, New Hampshire. From Manchester, goes to Rhode Island to visit Cora Clark Rice at Little Compton and Ellen Mason at Newport.

1881   Howells is succeeded as editor of *Atlantic Monthly* by Thomas Bailey Aldrich, with whom Jewett is also on friendly social terms. Jewett visits New York with Annie Fields in February. Attends, with Oliver Wendell Holmes, Howells, and Aldrich, a small private dinner in Cambridge, Massachusetts, given by publisher H. O. Hough-ton in honor of Henry Wadsworth Longfellow's 74th birthday. James T. Fields dies on April 24. Jewett spends the following winter with Annie Fields at her Boston home, 148 Charles Street. (Annie Fields, a poet and writer herself, remains an intimate friend of many of the authors and artists who have visited her home and of those she has met during trips abroad with her husband, including Ten-nyson and Browning; she is also active in various Boston charities.) *Country By-Ways*, a collection of nine sketches, is published by Houghton, Mifflin and Company (succes-sor to Houghton, Osgood), dedicated "To T. H. J., my dear father; my dear friend; the best and wisest man I ever knew; who taught me many lessons and showed me many things as we went together along the Country By-Ways." (All of the sketches, with the exception of "An October Ride," had appeared in periodicals from 1879 to 1881.)

1882   Jewett and Fields sail for Europe in late May. Whittier commemorates their departure with a sonnet, "God-speed," in honor of "my friends Annie Fields and Sarah Orne Jewett." Tours Ireland, England, Norway, Belgium, France, Switzerland, and Italy (where she renews friend-ship with Harriet Preston and witnesses pageantry and fireworks in Venice in honor of the Queen of Italy). Jewett and Fields visit Fields' friends, including Charles Reade (who takes them on a tour of Oxford), Tennyson, at his home on the Isle of Wight, Anne Thackeray Ritchie (Thackeray's daughter), and the family of Charles Dick-ens. They return to America in October and live at 148 Charles Street during the winter. (Over the next 20 years, with few exceptions, Jewett will spend spring in South Berwick, summer with Fields in Manchester, autumn in South Berwick, and winter with Fields at 148 Charles Street, where the two women entertain many friends and literary figures; she will also continue to make shorter vis-its to other friends.) Jewett and Fields begin practice of reading poetry and other literary works to each other.

1883   Continues writing, following established pattern of an-swering letters in the morning and working on stories in the afternoon. Does most of her writing in the "great house" in South Berwick. After day's work often goes for long walks, drives, or horseback rides. Vacations with Fields at Manchester and in July, with Whittier on Asquam Lake, Holderness, New Hampshire (they will return there in July 1884). Matthew Arnold makes extended stay at Manchester and 148 Charles Street during his October 1883–March 1884 lecture tour of the United States.

1884   *The Mate of the Daylight, and Friends Ashore*, collection of eight stories, published by Houghton, Mifflin, dedicated to "A. F." (Annie Fields). Contains one previously unpublished story, "Miss Debby's Neighbors," and seven stories that appeared in journals from 1880 to 1883. In April, Jewett and Fields visit Moravian settlement at Bethlehem, Pennsylvania. Visits Stowe in Hartford with Fields. Visits with great-aunts at Little Boar's Head near Rye, New Hampshire. Sees much of the Howells family, who are vacationing in nearby Kennebunkport, Maine. Novel *A Country Doctor* published by Houghton, Mifflin. Reads the last volume of Dickens' letters with great interest (will continue to read published letters throughout her life). Along with Fields, Celia Thaxter, and Mary Greenwood Lodge (Mrs. James Lodge), participates in séance with medium Rose Darrah.

1885   Corresponds with Marie Thérèse de Solms Blanc-Bentzon (pen name "Th. Bentzon"), French novelist and advocate of American literature who has translated works by Bret Harte and Mark Twain and written a long review of *A Country Doctor* in the February *Revue des Deux Mondes*. Novel *A Marsh Island* serialized in the *Atlantic* from January through June, then published by Houghton, Mifflin. Spends part of summer with sister Mary on Isles of Shoals; visits with Celia Thaxter. Author Mary Murfree (writer of tales about the Tennessee mountains under name Charles Egbert Craddock) visits Fields and Jewett in Manchester. Jewett visits with Whittier both in Danvers, Massachusetts, where he now lives most of the year, and Amesbury during his stays there.

1886   Continues to suffer severe rheumatic pains during winter. *A White Heron and Other Stories* published by Houghton, Mifflin, dedicated "To My Dear Sister Mary." Contains two stories never published before ("A White Heron" and

"The Gray Man" were rejected by Aldrich when Jewett submitted them to the *Atlantic*) and seven that appeared in periodicals between 1884 and 1886. Stays in South Berwick in July because of mother's worsening health. Travels in August and December to Richfield Springs, spa in New York State (goes there frequently to help ease her rheumatism). Through Fields, becomes friends with James Russell Lowell, who introduces her to Donne's poetry.

1887   Grandfather Perry dies January 11. *The Story of the Normans, told chiefly in relation to their Conquest of England*, a popular history for children, published in New York by G. P. Putnam's Sons, dedicated "To my dear grandfather, Doctor William Perry, of Exeter." Helps raise money in April to aid indigent Walt Whitman. Following the death of uncle William Jewett, moves with sister Mary and mother into the "great house," while sister Caroline, her husband Edwin Eastman, and their son Theodore (born August 4, 1879), move into the smaller house in the garden. Reads Thackeray's *Pendennis* and considers it far greater than Tolstoy's *Anna Karenina*. Publishes autobiographical essay, "My School Days," in the *Berwick Scholar* in October. Acts as secretary to committee arranging reading by various authors in the Boston Museum for the benefit of the Longfellow Memorial Fund.

1888   Reads *Katia*, story by Tolstoy and writes to Fields: "I never felt the soul of Tolstoi's work until last night." Travels with Fields in March to Aiken, South Carolina, Sea Island, Georgia, and then St. Augustine, Florida. *The King of Folly Island and Other People* published by Houghton, Mifflin, designed by friend Sarah Wyman Whitman and dedicated with "grateful affection" to Whittier. Contains one new story and seven that had been published in magazines from 1886 to 1888. Saddened by death of Matthew Arnold.

1889   Spends more time with ailing mother in South Berwick while sister Mary travels in Europe for five months. Visits artist friend Helen Bigelow Merriman at Stonehurst at Intervale, New Hampshire, in the White Mountains. Visits Alice Longfellow (daughter of Henry Wadsworth Longfellow) in July at Mouse Island in Boothbay Harbor, Maine; this is her first visit to the region she will later call the "country of the pointed firs." Goes rowing and sailing, and is impressed with Alice's strength and athletic skill. Howells and daughter Mildred visit Manchester in July. Houghton, Mifflin publishes *Betty Leicester, A Story for Girls* in December (it is dated 1890).

1890   In February Jewett and Fields travel to St. Augustine, Florida. Aldrich resigns as editor of *Atlantic Monthly* and is succeeded in April by Jewett's longtime adviser, Horace Scudder. *Tales of New England* is published by Houghton, Mifflin in May, containing eight stories that had been collected in earlier volumes ("A Lost Lover," "An Only Son," "The Dulham Ladies," "Marsh Rosemary," "A White Heron," "Miss Tempy's Watchers," "Law Lane" and "The Courting of Sister Wisby"). Remains at home in South Berwick most of the summer because of mother's failing health. *Strangers and Wayfarers*, published in November by Houghton, Mifflin, collects 11 stories that had appeared in periodicals from 1888 to 1890. The volume is dedicated "To S. W., Painter of New England men and women, New England fields and shores" (Sarah Wyman Whitman, a founder of Radcliffe College, a painter and book illustrator who designed four of Jewett's books, and a designer of stained glass windows).

1891   Reads Flaubert's *Madame Bovary* and writes to Fields: "It is quite wonderful how great a book he makes of it. People talk about dwelling upon trivialities and commonplaces in life, but a master-writer gives everything weight and makes you feel the distinction and importance of it, and counts it upon the right or the wrong side of life's account." Stays home in South Berwick to help care for mother, making only short trips away. Helps arrange centennial celebration of the founding of Berwick Academy in July. James Russell Lowell dies on August 12; Jewett writes to Fields, "How I treasure the last time I saw him, and the fringe tree in bloom . . . and he and I talking on and on, and I thinking he was really going to be better, in spite of the look about his face!" Mother dies after a long illness on October 21. Around this time Jewett writes to Fields: "Sometimes, the business part of writing grows very noxious to me, and I wonder if in heaven our best thoughts—poet's thoughts, especially—will not be flowers, somehow, or some sort of beautiful live things that stand about and grow, and don't have to be chaffered over and bought and sold." With Fields, visits Whittier on his 84th birthday December 17 (Whittier dies in September 1892).

1892   Publishes autobiographical essay, "Looking Back on Girlhood," in January *Youth's Companion*. Jewett and Fields leave for Europe in February, sailing with Robert Underwood Johnson, editor of New York's *Century Magazine*, and his wife, Katharine. Learns shortly after arriving in Rome that brother-in-law Edwin Eastman has died of peritonitis. Sees Mark Twain and his family in Venice, and in Paris visits Thérèse Blanc-Bentzon, with whom she has long corresponded. Goes to Aix-les-Bains in June. Spends July in the Barbizon area near Fontainebleau, where one of her favorite artists, Jean Françoise Millet, had lived. In England visits, among others, Mrs. Humphry Ward, the family of Matthew Arnold, George du Maurier, and Tennyson, whom she sees only a few months before his death (Jewett later writes that "he was far and away the greatest man I have ever seen"). Returns to America in October.

1893   Attends funeral in January of Phillips Brooks, Episcopal Bishop of Massachusetts, whom she had long admired. Rereads with pleasure Edward Fitzgerald's letters; particularly enjoys reading letters of Voltaire, George Sand, William and Dorothy Wordsworth, the Carlyles and Madame de Sévigné. By February, has completed five new stories. Visits World's Columbian Exposition in Chicago in April with Fields, sister Caroline, nephew Theodore, and old friend Sarah Woolsey, who, under the pen name "Susan Coolidge," has become a well-known author of children's stories (Jewett and Fields visit her annually at Newport). Thérèse Blanc-Bentzon, on a tour of United States, stays at 148 Charles Street. *A Native of Winby and Other Tales* published by Houghton, Mifflin, dedicated "To my dear younger sister, C. A. E. I have had many pleasures that were doubled because you shared them, and so I write your name at the beginning of this book. —S. O. J., August ninth, 1893." Volume contains one new story, "Miss Esther's Guest," and eight that had been published in periodicals from 1890 to 1893. In October, visits Forbes family at Naushon, island off Cape Cod owned by John Murray Forbes, for a few days before traveling to Manchester. Ill in November.

1894   Jewett, sister Mary, and Fields invite Oliver Wendell Holmes and Mark Twain to dinner at 148 Charles Street. Donates a memorial window designed by her friend Sarah Wyman Whitman to Berwick Academy, in honor of the young men from Berwick who would have been her schoolmates if they had not instead had to leave for service in the Civil War. Visits with Celia Thaxter on the Isles of Shoals. While in Richfield Springs, New York, for rheumatic treatment in August, receives telegram informing her of Thaxter's sudden death. *Betty Leicester's English Xmas*, a children's story, is printed privately in December by Dodd, Mead & Company of New York, for the Bryn Mawr School of Baltimore, one of whose founders is close friend Mary Elizabeth Garrett (story later serialized in *St. Nicholas*, Dec. 1895–Feb. 1896; issued by Houghton, Mifflin in slightly different form as *Betty Leicester's Christmas*, 1899). Suffers bout of pneumonia in winter.

1895   Unable to write as illness persists. Prepares and writes preface for *Stories and Poems for Children*, posthumous volume of Celia Thaxter's work (later writes preface to Appledore Edition of *The Poems of Celia Thaxter*, published in 1896). Jewett and Fields visit Lilian and Thomas Bailey Aldrich at Tenants Harbor on Maine coast in July; return to region in September for a month's rest in Martinsville. Jewett describes the area in letter as "all among the 'pointed firs.'" *The Life of Nancy*, a collection of ten stories, published by Houghton, Mifflin; all had appeared in periodicals from 1893 to 1895. Becomes ill in early December with symptoms of pneumonia.

1896   Jewett, Fields, and the Aldriches sail to the Caribbean on steam yacht, *Hermione*, owned by Henry L. Pierce, former mayor of Boston. After stopping at Nassau, Haiti, and Jamaica, Jewett and Fields travel to Florida, visiting Palm Beach and St. Augustine. Attends funeral of Harriet Beecher Stowe in Hartford in July. Rereads *The Pearl of Orr's Island*, and writes to Fields that she finds the beginning "classical—historical" and regrets that Stowe could not finish it in the same way, "but a woman made like Mrs. Stowe cannot bring herself to that cold selfishness of the moment for one's work's sake, and the recompense for her loss is a divine touch here and there in an incomplete piece of work." Attends memorial service given by Charles Eliot Norton in Ashfield, Massachusetts, in honor of author George William Curtis, whom Jewett and Fields often visited. Takes yacht cruise with nephew down the Maine coast in late August. *The Country of the Pointed Firs* (serialized in the *Atlantic* in four parts: Jan., March, July, and Sept.) is published in November by Houghton, Mifflin and dedicated to her friend of many years, Alice Greenwood Howe (Mrs. George D. Howe). In addition to enthusiastic reviews, she receives letters of praise for the novel from many friends including William James, Thomas Wentworth Higginson, and Rudyard Kipling (who ends his letter: "I don't believe even you know how good that work is!").

1897   Goes in March to Hot Springs, Virginia, with Fields, who has been ill. Sister Caroline Jewett Eastman dies of heart failure April 1, following surgery to treat an internal abscess. Sister Mary becomes guardian of nephew Theodore, who enters Harvard in the fall (he later will study and practice medicine). Hears William James speak at the unveiling of Augustus Saint-Gaudens' memorial relief in honor of Robert Gould Shaw and the 54th Massachusetts Regiment. Thérèse Blanc-Bentzon, on another American tour, stays with Jewett in South Berwick in June; they visit the Shaker community at Alfred, Maine (later visits the Shaker community in Canterbury, N.H.). Makes several visits to great-aunts in Exeter, New Hampshire.

1898   With Fields and old friend Susan Travers, sails for Europe in April. After stopping briefly in England, goes on to France; explores Provence in May, making a special "pilgrimage" to places Madame de Sévigné had lived during her last years. Meets Violet Paget, a British author who publishes as "Vernon Lee," and in June visits Thérèse Blanc-Bentzon at her country home in La Ferté sous Jouarre, east of Paris. Travels to Brittany in July to continue her Madame de Sévigné "pilgrimage," then joins Mary Jewett and Theodore Eastman in Paris. Visits in England, among others, Mrs. Humphry Ward, Edward Garnett, Rudyard Kipling, and (at Lamb House in Rye, Sussex) Henry James; also visits Haworth, in Yorkshire, where the Brontë family had lived ("a dreadfully sad old village"). Horace Scudder retires as editor of *Atlantic* and is succeeded by Walter Hines Page (Page leaves after one year; his successor, Bliss Perry, edits the magazine for the rest of Jewett's life).

1899   Makes visits in summer to relatives in Brunswick, Maine, to Alice Longfellow on Mouse Island, and to Susan Burley Cabot (an elderly friend whom Jewett visits for several weeks at her homes in Beverly, Massachusetts, and Boston every year). *The Queen's Twin and Other Stories* published by Houghton, Mifflin, with cover designed by Sarah Wyman Whitman, and dedication to Susan Burley Cabot. The volume contains eight stories published in periodicals or newspapers from 1895 to 1899. Charles Dudley Warner, during a visit to Berwick, urges Jewett to undertake a full-fledged historical novel dealing with Berwick during the American Revolution; she initially resists, writing to Scudder in December: "I have a great reluctance before the thought of turning aside into a new road."

1900   Sails for Europe in March with Fields and Mary Garrett; visits Pompeii in Italy, spends a month in Athens, Greece, and environs, makes a brief visit to Constantinople, and visits Thérèse Blanc-Bentzon in France. Returns in early June. "The Foreigner" published in August *Atlantic* (it is never collected by Jewett). Publication in Paris of Thérèse Blanc-Bentzon's translation of *A Country Doctor* (*Le Roman de la Femme-Médecin*) and nine stories (*Récits de la Nouvelle Angleterre*). Appointed a member of the examining committee by the Boston Public Library to report on the library's holdings. Historical romance, *The Tory Lover*, begins serialization in the *Atlantic* in November (continues through Aug. 1901).

1901   Works steadily to finish *The Tory Lover*. "I can see the wide difference there is between it and the *Pointed Firs*, for instance," Jewett writes to Katharine McMahon Johnson, wife of the editor of *Century Magazine*, in February. "One can't get the same immediate hold. It is certainly a dangerous thing to try to write something entirely different after one has been for years and years making stories as short and round as possible but I have long had a dream of doing this, as you know, and I suppose I had to do it." In

June, becomes the first woman to receive an honorary
Litt.D. from Bowdoin College. Commissions Sarah Wyman Whitman to design a stained glass window for Bowdoin College in memory of her father. Visits Alice
Longfellow at Holderness in the White Mountains. Sees
the Howells family when they vacation in York Harbor in
the summer. *The Tory Lover* is published by Houghton,
Mifflin in September and dedicated to her nephew, Theodore Jewett Eastman. The book receives good reviews
and sells well, though a number of friends (including
Henry James) urge Jewett to return to her more characteristic mode. In December Julia Ward Howe makes one of
her visits to Jewett and sister Mary at South Berwick.

1902   Meets and becomes friends with English poet Alice Meynell when she visits America in spring. On September 3,
her 53rd birthday, Jewett is thrown from carriage when
horse slips and falls; suffers spinal concussion which results in recurrent headaches and weakness; never recovers
sufficiently to return to writing. ("It is strange," she writes
to Sarah Wyman Whitman a year later, "how all that
strange machinery that writes, seems broken and confused.") John Tucker, the Jewetts' servant and friend of 30
years, dies in December.

1903   Annie Fields begins to recover in February from a stroke
that had partially paralyzed her. Jewett elected to the
Maine Historical Society with two other women; they are
the first women included in the membership. Finds recovery from accident very slow; writes to Dr. S. Weir Mitchell
in October that "I have either been staying in bed very
' Dumpy' and confined or creeping out into the garden
with a stick—walking zig-zag and swaying about (no co-ordination to speak of!) pain in my head, thickening of
meningeal tissue and all the rest."

1904   Visits Fields in Boston in February. "A Spring Sunday"
appears in May *McClure's*. Because of headaches and dizziness resulting from her accident, Jewett is largely confined
to the "great house" in South Berwick, and is forbidden to
read or write. Sarah Wyman Whitman dies in June. Accompanied by nurse, Jewett stays at Stonehurst, Helen
Merriman's house at Intervale in the White Mountains,
and later in the summer goes to Manchester. Visitors to

her home in South Berwick include Sara Norton, daughter of Charles Eliot Norton, who has become a close friend, and Howells, who has purchased a house nearby in Kittery Point, Maine. In December, feeling slightly better, goes to stay with Fields in Boston.

1905   Visited in South Berwick by Henry James and Howells in June. Goes alone to Poland Spring, Maine, in September in attempt to regain strength.

1906   Helps friend Frances (Mrs. Henry) Parkman edit *The Letters of Sarah Wyman Whitman*, and contributes short preface (published 1907). Still unable to write fiction, spends winter in Boston with Fields. Pleased to read appreciations of her stories by Newton, Massachusetts, high school students.

1907   Saddened by death of Thérèse Blanc-Bentzon on February 5. Thomas Bailey Aldrich dies on March 19. Vacations in July with sister and Mary Cabot Wheelwright and her parents at Mount Desert, Maine, and enjoys cruises on their yacht, *Hesper*, before going to Manchester. Birthday party in September given by Fields at Manchester includes Howells as guest (Jewett, according to Howells, calls it her "180th").

1908   Spends almost entire year with Fields. In March, Alice (Mrs. Louis) Brandeis introduces Willa Cather, visiting Boston on an assignment from *McClure's Magazine*, to Jewett and Fields; a friendship is formed immediately and Jewett, for the remaining year of her life, acts as Cather's literary mentor. (Jewett later writes to her: "your vivid exciting companionship in the office must not be your audience, you must find your own quiet centre of life, and write from that to the world that holds offices, and all society, all Bohemia; the city, the country—in short, you must write to the human heart, the great consciousness that all humanity goes to make up. Otherwise what might be strength in a writer is only crudeness, and what might be insight is only observation.") Delighted when Mrs. Humphry Ward and her daughter Dorothy visit in spring. With sister Mary, goes on two week-long cruises with Edith Emerson Forbes (daughter of Ralph Waldo Emerson and wife of William Forbes) on her yacht, *Merlin*, along the Maine coast. Willa Cather visits Fields and Jewett at Manchester. "The Gloucester Mother" appears in the October *McClure's*. Attends funeral on October 23 of Charles Eliot Norton. Writes to Howells: "And I thought that you in your friendship and I in mine with dear Mr. Norton know something together and hold them with dear love and gratitude for our very own that many of the old Cambridge neighbours, and cousins of varying degrees could never know. . . . How he said things about our stories—how he *didn't* say things; how quick his letters came when we were in trouble, how sure we were that he understood why some happy days and hours were so happy!" Elected a trustee of the Maine Society for the Prevention of Cruelty to Animals.

1909   Reads "The Hiltons' Holiday" to audience of 150 women students at Boston's Simmons College in January. Continues to enjoy reading Henry James's short stories, in particular "The Way It Came," "The Liar," and "The Jolly Corner." Suffers a severe stroke in March, which leaves her mind clear but the left side of her body paralyzed; she is taken by special railroad car from Boston to South Berwick, where she is confined to a wheelchair. Howells visits her in South Berwick on April 25 and finds her "smiling and joking" despite her paralysis. On May 20, writes to Annie Fields: "Dear, I do not know what to do with me!" Suffers another severe stroke on June 24; dies from cerebral hemorrhage at 6:40 P.M. in the house in which she had been born. After service in parlor of Jewett house, read by George Lewis, old friend and pastor of the First Parish Congregational Church, she is buried in the family plot in the Portland Street Cemetery.

Note on the Texts

This volume contains three novels by Sarah Orne Jewett, *Deephaven*, *A Country Doctor*, and *The Country of the Pointed Firs*, as well as a selection of 28 stories and sketches. Four of the short stories continue the story of *The Country of the Pointed Firs* and are placed in a separate section immediately following that novel. The short pieces are otherwise arranged in chronological order.

Deephaven had its beginning in three sketches Jewett published in the *Atlantic Monthly*: "The Shore House" (Sept. 1873); "Deephaven Cronies" (Sept. 1875); and "Deephaven Excursions" (Sept. 1876). With the encouragement of William Dean Howells, editor of the *Atlantic*, she revised, rearranged, and expanded the sketches for book publication. The novel was published in Boston by James R. Osgood and Company in April 1877, and reprinted from the same plates at least five times. An illustrated edition was prepared in 1894 with a few minor revisions in wording and punctuation, many of which may have been made by an editor or typesetter. The text printed here is that of the first edition.

A Country Doctor, published in Boston and New York by Houghton, Mifflin and Company in September 1884, was never serialized; no other edition appeared during Jewett's lifetime. The text printed here is that of the first edition.

The Country of the Pointed Firs was serialized in four parts in the *Atlantic* (Jan., March, July, and Sept. 1896). Jewett revised, expanded, and added chapter titles for book publication. Houghton, Mifflin and Company published the book in Boston and New York in November 1896. This edition went through several printings, but though Jewett wrote four additional stories using the same fictional town, Dunnet Landing, and the same characters, she did not include these later stories in the book. The text printed here is that of the first edition.

The four Dunnet Landing stories appear here in the order in which they were written. "The Queen's Twin" and "A Dunnet Shepherdess" appeared first in the *Atlantic* (Feb. and Dec. 1899), and were then revised for inclusion in *The Queen's Twin and Other Tales*, published in Boston and New York by Houghton, Mifflin and Company in 1899. The texts printed here are those of the book edition. The other two stories were never collected in a book by Jewett. The text of "The Foreigner" published in the *Atlantic* (Aug. 1900) is printed here. "William's Wedding," left unfinished, was published posthumously in the *Atlantic* (Aug. 1910), and that text is printed here.

Posthumous editions of *The Country of the Pointed Firs*, prepared by others, included these last stories as part of the book; but since Jewett herself never did, the four stories are published in a separate section in this volume.

Most of the other 24 stories and sketches selected for inclusion in this volume appeared first in periodical form and then were slightly revised by Jewett for inclusion in her collections of short stories. The texts printed here are taken from the collections, which were usually published soon after the pieces appeared in periodicals. Three of the stories and sketches were published only in book form, and two had their only appearance in periodicals. Five stories, "The Dulham Ladies," "Marsh Rosemary," "A White Heron," "Miss Tempy's Watchers," and "The Town Poor," were slightly revised after their first book appearances for inclusion in *Tales of New England* (1890), but because many, though not all, of these revisions appear to have been made by editors and typesetters, the texts of the first book publication are printed here. The following is a list of the stories and sketches, giving their periodical publication dates as well as the title of the book used as the source for the text in this edition. All of Jewett's collections of stories were published by Houghton, Mifflin and Company.

"An Autumn Holiday" (*Harper's Magazine*, Oct. 1880), *Country By-Ways*, 1881.

"From a Mournful Villager" (*Atlantic Monthly*, Nov. 1881), *Country By-Ways*, 1881.

"An October Ride," *Country By-Ways*, 1881.

"Tom's Husband" (*Atlantic Monthly*, Feb. 1882), *The Mate of the Daylight, and Friends Ashore*, 1884.

"Miss Debby's Neighbors," *The Mate of the Daylight, and Friends Ashore*, 1884.

"The Dulham Ladies" (*Atlantic Monthly*, Apr. 1886), *A White Heron and Other Stories*, 1886.

"Marsh Rosemary" (*Atlantic Monthly*, May 1886), *A White Heron and Other Stories*, 1886.

"A White Heron," *A White Heron and Other Stories*, 1886.

"Miss Tempy's Watchers" (*Atlantic Monthly*, March 1888), *The King of Folly Island and Other People*, 1888.

"A Winter Courtship" (*Atlantic Monthly*, Feb. 1889), *Strangers and Wayfarers*, 1890.

"Going to Shrewsbury" (*Atlantic Monthly*, July 1889), *Strangers and Wayfarers*, 1890.

"The White Rose Road" (*Atlantic Monthly*, Sept. 1889), *Strangers and Wayfarers*, 1890.

"The Town Poor" (*Atlantic Monthly*, July 1890), *Strangers and Way-farers*, 1890.

"A Native of Winby" (*Atlantic Monthly*, May 1891), *A Native of Winby and Other Tales*, 1893.

"Looking Back on Girlhood," *Youth's Companion*, January 7, 1892.

"The Passing of Sister Barsett" (*Cosmopolitan*, May 1892), *A Native of Winby and Other Tales*, 1893.

"Decoration Day" (*Harper's Magazine*, June 1892), *A Native of Winby and Other Tales*, 1893.

"The Flight of Betsey Lane" (*Scribner's Magazine*, Aug. 1893), *A Native of Winby and Other Tales*, 1893.

"The Hiltons' Holiday" (*Century Magazine*, Sept. 1893), *The Life of Nancy*, 1895.

"The Only Rose" (*Atlantic Monthly*, Jan. 1894), *The Life of Nancy*, 1895.

"The Guests of Mrs. Timms" (*Century Magazine*, Feb. 1894), *The Life of Nancy*, 1895.

"Aunt Cynthy Dallett" (*Harper's Bazaar*, Jan. 11, 1896, titled "The New-Year Guests"), *The Queen's Twin and Other Tales*, 1899.

"Martha's Lady" (*Atlantic Monthly*, Oct. 1897), *The Queen's Twin and Other Tales*, 1899.

"The Gray Mills of Farley," *Cosmopolitan Magazine*, June 1898.

This volume presents the texts of the original printings chosen for inclusion here but does not attempt to reproduce features of their typographic design, such as display capitalization of chapter openings. The texts are printed without change, except for the correction of typographical errors. Spelling, punctuation, and capitalization are often expressive features, and they are not altered, even when inconsistent or irregular. The following is a list of typographical errors corrected, cited by page and line number: 29.7–8, "The . . . blessed"; 36.33, surveyor's; 121.17, life?; 157.27, we' ve; 162.30, When; 163.17, I' d; 165.18, now."; 185.28, Jack-in-the box; 224.34, ancestors; 428.21, 'o; 435.22, word.; 451.19, wont; 458.4, trying'; 477.37, kind' o; 508.20, some; 532.2, aint; 673.3, creaturs; 677.30, villages; 702.24 em'; 703.26, strangers."; 705.11, thrif'less?; 706.25, gone."; 714.6, sterness; 755.10, seventeeth; 756.1, plank; 829.22, most; 834.36, wan't; 875.27, Why Martha.

Notes

In the notes below, the reference numbers denote page and line of the present volume (the line count includes story titles or chapter headings). No note is made for material included in standard desk-reference books such as Webster's *Ninth New Collegiate, Biographical*, and *Geographical* dictionaries. For further background and biographical information, see *The Letters of Sarah Orne Jewett* (Boston: Houghton, Mifflin, 1911), ed. Annie Fields; *Sarah Orne Jewett Letters* (Waterville, Maine: Colby College Press, 1967), ed. Richard Cary; Richard Cary, *Sarah Orne Jewett* (New York: Twayne Publishers, Inc., 1962); Josephine Donovan, *Sarah Orne Jewett* (New York: Frederick Ungar Publishing Co., 1980); John Eldridge Frost, *Sarah Orne Jewett* (Kittery Point, Maine: The Gundalow Club, 1960); F. O. Matthiessen, *Sarah Orne Jewett* (Boston: Houghton, Mifflin, 1929); and Sarah W. Sherman, *Sarah Orne Jewett, an American Persephone* (Hanover, New Hampshire: University Press of New England, 1989).

DEEPHAVEN

8.5   Littell] *Littell's Living Age*, weekly magazine of fiction and poetry founded 1864 in Boston by Eliakim Littell (1797–1870).

25.6   Hugh Miller] Scottish poet, author, and paleontologist (1802–56).

25.32   King's Chapel] Boston's first Anglican church, on Tremont Street.

40.6–7   conies of Scripture] Rabbits, in Proverbs 30:26: "The conies are a feeble-folk, yet they make their houses in the rocks."

40.9   embargo of 1807] The United States Embargo Act of 1807, passed in response to war between Great Britain and France, sought to prevent the combatants' violations of American shipping rights by banning all foreign trade. It failed to achieve its objectives and was repealed in 1809 after severely damaging the economies of American seaport towns.

42.8   Mrs. Betty . . . Cranford] In Elizabeth Gaskell's *Cranford* (1851–53), Betty Barker closes her millinery shop and sets herself up as a "lady," a position she maintains through deference to the more securely elite women of the town of Cranford.

45.25   Dundee] Hymn tune from *The Scottish Psalter* (1615).

52.18   the last war]   Probably the War of 1812 (see page 757.10 in this volume).

110.11   Parson Moody]   Samuel Moody (1676–1747) of York, Maine, Congregational minister and author of religious books.

122.10–11   "China," . . . funeral hymn]   Tune (1801) by Timothy Swan (1758–1842), to which, for example, Isaac Watts's poem "Why Do We Mourn Departing Friends?" (1707) has been set.

135.9–10   Ladies of Llangollen]   Lady Eleanor Butler (?1739–1829) and Sarah Ponsonby (?1733–1831) left their families, against strong opposition, in 1780 and made a home together in a Gothic-style house called Plas Newydd in Llangollen Vale, Wales; they were commemorated by Wordsworth in the sonnet "To the Lady E. B. and the Hon. Miss P." and by Anna Seward in "Llangollen Vale" (1795).

A COUNTRY DOCTOR

183.15   Fayal]   Or Faial, westernmost island of the central Azores.

213.33   'Lancet']   *The London Lancet*, prestigious medical weekly.

216.19–20   follow nature . . . no man.]   English physician and medical writer Thomas Sydenham (1624–89), who had little formal schooling, revolutionized clinical medicine by making detailed observation of patients the basis of treatment.

218.18   Buckle]   Henry Thomas Buckle (1821–62), author of *History of Civilization in England* (1857, 1861).

280.8   being strong . . . whale]   Cf. Christopher Smart, *A Song to David* (1763): "Strong against tide the enormous whale / Emerges as he goes."

THE COUNTRY OF THE POINTED FIRS

388.21   Countess of Carberry]   Frances, Countess of Carbery (d. 1650), the second wife of Richard Vaughan (1600?–86), second Earl of Carbery. Her exemplary piety was eulogized by the English devotional writer Jeremy Taylor (1613–67).

393.8   Parry's Discoveries]   Parry Islands, in the Arctic region north of Melville Sound and Banks Island, named for English explorer William Edward Parry (1790–1855), who made three voyages to the region in search of the Northwest Passage.

396.39   raised incessant armies]   Cf. *Paradise Lost*, VI, 138.

397.1   the ridges . . . retreat]   Cf. *Paradise Lost*, VI, 235–36.

397.2–3   Sometimes . . . air.]   Cf. *Paradise Lost*, VI, 242–44.

417.6–7   Antigone . . . plain]   In Sophocles' *Antigone*, the heroine, acting on her own, defies King Creon's orders and buries the body of her slain brother in the Theban field where it has been left as carrion.

428.8   bangeing-place]   Bangeing was New England dialect for idling, loafing; also, taking advantage of another's hospitality.

DUNNET LANDING STORIES

493.7–8   spies . . . Eshcol]   Cf. Numbers 13.

496.2–3   born . . . day]   Victoria (d. 1901; queen from 1837) was born May 24, 1819.

508.11–12   book . . . Highlands]   *Leaves from a Journal of Our Life in the Highlands . . . 1848–61* (1868); it was followed by *More Leaves . . . 1862–82* (1883).

508.25   her Jubilee]   Victoria's Jubilee, celebrating 50 years of reign, was in 1887.

513.14–15   Medea's . . . iron bulls]   In the legend of the Golden Fleece, Medea prepares a magic ointment that makes Jason impervious to the fire-breathing bulls that he must tame to win the golden fleece.

521.16–17   'Shepherd o' Salisbury Plain']   Popular religious tract (1795) by Hannah More (1745–1833) about a "Christian Arcadian" noted for his practical wisdom and piety.

543.25   fête day]   The feast of the saint for whom a person is named, celebrated in France like a birthday.

561.39–562.1   besmeared . . . Medea]   See note 513.14–15.

SELECTED STORIES AND SKETCHES

581.6   'Canterbury New']   "Canterbury," composed by Henry John Gauntlett (1805–76); the earlier "Canterbury" hymn-tune is by Orlando Gibbons (1583–1625).

598.5–12   Sheila . . . German fashion]   I.e., "Shyla."

600.10   marked . . . king's arrow]   Reserved, because of straightness and height, to become the mast of a ship of the Royal Navy.

617.40   Darby and Joan]   A loving, old-fashioned, virtuous, inseparable couple. The name originated in the poem "Darby and Joan" (1735) by Henry Woodfall.

631.14   heater-piece.]   A small triangular piece of land formed by a convergence of roads, so called because it is shaped like a heater, or flat-iron.

673.6   bangeing]   See note 428.8.

695.4   meechin']   Servile and humble.

696.25   cloud]   A large head scarf.

697.15   pudjicky]   Sensitive.

697.24   bangein']   See note 428.8.

717.23   omnipresent regicides]   At the Restoration (1660), the House of Commons specified that 84 men were responsible for the sentencing and execution of Charles I in 1649. Three "regicides" escaped to New England and were not apprehended; many locales claimed to have harbored one or more of the three.

720.4   Mason's settlers]   John Mason (1586–1635) a proprietor, 1622–29, of territory denoted Province of Maine, began sending settlers to the southern Piscataqua River region in 1623.

720.12   Frank Buckland]   A British naturalist and physician, Buckland (1826–60) was inspector of salmon fisheries and special commissioner on salmon fisheries in Scotland.

727.37   meechin']   See note 695.4.

736.12   Colburn's Arithmetic]   Warren Colburn's widely used *First Lessons. Intellectual Arithmetic* . . . (1821; 1826) or Dana Colburn's *Intellectual Arithmetic* (1859).

755.19–20   "the best . . . world."]   Cf. Matthew Arnold, *Literature and Dogma*, preface.

765.20–21   'Be ye . . . only,']   In James 1:22, "hearers only."

784.4   Grand Army]   The Grand Army of the Republic (1866–1949), an organization for Civil War veterans of the Union army and navy.

790.32   the Centennial]   The International Centennial Exhibition at Philadelphia, May to November 1876, celebrating the 100th anniversary of the signing of the Declaration of Independence, the first international exposition held in the United States.

810.24   gorpen]   Gawky, clumsy, slow-witted.

813.24   Copenhagen]   Game in which players stand in a circle holding a rope to form a ring; the player who is "it" stands in the middle and tries to slap a hand holding the rope. In the "kissing" version, the loser forfeits a kiss.

832.38   meechin']   See note 695.4.

897.21   croping]   Stingy, penurious, niggardly.

CATALOGING INFORMATION

Jewett, Sarah Orne, 1849–1909.
   Novels and Stories / Sarah Orne Jewett.
   Edited by Michael Davitt Bell.
   (The Library of America ; 69)
      Contents: Deephaven—A country doctor—The country
   of the pointed firs—Dunnet Landing stories—Selected
   stories and sketches.
      1. Maine—Fiction. I. Title. II. Deephaven. III. A country
   doctor. IV. The country of the pointed firs. V. Series.
PS2131   1994   93–24167
813'.4—dc
ISBN 0–940450–74–7 (alk. paper)

THE LIBRARY OF AMERICA SERIES

This book is set in 10 point Linotron Galliard,
a face designed for photocomposition by Matthew Carter
and based on the sixteenth-century face Granjon. The paper
is acid-free Ecusta Nyalite and meets the requirements for permanence of the American National Standards Institute. The binding
material is Brillianta, a 100% woven rayon cloth made by
Van Heek-Scholco Textielfabrieken, Holland. The composition is by Haddon Craftsmen, Inc., and The
Clarinda Company. Printing and binding
by R. R. Donnelley & Sons Company.
Designed by Bruce Campbell.

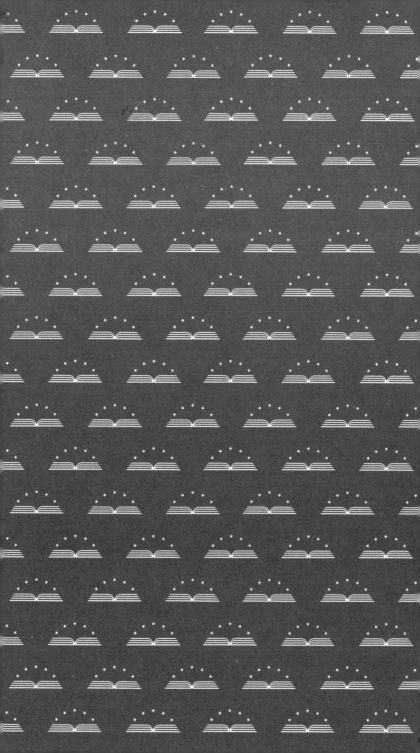